Also by the Same Author

Murder Moon
Dragons' Pearls
Land of the Firebird
The Jongleur

For Barney

1991 – 2009

Our beloved Maine Coon cat gave us 18 years of happiness
and companionship, may we see him again one day.

DARKEST
MAGIC

An Adult Fantasy Novel
by
ISABELLA LEAGUE

For more information, write to us at: **H E L E N E N T H A L   B O O K S**, 4191 Bradfordville Road, Tallahassee, Florida 32309-6401.

Visit us at: **http://galtman.books.officelive.com/default.aspx**

The Author encourages her readers' comments and may be reached via E-mail at: **helenenthal@hotmail.com**

FIRST EDITION

10 9 8 7 6 5 4 3 2 1

ISBN 13-978-1-888071-21-4

Artwork by *E..E. Coad*
Layout & Design by *Gregory S. Coad*

Credits: Copyright illustration from: *200 Decorative Title pages* by Alexander Nesbitt, Plate 11, Dover Books, 1964 Edition.
Title page and Cover Illustrations from: The Picture Book of Symbols, by Ernst Lehner, Tudor Publishing company, New York, page 65.

All other illustrations by E.E. Coad

prologue
the professor of ancient magics

The College of Merlin, Oxford, England, Michaelmas Term 1853

The room was not what they were used to; it was rather small and dark with no windows save those of a clerestory type, up near the ceiling. It seemed as if the windows were this style as if to keep everyone inside, or perhaps to keep them from daydreaming by looking out the windows. Mage lights would be needed to see by, even though out of doors it was a crisp, bright autumn day.

There were eight young men in Wizard's robes present, some of whom were complaining about taking yet another class in ancient magic, one moreover that was *required* if they were to take their *Magus Magistra,* the Master of Magic degree that was replacing the old fashioned test given to applicants by a consortium of Wizards, and if the rumors were true, a university degree would soon be required by law to practice magic at all in the Six Nations.

Alan Stillfield and his good friend Peter Huggin were the last to enter, bringing the total to ten. Alan had been at dragon-ball practice with his dragon friend Brendan and Peter never missed a chance to watch and help Alan care for Brendan. He hoped to have his own dragon one day.

"What is this class all about? I thought we had done with ancient magic. And it's really strange that we were told we could not bring our familiars!" Peter whispered to Alan as they took their seats, the only seats left, right down in front, where no sensible undergraduate ever sat, so vulnerable as it was to the professor's eye.

Alan shrugged. He could not imagine what other kind of ancient magic they had not already studied. Even should this prove to be deadly dull he would sit through it, for it was required and Alan had worked too long towards his *Magus Magistra* to jeopardize it by making a fuss over a required class. The powers that be, meaning the Dean of the College of Merlin, must have his reasons.

5

A young man that both knew slightly, John Tevington, leaned in closer as they sat down. "I say, chaps, I hear
this class is taught by a regular martinet, Professor Williamson. My brother Charlie had him and says he's tough and
surprising."

"Surprising?" Alan queried, frowning. "What did your
brother mean by surprising?"

Tevington said "Damned if I know. Charlie took this
class but it was one that he wouldn't talk about. He said I'd
find out if I made it this far."

Alan and Peter exchanged glances. This was beginning to seem and sound quite mysterious. What could be so
mysterious about a class in ancient magic?

Every young Wizard worth his salt had to study the
magic of the ancients, particularly that of Merlin Ambrosius,
the father of English Wizardry. Methods of magic had
changed a great deal over what was now nearly a millennia,
but the basic foundations had not and it was felt that a
thorough grounding in the past was needful for a full understanding of the nature of magic. Alan felt as if he had been
studying ancient magic forever. It was a topic often discussed
at home, for his grandfather collected old books and incun-
abula on ancient magic and was always sharing bits of
knowledge with the other Wizards in the family.

As a result Alan had done extremely well in his
classes on the subject, for he had an retentive memory and
learned easily. Indeed he had done well in all of his classes.
He was always at the top of his class in whatever subject he
studied. He would take his degree with highest honors.

Peter envied him this, Peter would take his degree
with honors, provided that he studied just as hard in this last
year as he had for the past three. He was grateful to Alan,
with whom he roomed, along with another young man, for
Alan was always willing to help him with his prep and offer
easy explanations for things that Peter could not seem to get
into his head right away.

They had been friends since they were children. Peter
had met Alan when his family moved to Dublin, Alan's family
home. Peter's father had a position working for Alan's uncle
and they had met at a party given by Alan's grandparents.

Peter had been rather a shy boy, for he was lame and

could not participate in the sports that other boys loved. But from the first Alan had made him forget his limitations and proved to like the same things that Peter did, books, magic and dragons, and they were fast friends from the moment of meeting. Alan seemed to understand how hard it was to be different from others.

For he too, *was* different, in looks. His mother, a Russian Countess, had the blood of the Tatars and it showed in her slightly slanted amber eyes. Alan's amber eyes, however, by some trick of inheritance, were so slanted as to make him look Chinese. Combined with the pale flyaway hair, dark Elfin brows he had inherited from his father and his slender height the was very striking looking, some even said *odd*. Peter, shorter, with ordinary brown hair and dark eyes, admired his friend tremendously and would correct anyone who called Alan a "Chinee" or a "Chink".

The ten young men in the room talked amongst themselves for a moment, waiting for the arrival of the professor.

They did not wait long. Precisely on the hour, the door opened and a tall man with an erect carriage entered the room, followed by a darkly handsome younger man carrying a stack of books.

Nigel Williamson was some fifty years of age and a full Fellow. He had a head of dark hair, now graying, with white wings at each temple and a silver streak over his brow. His face was thin, as were his lips and he had what some students called a gimlet eye, he gave the impression that his quick dark eyes, behind a pair of pinc-nez perched on the end of his long nose, saw everything. He wore a beard of the style that covered but his chin, which was beginning to be called an Imperial. It, too, was liberally streaked with silver. His was erect but not stiff; he moved like a much younger man. The students were to become familiar with his habit of arching one mobile brow in a question mark and even more familiar with his beautifully modulated voice that carried easily to every corner of the room and could gut one's pretensions to shreds with withering sarcasm. He was immaculately dressed in a dark frock coat and light trousers under a black Wizard's robe.

"Good afternoon gentlemen," he said briskly. "I trust

7

we are all here, ten of you? Good. Let us then proceed, we have a good deal of material to cover and not nearly enough time to do it in. Mr. Frayne, if you will be so good as to hand out the texts? Thank you."

"Mr. Peyton Frayne is my teaching assistant, gentlemen, and you will obey his dictums as if it were I issuing them. You will notice that your texts are completely in runes and I trust that you all can read them as easily as you can English for there is no translation of this particular book available. If you cannot easily read runes at this point in your career I strongly suggest that you are not best suited for Wizardry and might think of a more mundane career choice."

"The title of your text is "Forbidden Magics", a poor choice on the part of the publisher who seems more intent on titillation than any thing else. Its true title, the one that it should have, will be even more exciting to some of you, for it should be entitled "Sex Magic".

A murmur ran around the room and the professor smiled sardonically. "Yes, we will be talking about intercourse and various other sexual matters. Should we call this course by its true name we should have all the non-magicals in this University signing up to take it for purely prurient reasons. You will find yourselves unable to discuss this course outside this room until I ascertain that each of you is possessed of a certain amount of discretion and maturity, which since most of you are of age or nearly so, you ought to have reached by now." His eyes lifted to the back of the room and he said sarcastically, "Mr. Seeton, you give me doubts that you shall ever obtain any discretion or maturity."

All eyes turned to the back of the room where the Honorable Ronald Seeton tried to look innocent. He was a rather loutish young man, rich and spoiled, whom neither Peter nor Alan had ever had much use for. Alan could not understand how Seeton had made it to his fourth year.

"For those of you fortunate enough to be seated *away* from Mr. Seeton and therefore missed what he thinks is no doubt very clever, he made this gesture," The professor raised his hands and made a circle with the thumb and forefinger of the left hand and then poked the forefinger of his right hand in and out of it quickly. "Mr. Seeton is teaching us a hand gesture, gentlemen, the meaning of which is fucking. Really,

8

Mr. Seeton, your mind operates at the level of a nine year old. Do you still find shit and fart jokes amusing as well?"

By now Seeton's face was turning red and there were a few muffled guffaws and some gasps at hearing a professor use such language.

"We shall be calling a spade a spade in this class. This is a serious subject about a form of magic that is as dangerous, perhaps even more so than the blood magic and black arts that you have all learned of in every year that you have been here," the professor continued.

"Mr. Huggin, could you give us a definition of blood magic?" Williamson said, turning his gaze upon Peter.

Peter sat up straighter in his chair. "Yes, sir," he answered. "Blood magic is made by the subjugation of others, through pain and terror, torture and even death. These are emotional energies and can be gathered in by a blood magician and used for Dark powers."

The professor nodded. "Very good, Mr. Huggin. Succinct and correct. Mr. Stillfield, I am well acquainted with your grandfather, the Marquis of Keir. Has he ever talked to you of ancient fertility rites? I believe he delivered a paper on that subject to the Druid's Circle in London just last year."

"Yes, sir, I was the one who served as his amanuensis," Alan answered.

"Perhaps you remember the blessing of the fields? Could you tell the class about it?"

"It was a very ancient ritual," Alan began. "It took place on Plough Monday and was to assure the fertility of the crops in the coming year. The preceding autumn, at Samhain, a young man and a girl were chosen from amongst all the young villagers. They were to be virgins. All winter long they were treated as a king and a queen, with the best food and the warmest seat at the fireside and no work. On Plough Monday they would be ritually bathed and blessed by the priests and priestesses of the Horned God and the Mother Goddess. Their bodies would be anointed with oil and arcane symbols for fertility would be painted on their bodies with the blood of a sacred deer and the young man would be adorned with the horns of the stag. Then they would be taken out of doors, still naked, to the principal filed of the village, And there, to the beat of a drum and pipes, they would

9

represent the union of the god and goddess by making love. This was thought to be the god and goddess's blessing on the field."

"I say!" quailed Tevington. "In front of all the villagers? That's a rum go!"

Ignoring Tevington, the professor went on "That is an example, gentlemen, of *good* sex magic. There are many, most of you have no doubt attended the Vernal equinox dances, the dance of welcome to the spring that you have seen mothers, sisters and sweethearts perform in, their naked bodies covered in blue woad. We, raised in the traditions of Druidism and magic find nothing horrifying or lewd about this dance and we accept that the female members of our families, if they are Witches, perform a full two-thirds of their rituals sky clad, or naked. All of this is good sex magic, even though we do not call it such, for we live in a prudish age."

He looked intently at the class. "All magic is based on energy, and this good sex magic is as full of energy as the ley lines we use. Blood mages gather their energies through emotions and feelings, those of pain, terror and death, as Mr. Huggin told us. The sex magic that is akin to black magic and blood magic uses the energies of other, perhaps even more powerful emotions, humiliation, degradation, despair and shame. And you need to know this, right now, even in this country, there are brothels where girls and women are forced to perform sex acts under the power of a sex magician who with each act of intercourse can gather the potent energies generated for his own use."

"Here in England?" another young Wizard said in disbelief. "This is a Christian country, and such things are not possible here!"

Really, Mr. Marlowe? You are quite certain of this? Mr. Tevington," he said suddenly, startling John, who had been listening in open-mouthed shock. "Your brother Charles is now a Repressor, is he not?"

All eyes in the classroom turned to Tevington. A Repressor was a Wizard who suppressed and killed, if necessary, evil things, from bogles to black magicians. There were very few of them in all of the Six Nations. The general public were under the impression that all they did was kill bogles, but even that was not a job for the faint hearted for it took a powerful, knowledgeable Wizard with nerves of steel. "I am going to ask Charles to come in here and tell us some of his experiences," said the professor. "Just recently a brothel in Manchester was discovered to be harboring a sex magician and keeping more than thirty women in captivity. Charles was involved in capturing and killing the sex magician, a job well done."

Everyone looked at Tevington in awe and the young man blushed; he had not known that Charlie did anything save kill bogles.

"No doubt most of you have heard of Sir Francis Dashwood and the Hellfire Club as it is always a popular subject for the lurid, sex-drenched novels the young like to read. Contrary to popular opinion Dashwood was not just a hedonist but a powerful sex magician who was very difficult to destroy," Williamson went on.

"Why doesn't everybody know about this?" A young Wizard named Woodruffe blurted out.

"A long time ago, a decision was made, very high up, that the information must not be leaked to the general public. It was feared that people would be too afraid to go about their business, thinking that their wives and daughters might be kidnapped off the street to serve some monster's perverted magics by being put to every man that desired her. Our government is very good at hiding things from us that we really do need to know; witness the debacle of the Murder Moon several years ago. And in the present atmosphere of suffocating propriety we have to keep pretending that horrors like this do not exist. But every day women actually *are* kidnapped off the streets to disappear forever. Many end up in magic brothels in the Near and Middle East, especially in Persia, for sex magic is a very popular form there. It is a magic that requires little skill or study on the part of the magician. In this course you will learn how to protect yourself from Succuba, for you young men can be seduced by demon born spawn as well as a woman. I shall teach you how to fight sex magicians and how to rescue women from their clutches, because it is females who suffer the most from sex magic. I have yet to meet a man who suffers shame and humiliation from having too much sex."

A rather uneasy laugh swept over the class.

11

"Many of you will be going on the traditional Grand Tour of Greece and the Levant after you take your degree. And that area of the world too is where sex magic brothels flourish. It is an old magic and you will find that the magicians of that area prefer as their sex slaves women of the Western countries, for our women, particularly the non-magical women, are taught that nudity is shameful and the sex act is dirty, meant only for marriage and the procreation of children. Therefore, the shame a Western female feels at being kept naked, many times in chains, and given to all comers is far greater than a female in the cultures of say, Persia or India would feel. And I want you to remember one very important thing, gentlemen. Do not be self righteous prigs and blame the women who end in these brothels. It is no doing of theirs; it was not a choice they made. They have been forced into this subjugation, in fact, a woman who enjoys a loving sex act is of no use to a sex magician as the energies of pain and degradation are far more potent than those of enjoyment. A woman who lays with her husband or lover in the willing and eager act of love and in the enjoyment of such, generates only good sex magic, which is the magic of the Light which we all serve."

"But a good woman don't enjoy sex!" blurted out John Tevington.

"And if you believe that, Mr. Tevington, I should like to sell you some swamp land I own in the Fen country," said Professor Williamson dryly. "Now, gentlemen, open your texts to the first chapter. We shall be discussing Incubi and Succuba for the next half hour. I can see that I have an uphill road ahead of me."

Alan was not to know it, but what he was to learn from Professor Williamson was some of the most important material he would ever study.

the grass widow

On Board 'The Splendor Of India', March 1857

Rosamunde stood at the stern of the East Indiaman *Splendor of India*, gazing down towards the dragon deck. Overhead, canvas and ropes cracked in a brisk wind. On her shoulder was her familiar, the cat Sinéad, quiet now for once. Ever since the ship had entered the Mediterranean she had been talking about their new experiences and the sights and sounds of being at sea. Travel in Rosamunde's family was nearly always by dragon-back and Sinéad had never been in a ship this big before, only on a private yacht.

The Mediterranean was a vast improvement over the English Channel and the Bay of Biscay. Nearly everyone had been seasick. It was early February when the ship left southhampton and the winter passage had been rough.
But since Gibraltar had been passed, the entire aspect had changed and the ship ploughed through a bright blue sea under mostly cloudless skies. At times dolphins raced alongside the ship, leaping under the part of the bow beneath the figurehead that had been named for this dangerous habit of theirs – dolphin-striker. Amongst the dolphins Rosamunde could see Merchildren, wearing starfish in their greenish locks, attempting to see the dragon that was being oiled on the deck below Rosamunde.

Perhpas a steamer might nave been easier on the passengers, but none with the capacity for towing the dragon deck had been available until later in the year. Rosamunde fervently wished that she could have waited for a steamer, but her family would not hear of her going out to India by herself, not when Alan was going there as well and could escort her.

Another young woman might have felt that it was Alan's fault that she was going to India in the first place. Even now she awoke at night and wondered why she was going, indeed, how had this happened.

But she was far too honest with herself to not admit that she had acted on impulse, out of pain and disappointment, and the fault lay mostly with herself.

For since last October she had been Mrs. Raymond DeLacey, wife of a lieutenant in a Queen's cavalry Regiment, serving in India, by her own choice, and was not, as she had dreamed of since she was a child, the wife of her cousin, Alan Stillfield.

She could not remember not loving Alan – and she had thought he felt the same about her. Rosamunde had confidently expected that when she was old enough he would propose to her and they would be married. He was nearly four years her senior. It was entirely legal for first cousins to be married in the Six Nations although he was not *really* her cousin by blood as his father was the adopted son of Rosamunde's grandparents and there could be no objection to the union.

And since she was in her early teens she had hoped that marriage to Alan would not only make her happy, but would protect her.

Rosamunde's early adolescence had been made unhappy by a remark overheard from two chattering women. If Rosamunde had been older and wiser she would have realized that the two women were gossips of the worst sort. But at twelve years of age she could not know this.

Her father, a Wizard Healer, had taken his wife and eldest daughter to a medical symposium in Edinburgh in Scotland, where he had attended University. It was Rosamunde's first visit to Edinburgh and she had delighted in the many bookshops and shops for arcane materials. Her parents had allowed her, with her maid, to shop on her own. Rosamunde was a talented Witch, and with her maid and her familiar she would be quite properly chaperoned and Edinburgh was a safe, civilized city, considered the Athens of the north.

It was in a bookshop on the Royal Mile, while her maid and Sinéad were looking at other books, that she overheard someone mention her father's name – Stuart Delamar.

"Yes, my brother Henry was at school with him.

Henry mentioned at dinner last night that Dr. Delamar is here for the symposium and has his new wife with him. And his daughter by his first wife; Henry says she looks a bit like her mother," came a woman's voice.

"Wasn't his first wife Anabel Rossiter?" came another voice. The ladies sounded as if they were on the other side of the tall stacks from Rosamunde.

"Yes – I never could understand how a little slut like her could catch the heir to a Dukedom!" said the first woman.

"A slut!" exclaimed her companion. "Oh. Clara, she was of a good family! Her father was a most respected solicitor and her mother was one of the Campbells of Argyllshire! I can't believe..."

"She was completely promiscuous, Dorothy! It was well known that she would lift her skirts for anyone! Why, she even tried to seduce Henry! Her behavior was a scandal! It's to be hoped her daughter isn't like her; for some reason men clustered around Anabel like flies to honey. I never saw anything the least attractive in her myself. What a tragedy for the Delamar family if her daughter is as loose-conducted as her mother was!"

The two women had moved away, still gossiping and Rosamunde was left reeling with shock.

She was a very well-read girl and one more over who had been brought up to know the facts of life, unlike many of her contemporaries who were raised in an atmosphere of stultifying prudery. She knew all too well what 'promiscuous' meant. And her mother, her real mother, was like that?

For the last four years Julia, her father's new wife, had been "Mama' to Rosamunde – indeed, there were times when Rosamunde forgot that Julia was not her real mother, for Anabel had died shortly after Rosamunde was born.

She did not know what to do. She had been accustomed to talk to her parents about almost everything but one subject no one ever touched upon – Rosamunde's real mother. Rosamunde knew that her father had been unhappy when married to her real mother, and that no one in her entire family had really liked Anabel – she had heard that from tales told to Sinéad by her father's familiar, Dr. Foster. Out of love and concern for her father's feelings she had never asked much about her mother and Julia had never known her. Rosamunde had also felt that asking her grandparents or her aunt and uncle (who had never really known her either) would be disloyal to her father. And how could she ask anyone about something so vile?

Perhaps all of this would have faded in her memory save for one circumstance. While all of her classmates were still childish looking Rosamunde developed early and began to attract the attention of not only boys, but men. At thirteen, she had the figure of an older girl with slim but rounded hips, a tiny waist and full breasts. She was tall, too, the tallest of any girl in her class at Miss Ó Phaidan's Academy for the Daughters of Gentlemen in Dublin.

And she was quite extraordinarily beautiful. Even as a child she had been so but maturity had added a depth and an allure to her loveliness that seemed to stop men dead in their tracks. Her mass of silver blonde hair that curled naturally and seemed too heavy for her long neck, her enormous violet eyes with long dark lashes under delicately arched brows and a flawless complexion along with perfect features – all added up to a rare beauty. Added to these was a slim, graceful carriage for Rosamunde had studied dance for years. She loved dance almost as much as reading or music and her dancing mistress at school, who had studied ballet, had assured Rosamunde that had she not been the great granddaughter of a Duke she might have become a *prima* ballerina.

But Rosamunde could have never appeared on a stage, not once she began attracting unwanted attention wherever she went. Unlike some young girls who might have reveled in the glances men threw her way she became shy and self-conscious. She wore only the most modest of gowns and began to wear a shawl at all times to disguise her bosom. She stopped participating in the sky-clad rituals of her Coven and tried her best to keep away from strange men, all of whom showed a distressing tendency to pursue her. She was afraid and became more so over the years that this unlooked-for attention meant that she too, was promiscuous or could become so if she ever gave in to the pursuer's blandishments.

She had not wanted a come-out in London, but her great grandfather, the Duke of Chenevix, had insisted. Since she was ten years old they had become very close. He called her his 'sweet girl' and she gave in only to please him. He was inordinately proud of her beauty and accomplishments

Rosamunde had become convinced that her only salvation was in marrying Alan. Once she was married, and wed to an Adept class Wizard who could wither anyone who attempted to importune her with but a glance, men would leave her alone. She would be safe. She was tired of fending off eager suitors,some of whom tried to kiss her by force whenever they found her alone and she had to correct their behavior with her magic or Sinéad would offer to scratch their eyes out. She had not told her parents of these determined gentlemen, which was a mistake on her part.

She had dressed for her come-out ball in a glow of happiness. She was certain that Alan would propose tonight and she would come home from the ball safely betrothed to him. What could be more fitting or more romantic? As she dressed in an exceedingly demure gown of white tulle trimmed with bunches of violets made with almost no *decollatage* (much to her dressmaker's dismay) and a loose fit as well as a small hoop, she imagined how he would ask her to waltz and then would swirl her out to the terrace of her great grandfather's town house, drop to one knee and offer a beautiful diamond engagement ring, which she would immediately accept. Then they would announce their engagement at the ball and all the callers, the bouquets and the love notes would cease. She would be safe and she would never be labeled promiscuous like her mother.

But it did not happen; she danced the first dance with her great grandfather, then danced with her grandfather, her father, and all of her male cousins old enough to be at the ball. Her own favorite brother, to whom she was especially close, David, was only eight and too young to be present. Alan presented himself for the first waltz. He was a graceful dancer and their steps were well suited.

But his conversation had been about dragon-ball – dragon-ball! – when she expected words of love! He had not taken her out on the terrace, nor had he even paid her any compliments or indicated in the least that he found her a romantic interest. Indeed after he had danced with her, which he had seemed to consider a duty, not a longed for pleasure, he had disappeared into he library with a group of

17

Wizards who were discussing new spells. Alan, on leaving Oxford, had gone to work in his great great grandfather, the Marquis of Lyonshall's spell development facility.

Rosamunde stood it for nearly two more years, trying to avoid men who were insistent upon proposing and would not leave her alone, no matter how much she tried to dissuade them.

And then she heard that Alan was interested in a girl called Christine Chapman, a dark beauty from the Cotswolds where Lyonshall's laboratory was located. She also heard that Alan was coming back to Dublin, to set up a branch of the laboratory there and that he probably would be bringing Christine with him as his bride.

She could not bear it – she really could not bear to see Alan with someone else! She had to get away, as far as was possible. So she had accepted the proposal of Raymond DeLacey, a young Indian officer who had recently become part of her court. He was quiet and respectful; he never had much to say but just sat in the drawing room and gazed at her worshipfully, not even asking her to dance or to walk or drive out with him. He was very kind, she found out through the servant's grapevine. The servants thought highly of him and he was extremely attentive to his only living relative, an elderly aunt. Rosamunde told herself that she would learn to love him in time. Anything was better than watching Christine Chapman as Alan's wife!

She had found out what a mistake she had made on her wedding night.

And now here she was on a ship for India, leaving home and family far behind, to live with a man she scarcely knew. Most ironic of all, Alan was sailing to India as well and there was no sign of Christine Chapman.

Alan was under doctor's orders to take a long rest for he was suffering from overwork. He had roomed, whilst at Oxford with Peter Huggin and an young man from India, Ravi Chopra, from the small independent state of Ranijhat, which lay in the foothills of the Himalayas. They had become firm friends and Ravi had long been urging Alan to come out and visit him so that he could show his beloved country to his great friend. When Alan had written to Ravi of his near breakdown his friend had insisted that the clean, pine-scented air from the foothills was just the thing to restore Alan to full health.

Alan, of course, could go nowhere without his dragon friend, Brendan, but Brendan was merely making a stop in India. He was on his way to Tibet, to study at a draconic monastery on the Roof of the World. He was sorry to leave Alan but he was quite excited about this opportunity. Lakota, the dragon who was bonded to Alan's father Sir Simon Stillfield, had arranged it through a friend of his, a Chinese dragon named T'a Ming, who had studied there herself.

It could have not worked out better, Rosamunde's family declared. She could go out to India under Alan's protection, since Raymond had had to go ahead to rejoin his regiment soon after their marriage, thus leaving Rosamunde free to gather the household goods and clothing she would need for a sojourn in a hot country.

But continued proximity to Alan was just what she did NOT want. She wanted to leave him, and her disappointment behind. It still cost her a pang to even look at him and be natural with him. She had to make a new life with Raymond and she was going to do her very best to make it a good life, for both herself and her husband.

At least she would be joining Raymond at his post in Malabad, a district near the recently annexed state of Oudh, and not too far from Delhi in the area of northern India known as Hindustan, but far enough from where Alan would be headed to make visits from him difficult as he would not have Brendan with him to make traveling effortless.

Rosamunde's musings had taken her mentally quite far from the ship. Now Sinéad said in her ear, "They're after talkin' about ye, the chatterin' gossip mongers!" The little black and white cat hissed as she spoke.

On the deck below her sat five women. An awning had been set up for their comfort and to protect their delicate complexions from the sun.

Four of the women were young members of what was euphemistically called 'the Fishing Fleet', young women who had not 'taken' at home in the Six Nations of the British Isles and were going out to India, where white women were at a premium, to try and catch a husband. Those who failed to land a spouse even in India and sailed home in defeat were called, rather unkindly, "Returned Empties"

Rosamunde had had little to do with them so far. Most of them had been wretchedly seasick until Gibraltar, but since Rosamunde herself was a good sailor, she had helped the girls' chaperone, Mrs. Umphelby, with tending to them. Holding a basin while someone vomited into it was not conducive to forming friendships.

To Rosamunde's surprise she knew one of the girls, Mabel Clutterbuck, who had been briefly at school with her. Theirs could probably never be a congenial relationship, for Rosamunde's father had been instrumental in catching and convicting Mabel's father of murder.

The fact that Mr. Clutterbuck had been hung and his name made anathema had coloured Mabel's entire life. She was convinced that her father's guilt had given the whole family a bad name and that had ruined her chances for matrimony. Her own sullen disposition might have had more to do with it. She was a thin girl with stringy carroty hair and a face permanently marred by a frown.

The other girls were Susan Midthorpe, a little brown nonentity who was suffocatingly shy; Lavinia Baldwin, a sharp featured girl with dark hair and an equally sharp tongue, and Molly Fraser, who was sharing Rosamunde's tiny cabin, so that Rosamunde, a married woman, could serve as chaperone for her, while the other three girls shared a larger cabin with Mrs. Umphelby.

Molly, too was shy. She had a head of auburn hair and a sweet face. From what little Rosamunde had seen of her she seemed to have a sweet nature as well. She was from a poor family and was going out to India to join her brother, who worked for the East India company and was stationed in Calcutta. She was going to keep house for him there. Molly, however, was no match for Mabel's spite and Lavinia's nasty speech.

"What sort of cosmetics does she use?" Lavinia was grilling Molly as Rosamunde turned her attention to the group below.

Mrs, Umphelby, a large, stout, motherly woman who was returning to her husband in India after going to England to see her first grandchild, was frankly asleep, softly snoring. Elsewise she might have steered the girls to a more suitable topic – gossip, she had firmly declared, was un-Christian.

"I've only seen her use Olympian Dew on her face," said Molly uncomfortably.

"Oh, come now," Lavinia mocked in a rather drawling, nasal voice. "No one has cheeks and lips that colour naturally! And those lashes are surely darkened!"

"She looked like that even at school and she wouldn't have been allowed to use cosmetics there," said Mabel "even if her great grandfather is a Duke!"

"Which Duke?" said Lavinia sharply. "I'll not believe it – she dresses so plain! Why, look at the size of her hoop! My maid back home wore a bigger hoop when she went out walking with the footman! But she must wear her corsets very tight. Look at her waist!" This last was said with envy for Lavinia was rather thick- waisted. But she was wrong in this as Rosamunde did not wear corsets at all. Her father disapproved of them; he said that tight lacing was dangerously unhealthy

"The Duke of Chenevix," Mabel said in answer to Lavinia's question.

Lavinia drew in a sharp breath. "'Tis said he is the richest man in England! Why did someone with her looks and her money marry a mere Indian lieutenant? In her place I would be queen of society!" Contempt was in her voice.

Eavesdroppers hear no good of themselves, Rosamunde reminded herself and turned back to look at the dragon deck where Brendan now snoozed in the sunshine. Alan, who had been oiling his dragon friend, had finished this task and had disappeared. It was just as well for to watch him made her heart ache with longing.

Alan had seen Rosamunde standing above on the stern but rather than climbing the portable ladder to the deck above and joining her he had used the narrow walk that led down the side of the ship from the galley, there for the convenience of carrying food to draconic passengers.

Rosamunde had been strange lately, their old easy camaraderie seemed to have disappeared, He supposed this was because she was married now and she owed her first allegiance and friendship to her husband. He missed the old footing as he had always thought of her as his best friend.

Scampering along behind Alan was his familiar, the black-footed ferret Cathal. "Where are we going?" he called to Alan. "It's too nice a day to stay in our cabin. And at any rate, that subaltern Goodwinter stares at me as if he thinks you are throwing your voice and making me talk! I don't like it!"

Alan, like his cousin, was sharing a cabin with two subalterns, newly commissioned, who were going out to India for the first time. As far as Alan could tell a subaltern seemed to be a rank below captain, perhaps equivalent to an ensign in the Navy. The two sharing his cabin, Goodwinter and Jerome, were cut from the same cloth – young, eager, and naive. There were two other subalterns on board, Dunstan and Everard, and a Major Higby, an 'old India hand', who had been on home leave. Two missionaries, Mr. And Mrs. Ignatius Holloway, and a Eurasian gentleman, Mr. Laputa, completed the compliment of passengers.

Alan had largely ignored most of them. The army men had a tendency to talk shop and he disapproved strongly of missionaries for he thought that people should be left to worship in their own fashion, not have some one else's religion forced upon them.

He had had some interesting conversations with Mr. Laputa, who was able to tell him more about India. He was taking lessons in Urdu and Persian from Mr. Laputa. Years ago Ravi had taught him the basics of Hindustanee and it was coming back to him easily. Rosamunde was taking lessons of the pleasant little gentleman too. She wanted, as did Alan, to be able to speak to the Indian people they would meet in their own language.

Now in answer to Cathal's question Alan said "I left my lesson books in the ward room and the Captain told me that he was able to obtain some newspapers and periodicals in Gibraltar. Perhaps we can sit out here in the sun and drill each other on our lesson before we go to Mr. Laputa and find something to read as well." Cathal and Sinéad too, were learning the languages, although it had rather startled Mr. Laputa at first to teach animals to read and speak the tongues of his country.

"I have been missing the newspapers!" said Cathal

wistfully. "Do you suppose he was able to get the *Wizards' Times*?" There were columns and articles in this paper just for familiars.

"We'll hope so," said Alan cheerfully.

The officer's ward room had been made over for the sake of the male passengers, into a sort of salon. There had been card games in progress since the weather had changed for the better. This was another reason Alan had seen but little of his fellow male passengers. He did not like playing cards; he found it a bore, and in such fine weather he saw little reason to sit all day in a stuffy room redolent with an atmosphere of stale cigars and spilled liquor.

The usual game of whist was in progress as Alan entered the ward room; all of the subalterns and Major Higby were at the table, rowdy and noisy. A brief phrase or two, overheard, told Alan they were talking about women and boasting about their conquests.

Alan ignored them and quickly found his lesson books and began leafing through the pile of periodicals and newspapers. He found several issues of magazine he would like to read, among then *Punch* and the *Gentleman Wizards' Magazine.* He began to look through one and saw an article on "Higher Mathematics – the Final Solution to Dematerialization?" and, sinking into a chair, became engrossed in it.

Cathal was disappointed for there were no copies of the *Wizards' Times*, but there were copies of the *London Times*, which he decided to read. But before he could start, a name caught his sensitive ears and he looked up sharply at the men seated at the card table.

Major Bartholomew Higby was speaking. He was about thirty-five, considerably older than the subalterns, and from the looks they gave him, they much admired him. He had served in the Afghan War back in '42 and had distinguished himself, it was said. He was tall and broads-shouldered with a pair of glossy brown military whiskers, and dark eyes under hooded eyelids. His mouth was full and sensuous and he was said to be a devil to go with the ladies. At least three of the young ladies on board had cast him admiring glances when all the passengers had made their morning promenade around the deck this morning. He was a fine figure of a man in his regimentals and he well knew it. Cathal thought he was abominably conceited and thought the human females idiotic for admiring such a one.

"Now the females on board this old bucket, lads, are a poor lot. All save one – little Mrs. DeLacey. Now there's a piece I'd like to get my leg over! And I'll wager it won't be long before I am giving her a good rogering. All those grass widows are eager for fucking, they've gotten used to it and when they are separated from their husbands they find that they need a man badly."

"What's a grass widow?" Dunstan asked with a hiccup. Like the others he was more than a little drunk, even this early in the morning. Major Higby kept filling their glasses.

"Like a hunter when fox hunting is done, she's been put out to grass, not used until the next season." Higby said with a broad smile.

"But she's got no figure!" protested Goodwinter a man who never looked beyond the surface "Even today she's got on a lace shawl! Beautiful face, but –"

"I was out on deck once when the wind was blowing," said Higby "and saw her gown plastered to her body as that shawl was whisked away by the wind. I tell you, lads, she has the best pair of titties I've ever seen, and I've seen quite a few from London whores to Bengali bints, and that pair of titties is begging to be squeezed and suckled by me. Within the week I fully expect to be fucking her regularly – a little sweet talk and I'll be between her legs." He gave a malicious laugh and began to enumerate exactly what he meant to do to Rosamunde. Only Everard seemed at all disturbed by the fact that Higby was discussing a lady, and one who was married to a fellow officer. The others were too drunk and Higby outranked them.

Cathal listened in growing indignation. That was their Rosamunde this horrible man was talking about!

"Alan!" he said urgently, putting a paw on his Wizard's arm "You had better listen to this! They're talking about Rosamunde in a very nasty way!"

2

the cad and the missionary

Alan looked up sharply, his attention riveted at once on his familiar. "What did you say?" he demanded.

"That man – that awful Higby – is talking about Rosamunde as if she was a loose woman! He claims that he is going to lay with her!" said Cathal angrily. "How can he say things like that? She's a lady and a married woman, not a prostitute!"

"Some men think any woman is fair game," said Alan grimly, "but Rosamunde is not!"

At this moment Higby's voice came clear and loud. "A toast to Mrs. DeLacey's beautiful boobies, gentlemen! May my hands and lips soon be caressing them and other interesting parts of her lovely body!"

The magazine dropped to the floor. Alan rose and said in a carrying voice. "Anyone who drinks that toast is a dead man!"

All the subalterns turned at once to stare at him. At the sight of his angry face Dunstan and Everard hurriedly put down their glasses. Goodwinter, the drunkest of the lot, gave another hiccup and fell face forward onto the table, scattering the cards and knocking his glass, full of gin, to the floor. Jerome looked back and forth from Alan to Higby, uncertain as what to do. He was quite well to live as well and his eyes and senses were blurry.

Higby did not put down his glass. Instead he leaned back in his chair and looked up at Alan with a rather mocking smile on his lips. His whole attitude was one of amusement.

"You have an interest there yourself, Mr. Whoever-you-are?" he drawled. "I think you will find that the lady will chose substance over your desire. Are you even old enough to have had a woman? Do you know what to do with one?" His smile grew broader as Jerome tittered.

"The lady whose name and reputation you sully is just that, a lady," said Alan," and neither she nor her husband would appreciate your lewdness and foul suggestions. In the absence of her husband, it is up to me to protect her name."

"And how do you propose to do that, boy?" Higby said in derision, for to him, Alan looked to him to be no older than seventeen at the most and as if he had been ill at that. Alan's lack of fashionable facial hair made him look quite a bit younger than his twenty-four years. This youth was certainly no match for Bart Higby!

Higby raised his glass and drained it. "Go back to your nurse, boy. I wouldn't waste my time on an infant like you. And besides, I don't lower myself to fight with a *chi chi* — a half caste. Why don't you people stay in China or wherever you belong instead of trying to mix with white men? And get that little rodent out of here!" he directed, staring at Cathal with hostility.

The ferret drew in his breath sharply. He could feel the anger pouring of his Wizard. Alan had a hasty temper and Major Higby had managed in one short encounter to insult Rosamunde, Alan himself and Cathal.

A crack like thunder sounded. The subalterns looked about uneasily but sunlight still streamed in the ward room.

Alan raised his hand and a long whip of violet light ran off it so quickly that no one had any time to react to it. The whip seized Higby by the throat and slammed his head in to the table, repeatedly until the table upended, throwing the cards, coins and bills, the gin bottle and glasses all over the floor.

Higby was gasping, clutching at his throat with both hands as the subalterns scrambled to get away from the violet light. Only Goodwinter saw none of it, unconscious, he fell to the floor, smiling blissfully.

The violet light then held Higby up in the air. The Major's face was red from the pressure on his windpipe and his eyes were full of shock.

Alan walked up to him and said in a deceptively pleasant voice, "Now that I have your attention, you damned cad, I am going to tell you how it will be for the balance of this trip. You will not even so much as LOOK in Mrs. DeLacey's direction or else I shall repeat this treatment until you choke to death. Or I might feed you to my dragon. He will be very angry when I tell him the way you have been talking about my cousin. He's known her since she was a little girl and loves her dearly. Dragons are very protective of those they love. I may not be able to restrain him from flaming you. Another thing you might do well to consider – our great grandfather is the Duke of Chenevix. One word to him that you have been bandying my cousin's name about in your disgusting fashion and he will ruin you, Higby. You will be cashiered from the army and that would be the least of your problems if Chenevix takes you in dislike. You'd be left without a pot to piss in."

With this Alan let go and Higby fell to the ground, gasping and still clutching at his throat.

"I also expect an apology for the things you said. I had best never hear such filth again," Alan said, looking at the man with no pity. Why were such creatures allowed to live? He might be doing the world a favor to go ahead and kill Higby. If only killing such a man were considered justifiable homicide!

"And I am NOT a rodent!" said Cathal, sitting up on his back legs and staring down at Higby. "As a familiar I have as much right to be in here as you do, more, for I have better manners and do not get my companions drunk so I can fleece them at cards when they are too fuddled to think straight!"

Higby glared at him and looked at Alan with extreme dislike. When he spoke his was hoarse.

"Very well," he grated, "I'll apologize, you don't leave me any choice. But your 'cousin' " he said sneeringly, as if he doubted Alan could be related to Rosamunde, "has given me unmistakable looks – "

"As if she would look at you!" cried Cathal! "Sinéad told me Rosamunde thinks you are a bounder! The sort who pinches the maids in the corridors!"

Unnoticed by any of them the door to the ward room had opened. An astonished voice said "Why, what has happened here? Has there been some sort of brawl? This is most unseemly and most un-Christian!"

The speaker was the missionary, Ignatius Holloway. He was a gaunt man of medium height with graying hair and beard, worn in the fashion of the prophets of Biblical times. His dark eyes blazed with what Alan thought of as the light of fanaticism. He wore rusty black clerical vestments, old and shabby as if to emphasis his retreat from things of the world. And from the tone of his conversation and the amount of time he spent praying and proselytizing amongst the crew (many of whom were Muslim Indians) Alan very much feared that he was one of the Evangelical Christians that were becoming so numerous and were enemies to the practice of magic. They considered all magic, even Healing, the work of Satan.

Seeing Higby on the floor and Alan standing over him Holloway gave an exclamation and said severely to Alan, "Did you dare to raise a hand to your betters, you miscreant? Those of mixed blood should know their place! Dressing as if you were a white man does not give you the privileges that blood —"

"Oh, shut up!" said Alan in irritation. He was sick to death of these people.

"Alan's father is Sir Simon Stillfield! His mother is a Russian countess! His grandfather is the Marquis of Keir and his great grandfather is the Duke of Chenevix! He is related to half the noble families in the Six Nations! His breeding is far better than yours!" said Cathal in indignation.

Mr. Holloway looked at Cathal in horror. "What Devils' work is this ?" he cried. "An animal that converses as does a man? It is unnatural and unholy! I have felt ever since we embarked on this voyage that Satan was at work on this vessel!"

"Cathal is my familiar and all familiars talk," Alan could not believe this man. "Have you never seen a Wizard with a familiar before? Or have you spent your entire life in a cave?"

"And there is a dragon on this ship as well!" said the missionary, ignoring Alan as if he had not spoken. "A dragon! Another servant of Satan, a ravening beast that shoots the flames of Hell from its maw! We are none of us safe until the captain, as I have demanded, kills the beast and throw its carcass into the sea! "

"Of what denomination are you?" Alan asked, looking at Holloway with ill concealed contempt.

"I am a Methodist," Mr. Holloway drew himself up proudly.This he heard. He suffered from selective deafness.

"From the ignorant way you are going on I would

swear that you were an agent of the Inquisition," said Alan. "It is a mystery to me how any one of your age could live in the Six Nations his whole life and be so incredibly uninformed about Wizards and dragons and familiars."

"I am a man of God. I have kept myself away from such pernicious influences," said the missionary stiffly. "It is well known that magic and its practitioners and all the beasts of such practitioners are minions of Satan."

Higby had risen to his feet, still a little dizzy. With a look of intense dislike at Alan he mulled over whether or not he should complain of this behavior to the Captain. The mention of the Duke of Chenevix had given him pause. Everyone knew how powerful that rich old man was He held a Cabinet Post – Chancellor of Magic – and Lord Palmerston, the Prime Minister, was said to be a particular crony of his.

But India was a long ways from the Six Nations. This young man might be just an escort for his cousin, leaving her in her husband's care once they reached Calcutta. Higby decided that he would do some snooping and find out where the beautiful, desirable Mrs. DeLacey was to be stationed. Bart Higby was not used to being thwarted and he had conceived a strong desire to have Mrs. DeLacey, all the more so now that she had been forbidden to him. What he wanted, he generally got, particularly when it came to women.

And if he ever could find a way to pay back this *chi chi* for the insult and the humiliation he had just endured, he would do it.

Catching up his lesson books and the magazines he wanted to read, Alan said curtly to Cathal "It's time for our lesson," and walked out in the middle of a rant by Mr. Holloway about the evil of dragons and magic and the duty of every Christian to stamp out this wickedness.

"If I stay any longer I shall punch him in the nose," Alan added, loudly enough for the missionary to hear as they left the room.

"Alan," said Cathal as they went up the companionway onto the deck, " should we tell Rosamunde about that vile man and what he said about her?"

"No," said Alan decidedly. "She has to be in his company at meal times and I wouldn't wish for her to be completely uncomfortable with him around. We'll keep an eye on her, you and I. And an eye on him as well."

"Sinéad says Rosamunde does not like him at any rate. He frightens her," Cathal offered. Sinéad was his best friend.

"We'll make certain that he does not frighten her any more than just looking at him does. Given him looks indeed!" Alan fumed. "The man's an intolerable ass if he can't tell looks of loathing from a come hither stare! He sees what he wants to see."

He'd also have a word with Brendan, he decided as they went towards a small canopy on the deck where Mr. Laputa sat alone. The elderly Eurasian was very conscious of the proprieties and would not allow Rosamunde to join him until Alan was already seated. Cathal would run and fetch her and her familiar so that the lessons could begin.

Alan gladly gave his mind over to the intricacies of Urdu and Persian grammar, unaware that he had made two enemies.

"I know that you were eager to fly over land once we made landfall in Egypt," said Alan to Brendan later that day, "But I can't leave Rosamunde alone on this ship with that man. Mrs. Umphelby sleeps all the time; she isn't much of a chaperone. And I don't trust anyone else to watch over her. If that missionary were a clergyman like Mr. Gatewick back in Dublin I could trust him to keep an eye on her. But once this Holloway knows she is a Witch he'll be raving to her about her chances of burning in Hell forever or some such rot."

Brendan looked troubled. "Of course we can't leave her unprotected," he agreed. "I've seen him look at her, Alan, and I confess that I almost said something to you at the time. He has such a look of desire on his face – almost evil. Rosamunde is another man's mate. He should not be looking at he like that. It isn't right, no matter now beautiful she is! No dragon would ever behave like that.!" he added severely.

"Rosamunde? Beautiful?" repeated Alan looking at his dragon friend puzzled. "I daresay she's rather pretty..."

Brendan gave a long sigh, causing his emerald green

scales to ripple in the sunlight. "Alan , have you really looked at her since she grew up? She's a stunner as your brother Alex would say. She was one of the most sought after debutantes of the year when she made her come-out. Didn't you notice anything of this?"

Alan shrugged. She was just Rosamunde to him. He had known her forever it seemed and to him she had changed very little except to get taller, let her skirts down and put her hair up. She was still the same Rosamunde she had always been, save for this new distance between them. Alan realized something had to change when she was married, the same way that it would change if he married. A spouse might be jealous of their closeness. And he liked Raymond well enough. Like most of the family, Alan wished that Raymond were not taking Rosamunde so far away. But Rosamunde had made her choice and it was not Alan's place to interfere.

All the same, he would drop a word in Raymond's ear when they met him in Calcutta. One could not be too careful with a bounder such as Major Higby.

It was nearly dinner time on board *The Splendor of India*. Since this was an extremely civilized voyage most of the passengers changed for dinner.

Rosamunde was in front of the tiny mirror attempting to do something with her wildly independent curls. Since they had no maid, she and Molly had fallen into the habit of helping one another. It was not recommended that one bring servants from the Six Nations out to India as they were generally unhappy and dissatisfied and ended in going home with their employer having to pay their return passage. And native servants could be hired so cheaply that it was considered foolish to pay the wages of a British servant.

Molly, who generally chattered away, had been very quiet and Rosamunde, stealing a glance in the mirror at her as Molly sat on the edge of her very small bed, dressed and ready, saw a troubled look on her face.

"Is it true?" Molly suddenly burst out. "That Clutter-buck girl said that your grandfather is a Duke!"

"Great grandfather," Rosamunde said gently, putting

down the brush she had been using to try and control her wayward curls.

"It's true then?" Molly drew in a sharp breath." And I let you brush and dress my hair and button up my gown!"

Rosamunde turned to look at her a little surprised. "But you needed my help and there is no maid. What does it matter who my great grandfather is?"

"It matters a great deal," said Molly a little bitterly. "You will never have to leave your home and go to live in a strange place with a brother who is so much older that you can scarcely remember what he looks like. He doesn't really want me, you know. But my aunt and uncle did not want me to stay with them, either and no one offered for me so here I am, going to live with Theo, where I shall be his housekeeper and governess to his children, not treated as his sister and allowed to go about in society. His wife made that very plain in her letters."

"But we all thought –" Rosamunde began.

"That I was to be the belle of my brother's establishment?" Molly's mouth twisted wryly. "I could not bear to see how the others will sneer when they find out I shall be but an unpaid servant. They have sneered enough at my clothes," she looked sadly down at the limp brown worsted gown she wore, obviously made over from one meant for a larger lady. "Perhaps they did not take at home but they all have dowries and good incomes and might be able to make good marriages out here."

Rosamunde was appalled. Here she had been feeling so sorry for herself lately and poor Molly was going to a dismal future with little hope of escape. Rosamunde at least had a husband and family who loved her and so much more besides.

Sinéad, sitting on Rosamunde's narrow bed, said, "Rosamunde, ye should be after askin' Molly to visit us in Malabad an' be seein' if you can be findin' her a handsome husband, with a bit fortune."

Molly jumped, startled by the cat's speaking. She was unused to magic and magical creatures and still looked at Sinéad as if she could not believe that a cat was talking.

"That's an excellent idea!" Rosamunde said warmly. "I shall ask your brother to let you come out to me in Malabad once you are settled in and I have set up our house."

"She will never let me come," said Molly, although she felt a sudden surge of hope. "She is a terrible snob and will not let a servant go on a visit to a lady -"

"And ye are thinkin' that a terrible snob will not be lettin' ye go on a visit to the great granddaughter of a Duke so she can be boastin' to her friends of the connections ye've been after makin"?" queried Sinéad with a sniff. "Not bloody likely!" she added.

The two young women laughed.

"I should like it very much if you could come and visit me. I shall know no one save my husband and he has already warned me that he has many duties to perform and will not be able to be with me as much as we should like, for he is a junior officer," said Rosamunde warmly. "His garrison is not that far from Meerut, where I understand there is a theatre and amateur dramatics. He has promised to take me to the bazaar in Delhi, which is a beautiful old city that dates from the Mughal Empire. Malabad is almost precisely between Meerut and Delhi."

Molly accepted the invitation, and finally began to feel as if there was something to look forward to in her new home. They exchanged addresses, promising to write until Molly could make the journey to Malabad from Calcutta

Rosamunde was so happy at the thought of a new friend and a congenial companion, for she liked Molly more and more, that she barely noticed the hot glances accorded her at dinner by Major Higby. She was far more occupied in talking to Molly.

But the familiars saw the looks he cast Rosamunde's way when he thought Alan was not looking. Sinéad's fur stood on end as she looked at that besom, as she called him to Cathal under her breath.

Alan was unfortunately occupied with Mr. Holloway, who was joined by his wife, Maude, a plain little woman with an earnest manner, given to saying "Praise the Lord!" at every opportunity. They both talked about their mission to bring the joys of Christianity to their black brethren and of the burden the white man faced in their quest to lift the veil of ignorance and corruption from the minds and souls of the natives of India.

Alan had never before come across such closed-minded, bigoted people. They also insisted on treating him as if he were in need of conversion as well.

"Being a heathen Chinee yourself you can't understand what I am talking about," said Mr. Holloway condescendingly. "Perhaps if you could find your way to God. I would l be glad to pray with you as it is my duty and help you wrest the devil from your poor pagan soul and give up this foul pollution of magic. It is like a drug to the heathen, I am told."

"Praise the Lord!" said Mrs. Holloway fervently.

"Alan is a communicant of the Anglican church!" cried Cathal.

Mr. Holloway had decided that animals could not speak, therefore he could not 'hear' anything that Cathal or Sinéad said.

Captain Jackson a large, rugged man with tanned skin, blue eyes lost in smile lines and a salt and pepper beard, put in quietly but firmly, "Mr. Stillfield is in no need of conversion, sir. Whilst you and your wife were so ill earlier in the Bay of Biscay, he read the lesson every Sunday for our little church service. He is no heathen."

"You are in need of salvation yourself, sir," returned Mr. Holloway "as you employ many of the heathen Indians on this vessel and have made no attempt to bring them into the light."

"How they worship God is their own business, sir and I will thank you to keep away from my crew, interrupting their work and making them unhappy by forcing your tracts on them and subjecting them to exhortations and sermons!" The Captain was a tolerant man but far too many of his crew, all good men, had come to him complaining that since Mr. Holloway had gained his sea legs he was interfering with their work and insulting their religion as well..

"I wish we could have flown out to India," Alan thought suddenly. The thought of living for at least another month with these people was appalling. He liked the Captain and the crew and was growing fond of Mr. Laputa, who always ate in the tiny cabin he had to himself as he felt he would not be welcome at the table, but the rest of them. Rosamunde's new friend was all right but the other girls -!

34

He had been less than thrilled to find a Clutterbuck on board.

And as for the men, he had to stay to protect Rosamunde. He had offered to fly Rosamunde from Egypt onwards as it was only then that they could. land for supplies, away from the influence of the Inquisition since France held a large part of North Africa as a colony,and a dragon could not fly the distance from England to Gibraltar for the stops were too infrequent or in unfriendly hands.

But Raymond had grown huffy and said it would be highly improper for Rosamunde to fly alone with a man who was her cousin not even by blood, and so here they were on this ship with a group of perverts, gamblers, young women on the catch for a husband and bigots.

The time would pass very slowly.

3

from cairo to calcutta

Alan remained vigilant in watching Major Higby as did the two familiars and Brendan for the balance of their Mediterranean journey. The Major could go nowhere without eyes upon him, watching his every move and making certain that he did not go anywhere near Rosamunde.

The Major chafed under this treatment and only the memory of that violet whip choking away his air prevented him from doing anything. He had no defense against a Wizard.

But it made him all the more hungry for Rosamunde. He lay awake at night, sweating, thinking about her. He had never before been thwarted in his desire for a woman. He had always been able to cajole or pay his way into the bed of any woman he wanted, whether a lady or a whore. Almost as painful was the humiliation he had endured at the hands of a much younger man, and one whom he considered a inferior half-caste at that.

He had managed to find out from Mrs. Umphelby the final destination of the luscious Mrs. DeLacey – Malabad, where her husband was a mere lieutenant. Higby was returning to his own station of Meerut, which was less than twenty miles from Malabad, an easy ride. And once he had ridden over there on some pretext or another he intended to do more riding – on Mrs. DeLacey's lovely body.

He had also found out that the *Chi chi*, her cousin, would be leaving for the north once they reached Calcutta. That could not have not worked out better.

So he bided his time and dreamed every night of having his way with the woman he was becoming obsessed with. He would prefer her willing participation in her seduction but if he had to take her by force he would do so, with no hesitation. He had to have her.

With the brisk spring winds pushing the ship they arrived at their first port of call in the Mediterranean: Crete, where the *Splendor of India* took on fresh water and foodstuffs. The stopover was so brief that there was no time for sightseeing. However, the Captain promised, once they reached Alexandria in Egypt, there would be time before they started on the next leg of the journey to see the sights and the teeming bazaars of that ancient city.

Alan took care to remain at Rosamunde's side during their tour of the bazaars, where she purchased scarabs of dubious antiquity for her young brothers and sisters. "I shall be so sad that I have to miss David's birthday in April and I have already missed the twins' birthday in February, and shall miss Sabrina's birthday in June as well," she explained when he asked her why she was buying more presents for the children as she had already mailed them some treasures from Gibraltar. The Stillfield/Delamar family made much of birthdays and Rosamunde would miss her three younger siblings very much on their special days. David would be ten this year, the twins, Eden and Ellery, eight, while the youngest, Sabrina, would be six.

Thinking of her brothers and sisters made Rosamunde once more regret that she was going to be gone from home and family for so long; at least three years. Since Raymond was in a Queen's regiment rather than in the service of the East India Company, she hoped that he could put in for a home transfer as soon as was possible. In the meantime she hoped that the children would not forget her — they were so young! If she wrote to them often and sent them interesting things from India perhaps she would stay in their minds and hearts.

After the visit to the crowded, colourful bazaar they bade farewell to Captain Jackson and the crew, collected their baggage and boarded a steam barge. The Mahmoudieh canal would carry them to Cairo.

Alan had hoped to find a 'Ladies Only' compartment for Rosamunde and the other women, who seemed to be turning to him more and more for guidance and help in the intricacies of foreign travel, even though Mrs. Umphelby had been this way before and he had not.

But the steam barge was crowded to capacity and junior members of the parties on board were given short shrift as to accommodations. They ended in making do with the floor and the few available chairs. There was no place for dragons, so Brendan flew ahead to Suez.

They were to travel slowly, mostly by night and Alan, after a day spent trying to keep Mrs. Umphelby and the other young women out of harm's way (Lavinia in particular, had a habit of darting off on her own, in spite of Mrs. Umphelby's dire warnings about white slavers) fell into a deep sleep, in spite of his resolution to watch over Rosamunde all night. He did not like it that Higby was bedded down on the floor of the main salon, just feet away from Rosamunde. The salon was far too crowded to place magical wards around her and she would notice what he was doing and demand to know why he was doing such a thing.

Higby lay awake until soft snores and deep breathing told him that most of the passengers crowded so close together were deep in the arms of Morpheus. Even Mrs. DeLacey's protector, sleeping at her feet, was slumbering.

He had made up his mind that he was going to feel her breasts. The opportunity was there and he could claim that he had moved in his sleep and it was an accident if she were to complain of him to the *Chi chi*. He still felt that she would be open to his advance. Such was his conceit that he could not imagine otherwise.

Unbeknownst to Higby, two pairs of bright little eyes were watching him with deep intensity.

Carefully, he moved over, skirting Dunstan and Goodwinter, who slept very deeply, having imbibed a considerable amount of the cheap liquor kept for tourists at the bazaar, until he was almost close enough to Rosamunde to touch her.

"The wicked spalpeen!" Sinéad said under her breath to Cathal. "He's after tryin' to get near enough to work his wicked ways wi' me Rosamunde!"

"You mean to *mate* with her? Right here? In front of all these people and Alan?" said Cathal in a horrified voice.

"Oh, he'd be likin' fine to do that " said the cat. "but even he is not bein' able to manage that here. No, 'tis my guess he's after inchin' his way over here for a bit of slap an' tickle. Human males are likin' to be starin' at an' touchin' a woman's breasts, and me Witch has a finer pair than most."

Cathal could not understand this for breasts, like a female ferret's nipples, were for suckling babies. Why a full grown male found them so enticing he could not imagine. But there were still many things about humans he did not understand, including their penchant for wanting to mate all the time, instead of waiting for a female to be in heat, as was proper. Some of the young men Alan had been at University with thought of little else. Thank goodness Alan seemed to know that there was a time and a place for that sort of thing and did not talk about females and how to get them to mate with him to the exclusion of all else.

Higby was unaware of the animals as he moved ever closer to Rosamunde. She was sleeping on her side, facing him, her lace shawl fallen away from her magnificent bosom, looking more desirable than ever. He could just imagine how it would feel to have those beauties beneath his hands, to have her long legs wrapped about him as he lay atop her. He wanted her naked when he took her, none of this missish nonsense about merely lifting her petticoats and letting down her pantalets ... in anticipation he licked his lips and reached out his hand.

But no soft fabric covered breast connected with his groping fingers. Instead his hand encountered a furry little body which shifted rapidly beneath his touch and bit him in the thumb.

He almost screamed aloud. He snatched back his hand with a muffled curse and stuck the throbbing thumb into his mouth where he tasted the metallic tang of his own blood.

"That's after bein' a lesson to ye!" said Sinéad sternly in a penetrating whisper. "I'll be protectin'' me darlin' from the likes o' ye, so I will, and since I'm bein' nocturnal, I 'll be awake all night watchin' ye, ye divil!! Bad cess to ye! Ye've a cat's curse on ye, so ye do!" With this she glared and hissed at

Higby and backed up until she was right against Rosamunde's breasts. "'Tis not even a look ye'll be gettin'!" the familiar declared. "Come near her again and I'll be after scratchin' ye up so bad that ye won't be havin' enough money to pay the lowest of Dublin whores to lay wi' ye for the sheer ugliness of yer face!"

Cathal popped up over Rosamunde's head. " And I will be protecting her as well!" the ferret promised, showing his sharp little teeth in a nasty grin. "Keep your hands and eyes to yourself, or stare at those stupid enough to want your horrid attentions!"

Higby, with muttered curses, rolled away, completely thwarted. He had little experience of talking animals who seemed to think and react as did humans and it rather rattled him. He was used to treating animals as he did the *sepoys in* his regiment, his servants or his horses – with casual cruelty.

Until this trip he had naught to do with Wizards or familiars. Everyone who lived in the Six Nations was used to seeing dragons in the sky or hippogriffes bearing their Wizard Healers about their business but Higby's acquaintance and upbringing had been virtually all non-magical. There were almost no magical people in the armed forces, save for the Augury Corps, special defense corps, and in time of war, a handful of Wizard Healers, for Wizards took an oath to do no harm, which most interpreted to mean no unnecessary killing. Higby thought it just meant that in spite of all that power they were devout cowards.

His resentment grew as he rolled away from Rosamunde, still nursing his thumb. The cat had bitten him hard and it was still bleeding.

The animals would not always be there to protect her, any more than would the *Chi chi*, he thought savagely One day she would be alone and then he would have her and she would pay for keeping Bart Higby waiting.

Just before daylight they arrived at Boulac, on the canal. The groups of travelers were shown onto crowded donkey drawn omnibuses, proceeded by running Arab urchins, holding up flaming torches, and then driven to

Shepherd's Hotel in Cairo.

The hotel was full to overflowing with people going to an returning from India. They would stay here one night and then be conveyed to Suez, where they would board a Peninsular & Oriental (P&O) steamer for India, for the trip down the Red Sea, through the Gulf of Aden and on into the Indian Ocean. Then they would steam around the bottom of the subcontinent of India, past Ceylon and onto Calcutta, on the Bay of Bengal.

Mrs. Umphelby had explained that everyone had to go through to Calcutta, even though it had seemed silly to both Alan and Rosamunde that they go all the way to the far side of India and work their way backwards, rather than landing at Bombay or Goa on the near side. That was Company policy, said Mrs. Umphelby. The headquarters of the East India Company was in Calcutta and they liked to keep track of every person who went in or out of the country. Also, one landing at Bombay had to go through some very harsh country which was not in British hands – Rajputana; while to get to Hindustan from Calcutta was a pleasant river trip.

Rosamunde and Alan were fortunate, she had added, for when she was their age, and was first gone out to India, they sailed around the Cape of Good Hope in South Africa and the passage took well over ninety days in mostly stormy conditions all down the African coast.

Beds proved impossible to get for preference was being given to older and sickly persons and army officers of high rank and their wives.. Rosamunde made light of again having to sleep upon the floor and incurred Lavinia's wrath when she would not use Chenevix's name to procure beds for her little party.

Mrs. Umphelby, who was quite familiar with Cairo, knew where there were decent, private baths for females only, and suggested that they take advantage of them whilst in the city.

Since all of the ladies had grown tired of washing piecemeal in a basin this suggestion was greeted with enthusiasm. Alan, and several ragged Arab boys begging for 'baksheesh', escorted them, as did the familiars. Higby and the subalterns had gone off to find a place to drink and gamble with other officers staying at the hotel.

Alan felt safe in letting the familiars guard Rosamunde, since at the baths there was as well a stout, terrifying looking woman who kept all men far from the baths. She sent Alan about his business, pointing out where the men's bathhouse was located, a good ways away from the women's.

Clean and refreshed, the ordeal of sleeping on the floor was not as bad as they had anticipated. The hotel provided blankets and pillows and the men and woman were strictly segregated.

Alan, Rosamunde and Molly sat out on the steps of the hotel a while before retiring, watching the dozens of donkeys and donkey boys who offered their services to travelers who wished to see some of the ancient ruins in the area. Rosamunde wished that they might have stayed long enough to go out to Giza to see the pyramids of which she had read so much. But they were to board horse drawn vans just after dawn to be taken to Suez and there board the P&O steamer *Prometheus*.

Cairo and Egypt were so different from what Rosamunde had imagined: the glare of the bright sun during the day, the dry heat, the eye aching brilliance of the blue sky and the oriental strangeness of it all – she could scarcely take it all in. Would India be like this, or even more exotic and strange? Even the dry air here was so different from the soft damp air at home in Dublin.

Her dreams that night were of home and she woke up on the verge of tears.

There was no time for crying however, for just after dawn, when eyes were scarcely open, the vans that were to take them across the desert to Suez were at the hotel.

The vans were strange little conveyances, drawn by four horses, which seemed very ill-broke as they would not stand still in harness as did the well-trained horses at home, but were moving forward and backing up constantly. The driver, a burnoose clad Arab with a gap toothed grin who was carrying a long whip, seemed to have no control over them and shrugged when Alan demanded that he hold them still so that the ladies could get in safely. Each van held six persons and Alan had secured one for himself, Rosamunde and her friend Molly and the familiars. He also asked Mr.

Laputa to join them, causing Higby to say in a loud voice "All those *Chi chis* stick together!"

With great difficulty Alan ignored Higby. Alan had a quick temper and no one had ever accused him of being overly patient. It was the entreaty in Rosamunde's eyes that kept his tongue between his teeth.

After Cathal spoke to the horses and got them to stand still they were able to board. There followed one of the most uncomfortable parts of the trip.

The Arab drove like the Jehu of legend, madly and at top speed. The horses were ill-matched as well, with punishing gaits. Alan had read about the fabled steeds of this part of the world, the Barbs, the Arabs and their fleetness and beauty, but these horses would seem to be the local bonesetters.

Even judiciously applied magic could not make the ride much more comfortable. It took some eighteen hours of mind boggling discomfort to reach Suez. There were three halts made on the way there, in rest houses or *caravanserais* that were of the roughest type, mud buildings with little furniture, serving as refreshments very strong tea or coffee and dubious looking, unidentifiable food. After each brief halt it was back onto the beaten track that served as the only road across the desert, to be jolted along at a headlong gallop. The passengers in the three vans were glad indeed to see Suez at last.

Here at Suez they lost the Holloways who were to take a side trip to the Holy Land, so that they might, as Mrs. Holloway rapturously declared "We might walk in His footsteps. Praise the Lord!"

There was a handsome Eastern style hotel in Suez, where they were to get a decent meal of roast pigeon and very tolerable accommodations.

The next morning they boarded the small P& O steamer *Prometheus*. Alan had taken the precaution of bespelling their baggage so it could be neither lost nor stolen, but the Arab baggage handlers proved more than competent and everything was where it should be.

Rosamunde again shared a cabin with Molly while Alan arranged matters so that he shared with Mr. Laputa, much to the consternation of Goodwinter who could not be brought to believe that Stillfield preferred the company of an elderly Eurasian to his own self. Not that he had enjoyed being cabin mates with Stillfield, but it looked odd, to say the least.

The cabins were quite primitive, with beds screwed to the wall as was the tiny wash stand and the valises for daily needs had to be put up overhead, but it at last seemed as if they were finally nearing their destination.

It took six days to steam down to Aden, where the Captain pointed out, legend had it, that Cain, son of Adam and Eve and murderer of his brother Abel, was buried. But Rosamunde saw the barren rocks of Aden at dawn, when they were turned to bright gold by the rising sun, above a sea that seemed to be made of pale blue mother of pearl. She could not find the tall, rocky cliffs at all a fit tomb for a murderer.

Once out in the Indian Ocean, after an short stay in Aden, where they were much troubled by rats and mosquitoes in the night, they had an uneventful voyage to Pointe de Gaulle in Ceylon.

Once again Rosamunde wished that there was more time just to stop and look. The impression she received of Ceylon was one of endless beauty: a verdant, green jewel and lovely with tree covered hills, seas of crystalline purity and white shores, decked with flowers and coconut palms swaying in the tropic breezes – it seemed as if they had reached paradise.

Their first port of call in India was a disappointment after Ceylon. Madras was flat and uninteresting, a land of white houses on an endless white shore. The seas were running very heavy and it had been only with difficulty that they landed even near to the city for several of the passengers had Madras as their destination. The *Prometheus* anchored off the coast and natives in small boats and catamarans came alongside to take off those of the passengers and their luggage who were leaving the ship here.

Mrs. Umphelby insisted that the ladies all stay below while this took place as most of the men plying the boats were almost in a state of nature - they wore but a skimpy loin cloth. No decent Christian woman could look at such a sight without fainting. Mabel Clutterbuck tried to sneak up on deck and see, she had an endless curiosity as to what a naked man looked like. She had never been able to spy on her brothers, try as she might. But Mrs. Umphelby caught her before she got out the cabin door and gave her a shocked lecture on impropriety and how she would never catch a husband if she behaved in such a loose, immoral way.

As they approached Calcutta Rosamunde found that she was uncomfortably hot (it was not just the warm, moist air) and a strange feeling was growing at the pit of her stomach. She suddenly realized that this was it; she was going to be all alone with only her familiar which seemed a particularly apt term for the little cat at the moment. Alan was going north and Brendan, who had been flying over head while they steamed through the Indian Ocean and sometimes floating beside the ship, was going to Tibet. When would she see them again?

It no longer seemed so desirable to get away from Alan. He was all that was left to her and Sinéad of home. And her familiar would miss Cathal as well. The two had been friends for years and it was not the same as when Alan was in the Cotswolds, for it was a short flight over the Irish channel and there were frequent trips home or visits at Lyohshall, or lengthy scryed conversations and letters.

And suddenly she wanted very badly to go home.

4

calcutta at last

Rosamunde dressed with extreme care for disembarking at Calcutta. She put on one of her new gowns, especially made for the climate of India. It was of white muslin, trimmed in cornflower blue braided piping on the tiered skirt, three bands on each of the four tiers and about the high neckline. The fashion was for tucks and buttons and insets on the tight fitting bodice but Rosamunde always had her bodices made loose without ornamentation that otherwise might call attention to her bosom. The waist, again contrary to fashion's dictates, was not made tight down to the skirt but fitted in a relaxed manner. The pagoda sleeves were three quarter length and filled down to the wrist with insets called *engageante,* made of a delicate lace. With this ensemble she wore a wide brimmed hat trimmed with blue cornflowers, a necessity to protect fragile complexions from India's harsh sun, and carried a blue ribbon trimmed parasol. And of course, a lace shawl went over everything.

Molly had helped her into the crinoline, a relatively small one – they seemed to be becoming more enormous every year – sighing with envy when she saw that Rosamunde had one of the new light wire Thompson cage crinolines, rather than the hot and bulky contraption of horsehair pads and whalebone, weighed down by a multitude of petticoats that she had to endure.

Dressed and ready, with Sinéad on Rosamunde's shoulder, the two young women went up on deck to find Alan, Cathal and Mr. Laputa watching as the anchor was being dropped.

"But we're still out at sea!" Rosamunde said in dismay

"This is the Sandheads," said Mr. Laputa in his soft voice. "It is necessary that we wait here for the tide to turn and to take on a pilot, for the quicksands at the mouth of the Hooghly river and indeed, the length of the river are most treacherous. Many ships have been sunk there."

"Quicksand?" Molly repeated faintly.

Mr. Laputa pointed ahead. "Somewhere over there lies the most dangerous of the sandbanks," he said. "It is called the James and Mary named for a ship that struck the sandbar many, many years ago. Because of the quicksands the passengers do not escape – rescue is always unsuccessful. The sandbanks shift all of the time and it is very difficult navigation. I myself saw a most terrible wreck here – much loss of life!"

A green draconic head thrust itself up over the rail and Brendan said cheerfully "Hello!"

Molly gave a little scream and scrambled backwards away from the rail. She was unused to dragons and found the little she had seen of Brendan rather frightening.

Mr. Laputa too, was unused to dragons but he stood his ground, taking his cue from Alan and Rosamunde who moved closer to talk to Brendan.

"I've been up scouting around," the dragon announced "and I saw Ravi and Raymond waiting on the landing up the river in Calcutta. It seems to be a beautiful place, there are lots and lots of trees and flowers! I didn't see any other dragons, though."

"You will not be finding others such as yourself in Hindustan," Mr. Laputa offered timidly, unsure as how to talk to this gigantic creature who looked as if he could snap up a man in one gulp. "Such creatures have long been gone from the land."

"Then who carries the post?" Brendan wanted to know.

"The *dâk-ghari,*" answered Mr. Laputa and explained that this was a horse drawn vehicle, a high, four wheeled cart that sometimes carried a very limited amount of passengers as well.

"Well, that seems very inefficient to me,' said Brendan frankly, splashing a little as he floated in the warm water. "Dragons are much faster than a horse cart!" His head swiveled around suddenly. "Look! A boat is coming down the river, and the tide is turning, I can feel the current changing! If I had my saddle I could just fly you all to the landing place! And we would not have to wait so long," he added wistfully. But his harness was packed away in the hold. He would never

47

dream of carrying passengers without a saddle and a safety harness.

The boat, with some difficulty, made it through the brownish river water and came alongside the *Prometheus*. This proved to be the pilot, and he carried letters for some of the passengers, notably Major Higby.

Calcutta lay not on the shore but some ninety-six miles up the Hooghly on the eastern bank of that river. The Hooghly was a main tributary of the sacred river, the Ganges, on which they would travel to Allahabad, and from there they would journey on the Grand Trunk Road in horse drawn *gharis* while a transport company carried their luggage to Malabad and points beyond. Alan and Brendan, however, would take to the air once they reached Calcutta and met Ravi.

The voyage up the Hooghly to Calcutta took an entire day – it was nearly evening before they were docking at the quay.

Rosamunde had spent most of the day on deck, watching as they glided past bamboo thickets, thatched huts, with groves of mangoes, tamarind trees and custard apple, and many temples set in a low land that appeared uniformly brown in colour. The river too was brown and was broad, and more than once Rosamunde saw native crocodiles with their blunt noses that Mr. Laputa informed her were called *muggers*. They, he solemnly informed her, would eat a man as easily as a fish or an animal that strayed in to the water incautiously. They had cousins, long nosed *garrials*, who ate fish.

She was not certain that she liked the land, as it was so different from home and already she was feeling the oppressive heat and humidity of the low-lying, swampy country. It was well known that Calcutta was located in an area not considered healthy for Europeans.

But there were flowers in abundance, the foliage was rich and green and there were brightly coloured birds flying amongst the trees.

It was still light when the *Prometheus* at last docked,

which was actually an anchorage, small boats came out in abundance to greet the steamer and bear the passengers back to shore.

Rosamunde had already noticed that here in the tropics the sun rose and fell abruptly, as if someone had just lit or blown out the candle of the sun. It was rather disconcerting to one used to the lingering twilights of northern climes. Rosamunde had always loved twilight, the mysterious, softly darkening at evening and growing light in the morning. Missing that was just one of the many adjustments she was going to have to make.

Alan, too, had dressed for the heat in a white linen suit and a broad brimmed planter's hat. He had been keenly interested in all they had seen from the deck and had asked Mr. Laputa many questions. Brendan had at times floated beside the steamer for he had no worry about being attacked by *muggers*, and at other times taking to the sky, circling back to join them again. He was eager to get to Calcutta and be saddled, so that he and Alan could explore. He missed his friend and rider, it was a long time since they had flown together, for Brendan, always worried about his rider's safety, would not let Alan go up without the saddle and safety harness which due to its size, had been stored in the hold of each ship they had sailed on.

The two familiars ran back and forth from rail to rail, gazing in wonder at the passing scenery.

To Rosamunde's surprise, most of the Fishing Fleet stayed below in their hot cabins. At least up on deck there was a breeze created by the steamer churning through the water and Rosamunde could not understand why the other women did not want to see the land that was going to be their new home. Only Molly stayed on deck with her and Alan and Mr. Laputa. Even the subalterns and the Major stayed below, playing cards. "You wouldn't think that Higby had left them any money to still bet with," Alan remarked sarcastically. .

Once the P&O steamer had anchored off Calcutta and the boats began to arrive, all of the passengers finally came up on deck. The Fishing Fleet looked hot and cross, Lavinia remarking that it was time and past that they finally arrived and she only hoped that her cousins from Cawnpore, where she was going to be living, were there to meet her as they had promised. The Fishing Fleet was to be widely scattered – Lavinia to Cawnpore , Mabel to Delhi, where she was to live with an aunt, Susan to Meerut to stay with her father, Molly to stay in Calcutta, while Mrs. Umphelby was going to Mardan, up near the Khyber Pass, where her husband served in the Corps of Guides. And Rosamunde, of course, to Malabad. It was not inconceivable that she might meet both Mabel and Susan again as Malabad lay between Meerut and Delhi.

On one of the first boats out to the steamer was a tall figure clad in Indian dress, the tight-fitting, three quarter length collarless *achkan* coat over jodhpurs and worn with a turban. All were of silk brocade of a dazzling whiteness.

Alan shouted "Ravi!" and bent over the rail, waving at his friend. Ravi looked up and a wide grin split his face. His brown face was keen and handsome, with hawk-like features. He had broad shoulders and a fit, lean body. Rosamunde heard Mabel Clutterbuck, who was standing a short distance away, catch her breath as Ravi swung up a rope ladder to the deck where he and Alan fell into one another's arms.

"My brother," said Ravi in Hindustanee. "you have come at last!" He held Alan out at arm's length. " But what is this, you are pale and look worn, but we shall soon cure that!." he said joyfully.

A older, bearded man in a turban and dressed much as Ravi was, but in less fine fabrics, came up to them and bowed. "Shall I collect the *sahib's* things, *Hazrat?*"

"*Hazrat?*" Alan queried. looking at Ravi in surprise. "Highness?"

Ravi suddenly looked apologetic. "Well, yes," he admitted. "I'm afraid I *am* a Prince, Alan. I am the *Yuraraj,* heir to the throne of my father, the Maharajah of Ranijhat. I meant to tell you in a less public fashion but Ram Dass has let the cat out of the bag, as you say in *Belait.*" He looked affectionately at the older man who bowed low, hiding a smile on his dark features.

"But at Oxford – " Alan began.

"It was by my father's wish and command that I attended University as an ordinary undergraduate. He wished me to form true friendships and not be subject to the flattery and fawning that so often accompanies rank. He also thought that it would do me good to live as an ordinary person," he added ruefully.

Rosamunde, who had been leaning over the rail watching for Raymond, turned at the sound of his voice and said happily, "Ravi!" and ran forward to throw he arms around Alan's friend. Alan had brought Ravi home on the Long Vacations, as it was too far for him to return to India between terms. Rosamunde had grown to know and be fond of Ravi, as had the entire family.

There was a shocked gasp from Mrs. Umphelby as she saw Mrs. DeLacey embracing a native, even one so gorgeously clad, obviously of high rank.

Another voice was raised in shock as well. "Rosamunde!"

Unnoticed by Rosamunde as she ran towards Ravi, Raymond had scaled the ladder and was on board just in time to see his wife embrace a strange native as if they were on intimate terms.

Rosamunde turned when she heard his voice, but did not take her arms from around Ravi's neck. "Oh, Raymond!" she said happily. "It's Ravi, Alan's friend from Oxford! I told you about him."

Ravi took in the situation at a glance. He all too well understood the look on Raymond's face. He gently took Rosamunde's arms from about his neck and said: "Go to your husband, *Chota Moti* . It is not fitting that you greet me thus and ignore him."

Rosamunde obeyed and ran lightly up to Raymond and offered him her cheek. He was not a demonstrative man in public and would not wish to be extravagantly greeted with hugs and kisses as was the way in her family.

He was a good looking young man of nearly thirty, with sandy hair and bright blue eyes, but only slightly taller than Rosamunde. He wore a thick, sand-coloured mustache and a pair of military side whiskers. He made a dashing appearance in the light blue, gold-trimmed uniform of a Queen's Regiment of Cavalry, with a sword at his side and a neat white pith helmet.

He returned Rosamunde's embrace somewhat stiffly and said "What did he call you?"

"*Chota Moti* – Little Pearl," she explained. "He began

51

calling me that when first we met because of the colour of my hair. He thought that it shimmered like a pearl."

"It does not do to be over-familiar with natives, Rosamunde," Raymond said. "As the wife of an officer –"

"But I have known Ravi since I was a little girl!" she protested. "He roomed with Alan at Oxford and came home with him for the Long Vacation and even for Christmas!" She was honestly puzzled by Raymond's attitude, in her family there was no prejudice towards those of other races and cultures.

"We will speak more of this later," he said dampeningly and then drew her away from the chattering groups that were forming on the deck as more boats arrived and people began to disembark with friends and relatives.

"Rosamunde – did you tell anyone?" he asked urgently as soon as they had a modicum of privacy.

She looked at him in surprise. "No, Raymond, I gave you my word that I would not. I have not even told Sinéad and she is my familiar."

"Sinéad!" he exclaimed. "I had hoped that you would leave that cat behind!"

Rosamunde looked at him in surprise. "But why would I do that? She is my familiar, and my best friend, she goes where I go."

He bit his lip and turned away for a moment. "Are you certain that you did not mention – it – to any one, not even your mother or father? I should hate for your father to know –" He was rather afraid of Rosamunde's father, if truth be told.

"I gave you my word that I would tell no one," said Rosamunde, her temper stirring "and I did not. And if Papa were to know, he might be of some help, bring a doctor – "

"NO!" Raymond almost shouted. "No one must ever know, do you hear me?"

She stared at him in shocked surprise. "I gave you my word," she said again quietly, feeling as if he had slapped her.

"Females chatter so –" he said distractedly and taking off his helmet, ran a hand through his hair.

Rosamunde was about reply hotly to this when Alan joined them, causing the words to die on her lips.

"Hello, DeLacey," he said offhandedly to Raymond.

52

"Listen, I've just learned that the boat up the river takes a month, and then there is an uncomfortable trip in the *dâk gharis* for another longish time, over 400 miles. Why don't you both come with me dragon-back? We can be in Malabad in less than two days and Brendan can easily transport all of the household goods that Rosamunde brought with her as well. I've consulted a map and it is not that far out of my way up to Ranijhat."

"We could not take advantage," Raymond began.

"Don't be foolish, you're family! We've a six person saddle and fold out panniers and the breast harness as well," said Alan. "Think of the money you will save!"

It was this last that persuaded Raymond. His own private income was small, for he lived mainly on his army pay, which was by no means munificent. To do him justice, he had never thought of money when falling in love with and being fortunate enough to win Rosamunde's hand. He had been appalled when he found out the full extent of the incredible amount of her money – people would think he was a fortune hunter! So he had determined for his own scruples, to pay their living expenses with his money and let her use hers for the fripperies women loved so much and to be spent on their eventual children.

He had been worried about how he was to pay the transport costs as well as for the boat trip and then the *gharis*. He supposed that she had brought out trunks and valises full of fashionable clothing; most women did, as well as linens and china and silverware and other household goods to make everything look as much like home as was possible. There might even be furniture!

He accepted Alan's offer, but without enthusiasm and was even less pleased when he found that Ravi and Ram Dass were to be of the party, and the two familiars as well.

the road to malabad

When Alan first stepped out of the boat that carried them to the landing place he had a discomfiting sense of vertigo. His senses swam and his legs wobbled.

Ravi grabbed his arm and steadied him. "It is often thus," he said sympathetically, "when one has been on the water for a long while. I myself took two days to become used to the feeling of the land beneath my feet when first I returned from *Belait.*"

Neither Rosamunde or Molly, Alan noticed, seemed affected by this circumstance. But neither of them had been as ill as he had been earlier in the year. He supposed that Ravi was correct, and he just had to get his 'land legs' again. He was convinced once he could fly again he would feel a great deal better. The fresh air up above was always bracing

Before they had left the ship they had said farewell to the balance of the passengers, with many insincere promises to keep in touch on the part of the Fishing Fleet, and Rosamunde had met Molly's relatives, Mr and Mrs. Theodore Fraser.

Mrs. Fraser – Eudoxia – Molly's sister-in-law, proved to be as great a snob as Molly had feared, but she was as eager to let the unworthy Molly visit the great granddaughter of a Duke, as Sinéad had predicted. The visit would take place in early May, before the full heat of the summer, not really that far off.

Raymond was not best pleased that Rosamunde had invited a drab little nonentity whose relatives were in Trade to visit her, but although he grumbled, he did not become the autocratic husband over his wife, she was still a bride and must be indulged. He was also not happy that Rosamunde bade an affectionate farewell to their *munshi* or teacher, Mr. Laputa. Rosamunde had to learn, in his opinion, that one did not mix with people of that sort – one kept to one's own kind. But there were, he reflected, many ladies at Malabad Station, who would soon teach her how to go on properly.

They spent one night in Calcutta in extremely crowded conditions where Raymond ended in sharing a room with several other officers, while Rosamunde was asked to serve as a chaperone for several unmarried young ladies in another room.

Raymond was even less pleased the next morning when Rosamunde came down for breakfast in what he considered a completely indecent costume. It was of pale green linen and consisted of a loose fitting jacket over a white blouse made high to the neck. But the skirt was only mid-calf length, over high boots and when she moved, Raymond could see that the skirt was split. And there was no hoop, he could see the outline of her hips and *derrière*.

He had been seated at the table with Alan since Ravi had breakfasted early and gone to conduct some business in the city, and as Rosamunde approached the table Raymond noticed that other men, fellow officers, in the large, table-filled room cast admiring glances at her. Inwardly, he seethed.

He carefully folded his serviette and stood up. "Go above stairs at once and change out of that disgraceful rig out! People are staring at your limbs!" he said in a tight, low voice.

"Have ye never been after seein' a flyin' suit?" said Sinéad caustically. She rode on Rosamunde's shoulder as usual. Cathal sat on the table beside Alan's plate, sharing his breakfast.

Ignoring the little cat, Raymond continued "It is indecent to appear in public in such an outfit – or should I say such a *lack* of one?"

Rosamunde looked at him, completely baffled. "But how else am I to ride a dragon?" she inquired reasonably "There is no sidesaddle and I cannot ride dragon-back in a crinoline! Even my grandmother wears a flying suit like this one when she travels dragon-back!"

"Oh, for God's sake, DeLacey," said Alan in irritation. "You're acting as if she was naked! She's decently covered and, as she says, both our mothers and grandmother wear the exact same thing to fly! I hope that you are not going to tell me that our grandmother, the Marchioness of Keir, goes around in an indecent fashion!"

Raymond flushed and bit his lip. He had agreed to the dragon transport and in truth, talking to one of the officers the night before had pointed out to him that he would have been woefully short as to funds to get himself, Rosamunde and baggage to Malabad on his own.

So he subsided, with ill grace, but decided that he would make certain that the offensive garment would disappear from her wardrobe once they reached Malabad.

Brendan had flown relatively fast, rather disconcerting both Raymond and Ram Dass, the latter had never been on a dragon or even seen one before and Raymond had only been taken to Dragon Days (where children were introduce to the Post dragons and everyone had a wonderful time) as a child where he had flown low to the ground, slowly, on a small Welsh red dragon.

It was not quite eight hundred miles to Malabad from Calcutta and had Brendan flown at his top speed, they could have made it in about eight hours. But he was carrying a good deal of luggage as well as five passengers and Alan judged it better to do the trip in two stages, spending one night on the road.

The sight of Brendan in the air and during their necessary landings created much consternation amongst the natives, who ran, screaming, at the sight of him, snatching up their children and domestic animals as if he were about to swallow them whole. This saddened Brendan, for he was a friendly creature and had hoped to talk with some of the inhabitants and perhaps even give rides to children.

They stayed that night at a rest house, or *dâk* bungalow, which was a square-built house with a thatched roof. A verandah ran all around the outside.

Inside there were only four rooms, with a bathing room, the *ghosulhana*, attached to each and the most minimal of furniture; a table set in the center of the room, a bed, and two or three rickety chairs. No bedding was provided, it was expected that the traveler provide his own.

Rosamunde, whose trunks only numbered three, had taken the advice of an Anglo Indian lady whose husband had retired to Dublin and was in her Grandmother's charity Sewing Circle.

She had packed thin but comfortable mattresses that could be easily folded, with fluffy pillows. These were packed in the very top of one trunk, easily found and put on the beds, with the light linen sheets and blankets she had purchased as well. There were lengths of mosquito netting also, an absolute necessity if one were to get any sleep at all.

Raymond was amazed by how little Rosamunde had brought out with her. One trunk, the smallest one, contained her clothing and the other two were travel linens, books, her small harp, or *telyn* and the crystals and such she needed for her Witchcraft. She had left the bulk of their wedding presents, fine china, crystal and silver, behind, for when they had a permanent home in Dublin or somewhere in the British Isles. She fully intended to furnish their home in Malabad with locally made furniture and goods and have more gowns made up by a native seamstress. This was so contrary to what Raymond expected that he was almost stunned. Most *Memsahibs* brought a good part of home with them, including cuttings from English gardens, most of which died in the climate of India.

The food at the *dâk* bungalow presented no great choice, as the *khansamah*, or cook, informed then when he came out to ask the *husoors* (sirs) and the *mem sahib* what they fancied for their dinner. Since pork was forbidden to Muslims and Hindus could not eat beef, the menu consisted entirely of chicken-cutlets, curried, roasted and grilled, but it was prepared in a very short time and was served piping hot and proved delicious. There was no bread as they were used to at home, but there were fresh *chuppaties*, the flat unleavened bread of India that was made of coarse flour.

Rosamunde determined to try the curry, and she liked it at once, in spite of Raymond's warning that it was very spicy and really unsuited to a lady's palate.

Alan laughed when Raymond said this. "We have an international table at home," he said "We eat French, Irish, Russian and Chinese foods as well as British." He exchanged a glance of amusement with Ravi, who had been at the Stillfield or Delamar tables too often to not know this.

Ran Dass had refused to sit and eat with them, it was

not his place to do so, and Raymond had been surprised that Ravi would break caste by eating with non-Hindus.

"That is because I am not a Hindu," Ravi said. "I am a Musslman – a Muslim. My ancestors were Mughals who came here from Persia almost four hundred years ago in the train of Babur, the first Mughal conqueror, in the 13th century as you reckon it in *Belait.* My ancestor married the only surviving child, a daughter of the Maharajah of Ranijhat and took on his rank. However, like Babur's descendants and others of my race, we have intermarried with Hindus – my mother is a Rajput *Rajkumari,* a princess. So I have a foot in both worlds. And I have spent much time in England, taking my degree at Oxford and visiting my brother," he added, with a smile at Alan.

Raymond was somewhat taken aback for Ravi spoke pure Oxonian English, without the sing song inflection Raymond was used to in those he thought of as 'natives'. Indeed Ravi spoke better English than Raymond did Hindustanee. Raymond had passed the language examinations required of all the officers who wanted service in India but he had never learned to speak it idiomatically or with ease. He was rather chagrined when both Rosamunde and her cousin and those damned animals, proved to be far more fluent than was he!

After a dessert of ripe mangoes which were small and delicious and very juicy, they adjourned to the verandah to catch a cooling breeze before retiring.

Dusk had fallen and the moon had risen while they were inside eating. The moon was pouring a strong, pure light over the scene. The *dâk* bungalow stood by the side of the road. A *mango-tope,* or grove, lay near the bungalow and when they had arrived that afternoon Rosamunde had been delighted to see monkeys swinging and chattering in the branches.

Sinéad had not been as thrilled with the monkeys. They had called out abuse to her and she had called them *burchas*-ruffians and *bhainchute,* an insulting epithet that meant 'sister violators' and made Ravi break into laughter to see the little cat, fur all on end, hurl pejoratives remarks in the vernacular at the monkeys. The monkeys also asked Cathal what sort of mongoose was he?

The other aspects visible in the bright moonlight were a tangle of jungle, just beyond a compound wall that appeared to be doing a poor job of holding the lush vegetation back, for vines and leaves threatened to breach the wall everywhere. The jungle was dark and full of noise. Rosamunde could hear jackals howling and something roaring – was it a tiger? They were eerie, rather frightening sounds, and not too far off. Pariah dogs were adding to the noise by barking incessantly. Night birds called as well.

There were also open fields nearby under cultivation with sugar cane, the bungalow servant informed Rosamunde when she inquired.

And all around, people were edging closer to the clearing where the bungalow stood, to peer at the dragon. Brendan had made himself comfortable and lay quietly near the bungalow. Alan had procured a roasted goat for his supper and he had eaten this in the usual neat fashion of British dragons, digging a pit for the leftover bones. Usually a dragon would crunch the bones up for the good marrow and the calcium so necessary to draconic health, but would not eat the skull or the hooves.

But even Brendan's friendliest looks could not tempt the people from their safe places of observation.

Both Rosamunde and Alan had many questions to ask. Rosamunde turned naturally to Raymond, for he had been out here since he first joined the service, almost seven years now, but she was surprised at how much he did not know. Ravi was more help, but this area was not his homeland. That was in the foothills of the Himalayas, a far different landscape than this.

It was nearly ten before all retired to bed. Raymond told Rosamunde to go ahead and get ready while he smoked a *cheroot* out on the verandah. She did not care for the habit of smoking as she disliked the smell, but she went in to the tiny room with Sinéad and swiftly undressed and put on a cotton nightgown, long-sleeved and high to the neck. The night was sultry and only a sheet, if that, would be needed for sleeping. The servant had made up the bed and hung the mosquito netting over head.

"Ravi was after tellin' me that 'twill be even hotter in May until the monsoon is comin' in June. 'Tis said that the rain comes down in a solid wall, imagine that! Soaked in a minute I'll be!" said Sinéad in wonder.

A knock came on the door and Raymond entered. Rosamunde had already climbed into bed and sat up against the pillows.

Her incredible hair fell all around her shoulders and Raymond, looking at her, gulped audibly. "Rosamunde," he began hoarsely, and then spied Sinéad, sitting on the edge of the bed, washing.

"That cat is not going to stay in here!" he exclaimed.

'That cat' looked up. "No. "Tis sleepin' wi' me friends Brendan an' Cathal I'll be," she said. "But if ye're after plannin' what I am thinkin' ye are, ye'd best be thinkin' again - these walls are after bein' as thin as paper an' Alan an' Ravi are bein' right next to ye."

Raymond flushed. He hated the candid remarks the cat made and did not find her at all amusing as everyone else seemed to do. And why did she not try to at least speak the Queen's English instead of being so *Irish*? Better yet, learn to confine her speech to 'meow'.

"Sinéad!" said Rosamunde in reproach. *"Dún do bheal! Ná bac leis!"*

That was another thing that Raymond disliked; the two of them often spoke Gaelic to one another and he had no idea what they were talking about. It made him feel as if he were an unwanted third wheel.

With great dignity, and tail held high, Sinéad quit the room.

Outside, as the night deepened and stars burst into brilliancy in the deep velvet of the sky, Ravi and Alan stood near the dragon. Brendan's head was on Alan's shoulder as his friend scratched the sensitive eye ridges. Brendan sighed in bliss and closed his eyes.

Ravi was glad at last to be alone with Alan. "Rosamunde's husband is a *pukka,* a proper, *sahib,*" he said tentatively. "Do you know him well, my brother?"

"Not at all. We were all surprised when she accepted him. She must love him though, why else would she marry him? I own, I wish she had married another Wizard and stayed in Dublin. Aunt Julia and Uncle Stuart were more than a little upset that she would be going to live so far away – the whole family is. I thought Grandfather Chenevix would have an apoplexy!" Alan answered.

When Ravi made no comment but stared at the dusty ground, a frown knitting his brow, Alan said abruptly "What is it?" for this was not like his friend.

"It is not perhaps the best time for her to be coming out here," Ravi answered slowly. "There is something on the wind, Alan, something that frightens me. There is a prophecy, you know, that John Company shall only rule for one hundred years and it is one hundred years this very year since Robert Clive retook Calcutta and defeated Siraj-ud Daula at Plassey. In the hill country we have little of this disaffection; however, as I traveled to Calcutta I heard things. The Company anne-xation of Oudh has been much resented, as has the coming of all of these missionaries. Many are afraid that the British mean to forcibly convert us to Christianity."

"Mr. Laputa was telling me something of this," Alan said slowly, beginning to scratch behind Brendan's ears. "I have no liking for missionaries. I cannot discern why they feel that *they* have the right idea and everyone else is wrong. Surely there are many paths to God! Mr. Laputa also said that in the old days the relationships between the people and the *sahibs* was far warmer, that there was intermarriage and many *sahibs* who appreciated the culture and heritage of this country, not to despise it as so many seem to now."

"I fear that Rosamunde's husband is such a one. To him I am a 'dirty nigger'," Ravi added rather bitterly. "I could read his face as if it were an open book, Alan. He was horrified that Rosamunde hugged me in front of all the *sahibs* and *mem-sahibs* on the steamer. Not *pukka* behavior!"

"Rosamunde and I do not feel that way!" Alan said hotly. "You are our friend, my brother,Ravi, why, you're practically a member of the family!"

"We don't feel that way either, the familiars and I!" said Brendan, disturbing Cathal, who had been slumbering between the dragons' front legs. "If you ask me, the British have no right to tell the Indian people what to do and how to do it. They should mind their own business. How would they like it if the Indians were to come to the Six Nations and insist that everything be done their way ?"

"I wish that you had been Governor General of India, Brendan, rather than Lord Dalhousie," said Ravi, with a short laugh. "There would be no unrest at all." A new Governor general, Lord Canning, had recently arrived

"If I were, I should never have annexed Oudh! That was wrong, to depose the Nawab merely because the British Resident at Lucknow considered him debauched. And the Doctrine of Lapse is an ill advised policy," said the dragon darkly.

Ravi and Alan looked at him in surprise. "The Doctrine of Lapse?" Alan queried blankly.

Brendan looked at him reproachfully. "Did you read none of the books I recommended, Alan, that I took from the Collegium library out at Tara? I began reading everything that I could find on India once I knew that we were coming here and those on Tibet as well. The Doctrine of Lapse is a policy of the East India Company that allows the company to annex a state and put it under company governance if there is no legitimate heir. The company has decided that an adopted son may not inherit – only blood descendants. This has allowed the company to take over even more hapless states. And in the case of Oudh, since many of the *sepoys* and *sowars* in the Indian army are from Oudh, they feel as if their homeland has been stolen from them. This can only lead to disaffection!"

"You know more than many of the people in the government, Brendan," said Ravi in admiration. "Perhaps dragons should stand for Parliament!"

"I could do much better than some of the idiots in the government," said Brendan.

In the bedroom of the *dâk* bungalow, Raymond, after having undressed behind a handy screen and put on a loose cotton nightshirt, had climbed into bed beside Rosamunde, pulling down the mosquito netting over the bed as he did so.

He lay down well away from her and said stiffly "I had not intended to do what that cat suggested. I know well that there is too little privacy in a place such as this. We shall go on better in our own home. I am confident that there will be no problem at that time."

"I'm certain that you are right," Rosamunde agreed. She was quite happy that he had made no advances to her as she was quite out of charity with him at the moment. To make such a fuss over everything from her flying suit to the warmth with which she spoke to Ravi –! He was so conventional at times, so hidebound and so just *silly*. She would work hard to show him how ridiculous some of his ideas were and she hoped that once they were in their own home things would be better.

But she could not help but wonder if she had been sharing a bed with Alan, would they now be laying apart like this? Even if circumstances were the same and they had not enough privacy, surely Alan would at least hold her? She and Raymond had been separated since October; surely he wanted to kiss and caress and hold her, even if there was the Trouble between them? She sighed and turning over on her right side, away from him, chided herself for her disloyalty. Raymond had made it clear to her that he would welcome no advances from her – no lady behaved so.

Raymond lay flat on his back, listening to her quiet breathing as she fell into sleep. He wanted her so much, but it was never any good. He did not have this problem with whores, for his only experience had been with women he had to pay. He had even gone to a *bibi gurh*, or women's house, a term usually used by the officers for a brothel, once he had come back out to his station and he had no problems with the bints there.

It was only with Rosamunde that there was any difficulty. She was so damned beautiful, and a lady to boot. And she possessed an independence of thought and action that he was coming to deplore. He did not expect her to enjoy sexual relations, he would be shocked if she did, as a good woman was supposed to lay quietly and do her marital duty whilst thinking of the sons she was to breed for England. It would be enough if *he* were to enjoy it and what man would not enjoy possessing a woman of her beauty? One married to have a mistress for one's home and a mother for one's children, not for a bed partner that would be eager and willing – that was what whores were for. And they were eager and willing only because one paid them to be so.

Tomorrow he would make it clear to her that she had to be more ladylike and bow to his superior knowledge and his will. She was a trifle spoilt, having been raised with too much money and too much freedom and was too inclined to go her own way. And he much deplored the influence of her cousin. Stillfield was entirely too free and easy in his speech. Imagine saying 'naked' in front of a lady as he had that morning!

Stillfield would be leaving for the north the day after tomorrow, ending his malign influence, and Raymond would be certain to put Rosamunde in the hands of his Colonel's wife, who had already indicated a willingness to guide the dear little creature, as everything would be so new and strange to her. Mrs. Dalbeigh would soon have Rosamunde thinking the right way and doing the right things. And when she was more obedient and compliant he could finally make her his. He would be the envy of all the offices at Malabad to have such a wife.

With this comforting thought Raymond turned over, back to Rosamunde, and went to sleep.

6

there's no place like home

On the other side of the world from India it was raining in Dublin, Ireland. It had been raining most of the day; a cold, raw rain that seemed more like winter than early April. It was a good evening to be indoors in front of a peat fire that sent a smoky aroma into the room where Julia Delamar sat at the fireside, doing the homely task of mending children's stockings under a working mage light. On the hearth two cats snoozed; Julia's familiar Aithne and Stuart's Dr. Foster.

"I cannot fathom what those children do to their stockings!" Julia said. "Even Eden wears hers through at a fantastic rate, and you would think that being a girl she would be more careful of her things than Ellery is of his."

"Ummm," said her husband from his seat at a desk opposite the fireplace. His pen moved rapidly over a sheet of paper. The large desk top of shining cherry, was lit by a green shaded mage light and held many stacks of papers.

Julia allowed her hands to fall to her lap, the darning egg and the stocking sliding from her fingers. She let out a long sigh.

This attracted Stuart's attention and he said "What is it, Julia? That's an unhappy sigh if ever I heard one."

Julia moved restlessly in the comfortable chair. "I was just wondering where Rosamunde was and what she is doing. Do you think that she has reached Malabad yet?"

"I doubt it," Stuart answered and put down his pen, and removed the wire-rimmed spectacles he had begun to wear recently. As both Chief Forensic Wizard for the Dublin Police and a Wizard Healer who ran a free clinic for the poor three evenings a week, paperwork was the bane of his existence. He rubbed at his violet eyes, inherited by his daughter Rosamunde, in a tired fashion.

"I wish that she had married Peter Huggin or one of the other young Wizards who courted her!" Julia burst out.

"Then she would be living right here in Dublin and not so far away." Her eyes filled with tears. "I miss her, Stuart! She may not be the daughter of my body, but she is the daughter of my heart. I miss her every day! We were such good friends, as well as mother and daughter. I miss her at the clinic too. She was so good with the children and the very young mothers."

"That's the nature of things, Julia," Stuart said gently. "The young ones grow up and leave home and they sometimes end up far, far away from us. I don't like it any more than you do but whom to marry was her choice, not ours. I must admit, I wish that she had married a Wizard, rather than a non-magical person. I think that is going to be a conflict for them. From what I have seen of Raymond I do not think that he has much of an opinion of mages."

"I only wish that I could be certain that she was happy!" Julia said. "When they came back from their honeymoon she did not look, well, *satisfied*. And we did our best to prepare her. She knew all of the facts of the marriage bed and I stressed to her, as I know your mother and Tatya did as well how glorious and wonderful a union can be and how a woman can enjoy intimate relations just as much as a man."

"Raymond was not pleased the day I took him to luncheon at the Wizard's Club and explained to him our customs about the maidenhead," said Stuart on a sigh. "I think that he thought I was trying to tell him that she had been with another man and I was making up the story to cover her shame."

Among Wizards and Witches it was the accepted tradition for a young woman on the verge of marriage or contemplating a sexual relationship, to go to a Wizard Healer who specialized in such things, to have the hymen destroyed in order to make the wedding night or first time easier and less painful and have that first time be a good memory for a young Witch.

"Non-magicals are so stupid about that, Stuart!" Julia declared. "Our way makes far more sense. I have heard some horror stories at the Sewing Circle. We have quite a few non-magical members now and it is amazing the intimate things that are discussed in a group of women! The non-magical women seem almost *proud* that they suffered on their wedding night rather than enjoying intercourse from the beginning, although from what I hear most of them *never* enjoy it! And they are so mealy-mouthed! They are shocked so easily, and many of them refer to sexual relations as *IT* and even whisper the word *IT* as if it were shameful! Poor things, I feel sorry for them!"

"Raymond was not happy when I insisted on the contraceptive spell for Rosamunde," Stuart continued.

"Do you really think it was completely necessary?" Julia put her needle into the sock neatly.

"After her hymen was removed, Sir Harry Winston called on me and confided what he had found out in his examination," Stuart said. "he confirmed what I had suspected."

Julia remembered that procedure and examination very well. She had accompanied Rosamunde to the Wizard Healer's rooms in Dublin. Sir Harry Winston was a man of Stuart's age who had always specialized in female problems and obstetrics. He had delivered both the twins and Sabrina and Julia found him kind and knowledgeable.

Rosamunde had been nervous when she disrobed and put on the loose cotton examination gown. Sir Harry, a forward thinking man, employed one of the new, highly trained female nurses championed by Miss Nightingale and used so effectively in the Crimea only recently.

The woman was brisk and efficient and explained that there would be some pain but the healing magic would be much less painful than her bridegroom taking her maidenhead, particularly if he were not experienced. Rosamunde would be given an herbal drink for relaxation and her Mama could stay with her if she wanted.

"Oh, please stay with me!" Rosamunde had said, piteously, to Julia and Julia said that of course she would stay.

Rosamunde obediently drank down the sweet herb drink made of relaxants, choking a little, and lay back on the table waiting for it to take effect. Such things, mixed with magic, always took quickly and Julia had felt Rosamunde's fingers, which had been tightly clutching her own, relax slightly.

The nurse was watching for the signs and called Sir

Harry in when the patient was ready.

Sir Harry was of medium height and pleasant featured rather than handsome. He had very kind eyes and a reassuring manner. He asked Rosamunde some conversational questions about her up-coming wedding and the honeymoon as he held his hands above her pelvic area and 'read' her, seeing far more with his magic than he could with even a magnifying glass, and seeing her internal organs as well. An examination with the green Healer's magic was warming and comfortable.

Sir Harry looked thoughtful when he had concluded the exam and said, " I am afraid that this might hurt a bit more then normal. Your hymen is quite thick and it is a fortunate thing that you have decided to have the surgery, for else wise your wedding night would be extremely painful and it might have even proved impossible for your husband to make love to you."

Rosamunde looked rather frightened and Julia said soothingly, "You won't regret this, sweetheart. It will be over in a moment and it will make such a difference to both you and Raymond when the time comes for your first intercourse."

Sir Harry looked at Julia in approval. He admired the way she was so plain spoken about these matters and had taught this girl what to expect instead of raising her in ignorance.

Sir Harry wasted no time. He placed his hands over Rosamunde's pelvis and began the incantation. Rosamunde clung tight to Julia's hand and buried her face against her mother's breast. She knew that it was important that she remain still. but it was difficult, particularly once the pain started.

Sir Harry spoke bracingly, telling her that it was only a moment more and that she was being very brave. Rosamunde did not feel brave; she felt as if she were the greatest coward in the world for she wanted very badly to cry. If intercourse felt like this she wondered if she actually wanted to do it with any one, even Alan. But she had chosen to be married and she very badly wanted children one day. And for that one needed a husband.

There was a bit of bleeding, which Sir Harry Healed and advised Julia to draw a warm bath for Rosamunde as soon as they reached home, and use the packet of herbs the nurse would give her in the water. Rosamunde should rest for a day and then she could resume her normal activities. By her wedding night she would be completely healed.

Since Rosamunde was to marry a non-magical person, Sir Harry gave her a Certificate of Virginity, testifying that her hymen had been removed surgically. "Some of these young men get quite perturbed when the Witch they marry is not what they perceive of as virginal," he explained, signing the certificate with a flourish. "particularly the non- magical ones.

On the way home in the carriage she timidly asked Julia if being with a man felt like that.

"Of course not!" Julia said. "I will admit, when I had my surgery I wondered the same thing, but being with the one you love, so close, so intimate is indescribably wonderful. It was your aunt Tatya who explained that to me as I had no mother. And I had my surgery the afternoon before my wedding and had a special healing spell as well. But I did not regret it for one moment! It will be take a little getting used to, dear, as do all new things, but if you two truly love each other you will be pleased with each other, I am sure."

Now she sighed as Stuart said "She is so frail boned Julia, her pelvic structure is very small and I am very afraid that she will have extreme difficulty in bearing a child. Her mother never really recovered from her birth, you know. When Rosamunde becomes pregnant I want her here or in London, with a top of the trees Wizard Healer *accoucheur* to keep her under his eye, not out in a primitive country where there is, as far as I might ascertain, not a single Wizard Healer. I am very much afraid that she will have to be delivered by Caesarian section as do the Elves. Her Elfin blood is very strong, Julia, she even looks Elfin. The Elfin strain is very strong on my side of the family. Oberon, you know, calls my father 'cousin'."

"I think she has Elfin allure as well," said Julia thoughtfully. "It would explain why certain men are almost unreasonably mad for her, especially the non-magicals. She hates it, you know, Stuart, all the masculine attention. She told me once that she loathed the way men stared at her. Another young woman might have basked in the admiration but Rosamunde has become shy and won't even dress to show off her lovely figure. Her dressmaker practically cries when I talk to her about Rosamunde's clothes."

"She has become so self conscious that she will no longer go sky-clad, even though the Coven is only other women. And we miss her in the dances, as she was the best amongst us and her talent is a very suitable offering to the Goddess. But I never knew how to help her cope with her feelings. She could not seem to open up about it and I hesitated to intrude without her giving me an opening. Sometimes I think that is why she was married, to escape from all the men who wanted her."

"Unfortunately," said Stuart, "marriage will not protect her from certain men, as there will always be those who will want her, no matter whether there is a ring on her finger or not. But we have taught her well, she has her Witchcraft to protect her and Sinéad, and her husband as well." In spite of his confident words Stuart was worried – he, too, wished very much that his daughter was not going out to a strange place so far from home.

Julia still looked troubled and Stuart said bracingly as much for his own benefit as for hers, "She'll be home in no time at all. Three years will pass in the wink of an eye and it may not even be that long. Chenevix intends to use his influence, and he has a lot of it, to get Raymond posted here as soon as possible."

"I just want her to be happy," said Julia in a low voice, " And I wonder if she has made the right choice,"

"It's her choice, Julia and we can do naught about it. Worrying over her won't help," Stuart said. He rose and came around the desk to sit on a footstool at her feet.

"Let's give your thoughts another direction," he said "How would you like to get away from this dreary weather and go someplace warm and sunny, and go sky-clad on a beach with me?"

"You mean to go Underhill, to Oberon's kingdom and that lovely tropical domain where all we do is eat delicious food, swim, and sun, all without company or clothing? " She threw her arms around his neck, her mending slipping unnoticed to the floor. "When can we leave?" she demanded.

In Calcutta Major Bart Higby left the Residency with a smile on his face and a feeling that everything was falling into place for him. He had just received the promise of a promotion and a new assignment and it could not have been better, not even if he had put in a request for it himself. Fate was smiling upon him. He would soon have what at this moment he wanted most and it had been handed to him on a silver platter.

7

ā new home

It was with mixed feelings that Rosamunde watched Alan, his passengers and Brendan take off for the north the next evening. Part of her desperately wanted to keep them there at Malabad Station for they were a part of home and she was beginning to feel quite homesick.

But Alan himself was a constant reminder of the hopeless love she felt for him and she had made up her mind that she was going to be a good wife to Raymond. He had been her choice and if she worked hard at their marriage things would work out between them, even their problems in bed. It would be best if she tried to forget Alan and looked forward to her new life here.

They had arrived just before the early tropical dusk fell. Alan had refused to stay overnight since there was enough light from the moon that if Brendan flew quickly they could be in Ranijhat before dawn. A dragon landing at Malabad had made an incredible stir. Raymond's Colonel had not been pleased and Alan had not felt welcome, and neither had Ravi nor Brendan.

Therefore, between the oncoming dark and the farewells Rosamunde had not much chance to look about the cantonments, the military quarter, receiving only an impression of a large area full of public buildings, barracks and numerous small bungalows, bachelor officer quarters, most of which were thatched roofed, and larger bungalows of the same type for the married officers. A river lay nearby, unseen in the darkness. Sinéad said that she could smell it.

The jungle lay just beyond, full of strange trees and vegetation. Sinéad bristled as she sniffed the air coming from the jungle."There's after bein' wild things in there," she said darkly in Rosamunde's ear.

Raymond had requested and had received married quarters. This was a house in a compound near the cantonments and it was to this that he took Rosamunde immediately. The Colonels' wife had hired additional servants for them, as a household with a lady in it would require many more servants than did a bachelor household, and had sent her own *khidmatgar,* or butler to oversee the cleaning of the house, which had stood empty for almost a month. Even in that time there had been a notable incursion of both plant and animal life.

The house was built of brick and covered in white painted plaster. It was high in profile, but only of one story. A verandah, with shallow steps leading up to the front, ran all around it. Flowering creeper had covered the stone of the support columns and made deep shadows in the moonlight as Raymond showed Rosamunde up to the front door and said "Welcome home, my dear!"

The front door opened directly into the sitting room. Rosamunde had a confused impression of a sea of smiling brown faces waiting to greet her, in a room full of rather battered furniture of a European style.

By now she was so tired, for she had not slept well the two previous nights, and everything seemed unreal. A kind female voice said "*Sahib,* the *mem-sahib* sleeps on her feet! I shall put her to bed and in the morning she may greet all of us properly."

Rosamunde was taken to a bedroom and tenderly helped from her clothes and inserted into a nightgown. The woman, whom she correctly assumed was to be her maid, murmured soothingly to her, and brushed her hair out, even washing her face and hands as if she were a child. It felt so good to be taken care of while she was so tired and Rosamunde murmured her thank yous in her fluent Hindustanee.

The maid exclaimed in delight: "The *mem-sahib* speaks our tongue!" as she lowered the mosquito netting over her new mistress.

Rosamunde was asleep before the maid had finished putting away the discarded flying suit. She was unaware that Raymond came in and stood looking at her for long minutes.

The sound of a bugle woke Rosamunde. For one moment she was completely confused as to where she was and then with a rush, memory came pouring back. She was actually in Malabad at last, her new home, that had taken so long to reach.

She sat up and stretched. It was still dark out of doors. Why had someone blown a bugle in the middle of the night?

Raymond had obviously come to bed some time during the night, for the impression of his head was on his pillow, but he was not now in bed.

A murmur of voices beyond the mosquito netting attracted her attention and she lifted the white gauze and saw Raymond, dressed save for his jacket and sword belt, seated on a chair while being shaved by a turbaned native servant.

When Raymond was a bachelor, he had been shaved in bed, after a servant had brought him coffee, but he thought that this might offend Rosamunde's sensibilities, so he had determined to alter his routine to accommodate her. He had had his bath in the bathing room, the *ghosulknana,* which was paved with bricks, some of which formed a square above a drain built into the floor. Bathing consisted of standing, naked, over this drain, while a servant poured water over one from a series of porous red clay jars. These had been left to cool over night on the verandah in the shade of the creeper vines. There was no running water in any of the bungalows. Water was supplied from a well in the compound and every household employed a *bhasti*, a water carrier.

The room was lit by oil lamps and was full of furniture: one bureau, two wardrobes, the chair on which Raymond sat in front of, a shaving stand and a tiny dressing table. The walls were of white plaster and were adorned with a rack of guns and several heads of deceased animals. Rosamunde thought them singularly nasty for bedroom decor and seeing her glance at the heads, Raymond said "You can decorate the place any way you like. The furniture is ancient and in some cases fit only for retirement. It will give you some thing to do whilst I am at my duty."

"Is there something wrong?" Rosamunde queried, sitting up more against the pillows and pulling the *resai*,a light quilt, up over her chest. "Why are they blowing bugles in the middle of the night?" A glance at a small clock on a bedside table showed it to be not quite 4 A.M. "Is there some emergency?"

Raymond laughed indulgently. "It's necessary to rise this early in order to have our duties completed before it becomes too hot. Most of the ladies here rise early in the morning and ride before breakfast. I shall have to see about getting you a suitable ladies' mount so that you can join them. Mrs. Dalbeigh will call on you this morning, I daresay, and she will introduce you to the other ladies. You will have dozens of friends in no time at all."

The servant, the *nappy-wallah, the* barber, finished shaving Raymond and after wiping the *sahib's* face free of shaving soap, gathered the razor and the basin and departed with a bow.

Raymond stood up and shrugged himself into his uniform jacket. Normally a servant would do this for him but he wanted to talk to Rosamunde.

"I think it best," he said, looking at his buttons as he did them up and not at her, "that you mention to no one that you are a Witch. You will find that there is no liking for Witchcraft out here as many persons are devout Christians and would find it offensive. It smacks of paganism."

Rosamunde was taken aback. "But I *am* a Witch, Raymond! Witchcraft is as much a part of me as is breathing! And how am I to explain Sinéad, pray? Are there no other Witches here at all? No Covens?"

"No! And you will not tell any one that you have relatives who participated in such debauchery!" he said, his voice irritated. "I have heard what goes on at those *gatherings,* dancing unclothed under the moon and *orgies* no doubt, if you and your mother had not told me that you had not participated in that decadence I doubt I could have married you. The thought of a decent Christian woman cavorting in such a fashion is utterly repugnant." He finished with his buttons and looked at her, frowning. "And as for that cat - you must teach her to keep her opinions to herself and her mouth shut when guests are present." He picked up his sword and belted it on.

The door opened and a pleasant featured woman in a brightly coloured sari entered, carrying a tray.

"Ah, here is your maid, with your *chota haziri,*" said

75

Raymond in satisfaction. "This is what we call the little breakfast. Our full breakfast will be served at eight. I shall return then. The Colonel wants to see me now. I was to be on *chuti* – leave, for another month, but as we arrived back earlier ahead of schedule, he want me to resume my duties. He has promised that I may have leave later when it becomes hot to take you up to Simla in the hills where it is cooler. You will like it there. The society is very genteel."

Sinéad trotted in after the maid and leaped on the bed, purring, glad to be with Rosamunde again.

"I remembered that you prefer tea to coffee in the morning," said Raymond complacently, as the maid placed the try across Rosamunde's knees.

"Is he after expectin' a medal?" muttered Sinéad.

The little cat stared rather belligerently at Raymond as he strode towards the bed, spurs and sword jingling, and kissed Rosamunde on the brow. "I am certain that you shall find plenty to keep yourself busy," he said and left abruptly.

Rosamunde stared after him for a moment, smarting under the injustice of what he had said. Non- magical people had the strangest ideas about Witchcraft and Wizardry! Going sky-clad was necessary during the Rituals so that the body could absorb the goodness of the light of the moon. There was nothing in the least lewd or lascivious about it! If she had not become so self-conscious about her body she would have never given up the dancing in the moonlight. Even now she felt as if she had somehow shirked her duty as a Witch, but if she danced sky-clad in the rituals she would be expected to dance sky-clad at the Vernal and other festivals where men would be present and they would all look at her, perhaps lusting after her and that she could not bear.

She realized that he maid was waiting and with a sigh, she looked down at her tray. There were fresh chuppaties and cut up fruit as well as a pot of tea and a cup.

"Thank you, this looks wonderful," she said warmly to the maid, who beamed in pleasure at the sound of Rosamunde's Hindustanee.

"What is your name ?" she asked the maid.

"Sita, *mem-sahib*," she answered with a bobbing bow. She was a woman of middle age, with graying dark hair and smiling features. She wore a *sari* of blue, over a yellow blouse and on her arms were the bangle bracelets so loved by Indian women. She also wore a pair of heavy earrings.

"Thank you for putting me to bed last night Sita. I was so tired –"

"An' I was after bein' tired meself," interrupted Sinéad, startling Sita, who emitted a squeak of alarm and backed up hastily, her dark eyes wide.

"Don't be afraid," said Rosamunde coaxingly, "This is my cat Sinéad. She is magical but she is a *good* magical creature. May Sita pet you, Sinéad?"

"It's scratchin' behind me ears she could be doin'" the familiar suggested.

Sita, encouraged by Rosamunde, somewhat timidly advanced and placed a hand on Sinéad's head. "Soft!" she said in wonder.

The little cat began to purr as Sita stroked her head.

"I shall want to be introduced to the rest of the staff. I scarce remember them all from last night," said Rosamunde as Sita continued to pat the familiar, "and I shall want to see all around the house and grounds as well."

Sita nodded. "Shall you wish to bathe, *mem*? Shall I choose a gown for you?"

"Oh, yes, please," said Rosamunde. She felt hot and sticky already.

Shortly afterwards she was clean and dressed and ready to tour her new kingdom.

The *khidmatgar* assembled the rest of the servants on the verandah to meet their new mistress. He was a tall, thin, white clad Muslim of indeterminate years, with a somewhat lugubrious expression, but quick and efficient, Rosamunde was to find. His name was Alam Din.

He introduced the rest and Rosamunde was surprised to find how many servants were considered necessary to run such a small house.

There was Bulaki, the *bhasti* (water carrier); the *nappy-wallah*, (barber) Gobind; the *mali* (gardener) Gotama; a bearer called Akash; a syce (groom) Kashan; the *khan-*

77

samah, (cook) Anand; a sweeper, Prem; as well as a laundry man, several *punkah - wallahs* (fan fellows) who were only boys and several young women who were laundresses and maids. Raymond employed an orderly as well. There were also some who Rosamunde found, were employed sporadically, such as a *dai* - a nurse, and a *dazi* - a tailor.

Rosamunde greeted them all kindly and thanked them for making the house so nice for her. She did her best to remember all of their names.

Then Alam Din took her on a tour of the house. The rooms were larger than she had expected and the ceilings were high. As Raymond had indicated, the furniture was elderly and singularly bereft of decoration. The walls were largely bare, save for more animal heads, which seen in the light of day were more than a little moth-eaten.

Each room had tall windows with green shutters. On one side of the sitting room was the bedroom. The other side contained another room, which was empty at the moment. Alam Din explained that this could be another bedroom if the *mem* so desired. Rosamunde, however, decided to use this as her private sitting room. It had a view of the garden and of the *peepul* tree in the grassless square in the middle of the compound beyond.

There was another small room that Raymond had already claimed as a bookroom, a dining room, (here the furniture was of better quality) several store rooms and a room with a billiards table in it. The surface of this last was rather warped.

Much of the food appeared to be cooked out of doors on a brazier or in a small pit. Rosamunde supposed that this was because of the heat but she much disliked the swarms of flies everywhere and cast a surreptitious fly repellent spell. Oddly enough, she had to do it twice for it to take properly. Was she still tired from the long trip? Or perhaps she was just hungry, fruit was not much of a breakfast and spell casting on an empty stomach was not the best idea. Magic required strength.

She only had a brief time to see the out of doors before Raymond returned for breakfast. The house was set in front of a garden of jasmine, tuberoses and oleander which grew in profusion; the garden had been much neglected and was set in a long row of houses exactly identical to it, facing a square.

All were set within the compound of married quarters, which compromised three or so acres, surrounded by an earthen mound and an irrigation ditch. There were many trees unfamiliar to Rosamunde, palms of course, but also orchards of mango, guava and custard apple and the *peepul* tree, sacred to Hindus. A communal well in a corner was staffed by a wizened little man, who with the aid of a pair of yoked bullocks, drew skin fulls of water from the well that were then dumped into the irrigation ditch that kept the flower gardens and the kitchen gardens flourishing.

Behind each bungalow lay a cluster of rather wretched hovels, the servant's quarters. A vast amount of people seemed to live there including many children. The youngest ran around in the growing heat of the day *sans* clothing and smiled shyly at Rosamunde.

When Raymond returned he brought the Colonels' wife with him.

Mrs. Lorena Dalbeigh was a faded beauty of thirty-five. The climate of India and disappointment with her life had made her look older, with a sour, discontented expression on her features. She had always hoped that her husband would do better for himself than a small, insignificant Indian station such as Malabad, but as the Colonel was an indolent man, who hated to bestir himself for any reason, especially for his duty, they had remained in obscurity and Mrs. Dalbeigh's ambitions had remained unfilled. The Dalbeighs had four children, all of whom were in England, being educated, as the climate of India was considered unsuitable for children.

Mrs. Dalbeigh was a considerable snob and had at once consulted her "Bible" – *Burke's Peerage and the Landed Gentry* – when she had learned Rosamunde's maiden name from Raymond.

What she had read there had appalled her. She had assumed that the Lieutenant's wife would be some little Irish provincial nobody, not a girl connected to so many noble houses. Mrs. Dalbeigh's grandfather was a baronet and as such she had been the highest ranking lady in Malabad. And now she was to be displaced by a chit of a girl! It was past all bearing. But she had an obligation to be welcoming to the wife of a junior officer, moreover an officer on whom her husband depended greatly. Raymond did a great many of his superior's day to day tasks for him, allowing the Colonel to nap, play billiards or visit the women's house instead.

Mrs. Dalbeigh was prepared to dislike Rosamunde at sight. When Raymond introduced them and Mrs. Dalbeigh contrasted the bride's beauty with her own vanished looks, Rosamunde's figure with one showing the ravages of four pregnancies and the brilliant gold hair with faded blonde ringlets, her dislike was confirmed.

Rosamunde was taken aback by Mrs. Dalbeigh's brown eyes darting around the room, mentally assessing everything. She expressed surprise that Rosamunde had not brought out furnishings with her.

Breakfast was served on the old set of china that had been left in the house and Mrs. Dalbeigh made a *moue* of distaste as she refused a cup of tea.

"We have certain standards here, Mrs. DeLacey," she said "and you must do your part to hold up these standards. This chinaware will never do. I shall have to take you in hand and show you the better shops in Delhi where one can obtain tolerable wares but not as fine as at home, of course."

Raymond at the other end of the table was finishing a large breakfast and conferring with his orderly, a man named Manu Patel, and was paying no attention to the female conversation. There could be nothing there that would interest him, clothing and servant problems no doubt.

Mrs. Dalbeigh lowered her voice. "And if I may give you a hint, my dear young woman, even in one's own home it does not do to go about without a corset. It will give many people a very strange idea of your breeding and morals."

"My father is a doctor, Mrs. Dalbeigh, and he disapproves of corsets. My mother and I have never worn them. None of the ladies in my family do so," Rosamunde's voice was tight, she had had this corset conversation with far too many other women since she had left home. Mrs. Umphelby, among others, had been shocked at Rosamunde's lack of proper corsetry.

Much of the hauteur of which her great grandfather Chenevix was capable was in Rosamunde's voice when she said "I cannot conceive why my undergarments would be of interest to anyone save myself!"

Mrs. Dalbeigh wore a look of astonishment on her face. She was unused to the wife of a junior officer speaking to her in such a fashion.

Lowering her voice she said with a significant glance at Raymond, "You will do well to remember your position here, my dear, and take guidance where it is offered. It is far more pleasant if we all rub along in an agreeable fashion and do not put ourselves forward in unbecoming ways." Her voice was sugar sweet – the look on her face was not.

Raising her voice again, she said "Lieutenant, I was just telling your little bride that I shall give a tea for her tomorrow to introduce her to the other ladies."

"That's dashed kind in you, ma'am!" Raymond said heartily. "I told Rosamunde that she would soon have a score of friends!"

Sinéad had jumped up in Rosamunde's lap and now muttered "Sure an' if they are after bein' as this old besom we'd do better, so we would, to be collectin' enemies!"

Mrs. Dalbeigh took her leave soon afterwards, setting a time for the introductory tea.

"There now," said Raymond. "She's a pleasant lady and the leader of society here. You shall be well set if she takes you under her wing. She will show you how to go on properly."

"Me Witch is bein' fine just as she is!" said Sinéad, fur bristling. "An' if ye are thinkin' that a jealous cow like that one is after bein' a proper friend for a Delamar, well, 'tis out in the sun too much ye've been!"

Raymond glared at the familiar. "We are not interested in your opinions," he said in a stiff fashion that Rosamunde was beginning to recognize as extreme displeasure.

"Are all the women here like Mrs. Dalbeigh?" Rosamunde asked, disturbed. There had been more than one thing she had disliked about the Colonel's wife: the way she spoke to the servants, with never a please or a thank you, and saying disparaging things about the country in front of them, and her air of superiority with no justification.

Raymond failed to discern her true meaning. "Yes, she is very well thought of here and the natural leader of our little society. You will like her and her bosom bows. I am glad

81

to see you making friends,"

With this he was gone again, leaving her to her household duties.

She was left feeling a sense of deep depression. She was not to practice her Witchcraft and now it seemed that she was to have to endure that society of the type of women she had always avoided. The future seemed to stretch out endlessly before her.

8

ameera

Contrary to what she had hoped Rosamunde did not find each day easier and her marriage improving, in spite of her best efforts. She had to hold her tongue so many times. Sometimes she *had* to speak up when things became just too much to be borne.

She could not seem to please Raymond; he was critical of everything she did. An older woman, one with experience (she was only twenty), would have realized that this was caused by his continued frustration as their sexual problem failed to improve. The frustration manifested itself as anger at her.

And, too, the truth was that their upbringings had been so different that there was little common ground. He had been brought up in a strict, almost Evangelical atmosphere of black and white propriety. Her family was far more liberal in its outlook in everything from its attitudes towards other peoples to sexual mores.

They had a huge quarrel when Rosamunde told Raymond that she understood his problem as she had read about it in her father's medical books and if they only discussed it rationally...He had been horrified – no *lady* would EVER admit to knowing such a thing or try and talk about it! Her parents were depraved! He still grew heated and uncomfortable when he thought about that "Certificate of Virginity". If Rosamunde's father had not made him so nervous he would have forbidden the procedure and that contraceptive spell as well! Contraception was wrong, according to what he had been taught. One took all the children that God sent.

Another quarrel had followed when Rosamunde refused the nice, safe horse, a proper ladies' mount, that Raymond chose for her.

"A slug," was what Rosamunde said of the mare, "incapable of going above a tied in at the knee trot."

"Mrs. Dalbeigh"– Raymond began, but Rosamunde turned on him.

"I am sick of what Mrs. Daleigh wants and what Mrs. Dalbeigh does! If she likes that sloth of a horse she can have it! I'm going to find myself something worth riding! Kashan's uncle breeds horses and he is going to take me to see him."

"Kashan?" Raymond repeated blankly.

"Your *syce* – he has been in your employ for over four years and you do not know his name?" Rosamunde was contemptuous. As a result, a neat little black mare, spirited and fast, now stood in their stables, an animal that made Raymond's mounts look like dogsmeat.

Raymond had been angry about another circumstance as well, Rosamunde was far too chummy with the servants. That they had come to dote on her was apparent. She spent a great deal time in the servants' quarters, tending to their ills, spoiling their children and she was unnecessarily kind, always *asking* them to attend to their duties rather than ordering. She thanked them for performing their tasks as if they were not being paid to tend to the *sahib* and *mem-sahib's* every want.

She spent too much time with the troopers' families as well. When he protested, she said they were much more interesting that the ladies of the station and much better bred. She was actually teaching some of them to read!

Rosamunde despaired of ever being comfortable at Malabad or fitting in with the limited society. She tried to keep her opinions to herself but it was difficult, particularly when something was blatantly wrong and it could be easily fixed with a little application and thought.

Right from the beginning, at that first tea party, she had known that she would find no friends amongst the ladies of the station. They were a group of small-minded, petty gossips, who spent hours deciding on fabrics for new gowns, going to dinner parties and never seemed to read a book or have any original ideas. The only woman she liked at the station was the elderly wife of the veterinary surgeon who preferred animals to people.

As the heat advanced and the time headed towards May and Molly's visit, Rosamunde's days fell into a pattern. She rose when the bugle blew, had her *chota haziri* and then rode out, sometimes, at Raymond's insistence, with the other ladies, but most often with just Kashan, her syce, in attendance.

Upon returning home she conferred with Alam Din. He had become her confidante and co-conspirator. From him she learned what children were sick and which of the troopers, both English and native, had problems. To her disgust, the non-magical doctor at the station spent more time at the bottom of a bottle than he did in treating the sick. She had worked at her father's clinic often enough to know some medicine and she sent to Delhi for medical books to learn more.

From ten until three, after a cool bath, she lay on her bed in a darkened room, clad only in a loose cotton wrapper while the *punkah wallah* pulled endlessly on the cord of ceiling fan trying to keep her cool. Water soaked mats of woven fibrous roots called tatties hung in all of the windows. It was thought that the water vapors these gave off from evaporation cooled the air. When it began to grow cooler in the early evening they usually went out to dine or to a dance, both of which she found dull beyond belief as they saw only the same people who talked of the same things.

She also wrote endless letters home.

But her greatest pleasure was the bazaar.

When she was furnishing the house Sita had suggested that they go to the bazaar to look for nice things. It was the usual custom for merchants to bring their goods to the *mem sahibs*, but Sita thought that Rosamunde, who seemed bored and lonely to her faithful maid, would enjoy the colour and life in the bazaar.

And from the very beginning, she did.

Malabad was not a large city as was Meerut. It was rather a backwater and not considered a desirable posting. The post personnel was mixed; there was a Queen's Regiment stationed there as well as a native regiment of the East India company.

It was completely segregated. The native sepoys lived in squalid huts while the British troopers lived in barracks, which were equally squalid, being hot and close. Many British troopers had 'wives' and children – over half of these were native mistresses and illegitimate children. The children were known as "barracks rats".

The troopers spent much of their time either in the canteen, open all of the time, drunkenness was rife, or at the soldier's bazaar in the overcrowded area where the Hindus and Mussulmen lived, known as Black Town. It was a startling contrast to the open, broad spaces of the English section.

The bazaar was a loud, colourful place, teeming with life. One could obtain any type of goods that one wanted: silver bangle bracelets, beautifully tooled leather goods, food of all types, rugs, fabric, furniture; the merchants squatted outside their shops on woven mats, smoking hookahs, or fanning themselves, and waiting for customers. They made no display of wares as Rosamunde was used to in Dublin. When they inquired after goods Rosamunde and Sita were shown the poorest quality goods at first, and asked outrageous prices. Sita would not let Rosamunde buy the first thing she fancied. The maid kept after the merchant until he would produce better and better goods and then would bargain with him until the merchant would declare that she would bankrupt him. But Sita managed to get just what Rosamunde wanted for a quarter of the price Rosamunde would have paid on her own.

There were many things to see besides the merchandise. The people at the bazaar were endlessly fascinating. Besides the soldiers and *sepoys* there were Arab horse dealers, Parsee merchants in huge chariots, complete with outriders, Pathans from Afghanistan who looked as if they would slit one's throat for a mere *anna*, native ladies in curtained *jampans*, carried by eight men.... Noise was everywhere, the babble of many tongues and the endless beat of the *tom tom* drums. Strange music from stranger instruments sounded above the din of humanity, the blowing of a conch shell trumpet form a nearby temple, myriad bells and the call to prayer from the minaret in the town echoed over all.

There were the smells as well, the dusty smell of heat and the strong spices of curry, the smell of food and the vile smell of open sewers. Sanitation seemed to be very lacking; most mud huts had an open cesspit near the front door.

At the end of the bazaar stood a row of mud huts to which men seemed to be repairing with monotonous frequency.

"What is that place?" Rosamunde asked Sita.

"That is the *Lol Bibbees* Bazaar," said Sita matter of factly. "The prostitute's quarter."

As Rosamunde watched several women came out of one of the huts, laughing and hanging on the arms of some British troopers.

They were naked to the waist, clad in low slung gauze pantaloons, their arms and ankles loaded down with bangle bracelets and anklets. Their faces were heavily painted and they had bold, knowing eyes.

The younger ones were attractive in a hard fashion but some of them had no pretensions to youth or beauty at all, one woman's breasts sagged down to her waist and she was quite ugly. Nonetheless, she seemed to have a patron.

"In times past," said Sita sadly "the Company took care that the women were free of disease and were given a pension when too old to work. Now such things are deemed improper by the missionaries and the women are ill with many bad things. But still the soldiers go to them in spite of the missionaries. It is not natural for a man to do without a woman."

Rosamunde was grateful that Sita honestly answered her questions without telling her "such was not proper". Working in her father's clinic amongst the impoverished of Dublin had made her much more aware of how the poor had to live.

She could not imagine what it would be like to have to prostitute oneself in order to survive. The idea of offering herself to any man who had money to pay was horrifying; to expose her body to his gaze, to be intimate with him in ways that she could only imagine, it made her feel ill.

She was almost glad that nothing had happened between her and Raymond for contrary to what her female relatives had told her she did not think that relations with a man would be wonderful. She felt no thrill when Raymond kissed her. She often wondered if she would have felt like this

87

if *Alan* had proposed and they were married? She had found the whispered discussions at school uninteresting for she thought of marriage primarily as protection against men trying to kiss and touch her, and never considered the physical relationship that came with it.

Sita, looking at her face, which was all too easy to read, felt sorry for the young *mem-sahib*. The lack of a physical relationship between the *mem* and her husband was all too well known to the household, and also too was it known that the *sahib* had begun to go again to the *bibi-gurh* that was frequented by the officers. Sita, who enjoyed a satisfying martial relationship with her husband of over twenty years, found the relations of the *sahib-log* strange and sad. They took no joy in one another. Her young *mem* had more pleasure in buying things for the house and watching the people in the bazaar than she did in her husband.

For a long time Rosamunde had hoped to meet an Indian lady of her own class. As much as she liked Sita, there was always the constraint of mistress / servant between them.

She had asked Mrs, Dalbeigh what she knew of the life of an Indian lady and what she had seen of Indian ladies of rank.

"Oh, nothing, thank goodness!" Mrs, Dalbeigh had exclaimed, shocked that Rosamunde would ask such a thing. "I know nothing at all about them. Nor do I wish to. Really, the less one knows about the natives the better."

Rosamunde could not understand this attitude. She was endlessly fascinated by the differences in the culture and asked Sita countless questions. Some of the answers she did not like, particularly the subjugation of women, but she still found it very interesting.

She had just about given up on meeting an Indian lady when *kismet*, as Alam Din called fate, stepped in.

It was a warm morning at the bazaar. Bored with

shopping, Sinéad had stayed behind. Rosamunde had been looking for a light fabric with which to make draperies for her own little sitting room. She had seen nothing that struck her fancy and she and Sita had stayed longer than usual, searching in the various shops. Coaxing the merchants into bringing out their best wares took time.

The streets were crowded in spite of the heat. People jostled against one another and pickings were good for thieves and cut-purses.

Afterwards, Rosamunde could never reconstruct the chain of events with any degree of accuracy. A *jampam* swerved suddenly as a pariah dog, chased by a butcher from whom it had attempted to steal meat, ran in front of the litter. Two of the men carrying the *jampan* bumped into a man carrying a bowl of steaming curry and he tripped, sending the contents of his pot all over the person nearest to him - who was Rosamunde.

Sita shrieked as she saw the curry spatter Rosamunde's chest and spill all down the skirt of her light blue gown. Rosamunde gasped, for the curry was hot.

The curtain of the *jampan* opened abruptly, but only a crack, and a distressed female voice said "Oh, what has happened, Nilam?"

The head bearer said "A clumsy person has spilled his *tiffin* all over a *mem-sahib*, mistress."

The man with the curry said angrily "I would have not spilled my *tiffin* else you had not bumped into me, oh, stupid one !"

Several people in the crowd that was gathering agreed with this at the tops of their voices. Some showed a tendency to blame the butcher for chasing the dog, others took the side of the *jampan* bearers, while still others supported the man with the curry.

A slender hand with gilded nails, hennaed palms and bracelets on the slight wrist opened the curtain a little more.

"Oh, the poor lady!" came the voice from behind the curtain. "Bring your mistress here!" she called out to Sita, who was attempting to wipe down Rosamunde's skirt with a rag given her by a busybody. "She may be burned – I shall take her to my house, which is close by and we shall treat her and clean her clothing."

"Come, *mem,*" said Sita to Rosamunde, who was gasping from the pain of the hot curry soaking through her muslin gown. "A lady offers to aid you. You cannot walk to the compound in such condition."

Rosamunde was handed up into the *jampan* by the bearers who told Sita the identity of their mistress and where she lived, so that she might follow on foot.

A *jampan* was little more than a covered arm chair but this one was bigger than most. It reminded Rosamunde of the sedan chairs some older persons still used in places such as Bath.

A slender little lady in a red and gold *sari,* giggled and moved over as Rosamunde was helped beneath the curtain. "My husband's mother was extremely stout," she said in heavily accented but good English. "This *jampan* was made for her."

"How fortunate for me," said Rosamunde gratefully in Hindustanee.

The lady clapped her hands in delight. "You speak my language!" she exclaimed. "I am Ameera, wife of Sanjaya Sharma, a merchant of this city."

Rosamunde introduced herself and expressed her gratitude for the assistance.

"I have been so curious to speak to a *mem-sahib,*" said Ameera. "But they none of them will speak to me. Will you visit with me while my woman repairs your clothing? And my *dai* will have a soothing salve for those burns," she added sympathetically.

She was a slender, doe-eyed girl of about Rosamunde's age. Her complexion was a lovely coffee brown and she spoke with many fluttering hand gestures that were very graceful to see. Lustrous dark hair was pulled back into a bun at the nape of her neck and by the amount of very fine jewelry that she wore and the rich cloth of her *sari,* it was obvious that she and her household were quite well off.

She was interested to learn that Rosamunde was only a bride. Although they were almost the same age Ameera had already been married for six years and had given her husband two sons. She was a junior wife, a *khnuam,* and from what she left unsaid, Rosamunde deduced that the senior wife was unkind to her.

In no time at all they were at Ameera's home in the Indian section of the city. It was a surprisingly large edifice, which was called the *Hirren Mahal*, or deer palace. Once, before there had been a military facility here, it had been surrounded by jungle and it had been a hunting box. But the city had grown up around it in the last one hundred years and the only remnants of the jungle were the palm trees. And the hunting box had grown as well.

High walls surrounded the *Mahal* and shut out the noises of the city. Ameera took Rosamunde quickly through the public rooms and through the *zenana*, the women's quarters, to a small room overlooking a courtyard where a fountain spilled into a pool filled with water lilies.

"This is my own place," said Ameera proudly. "When I gave my husband his first son, which *she* could not do, he asked me what I desired most and I said that I most desired a place that was all mine. My maid and I, my sister-in-law and several others are the only ones admitted – not *her!*" she added, referring to the senior wife. "My husband visits me here, and he says that it soothes him, for the women in the *zenana* are always quarreling and gossiping." As she spoke she clapped her hands and several maids, bare-footed and jingling with bangles, came running.

Clucking in sympathy, they carefully drew the curry stained gown from Rosamunde. There were three burns, one on her right breast, another on her waist, with a third burn on her thigh where the curry had soaked through skirt, petticoats and drawers. A kind looking older woman, the *dai*, with her *sari* drawn up about her neck and face, followed them closely and clucked at the sight of the burns.

Rosamunde felt embarrassed to have all these women staring at her, for they had insisted on stripping her to the skin. Rosamunde gratefully accepted the *dai's* suggestion that she soak in the cooling waters of the lily pool while a fresh salve was mixed and the maids fetched a *sari* for her to wear. They had exclaimed at the sight of her pale body and had remarked to one another that such a lovely form must indeed please her husband. Rosamunde blushed at the thought. Raymond had never seen her form. From what he had said she had been given to understand that he thought nudity was disgraceful in a decent Christian woman. He expected her to bathe in a shift and always wear a high to the neck night- gown. He had let it slip that one of the things he found attractive in her character was the modesty and restraint in her dress. He disapproved of a show of bosom.

Ameera sat on the edge of the pool and chatted while Rosamunde soaked and her gown was cleaned. In no time at all they were talking and laughing with each other as if they had been friends all of their lives. When Rosamunde came out of the pool and had her burns dressed the other women enjoyed themselves, showing her how to drape herself in the *sari*.

Before Rosamunde left for the compound later that day an engagement had been made for another time. The next day she brought Sinéad with her.

Soon she was visiting Ameera almost daily and perfecting her Hindustanee, learning to wrap a *sari* properly, being taught how to make jasmine oil and make varying curry blends. She learned now to make *surma,* the black oil of antimony that was used for enhancing the eyes and how to apply it. Before too long she was shedding her hot English clothing when she visited and went about in a *sari* – so much more comfortable than that heavy hoop.

She told Raymond none of this. He expected her to spend time with her friends, well, she was doing that. They were not the sort of friends he expected her to have but she would far rather be with the women in Ameera's private *zenana* than with the so-called 'ladies' at the station.

What Raymond did not know would not hurt him. And as the gap between husband and wife widened almost daily, Rosamunde lost all of the feelings of guilt she might have felt for concealing part of her life from him.

9

ranijhat

In spite of the moonlight that night they could see little below as Brendan flew north. Conversation was impossible, for the dragon was flying at top speed and all they could do was lean forward over the saddle to try and protect themselves from the wind. Ram Dass held on for grim life. He would never admit it, but he was terrified by the speed and of being so far above the ground.

Brendan passed over the jungles, and into an area of rock strewn ground and from there into the foothills, rather high foothills as they were some 5,000 to 6,000 feet above sea level. Ranijhat was close to the fabled Vale of Kashmir, but was far smaller and inaccessible to the traveler. It was considered to be in the Lesser Himalayas, between these still formidable mountains and the Hindu Kush.

Ranijhat was neither as large, nor as rich as Kashmir. Because of this and because it was a quiet place that did not make war upon its neighbors, it had been left in peace by the East India Company. The same House had ruled the state since the time of Babur, quietly and peacefully.

It was also a difficult trip to Ranijhat for there were deep ravines, mountain trails instead of good roads and heavy forest all impeded the way, as well as a wild river which was a tributary of the meandering Jhelum. All of these obstructions made it easy to overlook. Many people who had been there didn't consider it worth the effort it took to get there, in spite of the beauty of the scenery and the hospitality of its contented people, for it was small and too far out of the world.

Alan and Brendan had inadvertently chosen the best way to get to this tiny, remote kingdom. Flight easily cleared the mountains and went over the thick forests and ravines.

They first saw Ranijhat as the rising sun touched the villages and city and set fire to the snow covered peaks of the mountains.

The capital, called Jhat, was a fortified, walled city and sat on the highest elevation in the kingdom. A long, narrow road ran up to the city from the white water river, the Ajit.

The palace, Ravi's home, sat on a rock that overlooked the city. It shone with a nacre-like luster in the morning sun. Ravi had told Alan that it was called the *Moti Mahal,* meaning 'pearl palace'. It had been rebuilt by the Mughal ancestor to resemble the domed and turreted architecture of Persia and proved to be a great deal larger than it looked from a distance. Brendan was easily able to land in the principal courtyard.

However, he startled the guards on duty who began to shout and run forward, lances leveled, at the sight of so fearsome a creature. It was not until Ravi and Ram Dass swung down and showed themselves, assuring the guards that the dragon was friendly, that they stopped their advance. But their postures showed that they were still wary of this strange beast.

Ravi's feet had scarcely touched the ground when the ornate door of the palace opened. This door was of heavily carved wood set in lacework tiles beneath a half circle roof supported by six slender white columns. It burst open and a man hurried down the steps. He was somewhat heavy set, and wore a graying beard. His clothing was of the finest silk and was edged with bands of beautiful gold and silver embroidery. He wore a triple strand of pearls about his neck, long enough to fall to his waist and ending in a large diamond. His turban was high and edged with pearls and another large diamond sat above his brow A white plume topped off the turban.

"Welcome!" he cried. "My son had returned and brought his friend, his *Angrezi* (English) brother whom we all have been longing to meet!"

His greeting was effusive – he hugged both his son and Alan as if they had just returned from a war and had not been expected to survive.

He greeted Ram Dass cordially and then turned with sparkling eyes to Brendan and Cathal. "I have heard so much of these creatures! My son's letters from *Belait* were full of their doings and sayings!"

Cathal, on Alan's shoulder, bowed and said he was glad to make the Maharajah's acquaintance and Brendan inclined his head.

"I am only sorry that I cannot spend much time in your beautiful country," the dragon said, " for I am expected in Tibet. But before I go perhaps your highness would like to take a flight? The aerial view is so interesting."

He could have not said anything that would have pleased the Maharajah more. Ever since Ravi had written home about his friendship with Alan and how he had flown on the dragon his father had imagined little else than what it would feel like to go up in the sky as did a bird.

It was agreed that after breakfast and a short rest Brendan would take his highness up before leaving for Tibet later in the morning.

The Maharajah ordered the finest meats brought for Brendan and expressed surprise when the dragon wished to have milk, honey, grain and fruit for his breakfast, not raw meat.

Alan stood to one side as the Maharajah talked to Brendan. He had staggered slightly when dismounting, feeling the world spin around him again. In the excitement no one, or so he thought, had noticed.

Cathal who had scampered up to his shoulder as soon as they were all on the ground, now said anxiously in his ear "Alan, what is it ? You're awfully pale and not quite steady in your feet! Are you having a relapse?"

Alan had been very ill in the autumn with a particularly virulent form of influenza. This combined with self-inflicted overwork had resulted in a near complete breakdown.

"I'm all right,"said Alan shortly. "Don't fuss,Cathal, and don't tell Brendan. I don't want him canceling his trip to Tibet. He's been looking forward to it far too long. You heard what Ravi said; it's just that I haven't gotten used to being back on land as yet and we flew a long way the last two days. I'll be fine. I came here to rest and recuperate and that's what I mean to do."

Cathal decided that, in spite of Alan's wishes, he would have a quiet word with Brendan before the dragon left. And perhaps he would write to Rosamunde as well.

A special stylus had recently been invented that fit over a paw and made it possible for a familiar to write. Cathal was proud that he could write letters to his friends and family and could even help Alan in the laboratory by taking notes, as well as reading instructions. His stylus was one of his most cherished possessions. He intended to write to Sinéad and she would write back, contrasting the two places they were visiting.

No one else noticed Alan's momentary dizziness. The Maharajah was fascinated with Brendan and ordered low tables and cushions brought out on the *chabutara,* the terrace,and clapped his hands, ordering *"Haziri lao,* to bring breakfast!" so that he could remain talking to the dragon.

Alan sank down on a cushion and thankfully accepted a cup of tea from a smiling, bowing servant. There was tea, fruit and muffins on the table as well as kedgeree, the popular blend of hard boiled eggs, dried flaked fish and boiled rice, flavored with curry that was to be found on almost every British breakfast table in India.

"We are having a British breakfast in your honor," said Ravi, "But we have muffins all the time now. I became addicted to them at Oxford!"

"I am looking forward to trying many Indian dishes," said Alan politely, but in truth, his appetite seemed to have deserted him lately. A headache had begun to nag behind his eyes as well.

His uncle had warned that he might be subject to minor relapses and had suggested pulling power from the ley lines which always a good remedy for a Wizard in a weakened state of health. Alan decided to do this as soon as he was alone. The ley lines in this part of the world were very strong, or so he understood, for they were largely unused. Five or ten minutes of pulling power and energy from the earth should set him up. He wanted to enjoy this trip, not be sick and weak and a millstone around his hosts' necks.

The Maharajah had his flight while Ravi took Alan indoors to meet his mother and three sisters and two younger brothers. The older ladies, of course, could not be exposed to the gaze of a strange man, a *feringhi,* a foreigner, but Alan was able to converse with the Maharani, Jyoti, and her two oldest daughters, with a carved stone *purdah* screen between them. The two eldest girls, Lakshmi and Sarika, who being fifteen and thirteen respectively, were of marriageable age, indeed, were more than a little old not to be betrothed. But the Maharajah and his wife were in no great hurry to lose their daughters and did not feel as if they had received any worthy offers for their hands.

The two boys, Chetan, nineteen, and Dhaval, seventeen, were eager to ride the dragon too, as was the youngest girl, Esha, who was ten, just a bit younger than Alan's little sister Irina. Esha was obviously the pet of the entire family and rather spoiled. She did not wish to stay in the *zenana* with the women, insisting that boys had all of the fun and it wasn't fair that girls had to be so bored. All of the family were very indulgent with her and she rode off with her father and the two boys in triumph, on the back of the dragon.

"If Brendan were to stay with us she would wear him out begging for rides!" laughed Ravi as they watched the dragon circle overhead from the piles of cushions on the terrace. He looked sideways at Alan, who had been very quiet since they had come back outside. "You will soon be well, my brother," he said abruptly. "I can see that you have been far more ill than you let on in your letters. We have a most skilled *Hakim* who will see you this very day."

"A *Hakim*, that's a doctor, isn't it?" said Cathal excitedly, sitting up, his black masked face eager. "Yes, Alan, you should see a doctor and eat a strengthening diet! Plenty of fresh air and no worry! Remember what your Uncle Stuart said! Stuart wrote a letter for any doctor that Alan would see out here, it's in our baggage," he exchanged a long concerned look with Ravi.

It had taken Ravi some time, whilst at Oxford, to become used to rooming with talking animals and seeing dragons and other strange creatures in the sky.

He would be eternally grateful to Alan and Peter both for befriending him, for his reception at University had not been a good one to begin with. More that a few of the young men had not wished to share a room with him, looking down their noses at a mere native.

Alan and Peter had first met him when he was sitting in the quadrangle, feeling rejected, alone and homesick, wondering what he was to do if no one here accepted him. After a brief conversation they offered to share their rooms as they were looking for a third flat-mate they explained. And there had begun a three way friendship that had lasted since that first day, strengthened by Alan's matter of fact statement that of course Ravi would come to stay with him at the various 'hols'; he couldn't expect to go back and forth to India several times a year, even if he had owned a dragon!

Alan's family had welcomed him warmly and it became an established custom for him to go to Dublin with Alan on every vacation or holiday. He felt as if he had another family in Dublin and wrote enthusiastically back to Ranijhat about his new friends and their magical doings.

Ravi had gone to University to study modern languages and history and had taken a double first. He had been barely aware before going to England that there *was* a College of Magic at Oxford. He had also been unaware of the fact that there would be dragons there as well. He had been cast into awe at the sight of his first dragon-ball game and had been excited beyond measure when in Dublin with Alan he was offered a chance to play.

Since he had left University Ravi had hoped to convince Alan and Peter to come out and visit him so that his family could return some of the hospitality he had been shown. He was glad that his friend, his brother, had finally come, but he was concerned. Alan did not look well and Ravi decided to have a talk with Cathal and find out just how serious the illness had been. Alan had been very reticent. At one time Ravi would have laughed in disbelief about discussing such a matter with an animal, but after knowing both Cathal and Brendan he no longer saw anything odd in it.

Several hours later, after biding Brendan good-bye and talking to the Maharajah about the many delights they had planned for his amusement. Alan was shown to a beautiful room that would be his for the entire time he would be here in Ranijhat.

It was a white, light and airy room, with the stone lacework that was typical of the architecture of the Mughals.

The floor was of a floral blue and white tile and the furniture inlaid with brass and mother of pearl. The *charpoy* or bedstead was covered with embroidered pillows of rich hues. A low table surrounded by more cushions graced the room as well as several European style chairs and a richly inlaid desk.

The plastered walls had been painted in places with designs of trees, birds and flowers in bright colours, echoed in the cotton *resai,* the bedspread on the bed in a pattern Alan was familiar with from home, the Tree of Life, that had originated in India many years earlier and was popular in England.

Most spectacular was the view from the *chabutara* that opened out from a large window/door. It was of the mountains, some of which, the servant who showed him to the room told him, were always in snow. *Himalaya* meant 'abode of snow'.

The servant informed Alan that his name was Jai and he would be Alan's servant while he was here. Perhaps when the *sahib* felt more himself he could climb the mountains with the *Yuraraj,* who enjoyed such sport. If the *sahib* needed fresh air as the *Angrezi Hakim sahib* had ordered, his bed might be moved out on to the terrace.

Alan, breathing deep of the fresh, cool air redolent of pine that swept down from the hills, thought that this might be a good idea. Surely he would sleep well in this bright, clean Mahal with the sweet air blowing over him! He had not slept well at all on the ships that had carried him to India.

He might be in a different world than that of the low lying Calcutta area or the heat of the plains. He thought fleetingly of Rosamunde, forced to stay in the dust and smothering hot air of the station at Malabad.

On further acquaintance Raymond had not improved. Alan had been taken aback at the Lieutenant's attitude towards Ravi and thought him condescending to his new wife. Rosamunde was a treasure and the man who was lucky enough to win her should appreciate his good fortune, not act as if it was his due.

DeLacey had brushed away Alan's blunt warning

about Higby as well. Higby was a fellow officer and officers had a code of honor that a civilian could not understand. Raymond was certain that Alan had misunderstood what Higby had said and he would not even listen to Cathal's testimony. It was quite the thing for officers to toast a beautiful woman in the mess – it was a compliment.

Cathal, angered by the stupidity of Rosamunde's husband, had retorted, "Oh, and is it a compliment for officers to speak of *fucking* another officer's wife and talking about *squeezing and suckling her titties*? I'm not human and I know that is wrong!"

But DeLacey had ignored him and Alan.

Alan had found out that Higby was stationed in Meerut, and hopefully, after having been on home leave for some little while he would stay in Meerut and leave Rosamunde alone. And after all, Alan consoled himself, in spite of a nagging uneasiness, she had her Witchcraft to protect her and Sinéad too.

Jai drew a bath for Alan in an incredible *ghosulhana*. Right off his bedchamber was a short flight of stairs that led to a large chamber with a high arched ceiling. In the center, under a dome held up by slender white pillars, was an enormous tiled bath, sunk deep in the floor. There were piles of towels to hand, jars of oils and soaps and sweet smelling soaps for the hair. The water was hot and steaming and Alan sank into it gratefully. It came up nearly to his chest, the first real bath he had since Egypt.

After the bath, Jai clothed him in a loose cotton *choga* - a long sleeved garment like a dressing gown, much more comfortable than his English clothing.

It was near to noon. At this time of day, even in the hills, all activity ceased and Jai suggested that the *sahib* rest until later in the afternoon, when the sun was declining and then he would be shown the gardens and the stables. The Maharajah was famous for the quality of his horseflesh, and they would ride out in the cool of the evening.

Cathal was already dozing on the bed when Jai left Alan to his rest, after laying out riding wear of an *achkan* and jodhpurs, with Alan's own boots, which he had shined to an incredible brightness while Alan was bathing.

Now that he was almost alone, with only Cathal

present, Alan decided to draw some power. He had had another spell of dizziness in getting out of the bath. Perhaps the water had been too hot, but magic would set him up, he was certain.

He went out on the *chabutara* and took another deep breath. The air was wonderful, so clean and fresh.

Then he opened himself to the ley lines and fell into a black void of pain. The room spun and he heard Cathal shrieking his name as he fainted.

10

cartridges and chuppaties

As the calendar drew on towards May and the hottest time of the year, Raymond was increasingly dissatisfied and unhappy.

His home life was not what he had dreamed of, for Rosamunde seemed to be doing her best to vex him. Every day she did something that was unacceptable or seemed designed to embarrass him rather than learning to please him, as a good wife should.

It was bad enough that she was playing at doctor in the barracks and teaching troopers to read but he also did not care for the way she had decorated the house. It looked more like a native bungalow than an Englishman's home, with swathes of fabric on the walls, cushions everywhere, low, soft furniture and bare floors. Where was the marble-topped furniture, heavy drapes and rooms full of what-nots laden with memorabilia? There were no heavy oil paintings in gilded frames the subjects being portraits of people or the ever popular fruit and dead game. Instead there were water colour paintings of Indian things such as temples and mosques and elephants. Many Anglo-Indians had tiger skins and statues they had collected but they were displayed on a good solid British background.

There was her sitting room, as alien as if it had come from another planet. Crystals hung in the window, her lap harp sat in a corner and she played strange things on that as well.

But the worst of all was the ballet *barre* she had had the carpenter mount on the wall. Every day she practiced at this, wearing a loose shirt and a short, mid-calf skirt and even stood on her toes! Raymond was terrified that people would find out and think that he had married an opera dancer. He had never seen her dance and thought that she would give up something that improper once she was married. He could not understand why her parents had allowed her to do something so unladylike.

And that cat! The relationship between Raymond and Sinéad, barely cordial to begin with, had disintegrated as the weeks went by. The cat had a quick wit and a cutting tongue and could make Raymond feel like a tongue-tied school boy with just one remark.

After one acrimonious argument, caused by yet another aborted attempt in the bedroom, Raymond had demanded that Sinéad be thrown from the house or sent back to Ireland.

"If she goes back to Ireland I am going with her!" Rosamunde had retorted.

"If you think that I shall pay for a return ticket –" began Raymond hotly.

And then it had come out that Chenevix had opened an account for her in the Bank of Calcutta, where he had an agent.

When Raymond pressed her, she showed him her bank book. The sum made him reel. £10,000! Just in case she needed a *little* money!

This led to another confrontation about her 'extravagance', which was completely unfair as she had furnished the house and ran it all within the small budget he had given her. She had been well taught to hold household as none of the women in her family believed in extravagant living. From the time she was a small girl she had been obliged to keep an account book and be responsible for a budget. She had paid for her own horse and the ballet *barre* out of the wedding money her parents had given her.

Raymond had other problems as well, for strange things were happening here and there and some of the reports that came across the Colonels' desk, most of which that the slothful Colonel did not even read, made Raymond rather uneasy.

Malabad was a poorly run station. In spite of his faults Raymond was a good and conscientious officer but he was one of the few that felt this way. Dalbeigh's lackadaisical attitude had filtered down to all levels. Discipline was lax and morale was low.

Raymond's professional frustration had something to do with the constant arguments with Rosamunde as well. It never occurred to him to confide in her about the situation and how the fact that the others on the post who were content to do nothing or as little as was possible made him so downhearted. That was not a woman's concern, and in his view, she could never understand how he felt. If he had had a friend or a confidante things might have been better. But Edward Grey, the one friend he had made in the regiment, was on detached duty on the Northwest frontier as a political officer and mail between Malabad and the frontier was spotty. And at any rate, he hesitated in committing either his professional or martial problems to paper.

Had Colonel Dalbeigh been a different sort of man, as the commanding officer in Raymond's first regiment had been, interested in all his men and the kind one could talk privately to on all sorts of problems, Raymond might have confided in him and the regiment would have functioned properly. Raymond's professional life, at least, would have been satisfying. That might have given him more ease and tact in dealing with Rosamunde.

She was at fault, too, in their relationship. She expected him to be more like her father and the other men in her family. And unconsciously, she constantly compared him to Alan, and Raymond came up short. She also chafed under what seemed to her the foolishness of what he believed to be 'woman's place' and his attitude towards Witchcraft and her familiar. She was used to couples who treated one another as equals and having magic be a part of daily life.

And now all the rumors and reports that were coming in, things he had observed, all were making Raymond increasingly nervous. Dalbeigh just waved them away as 'bunk' and went back to sleep or back to the arms of his native mistress.

First of all had been the business of the greased cartridges. The new Enfield rifles that were being issued were easier to load than the old rifles with the powder and the bullet in a single greased cartridge. But the end of the bullet had to be bitten off before loading in order to expose the powder to the source of ignition.

Somehow, and many thought that the trouble had begun in Dum Dum, the arsenal near Calcutta, the word had spread throughout India that the paper case of the cartridges were greased with animal fats, cow and pig to be exact. Grease from cows would break the caste of any Hindu who defiled himself by putting it in his mouth and pig fat was forbidden to pass Muslim lips.

Many of the native troops had demonstrated their deep distrust of the new cartridges and had refused to believe that the grease was of mutton fat and wax as many officers tried to reassure them.

At an evening parade of the 4th native Infantry in Barrakpore the native troops had made it clear that even if they were allowed to mix their own grease for the cartridges they did not trust that the paper was acceptable to their religious requirements. To them, it was just another incident of the British trying to break their caste or defile them and make then unclean so that they would *have* to convert to Christianity.

There had been a number of minor insurrections, quickly put down and severely punished, executing ringleaders, notably Mangal Pande in Barrackpore, and even disbanding some regiments. It had been decided that new cartridges would be issued that the men could smear with linseed oil and wax. It was felt that a crisis had been averted.

But now there was this strange business of the *chuppatties.*

Varying amounts of them, usually four to five at a time,were being passed all over India, or so it seemed. The watchmen of various villages had *chuppatties* delivered to them by mysterious means and were instructed to pass them on to the next village. No one seemed to know what this meant – was it a religious matter? A study was made and it was found that they were traveling all over the Northwest Provinces at the rate of a hundred miles in twenty-four hours.

Some people were convinced that this was a magical rite, to avert a coming disaster; some thought that it was another type of rite, appeasing the gods responsible for cholera epidemics. Even the natives themselves did not seem to know why a watchman had to run through the night to deliver the *chuppatties* but they were afraid to disobey and break the chain of communication. Some even thought that it was a British plot to make everyone in India eat the same food and therefore become Christian.

But the old men, the wise men, remembered that upon the downfall of Mahratta power, a sprig of millet and a morsel of bread had passed from village to village and that the distribution of the *chuppatties* was significant of some great trouble which was to follow.

And there was another disturbing incident. One morning, when escorting Rosamunde to the stables, Raymond had come across a mad looking man, naked save for a *dhoti* about his loins and a dirty turban on his head, squatting in the square, placing a stone *lingam*, smeared with red, at the foot of a *peepul* tree that spread over the dirt square. "*Sub lal hogea hai!*" he was murmuring as he sat before the lingam. "*Sub lal hogea hai!*"

Raymond was affronted. "Get that thing out of here!" he exploded. "How dare you place that where a *mem sahib* can see it?"

The man turned quickly and glared at him and then began cackling with laughter. He stood up and ran away into the jungle, still giggling. The insane cackle came back to them from the depths of the jungle. "*Sub lal hogea hai!*" he shouted. "*Sub lal hogea hai!*" He left the offending object behind.

"What did he mean, 'everything has become red?" Rosamunde queried. "And what is that piece of stone? Is that *blood* on it?"

Raymond flushed with mortification. "It is a religious symbol," he said stiffly. "And it is probably goat's blood. These people are ignorant and superstitious and will sacrifice animals to their pagan gods. And who can know what he meant; the man was obviously mad."

He refused to answer any more questions.

Rosamunde described the stone to Ameera, who stared at her in astonishment when Rosamunde told her how upset Raymond had become.

"That is a *lingam*," Ameera explained. "It is the symbol of Shiva, he who amongst other things is a god of fertility. It is a male member. You will remember that I taught you of Shiva's aspects as the fertile one and the destroyer." She had been teaching Rosamunde about the Hindu religion. "Why did it so upset your husband?"

"Among the *Angrezi* it is not proper for ladies to see these things," Rosamunde tried to explain.

"But do you not see his *lingam* when he copulates with you?" Ameera said in amazement. Truly, the *Angrezi-log* were very strange!

Rosamunde did not know how to answer this. Fortunately, it appeared to be a rhetorical question, for Ameera was more interested in resuming another kind of lesson – dancing.

They had discovered that they both loved the dance. Ameera had shown her new friend some of the symbolic and complicated movements of the *nautch,* the dance, for her mother had been a *nautch* girl, a professional dancer. Rosamunde had shared ballet steps, even bringing her *pointe* shoes to Ameera's private *zenana* and going up on her toes to the amazement of all the ladies therein.

They were learning a great deal from each other and having a good deal of fun as well, with much laughter. Ameera's friendship and her willingness to explain Indian culture and help Rosamunde become more fluent in her language skills had come to mean a good deal to both Rosamunde and Sinéad. They preferred the *zenana* to the drawing rooms of the cantonment.

To spare Rosamunde fighting so much with Raymond, the feline familiar had become silent when in company. She tried her best to be quiet but she chafed under the restrictions. She ended in spending a good deal of her time with the servants, who after an initial period of wariness, had finally come to accept her. She missed Rosamunde, though. She had been with her Witch since she was a kitten and Rosamunde was eight. At home in Ireland the familiars ate at table, attended church, parties, concerts and the theatre with their Witches and Wizards and were accounted part of the family. Here, Raymond expected her to just say 'meow', purr and chase mice and eat her supper on the floor like a proper 'pet'. He had been shocked when he found her reading a book and disbelieving when he saw her writing a letter to Brendan. It was unnatural, that is what it was, what if other people saw?

Both Rosamunde and Sinéad grew tired of the phrase

'what will people think?" And Raymond began to think that every transgression, as he termed any action that he did not sanction, was deliberate and part of a scheme to make him look foolish.

It was a household on the verge of an explosion and it finally came on a very hot morning in late April.

Rosamunde, with Sinéad on her shoulder, had ridden into town, where, unbeknownst to Raymond, she was spending the morning with Ameera. He thought that she was spending time with Mrs. Dalbeigh and the other ladies, who met almost daily to gossip, do needlework and dissect the character of any woman who did not attend their little conclaves. Rosamunde had never told him that she *was* attending the Dalbeigh gatherings. It never occurred to her that he would think that she was doing so, for he seemed to her totally uninterested in what she did during the day. If she told him about a household crisis or something that had happened in the barracks he seemed bored and said that such things were women's concerns. She was unused to accounting for her time to someone as well, for her parents gave her a great deal of freedom as they trusted her completely.

On this particular hot morning Rosamunde had left early for Ameera's house.They were going to put on a little dance for the other members of the household, combining elements of both Eastern and Western dance. Even the senior wife and her entourage were interested in seeing it.

At just after nine Raymond returned home, in a foul temper. His horse had cast a shoe whilst on parade that morning and the Colonel, who had also been in a bad mood, had dressed him down, right out on the *maidan*, the parade ground, for carelessness. When he returned to the stables he found Kashan missing and Rosamunde's mare was still out as well. All of the mounts belonging to the other ladies were in their stalls.

Raymond was more than a little annoyed. He thought that he had made it clear to Rosamunde that she was to ride with the other ladies and not go careering off with only her *syce* in attendance.

When he went back to the house he found Mrs. Dalbeigh in the *gol-kuma*, the sitting room. She looked impatient and demanded to know where Rosamunde might be.

"I have been calling for three days in a row!" she said in irritation. "It is Mrs. DeLacey's turn to host the Mutton Club and I have not been able to find her to iron out the details as she is so new to our ways she will no doubt need my guidance. Your servants are so stupid! All that they will say is that she is out riding!"

Alam Din stood nearby at attention, his face blank.

"Where is the *mem sahib?*" Raymond demanded of the *khidmatgar.*

"She rides out, *sahib*," said Alam Din.

"I know that!" said Raymond impatiently, "but where did she go?"

A new voice entered the conversation. Manu Patel, Raymond's orderly said sourly, coming into the room, "The *mem* visits a certain house in the Hindu quarter of the city, *sahib*, almost daily."

Alam Din looked at him reproachfully. The other servants were happy that Rosamunde was finding some enjoyment and it pleased them that her new friend was an Indian lady.

"Oh, my goodness!" exclaimed Mrs. Dalbeigh. "Do you think that she is meeting some man? Is that why we never see her on our rides or at any of our meetings?" She giggled like a schoolgirl.

Raymond was suddenly blazingly angry, both at Mrs, Dalbeigh for saying such a thing in front of the servants and at Rosamunde for putting him in such a position. Why was she not with the other ladies as he expected her to be?

"I would appreciate it, ma'am," he said stiffly to Mrs. Dalbeigh, "if you would mention this to no one until I have a chance to investigate. It is more than likely something totally innocent."

"I am the soul of discretion!" she said, with a simper. In truth, she was already deciding with who to share this lovely morsel of gossip.

"Thank you for bringing this to my attention, Patel," he said to the orderly. "Mrs. DeLacey is very young and does not know how to go on here. We must all keep an eye on her."

Patel bowed, his inclined head hiding a look of

contempt. "I am the *sahib's* to command," he said smoothly. Something in his tone made Alam Din look at him sharply. The look Patel tuned upon the *khidmatgar* was utterly bland.

It was at this inauspicious moment that Rosamunde entered. She was rather hot and disheveled from her ride, but there was a glow about her from the outcome of a successful and well-received dance exhibition. Even the sour senior wife had clapped and praised and gasped in delight.

Raymond made a grave tactical error. "Where have you been?" he blurted out, angered again at the sight of her. With a jolt he thought that she looked like a woman who had just been bedded.

"I was out riding," she said, placing her whip and gloves on a small inlaid table. She reached up and removed her riding hat as well and laid it down, revealing her hair to be falling from its pins and in wild disarray.

"Did you fall off your horse?" Raymond demanded.

Rosamunde stared at him. What was all of this? "What are you – an Inquisitor?" she flashed back. "If you have something to discuss should we not be private –?"

Sinéad sauntered into the room. One look at the angry faces and the flushed and avid look on Mrs. Dalbeigh's face and she well understood the situation.

"Have ye not the sense God was after givin' a flea?" she asked sarcastically of Raymond. "To be airin' yer dirty linen in front of this old cow who is bein' the biggest gossip in the whole of Hindustan? It's lost yer senses ye have, the both of yez!"

Mrs Dalbeigh's eyes ran out on stems as the cat spoke. She had never seen a familiar. She then screamed artistically and fainted, hitting the floor hard.

Alam Din leaped forward, yelling for Sita to come and burn some feathers under the poor afflicted lady's nose. Patel was sent to fetch Mrs. Dalbeigh's own maid. All was chaos for a brief while.

When at last everything had quieted down it was well into the heat of the day. Raymond in his usual stiff fashion said that they would have *tiffin* and bathe first and then talk. It was an uncomfortable meal. Raymond's manner made

Rosamunde felt like a naughty little girl. Her father had never made her feel so.

As he questioned her, Rosamunde freely admitted to seeing her Indian friend. Raymond could question Kashan if he doubted her word. Raymond, although relieved that she was not seeing a man, was nonetheless horrified that his wife preferred the company of a native to that of other Englishwomen.

After a long rant on impropriety and the probable damage to his career should it become known that Rosamunde was fraternizing with the natives, he finally said "Things are going to change around here! I don't want you to see that woman again. Matters are going to be different in this command as well for we are getting a new commanding officer, one who has an excellent reputation of pulling lazy regiments such as these right up by their bootstraps. He arrives next week. I think that you have already met him. I do not wish any of this nonsense going on under his eye! He can do a good deal for my future."

"Who is it?" Rosamunde queried, In truth she did not care. Perhaps if she placated Raymond by showing an interest in his career, she could go on seeing Ameera and the other women in the *zenana*. How could she bear this place otherwise? She had quietly let him rave at her, feeling as if she was being persecuted.

"Major, or as I should say now, Colonel Higby," said Raymond.

Sinéad let out a long, low hiss.

11

shadows

Cathal paused in writing his letter to take yet another concerned look at Alan, who lay on the charpoy that had been pulled out onto the *chabutara*. The Maharajah's *Hakim* had just left and had gone to make a report to his employer.

Ravi sat beside his friend, looking grave, while Alan himself, looking as if he was worn to the bone, lay back, eyes closed and unmoving.

Cathal looked down at what he had written to Sinéad.

...I thought that he was getting better but there have been dizzy spells that he has tried to hide from us. Today he collapsed and has just seen a doctor, who seems to be at a loss as to what might be wrong. All that Alan would say – he seems unable or unwilling to say much – is that the ley lines are 'wrong'. He tried to draw power from them and could not.

I wish that you will share this letter with Rosamunde. I think that perhaps Sir Simon should be notified. There is no telegraph connection here and the post is erratic. Indeed, this letter will be a long time in reaching you, for it must be taken by a servant to the nearest posting station. Perhaps you could telegraph Delhi from Malabad. I think there is a diplomatic hippogriffe express out of Bombay we could use to reach Ireland if we use the Duke's name. You and Rosamunde will know what to do, I am certain.

I cannot conceal from you, my dear friend, that I am extremely worried. The Hakim seems a good, competent doctor but he knows nothing about the ills that beset Wizards. I wish that I could draw on the ley lines so that I could ascertain exactly what Alan means by 'wrong'.

I am writing to Brendan as well, but that letter will take even longer to reach him. If I had any hopes that he would hear the dragon whistle I would blow it myself. But he is much too far away to hear it.

Alan does not want anyone 'bothered' by this but I

think that I am justified in ignoring his request where his health is concerned.

Cathal signed the letter and then slid the stylus that held the pen off his paw. As he shook sand over the ink on the sheet, a shadow fell on the paper and he looked up to see Ravi standing over him.

"He's sleeping," said Ravi, and perched on the balcony rail near the small table Cathal sat upon. "What does he mean by 'wrong', Cathal? When we were at Oxford or in Ireland I saw Alan and other Wizards draw upon the ley lines many times. I never saw any one faint from doing it."

"I really don't know!" Cathal said, spreading his paws in an eloquent gesture. "Wizards usually do collapse after a Great Working, but Alan was only attempting to pull a little power. The ley lines both empower and can drain a Wizard at home. But as far as we could find out there is little use of the ley lines in this part of the world, so they should not be draining since their power is not being depleted. When Alan's father was in China over twenty years ago, the ley lines were just brimming with untapped power. Are there Wizards here in India that our books don't tell us about that might have been using the ley lines?"

"Not that I am aware of. We have conjurors and *Faklirs,* who seem to have some magic," said Ravi. "I have seen some strange things in the bazaars but nothing like what I saw in *Belait.* There are always rumors that certain people are sorcerers, black magicians, such as the Maharajah of Jhaniput and Nana Sahib, he who is Dhondu Pant, the adopted son of the Peshwa of Bithur. But my father says that both these men are merely debauched sensualists. We are inclined to equate unbridled lust with magic, particularly when the man involved is so unprepossessing as to make one wonder why so many women offer themselves to him."

"There *is* sex magic, you know. Alan studied it at Oxford," said Cathal absently. "But it does not draw upon the ley lines." He sighed and then said "I have written to Sinéad and suggested that Sir Simon be notified."

"I agree," Ravi said, "and I know that my father will feel the same. He would wish to know if I were ill in a country far from home. Ram Dass shall take your letter to the nearest

113

posting house when it is finished."

He looked out towards the mountains for a moment and then said "If I had known how ill he really was I would have never suggested that he make such a journey. I thought that he was recovered –" he swallowed hard and stopped speaking, unable to go on.

Cathal went up to him and lay a paw on his arm. "We all thought he was recovered enough to come, even Stuart and the other Wizard Healer who saw him. They would have never approved the trip otherwise. Perhaps the *Hakim is* correct and he is just worn out and a good period of rest will set him back on his feet. He has worked himself into the ground, you know, since he left University. Lyonshall is not a taskmaster but once Alan starts a research project he cannot leave it alone until it is finished. It made for long hours with little rest, in spite of being urged to take time off by me and everyone else."

"He wrote to me of how much he enjoyed magical research and spell development," said Ravi, recovering himself a bit.

"It has become his passion," Cathal returned. "So many wonderful things have come out of the laboratory, things that help everyone not just magicians. There are common things like laundry wringing spells that make servants' lives easier to things such as spells that make roads and bridges sturdier and safer. Alan's last project was a spell to shore up tunnels to make digging safer for miners and navvies putting in the railways and permanently keep the ceiling and walls from collapse. It's important work."

Ravi nodded. He still felt terribly guilty as he truly thought of Alan as a much-loved brother and would have never done anything to harm him. He thought that this visit would be a pleasure for both of them. He had longed for years for his family to meet Alan and Peter. But he would never recover from the self-reproach he would feel should this sojourn prove the ruin of Alan's health.

Alan had eventually somewhat recovered as the weeks went on, but to both Ravi and Cathal he seemed quieter and rather withdrawn, although he fully participated in all that the Maharajah had planned.

But he tired easily, a fact that he attempted to hide. Both Cathal and Ravi learned to watch him carefully and diplomatically end the current activity. Alan went riding, on a tiger shoot, elephant-back, even climbed a little way into the mountains where he and Ravi and Ravi's brothers camped out and hunted for *gurrals,* mountain goats, although Alan's participation in the hunts was limited to watching.

Every day a *gop,* a milkmaid, delivered a full glass of fresh milk to Alan's room, which he drank down at once on the *Hakim's* orders and obediently ate all of the other concoctions the man prescribed of strengthening herbs and food.

In all of this time, as May approached, Cathal had had no answer to his letter to Sinéad. He had not had a letter from Brendan either, but he had not expected to as the monastery was high in the most remote part of Tibet, away from even trading routes, and they had been warned that mail was difficult both to send and to get. But he had expected at least a brief note from his fellow familiar. He wrote again and still received no answer. What was wrong? Cathal fretted over her lack of communication. Ram Dass assured him that the letters had been handed in at the closest *dâk* bungalow, which also served as the posting house.

And in Malabad, Sinéad was wondering why she had had no mail from Cathal, in spite of the fact that she had written once, sometimes twice a week. Nor had Rosamunde had any mail from Alan in answer to her letters to her cousin.

Mail had arrived from Ireland, which made Rosamunde weep as she read it The latest mail had arrived after a particularly acrimonious quarrel with Raymond over his latest edict. He had threatened to hire another groom whose duty would be to keep her from visiting Ameera.

Rosamunde had written to her friend, asking Alam Din to write the letter as her written Urdu was not as yet fluent. The sympathetic *khidmatgar* had delivered the note his own self, and taken Sita with him so that the *ayah* could explain what was happening to Ameera. The young Hindu woman was quite understanding. When the lieutenant *sahib* had recovered from his fit of unreasonable behavior she would see her friend again. Husbands must be humored. Men took these notions into their heads, as stupid and wrong as they were.

To Rosamunde, it was as if she had gone into a period of darkness. She still wanted to make a success of her marriage but lately she could not seem to make Raymond happy, from what she chose for daily menus to the continued failure of a physical relationship, he had nothing but anger and criticism for her.

She was flaring back at him more and more often as it was simply not in her nature to be meek and mild. She could not abide unfairness and most of what he criticized seemed beyond her control, particularly their sexual relations. She was ready, she was willing; he was the one who could not make it happen. How was this her fault?

She tried to be patient and pleasant and encouraging, but one evening, a very hot, stifling evening, in his extreme frustration he raised his hand as if he would strike her and she pushed him into the wall with a burst of Witchcraft.

He sat down on the floor with a thump, looking surprised. At first he looked thunderous but then said. "I suppose I deserved that! God, I'm sorry, Rosamunde! It's just that, just that – "

She said nothing.

"I want to love you so badly!" he burst out, not moving from the floor, "If I could just make love to you everything else would be fine, I know it! I just keep thinking over and over, what if people knew that we have been married all this time and I haven't taken you yet? What kind of a man does that make me?"

"It's nobody's business except ours!" she said angrily. "Why do you care so much what other people think?"

"I'm not the great granddaughter of a Duke with £10,000 in the bank who thinks she can do as she bloody well pleases!" he said bitterly. Of course one had to care what others thought! How could she be so silly? She was odiously spoiled.

He stood up and reached for his dressing gown that

was on a chest at the foot of the bed. "I think it best that I sleep in the book room tonight," he said. "I shall tell Alam Din that you have the headache from the heat and I do not care to disturb you."

He pulled open the door and did not notice that Sinéad ran past his feet into the room.

As Raymond closed the door behind him the cat leaped onto the bed where she headed straight for Rosamunde's arms.

Rosamunde put her furry little friend up against her cheek and sighed. "Oh, Sinéad, I don't know what to do!" She spoke in Gaelic, the language she almost always used when alone with her familiar.

"He's still after havin' his problem, is he?" said the cat. Like the everyone else in the tiny house she had come to know what their relationship lacked.

"Yes, "said Rosamunde in a low voice." Tonight I thought he was going to hit me!"

"As it were bein' yer fault because he is not bein' able to be havin' his way wi' ye!" Sinéad said indignantly.

"So I pushed him away with my Witchcraft and he should have bounced off the wall, Sinéad! I was *so* angry that he would dare to raise a hand to me! But he just went backwards with a thump and sat down on the floor. The power was not there! It was as if I was partially drained!" she shivered. "Every time I cast a spell, which is not often any more, it is as if my powers are waning!"

"'Tis because ye are not bein' happy," said the cat."or mayhap 'tis the heat here."

"I don't know what it is," Rosamunde said, her voice small,"but it frightens me."

"There's bein' somethin' else that has to be frightenin' ye as well," said Sinéad. "That besom Higby is after arrivin' tomorrow."

"Yes, and Mrs. Dalbeigh gives a tea to welcome him to the regiment. She is putting the pretty on the fact that Higby is replacing her husband and they are going to an even more obscure station than this in Gujerat. I am to help pour out."

Sinéad settled down in the crook of Rosamunde's arm. "Alan was not wantin' us to be tellin' ye this but it is bein' in my heart that ye ahd best be warned. On the ship, he was after speakin' about ye in a very bad way. He was talkin' about yer breasts and boastin' that he was going to be fuckin' ye."

Rosamunde looked confused. Her acquaintance with four letter words was slight. "What does 'fucking' mean?"

"Have intercourse," said the cat bluntly.

Rosamunde was horrified. "How could he say – or even think – such a thing? What kind of a lady does he think I am that I would ever even contemplate, oh, it's horrible!" she cried. "What else did he say?"

Sinéad told her everything that Higby had said and done. "I'll not wish to be frightenin' ye," the familiar said, "but 'tis best that ye know so ye can try an' never be alone wi' the spalpeen."

Rosamunde gave a long shudder. "Yes," she agreed. "Especially with my Witchcraft so diminished. I shall take great care never to be alone with that horrible man. He made me so uncomfortable, the way that he was used to stare at me! His glance was so hot and sometimes I felt as if he could see through my clothing! Oh, Sinéad, why are men so horrible? Why do they never think about anything else other than their lust?"

"Ye are after knowin' men who are not bein' like that, just be thinkin' of Alan an' yer Da an' yer uncles an' grandda."

"But they are all Wizards! Most of the non-magical men I have met seem to think of little else!" Rosamunde protested.

Sinéad was at a loss to explain this.

"I wish I was at home," said Rosamunde suddenly, with tears standing in her eyes. "I am so tired, Sinéad! Nothing I do seems to please Raymond. I can't seem to do anything right! I don't even speak properly. He corrected me the other day when I said can-<u>tone</u>-ments, he said it is pronounced can-<u>toon</u>-ment! And sometimes they seem to speak a different language here. They were talking about griffins at Mrs. Vernon's the other day and I began to talk about the griffins that live in the woods at Grandfather Lyon's estate and they laughed at me. Here a griffin is a newcomer to India, not an animal! No one tells me these things! I think they do it on purpose! If it were not for you and

Sita and Ameera I think I should run mad. And add to that this heat– !"

Rosamunde was finding the heat of India very difficult to cope with. Ireland was a cool country, but temperate, with temperatures seldom above 70 degrees Fahrenheit and barely ever below 40 at the lower end. Here, everyone kept saying that May and June, until the monsoon came, would be even hotter than it was now. And the monsoon would bring downpours and high humidity. It was unbearable.

"Since himself is sleepin' in the bookroom," said Sinéad, "it's cosyin' down wi' ye I'll be."

Rosamunde was quite agreeable to this. She did not want to be alone.

In the bookroom, Raymond sat at the desk, a sheaf of letters before him, illuminated in the glow of a single lamp.

There were quite a few of them: some had arrived from Ranijhat and one from Tibet and others were addressed to Cathal, Alan and Brendan had never been sent.

Raymond, orphaned at a young age, had been raised by an aunt and uncle who had very strict notions of propriety. One of his uncle's strongest beliefs was that he had the right to read and censor any mail that his wife or Raymond's cousin Letty received. This was for their protection and so he could keep an eye on their doings for any improper correspondence or thoughts. He had even read all of Raymond's mail until his nephew was of age.

Of course, Raymond thought that he had the same right. He had read all of Rosamunde's mail before he gave it to her, re-sealing it before he did so. The letters from her parents he passed on to her, as well as letters from other members of her family. He also read all of her outgoing mail before Alam Din posted it.

But those from Alan Stillfield, his peculiar little animal and from the dragon he had kept back from her. Nor did he let any letters written to any of them leave the bungalow. This was quite easy to do as Alam Din was under the strictest of orders, on pain of losing his position, to deliver all incoming and outgoing post to the Lieutenant *sahib* first.

119

(Alam Din had not considered Rosamunde's note to Ameera 'post'.)

Raymond felt no guilt in doing this. He considered Stillfield a pernicious influence on his wife and though much of her freedom of thought and speech had been encouraged by Stillfield. Her cousin seemed to have no idea of the proper relationship between men and women and insisted on talking to and treating women and natives as if they were equals.

He had attempted to read Rosamunde's diary as well, but here he was stymied, for it was a magical diary. To anyone save Rosamunde herself it looked as if it were full of blank pages. Raymond knew that she wrote in it for he had seen her at it, and he felt betrayed that she kept a spell on it so that he could not see what she had written. After all, it was his right to read it. Uncle had always read Letty's diary.

But radical changes were coming. The newly commissioned Colonel Higby was going to turn the regiment around and one of the bints at the *bibi-gurh* knew a *Hakim* who, she swore, could cure Raymond's problem with Rosamunde. It did not seem odd to Raymond that he had discussed his marriage bed with a whore. They knew about these things as that was their profession.

And once he was able to couple with Rosamunde and get her with child (he would order her to remove the contraceptive spell), she would settle down and become a proper wife like the others in the regiment, forget this native nonsense and Witchcraft, be obedient and help further his career, rather than impede it. He was certain of it.

the evangelicals

It seemed as if the summer season of 1857 would shatter all records for heat and for dust. The first week of May was blazingly hot.

Rosamunde visibly wilted. She spent most of her time laying on the bed in her wrapper, beneath the current of the *punkah* which seemed to do little besides move the hot air about and provide steady employment for the *punkah-wallah*.

Raymond was now sleeping almost entirely in the bookroom for this was a condition of his 'treatment' by the *Hakim* the bint had found for him. He was to stay away from the woman who caused him such sexual frustration until later in his treatment.

He tried his best, however, to be kind and thoughtful of Rosamunde. He felt guilty that he had nearly struck her and also felt badly that the heat was affecting her so. He bought her a Thermanidote which was a cylindrical device that stood against the exterior wall. It was filled with wet tatties and a revolving fan. A funnel from it projected into the room. The servants kept the tatties wet and turned a handle that then revolved the fan and then pumped the water-cooled air into the room.

Ordinarily, Rosamunde could have kept herself cool with Witchcraft, but as she had already noticed, that did not seem to be working properly.

She felt more and more depressed as each day passed.

She knew a large part of it was the heat, for her mind did not seem to function properly in the intensity of an Indian summer, and she was so tired all the time.

But she also felt deserted by Alan and Brendan. She had heard nothing from either of them since they had separated all those weeks ago. Alan was more than likely having a wonderful time in Ranijhat; too wonderful to bother with letters to his cousin.

She was also not eating well. The heat had destroyed

her appetite. Added to this was the lack of exercise, for she had given up riding to a great extent, only going out twice a week or so. Raymond insisted she ride with the other ladies and she found this so stifling and aggravating that she would rather not ride. A gentle walk around the cantonments, an occasional trot, not even a brisk trot, which irritated her little mare Devika as much as it did Rosamunde.

The servants viewed her lethargy with alarm. Anand, the *khansamah*, cooked every tempting dish he could think of and even resorted to creating several crisis in the kitchen to bring her out of her inertia.

One morning Sita insisted that her mistress come to the kitchen to see what that foolish fellow had done.

Rosamunde, caring little what had happened in the kitchen, nevertheless allowed Sita to bully her into her clothes and went to the kitchen where she found Anand straining the soup meant for the mid-day meal.

"Look, *mem,* look!" said Sita excitedly. "Only see what he has done, the stupid fellow! "

Obediently, Rosamunde looked, not seeing at first what Sita was so excited about. Her brain seemed very slow today.

Then she saw it – Anand was using a very unique soup strainer: Rosamunde's own silk stockings, the pair she kept for Sundays.

"Do not worry, *mem,* "said Anand in a placating fashion, a sheepish grin on his face. "They were not the clean ones!"

"It doesn't matter," said Rosamunde dully. "It's too hot to wear silk stockings. I'm going to lay down again, Sita. The next time you go to the bazaar please buy Anand a proper soup strainer." With this she left the room, leaving the servants staring at one another in consternation.

"Is it possible," said one of the laundry maids, "that the *mem sahib* is with child? My sister-in-law was so when she carried her first."

Alam Din snorted. "The *sahib* has never touched her! It would be a birth such as the infidel Christians prate of – that of a virgin mother!"

"Perhaps it is not the *sahib's* child," suggested Prem the sweeper, who was in the kitchen on sufferance as his profession was so low that it was generally performed by an Untouchable. But Prem was of the lowest caste, the *shudras,* whose function it was to serve the other castes.

Sita was affronted by this insult. "She is a good woman and obeys the laws of the *Angrezi* god! The cat has told me many things. Many men have paid her attentions but she pays them no mind." Her eyes filled with tears. "I care for her as if she were my daughter! And I do not know how to help her!"

"Perhaps when comes the monsoon," said Alam Din. "Many of the *Angrezi-log* suffer in the heat for they do not know how to manage. Only look at the foolish clothes that they wear!"

"The *sahib* once said that he would take her to the hills, to Simla, when the heat grew ill," said Gobind, the *nappy-wallah*.

Sita looked hopeful. "We must speak to Manu Patel, he may put the idea into the *sahib's* mind once more. Many of the *mem-log* will be going to the hills."

Unspoken was the knowledge that they all had - it was more than likely the ill relations between husband and wife that were troubling Rosamunde, not only the heat. They all knew that their employers no longer shared a bed and that the Lieutenant *sahib* was taking his pleasure with one of the bints at the house of women. Their employers scarcely even talked to one another any more.

Sinéad, too, was alarmed about Rosamunde, and wrote another agitated letter to Cathal. She also wrote a letter to her sister Aithne, in Ireland, asking her to share it with Julia and Stuart. The little cat had seen what Rosamunde was writing home, and it was more like a travelogue than anything personal.

Sinéad had another worry as well, Colonel Higby. The familiar, although uninvited, had infiltrated the tea party welcoming the Colonel to his new command. Except for one long look at Rosamunde, the Colonel had been quite circumspect and polite.

But that look had chilled Sinéad. It was a look of

gloating, of ownership. The man was supremely self-confident of eventual victory. And the cat was worried that Rosamunde, in her present mental state, might let down her guard. Her Witch was too apathetic lately.

Sunday, the 3rd of May, was another hot day. Rosamunde had slept very ill and was glad to see dawn coming. It meant she could get out of bed and bathe and be cool for a blessed few moments.

She lay in bed for a while listening to the sounds of the day beginning, from the city beyond the cantonments the call of the *Azams* from the minarets of the two mosques in the city, calling the faithful to prayer. Further away she could hear temple bells, and by the *ghat,* the steps or quay that led down to the water, there were shrines of various Hindu gods where people would be gathering. The devout Hindus would be going to bathe in the sacred waters of the river, and to make their first *pujas,* or prayers, of the day.

Birds filled the trees with strange song: the quarreling babblers, the chatter of the mynahs, the chipping of both rosy and of green parakeets as well as the scolding of the monkeys..

The door opened and closed and the mosquito netting lifted to reveal Sita. "Your bath waits, *mem,*" she said smiling at Rosamunde.

While Raymond preferred the shower bath, Rosamunde liked to bathe in a tin tub. In this climate the water was merely tepid as hot was unbearable. Sita poured a generous dollop of Rosamunde's favorite lavender bath salts into he water. Fortunately Rosamunde had brought a good supply of these and Julia had promised to send more when they were needed.

After a cool soak she was dressed and ready. Today she would attend church with Raymond. There were morning and evening services. In order to set a good example for the troopers Raymond always insisted that they attend both.

The Anglican church, which had been built in the style known to the irreverent as "disappointed Gothic", was at the moment bereft of a minister or *padre,* as a clergyman was called out here. A curate came from Delhi to conduct the services at the moment.

It was also stifling inside, even with the windows open. All those people packed together for a lengthy sermon made the temperature rise considerably. But no one would have dreamed of not attending church unless very ill. How would it look to shirk one's duty in so blatant a fashion?

Raymond sat at the breakfast table. On Sundays they did not have their 'little breakfast' but went straight to the main event.

The sheer amount of food on the table nauseated Rosamunde. For a slender man Raymond ate a great deal, heavy meals that made Rosamunde hot just thinking about putting such a large amount of food in her stomach,

There was the ever popular kedgeree which Rosamunde did not care for, beefsteak, eggs, toast, potatoes, curry, chicken, and fruit.

It was all that Rosamunde could manage to eat a slice of toast and a mango which Alam Din himself sliced for her, with an encouraging smile. To please him, she ate most of it. She drank all of her tea, which she had now learned to drink without milk and sweeten with *gur,* a coarse brown sugar.

Raymond was uncommonly talkative today. He had been complimented by his new commander and told he was deserving of a promotion, and indeed, the Colonel would see that he had it.

Rosamunde could see that she was going to grow very tired of 'the Colonel says'. Raymond approved everything that the new Colonel had done. He was shaking up these lazy dogs!

Sinéad, was on the floor beside Rosamunde's chair. Raymond had laid down the law on the cat sitting at table. It was unnatural! She listened sourly to Raymond waxing eloquent about Colonel Higby. Raymond was a gowk! Did he not realize that the Colonel was trying to get on his good side so that he could lift Rosamunde's skirts? The Colonel had already been sniffing around. He had questioned Alam Din as to when Rosamunde went out riding, and when she was alone in the house. Alam Din, as Sinéad had requested, had spun a farrago of nonsense about his mistress's habits.

Rosamunde was in no mood this morning to listen to a

sermon which over the weeks had become increasingly vehement about the duty of a Christian to lead his little brown brothers to the paths of righteousness.

It was therefore a horrible shock to find that, rather than the curate, who was bad enough, the Holloways had arrived and would henceforth be taking over the church, which was now to be of the Methodist affiliation.

Holloway's sermon was long, and spoke glowingly of the joys of converting the heathen and how their trip to the Holy Land had inspired the Holloways. They of course, were disappointed that the Holy land was not a *Christian* land, as it should be. Monday evening at the billiard hall (made available to them by the kindness of Colonel Higby) they were going to give a little talk about their trip and present some Magic Lantern views of the Holy Land.

"We shall definitely attend," Raymond murmured in Rosamunde's ear, at which her heart sank. Why had these horrible people had to come here of all places? Was there not another location in all of India they could have gone to spread their ignorance and bigotry? Most of the things that Mr. Holloway had said in this morning's sermon had set her teeth on edge. She had been raised in the Anglican church but she had also been raised to consider other's viewpoints and in respect for others' beliefs. Witches and Wizards also tended to believe in the old Celtic gods and goddesses in addition to their Christian doctrine and did not seem to feel that belief in both was contradictory.

The Holloways stood at the door, bidding their new parishioners goodbye and hoping to see then at evensong, as well as at the Monday lecture.

They professed themselves to be delighted to see Rosamunde again and even asked after Alan. But they did it in such a way that Rosamunde could feel her temper rising.

"And your heathen – er, "cousin", the Chinee?" Inquired Mr. Holloway, with his unctuous smile. "Has he found the path of righteousness as yet? I was hurt and surprised that he would not pray with me and let me save his soul "

"So good of your family to acknowledge him," put in Mrs. Holloway. "Praise the Lord! Although it is not quite proper to introduce him to the ladies in one's family."

Rosamunde stared at the complacent faces of the self righteous couple in front of her. "Do you think that my cousin Alan is *illegitimate?*" she choked out. "That's the most idiotic drivel I have ever heard, even from–"

"Rosamunde!" said Raymond sharply. "I am certain that Mr. And Mrs. Holloway meant no such thing! Don't make a scene, people are staring at us." Her hand had been on his arm; he now pulled her closed to him, in a gesture that looked affectionate but was actually one of censure.

"A most interesting and enlightening service, sir," he said to Mr. Holloway. "We shall be sure to attend the evening service and to see the lecture as well. I have always wished to see the Holy land."

In spite of her anger Rosamunde was suddenly conscious of being stared at. She turned her head slightly and met the eyes of Colonel Higby, who was heading towards them. He smiled at her, on the surface, a friendly enough gesture towards the wife of a fellow officer, but something in his look sent a chill down her spine. His look was possessive and again, she felt as if he had stripped her clothes from her back. With her free hand she pulled the lace shawl she wore despite the heat, up around her shoulders and forward over her breasts.

He smiled more broadly when he saw this. So she was quite conscious of him, was she? Her shyness made him desire her more than if she had responded to provocative glances.

As Higby was exchanging pleasantries with the missionaries he was watching her. He was biding his time, for she was a prize worth the wait. The time that had passed had not dampened his ardor. It had only served to increase it. Unlike some women he had known he had not been disappointed when he saw her again. She was still one of the most beautiful, desirable creatures he had ever seen.

And soon she would be his. Getting DeLacey out of the way would be no problem. Higby looked forward to a long and satisfying *affaire* with Mrs. DeLacey. If she was even half as lovely naked as he imagined, he would be a very happy man, especially once he had done teaching her what pleased him in bed. There was no better way to spend the long, hot afternoons than in bed with a lovely woman.

As Raymond drew Rosamunde away from the church

she decided that she was going to develop a very bad headache that very evening. She could stand no more of the Holloways or Higby.

Even in the hills it was hot this year. The cool winds that came off the mountains in the morning and again in the evening seemed to cease during the hottest part of the day. During the night it was fresh and sweet , the wind smelling of pine and the sound of the wind in the firs, the chestnuts, the rhododendrons and the *deodars* lulling one to sleep.

Alan could no longer lie out of doors on the *chabutara* in the strong sunlight but occupied the *charpoy* in his room, with split cane *chiks* blocking the sunlight from the windows. It was nowhere nearly as hot as it would be down on the plains but it was hot enough for someone raised in Ireland to feel the heat.

He kept to his room during the hottest part of the day, taking a cool bath after the morning's activities and not stirring until the sun began to decline. Usually he tried to sleep, but today he had company. The Maharajah and Ravi shared his room. Alan had been playing chess with Ravi's father, but the game had ended and the Maharajah was puffing on his *hookah,* an immense water pipe. The Maharajah was so fond of this that he employed a servant just to take care of it called, the *hookah-burdar*.

"I received a most interesting communication today," the Maharajah Zahallah said. He reached into the front of his *achkan* and withdrew a folded placard. "Are you able to read Persian?" he asked Alan.

"Cathal can read it better than I," Alan said rather tiredly. He was leaning back on the *charpoy,* with his eyes almost closed, feeling as exhausted as if he had climbed the tallest snow-covered peak of the distant *Dur Khaima.*

The Maharajah chuckled. He was constantly amused by the fact that Cathal could talk and read and write. "One day I shall go to *Belait,*" he said, unfolding the thick paper, "and see all of these talking and reading creatures for myself."

He handed the paper to Cathal who quickly scrutinized it. "It's calling upon 'all true Mussulmen to rise up and

128

slaughter the English!" he said in astonishment. "Where had you this, sir?"

"From a peddler who has just come from Cawnpore. These are all over the city there, he says. And there are as well, *fakirs* and *maulvis* moving all about the countryside, warning people that the *feringhis* mean to convert them to Christianity and exhorting them to resist all pressure and to fight if necessary for their faith."

Alan stirred restlessly. "Rosamunde," he murmured. He had been thinking of her quite a bit lately. Why had she not written to him as she had promised? His letters had gone unanswered. He had even written to DeLacey, wanting to know if Rosamunde was ill and that was why she had not written to him. But there had been no reply to that letter either.

He now opened his eyes and said "Is she in danger? *Is* there a real danger?'"

"She's probably in the safest place possible," said Ravi soothingly. "There are two regiments at Malabad at least. But I shall send Ram Dass to her if you like, Alan. If it should actually come to trouble, he can get her away in safety." He did not say: "You cannot go for you are too ill and would collapse before you had completed half of the trip."

"There are always malcontents that spread this sort of dissent," said the Maharajah. "Nevertheless, it might be a most excellent notion to send Ram Dass to the young lady. He is clever and trustworthy."

Alan felt a wave of despair wash over him. *What is wrong with me?* he thought bleakly. It was not just a physical illness. He was feeling his magic leach away day by day. It was terrifying and he did not know what was causing it or how to stop it. If he did not have magic he would not know any longer who or what he was.

13

ā fateful ride

In the following week the heat continued. It was very dry; the dust was thick and choking everywhere. At least a month would pass before the monsoon would arrive, bringing torrential rains and high humidity, a doubtful relief from the dry heat.

Rosamunde often thought longingly of the green softness of Ireland. The jungle was green, but it was different from her homeland, which had been so aptly named the Emerald Isle. The jungle was a strange, frightening place, with an overabundance of life and too many things that wanted to kill anyone who wandered into it. She often longed for the gray, rainy days so common in Ireland, rather than the harsh sun which beat relentlessly upon the baked earth.

At Raymond's insistence they had attended the lecture on the Holy Land which might have been interesting if not for the constant proselytizing of the Holloways and Mrs. Holloways oft repeated "Praise the Lord!" The Holloways had managed to obtain a set of hand-tinted, glass Magic Lantern slides, which were very well done.

Without Ameera to visit, or the bazaar, for Raymond had decided that it was highly improper for his wife to go there as well, Rosamunde had little to do. The small bungalow ran itself and she had read most of the books she had brought out with her. The station had a small library but the titles were very out of date and ran strongly towards fiction of the more lurid sort, such as *Varney the Vampire,* or the elderly novel *The Castle of Otranto,* which Rosamunde found overly melodramatic. Many of the volumes were sermons, or bound copies of *Sporting Life.*

This left little besides writing letters and needlework. She had been advised to bring silver needles to India as steel would rust in the humidity and from one's fingers sweating. But as a Witch, all of her sewing implements had to be of silver or copper for Cold Iron of any type was poisonous. In the heat she found it difficult to concentrate on needlework and the needle often slipped from her fingers.

Her days passed in restless slumber on the bed during the heat where she dreamed of home, and the evenings in the company of people she increasingly disliked with each passing day.

She tried to make friends amongst the other women but they seemed to have closed ranks against her. She could not know that this attitude came from their husbands, who resented the new Colonel who was making them tow the mark, and that resentment spilled over onto Raymond. They were calling him a toffee-nosed little sod because he was the new Colonel's right-hand man.

Writing letters was frustrating also, for the post took so long to get back and forth. For every five letters she wrote she got one back. The people at home had much more to do than did she. Rather unfairly, she thought that they were forgetting about her and did not miss her at all.

Sinéad was a little better off. She was free to make friends amongst the other animals on the station and had become particularly close to an animal that was a pet of one of the troopers, a mongoose named Hari.

Hari was a playful, bold little creature, short-legged, with a pointed nose and small ears. He was gray in colour, with specks of darker gray. He had five-toed feet and a long furry tail.

Sinéad had seen Hari kill a poisonous snake and had been much impressed. The mongoose, swift and agile, had darted in and bit the snake's head, crushing its skull. Coming from Ireland Sinéad was not used to snakes at all and she viewed then with deep distrust, especially when she found out that the bite of many of the snakes here in India was poisonous.

They often played together. The mongoose had a great deal of energy and one of their favorite games was chasing each other as fast as they could go. Generally they did this out of doors as Sinéad did not want to disturb Rosamunde or put the servants in a bad frame by having animals underfoot.

Sunday morning, the 10th of May had dawned blazingly hot. The air was suffocating with not a breath of air stirring and any activity sent dust into the air.

Raymond was on duty that day as even on Sunday there was parade and he thought it was important for discipline today, especially after what had happened at Meerut, so close to them, but the day before.

On the 24th of April eighty five men of the 3rd Light Calvary, all natives, had refused to take the new cartridges that were served out, saying that it would break their caste to touch the defiled grease of the cartridges. Nothing could move them from this stance.

A court of inquiry had been held and the men had been convicted and sentenced to be subject to court martial. That sentence had been carried out on Saturday, May 9th. Under a dark sky of storm clouds (which came to nothing) the men were stripped of their uniforms, their boots removed and their ankles shackled. The sentence was to be imprisonment for ten years with hard labor for all but a few of them, mostly those men who had served five years or less.

As the men had been marched away, carrying their boots, a number of them had thrown their footwear at Colonel Carmichael, cursing him loudly in Hindustanee. He had never been popular with the men. The convicted men had exhorted their comrades in arms not to forget them. There was a good deal of murmuring in the ranks and as it always did, the murmuring had spread here to Malabad.

Since the eighty-five men had been arrested, matters had been tense in Meerut. Almost every night there had been fires in one part of Meerut or the other. Flaming arrows had set thatch alight as houses and shops alike had been fired and the bazaar had been full of violent arguments.

It was this last that had prompted Raymond to ban Rosamunde's visits to the bazaar. Naturally though, he had not told her of the real reason for his word was law and he did not feel that she needed an explanation. At any rate, one did not needlessly frighten women.

Rosamunde, left to her own devices whilst Raymond was on duty, did not attend church that morning. She rose, ate very little and bathed, returning to bed with a nagging headache. She felt that she simply could not bear the

Holloways for one more minute. They had been present at every dinner party and gathering that entire week and the more she saw of them the more she was confirmed in her dislike of them. Nor could she bear the stifling church or the thought of her heavy hoop and a bonnet on her head. It was much better to just lie upon her bed, clad only in a thing cotton wrapper and let the slight hot breeze from the cooling device Raymond had bought to try to refresh her.

She only had to survive for three more days. On Wednesday, after Molly arrived for the promised visit, Raymond had promised he would take them to Simla, where they would remain until September, when the monsoon ended and cooler weather prevailed. Molly would then return home. Sita had already begun the packing for the trip.

Sinéad was out of doors, playing with her new friend. Rosamunde was glad that her familiar had made a friend, for the arguments the cat had with Raymond were becoming increasingly acrimonious.

Rosamunde had made a momentous decision the night before, alone in bed. If matters did not improve between her and her husband by the end of the year she was going home and seek a divorce. Ireland, next to Wales in the Six Nations, had the most liberal divorce laws, for current Irish law was based on the old Celtic laws. And at any rate, Rosamunde could easily obtain a divorce, an annulment, on the grounds of non-consummation. Grandfather Chenevix had the finest attorneys and he would gladly help her if that was what it came to.

This decision made her feel as if a great burden had been lifted and she slid into a doze very easily, hoping to sleep off her headache.

Sinéad had had words with Raymond that morning while Rosamunde still slept. He caught her reading yesterday's newspaper, the *Delhi Gazette*. That the cat could talk, and even worse, could read and write, infuriated him, as it went against every thing he had ever learned about the way things were. Animals were inferior; they were here to serve man as food and as beasts of burden and perhaps even companions, but not to express their own opinions and think for themselves.

She was deep in an article when he came upon her unawares and snatched the paper out from under her, almost sending her tumbling head over heels.

"Never let me see you doing that again!" he said, his voice shaking with anger. "You're a damned cat! Start acting like one! Go chase mice and earn your keep!"

"I do earn me keep!" she retorted. "I've me wages as me Witch's familiar."

"Rosamunde does not need a *familiar!*" he said, making of the word an obscenity.

Sinéad stuck her tongue out at him and scampered off before he could lift a hand to hit her.

So it was that by the time Hari showed up, wanting to play, Sinéad was in a foul mood. And when she and Hari were outside in the garden and saw the window to Raymond's book room standing open, she asked the mongoose if he would like to play indoors.

It was in her mind that she would create a mess in Raymond's room, muss up his papers, knock over as many things as she could – anything to pay him back for being such a gowk and making her beloved Witch unhappy.

Hari was agreeable and joined her in going up on the shelves and knocking things down. It was fun! It was fortunate for the two animals that the bookroom was far from the kitchen and that the servants that morning were deep in a discussion of what had happened at Meerut the previous day. Otherwise they would have been caught and stopped.

Hari found a drawer in the desk slightly opened. With his five-toed, non-tractile paws, so used to burrowing, he easily opened the drawer. "Oh look," he said to his friend, "It's full of the *sahib's* papers!"

"Let's be havin' them out and all over the floor!" said Sinéad vindictively. Bad cess to him! It would take him a long time to straighten out this mess, even should he have his orderly clean up the room. The sorting of his private papers would be up to Raymond himself.

With cheerful abandon Hari began digging and throwing the papers, which seemed to be all envelopes, out of the drawer and Sinéad for a while had a fine time pouncing and chasing.

Then by chance one of the envelopes caught her eye.

It was her own paw-writing.

Shocked, she began pawing through the other envelopes that Hari was so gleefully throwing out of the drawer.

There, from within Raymond's desk was all of the missing mail, letters from Cathal and Alan, even one from Brendan. And there were also her letters and Rosamunde's to Alan, Cathal and Brendan! He had kept their mail from them and had not allowed theirs to their family and friends to leave the bungalow.

Sinéad was so angry that she began spitting and hissing. The only words from her mouth were in the Gaelic with such venom in her voice that Hari stopped what he was doing and stared at her in consternation.

"D'anan do diabhal!" she swore. *"Do chorp don diabhal! Dannú ort! Loscadh is dó ort! Múchadh is há ort! Marbhfháise ort!"* "Your soul to the devil! Your body to the devil! Damnation on you! Scorching and burning on you! Smothering and drowning on you! A shroud on you!" Her fur stood up almost straight on end, making her look twice her size and her ears were flat against her head. Her eyes almost gave off sparks.

"Please be excusin' me," she said to Hari, "but I've got to be telling me Witch about this!"

"Why did he do this, Sinéad?" said Rosamunde, kneeling amidst the pile of letters on the floor of Raymond's book room. "I don't understand!"

She had not wanted to believe Sinéad when the familiar had come to her room and awakened her to tell her of the discovery. She was all too well aware of the ill feelings between the cat and Raymond.

But the familiar had insisted that her Witch come and see for herself, and the evidence of Raymond's perfidy was irrefutable.

Rosamunde was stunned. How could he do such a thing? He had no right to withhold her mail from her nor did he have the right to withhold her communications from anyone else – nor Sinéad's! She would have been stunned to learn that the law actually felt differently about that.

She could not imagine her father doing such a thing, nor any of her male relations. What she read, whom she wrote to, her mail, had never been censored. Her father, her uncle, her grandfather and great grandfather, even Great great grandfather Lyon, all trusted her good sense and judgment, considering her a mature person, not someone who had to be censored and coddled! It was an insult and a breach of trust so profound that suddenly she could stand the bungalow no more. She had to get out or start screaming.

She gathered up the letters and said "I'll read these later. I shall post the others that did not go out on the way to Ameera's."

"Ameera's?" Sinéad's ears poked up. "Himself is not wantin' ye yo be goin' there."

"After this he has forfeited all right to tell me what to do!" Rosamunde stood up with the letters in a pouch of her skirt held above the floor. "I have to get away from here, Sinéad. And Ameera's is the only place that I can go. Please run and fetch Sita. I shall need to change into my riding habit."

"Do not ride out today, *mem sahib*," Kashan begged as he tossed Rosamunde up into the saddle. "There is something in the air, a feeling, it is not good, you may not be safe. At least, let me come with you!"

"I am going to the house of Ameera Sharma, Kashan," she said, smiling rather absently at him. "If there is nay trouble I shall stay with her. I will be safe there, the *Hirren Mahal* is almost a fortress."

She took up the reins as he let go Devika's bridle. "Thank you for your concern, but I shall be fine."

She touched heel to the little mare's side and Devika,

under exercised recently, took off at a fast canter, Sinéad clinging to her Witch's shoulder for dear life. Kashan stood looking after them, a troubled frown on his face.

Halfway to the city Rosamunde was accosted by Colonel Higby.

He came out of nowhere, blocking the road with his rangy chestnut horse, an animal far larger and heavier than the dainty Devika, who was of an Arabian strain and delicate in build.

"Well, well," said the Colonel in some satisfaction. "Just the person I was looking for! And in such an excellent location to find her, too! There is a secluded copse just off the road here that is perfect!"

"Get out of my way!" said Rosamunde sharply. "I am going into town!"

"The only place you're going is into that copse and off your horse. And then I am going to watch you take off every stitch you have on. When I've had my full of looking at you naked I am going to screw you until you scream. I'll spend the rest of the afternoon teaching you what I like and then we'll practice what I've taught you. We've the whole afternoon for fucking," he said, looking her up and down in an insolent, leering manner. "And don't worry about your husband catching us. I've made sure he has enough duties to keep him busy until after evening parade!"

"You're mad!" Rosamunde stammered. "What makes you think I would – you're *horrible!*"

"Let me put it this way, my dear Mrs. DeLacey, Rosamunde –" he said threateningly. "Unless you open your legs for me whenever I want you to do so I shall see to it that your husband is demoted to private and spends the rest of his days doing night guard duty in Kabul!"

"Kick him," said Sinéad in Animal speech to Devika.

Devika did not have to be told twice. Although she understood very little human speech she could tell that her mistress was frightened. She was fond of Rosamunde, who had a light hand and a good seat and liked a gallop as much as she, Devika, did.

With a squeal of rage the mare whirled and kicked the chestnut gelding in the side. The gelding whinnied in protest and began to rear and plunge.

137

The Colonel went off over the horse's head as his mount began to buck, hitting the ground with a thud.

Devika laid her ears back and came down hard then went into a flat-out gallop. Rosamunde was thrown backwards by the force but, having a firm grip with her legs around the leaping head of the sidesaddle, managed to stay on and bent forward against the rush of the wind. She made no attempt to stop Devika's headlong rush.

"To the *Hirren Mahal!*" Sinéad shouted clinging with her claws for all she was worth.

14

in the zenana

It had been a difficult day for Raymond. Not only was the heat oppressive but everyone's nerves seemed on edge. More than once he saw a group of native *sepoys*, whilst not on duty, talking together in low, earnest voices. Even the British troops seemed perturbed by the happenings at Meerut. There was a feeling of uneasiness, of distrust and waiting for something to happen that was very trying to the sensibilities.

In spite of the fact that Raymond was rather proud to have been given so much responsibility by the Colonel, completing all of his assigned tasks did not allow him any time to go back to the bungalow and check upon Rosamunde.

Therefore he was quite perturbed when, shortly after *tiffin,* which he ate off a tray at a desk, Mrs. Holloway came to see him.

She was a rather vague woman, with her brown hair in an untidy bun and an air of otherworldliness which was helped by her faded, myopic blue eyes. She dressed in severe, plain gowns of sober hues and wore no jewelry other than a plain gold wedding band.

"I hesitate to bother you, Captain," she said, entering the office, ushered in by Manu Patel, who stood on duty outside. "but we must talk."

Raymond politely stood up at once. "I am not a captain as yet, ma'am," he said, and went around to the other side of the desk to pull out a chair for her.

She seated herself and spread her skirts so that her ankles would not show. "But from what Colonel Higby tells us, you very soon will be a Captain. He is loud in his praise of your work and had recommended in highest terms your immediate promotion. And my husband and I much appreciate your attendance at all of the services and at our little lectures. Such a good example for the men! Many of these British troopers, you know, are as heathen as the Hindus."

She then peered at him in her earnest fashion and

said "Mrs. DeLacey was not in church this morning. I trust nothing is wrong?"

Raymond was annoyed. He thought that he had impressed upon Rosamunde the necessity of church attendance.

He said carefully "She feels the heat very much. This is her first year out here and the adjustment is difficult for her. She has a friend arriving for a visit on Tuesday and I am taking both of then to Simla, in the hills, for the hot months. No doubt she was heat-sick this morning."

"It is particularly hot," Mrs. Holloway agreed. "I am used to it however, because my husband and I, before this assignment, had a mission is Africa and I have come to view the heat as perfectly natural." She looked down at her skirt and pleated it between her fingers. "One hesitates to interfere in matters between husband and wife, Lieutenant DeLacey, but from the first I have sensed that your bride does not feel as she ought towards her new duties as a wife and eventually, one hopes, as a mother. But, as your spiritual adviser, my husband felt that I had ought to offer my guidance to the poor young thing, for he considers me a shining example of Christian womanhood." She then looked up at him with her short-sighted, sincere gaze and withdrew a book from her skirt pocket.

It was a leather covered notebook. "I should like to lend this to your wife to read. It is a compilation of excerpts from various works by Christian writers, many of them women, penned in my own hand. It is only of those writers who know the proper sphere of women and her duties toward husband, family and God. I have found these works both inspiring and instructive. Once she has read it I shall be glad to discuss it with her and pray with her until her feet are firmly set on the proper path."

Raymond was grateful. He had hoped that Mrs. Dalbeigh would have filled this role in Rosamunde's life but this was even better. Rosamunde could not ignore the wife of the station's *padre*. And Rosamunde sorely needed guidance.

"Thank you ma'am," he said fervently. "My wife does indeed need direction. I do believe that her principles are sound, but she has been very much indulged by her parents and other members of her family and too much influenced by

140

her cousin."

"The heathen Chinee?" inquired Mrs. Holloway.

"Yes, but he is out of the picture now and I shall be doing all that I may to wean her from his hold over her." Raymond felt no compunction is discussing these matters with Mrs. Holloway; after all her husband was a clergyman and he would have discussed a problem such as this with his Vicar and the Vicar's wife back home in Hertfordshire.

Mrs. Holloway gave him the book and said "We are answering a call to another mission this afternoon, Lieutenant, so we shall not be conducting an evening service. Ordinarily, we would not travel on Sunday of course, but the need is great and we do not look to return until Tuesday week. We have already arranged for a member of our mission to come out from Delhi on the morrow to take our place during our absence. You will find him a good Christian, eager to spread the Gospel."

With this she took her leave, leaving the little book with Raymond.

Curious, he opened it at once.

It was a collection, as she had said, of writings about how a Christian woman was to comport herself. The handwriting was large and rather child-like, but easy enough to read.

Raymond's eye lit at once upon an excerpt that was obviously read often, for the notebook fell open naturally to the page and the words had been underlined.

It was essential to recognize, the writer, a Mrs. Sarah Ellis, said:

"the superiority of your husband simply as a man ...In the character of a noble, enlightened and truly good man there is a power and a sublimity so nearly approaching what we believe to be the nature and capacity of angels that ...no language can describe the degree of admiration and respect which the contemplation of such a character must excite. To be admitted to his heart – to share his counsels and to be the chosen companion of his joys and sorrows – it is difficult to say whether humility or gratitude should preponderate in the feelings of the woman thus distinguished and thus blest."

This was something like! Raymond exulted, flipping

141

through the pages and finding other little gems on the same line. This was how Rosamunde ought to be thinking and behaving, as a compliment to her beauty. He would insist upon her reading it, perhaps even writing a summation of it for him to show that she had indeed understood it. If she began behaving like this he would have no more problems making her his at last.

He lay the volume aside, unfortunately he had other duties to do, otherwise, he would go home at once and see that Rosamunde began reading this marvelous collection.

Rosamunde had arrived at the *Hirren Mahal,* with Devika covered in foam and blowing hard.

Concerned, one of the *syces* from the Sharma stables ran out to her and grabbed the bridle, thinking that Devika had run away with Rosamunde.

"What is it, *mem?*" he cried. "Has your horse been affrighted by something?"

"She saved me from a bad man," said Rosamunde, sliding down from the sidesaddle with a hand on Sinéad. "Look after her well, Kasside, and please make certain that she is well cooled-out."

The *syce* bowed his head. "I will, *mem,*" he promised.

Catching up the long skirts of her sidesaddle habit over her arm Rosamunde hurried into Ameera's apartments.

The Indian woman had been playing at *parchesi* with her two small sons, Kistna and Lalit. They were five and three years of age and sweet natured little boys who were very affectionate. When they saw Rosamunde they ran towards her, begging for her attention. Sinéad was a great favorite as well.

Rosamunde knelt on the floor and took them into her arms, making much of them. Sinéad, tail up, rubbed her head on them and purred, causing them to laugh delightedly.

"You should have children of your own, Gulab," said Ameera. Gulab meant Rose, a shortening of Rosamunde's name.

Rosamunde felt a pang. At this point she was not certain that she wanted to bear Raymond's children and it seemed a moot point now that he seemed to have given up trying to consummate the marriage.

When the little boys had finished greeting Rosamunde and begun to play with Sinéad, Ameera surveyed her friend critically. "You are hot and tired. Come, we will bathe in the pool and then my women shall clothe you in a fresh *sari* while your garments are cleaned and brushed." She clapped her hands for the children's *ayah* to come and take them to their own quarters so that she and her guest could have privacy. With a backwards look at Rosamunde, Sinéad trotted of with the boys. She enjoyed playing with them.

Ameera found it rather amusing that Rosamunde always insisted on retaining her shift while they soaked in the pool but she indulgently humored her friend. She was too glad to see her again. She assumed that her *sahib* husband had relented but forbore demanding an explanation. That would come in time.

Ameera was a most restful person, Rosamunde thought as she leaned back in the pool. She was not always asking questions or insisting upon reasons for things that happened. She accepted matters without demur. Rosamunde could either tell her the reason for her visit or not, Ameera did not need to know; she was just glad that Rosamunde had come.

"My husband has gone to Delhi this day," Ameera said at last when they had soaked in the cool water for a while. It was so restful in the *zenana*, with the sound of birds, and the tinkling of the small stream of water that flowed into the pool. It was cool as well from the high ceilings and tile floor, with the tall windows covered in *chiks* to shut out the sun. The windows of the *zenana* looked out on a high walled courtyard so that no one could gaze upon the women from outside the Mahal. "Why do you not stay the evening and the night with me? It is too hot to ride back to your home. Kasside may carry a note to your husband."

Rosamunde had always refused to do so before as she knew how much Raymond would dislike it, But this time she had no hesitation in accepting. She was still so angry with him! She realized that she could not expect Ameera, raised to a different standard, to empathize with her over the matter of the letters. Ameera accepted conditions that she herself would find intolerable, for Indian society seemed aggressively masculine to Rosamunde, even more so than her own male dominated world.

So she said nothing about Raymond's double-dealing. She was not certain that Ameera would condemn Higby's behavior either, as she seemed to feel differently about these things. She did not mind sharing her husband with another wife and Rosamunde had found out that several of Ameera's women were not maids but concubines for Sanjaya Sharma's use. This did not seem to bother Ameera at all. Her husband was a man and he had the right.

So she said nothing of why she had run away from home nor why she was suddenly free to stay.

Instead, she asked Ameera idly, "Does your husband object to your friendship with me, Ameera? "

Ameera laughed, a warm, low sound. "He says that it is good for business! Since you wore the gown made from the fabric from his warehouse he has had many orders from *memsahibs*! He says he shall have many fabrics to show you when he returns from Delhi."

"I am going to the hills in three days time and shall be gone until after the monsoon," said Rosamunde. "The monsoon ends in the month of *Asvin*, September/October, does it not?"

"Yes, you are an apt pupil!" laughed Ameera and then suddenly grew sober. "I shall miss you, but this is a good thing. I think that the heat does not agree with you, my friend. If you were to live in a place such as this you would not suffer so," said Ameera thoughtfully. "The bungalows are small and hot. I would not wish to live in one. You may write to me and practice your Urdu and Persian!" Unlike many Indian women, Ameera was literate and took great pleasure in reading, particularly the *ghazuls*, the stately Persian love lyrics of the Mughals.

The afternoon and the evening passed swiftly for the two friends. Once their soaking was done, they dressed in *saris*. Rosamunde was becoming adept at the wrapping, pleating and draping one needed to do to wear the long piece of fabric, in her case, seven yards in length, needed for one of her height, over a short bodice and petticoat. They talked of their homes. Ameera was from Lucknow and she told tales of that city while Rosamunde told her of Ireland. They practiced more dance steps and did needlework.

It was not until early evening that either of them thought to send Kasside to the station with a note for Raymond, for it had been difficult to write and Rosamunde had procrastinated as long as she could.

In the end, Rosamunde wrote, with no salutation:

I am staying the night with Ameera Sharma at the Hirren Mahal. I found the letters you hid from me in your desk and I am hurt beyond measure. We will talk about this and other things when I return. I need to be away from you at the moment

She signed it simply "R".

He would be angry, no doubt. She was in a forbidden place and she had not attended church, not because she was ill, but because she could not stomach the Holloways. But she did not care how infuriated he was. She was far more enraged with him.

It was too bad that she had not brought the letters with her. She had locked them in the little chest at the foot of her bed, telling Sinéad that they would read them when they returned.

Knowing, without even reading the letters, that Alan, Cathal and Brendan had not deserted her meant so much. But what must they think of her, not receiving any communication from her in all of this time?

Kasside was a long time in returning from his errand. They had eaten an evening meal of *bryani*, a meat and rice dish, vegetable curry and fruit, along with tea and sweets, *nuqul* – small hard sweets made of jaggery, cashews, almonds and sesame seeds.

Ameera was reading aloud, one of her favorite

ghazuls, when a great deal of noise was heard out of doors and Gauri, the *dai,* who had been Ameera's *ayah,* ran into the room and said "Mistress! There is terrible, terrible news!"

From out side the *zenana* there were shouts and more noise.

"What is it?" Ameera dropped the scroll she was reading from into her lap.

Gauri shivered and wrapped her arms around herself. She was a woman of over sixty, with a lined, worn, but very kind face. She was bent and stooped and her hair was nearly white.

"Kasside has returned, afraid for his life! He could not deliver the *mem's* note. The *sepoys* have risen at Meerut and have killed all the *Angrezi -log*! And they are on their way here to Malabad! They are even killing the *mem-log* and the *baba-log* as well!'

"Killing the women and children! Art thou certain of this?" Ameera cried, slipping into the intimate address that one used with family members and those much beloved.

"He *saw*, mistress, a group of men bore the body of an *Angrezi* child on a pike and had pieces of the dress of the *mem -log*!" Gauri said, her teeth chattering.

Ameera looked at Rosamunde. For the first time she used the intimate address "Thou art not safe here, my dear friend – not as an *Angrezi* woman! Gauri, I shall have need of your dyes for the hair and skin."

"What are you going to do?" Rosamunde said, exchanging a glance with Sinéad, who had been with them since supper.

"If they come here they will find no *Angrezi mem*, but my friend the dancing girl Gulab. We will change thy appearance so that even thy husband will not recognize thee! Come Gauri! Make haste! We have no time to waste. Gulab, remove thy clothing. Thee must be dyed everywhere and thy hair as well."

"My eyes –" Rosamunde protested, "I could never pass for Hindu!"

"If they see, we shall tell them that thou art from Afghanistan. Many people from that land have light or strangely coloured eyes. And do they come here thee will keep thine eyes downcast in modest fashion. We may well be safe here, but we must be ready."

"Kasside says that Meerut is burning. He saw the fires from the road. They will probably burn this city as well!" wailed Gauri.

"All the more reason to be prepared," said Ameera calmly. "Go and fetch the dyes, Gauri! You –" she pointed to one of the concubines "Fetch my sons. The rest of you pack such valuables as food and clothing such as we might need for a journey, should this madness spread. And any one who speaks word of my friend being *Angrezi* will feel my wrath, I promise that!" she added fiercely. "She is now Gulab – one of us."

15

night of blood

To the north of Malabad, where Meerut lay, a towering column of smoke rose. At eight o'clock that evening the moon had not yet risen and the smoke was becoming so thick that the light of the leaping flames burning the native lines and many of the English bungalows was obscured.

Earlier, in Malabad, evening church parade at 6:30 had been uneasy. There were sullen faces and mutterings in the lines and a disinclination to obey orders. Captain Wallace, the officer of the day, was forced to put several men on report.

Colonel Higby seemed to have disappeared. His horse turned up, sweat streaked, wild-eyed and dead lame. Under orders, Raymond took a detachment of troopers out to search for him. The horse had come from the south, although what they could find in the dark before moonrise Raymond was not certain. Naturally enough, they were unsuccessful in their search and returned to the station at nearly ten o'clock, weary and disheartened.

Within a mile of the cantonments it was evident that something was gone very wrong. The small troop could hear shouting and the sharp crack of musketry fire. As they rode closer they saw flames leap into the air and the smell of burning.

Mingled with terrified shrieking there were cries of "*Maro! Maro!* Kill! Kill!"

Raymond ordered the troopers, all British, to draw their arms and be prepared to fight. He drew his sword and led a charge into the cantonments.

A woman, in a huge hoop, ran straight at then, screaming in terror, chased by a group of sepoys, augmented by *badmashes* from the bazaar armed with *tulwars*. Slashing at her flying skirts with their curved blades they were shouting in frenzied fashion, their visages horrible to behold in their blood lust.

One of Raymond's troopers leveled his pistol and took

out the leader of the group. This only served to infuriate the maddened *sepoys* and they leaped on the poor woman, who Raymond recognized as Mrs. Wallace, and cut her to ribbons as Raymond and his troopers ineffectively fired at them. There were so many of them and more coming every moment. Several of the Raymond's troopers were pulled from their horses and hacked to pieces.

Raymond spurred his horse forward at a gallop, yelling for the men to follow him. The thought of Rosamunde and what had happed to her tortured him. How long had this been going on? He galloped towards the Bell of Arms, the conical brick and plaster building used to store arms, his first duty was to secure this from the insurgents. He saw more than one woman dead, children as well, and English bungalows in flames. Groups of *sepoys* and *sowars*, and the scaff and raff of the bazaar mingled in with them, were fighting English troops everywhere. All was chaos, confusion and shouting, whilst over all hung a pall of smoke in the stifling air.

Before Raymond reached the Bell of Arms, slashing and jabbing with his sword all those who tried to grab at his bridle, and with musket balls whizzing by his head, he realized that he was too late. The door to the building hung agape and it was beginning to burn. He wheeled his horse. He had done his duty, he had tried to save the arms but now he could go after his wife and try to save her.

As the horse spun on its haunches, knocking down several men who tried to stop its progress, a tremendous explosion shook the night. The ammunition magazine had exploded.

Raymond hoped that it was one of his fellows that had blown it up, rather than let all the munitions fall into the hands of the mutineers.

When he threw himself from the horse at their bungalow all seemed relatively quiet. He could smell smoke but nothing was burning.

Before he reached the door he found out why it was seemingly so peaceful for the rioters had been and gone.

He stumbled over the body of one of the *punkah wallahs* on the verandah. The *punkah-wallah* was little more than a boy and he had been savagely mutilated. His hands

149

were rigid about a broom as if he had tried to hold off men armed with knives with this frail defense.

"The world has gone mad!" Raymond thought in horror.

Worse was to come. In the sitting room he found the bodies of Alam Din and of the cook, torn and bloody amidst the wrecked and looted room. "Rosamunde!" Raymond screamed frantically, throwing open doors. He allowed his sword, still in his hand, to drop to the floor and ran into their bedroom.

She was not there. Her clothing had been pulled from the wardrobe and ripped to shreds, as had his uniforms and civilian dress. The bed cushions had been wrenched apart and hangings torn from the walls. Rosamunde's jewelry box was gone. Her shoes and hats were scattered all over the floor, most of them showing signs of ill usage, and one of her hoops, crushed and mangled, was atop the overturned bureau.

There was no sign of the cat either. Raymond ran to Rosamunde's little sitting room where broken crystal crunched beneath his feet. Her harp, its strings rent asunder, lay atop a stack of books that had been ripped apart quite violently.

It was a picture of rage, of hatred. Behind Rosamunde's little desk the other *punkah wallah* lay dead with an expression of shock on his young face.

A sound behind him made him spin around, hand automatically going to his hip where the sword no longer hung. For one moment he could not think where it might be and then realized he had let it fall beside Alam Din's body.

To his relief, the noise had been made by his orderly, Manu Patel.

"Patel," he said gratefully. "What has happened here? Have everyone gone mad? Where is the *mem sahib?* Did she escape?"

Patel said in a neutral voice, "It is the *sepoys* from Meerut and with them the ruffians from the bazaar."

"And the *mem sahib,-* where is she?" asked Raymond urgently. "I have to know, Patel! I have to find her!"

"You will not need to know that where you are going, *sahib,*" said Patel, and raising his hand so quickly that Raymond did not have time to react, shot his employer point blank between the eyes. "To *Jehanna!*" (Hell)

Raymond died instantly, falling amidst the litter of crystal, harp strings and ruined books.

Patel looked at the body in satisfaction. "Your time has gone, *Angrezi*! By tomorrow we will be in Delhi and proclaim Zafar Shah *Padishah,*emperor, of all Hind! Then our armies will drive the *feringhi* from our land. No more will we be servants and lackeys to be spit upon and to be made Christian dogs!! You all will die – the *sahibs* and the *mem sahibs* and their devil's get as well. This is *Jang-i Azidi!*" A war for freedom.

He turned on his heel and left the bungalow, for once, a smile on his normally sour face.

Nothing had gone as planned for Colonel Higby. Instead of enjoying a sexually satisfying interlude with a beautiful woman, he had been pitched from his horse and tossed into a ditch beside the road. He must have lost consciousness for a while because when he awoke it was full dark.

His head was throbbing and he could feel dried blood on his forehead. When he tried to stand up he was sick and dizzy and what was more, his right ankle throbbed and would not bear his weight.

He cursed all women and horses as he sat on the edge of the ditch, struggling to remove his boot. When he had it off at last his senses swam and he fell backwards, insensible once more.

The next time he awoke it was still dark, but in the direction of the station there was a curious light in the sky and the acrid stench of smoke in the air. Sharp crackling echoed in the distance and Higby recognized as musket fire. "What the hell?" he swore and managed to get on his feet, not without dizziness, pain and much colourful language.

A stout branch found in a nearby *tope* helped him walk. It was slow and painful progress, with his ankle pulsating and his head pounding. Savagely, he imagined what he would do to Rosamunde when he finally had her naked underneath him. And she was going to be there, never doubt it! She would pay for treating him so.

Coming up the road from Malabad at a run and on horseback, heading for Delhi, were the combined forces of the sepoys from Meerut and Malabad and the bazaar trash from both cities. In a state of high excitement they were screaming and shouting, firing their guns into the air and waving bloodstained knives and tulwars about. Some of them wore English clothing that they had stolen and many of the *sepoys* still wore their uniforms. Their numbers were swelled by the men they had helped released from both the Old and the New Gaols in Meerut, including the men that had been court martialled. Many carried loot: jewelry, extra guns, anything that they fancied valuable.

Slow and in pain, Higby failed to react quickly enough. If he had rolled into the deep ditch and stayed low in the dark he might have saved his life.

Higby was brave, but stupid. Drawing his pistol from his belt, he tried to face them down, ordering them to surrender. He had time to fire only one shot which went wide, before they were on him. When they finished with him, there was very little left to identify him by.

"*Mubank*, Gauir! Oh, well done!" Ameera clapped her hands in delight. "*Dekho*, Gulab! Look!" She pulled on Rosamunde's arm to lead her to a long European-style mirror that was normally hidden in a wall cabinet.

Gauri and Ameera between them had made Rosamunde, stripped to the skin, lie upon a bare table top and carefully applied what seemed like a cauldron full of dye to every visible inch of her. Gauri had carefully dyed her hands and feet as the skin of the palms and the soles was generally lighter. They had dyed her hair black as well, cutting its long length that hung nearly to her waist to just below her shoulders. The excess hair was burned, as was the riding habit.

The concubines, who entered into the spirit of the thing, fanned her dry until she could be clothed in a sari.

The one they chose was rather gaudy, of red silk, trimmed in gold over a yellow, gold embroidered *choli*, the

152

short bodice, the hem of which came just below the breasts. leaving the lower torso bare and had short sleeves that ended halfway between the elbow and the shoulder.

They made her up, for no Indian woman, particularly a dancing girl ,would be seen abroad without cosmetics. Her lips were painted vermilion, her eyes outlined with kohl and her cheeks rouged. Ameera, with a little brush, painted her friend's eyelids blue. Her nails, fingers and toenails, were gilded and henna applied to the palms and soles.

Gauri gathered her dry hair in to a bun at the nape of her neck and secured it with a brass clasp. All of the women ransacked their jewelry boxes and at Ameera's orders, took of their gaudiest, least expensive items and bedecked Rosa-munde. "Thou art now a dancing girl, a *pari*," Ameera explained. "Thou art not an artist of the *nautch*, for they dance and sing, play and belong to a troupe, but thou art not a naked *cumchunee* of the lowest caste. Thy jewelry should be of the type that a young admirer would buy in the bazaar,not the jewels given by a wealthy man or a Rajah."

Rosamunde ended in being laden with many brass and crystal bangle bracelets and anklets. She also wore chains set with freshwater pearls about her throat and a pair of large and heavy brass earrings that touched her shoulders. A *rakhri*, a forehead pendant, of peridot, hung low on her forehead. Hammered brass flowers on the tips of hair pins adorned her now dark locks, the curls having subsided from the thick dye.

What she saw in the mirror was an Indian woman. The red of the sari and the blue eye paint made her violet eyes look darker. The brown of her dyed skin seemed to change the shape of her nose and face as well and the dark hair made her into someone else entirely. The tight bodice showed off her breasts, for the *sari* draped loosely over only one shoulder.

"The *choli* should be transparent," said Ameera, frowning, "but we none of us have such a garment"

"She should remove the *choli* and leave one breast exposed," suggested one of the concubines.

But Rosamunde could not do this, even though it would be what a dancing girl would do. Many *paris* wore low hung gauze trousers that showed the hips and stomach, with little more than an embroidered vest above the waist that did little to hide the bosom. Remembering the prostitutes in the *Lol Bibi* bazaar, Rosamunde could not bring herself to be more authentic. She felt naked and exposed as it was.

"Now, thou must remember, Gulab is new come to the *zenana*. My husband has but recently purchased her. She is from a land far to the north, above Afghanistan," Ameera directed.

"*Purchased* me?" Rosamunde exclaimed. "But slavery is illegal – as is *suttee!*"

"*Angrezi* law," said one of the concubines, Unsa, a voluptuous, sloe-eyed woman, in scorn. "Think you that such laws are obeyed with regularity?"

"This is true," said Ameera. "The *Angrezi* law says that a man may not have more than one wife also! But here I am!"

"Now," she said, "we will wait for what will come. If they do not come, it does not matter. If they do come, they will find only women of Hind here. Gulab, let us dance for the others!"

Outside the noise was increasing. The walls of the *Mahal* were thick, almost fortress-like, but even here in the shielded *zenana,* they could hear firing and shouting. Dancing, with music and singing, with hand clapping, would drown out the terror lurking beyond the walls.

Several of the women could play instruments, a *shanal,* which was like an oboe, and a harp-like instrument as well as a tambourine. The rest clapped out a rhythm, shaking the bells on their wrists.

Rosamunde danced and whirled, using the ballet she knew and he sinuous movements taught to her by Ameera. Her mind was busy as her body moved. What had happened to Raymond? Was he looking for her even now? Would he not come here when he realized she was missing? Surely the British troops could subdue the riots! Meerut had more British troops than any other military installation in India. They could wire to Delhi or to Calcutta, there was another station at Cawnpore and one just beyond that at Lucknow, they would send help if necessary.

But the telegraph lines had been cut since four o'clock that afternoon. The mutineers were well on their way to Delhi, as none of the Meerut survivors had thought to blow up or hold the bridge across the Abu Nullah ravine that lead to the Grand Trunk road to Delhi. The lines had been cut another way as well, to Agra. No *tar* (wire) could get through.

And no one followed the Mutineers for reprisals or to stop them in their push to Delhi. The commanders at Meerut stayed put.

At Malabad there was no one left to go anywhere. A small station, it had been overrun and almost completely destroyed. Rosamunde was one of the few English left alive.

At the *Hirren Mahal* the women did everything that they could to keep from becoming completely terrorized by the increasingly violent sounds coming from out of doors.

And just after midnight, someone began pounding on the thick barred gate, shouting for them to open, or they would fire the *Mahal* and burn it down, with everyone in it.

16

wazid ali

There were too many of them. The mob outside the *Hirren Mahal* had grown moment by moment. Only Kasside, the elderly cook, and two boys, armed with one gun and staves stood between the women in the *zenana* and the blood-crazed throng outside the gates.

Ameera had gone out into the courtyard to consult with Kasside. Rosamunde and Sinéad followed her.

"Why do they come here, mistress?" quavered the cook, an elderly man called Venkata. He was very old, almost past his work, but he had been cook to Ameera's husband Sanjaya's parents and had been kept on out of sentiment. "Kasside says that they kill the *Angrezi-lo,* even the women and children! It is not right that they do so! Surely it is bad *karma!*"

Venkata carried a butcher's knife for a weapon in his frail hand. Kasside had the only gun in the *Mahal*, an ancient fowling piece, for Sanjaya was not overly fond of shooting and preferred to buy wild duck and game from dealers rather than hunt it himself.

The two boys, one a helper in the stables, Mutal, and a kitchen helper, Madhava, had bamboo staves to fight with. From the indiscriminate firing out of doors and the clash of steel, these weapons would be of limited use.

There were nine women altogether, counting Rosamunde: Ameera, the senior wife Swati, two concubines, Unsa and Neha, the children's *Ayah*, Darshama, the *dai* Gauri and two young serving girls, Pushpa and Asha. Earlier in the evening several other servants, who did not live at the Mahal, had gone to their own homes. Ameera's sister-in-law had gone visiting two days earlier and was now in Agra.

"Do you think that they are all dead at the station?" Rosamunde said in a low voice to Sinéad. "Do you think that Raymond is dead? Surely he would have come by now if he were not! He must have known that I would come here, even if Kasside could not deliver the note! Where else would I go?"

The little cat had been very quiet all evening since the news had come of the uprising. Now she said in tones full of self-reproach, "I was after cursin' him, ye must be knowin'. I was after sayin' *Marbhfháise ort!*"

"Sinéad, if he is dead, he is not dead because you wished a shroud on him," Rosamunde said reasonably, while inside she was sick with worry and dread. Between them had been very real problems but she never, ever, wished him dead! It was too horrible to contemplate.

What was also frightening Rosamunde at the moment was the fact that her powers seemed to have deserted her. She had tried to augment the bars on the gate and there was only the weakest stirring in her Witchcraft. Had it gone because she had not been using it these past months? Was it the heat as Sinéad had suggested? Or her desperate unhappiness? Whatever it was, it could not have chosen a worse time to leave. She would more than likely need her Witchcraft to protect herself and her friends. What was she to do without it?

The familiar shivered. "Me Ma is always after sayin' that a curse is bein' a powerful thing. I was after bein' so mad that I —"

What she intended to say was left unsaid. Kasside and Ameera had been conferring in low voices and now, straightening up to her full height Ameera said decidedly, "Lay aside your weapons and let them in! When they see but a houseful of women of their own land, they will go away and leave us in peace."

Kasside looked at her doubtfully but motioned to the other men to obey and then went to lift the bar from the now violently shaking gate.

Wazid Ali was a man on a mission.

He had a large commission from a valued client and the current situation that had happened today was much to his advantage. He could not prevent himself from chuckling in glee whenever he thought of it.

He had been in Meerut when the fighting broke out, both he and his brother Mohammed, who plied the same trade, although not as successfully, for Mohammed was far too soft-hearted. Wazid had a ruthless streak and one of cruelty as well. It was a nature well suited to his calling, that of a slaver, specializing in women.

The valued client wanted as many pretty women as possible, particularly *mem-sahibs,* even should they have to be kidnapped, and dancing girls and lovely native women as well.

The uprising had made filling his commission quite easy for rather than having to kidnap a struggling, screaming *mem* and subdue her with drugs or a gag, he merely offered refuge to those fleeing in fear of their lives. They gratefully climbed into his *palka-ghari,* a covered *purdah c*art pulled by two bullocks, and shed their Western hoops for the enveloping *bourkha,* the one piece head to heels gown that exposed only the face through a small square of coarse net. These belonged to his nieces, he explained in his avuncular fashion, even inviting the frightened women to address him as *cha-cha* or uncle. Amongst his stock in trade was a soothing manner and a demeanor that made him out to be a harmless, rather sweet old man, which was entirely deceptive, for he was no such thing.

By the time his *ghari* was full of thankful women and a few children as well, he met with his brother on the road, and collected there his confederates as well.

These were four Pathans: Akbar, Yakoub, Naskhs-band and Buzurg, all surnamed Khan, for they were cousins, hard, fierce men from Afghanistan who had worked for Wazid Ali for years. They helped in the obtaining of unwilling slaves and acted as guards for Ali, for his merchandize was very valuable and he did not wish to lose it to a competitor or worse, let it escape. The four Pathans also liked the extra pay which was the use of the women that Ali stole, any time they wanted them.

The fact that the *Angrezi-log* had outlawed slavery made little difference to Wazid Ali's business. Officials were easy to bribe. Many times all he had to do was offer the official the choice of any woman in his *palka ghari.* And if stopped by British officers, he claimed that the *ghari* was full of the female members of his *zenana,* on a visit to relatives.

He never actually bought slaves as it was far more

profitable to steal them. Many females who had disappeared, thought to have been eaten by a tiger, overcome by a *mugger* whilst bathing in the river, or run off with a lover had in truth ended up in Ali's *ghari* to be sold halfway across the country.

He now exchanged carts with his brother, for Mohammed as well drove a *palka-ghari*, and directed him to take the women to the client at once. Mohammed was to drug the women that night when he fed them so that they would not realize that they were not being taken to safety as they had been promised but rather into what would be worse than death for many of them. Under the driver's seat were ropes and chains that they could be secured with once they were drugged. Wazid could scarcely contain his joy at the thought of the huge purse of *rupees* that would be his when the valued client saw the contents of the cart.

And he was not done yet! Ahead lay Malabad and Delhi, full of both *mem sahibs* and young beauties of Hindustan. If he could only manage to get there before these fools killed all of the women. How stupid to kill what could be sold for much money!

Wazid arrived at the station at Malabad after the bazaar trash and the revolting *sepoys* had completed their deadly work and had departed towards Delhi or the city.

It was a scene of complete carnage. Bodies of women, of children British soldiers, servants who had remained loyal and had tried to help their British employers, and many *sepoys* and bazaar trash as well, lay everywhere, clearly visible in the lurid light of the burning native lines and British bungalows. Unlike Meerut, where a British force, with some still loyal *sepoys* lay entrenched, Malabad was deserted. It seemed as if everyone had died. But some few *had* escaped and headed to Meerut. It was these amongst whom Captain Wallace had survived, who would later identify the dead.

Wazid Ali surveyed the lifeless women in disgust. Some were so mutilated that it was difficult to tell if they had been attractive or not. Some had been stripped and raped, a certain sign that the worst scoundrels of the bazaar, the lowest dregs of all, had joined forces with the *sepoys*.

He would go into Malabad itself. Perhaps some of the *mem sahibs* had fled there and have been taken in by kindly folk, who could be persuaded to give up the women when the four Pathans, armed to the teeth, showed them the error of their ways.

Ameera gathered her household on a dais behind the courtyard fountain. Outwardly she showed no fear. Only her white knuckled hands on her eldest son's shoulders gave her away but no trace of terror showed in her face or posture. Nor would she allow any of the other women to cry or cower.

It should have been the senior wife, Swati, who was in charge, but she was a rather indolent woman of thirty-five who was naturally slow witted and prone to nervous hysterics. She persisted in moaning, asserting her conviction that the house would be looted and her jewelry stolen and they would all be violated by *badmashes* from the bazaar, many of whom were no doubt Untouchables. If the mere breath of an Untouchable broke one's caste, what would intimate contact do?

Rosamunde admired Ameera tremendously. She had taken charge, sensibly and without hand wringing. She was setting a good example for the others as well.

Rosamunde herself felt incredibly vulnerable. Not because of any lack of faith in her disguise or out of fear that one of the other women might betray her, but because of her loss of power. She had always had her Witchcraft to depend on for protection. But the sluggish, disconnected feeling she was now experiencing told her that she was now as prone to violence as any non-magical woman. And she could not stop worrying frantically about Raymond and the others at the station: her servants, the troopers and the other officers and their families. What had happened to them?

She hoped that none of this showed on her countenance. Sinéad, on her shoulder as was usual, was hissing under her breath, but Rosamunde could also feel the little cat quivering, whether with rage or with fear Rosamunde was not certain.

Kasside put down his gun and went slowly to the door of the gate, which was now bulging under the strain of the repeated assault upon it. Outside the crowd roared in

160

encouragement. to those who battered at it.

The two servant boys, obedient to Ameera's orders, lay down their staves and old Venkata was persuaded to give up his kitchen knife.

Kasside lifted the bar and was pushed aside by the mass of humanity that surged into the courtyard.

As Swati had feared, most of them were bazaar riff raff, using the *sepoys'* uprising as an excuse to loot and destroy the property of those that they envied. Most of the *sepoys* had gone on to Delhi.

When they had all crowded into the courtyard it could be seen that there were about twenty of them, most armed with *tulwars* or stolen knives. Guns were normally beyond the means of such poor people, but some had stolen guns at the cantonments. However they were now out of ammunition, having mindlessly shot the guns into the air as if in celebration.

They did seem to have a leader, a man of about forty, with a straggling beard, with a mouth full of missing teeth and a patch on one eye. He was clothed in dirty white *pyjamy* trousers and a tunic spattered with suspicious dark spots. His turban was askew and his eyes were alight with savage ferocity. "Bring out your valuables!" he shouted, looking at the group on the dais, and motioning to two men to begin searching the *Mahal*. He ordered two others to wrest their jewelry from the women.

"That will not be necessary," said Ameera cooly. She stripped the bracelets from her arms and the jewels from her ears and gave them to Kasside. "Here, give these to him. We will all give up our jewels."

The other women followed suit and Kasside went back and forth with jewelry until it all lay at the feet of the leader. It made a considerable pile, for Sanjaya was a prosperous man and generous with the members of his household. Ameera even took the tiny pearls from the ears of her sons. Jewels could be replaced, lives could not.

The two sent to search the house came back dragging *resais* full of jewel caskets and fine fabrics. "There are no *Angrezi-log* here," he reported, "but much good plunder!"

Not by the turn of a head nor a flicker of an eye did any of the women or the servants cast a betraying glance at

161

Rosamunde. Sinéad remained quiet, an Indian cat, of course, would not be able to speak.

"Since you have what you came for," Ameera said evenly, "leave us in peace, help yourselves to food and drink as well. Destroy the furniture but leave me and mine in peace. We have done you no harm and offered no resistance."

The leader's one eye gleamed as he looked at her and at Rosamunde. They were quite the best looking of the group, for even the two concubines were not as attractive. Swati was older looking than her thirty-five years and the two serving maids were both plain, while the *dai* and the *ayah* were elderly.

"Unless you wish to see these men and the *baba-log* killed, you will lay with us," he said, and pointed at Rosamunde, Ameera, Unsa and Neha. "There are five men for each woman. We will throw dice for your favors. I myself will have you !" he said to Ameera, his tongue licking at his lips.

A rifle spat and the one-eyed man fell dead, a bullet through his head.

Ameera gasped. Some of the others shrieked, grabbing at one another in alarm.

A man of late middle years stood in the open gateway, with four ferocious looking Pathans at his side. The Pathans all carried long barreled *jezzails*, (rifles) and wore ammunition belts, crisscrossed over their chests. *Tulwars* hung at their sides and several knives of varying lengths and pepper-box pistols adorned each belt. These men were hard-eyed and looked as if they would not mind killing everyone in the courtyard.

"To waste such beauty on bazaar trash!" the middle aged man said. "No, it does not bear thinking on! Most of them are dogs, the sons of diseased mothers."

There was a sudden motion as one of the dirty mob tried to throw the stone he held as a weapon at the man. Another shot rang out and he, too, fell dead.

"Must we kill all of you?" said the man plaintively. "Would you not prefer to remain alive? Take your spoils and go."

The Pathans raised their *jezzails* to their shoulders and cocked the triggers. Coldly, they dared the other men to challenge them.

162

Sullenly, the remaining mob picked up the loot and began to leave, much of their blood lust spent with the two deaths.

When the last one had gone, Yakoub Khan closed and barred the gate again.

"Allah is good!" said Wazid Ali piously. "Four beauties, two of them exceptional, have fallen into my hands!"

"What do you mean?" asked Ameera sharply. She had been about to express her gratitude to him but what he said and the tone he had said it in some how sent a *frisson* of alarm up her spine.

"You are my property now, *chabeli* (sweetheart), and will be sold to a most particular client of mine. I will garner many *rupees* for such as you," said Wazid Ali, his eyes sliding to Rosamunde and the two concubines.

"You are a slaver!" said Ameera in disgust.

"Bind those," Ali said to Akbar indicating Ameera, Rosamunde, Neha and Unsa. "The others are worthless."

As the big man moved forward, uncoiling a rope that hung at his waist, Rosamunde gathered what magic she had left in a desperate effort and Sinéad hissed and sprang full in his face.

All day long Alan had felt as if something, something terrible, was going to happen. He had woken from dreams of blood and horror, completely unrefreshed.

He was unaware that Cathal had spent most of the night awake, listening to his Wizard mutter in his sleep and watching as he tossed, sometimes violently, on the *charpoy*.

Jai too, looked worried a he served Alan with his *chota haziri*, which the *sahib* generally took in bed these days as getting up immediately was too much effort. To the servant, the *sahib* looked haggard and ill.

After several cups of tea but only a mouthful of fruit, Alan felt well enough to go down and meet Ravi's family for their morning exercise, a ride on some of the Maharajah's fine horses.

They had not ventured very far before Ravi pulled up beside Alan and said "What is it, my brother? You look far

163

from well!" Concern was in his voice. "All have remarked upon it."

Alan shrugged. He was more than a little tired of feeling unwell and even the solicitude of his hosts was being to grate upon his nerves. "I slept very ill last night," he said dismissively.

"I am worried about Rosamunde," he said, changing the subject abruptly. "I keep thinking about what your father told us, that the *sepoys* in the Native regiments are disaffected and feeling ill-used for such things as the new act that requires service overseas for Hindus and the ending of invalid pensions. John Company is being very petty, even requiring them to pay postage on their own letters, rather than having their officers frank them as they were always used to do. I daresay that the cost of the postage was putting the Company on the verge of insolvency!" he added sarcastically. "And there is this stupid business about the greased cartridges as well. It's a situation ripe for explosion and she could be in the middle of it."

It was difficult, if not impossible for a devout Hindu to travel in a ship as the religious law required him to cook his own food at his own fire and he of course could not use water from a common water butt that others of a different caste or even *feringhis* might have filled or drunk from it.

"If his journey has gone well Ram Dass should be with her in two days' time," said Ravi soothingly. "I have instructed him to bring her and Sinéad here, should he judge it the best action."

"I wish she *had* come here," said Alan irritably. "The more I saw of that DeLacey the less I liked him. I cannot understand what she sees in a jackass like him. She is generally not a stupid girl."

Ravi said nothing to this. He had seen Rosamunde look at Alan when she thought no one was looking, with her heart in her eyes. Although his friend was brilliant in so any ways, Ravi considered Alan to be foolish in matters of the heart. Ravi understood why Rosamunde had married Raymond as even in *Belait* there was little for a woman besides marriage and he had also observed how uncomfortable Rosamunde was with male attention.

He lightly turned the topic to the possibility of taking

out his latest acquisition, a falcon, that evening, for some sport, and resolved to keep an eye on Alan that day and see that he got more rest.

After a long wearing day, although he did little or nothing, Alan went out in the late afternoon with Ravi and Cathal. The friends were mounted on two of the Maharajah's finest horses. On Ravi's arm rode his new *shahin,* peregrine falcon, unhooded, as Cathal was talking to him in Animal speech. The bird, a magnificent raptor named Anil, meaning air, or wind in Sanskrit, looked about him with interest, but sitting quite still on Ravi's arm.

They were out a long time. Anil took several plump pigeons that Ravi tied to his saddle, saying that the *khansamah* could dress them for the evening meal.

In spite of the fact that the heat of the day had faded and a cool wind was coming from the mountains, Alan felt as if the oppressive heat still lingered. It seemed difficult to get a breath and he shifted restlessly in the saddle again and again, causing his horse to complain to Cathal that the *sahib was* riding like a novice this evening. She had carried him before and she did not remember him riding so badly.

Cathal told her worriedly, "He is ill. Should he faint will you stand fast and not run in fright?" He worried that if she was scared by her rider passing out she might begin to run and drag Alan if he did not fall clear.

The mare, Nila, tossed her head and said that she hoped she was not so silly as to let something like that frighten her. Cathal could trust her with the *sahib,* even though he had become such a poor horseman.

Ravi, taking care of his falcon did not see what suddenly happened.

Alan gave a choking gasp and to Cathal it looked as if his Wizard was having some sort of fit, for his eyes rolled back in his head and he convulsed, falling over sideways.

Cathal screamed "Ravi!" and jumped from Nila's back to where Alan lay crumpled on the turf. Ravi threw the bird into the air and vaulted from his mount, running to his friend's side.

And true to her word, Nila stood stock still. It was very well that he did so, for one of Alan's feet still remained in the stirrup.

17

laura

With a quick twist of his hand Akbar plucked Sinéad out of the air and flung her against the wall. The little cat struck the wall hard and fell to the floor where she lay, a crumpled mass of fur.

Rosamunde screamed in horror, the little magic she had managed to gather falling away from her as she tried to run towards her familiar.

Akbar caught her around the waist with one big hand, swinging her off the floor. Futilely, she shrieked and struggled, all of her attention on the little body that lay so still "Sinéad! Sinéad!" she sobbed, beating at him with her balled up hands. "Let me go! I have to go to her!"

"Quiet her!" Wazid Ali ordered, and with his fist, Akbar did so, and Rosamunde dropped to the floor, unconscious. Akbar produced a rope and tied her hands together. "Bind her feet as well, "Wazid Ali commanded. "Take care not to further harm my merchandise, Akbar Khan, or the amount I lose in her sale for damage will come from your pay! She will more than likely be bruised where you struck her."

"You may recoup the loss when you sell favors to many men on the way to Jhaniput," said the big Afghani carelessly. "I would have her too, Wazid Ali. She has spirit. She will fight me and the taking will be all the sweeter for the conquest."

Ameera had made no protest when Buzurg Khan bound her wrists. "Since I come with you willingly," she said "will you leave the children and my household alive?"

"I am no murderer, *chabeli*," he said with his oily smile. "There is no profit in it. And these men do as I tell them, for I pay their wages."

Ameera forbore pointing out that he had ordered his men to kill two others already. She wisely decided that her survival depended on her cooperation and she was determined to survive and return to Sanjaya and her sons. Sanjaya might even ransom them. She had already exchanged glances with Gauri. She knew that the old woman had taken careful note of the names mentioned, both of the slaver and his destination. Gauri would be able to tell Sanjaya who had taken them and where to look.

The younger of the concubines, Neha, had hysterics, scratching and shrieking when Buzurg bound her wrists. She too was silenced with a fist.

Unsa extended her wrists voluntarily and made no protest when Buzurg bound her as well. She held herself proudly, looking at the slaver and his men as if they were Untouchables.

"I will take this one," said Buzurg, running his eyes up and down her curvaceous body.

"That is what I like, Wazid Ali said approvingly. "Females should always be cooperative. I hope that you all will be as compliant when I put men to you. Those who please my customers will be well treated. Those who do not will be beaten."

With a last eloquent glance at her sons, who were clinging fearfully to their *ayah*, Ameera allowed herself to be led outside to the *palka-ghari*, followed by Unsa. Akbar picked up Rosamunde and draped her over his shoulder while Buzurg took Neha.

Yakoub picked up Sinéad and as they passed out the door, threw the little body on an ash heap.

The *palka-ghari* was a four-wheeled, high off the ground cart, with a canvas hood that was made with curtains on all sides so that no one could see the women within. It was pulled by two stolid bullocks, yoked to the axle.

Inside were benches on three sides, coved in a thin matting. At about shoulder level were rings hanging from the top edge of the *ghari* ,rather close together. Ropes hung from each one of these. To these Akbar attached the women's bound wrists. At their feet were more metal rings,and more ropes, to which he attached their ankles. He was rough and efficient, showing that he had done this many times before.

Ameera would have liked to tend to the two

unconscious women but she could not do so, tied to the sides of the *palki ghari.*

Wazid Ali came up into the *ghari* when Akbar had finished. "There will be no shouting for help," he said to Ameera and Unsa. "I doubt anyone would hear you on this night as there are far too many being chased and slain! Do you scream or call out, Akbar will first strike you and then gag you. It is in your best interest to be quiet." He nodded at Akbar. "You will ride with them. Your cousins are going to ride ahead looking for other women that may be on the road tonight. If Allah wills, we shall have a full *palka-ghari* of choice goods by morning with no effort on our part."

"When may we take them?" Akbar said, looking at Rosamunde's form with avid lechery.

"Not for a day or so, I wish to be well on our way before we halt and take the time to break them in. Don't worry; they do not want virgins in Jhaniput so there will be many chances for you to take your choice. Jhaniput is a customer who does not care how many times I have sold their favors before delivery!" Wazid Ali laughed and looked at the four women. "I shall charge an entire *rupee* for laying with these. They are exceptional, worth more than a few copper *pice* or an *anna* or two. Soon we shall see what their bare bodies look like before laying with them. You shall touch them as much as you like."

The look on Akbar's face indicated that he could scarcely wait.

Ameera shivered. At this point she saw no possibility of escape. She had but the faintest idea where this Jhaniput they spoke of might be. It sounded as if this despicable man might be going to sell them into a brothel and rape them beforehand as well.

How soon would Sanjaya return from Delhi? He had not known how long his business would keep him. She said a silent prayer that he would come soon and find her, and his concubines, before they were sold. Somehow she doubted that he would come before they had all been raped.

And if he had survived this night surely the Lieutenant *sahib* would come for his wife as well. Gauri could tell him where she had been taken.

Ameera fell into an uneasy sleep as did Unsa. It was very difficult to sleep with hands and feet tied, with no protection against the jolting of the cart. Only exhaustion allowed them to nod off.

Just before dawn the cart stooped and Ameera, rousing from a fitful sleep, heard voices outside and the clop of hooves. She looked about her. The others still slept or perhaps were unconscious as yet, she could not tell. Akbar was gone. Had they stopped for what little remained of the night?

As she watched and wondered, the rear flap of the *palka- ghar*i was lifted and another woman was thrust inside, with her arm held firmly by Buzurg.

Ameera stifled a gasp. Another *mem sahi,* this one dressed properly as an Englishwoman. She was disheveled, her hair straggling down around her face from coils over her ears, her face smudged with dirt and her gown of blur and green plaid torn in several places. She was without a hoop, for her gown trailed on the floor, tripping her up as Buzurg pushed her into the *ghar*.

He pulled her down onto the bench between Rosamunde and Ameera and tied her up in the same fashion.

"Do not scream !" he said in heavily accented English and made a gesture of throat cutting with a nasty grin on his face.

"Wasn't about to," she said in a quiet fashion, in English.

She was a tall woman, taller even that Rosamunde and had bright green eyes and dark auburn hair. She had an arresting face. She was not beautiful, her mouth was too wide and her features too strong for beauty, but it was a face that made one look at her again and again. Her figure was slim and athletic but quite womanly and her complexion rather tanned.

With a quick appraising look at the other women she leaned back and made herself as comfortable as possible, with an air of one making the best of a bad situation. There seemed to be no fear in her manner at all.

"Akbar!" called Wazid Ali from outside the *palka-*

ghari. "Come and drive the bullocks. I would take my rest. Your cousins go to locate more women. Allah has been good to us this night – five beauties! "

The newcomer snorted derisively. "Miserable old whore master!" she muttered.

When Akbar had left them alone and the *ghari* had started up, the newcomer looked at Ameera and pointed her chin at the others. "Drugged or beat up?" she asked in very rudimentary Hindustanee that she did not seem comfortable with.

"I speak English," Ameera offered. She had become more fluent since she and Rosamunde had made friends.

The newcomer smiled broadly which made her even more attractive. "Well, thank the Lord for that," she said. "My Hindoo is pretty bad. I was wondering how I was going to talk to anyone hereabouts. I'm Laura Fitzroy."

"I am Ameera Sharma," Ameera returned. "This old *boroowa* has stolen us from the home of my husband in Malabad."

"*Boroowa*," Laura repeated. "What does that mean?"

"I know not the word in English," said Ameera apologetically. "A man who sells women's bodies."

"A pimp," said Laura. "He looks like the type," she added in disgust. "A regular snake oil salesman!"

"Excuse me, *mem,* but you do not sound as do the other *mem sahibs* that I have heard," said Ameera carefully, not wishing to give offense.

Laura smiled again. "You mean all prissy and stuck-up? That's because I'm American. My Pa's a telegraphic engineer and I came out here with him and my intended Nate Connelly, who're working for the British. They'll be some old mad when they find out what's happened to me! And don't call me *mem* – I'm Laura to you and I'll call you Amy nice and friendly. If we're going to get out of this we've got to stick together and help each other. Now, who are these other ladies?"

Ameera felt her heart lighten a little as she explained to Laura who the others were. This was a strong, courageous woman, the sort of companion they would need to save themselves.

But all the same, she did not inform Laura that

Rosamunde was actually Irish and the wife of a British officer. That was Rosamunde's secret to divulge if she wished.

When Rosamunde awoke she could not imagine where she was. She was being painfully jolted and her arms were being pulled out of their sockets and she could not move her legs. Her face hurt and her head throbbed and suddenly, shockingly she remembered and cried out "Sinéad!"

"Hush,Gulab" came Ameera's voice in a loud whisper. "They will beat thee if thou make noise!"

Rosamunde painfully turned her head and realized why she was so sore and could not move. She took in the situation at a glance and then said to Ameera "What happened to Sinéad?"

Ameera looked sorrowful. "I think she is dead, my sister. They threw her on an ash heap before we were put upon this *ghari*." She knew how much the little cat meant to Rosamunde.

"Oh, no!" Rosamunde moaned as tears began to trickle down her face. "Oh, Sinéad! Sinéad!" she sobbed. Ameera implored her not to cry, to keep Akbar from coming in and perhaps hitting or gagging her.

"Who or what is shi-nayd?" Laura inquired.

Rosamunde turned her head again to look at Laura. "You're an American!" she said in amazement, tears still coursing down her cheeks. Inside, she felt as if her heart was breaking. Since Ameera begged her, she bravely tried to stop crying but her mind kept repeating in an endless refrain "Sinéad! Sinéad! How can I live without you? You can't be dead!" "

"And you're no Indian!" said Laura shrewdly "Not with eyes looking like violets and recognizing my accent hot from the bat like that."

"This is a disguise," said Rosamunde, sniffing and choking back more tears.

"And pretty damned clever too," said Laura in admiration.and laughed as Rosamunde looked at her, a little shocked at her language. "Don't mind my mouth. I grew up in a mining camp and I can cuss a blue streak. My Pa always says it's better to cuss than to kill somebody. No one's ever been hung for cussing that he recollects. Now, who or what is shi-nayd?"

"My cat, my familiar," she admitted, tears threatening again.

"You're a Witch?" Laura said delightedly. "However did they catch you? With Cold Iron? Not a Witch myself but I've known a few."

"My powers have gone missing," Rosamunde said miserably. "I couldn't even stop them from killing Sinéad. She tried to protect me. That's why I couldn't protect her." *I failed her*, she thought in self loathing. *When she needed me I was unable to do anything for her.*

"Well, don't that just frost you!" said Laura in disgust. "What's your real name, honey?"

"Rosamunde DeLacey," Rosamunde answered.

Laura grinned at her. "Sounds like something out of a serial novel! The Duke's daughter or something aristocratic. When I was a little girl I met a man everyone said was a Russian Count but they all just called him Sacha."

"Sacha Kustodiev?" said Rosamunde in amazement startled from her sorrow for a brief moment "He's my uncle by marriage, my aunt Tatya's brother. He was in America for a long time."

"Well, if don't that beat all!" marveled Laura and gave a low laugh, a sort of a chuckling gurgle. "Well, Rose, as I was telling Amy here, we've all got to stick together and see if we can't work our way out of this jam we're in."

Rosamunde gave her a tight, unhappy smile. The grief for Sinéad was too raw for at any other time she might have wanted to know the circumstances of Laura's acquaintance with Sacha, but now she could not bring herself to care. *"Sinéad, oh, my darling little one!"* was all she could think and pain was all that she could feel. That and a deep hatred of the man who had so wantonly taken the precious life.

"I am at a loss, *Hazrat,*" said the *Hakim,* Walayat Shah, spreading his hands expressively. "I know not what illness this might be or why the young *sahib* does not awaken.

I have not seen the like in all my years."

He was a precise, neat man of forty odd and a most accomplished physician who had studied extensively and mastered his craft. He was far more used to curing illness than to admitting he did not know what was wrong with a patient.

The Maharajah looked down at Alan, stretched out on the *charpoy* in his room. He had been unconscious since Ravi had brought him back to the *Moti Mahal*, holding him on the horse in front of himself with Cathal clinging to Ravi's shoulder and the falcon soaring above.

They put him right to bed and sent for the *Hakim*. That had been last night. Alan had alternated between laying as silent as an image on a tomb and feverishly tossing, muttering and crying out in a language that Cathal said was Gaelic and that he raved of blood. But he had not come to his senses. Both Ravi and Jai had spent most of the night by his bedside and the worry and anxiety showed in their faces.

"I like this not," said the Maharajah heavily. "Is this some malady that those of a magical turn are subject to?" he asked Cathal.

The ferret shook his head miserably. "I have never seen or heard of anything like this! Last night I consulted the emergency medical text in Alan's Wizard's bag and it said nothing about anything even remotely resembling this!" He looked up at the faces around him, the *Hakim*, the Maharajah, Ravi and Jai, looking as if he might cry any moment.

"Can ferrets cry?" Ravi thought bleakly. He himself had a heavy lump in his chest..

"I was thinking of sending for Brendan," said Cathal, "If worst came to worst we could fly up through Central Asia to St Petersburg. There is a family friend there – Anatoly Tcherepin, who is a Wizard, and there are Wizard Healers in Russia as well now in the Imperial College of Wizardry . But I had a letter from Brendan this morning saying that he is going high up in the mountains and will be inaccessible for weeks. He is already gone there, for the letter took some time in coming here."

"The post from the land of Bod comes in its own time," said the Maharajah with a frown. He had not taken his

174

eyes form Alan's now extremely still figure. "I will send someone to Cawnpore to telegraph Bombay and then from there notify his family in *Belait.*" He looked up at Ravi."You tell us that his uncle is a *Hakim.* Perhaps he will come out on a dragon very quickly and tend to our young friend."

"In the meantime, *Hazrat,* I shall try to bring down the fever to keep him alive and try to study on what this might be," the *Hakim* promised.

"I shall write to Rosamunde as well," said Ravi. "Perhaps she will have heard of this malady and know a cure."

Cathal hopped from the bedside table onto the *charpoy* and lay against Alan's side, putting his head on his Wizard's chest. He would stay right here and pray to all of the gods and goddesses he could think of that Alan would recover.

18

the mourning elephant

Sinéad stirred painfully and let out a piteous meow. She hurt all over! She meowed again, expecting to hear Rosamunde's voice and feel her soothing touch. But nothing came.

She became conscious that wherever she lay was not very comfortable nor did it smell very good.

It was a great effort to open her eyes for she wanted to drift back down into the comforting blackness of unconsciousness. But something was very wrong and she had to find out what it was.

The familiar was shocked when she finally managed to lever herself up and look about her.

She lay upon an ash heap full of rubbish and garbage. All about her was the smell of fire and she could see flames leaping in the sky from almost every direction.

And the streets were full of people, screaming in terror or shouting in excitement. Sinéad could hear yells of "*Maro! Maro!*" (Kill! Kill!) as the killing and looting spread all over the city, not just the cantonments.

Behind her, the gate to the *Hirren Mahal* stood open. Sinéad staggered to her feet, almost collapsing again as dizziness swept over her. She gritted her teeth, cursing in Gaelic underneath her breath.

On wobbling legs she went into the Mahal, only to find it empty of any life. There were signs that the occupants had made a hurried getaway. Sinéad could not know that Gauri had insisted that they all go into the country, to where her sister lived, surely much safer for the *baba-log* than in this city which seemed to have gone insane.

Where was Rosamunde? Sinéad shivered. That man was a slaver, Ameera had said. And the little cat had seen the way that the big Pathan looked at Rosamunde. He was as bad as Higby!

From the look of the sun, although it was heavily

obscured by the billowing and drifting smoke, the day was well advanced, perhaps even near or just past noon time.

Sinéad could not understand how things had come to such a pass. Where was the army? Had the army come and Raymond had taken Rosamunde away? She did not think that this was so, for Rosamunde would have never left her. Even if she had been dead Rosamunde would have picked up her body and buried it properly, with all the rituals that were needed to send her on her journey to stand before Bastet and her scales to account for this life before she started on another. No matter what Raymond said Rosamunde would have never allowed him to take her away without Sinéad, not unless Rosamunde was unconscious or dead herself.

Somehow Sinéad doubted that the army had ever come. There was no sign of it and she was forced to conclude that someone else, probably the slaver, had carried Rosamunde away. But where that was she had no idea. It made her sick to think of her Witch in the hands of slavers. She had listened to Sacha's tales of what happened to the slaves in New Spain in the Americas, and she could not imagine that slaves here would be treated any better.

She had to have help, and that meant finding Raymond. For that she had to get back to the cantonments.

At times she was certain that she would never make it. Her entire body seemed to be bruised and she could not move as easily as she normally could. Ordinarily, she could have run across country, for she had the cat's wonderful sense of direction and a loping cat could cover a good deal of ground quite easily. But she could not move above a walk or a stiff legged trot. She had to keep out of the way of people as well for they all seemed bent on pillage and killing. She even saw a group chase and shoot a pariah dog for what seemed little reason other than a fierce urge to kill something.

It was hard to breath as well. The air was full of smoke which only added to the stifling heat. Sinéad thought longingly of the cool greenness of Ireland. Right now it would more than likely be raining at home, the soft Irish rain that was so sweet. And if they were at home where they belonged,

177

since it was now Monday, she and Rosamunde would more than likely have just come back from the Sewing Circle and would be sitting in front of a warm peat fire, waiting for luncheon to be served. She would be in Rosamunde's lap, feeling her soft, gentle hands stroking and caressing...Sinéad cursed as she tripped because her eyesight was suddenly blurred, vowing that when she and her Witch were reunited she was going to do everything she could to persuade Rosamunde to go back to Ireland and never leave home again.

Halfway back to the station, tossed into a ditch, Sinéad came across what little remained of Colonel Higby.

She recognized his scent first and bristled at once. But it smelled also overwhelmingly of blood and she went to investigate.

A human would have been hard put to recognize him for he had been dreadfully mutilated, hacked to pieces and attacked far beyond what had been necessary to kill him.

Sinéad felt sick and emptied out what little remained in her stomach. This spoke of a savagery that was beyond her comprehension. Humans thought that cats were cruel because they played with their prey, but no cat would ever do something like this! As much as she had loathed the Colonel, Sinéad hoped that he had died quickly.

The closer she came to the cantonments the more bodies she passed, both British and native. Most had been violently disfigured, in some cases butchered, and most of these were English. Sinéad saw corpses of men, women and children, officers and troopers and their families. The rebelling *sepoys* and the *badmashes* from the bazaar had even extended their hatred to the native women who cohabitated with the troopers, killing them and their half-caste children as well.

Everything was burning or so it seemed. Most buildings lay in smoldering ruins. Clothing, household goods and even foodstuffs lay strewn about as well. Sinéad saw dead horses, bullocks, goats and pet birds amongst the human dead.

In all ways the station seemed deserted. There was no sign of human life, only the jackals and pariah dogs, snapping and snarling at each other as they looked for anything edible. Some of the jackals had already been gnawing on the bodies.

"*Dogs!*" Sinéad thought in scorn, picking her way carefully through the wreckage and remains. "*They'll be after eating' anything, so they will! 'Tis no decency they're havin'!*"

In the deep silence Sinéad heard a sound that she had become familiar with only since coming out to India, the trumpet of an elephant. But this was different from the sounds she knew for in it was mingled grief and rage and utter despair.

Curious, she followed the sound to the edge of the cantonments where she knew the elephants had been kept. This was the *sawaree,* the elephant stabling. Elephants were useful for hauling heavy loads, for felling trees and clearing undergrowth and for load bearing, as well as transport and carrying the *sahibs' howdah* during a tiger shoot.

Sinéad had never even spoken to one of them. She was rather intimidated by their size. One of those great feet could squash her flat. She got on well with horses and dragons. Although many dragons were far larger than an elephant, dragons seemed somehow tamer and friendlier than elephants. She had heard tales of the *must,* the madness of the rogue elephant from Hari the mongoose.

To her joy she found Hari on the same errand as she, curious to know why the elephant called so loudly and so heartrendingly. The mongoose looked a little dazed and his fur was slightly singed in some places. He was equally glad to see her.

"They're all dead," he told her when greetings had been exchanged. "They killed my people - Kimball *Sahib* and his woman Neela and their children and I don't understand why!" he cried in anguish. "Kimball was a kind *sahib* and loved his woman and their children. He would have married her if it had been allowed. And they loved me as I loved them! Those *goondas* (bad characters) killed them all, even the *chicos* (children)! They even tried to kill me! Why? Why?"

Sinéad had no answer for him, only her sympathy.

"Your *sahib* is dead, too," Hari told her. "I saw his body when I went looking for you and found him in your bungalow. Some of the *nauker-log* (the servants) were slain as well. But I did not see your *mem-sahib.*"

Very briefly, Sinéad told her mongoose friend what had happened, with her attention on the *sawaree* ahead, where the elephant bellowing had grown more frequent.

There had never been more than three elephants at the station, one old bull and two younger ones. Elephants had to be twenty before they could be trained and it was usual for young ones to be put with an older, experienced animal to help them learn. The cat and the mongoose saw one of the young ones laying dead, shot between the eyes, as they went on towards the *sawaree*. The other young one was not in evidence. "He's probably run off," said Hari.

The old bull was the one making all the noise. As they drew closer they could see the massive beast swaying from side to side, his trunk busy with something on the ground. Every few minutes he would lift his trunk and let out another roar that echoed amongst the ruins of the *sawaree*, which looked as if it had been reduced to rubble.

Bodies lay near the elephant, low class trash from the bazaar that appeared to have been trampled or thrown.

As they drew abreast of the elephant they could hear him sobbing and Sinéad saw that what lay on the ground in front of him was the body of a man in native dress.

"Why did they kill thee, O my beloved Nirav?" the elephant was saying in tones of anguish. "So kind to me thou wast, so fair and always thinking of me, thou gavest me the best food and never beat me." As he spoke he very gently drew the tip of his trunk over and over on the man's face in a gesture of profound love.

"His *mahout* (handler), no doubt," Hari said quietly to Sinéad. "Those *badmashes* killed too many of the *nauker-log*, their own people, because they served the *Angrezi!*"

The elephant's head came up sharply and he said belligerently, "Who seeks to disturb my dead? I warn thee, I shall kill thee as I did these others!"

Sinéad had seen elephants in the Dublin zoo but this one was different than those. His ears were smaller and he was not quite as big for he stood barely ten feet tall at the shoulder. He was gray, and, like the ones she had seen, had long, curving tusks of ivory. On his tusks, like on a dragon's horns at hone, he wore jewelry of brass circlets set with tiny bells.

"We are not come to desecrate your dead," called Hari in Animal Speech. "We are but a mongoose and a cat, with our own dead and lost to mourn."

"Come closer so that I might see thee!" the elephant commanded.

They obeyed, Sinéad in some trepidation. Hari was used to elephants while she was not. And the look of the dead people here frightened her. He had killed five of them. She tried to comfort herself with the thought that Hari would be equally nervous of a dragon but she had never seen a dragon kill five people or even one person.

When he saw that it was just as he had been told the elephant relaxed. "I do not know thee," he said, "Art thou of this station?"

Hari rightly decided that the elephant was at least fifty years of age, for he spoke in an old fashioned style not heard amongst the younger animals.

"I am Hari," said the mongoose, "I was beloved in the *bashu* (native house) of Trooper Kimball *Sahib,* of he and his woman Neela and their three *butchas* (young ones). This is Sinéad, she came out from *Belait* but recently with her *mem-sahib.*"

"I am Bharat," said the elephant. "And this," he said sadly, looking at the body on the ground, "was my *mahout,* Nirav, a Rajah amongst *mahouts.* And they killed him, those *burchas,* for no reason other than that he was *nauker* to the *Angrezi-log!*"

"At least you had your revenge," said Hari. "There was naught I could do to the ones who killed my people. It was all I could do to escape so that they did not kill me!"

"And me Witch is gone missing in the hands of a slaver!" said Sinéad."I am bein' fair worried over what they'll be doin' to her."

"If she is at all pretty she will be debauched," said the elephant in his old fashioned manner.

"She's after being beautiful!" said the cat.

"Then they will sell her to a Maharajah and she will adorn his *zenana* and his bed," Bharat said matter of factly.

Sinéad bristled. "I'll not be letting that happen to her! Sure and isn't she goin' home with me to Ireland!"

Since she had learned that Raymond was dead her mind had been working furiously. What could she do? Only one thing occurred to her. She had to get to Alan. He was an

Adept class Wizard and he could rescue Rosamunde very easily. But how was she to get to Ranijhat? She was not even certain where it lay. To the north, she thought. She could not write or telegraph as she was certain that regular communication had been disrupted, at least here, and who knew how far this madness had spread? But how could a small cat, injured as she was, and she was feeling her injuries more every moment, travel all that way?

"Are ye after knowin' where Ranijhat might be?" she asked the elephant. "It's there I've got to be goin'."

"It lies far to the north, a long journey," he replied. "Once, in my youth I took a bridal procession there, a Rajput *Rajkumari* was to be married. It was a long and arduous journey, and thou art far too little to go there on thine own. The tigers or the muggers wouldst make but a *chota haziri* of thee!"

"I have to be goin' there, for 'tis the only way I can be savin' me darlin' Witch," Sinéad insisted stubbornly.

"Then I had best introduce thee to the only one who can help thee, if thou wouldst help me honor my dead. I do not wish the jackals to have him." said Bharat.

Both Hari and Sinéad agreed, Hari even saying that he would go with Sinéad upon her journey as he had no reason to stay here any longer for the memories would be too painful.

"We shall properly care for our dead," said Bharat decidedly "and then I shall take thee to Koda Khan, who is the only one who may set thy feet on the way with safety."

19

violation

For two interminable days the *palka-ghari* traveled north. The heat inside it was intense. So that outsiders did not see his 'wares', Wazid Ali kept the canvas sides lashed down. Very little air circulated and the passengers suffered, tied as they were and unable to move about. Rest stops were few, only for meals and for the women to relieve themselves in full view of the Pathans, by the side of the road.

Wazid Ali had not been as fortunate as he had hoped. They had found only one other woman that he deemed worthy of selling, another *mem sahib,* a dark haired English girl, who could only manage to stammer out her name to Laura. Vera Hyde and then seemed to slip into a fever and dozed fitfully, waking them all by screaming in her sleep. From her nightmares they were able to discern that she had seen her father and mother cut down. In this fashion they learned of the fall of Delhi, for that was where Vera's father had been stationed.

"Poor little thing!" said Laura with a frown, watching Vera pull against her bonds in her sleep. "She can't be more than fifteen at the most. And she's goin' into shock, I reckon."

"She is afraid even of us," put in Ameera, "for we are of Hind, of the race that slaughtered her parents. Didst thou see her face when she saw us? It mattered not that we are prisoners as she is, only that our skin is brown."

Unsa, who understood a little English, said "She will suffer the same fate as will we. If it were not that this *boroowa* flees from the rebellion he would have given us to the Pathans long since. Do you see how they look at us, as if they were starving! I am very much afraid that the next time this *ghari* stops they will take us."

Yesterday they had stopped for a brief while, shortly after Yakoub had found Vera and brought her back to the *palka ghari.* She had been fleeing on horseback north to Rawalpindi where her uncle was stationed, in company with a still faithful servant. Yakoub had killed the servant and taken Vera prisoner.

Wazid Ali had ordered all of the women stripped, one at a time so that he might properly assess their value.

For Rosamunde this had been a particular horror. To be stared at, and what was worse, fondled by men who looked at her with hot eyes – it was her worst nightmares come to life. Akbar, clasping her bottom and pulling her against him, had said something in Pushtu that made his cousins roar with laughter.

And she could do nothing to prevent him touching her. She reached for her magic and it simply was not there. She could not even use her knee on him as Alan had taught her, her hands and feet were tied securely to the wheel of the *ghari*. When she screamed at him, he stuffed a dirty scarf in her mouth

Wazid Ali thought this highly amusing. "Are you certain that you wish to take such a termagent, Akbar?" he said, watching Rosamunde's ineffective struggles.

"My cousins will help me tame her," he said complacently. "Look at her body, Wazid Ali! Is it not exquisite? This one could be the favorite of a *Padishah!*"

"Yes, she and the tall *mem* have the finest forms. Tthey will pay well for them in Jhaniput! Until then, Akbar, you and your cousins my enjoy them, and I shall sell their bodies on the way for many *rupees*." Greedily, he rubbed his hands together, almost salivating at the thought of the riches that such beautiful women would bring. He gave no thought as to their unwillingness to be stolen away from their homes, sold and used as the receptacles of male lust. That was what women were for and they had no right to protest.

It was during this minute examination that Wazid Ali found out that Ameera was pregnant.

The old slaver was delighted. "I have a customer in Bangladore that wishes a woman with child, as his wife is herself to whelp shortly. And add that to the fact that this one is a beauty, he will be quite pleased, a wet nurse and a very pleasing concubine in one! For such beauty he will pay me double what he promised! And her child is an added bonus – two slaves for the price of one!" Ameera, he decreed, was not to be raped, given that the sexual congress might harm the unborn child and if she miscarried she would be of no use as a wet nurse.

In another day or so, Wazid Ali promised the Pathans, when they were well away from the scenes of the *sepoy* insurrection, they would stop for a rest and the Pathans could sample the women in the *palka ghari.*

Wazid Ali had grown increasingly nervous of what was happening in Hindustan. The stories circulating were frightening and he made a point of questioning every traveler they met on the road, most of whom seemed to be fleeing from death and destruction. The whole of northern India seemed to have gone mad. The *sepoys* and the bazaar trash were no longer just killing the *Angrezi-log,* they were attacking anyone that had something they wanted, and these women (and his cache of coins hidden in the false bottom of the *ghari*) might tempt any man, much less those maddened by blood lust. Therefore he judged it best to wait to get as far from the scenes of insurrection as was possible. The Pathans would be impatient, but as long as no real damage was done to the merchandise he did not care how many times they took his prisoners or how roughly the Pathans treated the women.

After three days of constant travel the *palka ghari* at last stopped. All of the women were hot and thirsty. Wazid Ali had not been generous with water, nor with food, which had consisted for the most part of stale *chuppallies* spread with almost rancid *ghee* (clarified butter) and a handful of sticky rice.

Rosamunde's appetite had fled. She was so afraid of what night happen that she could not eat and her stomach was tied in knots.

Laura viewed her with concern. "What is it, Rose honey? Are you thinking that they'll beat you?"

Rosamunde tuned her head away and said "Laura, they're going to rape us! Don't you know what that means?" She could not understand why the American woman seemed so unconcerned. Even little Vera, who slipped in and out of awareness, was afraid. Unsa and Neha were concubines; Unsa had been purchased from a brothel and Neha had been raised to be a concubine by her parents, who were very poor and saw selling their daughter for a man's use as a way to augment their meager income. They were resigned to their fate. And Ameera, by virtue of the fact that she was increasing, had been reprieved.

"Course I know what it means – and I plan to just lay there and let them do what they want."

"How can you say that, Laura?" said Rosamunde in a fierce whisper. "How can you talk about being violated as if it were nothing, to have a strange man doing intimate things to you? It was bad enough that they saw us naked and put their hands all over us!" She stopped abruptly, her breast heaving under the remnants of her bodice and *sari* – there had not been much left but rags once the Pathans had stripped them and Wazid Ali had grudgingly allowed them to crawl back into the remnants.

Laura gave a wry smile. "Because this has happened to me before, honey. When I was sixteen I joined a group that was helping to free slaves from the Inquisition in New Spain. On one of our raids something went real wrong and I was captured. I was sent to work in the mines and the men who ran the mines felt they had an obligation to rape me as many times as possible to teach me that we had no business trying to free the slaves. I was there for over a year, chained naked to an ore cart and grubbing in the dirt for gold. There wasn't a day went by when a whole bunch of them didn't grab me and do whatever they liked, and there wasn't a blessed thing I could do about it. Even the men slaves, they'd get so angry that they'd just take any available woman."

"Oh, Laura!" Rosamunde said in pity and horror.

Laura shrugged. "That's the way men, bad men, desperate men, are. And I learned there just to let them do what they wanted. It saved me a hell of a lot of beatings and even got me some better food. I knew Pa would come for me one day and he did, finally. It took him a while to find me as they had taken me to another place so's I couldn't be found."

Rosamunde shuddered. "I can't do that," she said finally. "I can't just lie there! The whole thing makes me sick! Why do people want to do that! Why are men so horrible?"

Laura looked at her curiously. "Thought you was

married," she said.

Rosamunde blushed. She looked over at Unsa and Neha – they were paying no attention, Neha did not speak English and Unsa's understanding was limited. Both Vera and Ameera slept.

"He could never consummate the marriage, he – he... " this was so difficult to admit! Raymond had stressed over and over again that no one must ever know. But he probably was dead, so what did it matter now?

"Couldn't get it up?" Laura suggested.

Rosamunde blushed again. "No, no, he said I was too beautiful and he, he – "

"Came without you," Laura finished prosaically. "And I suppose he blamed you for that. So you're still technically a virgin. How come Wazid Ali didn't find that out? He stuck his dirty paw up between my legs and poked around, must have done the same to you"

"I had surgery to remove my maidenhead. It's the custom with Witches," said Rosamunde hesitantly.

Laura whistled. "No wonder you're scared. Since they think you ain't a virgin they won't be as careful as they might be with Vera, that poor kid's in for another shock. All I can say, Rose honey, is to just take it, try and relax and don't fight them. I've seen the size of the whip that Nakshsband carries, you don't want that laid across your butt or back."

"It doesn't look like a whip," said Rosamunde. "It looks like it is made of bamboo..."

"It's a Chinese thing, the Inquisition used them. It won't leave a mark on you but the pain it causes is God-awful" Laura told her. "It's really bad when you're whipped with it on the backside and then they rape you. They used it on some of the women at the mine who fought them, and the screaming was awful. But Pa always told me when we were going on raids that if I was captured just let them do what they wanted, it didn't matter as long as I was alive, he'd come for me and I'd still be his gal even if I was to have a Spanish bastard."

Rosamunde gave a long shudder. Laura's voice, uttering horrors, was so matter of fact.

"I'm sorry about your husband, honey," said Laura in a kinder tone. "If you loved him a lot that must have been hard on you both, and a man who can't make love to his wife gets ugly tempered after a while."

"I miss Sinéad more than I miss Raymond," Rosamunde admitted. "I miss her every minute, and it hurts so much! That makes me a horrible person to miss my cat more than my husband."

"Well, no, " said Laura wisely. "I've seen Witches and familiars back home and it's kind of a special bond. And it sounds as if you and your husband had your problems." And at no time she said to herself, had the Irish girl ever used the word 'love' when she talked about her husband. Laura wondered if it had been an arranged marriage, for she had read that such things were common in Europe. The very idea appalled her. What she had with Nate, and what it would be like when they were married, was so different from what she was hearing from Rose.

Laura was completely confident that either she would extricate herself from the present situation or that Nate and her father would find her. They'd tear apart India if they had to. And it wouldn't matter to either one of them how many Pathans or Maharajahs or whatever had used her, they'd just be glad to have her back. Nate knew what had happened to her in New Spain and honored her for trying to help the slaves. He was an Abolitionist himself.

They did not have long to wait before Buzurg, who had won the first throw of the dice, came for Unsa, whose voluptuous curves he had much admired.

Rosamunde did not know how long the concubine was gone but when she returned she was completely unclothed and Buzurg gloated as he tied her up again. "You will be mine every day until you are sold to your new master," he promised. tightening the rope about her wrists.

"What happened?" Neha demanded when Buzurg had gone.

"He ripped my clothes off and took me," Unsa shrugged. "The old *boroowa* says we shall not need clothes any more and laughed, saying that we shall be cooler naked. They are throwing dice for the next one to be used now."

Vera was the next one to go. Nakshsband came for her and she struggled weakly, still ill. They heard her screaming for a while until the sound was abruptly cut off.

When they brought her back she was unconscious, and Nakshsband grumbled that she had been disappointing, but he would take her again anyway, for she could only improve with use.

Then it was Neha's turn, Yakoub wanted her and seemed quite pleased when he returned, slapping her playfully on the buttocks as he retied her.

A few moments later the canvas flap lifted and Akbar said to Rosamunde, "It is my turn, *larla* (darling). I would take you now for I have waited too long already." He then looked at Laura. "You are to be honored by the attentions of Wazid Ali himself. He has always wanted a *mem- sahib.*"

"Ain't I the lucky one," Laura drawled.

Akbar untied Rosamunde and she tried to kick him. He laughed. "Such spirit!" he exulted and threw her over his shoulder where she flailed with her feet and used her still bound hands to try and hit him about the head. She also shrieked at him to let her go.

All her struggles seem but to amuse him. "Hit me all you wish, little one," he said "I shall have you no matter what you do. You are no match for me!"

Laura said loudly "Do as he says, Rose honey!" but she was very much afraid that Rosamunde would fight to the end, as she was too afraid to take advice.

This time there was no escape for Rosamunde.

Hands were touching her. In a blind panic Rosamunde struck out "NO! Don't touch me!" she screamed.

"Hush, Rose honey, it's me, Laura. They're letting me take care of you and Vera. Let me see how much they hurt you, please, honey," Laura said coaxingly. "I've got water and some soft cloths. The old bastard even has some medicines."

Rosamunde could not stop shuddering. Arms clutched around her self and curled into a ball, she wanted nothing more than to die. She had cried so much that her face was swollen and her throat was raw.

"Open your eyes and look at me, honey," said Laura gently. "They knocked you around a little and I've got what looks and smells like arnica for those bruises. Come on, honey, it's all over for now."

Very reluctantly Rosamunde opened her eyes to Laura's soft-voiced pleadings.

"That's my girl!" said Laura, and at once wiped Rosamunde's face with a wet cloth. "That damned Akbar has a heavy hand!" she said.

They were not in the *palka-ghari*. Overhead stars shone in the night sky, and as Rosamunde moved slightly she heard the clink of a chain and a pull on her ankle. Vera lay some distance away in a crumpled heap. All three of them were naked.

"You, me and Vera are staked out here," said Laura. Rosamunde heard water falling and then felt the wet cloth on her face again. "That old whore master let me talk him into caring for you two. He was pretty mellow after screwing his first white woman. Fancies himself a real stud." Laura snorted in derision. "You and Vera are in the worse shape of any of us. She's still unconscious, that goddamned Pathan tore her up pretty bad. The damned jackass knew she was a virgin! So we've all three got chains around our ankles and those are attached to a stake pounded into the ground, strong enough to hold an elephant, I reckon. And I looked, the chains ain't iron they're some sort of brass but tough as nails. Now I'm sorry, honey, but I need to look down below and see if you're bleeding or need any arnica. You've been curled up tighter than a hedgehog."

"Oh, Laura –" Rosamunde said in a thread of a voice. " Hurt – it hurt!"

"I know, honey," said Laura sympathetically.

Rosamunde gritted her teeth for what followed. She knew enough medicine to know that treatment should not be put off.

Laura was very gentle, but Rosamunde still flinched away from her. "Done this more times than I can count for women who were brought to the mines," Laura said. "We all had to help each other."

When she finished tears were trickling down Rosamunde's face. Laura wiped her cheeks. "Just hold on honey," she urged. "Just get through each day. I know Pa and Nate are looking for me, and I'll make damn sure that they rescue all of us. And I might come up with a plan to get us

190

out of here too, I'm good with plans. There's that cousin of yours too, that you told me about - the Wizard. Once he knows you've gone missing it'll be hell or high water until he finds you. Don't give up hope, and don't let what these bastards do to you break you. Remember, you're still alive and there are people who love you, who'll be looking for you. Just hold on to that."

Rosamunde looked up into her face. On Laura's features was a look of compassion and loving concern, the first such look Rosamunde had seen since Akbar had tossed her over his shoulder back at the *Hirren Mahal*.

With a despairing shudder and a deep sob, she began to cry in gasping breaths and felt Laura's arms come around her.

"There, honey, you just cry it all out," Laura urged.

Rosamunde cried until she was exhausted. All the while Laura soothed her and held her as if she a small child until Rosamunde at last fell into sleep.

It was to be the last time she cried for a long, long time.

koda khan

"And who might be this Koda Khan?" Sinéad asked Bharat the elephant.

"He is *Rajnish,* the lord of the night," said Bharat. He refused to tell them any more until the dead were taken care of.

Hari and Sinéad helped the elephant honor his late *mahout.* Those of the Hindu faith were always cremated and the elephant piled up logs for a pyre, lifting them easily with his massive trunk. Hari's clever paws snatched a burning brand from the ruins of the Officer's mess and with it and the aid of some oil Sinéad located, set fire to the stack. The barracks where Hari's family lay dead were already aflame, that could serve as their funeral pyre.

As they watched the flames consume all that remained of Nirav, Sinéad wondered what she should do about Raymond's body. Cremation was not an English custom.

The decision was taken out of her paws by the arrival of a small contingent on horseback from Meerut, headed by Captain Wallace and the mere handful of men who had survived the attack. To them fell the horrible, painful task of identifying and burying the dead. The Captain was not the only one who had to face seeing a spouse or a child dead and dismembered. To bury the dead as quickly as possible was an utter necessity in the heat of India, for putrefying corpses could cause epidemics of disease.

Captain Wallace's little notebook, which he had divided into columns marked "dead" "survived" and "missing" (and was segregated as to British and natives) was soon full of dead. Sinéad saw him go into their bungalow and come out a few moments later, white-faced, scratching with his pencil in the little book. Like the others who had come with him, the Captain looked sick. There were groans of anguish as they saw the dead women and children and many of the men were forced to stagger away from the scene, emptying out their stomachs as they saw the butchery of those they regarded as innocents or found comrades and loved ones hacked to bits.

As the men were beginning to dig a pit – since burial had to take place so quickly there was no time for the niceties of coffins and funerals, no matter the feelings of the survivors, the animals were preparing to leave.

"The jackals and pi-dogs will snap thee up as a tender morsel," Bharat said to Sinéad and wrapped his trunk around her. She squawked in surprise as he swept her up and put her on his head where he still wore part of his trappings, a cloth headdress of red fabric. He put Hari up beside her and two little animals lay down and hung on.

"We shall leave before the *sahib-log* take notice and attempt to stop us," the elephant informed his passengers. Bharat was no fool; an fully trained elephant was a valuable commodity and the *sahibs* would hate to let him escape.

Quietly, they left the edge of the cantonments and slipped into the jungle. Sinéad was surprised at how quickly and silently the elephant could move. She thought of his species as slow and ponderous, making a tremendous amount of noise by virtue of their size alone.

The jungle was very still. Sinéad thought that this was very strange, for at home, the copses were full of birds, insects and small animals going about their business. She did not realize that the smell of burning (for fire was a terrifying danger) and the sounds of the Mutiny had scared the inhabitants of the jungle and they had fled, further in, to safety.

She had not dared to venture into the jungle on her own. Hari had teased her, saying that there was nothing to be frightened of if she kept her wits about her, but she had refused to go in. There was something very primitive about the jungle and Sinéad, being an extremely civilized cat, found it almost repulsive.

Now as she looked at the huge trees, the heavy vegetation and the tangled vines and creepers,she was glad that she was safe up on some thing the size of an elephant. And she was grateful to be laying down, for she ached in every part of her body.

Neither she not Hari spoke and Bharat was only intent on getting away from the station. None of the trio felt much like talking for their pain was too new, too raw. Sinéad reflected that she was the luckiest of the three; at least she had good reason to believe that Rosamunde was still alive but the people that Bharat and Hari loved were dead.

But how to find and get back with Rosamunde was the problem. She placed all of her hopes on Alan. She had found, on a quick trip to the bungalow, a small scarf of Rosamunde's and had asked Hari to tie it about her neck. Alan could use it to search for Rosamunde with his pendulum.

She had, however, avoided looking at Raymond's body, as the superstitious part of her brain insisted that her curse was responsible for his death. And he had not even the shroud on him, but would be thrown as he was in to a mass grave. The little cat gave a shudder as she thought of this. She would also have to tell Rosamunde that she was now a widow.

Sinéad fell into a light doze after a while. She was tired as well as being in pain. Her claws were well inserted into the elephant's headpiece so she did not worry about falling off.

Shadows of deepest blue were lengthening when, deep in the jungle, the elephant stopped.

Sinéad awoke with a start as Hari whispered right in her ear "Wake up!"

Bharat was standing quite still with his head lifted, and his trunk pointing upwards as well. Sinéad expected him to trumpet a call; she braced herself.

But the elephant called softly "Koda Khan! Koda Khan! I have need of thee!"

There was a rustling in the leaves of a *sal* tree and a small, black furry, rather cross face peered down at them."Who calls?" the animal said irritably. "Oh, it is you, Bharat! That is a very strange hat you are wearing!" he dissolved into laughter at his own humor.

"*A monkey!*" thought Sinéad in disgust, for she had no great opinion of monkeys. "*Light brained spalpeens, the lot of them!*"

"Sure, and if I was after thinkin' this Koda Khan was bein' a monkey I'd have stayed back at the station, so I would !" she muttered to Hari.

"I bid thee good day, Isha," said Bharat."My little friends have need of the guidance of Koda Khan. Is he about?"

Sinéad was very relieved, this was not Koda Khan. "And who would this monkey be, his secretary?" she muttered to Hari.

The mongoose chuckled at the thought of an animal having a secretary. He called to the monkey "My friend wishes to know if you are *sarishtadar* to Koda Khan!"

Isha the monkey frowned again. "Koda Khan, the lord of the jungle, is very busy. All sorts of animals come here, begging for his aid. And I am honored to help him."

"Peace, Isha," came a deep voice from above them. "My little cousin means no disrespect."

Sinéad turned her head and looked up. She gave a gasp when she saw what lay on a thick branch of an immense *banyan* tree above their heads.

It was an enormous black panther, lounging at his ease on a platform like branch of the tree. One huge paw hung down and his tail twitched slowly. His eyes were like brilliant yellow lanterns and his coat was sleek, glossy and black as ebony. *"He's after bein' as big as an Irish wolfhound!"* Sinéad thought in amazement.

The big cat rose and stretched and then like black lightning, sprang down to the broad trunk like roots of the tree and from there to the ground.

"Greetings, Bharat," he said to the elephant. "You are a long way from Malabad. We have not seen you much in recent times."

"Malabad is no more, Goondas have overrun it and killed all the *Angrezi-log* and many of the *nauker-log* as well," said Bharat sadly. "Including my Nirav."

"This is ill news," said the panther "I am most sorry to hear this, my friend. Nirav was a most unusual human - he truly understood animals."

"This explains why the vultures and the hyenas and jackals we saw were all leaving," said the monkey excitedly. "We wondered why they departed, but heard only rumors."

"It was no doubt the stench of carrion that drew them. Rumor has it that all over Hindustan humans have become *doolali* (insane) and are killing each other." The panther sat down at Bharat's feet. "You said you had need of me, Bharat. What may I do for my old friend?"

Bharat reached up and took Sinéad and Hari one at a

time from their high perch and put them in front of Koda Khan. He introduced them to the huge panther.

Sinéad immediately felt dwarfed by the sheer bulk of Koda Khan. She was the size of one of his paws.

" 'Tis bein' a great cat, ye are!" she said, looking up at him.

"By your speech you are not of Hind," he said, "though still related to me, however distantly. We are both cats."

"She is of *Belait*," explained Bharat, "and has mislaid her *mem sahib*."

Sinéad bristled. "I was not mislayin' her! She was stolen away from me by a spalpeen of a slaver! An' I am wantin' to get her back! An' to do that I am havin' to get to Ranijhat and find Alan. He's a Wizard."

"A Wizard?" the panther inquired. "I know not this word."

"A magician," Hari supplied. "A *Jogee.*"

"Have you then mislaid someone as well, mongoose?" the panther inquired.

"No, I go with my friend to help her on her journey. My people that I loved were all murdered at Malabad. There is nothing for me there now," Hari said, his voice low and sad as once again he realized he would never again play with the children or feel the kind hands of Kimball *sahib* stroking his fur or have a plate of food especially prepared for him by Neela.

Leaves shook and swayed in the large leathery leaves of the *sal* tree as the monkey came hurtling down.

He was revealed as a Hanuman Langur, largely gray, with a black face and front paws and a darker hind end and tail. He walked on all fours as he went up to Hari and said "It does not do to attach yourself to humans! Only heartache can come of it!"

Bharat ignored him. "We seek thy help, Koda Khan, to set this little cat on her way to the north. She needs to know how to proceed safely. She is so small she would be prey for many creatures in the jungle."

"Ranijhat. I know of this place. It is a long road that you will take, my little cousin." He looked kindly at Sinéad. "I think it best that you take her, Bharat. I shall give you my

196

safe conduct."

"*I* take her?" said the elephant, surprised."But Koda Khan –"

"You said that your Nirav is dead. There is naught to bind you to Malabad. Do you wish another *mahout* ? If you stay here the *sahib-log* will take you back and give you another *mahout,*" the panther pointed out. "And who can better protect her and guide her?"

"It is true, I have been there," said the elephant thoughtfully. "And I grow old, as thee knows, Koda Khan. My teeth wear out. I remember this Ranijhat as a pleasant place with sweet grass where I might like to spend my last days." He was lost in thought for a moment and then said decisively "Very well, I shall do it!"

"I shall send Isha with you," said the panther. "In spite of his distrust of humans he is a clever little soul. He will carry my safe conduct for you. Under the protection of Koda Khan you need fear no animal in the jungle."

Sinéad could not thank them enough. The elephant could cover far more ground in a day that could she and she had been afraid to travel on her own. This way she would feel protected. Having the monkey as a traveling companion, however, was not thrilling. She did not care for him. Not attach oneself to humans indeed! Nobody loved her more than Rosamunde!

Koda Khan's head suddenly came up sharply. "Someone comes!" he said sniffing the air. "A human in great haste and fear."

Sinéad heard it as well, a faraway crashing through the trees and then a loud roar.

"That is Rajiv the striped one!" said Isha. "Does he then chase human prey?"

Koda Khan frowned. "He will feel my wrath if he does so! He knows that to kill humans is forbidden!"

The crashing grew nearer. They could hear someone sobbing in fright and exhaustion, and then a disheveled figure burst into the small clearing.

It was a woman, an Englishwoman in a hoop skirt that now hung askew. Leaves and vines trailed from her tumbled hair and her gown of brown worsted was ripped in many places.

She stopped still when she saw the animals and uttered a little scream. Terrified, she looked around, trapped between the group in the clearing and what was chasing her. She shrank back against the whitish gray bark of a teak tree, and closed her eyes, her lips moving in a prayer.

Sinéad stared at her in amazement. It was Molly Fraser!

Another loud roar sounded and a large tiger bounded out of the jungle, heading straight for Molly. His yellow eyes gleamed and his large teeth snapped the air.

With an ear splitting roar and an Immense leap Koda Khan landed in front of the tiger and said "How dare you, Rajiv? You know my law! We do not hunt the humankind! Do you wish to bring down the hunt upon us? You know what they do to the eaters of humans!"

The tiger had halted in his tracks when he was confronted by the black panther. Now he bowed before the bigger cat, cowering a little. "Forgive me, O Koda Khan," he said. "I was hungry and hunger overtook my good sense."

"I killed this morning. You will find the remains in that tree," the panther indicated the banyan tree he had so lately occupied, "There is enough left for a good meal. Go and help yourself."

"Thank you, Great Lord," said the tiger humbly and sprang eagerly in to the tree.

"I am knowin' this human!" said Sinéad. "She's after bein' a friend of me Witch's."

Molly had watched in amazement as the tiger turned from her and the rest of the animals remained where they were. She looked as if she would faint at any moment and looked at the panther and the elephant in fear.

"It is to my sorrow that we cannot tell her that she has no need to fear us," said Koda Khan, frowning.

"I can be speakin' to humans," said Sinéad and went towards Molly.

"Molly!" she called, "'Tis me, Sinéad, Rosamunde's familiar. Ye need not be worryin' yourself. No one here will be eatin' you!"

"Sinéad?" Molly repeated faintly. She was still breathing very hard. She had been running forever or so it seemed and it was very hot.

Her legs suddenly gave out and she sank down beneath the tree. "I thought that tiger was going to eat me!" she said, leaning back and closing her eyes.

Sinéad climbed into her lap and proceeded to talk earnestly in a low voice.

"This is truly a talent, to be able to speak to humans!" said Koda Khan rather enviously.

Sinéad came back to the group. "She's been runnin' at least two days, the poor thing. She was comin' to visit me Witch an' when her guide was seein' what was happen' hereabouts, he up and left her on her own. She was after bein' scared by a gang o' rough characters an' took to her heels. She's been lost in the jungle ever since."

She looked up at the elephant. "We'll have to be takin' her wi' us. I am not knowin' what else to do wi' her, it is seeming as if there is no safe place for her to go here. 'Tis the army will be here soon, I am bettin', then there will be fightin', no place for a young girl!"

"I have no *howdah* for her to ride in," protested Bharat. "*Mem-sahibs* do not ride without a *howdah!!*"

"She can ride wi' me an' Hari. 'tis better than naught an' Molly's not one to give herself airs. Rosamunde would be wantin' me to look after her," Sinéad said stubbornly.

In the end it was the panther who persuaded the elephant to carry another passenger. Half an hour later, the oddly assorted group set off, Molly, the mongoose and Sinéad on the elephant while Isha swung ahead of them in the trees on their way to the north and Ranijhat.

21

under interdict

The morning air was soft and sweet and the sun shone in a blue, cloudless sky; a perfect spring day in Ireland.

Sir Simon Stillfield sighed as he leaned almost precariously far out of the window of his Wizard's Tower. Below him on the lawn he could see his wife Tatya and their thirteen year old daughter Irina playing with one of their red dogs. He could hear their laughter and the dog's excited barking drifting up in the clear air.

Out at the edge of his vision he could see the dragon pen near the stables and his second eldest son Jack, now two and twenty and a qualified veterinarian, talking to Simon's dragon Lakota, who had suffered a slight digestive upset yesterday. Soon seventeen year old Alex would be home from the Tara Druidry where he was studying to become a Druid, as it was the last day of term there.

How he wished that his desk were not piled high with correspondence! He had promised to write recommendations for several of his graduate students and there was an insistent letter from his publisher as his latest manuscript on *"Draconic Inhabitants of the North American Interior"* was overdue. He had end of term examinations to correct so that the grades could be posted before the students left University for the Long Vacation and there were letters from fellow Dracophilologists that needed to be answered as well. But this sort of day tempted one to be outside. It was a rare and lovely event to have such a clear, bright day in the spring. *"Sweet day,"* Simon murmured, taking a deep breath of the fragrant air, *"So calm, so cool, so bright, the bridal of the earth and sky..."*

He turned away from the window. Thinking about the work would not get it done. Resolutely, he sat at the desk and pulled a pile of examination booklets towards him and reached for pens and a double ink standish, containing bottles of both black and red ink.

He had time to finish only one booklet, which to his relief was excellent work, when a knock came at the door.

"Enter," he called absently, opening the next booklet in the stack. Recognizing the name of the student he sighed. This young man had never seemed to grasp the concepts of the study of dragons. Two years ago, a year of basic Draco-philology had become a required course for all Wizardry students as all Wizards eventually had some sort of a relationship with dragons. This had meant a heavier teaching burden for Simon, as well as for as it seemed there were many more rather poor students who had no wish to be in his classes but had to do so.

The door opened to reveal Ó Failbhe, the Stillfield butler. He looked perturbed. "Excuse me, Sir Simon," he said "but there is an urgent scry from his Grace, in the bookroom. His Grace was most insistent that he speak to you immed-iately."

"Urgent?" said Simon, putting down his pen, wondering what could be so urgent that Grandfather Chenevix would scry at so early an hour for it was scarcely eight o'clock.

"That was the exact word his Grace used, sir," the butler said. "He appeared to be extremely agitated."

"Oh, no," said Simon worriedly. "I hope this does not mean that Grandmother Lucie has passed away!" Lucie was in her nineties and being non-magical, was becoming increasingly frail.

He rose from behind the desk and went downstairs with the butler.

At Summerhills, the Stillfield estate, the scry bowl was kept on the first floor in the bookroom for the convenience of the household. As in most Wizards' homes a silver bell, called, like its counterpart in the ocean, a buoy, rode on the water's surface in the scry bowl. When a scry was coming in the slight boiling action of the water would cause the bell to ring out, alerting the footman on duty in the hall.

The French doors of the bookroom stood open to the beautiful day. Simon took another deep breath of the pure air, redolent with fresh cut grass as he sat down at the scry bowl.

There in the water's surface was an image of his grandfather, the Duke of Chenevix. Chenevix was now over one hundred years of age, but for a Wizard that was quite common. His hair was completely white and he expression was normally that of austerity. But his morning he looked haggard and anxious.

"Not Grandmama?" Simon asked worriedly as he took in the Duke's appearance.

"No," Chenevix said abruptly. "She is doing very well. This is something else," he paused and then said hurriedly, "I am on my way to Ireland, I am in London at the moment."

"London?" Simon queried. Usually this time of year found Chenevix at his principal seat, Chenevix Duchis in Dorsetshire, since neither he nor his Duchess cared much for the London social season any more.

"I should be with you in about three hours," the Duke continued. "A transport dragon is coming for me. I have already scryed Lyonshall and he is on his way as well."

"You scryed Lyonshall?" Simon repeated in amazement. The Marquis of Lyonshall was Simon's great grandfather by marriage and the Duke and the Marquis had never gotten along.

The Duke ignored this. "What I need you to do, Simon, is to get in touch with your father and brother as I shall want you all present. I am flying directly to Summerhills. I have not been able to raise either one of them. The police told me that Stuart was out on an investigation and your father seems to be from home as well."

"It's the last day of term at the Druidry," said Simon "He has classes today. It's the final dematerialization exam. What is it all about, sir?" he added curiously.

The Duke looked so bleak that Simon was suddenly afraid. "It is very bad news," he said heavily. "Very bad indeed. But I do not want to talk of it until I see you in person. Please, Simon, do as I say and make certain that Stuart and René are waiting for me. And please, do not tell the women or the children that there is anything out of the ordinary. I do not wish to alarm them."

With this the picture in the scry bowl abruptly disappeared.

Simon leaned back in his chair, both worried and mystified. What ever could this mean?

Then it struck him. TheDuke had actually said

'please' *twice.* Chenevix *never* said 'please'. He issued orders and expected them to be obeyed. And he had called Simon's father 'René', another thing that he never did. Ever since Simon could remember the Duke had called his son 'Keir', the name of his title as the heir to the Dukedom, the Marquis of Keir. For him to quit the habit of years, something was indeed seriously wrong.

He bent over the scry bowl. He would scry Tara first. His brother Stuart might be more difficult to locate if he was still out upon an investigation. Now for the first time Simon wished that there was an easy way to talk to people who were not near a scry bowl or a telegraph station.

Lyonshall arrived within the next hour, his Irish Emerald dragon, Tuathail, bringing both the Marquis and his Marchioness, Ninon, Simon's great grandmother. She had refused to be left behind. It was a short flight by draconic standards from the Cotswolds in England across the Irish sea to Summerhills, south of Dublin.

Both Lyon and Ninon were well into their second century of life but had not changed much since Simon had first met them over forty years earlier. Their hair might be more silver, their faces more lined, but their age had not seemed to slow them down at all.

As they waited for the others to arrive Lyon played his favorite trick of pacing up and down the floor of the bookroom. Simon had sent Lakota out to scout for Stuart as his brother's Hippogriffe, Gabriel, would be easy to spot from the air, and René's secretary had informed them that his lordship was just finishing up the last class and would be with them as soon as possible

"He didn't even drop a hint?" Lyon demanded of Simon, as he walked quickly up and down, passing his hands through his mane of hair. He looked like a worried, elderly lion. His familiar, an owl called Leander, had at first perched on his shoulder, but when Lyon's pacing became too much for him he flew to the back of a chair where he now clung.

Ninon's familiar, a snow white cat called Neige, sat in her Witch's lap. She was sister to Simon's black and orange cat Janus, who lay on the desk watching all of the proceedings intently.

"No,"Simon answered "he just said it was very bad, and not to tell the women or the children."

Ninon snorted. Her son-in-law tried her patience at times. "*Mon Dieu!* As if we are ones to need the protection! Where is Tatya?" she asked Simon. "Why is she not here?"

"It's Wednesday," he said "Her charity Sewing Circle meets this morning. Both she and Mama, and Julia too, will be there. I thought I'd find out what this was before alarming her."

"For all we know Palmerston's government has fallen and Chenevix is losing his position as Chancellor of Magic. Frankly I don't know how he's managed to hang onto it through so many administrations. He must spend a fortune in bribes," said Lyon. "But why would he scry *me* about that and insist I come to a meeting? After we had that blow up at David's birthday party I was very surprised to hear from him this morning!"

"You have always the blow-ups with *M'sieur le Duc*," said Ninon.

"No gathering would be complete without them," said Janus dryly. Leander, who had closed his eyes and drawn one foot up into the feathers on his breast, opened his eyes and winked at her.

There was a noise at the door and Stuart came in followed by his bespectacled brown tabby familiar, Dr. Foster.

"What's this all about, Simon?" he said after greeting his great grandparents. "Lakota said that I was to come at once, that Grandfather Chenevix had sent you an urgent message early this morning. What's happened? It isn't Grandmama Lucie, is it?"

"That's what I thought at first," answered Simon. "but he assured me that she is doing well. He would only say that it was very bad," he repeated his grandfather's words.

"We've been speculating as to what it might be," put in Lyon. "everything from the government having fallen to a resumption of the war with Russia."

"That would be very hard on Tatya and Sacha but scarcely calls for a family meeting," Stuart said, sinking into one of the armchairs near the fireplace. Dr. Foster joined

Janus on the desk top. They were old friends.

Janus, like the other cats, lifted her head. "Two more dragons arriving," she said.

"Two?" Lyon queried. "Aren't we waiting only for René?"

"If this is a family problem I thought Sacha should be here as well so I scryed him at the Incubatory," said Simon. "That is probably his Cynara, and Cerridwen with Papa, landing."

Cynara was an American Luna dragoness, bonded to Sacha Kustodiev, Simon's brother-in-law and she was in turn mated to Lakota. The two dragons spent half their evenings at Summerhills and the other half at Sacha's home so that they could be together. Cerridwen, a Welsh Red, had been with René for years.

Sacha was the Managing Director of the Dragon Egg Incubatory Facility in Dublin. Like Simon he had a doctorate in Dracophilology and until his recent marriage, had made his home with Tatya and Simon.

They heard voices in the hall and a few moments later Sacha and René entered the room. They were accompanied by their familiars, René's cat Rascal, brother to Neige and Janus, and Sacha's cat Anastasia, Janus's granddaughter.

Sacha was in his familiar buckskins, North American Indian dress that he had adopted while out there, declaring that they were far more comfortable than any other clothing he had ever worn.

René still wore the Druidical white robes he wore for teaching at the Druidry. These robes were stark white, made of the finest, purest linen and worn with a waist sash, the colour of which changed with the seasons. Today it was green, for the spring and for the just passed Beltane festival.

René was well over sixty but he looked far younger. His mahogany hair was touched lightly with silver and his face little lined. Not only practicing magic but the strong strain of Elfin blood in him had preserved his youth. His wife, Diana, had said in mock protest that this was not fair, *her* hair had gone completely silver.

"What's wrong?" said Sacha, looking at all the sober faces in the room. "What's the Duke up to?"

Simon again repeated what the Duke had said and

Lyon told how his Grace had roused them at the crack of dawn with the request that they join him in Ireland.

"*C'est mystérieux!*" said René. "But *mon père* is not one who becomes disordered easily, no? It is of a surety something not good."

Ó Failbhe appeared with a tray of sherry, to which all the gentlemen and Ninon helped themselves as they continued to talk about what might have prompted the Duke to call them together so abruptly.

"All this speculation is useless," said Stuart at last. "It's akin to trying to solve a murder by guesswork instead of solid forensic work and collecting hard evidence."

"Another dragon is coming!" announced Dr. Foster.

The driveway and the dragon pen were not visible from the bookroom which looked out from the back of the house into the garden. Simon put down his glass and went into the hall. A murmur of voices was heard and a just a few moments the Duke was with them, followed by his familiar, an owl called Minerva, who went to sit beside Leander on the chair back.

Chenevix looked terrible, haggard, old and ill. He looked from face to face and then passed a hand over his own face and said "Thank you, Simon, for getting everyone here, I don't think I can bear to tell this more than once."

Sacha sprang forward and pushed a chair behind the Duke, who sank into it at once as if his legs would not hold him up any longer. "I shall have to be logical about this," he said as if to himself. He then seemed to pull himself together and said "As you all know I have many business interests in India and employ several agents in the country. I gave Alan a letter of credit and set up a bank account in Calcutta for Rosamunde in her own name. I wanted neither of them to be in trouble because of lack of funds. Late last night I received a confidential express from my man in Calcutta. On Sunday past there was a native uprising in the 3rd Light Cavalry, a native regiment, in Meerut and the revolt has spread to Delhi. Most of the English have been slaughtered."

Ninon gasped, her hands flying to her throat. The men stared at him, horror-struck.

"As you probably know," he swallowed hard. "Rosamunde 's husband was stationed in Malabad, directly between

Meerut and Delhi. Preliminary reports indicate that Malabad was almost completely destroyed and all of its personnel and their dependents massacred."

"Rosamunde!" said Stuart in anguish. "No, it can't be possible!"

"I went to London immediately and badgered the War office and the Foreign Office until they let me see the first reports that have come in. I am not without influence still. Canning, the Governor General of India, has instituted an express messenger service with the fastest hippogriffes available. There is already a death report from Meerut and Malabad, and they were hoping for one from Delhi today, but everything is all chaos out there. The telegraph wires have all been destroyed in many places and there never has been a hippogriffe service in the interior. But I did not see Rosamunde's name on the list of the dead. Her husband's name I did see. Rosamunde is listed as missing."

René had gone to Stuart at once and put his hand on his son's shoulder. Stuart stared at the floor blindly , as if he could not comprehend what had happened. "Not my Rosamunde!" he said hoarsely.

"What about Alan?" Simon said sharply. "How far has this revolt or whatever it is spread?"

"As far as the FO knows, it is confined to Hindustan. According to a map I saw Alan is far away from the area, up to the North in Ranijhat." said the Duke and suddenly his face blazed with anger. "But both those children are in terrible danger! They should have never been allowed to go out to India, either one of them! India is under Interdict!"

"What!" Lyon exclaimed. He had gone to hold Ninon's hand. Tears were streaming down her face.

"What does that mean?" queried Sacha, as worried as any of them over the fate of his sister's son and niece by marriage.

"Under Interdict means that no Wizards or Witches are usually issued passports to go to a certain place," Simon explained. "Usually because of some magical danger. Did they tell you why India is forbidden, sir?" "*Oh, my God – Alan – my son!*", his mind was screaming under his calm exterior.

"The ley lines are polluted," said the Duke grimly. "With black magic. They have managed to contain it with the borders of India. There have been teams of Repressors out there for some time, but something or someone is using the ley lines for the blackest of the black arts!" He took a deep breath and said "I knew nothing of this - nothing! When I protested this morning that as Chancellor of Magic I should have been told of this I was informed that it was under the purlieu of the FO! They implied it was none of my business! None of my business when those children of ours are out there, with no defenses, for they will be drained of their magic – it is as inevitable as the sun rising in the morning!"

"How did they slip through the cracks?" Sacha queried. "Don't they keep lists of Witches and Wizards? Doesn't the FO at least have a copy of *Registratum*? When I got my passport to go to America they knew I was a Wizard." Sacha referred to *Registratum Magii Britannae*, the Registry book that listed all of the Witches and Wizards in the Six Nations and their rankings.

"Alan only had to have his passport renewed," said Simon. "We've been back and forth to America so many times, but he had not used it since he was in his teens and his magical ranking would not have been listed then, not while he was underage and not fully qualified. And I remember him laughing about the inept young man who was in the passport office. All the seniors were out ill with the same influenza that struck Alan down. You remember, Stuart, Alan and Rosamunde went together to get their passports...the official must not have checked the lists for either Alan or Rosamunde's names."

But Stuart was past listening or understanding, so great was his terror for Rosamunde. His mind was going around in helpless circles.

"This would not have happened in the old days, when we were all obliged to wear a lapel pin or a brooch indicating our Wizardry and ranking!" said the Duke savagely. "That damned reform bill –! Now there is no knowing who is a Wizard and who is not! And most of these young degenerates don't use a proper wand any more!"

Stuart stood up abruptly. "Simon, I want to borrow Lakota. I am going out to India immediately! I have to find her! When I think of what could be happening to her..."

"You can't go," said the Duke. "It's forbidden –"

"Do you think I care a rap for that?" Stuart cried.

"Do you think *I* don't care?" the Duke retorted angrily. "The FO told me that women were being raped and mutilated! I want my sweet girl back as much as you do, even if she has a Hindoo brat in her belly! But when I left London they were erecting an etheric barrier to prevent just such a thing happening. No one save those with official government business will be allowed to fly in or out. It will be in place by now, three miles high, Stuart! You cannot fly over that without killing yourself from cold and icing up the dragon's wings. The news of this revolt will be given to the press later today and the government is afraid that people, not just magicals, any people with loved ones in India, will take any means to get out there. Only troop ships will be leaving the ports as well."

Stuart sank back down into the chair and covered his face in his hands, his shoulders beginning to shake. René, tears in his own eyes, bent over him once more.

The others were as grief stricken as were they. Simon thought of Alan with immense pain. They had received only one letter from him, and it had been full of a blissful description of the beauties of Ranijhat and of the kindness of Ravi's family. How was he to tell Tatya of this, how was Stuart to tell Julia? Or how to tell any of the rest of the family? What could they do, so far from the scene and forbidden to go to the aid of their children? All they could do was pray and right now that did not seem like enough.

Jhaniput

Rosamunde completely lost track of time. Her world had narrowed down to the *palka-ghari* and its irregular movements. Sometimes they traveled by day, sometimes by night and one day was almost exactly like the one before it, tied in the hot ghari, stopping briefly for food and necessary functions, and offered to and taken by men, always under the watchful and lustful eyes of the Pathans.

Wazid Ali was disappointed for he did not make as much money on the road, selling the women as he had hoped. In fact, he decided it was best to avoid the bigger villages and the main roads as much as ws possible, for people seemed to be on the move everywhere. Everything was in ferment. The unrest was spreading but the news they heard was mostly rumor and speculation.

Once a day at least Akbar would come for Rosamunde. It never became any easier for her and she usually fought him, contrary to Laura's advice. The big Pathan never failed to be amused by her spirit and would not hear of Wazid Ali beating her. The slaver wanted compliant women and the others were more accepting of their fate. In spite of their 'good behavior' Wazid Ali kept them tied up. He was not going to take a chance on any of his valuable property escaping.

In Bangalore, which was to the north of Delhi on the way to Jhaniput, Ameera was sold to a fat merchant who, as Wazid Ali had hoped, rewarded the slaver with two heavy money bags. He was more than pleased with her beauty and the fact that he ws getting two slaves and a wet nurse for his wife's coming child.

The other women watched her go with tears and regrets. Laura said fiercely "When Pa and Nate come for me I'll tell them where you are too and we'll come and get you!"

Rosamunde was dry-eyed when Ameera went to her 'master' but she had an enormous choking lump in her breast but as much as she wanted to cry she could not seem to raise any tears.

That night, after yet another encounter with Akbar, she lay awake a long time, breathing hard and staring with hot eyes at the roof of the *ghari,* a mass of conflicting emotions; anger, resentment, terror and dread and hatred.

A few days later Wazid Ali sold both Neha and Unsa to a *zemindar,* a large landholder, who wanted bed mates for his two sons. That meant that Laura and Rosamunde were the only two left to 'entertain' the four Pathans.

For somewher between Bangalore and the sale to the *zemindar,* Vera had quietly died, much to Wazid Ali's dismay. She had never really recovered from the shock of seeing her parents killed in front of her, and her will to live had ebbed away, particularly after the rape. She had stopped eating and showed no interest in anything.

Laura nearly got a terrible beating over Vera's death for she made a furor over burying the girl, rather than tossing her body into a ditch as Wazid Ali thought was suitable.

It was Yakoub who finally dug a shallow grave for the girl. He had taken quite a fancy to Laura and was highly amused at the way she stood up to Wazid Ali. He was of a temperament that delighted in doing exactly the opposite of what was expected of him and he enjoyed enraging his employer.

Laura said a short silent prayer over Vera's resting place and vowed to Rosamunde that she would remember exactly where the girl was buried and one day would come back and see that she had a proper burial and a marked grave.

Rosamunde found it unreal that she stood naked over a grave site, saying prayers that she was beginning to think were useless for some one she had barely known at all.

Afterwards, Akbar took her under the shade of the *palka ghari,* out of the glare of the sun and as usual laughed at her struggles. He was very strong and had no trouble subduing her at all. They were joined by Yakoub and Laura and then the other two had to have their turns as well. Wazid Ali seemed to be able to exist without a woman for a long period of time but the Pathans wanted their 'bonus pay' at least once a day.

After being out of doors, even in the morning sun and being used by the Pathans, it was an extreme hardship to be put back into the stifling *ghari* and tied hand and foot.

"Lord, it's hot!" said Laura when Buzurg had finally left them, closing the canvas flap. He had spent some time running his hands over them and whispering obscenities, which fortunately were all in Pushtu. "Never thought I'd be happy to be as naked as a jay bird but it's so damn hot. I can't imagine what it would be like to have to be still wearing a hoop skirt!"

"I wish I could be more like you, Laura," said Rosamunde in a low, dull voice. "Nothing seems to bother you, even what happened today, Vera dying and then beneath the cart..." her voice died away.

"You think I'm not bothered by those rat bastards banging away at me?" Laura retorted. "I hate it just as much as you do, I hate it like poison! What I wouldn't give to have my Colt revolver or my Bowie knife and carve out their entrails! But I ain't going to give them the satisfaction. They *like* it that you fight them, Rose! It makes 'em feel powerful. And as for Vera, that poor little kid! She just gave up, and don't you go thinking that she's better off dead, Rose – you hear me? Dead is never better, there's always a chance, always hope, always! I ain't going to badger Yakoub into digging a grave for you, so don't you go dying on me!"

Rosamunde had to admit that she had thought about killing herself after the first time Akbar had raped her. She had thought that she would never get over the pain and the shame. What he did to her was degrading and humiliating and it violated every sense of modesty, every feeling of personal privacy that she had. Her body was no longer her own; he used her when he felt like it and her wishes had nothing to do with it. The feeling of being powerless was overwhelming.

But something in her *wanted* to live, wanted to fight, in spite of the shame and the pain. She wanted to survive, to hope that this would end, that she *would* get back to her own life, that she could go home one day.

Now she said to Laura, "I don't want to die, I don't

know why,though. I always thought that I could not survive being touched and looked at, that it would be better to be dead than shamed, but somehow, in spite of everything, I want to live."

"That's the ticket!" said Laura approvingly.

"I'm not as brave as you, Laura," Rosamunde admitted."I feel sick every time one of them touches me and when they are on top of me..." she broke off. "Oh, I hate having no defenses and not being able to prevent them from doing just what they want to me!"

"That's the worst of it," said Laura. "When I was first captured back in New Spain I was just like you, I wanted to die too. I thought I'd never get over the shame of it. We're raised to think having a man take you against your will is the fate worse than death and no good woman would allow it, well, there's a lot of things that are done to you that you wouldn't allow, people cheating you and lying to you and hurting you. And men like these don't even think of us as people, we're just things to use. But I really believe, Rose, that even this is better than being dead. Never give up, is what I say."

"I keep thinking," Rosamunde said "If only I had not lost my powers, this would not have happened!" She also thought that if only she had not married Raymond this would not have happened. "I hate being without my Witchcraft!"

"You still haven't figured out where it went?" Laura inquired.

Rosamunde shook her head tiredly. She had been over and over this in her mind. She could think of no reason why this loss had happened to her. It made no sense. Like a Wizard, a Witch only was weak in power when she had done a major working. But this was as if she had been drained of all her power, a steady draining ever since she had arrived in Malabad.

"Perhaps I can gain some power from the moon at night she said, thinking aloud. "If Wazid Ali keeps staking us out at night perhaps the moonlight that my body absorbs may help bring my powers back."

"That old whoreson is staking us out at night so anyone coming by and feeling a little horny can give him a *rupee* for which ever one of us he fancies," said Laura. "And yes, horny means what you think it does," she added, seeing the look on Rosamunde's face.

Laura had an extensive and very colourful vocabulary and Rosamunde was learning words and phrases she had never known were in existence.

In turn, she was teaching Laura Hindustanee. "I need to be able to understand what they're telling me to do," she had said. "Back in the mines I got hit a lot because my Spanish wasn't too good until I buckled down and set myself to learning it. It's bad enough being banged by all these bastards, no need to be beat up as well."

She was a very determined pupil. Although she had no natural facility for languages as did Rosamunde, she asked for a lesson as many times a day as was possible.

During the next few days they were left largely alone during the hours of daylight. The roads had become emptier and the villages further apart on the back roads that they traveled. And the heat was more intense.

Every evening as soon as they had stopped for the night the men would pull them from the *ghari* and share their favors. Then Wazid Ali would order them staked out and they would be fed.

The food was better now. One or the other of the Pathans went out for game almost daily and they ate duck and other birds. The men, of course, took the lion's share.

Rosamunde still had little appetite but she allowed Laura to bully her into eating. "You can't make a break for it if you're too weak to run," she said.

Laura was always on the lookout for a chance to escape. She had tried to untie their ropes in the *palka ghari,* futile as they were strong and tough and tied in intricate knots, and even tried pulling up the stake. She watched the Pathans carefully to find out their weaknesses and mistakes as well.

But Wazid Ali and the Pathans had been at their trade too long. They never became careless and one of the Pathans always guarded the two women, no matter whether they were eating, being used by one of their cousins or 'entertaining' the few 'clients' that Wazid Ali managed to find.

Morning after morning the brassy sun rose in a sky that made the eyes ache to look at it. Dust coated the roads and the stolid bullock's slow moving hooves raised a great deal of it. Laura and Rosamunde became almost grateful for the hot canvas walls of the *palka ghari,* for a large quantity of the choking dust was shut out. Enough crept in though, to dirty everything.

They began halting at ten in the morning and resting until the sun was lower in the sky. Laura and Rosamunde were tied beneath the *ghari* in the shade and to their relief were largely left alone. It was simply too hot for any kind of activity. Wazid Ali grudgingly gave them more water.

"I'd give my eyeteeth for a bath," Laura murmured one particularly scorching morning as she and Rosamunde were imprisoned between the wheels of the *ghari.*

Wazid Ali, standing nearby, bent down and smiled at her with his oily grin. "And you shall have a bath tomorrow, my fair flower. For tomorrow we reach Jhaniput and my most excellent establishment. The important customer, who will swoon at the sight of your lovely forms and give me many, many *rupees* for you, would find your present state of cleanliness quite offensive. You will be cleansed and brushed."

"And given clothes?" Laura inquired.

"Whatever for?" said the slaver. "My customers wish to see what they are buying; they will probably try out your paces as well! After all, one does not buy a horse without riding it first!" He chuckled at his own wit and turned away, walking towards the palaquin that the Pathans had set up for the hot part of the day. They were smoking their hookahs and idly tossing dice. When it became cooler they would come for the two women.

Laura gave an angry twitch at her bonds. "Don't they overdo this just a little bit?" she said sarcastically. Their hands were pulled above their heads and tied to one wheel while their ankles were tied to the opposite wheel. There was little play in the ropes; they were forced to lie flat on their backs, mostly unmoving. It was painful and completely uncomfortable. "And that damned Buzurg will probably be over here in a minute or two and start rubbing his damned paws all over us. God, I'd love to kick him in the balls!"

215

Rosamunde thought longingly of what she could do to all of them had she only still had her Witchcraft.

"Sorry, honey," Laura said after a moment. "I didn't mean to be so irritable. It's this damned heat, that, and not knowing what's going to happen tomorrow."

"I hope we can stay together," said Rosamunde in a low voice. Laura gave her strength.

"'Pears to me as if old Wazid is talking about the same customer for both of us, more than likely some whore house," Laura said. "Let's hope it's a high class place, not some dime a screw crib."

She sighed heavily. "Teach me some more Hindoo, Rose honey," she said. "Don't suppose you know how to say "You're a lousy lay", in Hindoo? I'd LOVE to say that to Nakshsband! The bastard don't know enough English to know when I'm insulting him!"

The next day was blisteringly hot. Wazid Ali roused everyone long before dawn and, after a sketchy breakfast, got the *palka-ghari* on the road. He wanted to be in Jhaniput before the sun was high in the sky, the thought of all those *rupees* driving him onwards.

Both Rosamunde and Laura dozed uneasily. The Pathans had kept them up late, as this would be the last might that the four of them could enjoy these particular women. Wazid Ali confidently expected that this evening would see them the property of their new master.

Rosamunde roused briefly when the cart stopped at last. She looked up to see a strange bearded face peering in at her. He looked her up and down with an insolent leer.

She shivered. From what she coudl see he seemed to be wearing some sort of uniform.

There was all sorts of shouting outside and then the *ghari* moved forward. A huge boom, as if there were something heavy being dropped, sounded behind them.

A few moments later Laura stirred and woke up. 'Where are we, honey?" she asked on a yawn. "Damn! I wish I could stretch!" She moved the little that their bonds allowed.

"I think we are in Jhaniput," Rosamunde said. "A

soldier just looked in at us."

The *ghari* stopped and a few moments later Buzurg entered and untied their feet and then released their hands from the rings. This still left their hands tied and he bent down to put what Laura called hobbles on their ankles.

He lifted each of them from the *ghari* taking the opportunity to run his hands over them as he did so.

They could see little outside. They were in a rather mean alley in back of a low building. Buzurg pushed them along ahead of him. laughing when they stumbled, for their limbs were cramped and the hobbles made walking difficult.

Inside it was cool and dark and Wazid Ali awaited them. "Take them to the bathing room," he ordered. "All is ready. Remove the ropes and lock them in. Then I shall have other tasks for you, Our customer will be here soon!" He rubbed his hands together in gleeful anticipation.

The bathing room was huge, all of gleaming pale blue tile, and in the center sat a large sunken tub, steaming with hot water and smelling of roses. There piles of towels and soaps of all kind.

"Wash yourselves well," said Buzurg, untying then one at a time. "If you do not wash yourselves well the eunuchs will scour you with twigs. Wash everywhere and your hair as well." Then he grinned, showing very bad teeth. "You cannot drown yourselves here, for the water is magiced."

With this he was gone, taking the ropes and hobbles with him. The door clicked shut behind him and they heard the key turn in the lock.

There was no way out of the room. There were no windows, no ventilation save for some tiny air slits, very high up.

"God, that looks good!" said Laura and went to the tub and put a toe in. "Perfect!" she said and walked down a little flight of steps in to the water. She sank in it, up to her neck. "Come on in, honey," she called to Rosamunde. "There's room for us both and a whole lot of other folks besides."

Rosamunde obeyed and sat down opposite Laura. The hot water did feel good. She had been dirty in more ways than one for far too long.

"This is wonderful," said Laura, leaning back. "My Pa has always said when you're in a real bad situation look for the little things that can please you and hold onto those. This is one thing that pleases me a lot. In a few minutes I'm going to wash my hair and then I am just going to lay here until they come and drag us out!"

They were allowed to spend quite a long time in the bath. They washed each other's hair and soaked.

When they had wrapped towels around their wet hair and gone back into the tub Laura said "Nobody knows you're English, do they, Rose.?""

Rosamunde shook her head. "Ameera thought it was best that I maintain this disguise. It won't wear off because I did manage a 'stay' spell of the dye before Wazid Ali came and took us away. It's a simple spell that requires almost no real power."

"I wouldn't let them know. You'll be safer if they think you're a native."

"But what about you, Laura?" Rosamunde asked, frowning.

"I'm not English, I'm American. I'm not the one coming the lord and master over the oppressed natives."

This was a fallacious argument for they would see her as a *mem sahib*, no matter if she were American or British.

But Rosamunde was given no chance to argue with her friend as the door was unlocked and Wazid Ali entered, followed by a very large man and two women.

"Out of the water! Out! Out!" he commanded, clapping his hands. "Hurry now!"

Laura and Rosamunde climbed out of the bath and stood dripping before Wazid Ali. He snatched the towels from their hair, allowing their wet locks to fall down around their shoulders.

"What did I tell you, highness?" he said proudly. "Are these not just the sort of *bibis* that you desire? And this one," he pointed at Laura "is a *mem sahib*!"

The big man wore an *achkhan* and *jodhpurs,* and his turban bore a huge jewel, a ruby. His face was dark and bearded and he stood with crossed arms, slightly behind a very short woman.

This woman was clad in a brilliant red sari, richly embroidered with gold thread. She wore so much jewelry that she seemed in danger of falling over from the weight of it. A huge ruby adorned her forehead.

She was also one of the most ugly, repellent women Rosamunde had ever seen.

Her features were heavy, her complexion muddy. A large mole disfigured one cheek and she had heavy bushy eyebrows, a crooked nose and a narrow little mouth. But what made her completely repulsive were her eyes. They were cold and lifeless and heartless as a snake's and no expression whatsoever crossed her face. Her figure was thick and she had no female curves, being built more like a beer barrel than anything else.

The other woman was in complete contrast to her. She was taller, and lushly feminine. This was readily apparent for she wore a pair of extremely low slung gauze pantaloons of red, trimmed in gold. They clung tightly to her legs until just below the knee, where they flared out in a bell shape. Laura wondered how they stayed up, for they were extremely low on her hips. Above the pantaloons she was bare, save for a collar of rubies and gold. She also wore a multitude of bangles and gold shoes with up curved toes. Her black hair was clubbed back and her gold and ruby earrings were quite large. Like the short woman she wore a ruby on her forehead, and one in her navel as well.

Over one shoulder she carried a coiled whip. She bore herself proudly, thrusting her large but firm breasts forward. Her hard, handsome face showed cruelty and greed. Her eyes as she looked at Rosamunde and Laura were speculative. "These are fine specimens, *Hazrat*," she said to the short woman. "See how she shrinks!" she pointed at Rosamunde, who wanted nothing more to get as far away as possible from these horrible people who gave her a very bad feeling.

"We shall see," said the short woman in a frosty voice that made shivers go up and down Rosamunde's spine.

Turning to the large man, the woman said "Take her, Kumala Jha," pointing at Rosamunde.

"I told you that they would wish to try your paces!" giggled Wazid Ali.

23

the purchase

When he had finished with Rosamunde the big man stood up, leaving her sprawled on the floor, glaring at all of them and shaking with rage. "A *tung bibi*, a tight lady," he announced, "and she feels much shame, much anger and humiliation at being used."

"This is well, but she needs to learn obedience," said the bare breasted woman. "She fought you, Kumala Jha, and that is not acceptable." She stroked the soils of the whip as she spoke and licked her lips.

"She will be trained to accept men in the proper way," said the short woman. "if the whip does not convince her I shall give her to the *Bhutas*. We will purchase this one," she said, turning to Wazid Ali and nodding at Rosamunde. "Kumala Jha will give us his opinion of the other one as well as her form is also pleasing."

Kumala Jha reached into a pouch that hung from his belt and drew out a pinch of what looked like snuff. He snorted it up his nose and then advanced on Laura.

She had expected a short reprieve after his attentions to Rosamunde, for in her experience men needed a recovery time before they could perform again, but to her amazement whatever it was he had sniffed made him virile yet again and he took her as well. He was immensely strong and she could understand how he had so easily subdued Rosamunde. As usual, she just let him do what he wanted.

"An excellent *yoni*, deep and slick," he said. "This one is more accepting of use, but she still hates and fears and feels shame deep inside."

"*How the hell do you know that?*" Laura wondered. She prided herself on not letting her real feelings show to these bastards. But he had described her emotions precisely.

Laura could hear Rosamunde, still laying on the tiles, breathing hard as the short female said to Wazid Ali "We will take this one as well. You have done well by us, Wazid Ali.

The slaves your brother brought us are proving to be some of the best for our purposes. I will buy all that you procure, in particularly the *mem-sahibs*. You will be amply rewarded. You may call upon the *Diwan* later in the day for your payment."

"I make another trip south, *Hazrat,* the day after tomorrow," he said in his unctuous fashion, bowing so low that his nose almost touched the floor. "I will bring you the best of what I find."

The large Kumala Jha went to Rosamunde and pulled her to her feet. He removed a coil of wire from his pouch and wrapped it around her wrists and slapped her hard when she tried to kick him.

"That one will need much discipline," said the woman with the whip.

"She will prove all the better for our purposes, Hussaini," said the short woman. "When she does finally obey, so as not to be punished, she will be resentful and feel much shame that she was obliged to give in."

Laura allowed Jha to bind her as well. With no effort the big man took one of them on each shoulder and took them out through the front of the establishment.

It was difficult to see hung upside down but Laura got an impression of a large room, filled with people of all types, men, women and children of all ages, most of who were chained to either posts or the wall.

Outside in the street were three horses, gorgeously caparisoned. Their large saddles were of red velvet and gold brocade, heavily embroidered, and chains of jewels adorned their heads and necks, with bejeweled breast plates and cruppers. The smallest horse was white and wore a plume on its head and tassels swung from the bit of the golden bridle. A ruby adorned its forehead as well.

With a long rope Jha tied Laura and Rosamunde to hooks on the saddle of a gigantic black horse. He then gave the short woman a leg up onto the white horse.

"This is your new mistress," he said to Laura and Rosamunde. "she who is her Divine Highness the Maharani of Jhaniput. You will obey her in all things and be humble before her greatness. Your lives will be but to please her and do as she wishes."

221

Hussaini leaped up onto her chestnut horse her own self. *"It's a wonder to me that she don't lose those pants!"* Laura thought.

Hussaini uncoiled the whip as Laura watched. "If you lag behind I shall urge you on with this," she said. "There is near a *kos* to traverse to reach the *Kala Mahal* and we shall not wait for you."

From her travels around India with her father Laura had learned that a *kos* was accounted about a mile and a half or so. That was a long way to be dragged behind a horse in this heat, she though as Jha swung up onto the big black and they moved out.

She was worried about Rosamunde as well. Rose had not looked at her or at anyone since Jha had slapped her so hard. Laura was worried that she might be a little dazed but she was on her feet steady enough. She kept her head down and looked at the ground though.

Laura had been in many Indian cities and they all shared some similarities. Many of then were walled and sprawling, with twisting, narrow streets but they all teemed with life and noise. There was music, laughter, talking, bargaining in the bazaar, merchants crying their wares, the call of the *muezzins* from the mosques...but in this city an unnatural stillness hung over everything. The streets were largely empty and the few people that they passed, a sweeper, a *bhasti* with his water cart, a *bal-ghari* with a load of melons, looked at them with apathy, not finding anything odd in the spectacle of two naked women trotting along behind a horse.

It seemed a great deal longer than a mile and a half, almost running to keep up with the horse in the heat and the dust. The last of it was uphill as well to where a huge palace stood on an escarpment over a river.

Under any other circumstances Laura would have found the palace beautiful for it was of a shining whiteness with domes and turret seemingly made from lace as delicate and airy as if they were not carved from stone but were fashioned from the daintiest of fabrics.

But as they went inside a gate into an interior courtyard she could see that it was more of a prison or a fortress than a Faerie tale castle. The walls were high and ended in spikes. On a catwalk along the edge of the wall guards walked, armed with *tulwars*, pikes and pistols. All the arched windows she saw on the façade of the palace wore bars, painted gold, and there were heavily armed guards everywhere, not only on the catwalk.

As the horses halted, several servants, all male, came rushing out and helped the Maharani dismount, and took the women's horses. Without a backwards glance at her new property the Maharani went into the palace.

"Clean then up," Hussaini ordered Kumala Jai "There will be another ruby ceremony tonight for the others we purchased yesterday and these might as well be readied for that. They will go to work in the Joy House after their training tomorrow."

"Yes, mistress," said the big man. "I hear and obey. They shall be ready for your pleasure." He bowed deeply to her.

He then untied Laura and Rosamunde from the saddle of the huge black horse, leaving the wires round their wrists, and as before, put then over his shoulders.

Again it was not easy to see. Laura thought that they traveled endless corridors, all of highly polished black marble. Guards seemed to be on duty every where she looked even though Laura only could see their booted feet but sometimes she saw the bare feet of females, all with anklets of bells and gilded toenails.

At long last they went to a room that was completely covered in blue and white tile. Several tables of stone stood at the edge of the floor and what looked to be large meat hooks, quite a few of them, hung from the ceiling and beneath each was a drain set in the floor and two large rings to which ropes were attached on either side of the drain.

Another large man, this one in baggy pantaloons, a short vest over his immense bare chest and a intricate turban on his head, again adorned with a ruby, stood to the side and bowed as Jha entered with his prisoners.

With effortless ease he plucked Rosamunde off Jha's shoulders and wrenched her arms up above her head, and slipped the wire binding her wrists over one of the meat hooks. He lowered the hook with a winch arrangement and then, tied her ankles to the rings in the floor, set so that her legs were forced wide apart. Jha did the same to Laura.

"Wash and pluck them for they go to the ruby ceremony this very evening," Jha told his confederate.

"It shall be as you desire, Master," said the man in the baggy pantaloons, with another bow as Jha exited the room.

"Feel as if I'm a slab of beef in the Chicago stock yards," Laura muttered.

"*Chup*! Be silent!" roared baggy pantaloons. "You will learn to speak only when you are given permission! I am the chief eunuch Pramoda Tandon. You are in my charge and I shall clean you and enforce your training. I shall also record how many men use you each day. You will learn to do exactly as I say. Your will, your desire are as nothing here. You are here but to please the men who use you and to do the will of the Divine Maharani and her son the Maharajah. Their will is law."

He then inspected them carefully and intimately, murmuring to himself.

Rosamunde had never felt so ashamed or humiliated. In many ways his poking and prodding and comments were even worse than the many times Akbar had raped her or what had happened in Wazid Ali's bathing room. She gritted her teeth until he was finished and turned his attentions to Laura. Her friend, she could see, was almost as upset as she was for the eunuch seemed to delight in poking, pinching and squeezing and at the smallest, slightest sound he smacked them. "You will learn to be silent no matter what is done to you! A receptacle does not utter noise!"

He then stood back and clapped his hands.

Three more men came running into the room, dressed much as he was but far more plainly.

Laura and Rosamunde were thoroughly washed and scrubbed down by the four men and then tied to the tops of the tables, laid on their stomachs. With two men working on each of them all visible hair was plucked or shaved from their bodies, saving only the hair on their heads and their eyebrows and eyelashes. This was repeated on the front of their bodies, even in their intimate places.

"*We're going to be a naked as plucked chickens!*" Laura thought.

Then they were turned backside up again and one of the men disappeared and returned with a bucket of foul smelling yellow stuff. This was slathered all over their backsides, from the neck down to the toes, in every crack and cranny.

"His highness find hair on the bodies of women offensive," said the eunuch, smearing the vile concoction heavily on Rosamunde's bottom. He spoke to a young man that appeared to be perhps an apprentice. "This insures that no hair will ever grow upon their bodies again so that his highness will never be displeased with their appearance."

A large hour glass with red sand stood in a corner and as the other men gathered the sponges, towels and the bucket, Tandon said,"In two hours we will return to paint their other sides." He turned the hour glass over and left the room with the other men, closing the door behind him.

"Goddamn, this stuff stings and it stinks!" swore Laura. "I guess we can talk now that he's gone?" she said a little sarcastically."I didn't get all of what they were saying. What kind of ceremony were they talking about?"

"A ruby ceremony," said Rosamunde in a low voice.

"Already noticed how much they like rubies. Got them on their heads, horses and hats, even in that bitch's belly," said Laura. She was very relieved that Rosamunde was talking rationally, considering what had happened to them today. She had been afraid that the younger girl would slip into the state of uncaring that had killed Vera. But Laura was beginning to think that Rosamunde was a lot tougher than she herself thought. "What's a ruby ceremony?"

"I wish I knew," Rosamunde continued, wincing and gasping a little at the pain of the foul potion that coated the back of her body. "Laura, this is a bad, bad place, wicked and *wrong*! There is black magic here, I am certain of it! I felt such a wave of *evil* coming off these people, that man who raped us at Wazid Ali's slave market, he was an Empath. I could feel him probing my emotions."

"An Empath?" Laura inquired.

"It's a person who can project themselves into the emotions of another and in effect, read their true feelings," Rosamunde explained.

"That's how he knew what I was really feeling then,"

said Laura. "Don't that just beat the Dutch!"

"I have never before heard of an evil Empath," said Rosamunde. "They are usually Healers, especially of the mind. I'd like to look at them with my Othersight, if it was still working that is," she added a little bitterly. "Did you understand the part about setting us to work in the Joy House? Do you suppose that means a brothel?"

"It's dollars to doughnuts that what it means. It ain't no joy for the women, that's for sure. I did understand, Rose honey, your lessons have been damn good. It's what we expected, ain't it?"

"Yes," Rosamunde admitted. "But, Laura, if we had to be sold to pleasure a man why could it not be just *one* man, not many?"

"As my Pa always says, you usually get what you don't want unless your name is Vanderbilt or Astor," said Laura philosophically. "Just remember, Rose honey, try not to fight them. They'll whale the tar out of you if you keep it up, I've seen women like that bitch with the ruby in her belly before and there's a look in her eye that tells me she enjoys laying that whip of hers on other women. She'll be waiting for you to step out of line."

"I'll try, Laura," Rosamunde promised, "But when a man comes at me and I know he is going to rape me, I panic, and I *have* to strike out."

"Just try your damndest, honey, to lay there and take it," said Laura. "I don't want to see you with a bloody back. If this is anything like the mines they have people here who know just how to handle a whip, just enough to hurt real bad but not enough to maim and kill. You're a valuable property and they ain't going to permanently damage their own property. But they'll put men to you even if your back is raw, and believe me, that hurts like hell."

Their talk fell off after this exchange as the pain of the hair remover began to intensify.

Two hours later, Tandon was back again and the painful process was repeated upon the front of their bodies. After another two hours they were rinsed, again hanging from the meat hooks, as Laura called them, and then conducted to a tiny cell, with a narrow window high up. A bucket for their sanitary needs stood in a corner and there was a red clay jar of water with a dipper. There was no bed, no blankets, not even any straw on the rough limestone of the floor.

"You may have no food until after the ceremony," Tandon said as he left them in the room and locked the door behind himself.

"Never seen such people for locking us up and tying us down!" said Laura in disgust. "Look at us, we're as bare as billiard balls! What kind of man finds a woman's hair 'offensive'? We've all got hair here and there! Bet you ten to one *he* ain't shaved! Probably as hairy as an a dog's bed!"

The removal of her body hair had left Rosamunde feeling even more naked than she had before. She felt completely exposed. After the second washing the men had again gone over them minutely, looking for even the smallest hair that might have been missed. But now as Laura said 'hairy as a dog's bed' she began laughing almost hysterically. Laura looked at her in concern but let her laugh herself out.

When she gained control of herself again Rosamunde said "I'm so glad you're here with me, Laura!"

"Less'n they separate us, I'll be here for you, Rose. I think of you like you were the little sister I never had. Now I guess we could call ourselves the Hairless Sisters and do an act for the freaks tent at the sideshow! Old P.T. Barnum would snap us up!" Laura said with a grin. She went over to the water bucket and dipped in the gourd that served as a ladle and took a long drink. "Leastways the water's cool and fresh," she said. "Have some, honey. God, the taste of that foul crap is even in my mouth!"

Rosamunde took a long draught too, and then they sat down side by side on the rough floor to wait.

It had to be at least four or five hours later, and they were both very hungry, when the door opened and Pramoda Tandon returned, with two massive menservants. Each grabbed one of the women and pulled them to their feet and slung one over his shoulder, then hurrying through what seemed like miles of dark corridors.

They were thrust unceremoniously into a windowless room lit by torches. All the walls, the ceiling and the floor were of black marble so highly polished that it was almost mirror-like. On the floor in various attitudes of despair, pain or defiance were three other women. All of them were naked and hairless, having obviously undergone the same treatment as had Rosamunde and Laura. All three were *mem-sahibs,* judging by the light colour of their skin.

At the far end of the room was a massive brass bound door, with a torch on either side of it, burning red of flame.

Seeing that flame colour Rosamunde shivered. That was a *very* bad sign. She knew for a fact that red flames meant bale fire, black magic.

The door opened and the short, squat figure of the Maharani appeared and Rosamunde gave a barely suppressed gasp.

The woman was as naked and hairless as were they, but her body gleamed with oil and dark red arcane symbols had been painted on her heavy abdomen, thighs and her childishly small breasts.

Rosamunde knew at once what the dark paint was,– it was blood.

The Maharajah was a black sorceress and whatever the "ruby ceremony" was, it involved black magic.

the sacrificial goat

The first day of the journey to Ranijhat they did not get very far. They had started late in the day, and save for Isha, all of them had experienced an emotional or physically challenging day, or both, and were only to ready to rest as darkness fell abruptly.

Sinéad was very grateful to have the companionship of the other animals and Molly; especially to have the large bulk of Bharat between her and the night terrors of the jungle. The heavy vegetation echoed with strange noises and even Molly, though initially afraid of the elephant, was grateful to curl up against him at Sinéad's suggestion, and take the familiar into her lap, with Hari close beside them. They all drew comfort from one another. Only Isha kept his distance, preferring to sleep in a teak tree.

Molly stroked both Hari and Sinéad, although she had to be coaxed to touch the mongoose at first. The familiar explained to Molly that Hari had lost his people as well and would be all the happier for a bit of petting

They lay down to sleep, most of them, without any food. Feeding themselves was going to be a problem. Hari stared at Sinéad in disbelief when she admitted that she had never in her life hunted or killed anything. A familiar ate at her Witch's table. Hari looked at her as if she was lying when she told him of restaurants in Dublin where familiar animals were welcome, even having their own menus.

Bharat ate grass and leaves. Isha ate fruit, insects and even tree bark and gum when necessary. Hari was a predator. His normal diet included small mammals, birds, reptiles, lizards, eggs and sometimes fruit.

Molly and Sinéad were the problem.The cat was not even certain that she could bring herself to kill and eat something. For one thing, all of her life she had eaten cooked food; raw meat, freshly dead, did not even appeal to her and the thought of tearing apart a dead rodent or other creature was rather nauseating. And Molly could not live on only fruit for she would become ill.

Before they went to sleep Molly told Sinéad what had happened to her before they found her. Molly's brother had sent her on the first leg of her journey by herself, putting her on the steamer that went to Allahabad with little money in her purse and no companions and speaking very little Hindustanee. That had been bad enough but in Allahabad she had been put in charge of a shifty-eyed native in a rickety *ghari,* who abandoned her, taking all her money and most of her possessions suddenly, after talking to a group of men they had met on the road. "We were nearly to Meerut," Molly told the familiar as she stroked the fur of the two animals. Hari by now was in her lap as well. Behind their backs Bharat dozed, a gigantic comforting cushion.

Molly had tried to walk to Meerut, thinking that from there she could obtain transport to Malabad and could ask Rosamunde to loan her the money to pay for it. But she had heard guns firing and there had been men on the road, running and shouting and she had been so frightened that she had fled into the jungle, promptly becoming hopelessly lost. She had been sent running from every noise, finally ending in being chased by the tiger.

She was still hot, tired and dirty and hungry as well.

Sinéad told her story and Molly was horrified that Rosamunde was in the hands of slavers.

"And that is bein' why we must be after gettin' to Alan," the familiar concluded. "He can be helpin' ye as well," she said to Molly.

"It's a long way from here," said Molly doubtfully. "I saw a map of India in my brother's study and I looked for all of the places that the people on the trip out had mentioned and Ranijhat seemed as if it is very far to the north of this area."

"There's naught else we can do," said Sinéad. "Alan will be able to find me Witch wi' his pendulum an go an' rescue her. He's Adept class and can wipe the earth wi' anyone who is after darin' to hold her!"

Molly, who did not know what else to do, allowed Sinéad to talk her out of the very real doubts that she felt. Going back to Calcutta was not an option. After she heard what Sinéad had seen in Malabad, Molly was terrified of going near any habitation in the locality.

And the plain truth was that she knew both her sister-in-law and brother were not keen to have her back. They had decided to send the children back to England and therefore had no use for a nursery maid and the post of companion to Eudoxia was already taken by another poor relation. There was no place for Molly. The very last thing that Eudoxia had said to her was an exhortation to make herself useful to the Duke's great granddaughter and perhaps she would be taken on as a companion. Molly was frightened in more ways than one for the future stretched out before her, barren and friendless as well as dangerous. She had counted heavily on Rosamunde and now even that lifeline had disappeared. She really had no other recourse but to do as the cat suggested.

After some more desultory talk they all fell into an uneasy doze. Both Molly and Sinéad were hungry and Hari kept dreaming about seeing the bodies of his people, while Bharat moaned "Nirav! Nirav!" in his sleep.

It was the silence that awoke Sinéad. There was not a sound in the night; not of night birds, nor of insects, nor of the many night hunters that prowled the jungle. This was abnormal and it made her fur stand on end.

Beside her, still in Molly's lap, Hari was awake and alert. "Something is not right," he said in a low voice.

Sinéad strained to see something – anything! – but the darkness of the jungle was profound. Never had she seen such inky blackness. The moon was just past the full but the moonlight made no impression upon the darkness of the jungle, even though the night sky was clear.

"It's as if somethin' else is makin' the dark," she whispered to Hari.

"What else can make it dark?" he returned a little scornfully. "Besides the lack of light?"

Sinéad shivered. "Black magic," she said.

Bharat stirred and raised his head, Molly still slept the sleep of exhaustion. And she, being human, did not have

231

the acute senses of the animals. "I feel that there is evil abroad tonight," the elephant said quietly. "Black evil, blacker than that which took the life of my Nirav."

A gray, ghost-like form came out of the darkness and Isha joined them. "There are men coming," the monkey said in a low voice. "Men with torches. There is a human place of worship not too far from here and I think that they go there."

"Show me," said Sinéad and crept off Molly's lap. Molly stirred a little and sighed in her sleep, nestling against Bharat's flank as the elephant lay on the ground.

"Go," said the elephant. "I shall stay and guard the *mem-sahib*."

Hari seemed a little reluctant to go with Isha and Sinéad but at last trailed after them. The peculiar quiet of the night had made him very anxious as well.

Walking on all fours, the monkey stayed on the ground so the other animals could easily follow him. On his own he would have swung through the trees.

Sinéad's acute hearing began to recognize a low rhythmic murmur ahead of them, a murmur she had heard only too often back home in Ireland. Men were chanting, chanting some sort of ritual. As she listened a drum began to beat, underscoring the rhythm of the chant.

Isha led them up to a huge banyan tree, and they hid amongst the twisted roots of the trunk. Here, well hidden, they could see what was happening.

The stone structure in the small jungle clearing was ancient and vine covered. Parts of it had fallen to the ground. It did indeed seem to be some sort of a temple and a curtain of vines had been lifted from the front of it to reveal a statue.

"They came from every direction," said Isha "There are no clear paths through the jungle to this location. It has been long unused, I would say."

There were perhaps ten or fifteen men in the clearing, all dark cloaked as if they wished to be hidden. As the little animals watched the chant grew in intensity and Sinéad could make out what they were saying:.

"Kali! Kali! Drinker of blood! Hear us, O great Kali!"

Torches were placed in brackets on either side of the statue beneath the curtain of vines and the statue sprang into view.

Sinéad was immediately repulsed. The statue was of some black stone and a red tongue protruded from its mouth. It was a buxom, hedonistic female figure with many arms. In each hand was a weapon or a severed human head. Around her neck she wore a necklace of human skulls. As the animals watched someone brought forth a brazier on three legs and lit it, throwing handfuls of a powder on the glowing coals so that an acrid stench began to rise and the smoke from it billowed around the black statue. Sinéad sniffed. The stench was somehow familiar but she could not place it.

Another man came forward and withdrew a chain of marigold flowers from under his cloak. This he draped about he statue's neck, with much bowing and respectful gestures, backing away when he had finished his task.

The chanting grew in intensity and from out of the jungle came an old human dressed as a holy man, wearing a *dhoti* about his skinny hips and little else. Wild, graying locks that matched an unkempt beard strayed from beneath the turban. He had gone long unwashed. Sinéad could smell him easily from their hiding place and she wrinkled her nose in disgust. In the torchlight she could see that his dark eyes held almost insane light.

He went to stand in front of the statue and raised dirty hands for silence.

The chanting stopped abruptly.

"*Baiyan!* Brothers!" he said in a shrill, penetrating voice. "We gather here tonight to give ourselves to Kali, to promise her the blood of the *feringhis* for which she thirsts. Our brothers in Meerut, in Malabad and in Delhi have killed many, but there are many more of the devil's get to die! Kali will help us, she will make us strong! She has promised that those who are high in her favor will soon be invincible and we shall drive the *Angrezi-log* out of our land and proclaim Bahadur Shah Zafar our *Padishah!* We will return to the glory of our golden days! The *shaitan ka hawa,* the devil's wind, blows across all Hind and the *feringhis* flee before it! And Kali drinks their blood!"

The men roared their approval and repeated "Kali drinks their blood! *Shabash! Shabash!* Well done! Well done!"

"To seal our bargain with Kali we offer sacrifice!" the holy man shouted.

233

Plaintive bleating was heard and from the shadows at the edge of the clearing came a young boy, not more than twelve or thirteen, leading a white kid.

One of the men nearest to the *Sadhu,* the holy man, stepped forward and offered a long knife. The *Sadhu* raised it, to more cries of approval from the men, and then with a swift movement, drew it across the kid's throat.

The little goat buckled and fell, its life's blood spurting everywhere. Almost gleefully the *Sadhu* dipped his hands in the warm red tide and lifted them, dripping, above his head. "*Khuri!* Bloody!" he shouted.

"*Shabash! Shabash!*" exulted the others.

Sinéad felt sick. The little goat ahd been bleating, terrified, "Mama! Mama!" in Animal language.

"I've been seein' enough of this," she said in a low voice to Isha and Hari.

Silently , they slipped away from the scene, not saying a word each lost in his or her own thoughts about what they had seen.

Molly still slept. When they told Bharat of what they had seen the elephant looked very troubled and said "So it begins again! The drinkers of blood have risen."

"What do you mean?" Hari asked.

"Thou art too young to remember but when I was not quite half this age I am now these blood drinkers roamed the land at will," said the elephant. "They robbed and killed all who would venture forth on the roads in Hindustan. They were of the *Thuggee,* the Thugs, worshippers of Kali the black one, she who is goddess of destruction and death. These Thugs were born into this way of life and they had even their own gravediggers, the *Lughais,* who put the unfortunates they murdered so that their foul deeds would not be found out, in the *bhils,* the shallow graves. They much used a noose to strangle their victims but also carried a *Khusse,* a short handled axe. They were very evil. It was Sleeman *Sahib* who stopped them. The *sahibs* made laws that if man was found to belong to the band of Thugs he could be convicted of a crime, for this was easier to do than to prove murder," he paused and said "This is very bad, very evil that they are come back!"

"I've never been seein' a piece of rock I was more dislikin'!" said Sinéad candidly. "Why is she after stickin' her foul tongue from out her face?"

"Of this I am not certain," said Bharat. "It may be to lick the blood of her enemies or sacrifices. I only know of what I heard the men speak in whispers. Nirav never worshipped Kali. Of *this* I am certain, however, thou wouldst do well to have naught to do with the blood worshippers lest they sacrifice thee!"

Sinéad suddenly recognized the smell of that incense or whatever it was that had been thrown in the brazier in front of that obscene statue. It was the smell of spilled blood.

the ruby ceremony

The Maharani looked about her with her cold, flat eyes, paying particular attention to the five women on the floor. "That one," she said at last, pointing to a dark-haired woman with very fair skin, who wore an expression of outrage and had been muttering angrily until one of the big men had slapped her hard. She was bent over, in a tight ball, attempting to cover herself.

She began shrieking as the men lifted her from the floor, arms and legs striking out at random, ordering them to put her down and leave her alone.

The screaming was abruptly cut off as the Maharani followed the men into the room beyond and the big door closed behind her with a hollow thud.

Rosamunde, sitting as still as she could beside Laura, took a furtive look at the other two women. One was a plump and pretty blue-eyed blonde, who was a bit older than the rest. She was sitting with her legs drawn up to her breasts and her arms folded across her knees. She wore an expression of anxiety and kept casting fearful glances at the guards.

The other woman was much younger; to call her a woman was stretching a point for she could hardly be more than sixteen. She was rather small, with fine bones and a slight, immature figure and flyaway brown hair. She sat quietly, with crossed legs making no attempt to hide her underdeveloped breasts. Her expression was almost a blank, her eyes downcast so that they could not be seen.

Laura, like Rosamunde was sitting on folded legs, with no attempt to hide their bodies for they had learned from Wazid Ali that this was an exercise in futility. If these men wanted to look they were going to look as they all seemed chosen for their strength and their utter indifference to the women's shame or pain.

It was probably twenty minutes before the first woman was carried out again, semi-conscious. She was dumped on the floor and sprawled out limply, face up. Something had been done to her, Rosamunde could see, for there was a large ruby in her navel. Unlike the horrible Hussaini, whose navel adornment was held in by piercing, the ruby seemed merely to sit in the dark haired woman's belly.

The slight girl went next, and as the men lifted her she opened her eyes to reveal them as large, frightened and deep brown in colour. As the men took her into the room the only sign of her agitation was the spasmodic clenching and unclenching of her hands as she was lifted and borne away. She uttered not a sound.

In another twenty minutes she too was back, again appearing stunned and wearing the large ruby.

The older blonde woman was the third to go into the room. She uttered a squeak as they bore her away, still trying to hide her body with no success.

Laura went quietly when it was her turn, silently mouthing to Rosamunde "Don't fight it!"

Rosamunde had no intention of fighting, for she was nearly paralyzed with fear.

All of her life she had been taught how bad, how wrong, black magic was. She had been raised on family stories about the battles against the dark arts various members of her family had fought. She had always thought that she could never be as brave as they had been, that she would fail miserably if she had ever had to come up against a black magician. And that was when she had still had her Witchcraft!

Now she was bereft of powers and was soon to be exposed to the dark power of a sorceress.

She could not even scream or cry, so great was her fear. Inside she was shaking and terrified, for unlike the others, she knew what black magic meant. What was going to happen? What was this ruby for? It would give the sorceress some arcane hold over them, she knew.

When Laura was brought out and the men picked her up, as easily as if she had weighed nothing, she made no protest, with no kicking or struggling. She took a last look at Laura's still form on the floor.

The interior room was shrouded in darkness. It was also cold and Rosamunde began to shiver as the men lay her face up on a slab of stone, tying her down yet again, by wrists stretched up over her head and ankles spread wide.

Torches on the wall suddenly flared into light, burning red, as the Maharani walked forward.

Rosamunde could not see very well, for she was tied down so tightly that even raising her head was difficult. But she suddenly was aware that *something else* was in the room with her, besides the Maharani and the two menservants. Something not human – something evil.

The Maharani came to stand beside her, the barrel-like body gleaming in the torchlight from the oil she had been anointed with. It had a fetid, cloying odor, as of something rotted. Although Rosamunde did not recognize most of the arcane symbols painted on the woman's body, she could feel their wicked intent.

The Maharani lifted her hands and a huge ruby caught the light of the torches. She held this above Rosamunde and began to chant in a language that Rosamunde was unfamiliar with.

The air in the room seemed to pulse as the chant grew louder. The two men-servants began to stamp upon the floor in rhythmic counterpoint to the Maharani's harsh voice. Above Rosamunde the ruby seemed to reverberate to the beat of the chant. She could not take her eyes from it, drawn against her will to watching it.

And in the shadows behind the Maharani something stirred and a wave of blackness seemed to envelope the room.

"Now!" shouted the Maharani and brought the ruby down hard into Rosamunde's stomach.

Rosamunde convulsed and screamed. She could not help it, for the pain was intense.

The blackness invading the room seemed to fill her as well and she lost her tenuous hold on consciousness. The Maharani's cold face was the last thing she saw before she was catapulted into nothingness.

She awoke about an hour later, again on a *kunkar* floor of coarse limestone. Her stomach felt as if she had been punched and her left buttock stung. As her awareness became more acute, she smelled food and she struggled to sit up. In spite of everything, her body demanded sustenance.

She looked up and saw that she was still with the other women who had undergone the ruby ceremony, although in a different room. Laura was close by her, obviously waiting for her friend to awake.

As Rosamunde looked into Laura's face and opened her lips to speak. Laura gave a short shake of her head. Correctly identifying this as the signal to remain silent. Rosamunde looked past Laura and saw the woman Hussaini seated cross legged on the floor, whip in hand, a rather nasty smile upon her face.

"The last one awakens – good!" she said. "I am here to tell you how you will go on for the remainder of your lives, which will be spent here serving the needs of her highness the Maharani. I am Hussaini Kaul. You will address me as 'mistress' and obey my every order with speed and obedience. When I give you an order you will say "yes, mistress" and do as I tell you without demur. Those who do not will feel my whip !" she paused and looked with a stern eyes at all of them. She stroked the coils of the whip lovingly .

"You shall be fed shortly as you cannot undertake your duties without nourishment," she continued. "And the men will not find you pleasing if you are too thin! What man wishes to copulate with a rack of bones?" She gave a short mirthless laugh. "Tomorrow after a short period of training you will be put to work pleasing our men. That is your primary function here, to be used by many, many men. We have a large army and our men are allowed as much copulation as they desire. Indeed, once a day at the very least is required of them, and they delight in fulfilling this requirement. Later on, after you have spent enough time in training and have been properly broken in by much usage, we shall determine what else you will do here in the *Kala Mahal*. Some of you, if you are tall and strong", she glanced at Laura, "may have the honor to become guards for his highness, as he prefers women to guard his person. Others may become dancers or entertainers to amuse his highness. Still others will be sweepers or laundresses or cleaners. But whatever your other duties you primary one will be to take as many men as you can into your *yoni*. You will offer yourself to every man that approaches you and do whatever he wishes. If you do not take enough men you will be severely punished, for we will know if you do not comply with this duty. The ruby will tell of your every encounter. Is this understood?"

She had been speaking in rapid Hindustanee and Rosamunde blessed the fact that she had learned to speak it when first Ravi had started coming to visit them and had taken additional lessons on the trip out, learning from Ameera as well. She was certain that Laura had understood much of what had been said and the blonde had as well. But the slight girl looked confused and the dark haired woman did not understand at all for she suddenly burst out "Don't sit there and jibber jabber that heathen rubbish at me, you brazen hussy! I demand that you release me, and provide me with decent garments! I am the wife of an officer in Her Majesty's service, Colonel the Honorable Hugh Montmorency! My father is Baron Inglis! I will not be treated in this fashion! Nor will I consent to remain in a vile little room unfit for keeping cattle with a dirty nigger wench," she looked at Rosamunde in scorn, and a trooper's wife!" She looked a with equal distaste at the slight girl.

"Jesus H. Christ!" said Laura under her breath.

"*Chubbarao!* Shut up!" snarled Hussaini and her whip suddenly flicked out and caught the dark haired woman on the arm she had raised to emphasize her points and pulled her forward so that she fell onto her face. Her back was thus exposed and Hussaini lashed her three times, leaving bloody scores. " You –" she pointed at Laura. "You understood me. Since this slave understands me not, you will tell her what I have said. She had best learn to understand me or it will go very hard with her, tell her that."

"Yes, mistress," said Laura. She had learned the lesson of obedience in the mines.

"If she disobeys me again I shall whip her raw and then give her to an entire regiment of large, lusty men," Hussaini said, coiling up her whip. her eyes gleaming as the bloody thongs passed through her hand.

"Before the eunuchs bring the food I will tell you one thing more," Hussaini continued, ignoring the dark-haired woman who was curled on the floor now, sobbing hysterically. "You will no longer use the name given to you by your parents. You have been renamed and remember these names well, for if you do not respond to them you will be punished. You" she pointed at Laura, "will be known as Pice, for your hair is the colour of a copper coin." "You," she pointed at Rosamunde, "are Serai, for that is a house of accommodation and you will be accommodating many men."

The slight girl was to be Poshteen, which was a hairy coat, as the eunuchs had found her body particularly hairy, while the plump woman was now Mussock, the name of the inflated sheep's bladder that men floated on in the public bath houses. The dark haired woman now crying on the rough floor was to be Dubh, milk, for the extreme whiteness of her skin.

When she was done renaming the women, Hussaini stood and clapped her hands. The door opened and the eunuchs appeared with the food that smelled so good. It was hot and there appeared to be plenty of it.

"Eat well and sleep," said Hussaini with her cruel smile, "for tomorrow you have lessons to learn and will be put to hard usage. After your sleep eunuchs will come for you and will wash and oil you and then deliver you to me."

When the door closed behind her and a key grated in the lock, the plump woman went to the dark one, who by now had subsided to moaning. "Hush, hush," she said. "Crying won't solve anything. Judging by what that awful woman said she'll delight in hitting you as much as possible. There, there," she said and stroked the dark one's hair. "Let's introduce ourselves' she said, looking up at the others, "as it appears we are going to be room-mates. I'm Margaret Broadbent. I was visiting my sister in Delhi when this madness broke out, I saw her killed. My husband is Major James Broadbent of the Guides. I hope that this revolt has not spread all the way up to Mardan. Jim may still be alive." Mardan was on the northwest frontier near the Khyber Pass.

"I'm Laura Fitzroy," said that lady impressed by Margaret's now calm demeanor. After the initial shock she seemed to have gained her footing. Laura looked a question at Rosamunde, who nodded.

"This is my friend Rosamunde DeLacey – she ain't really a native, her friend who *was* a Hindu lady disguised her so that the bazaar trash wouldn't kill her." said Laura.

"My husband is a Lieutenant in the Queen's 17th

Cavalry in Malabad," said Rosamunde.

"He's probably dead, my dear," said Margaret gently. "Even in Delhi we heard that Malabad was completely destroyed and almost all the personnel and their dependents slaughtered."

" I thought so," Rosamunde said in a low voice.

"And you are?" Margaret said to the slight girl.

"Ivy 'iggins," the girl said. Me 'usband's a Corporal 'in th' 14th Infantry, in Delhi I dunno if 'e's alive or dead." She spoke with a Cockney accent, dropping her aitches and articulating vowel sounds as if they had an H in front of each – 'in' came out as 'h'in' while 'alive' was 'h'alive.'

The dark haired woman had stopped crying and when Margaret kindly questioned her she said that her Christian name was Henrietta.

"I wish that I had some cloth and some water to treat that back of yours," said Margaret worriedly. "and some calendula ointment as well. Perhaps when they give us some garments..."

Laura snorted. "That ain't likely, Maggie. The slaver that caught me and Rose told us we wouldn't be needing any clothes where we were going. And I ain't never seen a crib that bothered clothing the inmates."

"A crib?" Margaret repeated, looking confused. She helped Henrietta sit up.

"Low class whore house," said Laura. "Plenty of those in San Francisco where all they care about is quantity."

Henrietta winced, not only from her pain but from Laura's speech. "You're an American!" she said accusingly as if being American was somehow a crime. "A Colonial!" she added in disgust.

An' what are you, a bleedin' Duchess?" said Ivy sarcastically. "Thinks she's better than the lot of us, does she?"

"Please," pleaded Rosamunde "hadn't we ought to do our best to get on with one another? We're all in the same terrible situation and must needs make the best of it!"

"And let's eat this food before it gets cold!" said Laura.

This was agreed to and Laura, who seemed to be falling into the position of the group's leader, parceled it out.

There were enough rough made bowls and cups, with

stone bottles of hot tea. There was a large pot of curry, made with plenty of vegetables and chicken and fresh *chuppatties* to serve as both bread and spoons with another bowl full of hot rice.

"At least the food's good and there's more than enough," said Laura while everyone satisfied their appetites. Even the haughty Henrietta had been hungry, after declaring at first that she could not eat that native trash, only fit for pig's slop!

While they were eating they talked about what the ruby might be for as all of them tried to pry it out with fingernails, only to find that it was in their navels as firmly as if it had been glued in. Even Rosamunde had no idea what it was for. She only knew that it was bad magic and that touching it made her ill.

When Ivy remarked that "me bum stings" they discovered that a line of Hindi script had been tattooed on their left buttocks. This, as Rosamunde and Margaret, the only ones who read it, found, was the slave name that they each had been given.

There might have been some sort of sleep aid in the food, for not long afterwards they were all asleep, stretched out on the rough uncomfortable floor, not to awaken again until the door opened in the morning and several eunuchs appeared with a breakfast of fruit, boiled grain and the inevitable *chuppatties*.

The eunuchs made much of handling them as much as possible after they ate. Henrietta screamed and struck at one who handled her breasts and he slapped her hard. "It is our right to handle you as we please!" he said.

Laura had told Henrietta, whose name she shortened to Hetty, while they were eating the night before what lay in store for them and advise her to start learning Hindustanee.

"They would not dare to treat me so!" said the outraged Mrs. Montmorency, "Why, my husband is a Colonel, I am a lady!"

"They don't give a goddamn about your husband, Hetty," said Laura bluntly. "All these people care about is that your're a whore that can be screwed. My advice is to just stop fighting and take it, unless you want to spend all your time with your back in stripes. I told you what that Hussaini said, and believe me, that bitch will enjoy beating you."

But Hetty had not taken Laura's advice.

Rosamunde was trying her best to take Laura's excellent advice but when one of the eunuchs stuck his hand up between her legs she kicked at him. He hit her hard and said to the others "This one needs discipline. Perhaps she and the other one should go to the *Bhutas.*"

What were the *Bhutas*? This was a word that Rosamunde was completely unfamiliar with. She searched her memory as they were taken to the room with the 'meat hooks' where each woman had her wrists bound and was hung on a hook, feet tied, and thoroughly washed. Then they were oiled completely, even to intimate places, with a musky smelling oil that made their skin glow. "This will attract men," one of the eunuchs explained to the apprentice. "The saffron in it makes the skin shine alluringly and the scent inflames the senses so that a man lusts after a woman so adorned."

Then they were taken to a third room where Hussaini waited them. Today she wore transparent black pantaloons heavily embroidered in silver and her jewelry was all of silver as well, with what seemed like dozens of bangle bracelets on each arm. She was still bare-breasted. They were to find out that she never wore anything on her torso. The pantaloons as usual looked as if a deep breath would cause them to fall off.

This room was almost pleasant, save for the gold painted bars on the arched windows. There seemed to be a garden outside.

The tile floor was cool when they knelt upon it at Hussaini's direction. When Margaret attempted to cover herself Hussaini flicked the whip at her. "That is not allowed! The men must be able to see your body at all times. Slaves have no need for modesty for their bodies belong to their master, not to themselves."

She walked up and down in front of the kneeling women, who she had directed to sink back on their heels and sit up straight. "Today before your first turn in the Joy

244

House, you will learn to assume the correct position in approaching a man or in the presence of her highness, myself, the eunuchs, or one of his highness's guests, many of whom you will be offered to. You shall also learn the correct position to take when a man is using your body."

At Hussaini's direction, Laura translated this for Henrietta and Ivy. A look of disgust spread itself over Henrietta's proud features and Ivy looked frightened. Margaret seemed resigned.

"One of the slaves shall come and show you the proper way to do this, and you would do well to profit by this slave's example. She has been here but a little time and already she takes more men than many who have been here for much longer. She makes no demur no matter how many men use her. She is obedient and does as she is told. Come, Lali!" Hussaini raised her hands over her head and clapped hard.

A few moments later a woman trotted into sight and cast herself at Hussaini's feet. Like Rosamunde and her companions she was naked and had a huge ruby in her stomach. "Yes, mistress?" she said eagerly. She was a white woman, with red hair and very large breasts.

Rosamunde almost choked. "Lali" was Mabel Clutterbuck.

26

the red one

Mabel Clutterbuck had hated Delhi as much as she had hated London and Dublin before that.

Aunt Forrest, her late mother's sister, had a long list of rules, all of them to do with proper, ladylike behavior. Mabel was expected to sit about in her hot clothes, pretending to be interested in her aunt's boring friends. There were very few parties, or young people and when Mabel found out that she had been brought out to India to marry her second cousin, a stout bald, boring widower with children almost as old as she was, everything in her rebelled.

She was sick of being told what to do and how to live. She was also tired of the hot, heavy corset and the horsehair padded hoop. Aunt Forrest thought the new wire hoop suitable for only women of easy virtue. And most of all Mabel was sick of Mrs. Lillyvick's Patented Bosom Suppressor.

Mabel had begun to develop early and from the beginning her breasts had been lush and full. First her grandmother, then her sister-in-law had been horrified by Mabel's large breasts. They were so vulgar in a young girl, like an actress or a courtesan!

So at the age of twelve Mabel had been forced into the Suppressor. It flattened the breasts and was supposed to reduce their size but it never seemed to work. Day and night Mabel had to wear the horrible thing, for there was a special night model as well and the women in charge of her made certain that she wore it each and every day. Even Mrs. Umphelby, on the trip out to India, had checked that she was strapped into it all of the time .

Within a fortnight of her arrival in Delhi Aunt Forrest was talking about invitations to the wedding between Mabel and Darin Hepworth, or the old man, as Mabel thought of him.

Mabel could not bear it so she ran away.

It was an ill-conceived idea from the start. She had

little money, and could not speak Hindustanee. She had no idea where to go but anything had to be better than becoming a brood mare for the old man. Lots of little Hepworths was all he talked about even though he already had seven children but he wanted at least seven more.

After a series of petty misadventures she fell in with a half-caste horse trader called Sirkan Jenkins, who said that he would take her to Calcutta, where she could catch a boat for England, if she would sleep with him. Naively, she thought that was literally what he meant, for as little as she knew what a naked man looked like, did she have any ideas of sexual relations.

The horse trader did not let her remain ignorant long. He literally ripped the clothes off her back and ravished her.

She felt none of the fear and loathing that Rosamunde had. She thought it was an interesting experience and at last she was able to satisfy her curiosity about what a naked man looked like. When he wanted to repeat the experience she was nothing loathe, because she liked it better and better each time and because he gave her something she had always longed for.

For Sirkan had admired her. He was loud in his praise of her breasts and narrow waist and slender thighs as save for her breasts she was on the thin side. He spent hours stroking her bosom and buttocks and made up very bad poetry about them.

No one in her life had ever praised her before and she basked in his adulation, even to the point of not balking when he began to sell her favors to his 'friends'.

Eventually, in need of money, for he was a heavy but untalented gambler, he sold her to a slaver, Wazid Ali's brother Mohammed, who knew just where to resell this delectable morsel.

From the beginning Mabel had no objections to Jhaniput. She had learned enough Hindustanee from Sirkan to get by and when she learned that she was to be kept naked, with no more Bosom Suppressor! No more corsets! No more heavy awkward hoop! – she was extremely happy.

She liked the brothel. The quantities of brown men that used her each day gave her a thrill that only one other thing ever had – shoplifting. In London she had stolen vast quantities of inexpensive things and every time she had done so, and not been caught she had felt a heady rush of adrenalin and a marvelous glow of self satisfaction. She had done something very wrong and had gotten away with it! Now she was very aware that what she was doing was wicked and wrong. She was now a fallen woman and taking native men into her body, and quite a lot of them. It gave her the same feeling that stealing had done, and she loved it.

She was also heavily praised, Hussaini was pleased with her. Mabel was very popular with the men and many times there would be a line of soldiers eager for the services of Lali , the Red One, as she had been named for the colour of her hair. Mabel lapped it all up.

Now Hussaini was using her to show the new women how to act. Mabel was quite certain that all of these women envied her and her position in the *Kala Mahal*. Hussaini had told her that she would never have any duties other than pleasuring the men, as they liked her so much.

Mabel too, loved the admiring glances of the men and their lust when they lay on top of her, calling out "Lali! Lali!" and afterwards praising her body and eagerness to please them. She liked walking about the palace and seeing her body reflected in the marble floor and walls and knowing that each man who saw her liked what he saw, and when she offered herself they were eager for her, almost as eager as she was for them. She had become addicted to sex and craved it constantly. She never seemed to have enough.

She only wished that her family could see her, could see how all these men admired her so much and were so eager to lay with her. She would relish the looks of horror on their faces. For the first time in her life she felt powerful, and the praise was intoxicating, from her eunuch boasting about how many men Lali had taken in a day's time to Hussaini and the Maharani praising her for her obedience, and the few times she had been taken before the Maharajah, the way he had looked at her and touched her – it was all marvelous. When the other white women in the brothel talked about being rescued or escaping in low voices, she thought them fools. Here was where she wanted to be, doing just what she was doing. She had never been so happy in her life, and she did not even miss stealing things.

Now she happily knelt before Hussaini, with her legs apart, and leaning backwards with her arms behind her so that her breasts were thrust forward.

"Very good, Lali," said Hussaini with an approving glance.

"If that girl was a dog she'd be wagging her tail," thought Laura and stealing a glance at Rosamunde, she was surprised at the look on her friend's face. Rosamunde looked shocked. Laura could not imagine why. Surely some of the positions that Akbar and his cousins had put them in were no worse than this?

"This is the position of submission," Hussaini announced. "This is the position you will take whenever you are approached by a man or any of us in authority. This position shows a man what you offer him and it shows your humility and obedience as well. You will be expected to fall to your knees exactly like this. Lali is very talented – she makes a fine example."

Rosamunde could only feel sick as she watched the Clutterbuck girl abasing herself and looking quite pleased to do it. She had never before seen Mabel Clutterbuck with such a pleasant, pleased expression. The girl had always looked sullen. Rosamunde was surprised in another way too as she had always thought Mabel rather flat chested. However had she kept these very large breasts hidden?

"Now Lali and Kumala Jha will demonstrate how you are to take a man," said Hussaini as the large Empath joined them.

"Damned if I ever saw such a bunch of people for tying a body up!" said Laura three hours later.

They had been returned to the locked room with the *kunkar* floor after their first stint in the brothel .All of them now wearing bracelets on their wrists and upper arms, anklets and a brass round just above each knee as well. These were covered with little bells that rang out with every movement and each piece of jewelry had a good sized brass ring hanging from it.

These had been used as each woman was tied to a

charpoy in the 'proper position' of arms above the head, and knees up with legs spread wide.

"They didn't do that even in the mines," said Laura in disgust, although what followed, one man after another, *had* taken place in the mines.

After two hours of this they were released and taken back to the room and fed.

Laura was the only one with any appetite for the others were too horrified at what had happened to them and looked at her with dull eyes when she tried to badger them into eating. Their limbs were aching and cramped from being tied and they were every sore in other places as well. Henrietta had had hysterics and the eunuchs had gagged her. Margaret and Ivy were crying silently, compared to Henrietta's angry sobs and moans.

Rosamunde was dry eyed. She had fought them again and had been hit rather hard. She said in a low voice, "Why do they tie us up, Laura? Isn't it enough that they are using us –" her voice broke off.

"There's two reasons for it, honey, these people, like the ones at the mines who kept people and dragons chained to the ore carts had the idea that keeping the body in one position trained it to fall that way naturally, not that it works all that well. And they want to teach you to be humiliated and obey them. You watch, they'll start offering 'privileges' for the cooperative ones soon and a lot more punishment for the ones that don't do as they are told. Damn,but I wish you'd stop fighting them, Rose! You and Hetty both. They're not going to put up with it much longer. You ain't got to like what they're doing to you, but try not to make 'em mad at you."

"They said that they will give me to the *Bhutas*. I don't know what they mean," said Rosamunde. "I wish I could stop fighting, Laura, but something just comes over me and I have to fight, I just cannot accept being treated like that, as if I was just a *thing* for men to use."

Margaret, wiping her face with the back of her hand, came over to them, trailed by Ivy. "Henrietta's asleep," she said. "She's in a lot of pain from her back, those lashes are deep, and what was done to us this afternoon aggravated the pain. I got her to drink some tea, but she wouldn't eat."

"Maggie, you told us your pa was in the Indian army too, and you grew up here. Have you ever heard of *Bhutas*?" Laura inquired.

Margaret wrinkled her brow. Finally she shook her head."I don't recognize the word at all," she admitted. Her Hindustanee was extremely fluent.

"You knew that woman who demonstrated for us this morning, didn't you?" she said to Rosamunde, changing the subject.

"Yes, her real name is Mabel Clutterbuck and she was at my school for a while. She was also on the boat when I came out to India. She was joining a relative in Delhi." Rosamunde answered. "I don't think that she recognized me, but I remember her all too well."

" 'ow could she do that, lettin' that man take 'er in front of us all?" Ivy burst out, "It weren't decent! I comes from Whitechapel in Lunnon an' every other girls' a whore 'cause otherwise you don't gets enough to eat, but not one of 'em would do that!"

"Reckon she's either decided to cooperate with these bitches or else she was forced –" Laura said. "Don't go judging her, Ivy, We don't know what they did to her."

"It could be this ruby," said Rosamunde slowly."It is something arcane, I am certain, I just have not been able to determine what it might be. Perhaps they can control us with it and Mabel is not responsible for what she is doing."

"What do you mean' arcane'?" Margaret asked, frowning. "Do you mean magical?"

Rosamunde nodded. "When the Maharani performed the ruby ceremony she had arcane symbols painted on her body and there was something inhuman in that room as well – something very evil."

Margaret smiled a little indulgently. "Magic does not exist my dear!I know that there are supposed to be Wizards and Witches in the British isles but I never met any and am inclined to think that it is all nonsense." Margaret had never lived in England. She had been born in India, married there and spent her entire life as either the daughter or the wife of an Indian army officer. "Don't tell me you believe in magic!"

"I not only believe in magic," said Rosamunde "for it is very real, but at home I am a practicing Witch. Something

251

here in India has drained my powers."

"There's Witches and Wizards in America too," Laura offered. "it's as real as we are, Maggie – magic, I mean. There's something else real strange going on here besides these damned rubies! Did anybody look at the men that were banging us?"

They all looked at her a little shocked. The others had all kept their eyes tightly closed as if not seeing what the men were doing would make it less real.

"I gained the impression that they were all lower caste *sepoys* and *sowars*," Margaret said.

"They also look like they been drugged," said Laura. "All sweaty and shaky, and that's not just from lust!" she said as Margaret opened her mouth to speak. "I looked at least four of them who used me, and their eyes were all dilated and glassy, like they'd smoked opium or taken a big dose of laudanum." "

"They drink opium here in India," said Margaret absently."I can think of one reason the men might need to be drugged. If they are Hindu it would be a defilement for them to sleep with a non-Hindu woman. It would not matter to a Muslim. But why drug them at all? The horrible Hussaini said the mean are encouraged to make use of the women and surely the Hindu men could find Hindu partners here. It sounds as if there are a great many female slaves here."

"That's what I aim to find out," said Laura. "I think there's something going on here other than just a big whore house and I think Rose is right too, this is black magic. But I can't figure out why, not yet anyway. But I will!"

"Why does a wealthy Maharani need to operate a bawdy house?" Rosamunde asked. "Is that how they make their money? Did anyone see any money exchanging hands?"

No one had. The whole of Jhaniput was a mystery.

It was difficult to do any 'snooping' as Laura called it. Every day they spent a stint in the brothel, two hours on, two hours off, three times a day. Rosamunde guessed rightly that this was to prevent their bodies from cramping up too much while tied down.

Every morning, after the baths in the 'Chicago slaughter house' as Laura called it, they had more 'training' with Hussaini. She took great delight in informing then them that it was now impossible for them to ever again wear clothing as one of their "gifts" given during the ruby ceremony was a spell that would make any fabric they put on burst in to flame and immolate them. She demonstrated this with a little Untouchable girl who was bespelled and burned to death when a cloak was thrown around her. Laura said the child was drugged, probably with *bhang*, but Rosamunde, as did they all, had nightmares about what the child had suffered and her horrible death.

The soldiers wore special cloth that was magiced so that it would not burn if they had an encounter with one of the female slaves and even guests were given gifts of special clothing for them to wear. *Charpoys* and cushions alike were bespelled against fire.

Very often Mabel or "Lali" came to demonstrate some movement or technique to them. It was obvious that she was Hussaini's prize pupil. There was not a flicker of recognition in her face as she looked at Rosamunde. She saw only a dark-skinned native girl, not the great granddaughter of an English Duke.

The five women were also told that the Maharani had kindly arranged that they would not become pregnant, no matter how many men used them, nor would they have their monthly bleeding, for both Muslims and Hindus would not lie with a menstruating woman and a woman in that condition was of no use to the *Kala Mahal*.

There were no days off for any of the women in the *Kala Mahal*. Everything that they learned was to attract men. Eventually, when they had finished a stint in the brothel and they were judged to know the positions well enough, they would be sent to the *zenana* and allowed as much freedom as a barred fortress might offer, as long as they took great care to attract as many men as was possible.

To this end they were taught to walk in a peculiar swaying fashion, and to sit, lay and stand in seductive postures. Eunuchs made up their faces every morning and painted their palms and soles with henna.

And still Rosamunde fought with them every time

they came for her and tied her down to the *charpoy* in the brothel. She earned many whippings, much to Laura's dismay, but something in her would not give in. Even Henrietta had given up, falling into a depression that alternated between despair and rage. Margaret seemed resigned; she still lived in hope that her husband lived and would come looking for her. Ivy, a Stoic little soul, gritted her teeth and bore it, while Laura kept her wits about her and tried to snoop as much as was possible. She was determined to get to the bottom of the mystery of Jhaniput.

One morning, in between men, Hussaini came and stood over Rosamunde, and looked down at her contemptuously, "You still think that you can fight us, you stupid slave? There has been enough of this foolishness. This afternoon you go to the *Bhutas!*" She turned to the eunuch standing near by. "Make certain that this one takes the bulk of the men waiting and then take her to the room of the *Bhutas* when her time here is over."

The eunuch bowed. "I hear and obey, mistress. It shall be done as you command."

Rosamunde did not join her companions in the little room afterwards; instead, two burly man dragged her away, down a long corridor and down a flight of stairs, going down, down, until the air temperature was suddenly cold and Rosamunde realized they were underground.

The narrow dark corridor was lit but by torches which flickered drearily, doing little to relieve the darkness.

"Where are you taking me?" Rosamunde asked fearfully. The atmosphere in the corridor was making her skin crawl. and she began to be very afraid.

"*Chup!*" said one of the men and gave her a vicious shake. "You are being punished for disobedience. You have no right to question us."

At long last they came to a huge door, bound with iron and closed with a huge lock.

Rosamunde began to feel the effects of the unpainted Cold Iron immediately. Everywhere else in the *Mahal*, the iron bars and locks had been covered in gold, which had served as a protection for her against the poison of Cold Iron, that her Elfin and magical blood laid her open to.

One eunuch took a gigantic key from his belt and unlocked the lock, while the other retained a tight hold on Rosamunde.

She was shivering badly, not just from the penetrating cold on her bare body but from dread. What was going to happen to her?

The eunuch with the key opened the huge door only a crack and they shoved her inside, slamming the door behind her.

Rosamunde was effectively blinded. The darkness in the room was complete. Not even the most minute particle of light showed anywhere. There was an odd, unpleasantly pungent smell in the room.

Her bare feet felt a rough surface and when she put out her hand the wall ran with damp.

And then something moved in the darkness.

27

muggers

Sinéad and Molly soon found that it was just as hot amidst the trees of the jungle as it was out in the full sun. Even the deep shade provided little relief from the heat.

For the weather continued brutal. Bharat spoke of the monsoon that would come in June bringing rain that would put a halt to the heavy dust that cloaked and choked everything but it might slow down their progress.

"*Slow down our progress!*" thought the cat. "*If we were moving any slower we'd be after standin' still!*"

Sinéad had been ready to spit and hiss when she had asked Bharat how long his original trek to Ranijhat had taken and he had replied that he remembered it as nearly six moons of journeying.

"Six moons!" the little familiar had exclaimed in dismay. "That's bein' about six months! What will be happenin' to me Witch in six months!"

"It will not take as long from where we have started this time," said the elephant. "For I came from Rajputana that first time, not Hindustan, and the heat was intense on the plain. We could not move as quickly."

"The heat was intense?" demanded Sinéad "An' what are ye callin' this – a bloody snow storm?"

She was finding out more and more that a deep gulf seemed to separate her from other animals, those who were not familiars.

For she now thought in human terms. She wondered what time it was by the clock and it bothered her that she had become muddled as to what day of the week it was and she no longer knew the date.

To Hari, Bharat and Isha, to count time in such fashion was meaningless. Darkness and light indicated when it was time to sleep or eat or hunt for food and knowing the day of the week or the month was useless to them. They could not understand why she wanted to know these things and why she also fretted over the lack of a newspaper and their lack of a map. Indeed, they found the very concept of a picture of where they were going highly amusing.

Only Molly shared her anxiety and her distaste of raw food.

Both Sinéad and Molly were living largely in fruit and this diet suited neither one of them. Molly had never eaten half the fruits that Isha brought from the trees for them and had more than one stomach upset as a result. Sinéad, too, was sick on and off, but was sicker still when Hari brought her a dead gecko to eat. "I can't be eatin' something' that's starin' at me," she said with a shudder, looking at the dead lizard's glazed eyes.

"It's not staring at you," said Hari with a laugh."It's dead!" He tore into the lizard with relish, and Sinéad had turned away, repelled.

It had never been the custom in Sinéad's family to eat an intact fish as was fashionable. It was always filleted.And she found the dead eyes of things Hari killed and ate rather accusatory. It was one thing to eat things that had been carved up and humanely killed beforehand, but to track something and kill it, that was too uncivilized for the familiar. If someone else had caught and killed it and prepared it, that would be one thing. The other animals laughed at her for her scruples. They expected this silliness from Molly, for she was a *mem-sahib* after all.

None of the other animals had any idea how far it was to Ranijhat in miles or how many miles they might be making in a day. They did not understand why Sinéad worried over this. They would get there when they got there. Even Molly did not share Sinéad's anxiety, for the end of this strange trip meant thinking about what she was to do and where she was to go and she had no answer for either of those questions. Her only concerns were the lack of good food and the horrible heat.

The heat became very much a problem for them one morning, when after a short rest stop, when Molly, in attempting to climb back upon Bharat, fainted dead away.

"Molly!" cried Sinéad in distress, running to her friend.

Molly had fallen face down, very suddenly. "Help me get her over on her back!" Sinéad said urgently to Hari.

But it was not until Bharat helped with his trunk that they tuned her over, for she was heavy and limp and could not help them.

"What happened?" said Hari anxiously.The mongoose had become fond of Molly. Every evening when they had stopped for the day he climbed into her lap for some stroking. "Her face is very pale, even paler than that of most *mem-sahibs*."

" 'Tis the heat," said Sinéad, patting Molly's face with a soft paw. "The heat an' this heavy gown. An' what I am wonderin' was that besom of a sister-in-law thinkin' to send her out in a gown of worsted, for 'tis after bein' criminal neglect!" she fumed.

The gown in question was of a heavy brown worsted, which was a fine, closely woven wool. It was made high to the neck and had long, close sleeves. Molly had been obliged to drop her hoop, for sitting astride the elephant was not possible with the hoop on. She had torn one tier from the very bottom of the gown and from the three heavy petticoats she wore underneath so that the length, no longer held out by the hoop, would not trip her up.

"Why do humans cover themselves with such things?" Hari said.

"It is their way," said Bharat, "but the *sahibs* clothe themselves foolishly, Nirav said, in a manner unsuited to the climate."

"We are after needin' to get this thing off her," said Sinéad decidedly, putting a paw on the heavy gown, "before she is gettin' heat stroke." Experimentally, she unsheathed her claws and nicked a seam. The gown had suffered much abuse in the recent past and had not been new to begin with. Nor had it even been made for Molly. "When I've ripped this, you pull it away," she directed Hari.

Isha watched this with a pained expression. "I knew that the human would cause problems!" he said ."They always do!"

"Cease yer jabberin' an' come an' be helpin' us! Ye've got hands and fingers like a person's, so ye can be unlacing her corset!" Sinéad commanded the monkey.

With ill grace, and much grumbling, Isha went to help.

Bharat lifted his trunk and sniffed. "There is water nearby," he announced, "I shall go and fill my trunk and bring it back to cool her."

Leaving the others to finish pulling the hot fabric off Molly, the elephant headed towards the sweet scent of water.

As he went through the jungle Bharat thought longingly of a bath, of water sucked up in his trunk sprayed and trickling down his back and sides. If the *mem* was feeling the heat they would do well to stop and let her rest, and then there would be time to go to the river and bathe.

He heard the noise before he saw it: splashing in the water and the voices of *muggers*. "He is mine!" "No, mine!" And then a young voice, a human voice, crying in Urdu. "Help me! Help me!"

Bharat charged forward.

There on the river bank, a man in native dress was trying to climb from the water. An overturned boat floating nearby told the story of what had happened to put him at the mercy of the *muggers*. Three of them snapped and lunged at him. He was a strong swimmer and he had a knife, but he was tiring rapidly.

Bharat ran forward and grabbed the man with his trunk. He had almost made it to the bank and it was little effort for the large elephant to swing the man up behind his head to safety.

"That human is ours!" yelled the largest *mugger*. "He is in our river! He is our prey!" He clacked his teeth, gleaming in his long snout, together.

Bharat felt the man settle into place behind his head and droop in exhaustion, breathing heavily. The elephant back away from the edge of the bank knowing that the muggers were at a disadvantage on land. "Water belongs to no one," he said evenly. "And Koda Khan's Law is that none of us eat humans, not the striped ones, nor the lion, nor the cheetahs, and not thou, O *muggers*."

"Koda Khan!" said one of the smaller *muggers* impressed. "He who is lord of the night?"

"He who is also *Malki-la,-* the lord of the land. It is his *hukkum,* his order that no animal in the jungle kill a human, for the vengeance of the humans is swift and terrible and they do not kill but the one of us who took human life, but all that they can find," Bharat stated.

"Is it a true tale, that once Koda Khan killed a *mugger?*" called out the third of the creatures.

"Yes, I myself saw it. He killed, for breaking the Law, a *mugger* of the Ganga, one called Kishor," Bharat answered.

"Kishor was a giant amongst *muggers!*" cried the smallest *mugger*. He could give thee three lengths, Partha!" he said to the largest *mugger*. "I for one will obey the Law of Koda Khan!" He dived down into the water and swam away.

"I, too," said the second *mugger* and followed his friend.

The large one muttered to himself, but after a few moments he, too, swam away.

Bharat went to the edge of the water and filled his trunk.

The man on his back sat up and said in Urdu, "I do not know from where you have come, elephant, or why you have rescued me, but I thank Allah for sending you! Nor do I even know where you are taking me!" he added as Bharat, trunk full of water, headed purposefully back into the jungle.

When the man saw Molly stretched out on the ground with the animals around her he slid off the elephant's back at once and went to her. "A *mem-sahib!*" he exclaimed in surprise.

The three animals had ripped and pulled her dress off and Isha had managed to untangle her corset strings so that she was in but chemise, petticoats, pantelettes, stockings and shoes.

"What has happened here?" the man said as if to himself.

"She fainted from the heat, ye gowk!" said Sinéad impatiently.

"Ai!" exclaimed the young man, his eyes starting from his head. "It is a djinn!" He made the sign for the evil eye, and, still kneeling, backed away from Sinéad

"I'm bein' a Witch's familiar!" said the little cat in exasperation." Have ye never been hearin' of Witches and such?"

"There was a *Angrezi* trooper who told tales of Witches and Wizards in *Belait*. We all thought that he was but a *dastan-go,* a storyteller," said the young man."These tales were true? There are dragons and animals that speak as do men and those who can do magic?" From being afraid he had suddenly become eager and excited.

"As true as I am after standin' here speakin' to you," said the cat.

"And these others, they can speak to me as well?" he queried, looking at the mongoose, the monkey and the elephant .

"I'll be havin' to translate for ye," said the familiar. "They're not bein' magical."

The young man stood up and bowed. "I am Niaz ul Mulik," he said. "I owe you a life debt, for this elephant saved my life. *Muggers* were about to eat me."

Sinéad looked him over carefully as she told him her name and that of the others. She liked what she saw.

In spite of a short dark beard he was very young, she thought, not much more than twenty-one or two. He was a little more than medium height, very slim and supple and had dark expressive eyes and the rather aquiline features common in men of the Middle East , for she perceived by his mention of Allah and by his name that he was a Muslim, a Mughal. He wore native dress of a tunic, a waist sash, a *pagri* or turban, and loose *pyjamy* trousers, now wet and rather the worse for wear. One straw woven sandal was missing.

While Sinéad and Niaz were talking, Bharat had gently begun to dribble water on Molly's face and body.

She began to rouse at last, waving her hand at the water that trickled from the air onto her face. "Oh," she moaned and opened her eyes, only to scream when she saw Niaz standing close by and realized that she was in her petticoats.

"Hush, hush, Molly!" said Sinéad. "He's a friend, an' do ye think that we'd allow anyone to be ravishin' ye?"

"I am the *mem-sahib's* to command," said Niaz, in good English. He bowed deeply to her, and placed his hands together, palm to palm. "*Namaste*," he murmured.

Molly pulled what remained of her gown towards herself and covered her chest with it, still a little uncertainty about this stranger, looking worriedly from the cat to Niaz and back again.

"Fear not, *mem*. I am not one of the murderers of

Meerut," said Niaz. "I fled them myself, they killed Anderson *Sahib*, he who was like a father to me, who took me in and educated me when my parents died else I, once a man of rank, would have lived on the streets and ended in being an outcast. But instead I became a *Jemadar*, a lieutenant, an officer in the cavalry. But my own men turned upon me when I would not join in their killing. It was wrong! A curse be on them – and it will be – to take the innocent lives of women and children!"

"Molly was bein' on her way to Malabad to visit a friend, me Witch," said Sinéad and recounted Molly's trials.

"Ah!" said Niaz. "And you are perhaps going after your friend?" He swayed suddenly. "May I sit, *mem?*"

"Oh, yes!" Molly said hurriedly.

He sat down rather abruptly and said "I was chased by muggers and swam a long way..."

"And it is lookin' as if one of them was gettin' ye,' said the familiar, for a red stain was beginning to appear on his left sleeve.

"That is from a *tulwar,* one of my own *sowar,* " he said.

"Let me see," said Molly and forgetting her trepidation, tore open his sleeve and laid bare a long, ugly gash.

Bharat dribbled the rest of the water over it and Molly tore strips from her petticoat and bandaged it.

While she worked, Sinéad explained where they were going and why. "Are ye knowin' where how far we are from Ranijhat?" she asked Niaz hopefully.

"I have never been there but I once accompanied Anderson *sahib* to Rawalpindi on the frontier. He said at that time that the road to Ranijhat lay between Peshawar and Rawalpindi. He also said that the road was but a goat track, for in the early days of his service to the Company he was sent there upon a mission," answered Niaz, wincing a little at Molly's ministrations...

"And are ye rememberin' how far it might be?" Sinéad urged.

"It is some two hundred and fifty *kos* to Peshawar from Delhi, " he answered and gave a quick smile of thanks to Molly, who had finished the bandaging.

"That's bein' over four hundred miles!" exclaimed

Sinéad in dismay.

The other animals had been sitting quietly, listening, although they understood but little of what was being said, for the conversation was in English. Only Isha sat apart. He had climbed a nearby tree and seemed to be sulking. He looked as if he disapproved of Bharat's having saved the human's life.

Niaz looked at the cat, and then looked at the other animals and Molly. "May I come with you?" he inquired abruptly. "I can be of service to you. I am wise in the ways of living off the land. He reached into his sash and pulled out a knife and a fish hook. "And the *mem* requires new garments, I have even a little money, a few *rupees,* I may purchase a *ghagra,* a skirt and a tunic for her in a village, and perhaps food as well, if I cannot catch any fish. And I have no place else to go," he admitted, staring at the ground. "My regiment has rebelled. It has been dishonored. It will be disbanded and the *sahib-lait,* the great men, will never believe that I did not rebel with my men..." his voice trailed off, sounding as if he was overcome with emotion.

"I'll have to be askin' the others," said Sinéad, but Molly, who some how trusted this man, was all for it. She would feel safer with a male presence, even though his weapons for her protection consisted only of a small knife.

The only dissenting voice was that of Isha. "Never trust a human!" he snapped. "They're treacherous, the lot of them!"

But he was overruled and Niaz was asked to join the little party.

He quickly proved his worth that very afternoon by finding a nearby village and purchasing a colorful skirt and tunic for Molly, making her much more comfortable, for they were cool cotton. He also caught a string of fish with a line made from the remnants of Molly's worsted gown , and cooked them over a fire he put together and lit with a flint, which was amongst the other useful objects in his sash pockets. He cut grass for Bharat and took off his trappings so that the elephant could bathe in the river.

Both Molly and Sinéad were pleasantly full that evening for the first time since they had started upon this journey. Even Hari had enjoyed some fish and Bharat, tired at his age of the long trek and the endless search for food, gratefully ate the choice grasses that Niaz brought to him.

Only Isha stayed apart, scowling and resisting all of Niaz's attempts to be friendly.

28

cunchunee

Rosamunde was not returned to the company of the other women for a night and a part of the following day.

Laura was growing extremely worried, almost frantic, and even went so far as to ask the eunuch Pramoda Tandon where was the one called Serai. She earned an open-handed slap across the face and was told brusquely that the disobedient slave was being punished and unless 'Pice' wanted the same punishment, she would not speak without permission.

Laura had to subside at that, as Margaret, worried that Laura, who they all depended on, would be dragged away as well, begged her to hold her tongue.

It was after their second stint in the brothel that the returned to the little room and found Rosamunde there, lying on the floor on her back, staring at the ceiling.

"Rose honey!" said Laura and ran forward to kneel beside her friend.

Rosamunde turned dull eyes on her and said in a voice that was hoarse and flat, "You were right, Laura, I should have just let them do what they want. Fighting it was wrong. I will never fight them again. They can do anything they want to me, (her voice broke), as long as they don't put me in that *tykhara* again!" She gave a long shudder and her lips quivered but no tears came. She raised no objection when Laura helped her sit up and put an arm around her shoulders.

"What's a *tykhara?*" Laura raised her head and looked at Margaret.

"It's an underground room," said Margaret. "Many of the *Mahals* have them. When it becomes very hot the people in the palace retreat to them to cool off as it can be as much as fifteen degrees colder below the ground."

"What did they do to you, honey? What were those *Bhutas*?" Laura asked anxiously. She could see no signs of a beating on Rosamunde. If there had been a beating, she thought, it would have had to been a hell of a whaling to make Rose say that she would never fight again. Rose was feisty, too feisty for her own good.

Rosamunde shivered and her eyes suddenly looked haunted. In a voice so low Laura could scarcely hear her as she murmured some thing about scales and claws and then seemed unwilling to go on. Laura suspected that it was more that she was *unable* to go on.

"It's all right, honey," Laura said soothingly when Rosamunde began to struggle to articulate. "you don't have to tell us. It was something awful, real bad, I reckon. What ain't real bad in this damned place? Maybe some day you'll tell me, but it don't really matter. I'm just sorry you had to go through it, that's all. But at least they let you come back here with us."

Rosamunde looked at her gratefully. In Laura's face was the same compassion and concern that she had seen after the first time that Akbar had raped her. What had happened in that room was worse, far worse and she really did not want to talk about it. Perhpas one day – but not now.

But it was noticeable that when the eunuch came for them for their next turn in the brothel, Rosamunde was obedient and did exactly as she was told with no fight or struggle, and did it quickly as well.

When Hussaini gloatingly stood over her and taunted her about her punishment and her humbling Rosamunde said no more then "Yes, mistress," with an expressionless voice and face.

Laura was worried that her spirit had been broken, but that evening, after they had been returned to the room and the others slept, Rosamunde informed Laura that in spite of her new obedience, she was determined that somehow they were all going to get out of this awful place.

"No one should be allowed to treat people like this, Laura! No one!" she said in a fierce whisper. "The Maharani, that evil Hussaini, the eunuchs, they all should be destroyed and go straight to Hell!"

"That's the spirit!" said Laura approvingly. "We got to study the situation, Rose, and find out as much as we can about this operation. That means keeping our eyes open and ears to the ground. Once we get moved into the *zenana* and have more freedom it'll be easier to spy on them."

"When will that be?" said Rosamunde.

"I don't rightly know. That bitch Hussaini said when we were obedient and well used," Laura answered. "We certainly have been well used," she added ruefully. "Every night that damned eunuch reels off how many men banged us that day and that's something I could live without knowing, but it's probably the only pleasure the poor bastard gets any more, watching and counting."

"How long have we been here, Laura? I've completely lost track of time," Rosamunde asked.

"So have I," Laura admitted. "that's done on purpose, I reckon. Have you noticed that sometimes when the eunuchs take us to Hussaini it's still dark and other times the morning is half over? I been watching the sky over that garden we can see out the window in that training room. That's deliberate. They do it to us to keep us off balance. After a while you begin to doubt your own senses." She snorted. "They still ain't as bad as those bastards in New Spain, Hussaini could learn a thing or two from Señor de Alvarez at the Orinoco Mine, that man had a real bent for torture and Hussaini ain't even in his class. Course, he didn't tie us up as much as they do here. They're over fond of that, if you was to ask me."

Rosamunde wondered if she could still have the outlook that Laura had if something like this had happened to her *twice*. Laura never gave up and she encouraged the others in their group to hope also.

"The monsoon hasn't started yet and they always says that is in June," said Rosamunde thoughtfully. "Might it still be May?"

"I don't think so," said Laura. "'Pears to me the time is a little further along than that." She gave a sudden growling noise, "Damn, but I miss newspapers! I wish I knew what was going on out in the world! Nobody here ever talks about what's happening outside. It's as if the rest of the world don't exist!"

"Perhaps when we get to the *zenana* we will hear more," said Rosamunde, and suddenly yawned.

"We'd better get to sleep, honey," suggested Laura. "Wouldn't think that being flat on your back most of the day would be so damn tiring but it is. That Hussaini would have a cow if we was to fall asleep while some man was humping us."

Rosamunde expected to have nightmares about what had happened to her in the *tykhara*, but she did not. Instead, she dreamed about Sinéad. In the dream, which was extraordinarily vivid, the little familiar was looking for her but could not find her. Rosamunde awoke feeling a deep sense of loss. She wished that she could cry but still no tears would come, not even for Sinéad.

They were never certain exactly how much time had passed, when Hussaini finally came to them and told them that when they had finished the third of today's sessions in the brothel, they would be taken to the *zenana*.

"Your bodies have learned the positions and you are all obedient. Let this continue and you will have more freedom and for now you will no longer be tied in the positions. But be warned, you must still take as many men as possible. You must attract those who come to the *zenana* to choose a woman and make them want to lay with you. There are rewards for those who attract men and punishments for those who do not. We shall also be deciding what your other duties will be here," she added.

"I think that you shall become a guard," she said to Laura. "You are tall and strong with broad shoulders and full breasts, such as his highness likes. You will probably be a maidservant," she said to Ivy "you are too frail for anything else. The others we have yet to decide upon.

But Rosamunde was to learn her future that very evening.

The *zenana* was quite different from the little room they had shared for so long. It was very large and even attractive, with tile and lace work stone carvings, not for the women to enjoy but for the men, who, contrary to the rule of most *zenanas*, were allowed in to pick and choose what women they wanted. The walls of polished limestone were covered in erotic murals of positions taken from the *Kamasutr*, the manual of the amatory arts. There were also many *maithuna* sculptures, which were, to Western eyes, obscene. There were other suites of rooms for the 'use' of the women, private cubicles for officers and a long, low ceilinged room for the *sowars* and *sepoys* to take their choices and bed them, if they were so inclined. Otherwise they could choose to take any female they desired right in the *zenana*, to their quarters or in one of the many gardens. The zenana never closed. Hussaini informed them that they were available to men all day and all night, even to be woken from sleep if a man wanted one of them.

"At least there's cushions here," said Laura *soto voice* to Rosamunde as they were shown into the large room. Hussaini had informed them that the cushions were for the benefit of the men and had been bespelled so that they would not burst into flame when the women were laid upon them. "*Big of them*," muttered Laura to herself.

The room was full of women, perhaps as many as thirty or more, each with a ruby in her navel and all wearing the same hairstyle. Early on, all of their hair had been cut to the same length, just below the shoulder. It was then center parted, and clubbed back and fastened with a brass clip.

The main difference in the women, besides skin, hair and eye colour for there seemed to be women of almost every race present, ranging from merely pretty to exquisitely lovely, was in the jewelry. Many had nose jewelry, earrings. collars and other body piercings. Some wore a few bangle bracelets others, many of them. All had the same belled jewelry that Laura, Rosamunde, Ivy, Margaret and Henrietta wore but had added to it considerably. But in no case did the jewelry cover what was considered vital for the men to see.

Hussaini took them to a corner with some cushions on the floor and said "You will live here. You will also take men here if they so desire. Pramoda Tandon will come each

269

day and take you to be washed and oiled. Food will be brought to you and through there," she pointed to an arched door with a beaded curtain, "is where you may relieve yourselves. Food will arrive shortly and in a little while the men who were on duty during the day will be coming in to choose a companion for the evening." She looked at them and took the whip from her shoulders and snapped it open. "These are the rules: You must go with the first man who wants you. You must do *anything* he orders you to do. You may not speak unless he gives you leave to do so. You will stay with him as long as he wants you, even should he desire to share you with his comrades. When he has dismissed you, you will return here and attract another man. Only when no more men want you may you sleep. Later, when you have duties, there will be different rules. Do you understand?" She snapped the whip again.

"Yes, mistress," they all chorused, even Henrietta, who had been looking as if she was going to be ill.

"See that you abide by the rules and you will not taste my lash," she said, with a look, as Laura said later, as if she hoped they would be disobedient so that she could use that whip.

She left them alone and they all sank to the floor to sit on the cushions.

"Well," said Laura, "My ass is grateful for the cushion at least."

"Whatever will we do if we can't get no men to take us?" said Ivy, shivering slightly. "I don't wants to be 'it wi' that whip o' hers! An' I ain't as 'andsome as the rest of you. Me titties is small and me bum don't even exist."

"I'm certain that there are men who will find you attractive, dear," said Margaret. "Not all men have the same taste in females – "

"I can't believe this!" Henrietta burst out. "Here we are sitting about discussing *whoring*, hoping to attract *native* men, as if we were at a tea at the Vicarage discussing our chances of making a good marriage! All I keep thinking about is that even if we are rescued Hugh will not wish to have me as his wife any more. I have been dishonored too many times!" She angrily wiped away a tear that trickled down her face. "And you," she turned to Laura, "you are so casual about this!

What do you think that *fiancé* of yours will say when he finds out how many men have had you? He'll break the engagement!"

"Nate was in the party, with my Pa, who rescued me from the mine. First time he saw me I was naked as a jaybird, chained to an ore cart and was lying there with a dead Spaniard on me. Actually the bastard was *in* me. Someone shot him in the back while he was banging me. I don't think this'll upset him none," Laura said evenly.

What can one expect from an American! the look on Henrietta's face seemed to say.

"How can any of us ever have a normal life again?" Margaret said thoughtfully. "I am not really certain that I ever want a man to touch me again after this, even Jim, as much as I love him. The thought of becoming a nun is becoming immensely appealing, and I am not even a Papist!"

Rosamunde had not taken part in this conversation as she had begun to do her exercises which were based on ballet. She ws determined now, more than ever, after the night in the *tykhara*, to be ready to escape and that meant being strong and fit.

Being tied in one position for sometimes six hours every day, even with respites in between, was bad for the muscles. The others all had trouble with terrible cramps but Rosamunde, due to the command she had over her body from her ballet training, had not been as badly off as had they. Even in the little room they had shared she had made a ritual of exercising. Laura and Ivy sometimes joined her but Margaret said that she was too old and Henrietta thought it undignified and unladylike, repeating what Raymond had said, that only an opera dancer did things like that.

Rosamunde ignored her. She began every workout with the five positions, holding each for a minute or two and then went on to *Demi-Plié*, the basis of everything that was done in ballet. She missed her *barre*, however, as facing it aided in posturing. She did *Demi-Plié*, a half bend at the knees, in each of the five positions, counting two counts to herself for each *Demi-Plié* Then onto the *Grand-Plié*, a full bend at the knee, four counts going down and four coming up again in all five positions and here she really missed her *barre*.

She then did *Battements, tendues, de jambe á terre, frappes, glissades* and *sautes*, where she jumped into the air, and then the three *arabesques*. She went through this routine several times until her muscles felt limber and the cramping had stopped. It seemed very strange indeed to be doing these exercises naked, strange and so shocking, but she persevered.

The others had grown used to her and paid no attention to her any more, unless Laura or Ivy felt in need of stretching their muscles. But today she exercised alone.

She was just finishing when she realized that someone was staring at her and she looked up to meet Hussaini's eyes. She dropped to her knees in the 'position of submission' as she could see the others in her group were already doing.

"You are a *cunchunee,* a dancing girl!" said Hussaini. "I have never seen dancing such as that, but his highness may like it." She turned and gestured to someone behind her. "Come!" she said imperiously.

An Indian woman, covered in bangle bracelets but otherwise looking like any of Rosamunde's group came forward dropped into the position. She wore hoops that pierced the aureoles of her breasts, with bells upon them. She was very beautiful, with large soft eyes, and a smooth dark skin and a graceful yet voluptuous figure. She also had an expression of sweetness and kindness.

"This is Chowki," Hussaini said. "She is the principal dancer of his highness's *nautch,* his dance troupe. You will be in her charge and beginning tomorrow you will train with her to be a part of the *nautch*. This does not mean that you will not have to take men!" she added. "You will still be expected to take as many as possible, no matter what else you are doing. No one escapes that duty. Chowki, you will show this one what her new duties will be and train her in our dances. Perhaps you and the other *cunchunees* will learn her dances as well if his highness finds them pleasing."

"Yes, mistress," said the newcomer.

"Yes, mistress," echoed Rosamunde. The last thing she ever thought she would be doing here at the *Kala Mahal* was dancing. Perhaps she would end in dancing more than in servicing men!

"And tomorrow," Hussaini said to Laura," you will be

fitted with arm and leg gyves and a mace and you will be trained to guard his highness. You will remain bare other than the arm and leg protection, for his highness will wish to look at you and touch you whenever he desires."

Only arm and leg protection will do real good if the rest of me is as bare as a baby's butt and I have to do any actual protecting, Laura thought in disgust. But she said "Yes, mistress."

"You others will receive your assignments tomorrow as well," Hussaini continued. "Everyone will be needed to work, for a great future lies in front of us and you shall all be needed, both to take as many men as you can and to work hard at your assigned tasks." Her eyes seemed to glow as she looked into a vision that only she could see.

"Yes, mistress," they all said.

parminder

When Hussaini had left them alone, they stood up and moved to the piles of cushions, the Indian woman going to sit beside Rosamunde, who was to be her pupil.

"Do - you - speak - English?" Henrietta said slowly and loudly as if she was speaking to a very small child or an idiot.

The newcomer looked at her, puzzled. "I grew up in Bombay, a most international city," she said in English. "I not only speak English, but Portuguese as well as Urdu, Pushtu, my native Hindee and even French. Do you actually speak English?" she asked Henrietta.

Laura snorted and gave a great guffaw and even Ivy hid a smile.

The Indian woman said to Henrietta, who was looking distressed. "Please, I did not mean to hurt your feelings," Her sweet features were equally distressed. "but one becomes tired –"

"But Hetty needs to learn not to assume everyone's a dummy just because they ain't white!" said Laura.

"You name is not really 'chair', is it?" Rosamunde asked the newcomer, for Chowki meant 'chair' or 'shed' in English.

"No, of course not. All the slave names we are given here are chosen to be demeaning. They were used to call everybody by the name of body parts. You will find that there are women here called Breasts and Buttocks and so forth. But they have brought in so many new women lately that they have had to devise new names. My real name is Parminder, Parminder Mehra. We may use our real names when we are alone but in front of Hussaini or the others, if we are allowed to speak, we must use the slave names. This is very important, for they will beat you most severely if they hear otherwise," she said.

"Well, then," said Laura, "we need to make double

introductions."

Parminder carefully repeated each woman's real name as well as her slave name as Laura told them. She smiled shyly at Rosamunde and remarked that her real name was very pretty.

"My father told me that it meant 'Rose of the world,'" Rosamunde offered. Parminder repeated this as well.

"You said, Parminder, that they have brought in many new women lately," said Margaret. "Is there some reason for that?"

"I do not know," the Indian woman said. "but not only has the amount of women increased substantially but the Maharani and her son meet with many important men from all over Hind. We see them at *Durbar*, where we dance or go to be a fondle toy for his highness."

"A fondle toy? What the hell's that?" Laura asked.

"His highness must always have a woman's body to touch and play with while he sits in *Durba*. That is my term for what he does to us," Parminder explained. " Without this kind of stimulation and watching others couple, he cannot use his brides. He cannot use the dust of Kali to excite himself, as it makes a man lusty, but also renders him sterile while he is using it. They badly want an heir to the throne."

Durbar was a royal audience, to conduct business, or celebrate festivals, among other functions. It was usually held in either the *Diwan-i-Am,* the Hall of Public Audience, or in the *Diwan-i-Khas,* the Hall of private audience, but it was not unusual to hold *Durbar* out of doors or other places such as a tent.

"That's disgusting!" said Henrietta. "These people are completely depraved! Will he do that to us?" she asked, suddenly worried, actually meaning "Will he do that to *me?*"

"He prefers to use the dancers," Parminder. "When you become a dancer, Rose of the World, he will wish to fondle you."

"He's not the only one to behave like that," said Margaret. "One of Jim's friends who was in Bithur said that the ruler there, Nana Sahib, keeps a naked courtesan at his side all of the time and has his hands all over her, right in front of his guests. It's also said that he has secret galleries full of the most indecent works of art."

"Sort of like those," Laura said, waving her hand at a nearby *maithuna* statue that showed two lovers entwined in a position that one would have to be a contortionist by profession to emulate. "Only these ain't secret."

Parminder was able to answer many of their questions. In case Hussaini or any of the eunuchs was keeping an eye on them she and Rosamunde stood and she began to show dance moves to the new pupil, concentrating on the arm movements and how to move the stomach muscles so that the jewel imbedded in the navel flashed in the light.

The amount of jewelry worn, said Parminder, was for rank. It told Hussaini and the eunuchs exactly what function each woman had in the *Mahal*. All newcomers wore but what their little group wore, the anklets, bracelets on wrists and upper arms and thigh bracelets which served three functions: to make tying down easier, to identify them as new to the *Mahal*, and the bells were also to both attract men by letting them know that an available woman was near and to let the eunuchs know where they were, as the bells could be made to rung magically from a distance by the Maharani. When Rosamunde became a dancer, Parminder told them, her breasts would be pierced as hers were. As a guard, Laura would be provided with a brass and enamel collar and matching large earrings, as well as her gyves, while if Ivy became a maid, she would get three bangle bracelets, with chimes, to wear on each arm and ankle. And none of this jewelry could be removed. "I have tried many times," said Parminder, "especially to remove these," she looked down at the loops that passed through her breasts.

"How are those put in there?" Laura said "Don't see no holes, 'pears as if they just grew there, natural like."

"It is done by the Maharani in a ceremony before the shrine of Kali," said Parminder. "As are all body piercings. You will have only once before been in the room of Kali , when you were given the ruby. She collects the power from your stones while you sleep now, since you lay with but *sepoys* and *sowars* of no position or caste, but when you sleep with men who they themselves have power, such as officers and the guests who come here, you will have to go to the room of Kali and have the power drained."

Rosamunde gasped and stopped in the middle of a

movement."Blood magic!" she said in horror. "She's collecting power through the stones! Oh, why didn't I see this before! Blood magic is collected not just from torture and death but from pain and suffering and that certainly has been what has happened to us!" Inadvertently she touched the stone in her stomach and recoiled as if stung by a scorpion.

"What is it?" said Laura sharply.

"I saw *myself* – with all the men, and those *things* –" she gave a convulsive shudder.

Ivy touched her stone and then looked up a confused look on her face. "I don't see nothin'," she said.

Neither Margaret or Henrietta could see anything either and Laura got only a blurry impression of something. Parminder had never been able to 'see'.

"Stands to reason Rose would be the only one to see anything," said Laura. "She's a Witch and we ain't." She thought for a minute and said slowly "Bet I know when she came and stole that power! Did you ever notice how some nights we slept so sound and nodded off right after supper? We was just thinking how tired we were, but I bet that grub was drugged!"

"Dance again, Rose of the World!" said Parminder in a low voice, "A eunuch looks this way. And they are beginning to bring the food. Soon after this the men will come and choose the women they want. You all must try very hard to attract a man this night for Hussaini will be watching. You do not wish to be punished for not trying."

In the end they had little to worry about in this regard. Even Ivy was chosen by a very young *nauk*, a corporal, and they all went in different directions, not to meet again until dawn.

"This is the room of the dance," said Hussaini to Rosamunde as they entered the room. "Here you and Chowki will practice this afternoon until you are ready to go before his highness this evening."

Parminder was already present, in the familiar 'position', eyes downcast.

Rosamunde joined her after stealing a quick look

around the room. It was white and spacious and one wall had European style mirrors, floor to ceiling. On the opposite wall from this was a small raised dais and on one long wall a series of arched windows, barred, overlooked a garden.

"Practice hard. I shall expect to see sweat coating your body when I return," said Hussaini. "Her highness is pleased with you, Serai, and you shall have extra rice at your evening meal. You had a goodly number of men last night and this morning and already the *Halvidar* sergeant of infantry Om Singh has asked for you again this evening. You learned your lesson well from the *Bhutas!*" she laughed.

"Yes, mistress," said Rosamunde.

"I shall summon the musicians. Be certain that you pay them well!" With this Hussaini let them alone.

"Pay the musicians?" Rosamunde queried, as she and Parminder stood up.

"We must lay with them every time we wish to practice," Parminder explained. "Now that you are free to go about the *Mahal* you will find that everything must be paid for with the only coin we have, our bodies. I must warn you, Rose of the World, that Gopala, the *tabla* drum player, is a man of vile and perverted tastes. Show no emotion at any thing he asks you to do. Only try to do exactly as he orders you without reaction and he will soon cease his vilest tricks. He much enjoys your fear, loathing and disgust more than the act itself."

It seemed to Rosamunde that everyone here was a man of vile and perverted tastes.

"The three others will ask nothing other of you than regular usage. Indeed, the sitar player, Laxman, is elderly and sometimes will just touch your breasts and buttocks. It is required of the men here that they engage the women as much as is possible."

"Why?" Rosamunde asked. "I don't understand, what is all this power for? "

"It is to keep the throne, I think," said Parminder slowly. "Fifty years ago, the Maharani's grandfather stole this throne from its rightful holder, the Maharajah Mukesha Srivastava. The Rawits, her family, are not *badshahi*, royal, for her grandfather was only a *chobda*, a ceremonial mace bearer, but his daughter was very beautiful and she enticed the rightful Maharajah, over the objections of his family and his senior wife, to marry her, even though she was of low caste. It was said that this was done by magic. And this is how they have held the throne, both by magic and murder. The Maharani is the product of an incestuous union," she said, leaning close to Rosamunde and lowering her voice. "And she herself lay with her own brother and became with child by him. That child is the Maharajah. And as I told you, the reason that he must fondle beautiful women is that he finds it difficult to mount his virginal brides without previous excitement. He does that and watches his guests as they take the dancers and guard women. They want an heir badly but his highness cannot seem to impregnate his brides, even with all of his mother's magics. The few whose wombs have quickened have miscarried. One child was born dead. It was a boy and his highness had the mother killed because the child died."

"What happened to the family of the rightful Maharajah?" Rosamunde asked with a shudder. These people were horrible!

"Poison, accidents; in very little time there were none of them left. The Rawits are an evil race," said Parminder. She suddenly tensed at the sound of a door opening. "Here are the musicians. I am very sorry, Rose of the World, but the vile Gopalas will want you because you are new. I would take him for you if I could." Her eyes and voice were completely sincere.

Rosamunde felt drawn to Parminder. She felt that the Indian woman would become a friend. Parminder reached for her hand and gave it a reassuring squeeze as they turned to face the four men entering the room.

"Don't know who ever thought up this outfit, but he must have been blind drunk!" said Laura in disgust. She was modeling her guard's uniform for the rest of them while they were waiting for supper to be served.

It consisted of metal lower arm and leg protectors and a 'helmet' that was more decorative than useful. All were of beaten and chased highly polished brass with blue enamel work in a peacock feather design. A collar of the same material and design was about her throat, with a long teardrop of brass so polished that it looked like gold hung between her breasts. Long, heavy, matching earrings hung from each ear lobe. Real peacock feathers adorned the brass helmet.

"I can take these arm and leg things off and the earrings too, but the collar's permanent," said Laura."It won't budge a hair and that ain't for my sake, it's so they won't get in the way of the men's wants, Noori says." Noori was another of the guard women.

"These won't come off either," Margaret remarked. She now wore three bangle bracelets on each wrist, the lower one attached to a ring on her middle finger by two thin chains. She had been made a maid, as had Ivy, who wore the same jewelry.

Henrietta was completely disgusted about her 'job'. She had been made a laundress and would be going down to the river every morning to scrub laundry at the *ghat*. Hussaini assured her, maliciously, that she would still be able to take many men, for most of them swam there, or visited the shrine to Yuma, the river goddess. Henrietta now wore heavy anklets of brass bells and a narrow collar of bells as well.

Rosamunde's jewelry had changed the most. She now had a vast quantity of belled bangles on each arm and ankle. And in a ceremony through which she had been mercifully unconscious that afternoon, the Maharani had inserted the hoops into the aureoles of her breasts. These had bells upon them also: one large bell in the center and five gradually smaller bells on each side of it. The hoops were about fourteen inches in diameter. And tomorrow Parminder was going to start training her to make each hoop ring separately as she danced as this was one of his highness's favorite movements. In fact, it had been his idea.

"That must hurt," said Laura, looking at these hoops. "Can't imagine how they do it 'cause there ain't no entry and exit holes, it's just there like it was born part of you."

It did hurt, Rosamunde acknowledged, but Parminder had assured her the pain would fade in time. What would be far worse, Parminder now said, would be the attentions of his highness.

"For since you are new, he will want to study and to touch you," she said. "He will not take you, for his mother insists that he save his seed for his brides. But he will squeeze and pinch and poke and he has a particular fondness for breasts."

"I heard from Noori that he don't have any idea of how to touch a woman and thinks squeezing hard is what we like," Laura put in.

"This is true," said Parminder. "and, Rose of the World, you must not react to any of his fondling. If you pull away, or even murmur, he will be affronted and have you whipped badly. You must learn to control every facial movement for he likes us to be expressionless, particularly for the game of statues. And you too, Laura, for he will fondle you as well."

"Game of statues, huh? This is sounding like more fun by the moment!" drawled Laura. "Ain't we the lucky ones Rose? I get to guard the little bastard tonight and you get to dance for him and we both get to have the little jackass's hands all over us! I get to 'guard' him with this big old peacock fan, 'bout as much use in a fight as a feather. If someone was to attack him I could maybe tickle them to death."

"You must both, if he gives you permission to speak, lavish praise upon him, tell him how much you like for him to fondle you and that you much regret you cannot lay with him," cautioned Parminder.

Laura rolled her eyes.

"I am very thankful that I was made a maidservant!" said Margaret fervently.

"I only hope that he likes the new dance we have devised from he dances of your country," Parminder said worriedly. "He will have us whipped if he does not. Tomorrow I shall begin teaching you his favorite dances."

"Whot kind o' dancin' does 'e like?" asked Ivy.

"Need you ask?" demanded Henrietta. "Naked dancing girls? It will be obscene of course."

Parminder nodded. "The dances are very lewd."

"I don't know if I can," said Rosamunde. What she was going to do tonight was distressful enough. The ballet steps, done naked in front of the big mirror, had seemed very lascivious indeed.

"You have no choice," said Parminder sadly. "You must do as you are told or suffer the consequences."

Did she mean the *Bhutas?* Just the thought of that underground room and what had happened there was enough to make Rosamunde resolve that no matter how filthy and degrading the dance she would do it and do it as well as she was able.

"Dances with the male dancers are not done very often, for her highness and Hussaini keep the dancers busy in their beds," said Parminder. "Many of the eunuchs were bed men, former dancers, that the Maharani has tired of."

"Male dancers? With us?" repeated Rosamunde faintly. Oh no! She could only imagine what those would be like.

Parminder nodded.

"No wonder the eunuchs are such bright, happy little rays of sunshine!" said Laura. "Cut off in their prime 'cause someone got tired of 'em! God, what a place this is!"

"Perhaps you can hear some useful information in the *Durbar* room", Margaret suggested. "something that might be of help to us".

"That's if I don't end up killing the little bastard with his own fan. I hate him already and I ain't even met him yet," declared Laura.

Rosamunde could only hope that they would get some good from this new development. Otherwise it sounded as if her life was changing for the worse, although as Laura said, it couldn't seem to get much worse than it already was. Parminder had informed her that the Maharajah would offer her to all the men who frequented the *Durbar.* Another spell had been put on her this afternoon as well, a spell that would enable her to stay very, very still for a long time. She could not imagine what this could be for.

She could only view the coming evening with fear and loathing. She had never imagined that the time would come in which she would *not* want to dance.

30

jaganatha rawit

When Rosamunde first saw Jaganatha Rawit, the Maharajah of Jhaniput, all she could think of was a giant toad.

He was very short, shorter even than his mother. He would barely come up to Laura's shoulder. He had bulbous eyes that protruded from his head and a flat broad face with thick, fleshy lips. He looked, and so did the front of his coat, as if he very often drooled. His body was corpulent and encased in a too tight *achkan*, made of *kinkhwab*, a beautiful brocaded fabric of silk interwoven with gold and silver threads, adorned with ruby buttons, but pulling away from the bulging stomach. His high extravagant turban had a *sarpeche*, a turban jewel ornament, of a huge ruby surrounded by gold filigree. A white plume stood straight up from behind the *sarpeche*. Ropes of pearls and rubies set in gold adorned his almost non-existent neck and rings of rubies and diamonds covered his stubby little hands.

The *Diwan-i-Khas* that she was taken to that evening was a small, private hall, with the inevitable walls of black marble with limestone insets of extremely erotic murals and the acrobatic *maithuna* sculptures. One wall was open, held up by slender columns, opening in to a lush garden where stars gleamed on a formal *Cha Bagh,* a Mughal garden divided into 4 quarters, or *char*, by a cross of runnels and fountains.

From where Rosamunde stood with Parminder in a curtained alcove waiting to dance, she could hear the sound of the water in the fountains and smell the sweet scents of the flowers. She realized that it had been a long time since she had been out of doors, since she and Laura were tied out at night under the aegis of Wazid Ali.

It was late in the evening, sometime after midnight perhaps. A *ghurry*, a water clock, had just sounded, the gong ringing out above the noise in the *Diwan-i-Khas*. The

Maharajah liked his entertainments in the cool of the evening for he was a creature of night, Parminder had explained. His public *Durbar* took place in the late afternoon, when it was cooler, then he returned to bed for a few hours before rising again and expecting to be entertained. He remained in his bed or in a cooling pool during the heat of the day.

Rosamunde saw the moon rise as she waited and saw that it was full. As a Witch, Rosamunde was sensitive to the moon and all of its phases, but this was the first time she had seen it since before arriving at the *Mahal*. It had last been full, for her to see, on the 9th of May, the day before the world fell apart. Doing some calculations she realized with a jolt of shock that this meant it must be about the 7th of August. She had been a captive for nearly three months! This was somewhat of a surprise but she reflected that at times it seemed even longer.

The wait to perform seemed interminable. They stood there as a man who appeared to be some sort of Court jester imitated a British officer's stiff walk to giggles of glee from the Maharajah. His highness seemed very easily amused. There was also a puppet show, very simple, but greeted with squeals of joy and hand clapping, for it was extremely dirty in spite of its simplicity. A juggler, as well as a snake charmer, and a man who swallowed swords and breathed fire performed.

From where she and Parminder stood Rosamunde could see the *musnud,* the low dais of cushions and bolsters that served as a throne for the toad-like Prince. Two women, clad in the guards' 'uniform' each holding a peacock feather fan, stood on either side of him, and when he was not clapping or stuffing his face with a wide assortment of foodstuffs, he was fondling the one on the right.

It was Laura. Rosamunde admired how still her friend was remaining as those never motionless little hands squeezed and stroked her. Not a flicker of distaste showed on her face.

On a *gaddi*, a highly embroidered cushion, on a throne-like chair behind the *musnud,* sat the Maharani, with Hussaini on a low stool beside her. Hussaini wore tonight her usual low cut pantaloons, this time of silver, with red embroidery set with pearls and crystals in intricate patterns of florals and vines. She wore breast adornment of tassels, immense and of silver, which swung from nipple clamps and her jewelry, a multitude of bangle bracelets, a silver and ruby studded collar and matching arm and ankle jewelry, glittered in the flickering light of the torches.

The Maharani wore her usual red silk with a multitude of gold jewelry but tonight she wore a headdress like a golden helmet set with a huge ruby right over her eyes, looking as if she had a huge, glaring third eye. At no time did the cold, hard expression on her face change, no matter what entertainment was presented. She neither clapped nor laughed. Hussaini watched avidly, but with her eye on the Maharajah more often than on the performers.

At Hussaini's feet crouched Mabel Clutterbuck, taking it all in with a look of pleased excitement. Rosamunde felt sick when she looked at Mabel. How could that girl enjoy this so much? She was like an eager puppy with Hussaini, and looked up at the woman adoringly as the 'mistress' dropped an approving hand on her head for a brief moment. Laura had pointed out how puppy-like the Clutterbuck girl was and the resemblance was heightened when Hussaini threw a piece of *misre,* sugar candy, at her and Mabel caught it in her mouth out of the air, and looked pleased with herself when Hussaini laughed and said something to her. "*She is no doubt telling her what a good dog she is!*" Rosamunde though in disgust.

"I am next," Parminder whispered, interrupting her thoughts. "The *Nazir* beckons to me."

In most courts the *Nazir* was the one who served processes and other matters, but in the court of Jhaniput the *Nazir* was as well in charge of the entertainments, as his highness needed constant amusement.

He was a fussy little man called Abhay Baqar, who in addition to seeing Rosamunde dance and approve her appearance before his highness, had also taken her to his bed and told her that he expected her there every day that she performed. One of the prerequisites of his job was to bed all of the entertainers and he took full advantage of this.

The four musicians, old Laxman on the *sitar,* Harenda on the *sarod* resembling the large lute-like *sitar* but more resonant in tone, Dipake on the *tampura* which was an upright instrument which reminded Rosamunde of a bass and the *tabla* drum player, the vile Gopala, played music that to Western ears was very odd indeed. The *tampura* played a drone to establish the tonic note and the drum kept the *tala* or rhythmic cycle, which could arrange from 3 to more than 100 beats. Although there were many styles of *ragas*, which meant 'colours' or 'passions', each with its own mood, and many very ancient indeed, Indian music could be largely improvisational. The sound was exotic and since the *sitar* and the *sarod* resonated the sound seemed to linger in the air. There were also at the *Kala Mahal* players of the *bansuri* , a bamboo reed flute; *shehnai, which was* oboe-like, and the *sarangi,* a bowed instrument 'of a hundred colours', but the present quartet was the Maharajah's favorite, particularly when the members of his *nautch* danced for him.

Parminder ran out onto the floor and the musicians struck up.It was a fast beat, one to which she twisted and turned, moving her hips up and down rapidly and thrusting her breasts forward and making each belled hoop ring out. She leaned far backwards with her legs spread wide and thrust her hips up and down to the sensual, savage beat of the music. The bells on her arms and legs rang out in perfect time to the beat. She fell to the floor, still gyrating, and sensuously moving hips and breasts.

The Maharajah was almost hopping up and down on his cushion and clapping loudly as Parminder finished in the attitude of submission. "Marvelous!" he said in a high shrill voice. "Wonderful! She moves her body so well – it enflames me! Come here, girl," He beckoned to Parminder. "I would have you by me."

Parminder rose and went to kneel beside his cushions. He at once reached out and began feeling her body. "Mother! Only see how she sweats as if she had really been in bed with me, unlike my silly brides who can only scream and sob. This one would make a lusty bed mate!"

"No, my son," said the Maharani in her cold way." You cannot bed her. She cannot bear you a child."

He looked sulky at this, his lower lip stuck out like a small boy about to pout, but he continued to fondle Parminder.

"We have next a new *nautch* girl for your highness's pleasure and she will perform a dance of her homeland, a place from far to the north of Afghanistan," announced the *Nazir.*

Rosamunde wore a costume of sorts. After being oiled with the saffron based cream she had been lightly dusted with a gold powder so that she gleamed. Other than that the dancer's jewelry was her only adornment.

After a d*emi-plié,* she went out onto the floor in a series of *jeté,* the throwing step, in which the working leg is thrust into the air and appeared to have been thrown. She was very light on her feet and she appeared ethereal and almost airborne. Her elevation, or ability to attain height had always been great. She followed this with *glissades,* gliding steps, done rapidly, and then *entrechat,* interweaving, jumping into the air and rapidly crossing the legs before and behind one another.

She took great care, as Parminder had told her, to exhibit her body, which was not the aim of ballet as she had learned it. The beauty of the dance and the dancer's control and skill was everything.

But the Maharajah wanted everything to be lewd. He had to be sexually excited.

He made no noise as she began to do a series of *jetés grand,* throwing the legs ninety degrees with a corresponding high jump and she was afraid that he did not like what he saw. She dared to steal a look at him as she began the next movements and saw that his attention was riveted on her, his mouth open in a 'o' of astonishment.

When she finished, she sank to the ground in a graceful attitude and bowed her head.

The Maharajah came to his feet, clapping loudly. "Wonderful! Wonderful!" he called out. "Mother, was that not wonderfu, all of those leaps and bounds, I thought that she was flying! And her body is so beautiful. She looks as if she is the statue of Yuma at the *ghat* come to life! *Ideroo,* come here, girl!" He beckoned imperiously to Rosamunde after telling Parminder, "*Ijazat hai!* You may go!"

Rosamunde stood up and walked to the pile of cushions where she sank down in the proper attitude before his highness.

"You're even more beautiful close to me," he said, licking his lips. He reached out and grabbed her breasts with his hands. "See how high and firm they are!" he exulted "And they fit my hands perfectly! Hussaini!" he called out.

"Yes, highness?" the 'mistress' said.

"I shall want this one to be at my side at the *Durbar* tomorrow. We have many important guests there and I wish to see their faces when they see this beauty! Perhaps I shall allow them to throw dice for her favors and I shall watch them take her."

"That is an excellent idea, my son," approved his mother, "for you take a new bride tomorrow, and you will wish to be at your best for her."

"Am I to be rid of that whining Shoba at last? All she does is scream whenever I use her!" he said in disgust, squeezing Rosamunde hard. It was all she could do not to gasp. "Make certain that her new position is lowly, mother and that many lusty men use her, to teach her what privileges she no longer has, for failing to be pleased with my attentions and for failing to give me a son," he added viciously and inserting his pudgy fingers into the breast hoops, pulled on them until the chimes rang out. He giggled. "I shall keep you by me for the remainder of the night! Later you shall dance again." he said, leaning close to Rosamunde and revealing that in addition to his repulsive appearance his breath was also offensive, and his teeth were dark, due to endlessly chewing *betel* nuts.

"Shoba shall become the lowest of the low, a *mehterani,* a disposer of filth," said the Maharani, "and she will be put to the Untouchables and lowest caste men. She will be much shamed for she is a Brahmin."

"But barren!" said the Maharajah. "Such punishment is what she deserves, for we were assured that the women in her family are very fertile. But in four months her womb failed to quicken, even though I coupled with her many, many times."

"I do like this one!" he said very low, his hands beginning to roam. "Shall I tell you what I would like to do to you if I were able to take you to my bed, which I shall do once I have a son," he promised and began to enumerate every thing in that same low, excited voice as he kept touching.

"Goddamn frigging miserable little turd!" swore Laura forcefully. "Thank God his Ma won't let him bang us. I heard from Noori that he's hung like an elephant and has no idea what to do with –"

"Laura!" Margaret exclaimed, shocked. "I know we are living in a brothel and being used by countless men, but your language –!"

"Sorry, Maggie," said Laura with a rueful grin, "I sometimes forget I ain't in a mining camp. I ain't never been so poked and squeezed as that little bastard did me and once he had Rose in his slimy paws he was on her for hours!"

They had been brought back to their own corner of the *zenana* sometime around three in the morning and had managed a few hours sleep until being awoken by Pramoda Tandon and taken for their morning wash in the 'slaughter house'. They still were not allowed to wash themselves, for as Parminder had explained, everything here was done to humiliate and show how low their position was.

Rosamunde lay back on the pillows with one hand across her forehead. She was worn to the bone. All night long she had knelt or lay beside him, as he violated every sense of decency and modesty she possessed. At his command she had danced twice more, which had only served to exhaust her and excite him. Only when the Maharani decided that the court should go to bed was she allowed to escape and come back to the *zenana* with Laura. Now, washing and breakfast over, they were waiting for the guards who had been on night duty to come in after their meal. Although Rosamunde herself was only to be there three hours, for she was to go to Parminder to learn the game of statues, whatever that was, Hussaini had told her she had at least four men who wanted her before she could go.

"Last night, I was able to compute that it is now August 8th," she said, her voice flat and tired. "It's a Saturday."

"How could you do that?" said Henrietta suspiciously. She had already been at work, woken before dawn to go down to the river and wash clothing, where a number of men, bathing in the river, had found her attractive.

"The moon. It's at the full and by my computations if

it was rising almost half after midnight last night, it has to be August 8th today. The moon was at the full on May 9th at about 8 AM, on June 7th at a little after 11 P.M., on July 7th at 12:30 PM and now if it is rising full half after 12 AM, it had to be August 7th yesterday," said Rosamunde. She had learned her lunation well since she was a small child for every good Witch knew where the moon was in the sky, what phase it was in and the times of rising and setting and knew how to calculate it.

"But the Monsoon – !" Margaret objected, "How could we have missed seeing the Monsoon?"

"Because they made damn certain that if we were anywhere near a window it wasn't raining," said Laura viciously. "Told you they wanted to get all mixed up like! Noori told me that Monsoon was real late this year, the end of June. I knew that the time had gone along but I had no notion it was that far along! Three months in this hell hole!" She looked utterly disgusted. "And now we've got Mr. Hands to look forward to every night. And, Rose, you've got to go be fondled in front of his guests in *Durbar* this afternoon while I guard the slimy little rat. *Guard!* I'd like to *kill* him!" she snorted angrily. Then her tone changed. "I wished I knew where Pa and Nate are! Thought they'd be here long afore now!" she said wistfully.

Not even Henrietta wished to suggest to her that her father and *fiancé* might not be in a position to come looking for her, and even if they did come, what could two men do against an army the size of the one here?

Rosamunde wondered if Alan was looking for her. How would he ever find her? But if Alan came he could send all these people to Hell with one sweep of his hand for he was Adept class, one of the very few in the Six Nations, a powerful Wizard indeed. Even the Maharani's black magics could not stand up against him. He only had to find out where Rosamunde was and come and get her. He could rescue them all.

31

cruel awakening

Cathal had stayed with Alan every minute, faithfully and lovingly watching over him, supervising his care. When Alan lay quietly the familiar was with him, his head on his Wizard's chest, and when Alan tossed violently Cathal stayed on the pillow, but always near enough to put a paw on Alan to try and soothe him.

Remembering the many times that Peter Huggin had had to remain in bed after one of the many surgeries he suffered on his lame leg, Cathal insisted on Alan's limbs being massaged so that his muscles would not atrophy. He took recipes from the Wizard's Medical Emergency book for building a Wizard's strength up after a Great Working, which very often caused weakness and collapse, and had the Mahal's cook make them up. He directed Jai and Ravi in making herbal potions and told them how to get them, and food, down Alan's throat.

Therefore it was Cathal who was with Alan when he first showed signs of rejoining the world after a terrifying thirteen weeks of wandering somewhere beyond their ken.

And it had not been a pleasant wandering. His mutterings were always of blood and violence and horror. Only Cathal understood what Alan said, as for some strange reason he raved mainly in Gaelic.

It was early in the morning and an exhausted Jai lay on a mat near Alan's bed. Cathal had insisted that Ravi, who spent a great deal of time at the bedside, go to bed earlier in the evening, for he too was tired out from watching and worrying.

Cathal was laying close beside Alan, his head on his Wizard's chest. Alan had been very quiet recently, with little of the violent outbursts that had so frightened them earlier. The outbreaks on both June 27th and two weeks again after that date had been particularly ungovernable.

The ferret was half asleep when he felt Alan stir and

half articulate a sound and then as he sat up,wide awake now, the familiar saw Alan's eyes open, very briefly, and then fall shut again as if that small movement had exhausted him.

"Alan?" said Cathal hopefully. "Are you awake?"

'What's wrong?" Alan said on the thread of a whisper, rolling his head on the pillow and then wincing as if the movement hurt him.

"You've been very,very ill," Cathal said. "We've been so worried —"

Alan opened his eyes again and flinched as thunder pealed and lightning followed it almost immediately out of doors. Even through the lowered *chiks* the lightning lit up the sky. The rain was torrential in volume, a true Monsoon rain.

"Where are we, Cathal?" Alan said in confusion. "This isn't my room."

"We're in India, at Ravi's home," Cathal said in worried tones. Alan sounded as if he had no idea where he was or what had happened to him.

"India —" Alan repeated as if he had never heard the word before. "How long —?"

Cathal correctly interpreted this inquiry to mean "How long have I been ill?" and he answered "Almost three months."

Alan moved restlessly and painfully. "Three months!" he repeated, still in a hoarse whisper. "How could I have been ill for three months?" He frowned and said "Cathal, I remember now. What about Rosamunde? Is she here? Did Ram Dass bring her back? Can I see her? I dreamed about her, she was in terrible danger! Please, go and get her!" He turned his head and looked at his familiar anxiously.

Cathal did not know what to say. All the inhabitants of the *Mahal* had been in a sate of extreme distress since Ram Dass had returned from the south with unbelievably grim news. The servant had taken so long to return that Ravi and his father had almost given up on seeing him again.They were certain that something fatal had happened to him.

"I think I had better go and get Ravi," the ferret said. "I'll wake Jai and have him make you some tea. We'll talk when I get back with Ravi,"

"The whole of Hindustan seems to have gone up in flames," said Ravi, watching Alan's face carefully. When told that Rosamunde had disappeared, his face had gone completely blank and it was as if he had gone somewhere else for a moment, some place that was not at all to his liking. He had then seemed to recover and asked for all of the news.

None of it was good. Ram Dass had brought back the news of the massacres at Meerut, Malabad and Delhi, and the news of more revolts in Muttra, Lucknow, Cawnpore and Allahabad, of the massacre at Jhansi, and the first massacre at the Satichaura Ghat in Cawnpore and two weeks later Nana Sahib's slaughter of over two hundred women and children in the Women's House in Cawnpore. Alan heard how Lucknow was under siege, and how Sir Henry Lawrence, Chief Commissioner of Oudh and recently appointed Brigadier General, had died there. Nana Sahib had been defeated in battle at Cawnpore on July 16th, by Henry Havelock's forces, but the Nana had not been captured. He had disappeared, and, it was said, was gathering a huge force to drive the British from India. Nana Sahib was a black magician, the whispers ran. Delhi was still in rebel hands and the madness of the *shaitan ka haw,* the devil's wind, still blew hot over the land.

The Maharajah and his two other sons sat in on this recital, looking grim. Ram Dass, who seemed to have aged ten years since Alan last saw him, stood quietly, waiting to speak to Alan when Ravi had finished.

"I have issued a *parwana,* an edict," said the Maharajah Zahallah, "that no one in this kingdom is to begin *Jihad* or to attempt an assault upon any *feringhi,* else he will die a most horrible death. This stupidity will not come to Ranijhat! With the killing of the innocents at Cawnpore Nana Sahib has made certain that Allah will turn his face from his cause. They cannot win against the might of *Belait.* Ravi has told us of the mighty factories that can produce many weapons, and the amount of soldiers that can be drawn from Canada and other places." He shook his head. "No, peaceful negotiation is the best thing, to seek to redress grievances in dialogue, not bloodshed. Things will be all the worse for my country after this madness has passed."

With great difficulty Alan had been propped up upon

a stack of pillows so that he could watch the speakers. He was terribly weak. He could not even hold the cup of tea that Jai had made for him, the servant had to hold it to his lips as raising his hand had proved impossible for Alan. He had to carefully concentrate on what Ravi had been saying as his attention seemed to wander off and his body wanted to seek oblivion in sleep.

He had to know about Rosamunde. Ram Dass had only so far said that he had been unable to find her. He had found out hat her husband had been killed. His orderly, Manu Patel, had boasted of doing the deed.

Now Alan looked at Ram Dass, his heart in his eyes, "Tell me," he said "please, Ram Dass, tell me what you found out about Rosamunde."

Ran Dass bowed his head as he stood at the foot of the bed. "At the first, Stillfield *Sahib*, I could find no trace of her. She was not with the dead at Malabad and I talked with all of the people I could find who had fled that cursed place. I spoke to her *ayah*, a woman called Sita, who said that the *mem* had ridden towards the city. I found her *syce*, half dead from trying to defend some troopers' children whose only crime was that their fathers were *Angrezi*, and he confirmed that the *mem-sahib* had gone to the home of her friend, Ameera Sharma who dwelt in the *Hirren Mahal*. The *Mahal* was deserted and had been looted but the *mem's* horse and her saddle were in the stables. A neighbor saw four women taken away by the slaver Wazid Ali. None of them were *Angrezi* but there was one whom the neighbor had never seen before. This woman seems to have little to do other than watch her neighbors." He paused and then continued. "I had been hearing tales of how the *Angrezi-log* were disguising themselves to try and avoid slaughter by passing as persons of Hind and I wondered if the *mem* had done so. I called upon my cousins on my mother's side to help me find the slaver and when we found his trail we began inquiring for a woman of Hind with eyes the colour of the flowers of the *Nar Kachura* the black turmeric. To the north of Delhi we found a man who well remembered her and I am sorry to tell this, *sahib*, but he remembered her because he paid an entire *rupee* to lay with her. She fought him like a tigress, he said, and wished to buy her for his *zenana*, but Wazid Ali said that he had not enough money to buy her for she was to go to Jhaniput where she would fetch a *lakh* of *rupees.*"

Alan closed his eyes and seemed to sink deep into the pillows. For one moment Ravi though that he had fainted, but Alan at last said "God! Rosamunde!"

"Jhaniput! This is ill news!" said the Maharajah. "It is a bad place if even half the rumors one hears are true. The Maharajah lives for sexual pleasure I have heard and he has a monstrous *zenana* and has debauched many an unwilling woman."

"Father, did you not tell me that the Maharajah Jaganatha's father tried to arrange a marriage between you and his daughter?" said Dhaval.

"Yes, I was no older than you are, my son, when the marriage was proposed. At seventeen it was time I was married and at first my father looked with favor on the match, for the dowry was large, until we journeyed to Jhaniput. He discovered that he did not care for the Rawits and did not wish for their blood to pollute ours. I found the *Rajkumari* repulsive as well. It was not only that her face and form were not pleasing but she had a cruel, ugly soul. I saw her whip a serving wench for tripping and spilling a tray, and it was the *Yuveraj* who tripped her up. The *Rajkumari* beat the girl until her back ran with blood and she was screaming. I tried to stop her and she turned the whip on me. If her father had not come into the room...this Dipti Rawit was as cold as the snows on the top of the mountains and I thought then that I would l rather lay in the embrace of the snows. I heard later, though I do not know how true this is, that she lay with her own brother in order to get a child, for no man would have her, save those she commanded to her bed and they were all of low caste and not royal."

And Rosamunde had fallen into the hands of these people? Alan thought in despair.

Ravi, looking at his friend's face, was suddenly worried. Alan's eyes were enormous in his now very thin face and his expression was one of immense mental pain. "I must get from this bed!" he said "I have to find Rosamunde and take her away from them."

"My son," said the Maharajah heavily. "I will give you the advice I would give my own sons in like circumstances.

Forget this woman. If she is in the hands of Jhaniput she has been ruined in more ways than you can imagine. She has more than likely been completely debauched by the Maharajah and may be part of his *zenana* now; she may even be with child by him, or by one of his minions. It is known that he shares his women with all who come to his *Durbar*, and that women are used in open *Durbar* as a form of sport. I have heard tales that they are kept naked and subjected to the grossest indecencies."

"All the more reason I have to rescue her," said Alan, closing his eyes as a wave of weakness and despair, swept over him. "I can't leave her to that! She is my cousin. I love her." he added in an almost inaudible voice.

He had to get well – he had to get strong – and hope that his magic returned as he healed. Right now he could feel only the vaguest stirring of the power that had once been his to command. He could not leave Rosamunde to that fate – he could not!

The rain had ceased, leaving as a violent storm so often does, a crystal clear sky. Now the sun was setting in a beautiful palette of brilliant colours, turning everything it touched to fire. From the city below drifted up the call of the *muezzin* from his perch high in the *minaret,* the tower of a *Musjid,* a mosque, borne on the evening breeze: *"La Ill-ah ha! il-ah ho*! There is no God but God!"*, calling the faithful to prayer.

Save for Cathal, Alan was alone. He had dismissed Jai so that he young Mussulman could make his devotions.

He had been able to eat only a little of a strengthening meal made for him especially by the Mahal's cook, who had delivered it to the young *sahib* in his own hands. To his consternation, Alan was unable to feed himself. He was so weak that lifting his head or his hands proved impossible. Looking down at his hands he thought they belonged to someone else, pale, feeble and transparent. He could only imagine what he looked like, for Ravi had refused to give him a mirror. He hadn't much beard, for the Elfin blood that came to him through his father's birth mother, Elfrida Westhame, kept his whiskers sparse. There was no such thing as a bearded Elf.

His body felt wasted and his legs were weak as well. He had blessed Cathal for ordering the daily massages, otherwise he might be in even more trouble.

All he could think of was Rosamunde, and what she must be suffering. Did she imagine that he had deserted her, that he cared nothing for her plight? That because she had more than likely been raped he would abandon her to her fate, casting her aside because she was now what their society termed a fallen woman?

All he wanted to do was to find her, to take her away from anyone who would hurt her and protect her from being hurt ever again. He thought of what the Maharajah had said, of the depravity of the court of Jhaniput.

In his mind's eye he could see her face, imagined how badly she had been treated and a choking lump seemed to settle in his chest, making it difficult to breathe. His eyes pricked with tears and he began to shudder, as sobs he could not stop began to overtake him. It was not only the easy tears of the invalid, but a deep anguish.

Cathal, who had been dozing, stirred and awoke to find Alan on his side in the pillows, wasted hands brought with effort up to his face, moaning one word over and over. "Alan!" said the ferret, appalled.

The word he was repeating in grief was "Rosamunde".

The ferret lay a paw on his Wizard's shoulder as Alan gave vent to his emotions. Cathal said nothing, only tried to make his sympathy felt.

At long last Alan began to regain his control and said, drawing the sleeve of his nightshirt across his eyes, "I'm all right Cathal, I just thought of her –"

Cathal went to the bedside table inlaid with mother of pearl and picked up a handkerchief in his mouth and offered it to Alan.

"Thank you," said his Wizard. When he had, with difficulty, dabbed at his face he said, "I'm a stupid fool, Cathal. I've just had an epiphany, when I realized that Rosamunde might be lost to me I knew that I love her, not as my cousin, but as a woman, the woman I want to marry, to spend the rest of my life with. I want to go and save her and look at me! I cannot sit up in bed without feeling faint!" In his voice was self loathing.

"If I was not such a stupid fool she would have been *my* wife by now, not DeLacey's, and she would be safe here with me in this beautiful place instead of being in the hands of a slaver! I should never have left her there! I shall never forgive myself for that. I ought to have known better! How could I not know until just now that I love her? "

Cathal had no answer for this, he had often discussed the vagaries of their humans' behavior with Sinéad and Brendan. All three of the animals were aware of Rosamunde's feelings for Alan, only Alan himself, they had decided, was blind to her love for him, and she had forbidden them to tell him of it. They thought it ludicrous that she did not just tell him how she felt, but she said that this was impossible, a lady did not do that. Humans, they had decided, had a tendency to complicate what should be the simplest and most natural of matters.

"I have to get well," Alan said in a determined voice. "I have to go and find her, and I have to get my magic back."

Cathal had the feeling that the first two on this list were going to be far easier to accomplish than the latter. But now, looking at Alan, he was not even certain that the first item was realistic. Alan was a shadow of himself and getting back on his feet was not going to be easy.

32

coping

Sacha Kustodiev left his dragon, Cynara in the lot provided for dragon traffic to the side of the Dublin Police Station. "This won't take long, sweetheart," he said to Cynara as he swung down from her saddle and slid down her foreleg.

"At least you hope it won't," she said dryly.

Sacha grinned. Cynara was a far different dragon than the frightened, shy creature he had rescued from the mines in New Spain some thirteen years ago. Being treated with love and respect and mating with Lakota had given her confidence and made her unafraid to speak her mind.

"I'm just glad he had the good sense to scry me, and not his father or uncle," he said "They've enough in their dish at the moment." He patted the front of his buckskins to make certain that he had not gone off without his cheque book. "We'll go home after this. There's not much going on at the Incubatory today and MacKenzie can handle anything that comes up. He can scry me if there are any problems. And I am going to have to have a long talk with certain persons which is best done at home in private"

Cynara nodded. There was a rather rare Manx Yellow due to hatch soon, but the egg had assured her that he would not be emerging for another week.

Leaving her behind, Sacha entered the police station, hoping that he would not meet any of those on the force that he knew. He would just as soon keep the current problem as private as was possible for the time being.

He was in luck. The desk sergeant was someone new, and after ascertaining that Sacha was who he said he was, allowed the wheels of justice to proceed.

Fifteen minutes later, after paying a stiff fine to the Clerk, Sacha's nephew Alex Stillfield was released into his care.

"Ye're being in luck, young sir," said the constable who brought Alex out of the cells, as he unlocked the silver handcuffs, "'Tis being said that the law will be takin a dimmer view of your crime very soon and ye might have had to be after doing a stiffish sentence!"

Alex looked both abashed and rather scared as he rubbed at his wrists where the cuffs had been. One sleeve of his blue jacket was torn and his cravat was missing. He looked at his uncle swiftly and then lowered his head as he saw Sacha's face and said in a low voice, "Thanks for coming, Uncle Sacha. I couldn't scry Papa."

"No, because you knew he'd be over the roof about this!" Sacha interrupted. "Cynara's waiting. You're coming home with me for a bit. We'll get you cleaned up. That's a beautiful black eye you're getting, by the way, and I want to have a little talk with you."

Alex flushed and hung his head. He now realized that what he had done was foolish but it had seemed at the time to be the only answer.

He was just about to turn eighteen and while he had the height of his father, he bore no other resemblance to Simon, for he was very dark, with deep brown hair that seemed almost black, and green eyes. He had extremely Elfin looks, even to slightly pointed ears that he allowed his curling hair to cover most of the time. He had just graduated from the Tara Druidry and was to go to Oxford, to the College of Merlin, in the coming autumn.

Since Sacha did not seem predisposed to speak any further, Alex followed his uncle in silence and greeted Cynara slightly shamefaced. She gave him a look but did not say anything, and they mounted and flew out to Sacha's home in silence.

Like most of the family, Sacha, when he married, had built a house to the south of Dublin. He and his wife called the villa, built in the now rather old fashioned cottage *ornée* style, Mikhailovskoe, after his childhood home in Russia. It was a simple, unpretentious place, built more for their comfort than for fashion and set amidst nature, with many trees, lovely vistas and informal gardens.

Cynara landed near the dragon pen, and informed Sacha that she would ask one of the grooms to unharness her and order some hot tea for her. Even on this August day the air was chilly for it had been raining since yesterday and although the rain had just stopped the damp still lingered.

The dragon pen was separated from the house by several flower beds, now at the height of summer splendor. A narrow gravel path ran through the flowers, up to the house. Sacha led Alex up this way, for it went to the back of the house where French doors stood ajar looking out on to a terrace that on a sunny day, was most inviting for sitting out of doors, with basket chairs, umbrellas and low tables, set amidst pots of flowering plants and lush greenery. The chairs were magiced so that they were always dry and the wicker never squeaked from being exposed to the elements.

Sacha had been married now for not quite two years, and his choice of a bride had surprised everyone, but made them quite happy as well.

A quick step sounded and Sacha's wife, in a fashionable *basque* gown and wearing a pretty lace cap over her dark blonde ringlets joined them, looking disturbed. "Sacha! Is something wrong? You're home so early!" Then she caught a glimpse of the young man behind her husband, who seemed to be trying to hide behind Sacha and she gave a startled gasp. "Alex! You look as if you've been in a fight!"

"Hello, Aunt Holly," Alex said rather awkwardly. "I was in a kind of fight," he admitted as she came up to him, much distressed and look at his rapidly blackening eye and the torn sleeve of his jacket and missing cravat.

It had taken Sacha a long time to convince Holly that he loved her and could think of no greater happiness than to marry her. She was older than he was, and she had for a long while considered herself on the shelf, too plain and shy to attract a man. But she had at last admitted that she had loved him since he was eighteen and she was twenty two. Now they had been most happily married for nearly two years and upstairs in the nursery resided six month old Mikhail Alexandrovich Kustodiev.

"This young idiot," said Sacha, "tried to enlist today, Holly, to go out to India."

"But didn't they forbid magical persons from enlisting? " Holly said, surprised. "How did you ever hope, Alex, to pass yourself off as a non-magical?"

"I didn't know they'd have an aura reader there!" he said defensively. "I thought I could give them a made-up name –" adding as his aunt and his uncle looked at him in disbelief at his foolishness. "Well, I had to do *something*! You can't imagine what it is like at home! Papa and Mama barely speak and Mama cries all night long and Jack is so short tempered. Irina spends all her time in front of the *iconostasis* praying! Even Lakota and the dogs and the familiars...I just couldn't bear it any more! I had to try and do something to help and try and find Alan and Rosamunde!"

"And your familiar didn't try to talk you out of this? If they had accepted you in the Army what were you going to do with Grendel? Leave her behind? It would have killed her, Alex! She is most particularly attached to you!" said Sacha severely.

Grendel was Alex's hedgehog familiar. He had the grace to look conscience stricken as he thought of her. "I didn't tell her," he admitted. "She was going out to see her family today for a long visit before we left for Oxford."

"And that's another thing," said Sacha sternly. "what about your education? The term of enlistment in the army is ten years! Did you think that you could l just go out to India, heroically find your brother and your cousin and come home?"

Alex hung his head. He had not really thought this through and everything that Sacha said was right. It had been a purely emotional response.

"Stop berating him, Sacha," said Holly. "I think he knows now how silly he was."

Turning to Alex she said "Let me get you something for that eye, Alex, and I shall try and mend your coat. I don't know what to do about your cravat, as Sacha never wears one! Perhaps one of the menservants...I shall ask Mac Conraoi." She rang the bell as she spoke and when the butler appeared she asked him to fetch her medical box and some tea for everyone and what could they do about Mr. Alex's cravat? A few moments later Alex was sitting in a wing chair in front of the fire in his shirt sleeves, while Holly took his coat and opened her sewing box.

Alex looked uneasily at his uncle. There was another matter that had to be spoken of. "Did you have to pay a fine, Uncle Sacha?" he asked hesitantly.

"Two hundred and fifty pounds," said Sacha as Alex gasped and looked a little sick. That was a great deal more than his allowance and he could not ask or expect his father to pay this fine. And he knew that his father would *not* pay it, not for something so foolish.

"You're very lucky, Alex," Sacha went on "for the sergeant was telling me that a new law is shortly taking effect that is going to make it a criminal offense for persons on the forbidden list to try and join the services, stiffer punishment than a fine! You are only just shy of serving a prison term. Even Chenevix would probably not have been able to get you off."

"I'll pay you back," his nephew promised, blanching at the thought of going to prison.

"You most certainly will!" Sacha stated. "Resign yourself to working for me at the Incubatory until this is paid off, and that means every holiday and the Long Vacation as well."

"How did you get the black eye, Alex?" his aunt asked, putting her small neat stitches into the sleeve of his coat, which had fortunately ripped along the seam.

"The recruiting sergeant didn't like the fact that I lied to him," Alex admitted. "He said he was going to teach me a lesson and as he was a non-magical I couldn't use magic on him."

"A fact that the sergeant was no doubt acquainted with," said Sacha dryly. He then said, far more gently, "Believe me, Alex, we understand what you are going through. We're just as upset as you are. The whole family is. Julia scryed this morning and told us that Stuart has been ordered to take an indefinite leave, as he is completely ineffectual at his job. Your grandparents are beside themselves and as for Chenevix, he's had another heart attack, the first in years. He's fine –" he put up a hand as Alex started from his chair, a look of horror on his face, "but the last thing any of us need is you or Jack haring off to India on a foolhardy quest!"

"Jack?" Alex said in surprise. "Jack tried to go out as well? He's non- magical –" He sank back down into his chair.

"Even though he gave up studying Wizardry he still has a magical aura and could be affected by the polluted ley lines. He told me that he volunteered his services as a veterinary surgeon but they turned him down, not only for his aura, but the for fact that he knows nothing about camels or elephants. Jack's practice is mainly cats, dogs and horses, familiars, and dragons, most of which is not needed in India."

The door to the room opened and the butler entered, followed by two footmen. One bore a laden tea tray and placed this on a low table in front of Holly. Another footman carried a wooden chest which he gave to Holly as she put aside the now mended jacket.

Across his arm the butler bore a strip of linen. "I have taken the liberty, my lady, of supplying Master Alex with one of my own cravats. I trust he will find it satisfactory."

Marrying Sacha, who was her adopted brother Simon's brother-in-law, had made Holly a Russian Countess, although Sacha seldom used the title. But the butler was most conscious of all the proprieties and never failed to address his employers as 'my lord' and 'my lady" and made certain that the other members of the household did so as well.

Holly took a small jar out of the chest of arnica, with a touch of magic. She went to Alex and tilted his head up to the fire light so that she could see to apply the cream to his damaged eye. "This should make it fade well before you have to go home," she said.

Alex winced. in spite of her gentle touch "What shall I tell my parents?"

"Nothing," said Sacha. "They don't need any more worries, Alex."

"But how can I go off to Oxford if Alan and Rosamunde are still missing?" Alex asked.

"And how would sitting around here help them? I've actually had an idea, Alex, I haven't talked this over with your father or Stuart as yet, but it may work. I wrote to Anatoly Tcherepin in Saint Petersburg and asked him to write back, demanding my presence in Russia for some urgent reason. Since I have a dual citizenship here in Ireland and Russia I should be able to get a diplomatic pass to fly out to Russia. From there I plan to go to India," Sacha helped himself to a slice of Dundee cake.

"But the ley lines!" Alex protested. Holly had finished applying the ointment to his eye and a tingling sensation told him that already it was doing its work. Alex absently accepted a cup of tea from his aunt as he stared at his uncle in surprise.

"I am willing to wager a very large sum of money on the fact that they will not effect me," said Sacha calmly. "I am completely immune to Cold Iron and when I was out in New Spain there were a lot of magical traps set by the rogue Wizards of the Inquisition that harmed everyone but me."

Alex's mother Tatya was also immune to the poisonous effects of Cold Iron that was so dangerous for Wizards and Witches who had the Old Blood, Celtic mingled with that of the Elf folk, the *Sidhe*. No one understood why this immunity but Sacha and his sister were Russian, not Celts, and it was not even understood where their magic came from. Alan had been slightly immune when he was younger, but this protection had diminished as he became older. To Alex's dismay, he himself had no immunity at all and as far as they could tell, neither did Irina or Jack.

"I'm the logical person to go out there, as there isn't anyone else," said Sacha, biting into another thick slice of cake, having made short work of the first one. "Stuart even asked Oberon for his help –"

"Uncle Stuart asked the Elves for help?" Alex's eyes grew round. "What did the Elf King say?"

"That polluted ley lines were even more poisonous to Elves than they are to us. Otherwise, he said, he would be glad to help. Oberon thinks highly of both Alan and Rosamunde. That's another thing you did not think of, Alex. The Elfin strain is very strong in you. You even look more Elfin that most of the others. You might be far too ill to help anyone out there in India. That's why it is best that I go. Not a word of this to anyone else, now," Sacha cautioned. "I have to hear from Anatoly first and arrange for a diplomatic passport and probably be obliged to get permission to travel outside the country. Thank goodness the war with Russia is over!" The recent Crimean war had been difficult for Sacha and Tatya, to have their native country and their adopted country enemies.

"Do you think they are still alive, Uncle Sacha?" said Alex in a low voice. "I've been reading the papers every day and the news out of India is terrible! Atrocities, murders, rapes, women and children slaughtered...Papa keeps urging Mama not to read the journals but she cannot stop reading them any more than I can."

"I don't know, Alex," said Sacha honestly. "We've heard nothing from either one of them. Rosamunde was in the thick of it but Alan was far to the north. But we have been unable to get a message to him or from him. She is officially listed as 'missing', which could mean that she is in hiding someplace, waiting for this madness to blow over. Rosamunde is a very clever girl. And I am willing to hazard a guess that Alan is out looking for her at this very minute."

What Sacha did not tell Alex was what he had read about the effect of poisoned ley lines: the draining, the illness they caused in a Witch or Wizard. Sacha was very much afraid that even if Alan and Rosamunde lived they would be extremely ill, or even, if not murdered by mutineers, then dead of exposure to the pollution.

Sinéad looked out at the pouring rain and sighed. The Monsoon had slowed them down further.

The rivers were numerous in this part of the world and were all swollen with heavy rain. The earlier dust, so choking and cloying, had turned to mud, thick, filthy mud that slowed even Bharat's mighty legs.

Thanks to Niaz they now had a little tent. He had been able to trade some of Bharat's harness, no longer needed, for it. And thank goodness for it as else wise they would have been drenched to the skin and like most cats, Sinéad hated being wet.

She shared the tent with Niaz, Molly, and Hari. It was too small to contain the elephant. At any rate, he claimed to enjoy being out in the rain and moved beneath the leaves of a tree when he grew tired of the torrent of water that poured from the sky.

Isha remained stubbornly apart from the humans. He would rather stay wet and miserable in a tree than share the tent with them. Sinéad though he was mad and told him so. She only received a sour look for her pains.

Sinéad turned back to the map she had been perusing. On one of his forays into villages near the jungle Niaz had found a deserted bungalow and brought back the map. This was a true treasure as far as Sinéad was concerned. Being able to see where they had been and were going was a great comfort. She was also able to compute how far they had come.

It was a pathetic total, she thought in despair, only a little over two hundred miles. They had been lost more than once, mostly due to running and hiding from men on the move, who were going south to join the ongoing fighting.

And these had not just been native troops but British as well. Niaz had heard in one village that the Corps of Guides was marching from Mardan in the Punjab to the relief of Delhi. Molly did not want to meet native troops, while Niaz wanted to avoid the British. Many times they had been forced to hide, and then making only a mile or two in a day's travel.

The landscape was changing as well for they were getting near to Jullundar, where, if Sinéad was reading the map correctly, the terrain would start to become mountainous and their route would probably take them through the Khyber Pass. That would further slow their progress, for it was rough terrain.

It was another 234 miles to Rawalpindi from Jullundar, beyond which lay the 'goat track' to Ranijhat. Ranijhat was not even marked on this map.

Sinéad was tortured as to what might be happening to Rosamunde. She felt that her Witch was in terrible trouble somehow and had nightmares about what might have happened. She was also worried that Rosamunde thought that she, Sinéad, was dead, for the familiar had awakened on that rubbish heap, as if tossed away like a carcass. What if Rosamunde had seen that? What must she have thought?

What too, if Alan had heard about what had happened at Malabad and had gone to look for Rosamunde? Sinéad had important information for him about who had taken Rosamunde away. And she wanted to go with Alan when he set out after Rosamunde. She *had* to go with him! But at this pace, they might never get there. And she had no idea as to how to go on any faster.

jehan the magician

In the end it was nearly another month before Alan could even begin to try and rescue Rosamunde.

His recovery was slow. It took days before he could sit up by himself and almost as long before he could hold a cup to drink from for more than a moment. It was above a week before he could try and walk and then he would have fallen if not for the support of Jai's arm. The room showed a distressing tendency to do Catherine wheels around him.

Ravi watched anxiously as Alan forced himself beyond what the Prince considered wise. The *Hakim* shook his head over the young *sahib*, saying that he would put himself into his grave.

But always the thought of Rosamunde was driving him onwards. The news they had from the outside world was sporadic at best and little was encouraging. They did hear that Henry Havelock had a victory against the rebel forces at Unao, and had triumphed in another engagement at Bashiratganj, and that a detachment of the Guides had reached Delhi, having marched 580 miles in just under twenty-one days. But Delhi was still in the hands of the rebels and Lucknow was still under siege. All Hindustan seemed in the grip of chaos.

The Maharajah had sent a servant to Bombay, hoping to be able to contact Alan's family from there. The man had not returned as yet for it was a long way to go, under hazardous traveling conditions. And there was very little mail coming to Ranijhat.

At night, when he was alone with Cathal, Alan tried to recapture his magic and this was even less successful than his recovery of health.

He had a little left: he could make a mage light and warm or chill things and he could fetch objects and send them across the room, and create colours in the air and a few other minor things as well as cast illusions but the major arcana were beyond his strength.

"It's as if I were just a rank beginner, just starting out to learn magic!" he complained to Ravi one day as they sat out of doors in the *baradai*, a Mughal style open pavilion with three doors on each side. This sat in the *Mentab Bagh*, the moonlit garden, which was lovely by day, but extraordinary by night.

Alan had been practicing waking a distance all morning, so much so that his hair and shirt were wet with sweat, his shirt plastered to his body. Jai had hovered anxiously as Alan forced himself to walk further and further about the garden. Cathal had put his paws over his face each time it looked as if Alan would fall.

Ravi had finally managed to persuade Alan to sit down and rest and had sent Jai for tea. Now he said carefully, "Alan, perhaps you are pushing yourself too hard? Perhaps you need more time?"

Alan shook his head, and pushed his damp hair off his forehead. "I can't! When I think of what might be happening to her, I *have* to get well! I *have* to get strong and go after her! There's no one else who can do it." He had already refused the Maharajah's offer of an armed force. The Ranijhat standing army was small and made up of elderly retainers. At any rate, Alan did not want to start another war. It was best that he do this himself.

"I've given a great deal of thought to what I might do and I shall first offer to buy her freedom," Alan said.

"I have hesitated to tell you this," said Ravi, in a low voice," but my father sent a courier to Jhaniput a week since with an offer to buy several women, not wishing to let them know that we were particularly interested in Rosamunde, and it was flatly refused. None of the women are for sale for any sum. "There are not enough *rupees* in all of Hind", was the way the Nazir refused the offer."

Alan stared at him in consternation. "But why? Why would they not sell, if I were to offer a handsome sum? I can pay anything that they want. Grandfather Chenevix gave me a letter of credit and I know that he would pay any sum for Rosamunde's safety, even a million pounds sterling if needs be!"

Ravi spread his hands helplessly, "I know not," he

said. "but I shall tell you of several matters the courier observed whilst at *Durbar*. The Maharajah needs constant amusement. He pays little attention to the petitioners and the governing of his principality. It is the Maharani, his mother, who is the power. His highness plays with a naked courtesan all the while the *Durbar* is conducted and offers her to any man who desires her. He then watches as the men take her with avidity, for it is a condition of her use that she be taken in public and that he watch. He also favors child-like entertainments. The courier was told that he will watch the same puppet play or jests again and again as long as it is amusing or lewd. Women seem to be his only adult interest."

Alan looked thoughtful and then said slowly, "What if I were to go to Jhaniput as an itinerant magician? I have enough magic left to do parlor tricks and if he is as simple as you say I am certain that I will be able to please his small brain. I shall need a disguise–."

Cathal, who had been listening to this exchange in silence, now sat up and said eagerly "And I could be your trained animal! You can tell them I am a type of mongoose! I could juggle and do acrobatics and act as magician's assistant!"

"It's too dangerous," Alan began, but Cathal said "I can be of great help, Alan! I can go about the *Mahal* in tiny places you cannot and find out secrets! I can talk to the other animals there."

"He is correct, my brother. He would be invaluable as a spy, particularly if no one knows that he can understand and speak human speech," Ravi said. "And I have a mind to accompany you as well –"

But this Alan would not hear of. It was bad enough that Cathal would go into danger with him but he could not in good conscience let Ravi go for something that was not his problem. "Besides," he said "why would the *Yuraraj* of Ranijhat be traveling about the country in the company of a poor traveling magician? What if we were to meet someone who knows you?"

This was a distinct possibility for Ravi had spent time only recently traveling to other courts in Hindustan, the Punjab and Rajputana, in search of a bride.

"How will you affect her rescue?" Ravi asked, he

wanted to do *something* to help.

Alan smiled wryly. "I have no idea, I shall have to locate her and study the situation and then plan. I wish that Brendan were here. We could just swoop in and take her by force if necessary."

Brendan! This was something he could do, Ravi thought. He would go in search of Brendan! Alan was right. The dragon would put all of the advantage on their side.

And thus was born the persona of Jehan the magician. With Ram Dass's help, Alan, like Rosamunde before him, dyed his skin and hair dark. He could not disguise his amber eyes, for sustaining that amount of *glamourie* any length of time was beyond his powers, so they concocted a story of a faraway land that was Jehan's original home.

He practiced a magical act that used what little magic he had left; mage lights, sending and fetching, small illusions, using balls and ribbons and cups. The younger members of the *Moti Mahal* adored it and even the Maharajah clapped enthusiastically. Cathal juggled with glass beads lit with different colours of mage lights and climbed a rope to disappear into a illusion of nothingness and fetched the balls and ribbons and a "magic box" Alan designed. "Jehan" ended up with nearly two hours worth of clever tricks.

The Maharajah gave him a horse, a sturdy gray gelding named Akhil, who was not as good looking as some of the horses in the Maharajah's stud, but was clever and very fast. What was more important, Akhil had an equable temperament and was not easily perturbed. Cathal established a friendly relationship with him at once.

"Jehan's' clothing, equipment and saddlery were carefully chosen, not too plain as they did not wish to have him appear so unsuccessful that the court would not allow him to appear before the Maharajah, but not so fine as to make anyone wonder why he was not court magician in some rich place such as Hydrabad.

"You may use the excuse of the rebellion as your reason for going to Jhaniput," said Ravi as he watched Alan pack the last of his saddle bags the evening before he was to leave.

Ravi had his doubts as he thought Alan still too weak to undertake such a journey. He himself, without telling Alan, was leaving immediately after his friend, to go to the land of Bod, or Tibet, where he was going to find Brendan and tell the dragon of Alan's need of him.

Alan tightened the strap on the last bag and sat down on the *charpoy*, where Cathal sat, watching him rather anxiously. Alan was still subject to bouts of dizziness and weakness but he was determined to go. He could not wait any longer.

Alan said slowly "I've realized something, Ravi, after listening to everyone's accounts of what has been happening in Hindustan. You told me that my most violent outbreaks were on the 10th of May when I first took ill and on the next day. And then there were bad episodes on the 8th June, the 27th of that month and then two weeks later. Those are all dates of the massacres, Meerut and Malabad, Delhi, Jhansi, the Satichaura Ghat at Cawnpore, and Nana Sahib's slaughter of the women and children at Cawnpore. During those times I dreamed of blood and killing, of anguished, terror filled faces and it was as if in the worst type of nightmare when horror is happening all around and you are completely helpless to stop it." He shivered suddenly. "It is almost as if I was *there,* at those places, seeing those people die." he added in a low voice. "The rest of the time it ws as if I wandered in a black, ruined landscape with no way out and not knowing where I was or how to get home."

"It sounds horrible," said Ravi, shuddering himself. How could his friend have seen those horrors, so far away?

Alan stood up and walked to the mirror and studied "Jehan'. "My own mother would not recognize me," he said ruefully.

There was no trace at all of Alan Stillfield, Irishman. The man that looked back at him was gaunt and tall, looking far older than Alan's twenty four years as a result of the prolonged illness. He was stripped down to skin and bone. His skin and hair were dark as was the very short fringe of beard on his face. It would never be much of a beard, but in India, most men wore beards and he would stand out too much clean shaven. He wore a slightly shabby *achkan*, worn *jodhpurs* and well broken-in boots. A *puggaree* turban covered his hair. Ravi and Jai had spent hours drilling him in how to tie this properly.

Since there had not been enough time to teach Alan how to conduct himself as a Hindu or a Mussulman it was agreed that Jehan would have his own gods from his faraway country, even though this would make the magician a *feringhi.* "With these eyes I cannot be anything else," Alan said.

Ravi wanted to tell him that he should not count too heavily on finding and being able to rescue Rosamunde as only Allah knew what Alan would find in Jhaniput. But he could not bring himself to do so. Alan had confessed his new found love and Ravi could not bear to cast stones in Alan's path. If he, Ravi, loved a woman like that, he would do the same, foolish as it might be.

It was 420 air miles from Rawalpindi to Delhi, for Alan still thought in terms of dragon flight. Fortunately Jhaniput was not as far south as Delhi, but first of all Alan had to get to Rawalpindi through some treacherous mountain terrain. He pushed himself and Akhil as far as he dared each day, sometimes nearly falling out of the saddle at the end of the day, only able to see to the horse's needs before collapsing in exhaustion.

He stopped occasionally in a village or small town to give a magic show. He wanted to refine his act and he also wanted there to be traces of Jehan here and there should any one inquire. The Maharajah had well supplied him with *pice, annas* and *rupees* even some golden *mohurs* which he wore in a money belt about his waist. When he purchased supplies he used the smallest coins he could, for here on the Northwest Frontier, so near to the lawless Afghanistan, there were many *dacoits,* robbers, and he did not wish to draw attention to Jehan, especially with no magic to defend himself.

He had to learn some rudimentary Punjabi, as many of the people in this region spoke little else. Cathal had picked it up far more quickly than he had, for his brain still seemed slow and muddled at times, as if the nightmare had not given up its grip on him.

It was sometime in early October, he thought, when he finally rode into Jhaniput, for the Monsoon had ceased and the days were cooler under a cloudless sky. He had passed through a village that was celebrating Dursheera , the end of the ten day Hindu festival that celebrated Durga, the mother goddess, in all of her aspects and names. That festival, he knew, took place at the end of September, into early October. It was going to be some time, Alan thought, before he recovered his sense of time, for a large chunk of his life–three months! – was missing.

Jhaniput lay at the far edge of the plain of Tarrai, north of Delhi. A great battle had been fought there many years earlier. It was a desolate place, lacking the charm of the mountains in Ranijhat, a flat place of low vegetation, but with the mountains in the far distance. A narrow muddy river,the Yuma, a tributary of the Sutlej, ran near the city, which stood upon a elevation that did not even deserve the description 'hill'.

In the brilliance of the setting sun the city seemed a place of enchantment as Alan, with Cathal on his shoulder and on a tired Akhil, approached it.

Towers and domes reached into the sky, their white surfaces, lace carved in stone, gilded with the declining sun. Going down to the river in front of the city were cultivated fields of sugar cane, and grains, looking as if harvest was nearly complete. As Alan rode by, he saw a gang of laborers, hoes and scythes on shoulders, clad only in turbans and *dhotis,* heading towards the city. As he passed by he heard the unmistakable clink of iron and realized that the ex-hausted looking men were chained together and the man that rode behind them held a heavy coiled whip in his hand. None of them glanced at him as he rode by for they all seemed to be in a sort of dull stupor. Their overseer did look at Alan, with a hard, suspicious eye.

"Oh, I don't like this!" said Cathal in Alan's ear.

There was even less to like when they reached the city gates.

There was but one gate. Usually in an Indian walled city there were many and most stood open for traffic to go in and out. They were usually named for the direction towards which they were aligned, such as Kashmiri gate, Lahore gate and this one could have been the Delhi gate, for that was the direction it faced.

But it was also the Suttee gate, for on the arches of the gateway were countless little red hand prints of the widows who had left them there on their way to burn on the funeral pyres of their husbands.

And this ghoulish gate was barred and guarded with two men in native uniform, with brand new rifles on their shoulders, standing stiffly at attention.

Alan was stopped and made to account for himself, presenting his papers.

His way was smoothed when he produced a letter to the Nazir, Abhay Baqar, from the Maharajah of Ranijhat, introducing Jehan the magician as an accomplished entertainer.

The guards had standing orders to admit any entertainers and send them to Abhay Baqar. The fussy little man was at his wits' end at times, trying to provide enough entertainment to keep his highness amused. Although his highness did enjoy the same things repeatedly, at times he yearned for something new, like the petulant child he so resembled.

Not many entertainers came to Jhaniput voluntarily. The new *nautch* girl had been sent by Allah. Her dances were so new and strange that his highness was endlessly entranced with her. And she had become his favorite for fondling and the whispering of obscenities, as well as for watching her in the sexual act with other men. Baqar enjoyed her as well; she was so beautiful with those odd coloured eyes and a goddess like body. Just this afternoon after the *Durbar* when his highness had retired to be with his bride and hopefully fill her womb with child, Baqar had called for the new girl to come to his room and satisfy him. Like his royal master, watching men take her excited him. There was something about her that seemed to drive some men almost mad until they had her.

When the guards escorted the magician to his rooms, Baqar was very pleased. He was even more pleased when the magician showed him what he could do. The trained animal that seemed to understand his master was an excellent touch as well.

"I shall introduce you to his highness this very night. We have no guests and that is very often the time that he most desires novelty." Baqar said to the latest acquisition, who bowed gracefully and said that he was pleased to be of service.

"I shall have you shown to a room. You will find, Jehan, that we do very well by our entertainers here with a fine room, good food and all the women you desire. The pay is excellent as well and if his highness is pleased with you he will often gift you with a piece of his own jewelry. All you must do is entertain him."

"I shall try my very best," said the magician, with another graceful bow.

"Very well! Just show him the tricks you have shown me and he will be quite happy," said Baqar. He clapped his hands and a eunuch came into the room from a small antechamber.

"The *husoor* requires?" he asked.

"This *husoor* is Jehan, his highness's new magician. Show him to a chamber, the Moonlight chamber, I think, and make certain that he is well tended," Baqar ordered.

"It shall be as the *husoor* desires," said the eunuch and gestured to Alan to follow him. "A stable slave shall bring in your bags, *husoor*."

Alan and Cathal followed him down endless corridors. On every wall were erotic murals that left nothing to the imagination and in every niche was a *maithuna* statue in a couple in three dimensional lascivious embrace.

Alan could hear Cathal on his shoulder, muttering under his breath such things as "Good heavens! By the Great Ferret, how do they –?"

The room they were shown to was handsome, wide and high with comfortable Indian style furniture. Sheer draperies screened a *chabutara* that jutted out into a garden surrounded by a high wall.

"Does this meet the *husoor's* requirements?" the eunuch inquired.

"Very nice," Alan said, looking about in approval.

The eunuch bowed. "A maidservant shall be sent with towels and bed linens. Ask anything of her that you desire." he left, backing out of the room bowing all the way.

Alan sank onto the *charpoy*. He was so tired he only wanted to perhaps take a bath and wash the dust of the road from his person and then sleep until he was summoned to his performance. Even food would be superfluous. When the maid came he would ask her where one went to bathe.

He lay back on the charpoy as Cathal began to explore the room, and fell into a half doze. He heard, vaguely the door open and someone walking about, with the jingle of bangle bracelets.

He must have fallen into a deeper sleep. It seemed but a few moments later when Cathal was saying in his ear, in a sibilant hiss "Alan! Wake up! This is, this is –!" Words failed him as a female voice spoke.

Alan opened his eyes and slowly sat up, staring in astonishment at the maid. "What did you say to me?" He certainly could not have heard that correctly.

"Does the *husoor* wish to make use of this slave's body?" she repeated. She was in the strangest position, kneeling, with legs spread rather wide so that he had a full view of her private parts and leaning back so that her arms were behind her back, thus thrusting her torso forward. She wore a ruby in her navel and bangle jewelry but otherwise was completely naked, and without body hair of any type.

"Make use of your body?" he repeated, feeling stupid.

"To couple with me," she said in a resigned, dull voice.

She could not have been more than fourteen years old.

317

34

the performance

Alan could not speak for several moments; he was so shocked. She did not look at him but kept her eyes downcast.

"Child," he began but she interrupted him in a low, urgent whisper.

"Please, please, *husoor*! If you do not use me I will be beaten!" Her downcast lids lifted for a brief moment and he saw anguish in her large brown eyes.

"Who will beat you, the eunuch?" he asked gently.

She nodded briefly, in a furtive way.

"I cannot, child, for I am tired beyond belief. You may tell your eunuch that he may come and see me if he doubts that. Also tell him that you are lovely and desirable and that in any other circumstances I should be more than happy to share my bed with you." This was a lie. As if he would ever debauch a child of her age! "But I am no longer young," This was true for at the moment he felt older than Grandfather Lyonshall, who was 117 years old. "and I have ridden far today. I need to sleep more than I need to take a woman. But I should like to bathe before I sleep. Could you show me where I might do that?"

She lifted her eyes again briefly and he thought he saw gratitude there. She jumped up and said. "There is a bath through here," She pointed to the back of the room where an arched door showed in the wall. "Shall I draw the *husoor's* bath?"

"Thank you," he said as she trotted off. As she turned away from him he saw that there was a line of Hindi script tattooed on her left buttock.

"*Gulam*," read Cathal. "That means slave!" he said indignantly. "Alan, what sort of a place is this?"

"A very bad one," he said in a low voice so that the girl would not hear him conversing with an animal. "From the moment we came near this place I have felt such waves of pure evil pouring off everything," he broke off as the girl came back in and cast herself at his feet in that same strange position. "The bath is filling, *husoor*. Do you desire that I bathe you?"

"No, thank you," he said. " You may go."

She rose and left the room as the eunuch had, backwards and bowing until she slid from the door.

Alan changed from his dusty clothing to a loose *choga* and, followed by Cathal, went into the *ghosulhana*. While not as elegant as the bath in Ranijhat, it too was tiled and had an immense sunken tub. It was filled with water by a most ingenious arrangement of a spigot coming from the roof that could be turned on and off and allowed sun-warmed water to drain from a tank and fill the tub. With a touch of his remaining magic Alan increased the temperature of the water, which was now only slightly warm, to steaming.

"Look at this!" Cathal stood on the edge of the tub and went up on his hind legs, amazement in his voice. "Do humans really do things like that?"

Over the tub was a mural of two lovers, in a very strange position. The woman stood on her hands, with her legs bent forward over her chest so that she was looking at her own heels. A man was mounting her, his left leg lifted over her back.

"Not if they have any intelligence, no," said Alan dryly, taking off his *choga* and slipping into the water. "If it were not for the fact that they are clearly having intercourse, I would say that was a circus act. It's probably from the *Kamasutra*, Cathal."

"That strange book that the Maharajah showed us with all the odd positions? What's wrong with the normal positions? Humans like to complicate everything!" said the familiar in disgust. "Alan, *you* don't – ?"

Alan lay back in the water and closed his eyes. "No, Cathal, I have no desire to put out my back when there are easier, far more pleasant ways to do it."

"I'm sorry," said the ferret, "It's none of my business, but I don't understand why humans do some of the things they do!"

Alan opened his eyes and gave the familiar an affectionate glance. "You may ask me anything you like if it will help you understand us. Although I warn you, I don't understand some of the things humans do and I am one!"

Cathal laughed with him. "I'm going to explore," he then announced. "I'll come back before we have to go perform. Perhaps I can find out where they are keeping Rosamunde! I saw some old rat holes in the wall near the *charpoy* and I will try those first." He scampered off, leaving Alan to soak.

He must have fallen asleep for a while after his bath, for when he awoke on the *charpoy* it was full dark and a eunuch was setting up a table of dishes from which savory smells were coming, in front of the door leading out to the *chabutara*.

He bowed low when he saw Alan looking at him. "Your evening meal, *husoor*," he said. "In two hours his royal highness requires your presence in the *Diwan-i -Khas*. I shall come at that time to conduct you to him. Your clothing has been cleaned and is ready for your use. Does the *husoor* require aught else?"

Alan sat up, feeling the familiar dizziness as he did so. "No, I thank you. I have all that I need."

The eunuch bowed himself from the room.

When his senses had steadied, Alan stood slowly and went to the table where a supper had been laid out.

Baqar had been right. The food looked good and the portions were generous. There was chicken *tikka,* boneless chunks of chicken cooked in yogurt and spices, ginger, garlic turmeric, chilies and lemon juice, in a *tandoor,* a clay oven, with sides of cumin scented vegetables with toasted almonds, cabbage, *mangetouts* or snow peas, and tiny little ears of corn with dried red chilies. Mushroom curry with mushrooms and tomatoes, seasoned with garlic, cumin, cardamom, turmeric, coriander, *garam masala,* ginger and garlic completed the meal. This last was surprising, for Alan had been told that mushrooms grew only in Kashmir, which meant that they had to be imported. To compliment the meal was *naan* bread, the light, puffy teardrop shaped bread that was made from flour, yogurt and yeast. There was hot tea to wash it down and a tray with several sweetmeats and sliced fruit for a dessert. In a covered dish with ice about it was a glass of fruit sherbet.

Alan automatically put aside food for Cathal. He would have to see about getting some milk and perhaps some eggs for the ferret. In the wild ferrets ate rodents, much as did feral cats, but Cathal, being a familiar and used to eating with humans and sharing their diet, had learned to eat and to like vegetables. He even liked the spicy food here in India. Alan knew he would like the little ears of corn in particular. He had loved the roasted ears of corn they had eaten whilst in America.

But before he ate he conducted a small ritual. Around his neck on a chain hung a piece of horn and he took this out and passed it over the food. A blue light shone faintly and then died.

This was a unicorn horn, the very tip of one, the spiral surface edged in gold. The tip was the most powerful part of the horn and had been given to Alan's grandfather René by a unicorn friend called Cluny. Alan and Rosamunde both had been gifted with a piece of horn in hopes that it would prevent traveler's distress when eating strange food and water. Alan had thought tonight that it might be a good idea to use it on the food given him in this strange place. He was glad that he had, for the blue light meant that something indeed had been added to the food. The horn had purified it and it was now safe to eat. Whatever had been added would have no effect upon him, for the horn had negated it.

But he had scarcely started eating before Cathal returned, emerging from the rat hole in a somewhat dusty condition, but full of news.

"Oh, good, supper!" the ferret said and hopped up on to the table.

Alan pushed the plate he had prepared for his familiar towards him. "I'll have to brush you before we go to the *Diwan-i-Khas*," he said.

"This looks good!" said Cathal, and picked up a small corn cob between his two paws. "I didn't find Rosamunde yet," he said "But this is the strangest place! There are spy corridors and spy holes behind all of the walls and, Alan, you would not believe it but I saw no less than fourteen pairs of humans mating! Just in this part of the Mahal! All of the woman are like the little girl who was in here, naked, with bangle jewelry and a ruby right in their stomachs. I saw no women wearing clothes at all! I met a mongoose who has offered to show me about. She is called Kaveri and she is no one's pet although she says some of the women in the *zenana* feed and pet her when the eunuchs are not looking. She is kept here to keep the snakes away. She is going to take me to the *zenana* later, after our show." He took a bite out of the corn and then said in troubled tones, "Alan, Kaveri told me that all of the women here are used constantly by men. She called this place 'a gigantic *lol bibis* bazaar'."

Alan suddenly found that his appetite had disappeared. He put down the wooden spoon with which he had been eating. "The Maharajah warned us," he said, thinking of Rosamunde and what had more than likely happened to her, with intense pain. What must she be feeling?

Alan was perhaps more sensitive to what a woman felt in these circumstances than were most men, for his mother had sat him down and explained to him what had been her emotions when she was nearly raped, and how a woman would like a man who loved her to react if she *was* raped. His father as well had discussed with him quite frankly how he had felt about his wife almost being debauched. Alan had also been influenced by the attitude of Professor Williamson at Oxford, a man he had come to admire tremendously.

But he had to admit, the thought of a good many men being intimate with Rosamunde made him want to kill someone, and it made him more than a little sick. Just seeing this place made him realize that there was very little chance that Rosamunde could have escaped being molested even with magic to protect her. If they had restrained her in Cold Iron she would have been too sick to fight them off. She might have been drugged, or even just over powered by sheer strength or defeated by black magic. He had to get her away from here! And he had a duty to try and rescue as many of the other woman as was possible.

"Cathal, I think that this might be a sex magic brothel," he said slowly.

Cathal nodded, busy with a piece of chicken. He swallowed and then said," I wondered that myself." He had read Alan's text book on the subject and had joined in the talks with Peter and his familiar once the Professor had lifted the spell that kept them from discussing the subject outside the classroom and had allowed the familiars to join the class. Although Cathal could not perform magic he had always made it his business to read it and study it as much as possible so he could understand what Alan did and understand his own duties as well.

"They are probably gathering the power made by the sex acts in those rubies," Alan said.

"They're a sort of focus stone, aren't they? But they would have to be drained eventually," said Cathal, taking another little ear of corn. "You need to eat some more of this, Alan!" he scolded. "You can't keep your strength up, eating the way you've been doing!"

Cathal was right and Alan picked up his spoon again. "But what is all the power *for*?" He asked thoughtfully, taking a spoonful of the chicken *tikka*. "If it is the Maharajah who is the magician, he is already rich and powerful. And we have not heard that Jhaniput is in any way involved in the rebellion."

"I am going to be able to go all over the *Mahal* and listen to people," said Cathal. "Kaveri says this place is riddled with secret passages and that the Maharajah sneaks about in the passages, spying upon his guests when they are with a woman."

Alan was revolted. "What a pervert!" he said, "Could someone be watching and listening to us right now?" he asked.

"I'd know," said Cathal simply. "And since we decided to speak only in Gaelic to each other I doubt that there would be anyone here who could understand us, even if they believed that I could actually speak."

With Cathal's affectionate urging Alan made a better meal and then brushed his familiar until his fur shone. For the performance, he put a collar of coloured crystals about the ferret's neck, and he changed into his own clothes, an *achkan* of white surrah silk with matching *jodhpurs* and gold curly toed shoes. His turban was decorated with a large moonstone from his Wizard's kit and another moonstone hung around his neck.

All the impedimenta Alan needed was in a cleverly designed box made in the City of Jhat. It was a beautiful thing, carved and inlaid with nacre, and had fold- up legs that turned it into a table. Alan could carry it by a wide shoulder strap.

When the eunuch came they were ready. With Cathal riding on one of Alan's shoulders and the box slung from the other they followed the eunuch through seemingly endless halls.

The closer they drew to the *Diwan-i-Khas*, the more guards they saw and it was not uncommon to see three guards on duty while a fourth was on the floor with a woman, 'mating' as Cathal put it.

"Here within the *Kala Mahal* it has been recently decided that as long as three remain in duty at one time they may share a woman," the eunuch explained, seeing Alan's glance. "His highness has decided that it is not in the best interest of the men to make them wait for the use of a woman. Those four will share her, and then will be free to go to that *zenana* and take another each when they are off duty. His highness is a generous master."

"I daresay the women don't think of him that way!" Cathal murmured in Alan's ear.

The *Diwan-i-Khas* was soon reached and Alan was instructed to wait while the Nazir announced him.

Alan looked about him with interest. The walls were covered in erotic murals, and there were the usual *maithuna* statues. Whoever had chosen the decor for the Mahal had very little imagination, Alan decided. It was obvious that the *Kala Mahal*, the Black Palace, had been named for the walls and floors of black marble, polished to a brilliant shine. One wall opened out into a garden where a fountain played.

Behind the repulsive little Maharajah, who sat on a bank of cushions, was a throne like chair with a woman in it that Alan correctly assumed to be the Maharani. She was as repellent as her son. Another woman, bare to the waist, sat beside her on a stool while a third, a white woman with red hair, knelt at her feet, naked, with a ruby in her navel as were the other women they had seen that day. She was being fed bits of sweetmeats by the bare breasted woman as if she were a pet animal.

"Good God!" said Alan under his breath, suddenly recognizing the red head. Mabel Clutterbuck!

On either side of the Maharajah stood a woman in ridiculously ornate and incomplete sets of peacock decorated armor that left most of their bodies bare. Like all the others, rubies sparkled in their navels and they were free of body hair. Each held a peacock feather fan.

The Maharajah was busy watching an extremely lewd puppet show, jumping up and down on the cushions and clapping his hands in glee. He was also busy eating *halwa*, sweetmeats, mostly *jellabies* which were fried sweets of honey and butter, and the evidence of this showed on his face and clothing as well as his hands. These were sticky and greasy and since between clapping and sweets he was handling the bodies of the guard women, they too were covered in candy detritus.

A little to the side of the *musnud* where the Maharajah sat (Alan thought it would be more suitable if he squatted on a lily pad) was a statue, unlike Alan had ever seen in India. There were many statues of stone and of bronze, and many of them voluptuous female nudes but this one was of wood and painted wood at that and painted very realistically.

This carved woman was in the same strange position that the naked child had been in his room. However, since this statue was of a full grown woman and not an half formed child the effect was a great deal more erotic. The statue had been equipped with bracelets on forearm and upper arm and a multitude of bangles as well. She also wore hoops of bells through the aureoles of her nipples, each hoop a good foot in circumference. On her head was a helmet type headpiece decorated with enamel work and the ubiquitous ruby shone in her carved navel.

The skin had been painted a warm *café au lait*. The statue was slimmer and smaller bosomed than most Alan had seen. Most of the female statues had 'watermelon' breasts of inordinate size. She had been carved with her eyes closed, but the eyes heavily outlined in kohl, the lids painted blue and the sculptor had given her eyelashes darkened with antimony as well and the lips were vermilion.

The painting was superb: the darker brown of the nipples, the way the skin on the knees was slightly darker, the colouring of the private parts that showed between her wide spread legs – it was a masterwork of realism. The statue had been highly polished, gleaming with oil.

Abhay Baqar appeared at his side. "Come!" he said "You shall perform now! All your best tricks, mind you!"

Alan followed him out in front of the *musnud* and bowed low to the Maharajah as the Nazir introduced him.

"I hope that you are a good magician and can show me something new," said the Maharajah, sulkily. "The last fellow could only charm snakes! That is not very magical. Why, every *fakir* in the bazaar can do that!."

Alan put down his bag and stood up. He made a complicated pass in the air and suddenly a shining ball hung there, spinning and gleaming in the torch light. He put his hand over it and all around it to show that no strings held it up and then lowering his hand to the top of it made it slow to a stop. It was then seen to be an eight-sided ball.

"A gift for your highness, to while away an idle hour," he said, and handed it to the still waiting Nazir to give to the Maharajah.

"For me?" His highness exclaimed and took it a little gingerly from Baqar.

"If your highness will but put your eye to any one of the sides," Alan suggested.

The Maharajah did so and then squealed in delight. "Why, they're coupling! A tiny naked male and female, copulating!"

"You will see a different position on each side of the ball," Alan suggested.

Nothing would do but that the royal pervert had to see each view that very minute. He was utterly charmed by this and Alan silently blessed Ravi's worldly wise father for suggesting an erotic gift and that he had enough magic left to create this illusion. Caught in glass, the illusion would last six months. It predisposed the Maharajah to like 'Jehan's' offerings.

And like them he did. He sat in awe as the glass beads, each a different colour, winked on and off and made fireworks-like displays at Alan's command. He stared like a wide-eyed child as Cathal juggled a multitude of beads, whirling them faster and faster, helped by a touch of magic. Ribbons flew around the room, tying themselves into intricate knots, while a flock of doves erupted from Jehan's turban when he doffed it, only to turn into soft feathers that rained from the sky and tuned themselves in to white flowers before they dissolved in smoke. Things disappeared and reappeared in a another part of the room right before his fascinated gaze. The magician made it rain pearls which changed into white mice which the trained animal 'herded' into a group and then they vanished in a puff of coloured smoke. Blue fire spurted from the tips of the magician's fingers and he conjured up a most fearsome creature, enormous, with a mouth of shining teeth, a huge reptile with wings like a bats and it spat flame!

By this time the Maharajah had a cushion stuffed into his mouth and his eyes were as round as pebbles. He had not eaten a sweetmeat nor touched either of the guards since the very beginning of the performance.

When the show was complete and the magician bowed, the Maharajah just sat and stared at him for a moment, stupefied.

Then the silence was broken by the sound of clapping and the Maharajah turned to see his mother, who never indicated pleasure or displeasure in any of the entertainments, clapping her hands.

Not to be outdone by her he began thumping his hands together enthusiastically. "Wonderful! Wonderful !" he shrilled.

"This man has real magic," the Maharani said in a low voice to Hussaini. "We must put a woman to him as often as possible. Only think of the power she will gather!"

"Come, magician, come and sit by me!" the Maharajah ordered. "*Nazir*! Wine for the magician who has entertained us so royally!".

Alan was glad to sit down as he was exhausted and a little dizzy. The illusions had taken a lot out of him. With Cathal on his shoulder he bowed, Cathal doing likewise, and took a seat on the cushion that the Maharajah patted with one stubby, jewel covered hand.

The Maharajah had many eager questions and wanted to see Cathal juggle again. He took a heavy rope of pearls and diamonds from around his neck and threw them over Alan's head. "I reward those who please me!" he said.

He then giggled. "Now I think that I may surprise you!" he said." I noticed that you have been admiring my statue!"

Alan indeed had been studying it again. There was something quite fascinating about it. "It is a true work of art, highness. The artist has much skill." he said.

Another piercing giggle followed from the Maharajah. He raised his hands over head and clapped. At once music began to play from an alcove Alan had noticed earlier, half hidden by curtains.

The statue sprang into the air and with a great leap, landed on the dance floor and began to exhibit herself in perhaps the most lascivious, lewd dance Alan had ever seen.

He was no prude. He was used to living amongst Elves who spent much of their time naked, to seeing sky-clad dancing amongst the Witches. Even in Ranijhat he had watched the Maharajah's Zahallah's troupe of Kashmiri dancing girls who were naked to the waist and wore but narrow gold belts low on their hips with handkerchief sized pieces of gauze attached to them and had performed most suggestively.

But this–! There was no doubt as to what she was parodying, as she bent backwards from the waist, running her hands up and down her own body, thrusting her hips in and out, with widespread legs, and making the bells in the breast hoops alternate in ringing out as she rolled her arms and shoulders. All the while the sitar and sarod rang out, the drum thudded and a drone echoed a sensual beat to her writhing. When the dance finished she fell to the floor directly in front of the Maharajah in the same attitude she had occupied as a statue.

He giggled again and reached out to pull hard at the breast rings. "Is that not exciting, magician?" He dropped the rings and began squeezing her breasts. "This one is my favorite. I try and keep her by me always so I may touch her whenever I like. I never tire of her body. I would dearly love to couple with her, but it would pollute me to do so because she has been used by so many men. I shall have her eunuch in here to tell you just how many. I cannot remember, for of course the tally grows daily." His voice grew dreamy. "She is so beautiful! There is a statue of the goddess Yuma by the *ghat* behind the *Mahal* and this girl resembles it to a marked degree, tall and slender as a young cypress with breasts like ripe melons and a bottom like a peach! Once I have a son, though, I shall take this one to my bed and couple with her again and again! I may never let her from my bed!" He giggled once more.

Alan was growing to hate the sound of his giggles. He felt desperately sorry for the girl, who was having to endure not only being manhandled (now the little hands were stroking her thighs), but being talked of as if she was some sort of thing, a toy for his pleasure.

"We call her Serai," the Maharajah said. For some reason this sent him into a perfect cascade of giggles. He looked at Alan's face closely and then said, "You have very odd eyes, magician! And so does she! Look at this! Open your eyes, girl!"

The dancer opened her eyes, showing a dull gaze, as if she were not really present.

Amber eyes met violet. The dancing girl was Rosamunde.

35

ṣєraї

Alan could not suppress it. He gasped aloud.

"Have you ever seen the like? Purple eyes!" said the Maharajah, giggling again, those hands all over her.

Alan clenched his fists. He wanted to scream "Get your hands off her, you little pervert!" and then throttle the bastard until his eyes bulged even further from out his amphibian face. He heard himself saying though, "Such eyes are quite common amongst the women of my country, highness,"

The Maharajah looked at him in surprise. "Is this slave girl a countrywoman of yours?" His hands had moved again, he was now stroking Rosamunde's buttocks. "If all of the women there are as beautiful as this one I wonder that the men ever rise from their beds with such partners to couple with!"

"Might I have your permission to speak to her in my own language and find out if she *is* from my homeland?" Alan inquired, marveling at his own self control. How was he managing this? It was almost if someone else was speaking through his mouth, someone calmer, without the murderous impulses he was feeling. He could feel Cathal staring at him.

"You may have my permission," said the Maharajah." And you have my permission to speak to the magician, girl." He went back to her breasts again, pulling hard on the hoops that pierced her.

"Rosamunde," said Alan in Gaelic, trying hard to keep his voice on an even keel. "Rosamunde, look at me. It's Alan." He was frightened, for she seemed to be someplace else, a place that no one else could see. She did not even appear to notice what the horrible Maharajah was doing to her.

Her eyes seemed to come into focus and she finally looked at him. The only sign of recognition was a slight widening of her eyes. Her facial expression, her body posture, all remained the same. "Alan –" she said .

"Have you come to take me away from this horrible place?"

"Yes, as soon as I can," he said.

"You look so strange," the Maharajah gave a particularly hard tug on her breast hoops, giggling in his inane fashion, but only a slight tightening of the lips betrayed her and only Alan, who knew her so well, would have noticed it.

"I haven't much magic," he confessed, "But as soon as I can figure out a way... "

"My magic is all gone. I cannot even make a Mage light," she said. Her voice was expressionless but he saw, deep in her eyes, a sudden anguish.

"Well, is she from your country?" interrupted the Maharajah, still tugging on the hoops.

"Yes, your highness, it is quite amazing. She is actually from a village in the hills quite near to my old home," Alan answered him in the same unemotional voice and how he was controlling it he could not understand. Inside he wanted to scream and to do extreme harm to all of them. If he had had his full powers these people would no longer be alive and this hell hole would be razed to the ground.

A female voice came from behind him, a rather unattractive, raspy voice. "Would you like to couple with your countrywoman, magician? Your performance tonight deserves another reward and we strive to see that our entertainers are happy, including providing bed mates."

Alan turned and saw the Maharani looking at him. Hastily, he bowed and heard himself saying, "Your highness is most gracious, to allow me use of such a valuable slave. I would indeed like to taste her charms. It is far too long since I lay with a countrywoman and there are certain skills that she will possess for pleasure that are not found in the women of Hind."

"Very well," said the Maharani. "Hussaini, how many others is she promised to for this evening?"

"Only three, highness, for we have no guests. The General wants her as does a Captain and the *quiladar,* the fort keeper," Hussaini answered.

"She shall be used in order of rank," said the Maharani. "When the Captain has finished with her, take her to the magician. You may have her the rest of the night, magician, after she has been with the others. Make certain that you make good use of her. If she does not please you she will be beaten."

"I thank your highness most sincerely for the honor," Alan bowed deeply. His hands were still clenched and when he returned to his room he found that he had squeezed his fists so tightly that four bloody half moons adorned each palm where his nails had dug into his flesh. He had not even felt it.

When the eunuch came to escort him back to his room the last thing he saw as he bowed himself away was the vile Maharajah, still stroking Rosamunde's body and drooling over her.

It seemed an age, but in fact it was three hours, before they delivered Rosamunde to his rooms.

In the meantime Alan raged and fumed, pacing up and down angrily until a wave of dizziness forced him to sink on to the *charpoy*.

Cathal watched him anxiously. He had been as horrified as Alan had been at what was being done to Rosamunde and he well understood his Wizard's frustrations at having no power to draw upon to punish these creatures as they deserved. He was amazed that Alan had been able to so well control himself in the *Diwan-i-Khas* and said so.

"I was amazed myself," Alan said, wrapping his arms around himself as if he were cold, although the evening was warm. He was wearing the *choga* and loose *pyjamy* trousers, the *Mahal* had provided, for as Cathal had sensibly pointed out, the eunuch would expect him to be clad for bed, as that was why Rosamunde was being brought here, so that he could bed her. "Cathal, it was as if someone else were speaking through me, it was the strangest thing. My own words would have been for him to get his hands off her or I would kill him! And God, I wanted to kill him! With my bare hands! I could just see his fat little face turning purple as I strangled him!" he stretched out his hands and looked at them, flexing his long fingers. Cathal had doctored the wounds left by the pressure of his nails.

"I was looking at his face as his mother offered Rosamunde to you and he was not best pleased, but he made no objection. Kaveri told me earlier that the Maharani rules in this *Mahal* and I could see that. He is firmly under her thumb," Cathal said.

"I'm reasonably certain that she is the magician, not him," Alan stated. "The sense of *wrongness* about her..." He shivered in revulsion. "Cathal, I can't understand a woman allowing these horrors to be done to other women! At Oxford, the sex magicians we studied were all male. Not one woman was in the texts, other than as victims."

"I've read about people such as her," said the ferret. "They are completely amoral, with no conscience and can do any horror to anyone else, as long as it furthers their own ends. I forgot to tell you that Kaveri told me that what the Maharajah Zahallah thought was true, she did sleep with her own brother to get a royal child and as soon as the present Maharajah looked as if he would grow and be strong, she murdered her brother. She poisoned him."

"Oh God!" said Alan fervently, closing his eyes at the thought of this loathsome, ruthless woman. A few moments later he said, "Go about and listen as much as you can, Cathal. Somehow I have got to find out how strong her magic is, so I know what I am up against,"

Neither of them stated the obvious! That the parlor tricks he was capable of now would be of very little use in defeating or even challenging a black magician.

A few moments later the door opened and a large eunuch entered, with Rosamunde. over his shoulder.

Alan stood up quickly and moved aside as the eunuch headed for the *charpoy*. The big man dumped his burden on the bedstead and said to her, in a rough tone "Assume the position!"

Without a glance at Alan, Rosamunde lay on her back, put her arms over her head,and arching her back up that her breasts were thrust up. She opened her legs wide and bent her knees.

"This slave has been well trained in the art of pleasing a man, *husoor,*" said the eunuch. "If she does not satisfy your every desire, you may beat her and I shall beat her again when she leaves you," He pointed to a cabinet by the bed. "There are oils to use and pleasure devices as well. You will also find whips and lashes. She has also been trained to assume many of the positions of the *Kamasutra* and she will obey whatever you tell her to do. Does the *husoor* wish her tied in the position or does he wish her oiled before he uses her? Or perhaps wishes to beat her first?"

Alan wanted to be sick. He could not look at Rosamunde and again was conscious of an all consuming rage that wanted to destroy.

But again he heard himself saying calmly, "Thank you, no, but it is the custom of my country to do these things for oneself."

"As the *husoor* wishes. Her highness directs that you may keep her by you until mid morning."

"Her highness is most gracious," Alan said.

The eunuch bowed himself out and Alan, with his back to Rosamunde, picked up his discarded *achkan*. He heard the *charpoy* squeak as she moved and sat up, and he said, without turning around, "Here, you can put on my *achkan–*"

"No, I can't," she said , an undercurrent of bitterness in her voice. "I've been bespelled. If any cloth not especially bespelled touches my skin I shall burst into bale fire and be consumed. I've been kept naked since the middle of May, Alan. I am beginning to forget what it is like to wear clothing or be modest. But I don't blame you for not being able to look at me, it isn't often you have to look at your cousin the dirty whore."

He whirled around, his eyes blazing and he dropped to his knees in front of the *charpoy*, where she sat on the edge of it, and taking her by the shoulders said fiercely "Don't you EVER dare to refer to yourself like that!" and gave her a slight shake. "Do you hear me, Rosamunde? I was trying to be a gentleman! You are NOT a whore, no matter what these vile people have done to you!" He pulled her against him and wrapped his arms around her tightly. "I thought I'd lost you!"

She was stiff in his arms for a moment and then suddenly relaxed, allowing her head to drop onto his shoulder.

They stayed like that for a few moments.

She laughed shakily and said "I kept hoping that you would come!" She could not believe he was actually here for in the last month she had begun to despair, thinking perhaps that either the rebellion had spread to Ranijhat and he had been killed or he had found out what had happened to her and had left her here in disgust for what she had become.

She raised her head and looked at him, but not seeking to escape from the embrace in which he still held her. "You look so strange Alan! You said you hadn't much magic? How will we get from here without magic?"

"Ravi's gone to fetch Brendan," interrupted an animal voice.

"What?" said Alan, turning his head sharply but still retaining his grip upon Rosamunde.

"Ravi left for the land of Bod the day you left Rani-jhat," Cathal repeated. "He's going to locate Brendan and send him here. They've got nothing here that can hurt a dragon and Brendan can knock down walls and flame as many men as he needs to in order to rescue you! Hello, Rosamunde," he added shyly. "I'm so glad to see you are still alive!"

"Hello, Cathal," she said, smiling tiredly.

"Where's Sinéad?" the ferret asked eagerly.

Rosamunde winced and slid out from Alan's arms. He rose and went to sit beside her, still careful not to stare at her nudity.

"I think she's dead," Rosamunde said bleakly and told them the story of that last night in Malabad and from there how she had come to be in the *Kala Mahal* as a slave. "It's blood magic, Alan," she finished. "They are collecting our pain and suffering through the rubies and using it for I don't know what. Laura and I have been trying to find out."

"It's not blood magic, it's sex magic," said Alan. "It's the same principal as in the gathering of blood magic but it draws its power from the humiliation and degradation of a unwilling participant in the sex act. They seem to be very good at humiliation and degradation in this place," he added in disgust.

"Did it take you all this time to find me?" she asked. Cathal, grief stricken for his best friend, had slipped away to sit in the window and stare blindly out at the garden.

Alan explained to her what had happened to him as briefly as he could. "We neither one of us have fared too well in India," he said, and then remembered a fact he had omitted. "Oh, God, Rosamunde, I'm sorry, but Raymond is dead. Ram Dass confirmed it." He took her hands in his, deep concern on his face.

"I know," she said "One of the women in here was from Delhi and they heard that the entire station was wiped out. It's probably just as well, for he would never want me as his wife after this. What decent man would?"

As he began to protest she smiled sadly and said "Alan, I have been with literally hundreds of men. I could probably tell you exactly how many, for the eunuch keeps count and I am beaten if they are not satisfied by how many I service in a day."

Alan wanted to tell he that *he* wanted her, even if she had been with thousands of men, millions! He was conscious of a feeling of jealousy that she had been anyone else's, but his main emotions were pity for her, anger that such a terrible thing had happened to her and a grim determination to take her out of this and spend the rest of his life making her happy.

But he sensed that now was not the time to tell her that he wanted to marry her, that he loved her, for she would never believe him; she would think that he was offering his name to cover her shame, out of pity of the worst kind, not out of love. He would have to show her that he was not concerned over all of those men who had used her. This would be hard, for he *was* concerned. He wanted to kill each and every one of them!

"I had to rouse you from some sort of stupor," he now said "I was frightened, for you seemed as if you had gone away."

"I've learned how to do that, I do go away, to home, in my mind, when I have to tolerate him touching me and the horrible dances I have to do or when some man is..." she broke off. "It's the only protection I have. It's a form of *yoga* meditation. My friend Parminder taught me. And there is another spell on me to enable me to remain in the same position for a very long time, so that I can play the game of statues," she explained.

"I was surprised when a statue came to life," he admitted.

She made a face. "That is his very favorite jest. He never grows tired of it. Sometimes he has the whole dance troupe, male and female, arranged around the room, most of them arranged as *maithuna* statues and at a given signal they all spring to life. He never tires of seeing the surprise on people's faces. You will find out that he will want to see you perform the same tricks over and over."

"I don't intend to be here long enough for him to get used to me," said Alan decidedly.

Rosamunde looked at him sadly. "Have you looked about this place, Alan? There are walls 15 and 20 feet high, all topped with spikes set close together. There are guards everywhere and the one gate in and out of the city is guarded. No one goes in or out without permission. The rest of the gates that used to be here have been blocked up. Even the men who work the fields are taken in and out in chains so that they cannot leave. The garden outside this room has a high retaining wall as well and all of the windows are barred. I cannot leave because where would I go, naked? I can never wear clothes again unless this spell is lifted and none of this jewelry will come off, particularly these horrible things," she looked down at the large hoops through her breasts.

"Those must hurt," he said sympathetically.

"They do and they hurt worse because he has been pulling and pulling at them since they were put in by her magic and he will not leave them alone. He squeezes and pokes and prods at every part of me! I sometimes think I would rather be back in the brothel being used by one man after another!" She put her hands up to her face.

Tentatively he put an arm around her shoulders.

She did not reject him, but sighed and allowed her hands to drop and leaned against him.

"I am glad you are here, Alan, even though it means that you are now as much a prisoner as I am, for he liked you too well. You will never be allowed to leave now. And now you must lay with me as many times as you can manage so that I will be given to you again and we can see one another," she said.

He stared at her, appalled by her matter of fact manner and her assumption that he would use her so.

It had been a bad day for Laura. First thing in the

morning she had been taken by a group of rowdy men out to the garden, and they passed her around as if she was some sort of cake tray full of goodies, egging one another on. Then she had done a double shift on 'guard' duty; as one of the guests had roughed up the afternoon 'guard' woman something awful before the eunuchs could pull him off her. The guests were allowed to beat the women if they wished, but not so badly so that they could not be used by other men.

She then had to bear the attentions of a guest who was excited beyond measure to have a naked woman he could do anything he wished to and had done them right out in the open in front of the whole court. The Maharajah had watched with hot eyes, his hands all over Rosamunde.

Laura always felt sorry for Rose the way that slimy little turd pawed her and pulled at her breasts. The poor kid was sore all the time and then having to exhibit herself in those godawful filthy dances and on top of that, kneel in the position of submission while guests threw dice to see which one of them got to take her first. Being a guard was bad enough but Rose had it worse, as did Parminder, who alternated with Rose as the Maharajah's favorite fondle toy.

The only good part of Laura's evening had been getting to see the magic show. The magician was good, as good as any she'd ever seen in the States. She'd been surprised when he said that Rosamunde was his countrywoman and had spoken to her in a strange language and she had answered him.

Laura, for the first time in a while, felt a stirring of hope. Was this Rose's cousin, the Wizard? When she heard that Rosamunde was to be given to him she hoped that they would come up with a plan if he was indeed her cousin.

To her surprise a eunuch came and took her away early and she was taken to be washed and re-oiled, her body sprinkled with gold powder, and her cosmetics reapplied, which meant she was to have a special 'customer'.

Pramoda Tandon then came for her and took her to one of the more private rooms and made her sit upon the *charpoy*.

"You are to have a singular honor," he said. "It is the natal day of the *Daffadur* Gautauma Sarin and his fellow officers have decided that you shall entertain him. He was heard to express an interest in having a woman with hair your colour and wonders if the *yoni* of a *mem sahib* is different than that of a woman of Hind. The *Daffadur* is a very brave soldier and comes to us with the highest of recommendations. You should be grateful that he has decided to use you and I expect that you will be obedient to his every wish and do exactly as he directs you."

"I hear and obey," said Laura as she had been taught, wondering meanwhile all of these jokers always thought her equipment was different just because she had pale skin.

"But first you shall be used by his fellow officers, for they would not wish their comrade to lie with an inferior woman. "There will be five of them. Assume the position."

As Laura lay back on the charpoy she thought ruefully that they would expect her to be grateful that she was moving up in the world, being screwed by officers and the Maharajah's guests rather than just common soldiers. A *Daffadur* was a commander of calvary, a commander of at least ten men.

The *Daffadur's* fellow officers were a young, rowdy, lusty bunch and seemed to have no inhibitions about sharing her with each other. They called out instructions to each other as each took his turn on her body, laughing uproariously. They had been drinking, and continued to drink, mainly *puggle*, a potent native drink.

The *Daffadur* came at last, just as his fellows were beginning a second go-round. They greeted him heartily and told him that Laura was well warmed for his attentions and a worthwhile couple.

Laura stole a glance at him. She usually paid little or no attention to the men who used her, barely even looking at them, but she was always a little insecure when they had been drinking. Drink made some men incapable and they had a tendency to take out their frustration on the woman.

He was a tall, broad shouldered man with the flat stomach and slim hips of the horseman. He had a dark face, largely hidden by an enormous black beard and a *puggaree* that was wrapped around a conical striped hat and hung down his back. This was usually done for protection against the sun.

He looked fairly sober to Laura and she closed her eyes as he moved towards her and she heard him drop his *achkan* upon the floor and open his *jodhpurs*. The women had been told that all the clothing of the men had been made from special cloth to allow them to use the women without starting a bale fire.

Then he was on top of her and she tried to do as Rose and Parminder had been teaching her, to think of something else, to go away in her mind. She was becoming reasonably successful.

She usually thought of Nate and the little farm in Connecticut they were planning to buy there to raise horses.

Therefore she thought she was dreaming when a voice, a familiar, well-loved voice said, close to her ear, "Hello, Laurie honey."

Only Nate called her Laurie, not even Pa did so –! She opened her eyes and with a gasp, recognized the man on top of her.

It was Nate.

36

nate

To the ribald calls of his fellow officers Nate finished taking Laura, calling out *"Hai!"* as he did so, and then rolled off her.

"A worthy couple indeed!" he said in Hindustani, staying in character and ignoring Laura. "I would have more of her."

"Gautama Sarin is a lusty man!" hiccupped one of his fellows, far gone in drink.

The eunuch, who had stayed just outside the door of the room now came in and bowed to Nate. "Would the *Daffadur* care to take the slave to his quarters and use her again? She is not needed for her other duties until late afternoon, and in that time the *Daffadur* could enjoy her many times. Food and drink may be brought as well..."

"I shall do that and see that you bring much food and drink! My appetites are all large!" said Nate, a white grin splitting his dark beard.

The other men roared with laughter, calling out coarse suggestions as to what the *Daffadur* could do with the female slave to satisfy his large appetite. He tossed back equally crude comments as to what he was going to do to her in fluent Hindustani and thanked them for a fine gift.

Laura still lay in 'the position', as they had been taught they could not alter this posture until given permission. The eunuch came to her, gave her leave to put down her arms and close her legs and then picked her up, slinging her over his shoulder, the approved method for transporting female slaves, as it allowed the eunuch to fondle her buttocks.

He followed Nate as Laura's *fiancé* led the way towards his quarters in the barracks.

Laura was so filled with joy that she wanted to shout and sing and dance. Nate was here! That probably meant that Pa was nearby and that her days in this hell hole were numbered!

Laura had never been near the barracks before. They were behind the *Mahal*, still within the retaining wall. By now she had perfected the art of seeing while being slung over a shoulder and noticed with interest that there were indeed an enormous amount of men here, more than she and Rose had reckoned. She could hear the shouts of a *havildar* a sergeant, drilling some troops and even the firing of weapons as if artillery practice were taking place. She also saw men wrestling and heard the thump of arrows going into butts.

And this was going on at night, under torchlight, although dawn was probably not that far off.

The officers' quarters lay at the top of the three storey barracks, up a flight of narrow stairs. There seemed to be construction of a new wing going on as well. The eunuch stuck close to Nate's heels and followed him into a mid-sized room with a good row of windows.

It was lit by torchlight and Laura did not see much at first, for the eunuch deposited her upon the charpoy and commanded her to assume the position, chiding her for not thrusting her breasts up higher, pushing at her with a rough hand.

Then he turned to Nate and bowed, saying that the food and drink would be delivered shortly and that he was the *Daffadur's* to command, should he wish anything further. "For their highnesses are much pleased that a soldier of such renown has taken service with them and wish to do everything that will insure a satisfactory relationship. Should the *Daffadur* enjoy this particular slave it may be arranged that she be yours for a certain length of time every day."

"I shall decide that after I thoroughly use her this day and determine if she is obedient and skilled," said Nate.

The eunuch bowed and left the room, closing the door behind him.

Nate turned to Laura and laid a finger on his lips, in an alert listening posture.

She lay still, not moving, until he said "The coast is clear."

She sat up and said "So you've got to see if I'm obedient and skilled before you decide if you want me again or not, Nate Connelly?"

Nate's wonderful grin flashed over his face and he

bounded forward. He picked her up easily, for he was a big man, and swung her around.

"Laurie! Laurie!" he exulted and then kissed her – hard.

"Whew!" she laughed when he had finished. "Did you miss me or what?" She had returned his kiss with equal enthusiasm.

He put her feet on the floor. "God in heaven, Laurie, I thought I'd never find you!" His face grew suddenly sober and he said, his big hands tightening on her upper arms, "I'm so sorry, Laurie honey, that I had to use you like that in front of all those rat bastards. I didn't know how else to get to you."

She shook her head. "Don't be sorry, Nate, I thought it was damned clever of you! I was almost like to faint when you said hello, though."

He laughed. "My Laurie swoon away like a prissy little society miss? It ain't going to happen! Not when the very first time we met you were stuffed with dead Spanish sausage, yelling to get the bastard off you!"

He hugged her a few moments longer and kissed her again and then sat down on the *charpoy*, taking her into his lap. She put an arm around his neck and he kept his arm about her waist.

"Is Pa here too?" she asked eagerly.

He smiled. "There's no way your Pa could ever pass himself off as a Hindoo! He's got 'American' writ acrost his forehead! 'Sides, he don't speak the lingo too good. But he's around, trying to scare up more support to rescue you."

"How did you find me, Nate, and how come you're a *Daffadur* of Cavalry calling yourself Gautama Sarin?" she inquired, once satisfied that her father was safe and well.

There was a noise at the door and Nate bent Laura backwards, his hand going up to cover one breast and locking his lips on hers.

He paid no attention as two eunuchs entered and set up a table with food and drink and then withdrew. He continued to fondle Laura as if they did not exist.

When they left he let her up and said "No reason we can't eat while I tell you what happened," and set her on the floor.

The table as were most in the *Mahal*, was low to the

floor and they sat on cushions around it.

"There's only one plate and one spoon," said Nate, frowning down at the array of food.

"I ain't supposed to eat," she said. "Female slaves live on air and banging."

"Thought you felt a little skinny," he said. "Never mind, there's enough for both of us. I'll eat out of the bowl and use one of these *tortilla* things for a spoon," he added, picking up a *chupapatti*.

Laura was very glad to eat. It had been a long while since her last meal. The eunuchs gave little thought as to whether or not the slaves ate at regular hours. If they were not in the *zenana* at meal time they went without. And this food was far better than the fare in the *zenana*

When the first pangs of hunger had been satisfied Nate wiped his mouth and said "When you didn't arrive back at Udagore when we expected we went looking for you and ran into a bunch of folks running aways from Delhi. Christ, Laurie, your Pa and me was so scared that you'd been killed by those sons of bitches!"

Udagore was a small city some ten miles to the northeast of Delhi. Nate and his future father-in-law had been overseeing the construction of a new telegraphic line on the 11th of May. Laura, in a little *eka*, which was a light, two wheeled trap pulled by one horse, had gone into Delhi to fetch supplies and ran straight into revolting *sepoys*.

"I turned myself right around and whipped up that horse and got the hell out of there," she said, remembering. "I was heading back when this big old Pathan stopped me," she told him how she had come to be in Wazid Ali's *palka-ghari* and all that had happened since.

"We looked all over, me and your Pa, until we found the *eka*. And since there was no sign of blood I figured you was still alive, and after that it was only a matter of tracking," said Nate. "The man who took you off, his horse had shoes that gave him away easy, left a mark a blind man could follow."

"And you're the best," said Laura admiringly.

Indeed he was. For years Nate had been a cavalry scout. His father had been half Cherokee, and his mother an African woman, a Berber, rescued from the mines of New

344

Spain. He had grown up on the frontier of New Spain where life was rough and hard. He had learned survival skills at an early age. He was also one of the finest horsemen Laura had ever seen. There was nothing that Nate could not do with a horse. Laura had seen him take a wild, unbroken mustang and have it gentle enough to serve as a lady's mount in less than a day, all without force or whips or cruelty. With his naturally dark complexion and horsemanship he could easily pass as an Indian *Daffadur.*

"How'd you come to be Gautama Sarin?" Laura wanted to know, as she polished off the last of the rice and curried vegetables.

"That part wasn't too hard. Remember that Rajah who took such a fancy to your Pa, old Mayur Kapoor up in the Punjab? Well, this Gautama Sarin was a *Daffadur* in his private army and it chanced that he was killed recently. Your Pa and I went up there to see if old Mayur could help us rescue you and to find out what he knew about this Jhaniput place. It was that old fox's idea that I take Sarin's place. Mayur's disbanding his army. Most of the men are damned old, and he says the British will squash this revolt and then the Princes won't be allowed to have their own armies any more, so all his officers would be looking for new places. And with this beard I look enough like that Sarin to fool his own Ma. Mayur heard that Jhaniput was looking for officers, especially and he wrote me a recommendation. So I grew my beard, practiced my Hindoo, learned the ways of the army here and studied up on the religion. When I came here they snapped me up."

Nate made this sound as if what he had had to do was nothing, a snap of the fingers. Laura looked at him with pride and appreciation. He had gone to a great deal of effort and was in constant danger. All because he loved her and wanted her back. Her heart glowed.

"This is the damndest place I ever saw, Laurie," he said, taking a slice of fruit from a dish.

"One big old whore house," she said.

"Why? That's what I want to know. They put lust dust in the enlisted men's food, did you know that? They call it the 'Dust of Kali' and it makes the little bastards as horny as all get out. They have to go hump a female at least twice a day

345

or they'll bust! Since I'm an officer I get to give it to myself. One of the first things they told me was that when I was off duty I could have all the women I wanted. In fact, they pushed me to visit the *zenana* often and take my pick and I could use the dust. You snort it up your nose, and be able to take as many women as you wanted without worrying about wearing yourself out. Why?" Nate asked, "are they doing this?"

"It's some sort of black magic. Laura answered. "Rose says this stone in my belly is gathering power. And they drain it off. 'Bout once a month now we have to go to the Room of Kali and have a little ceremony in front of a big old statue of Kali and pull the power out. That Maharani, Parminder told us she changed her name from Dipti to Kalidassa."

"Servant of Kali," Nate translated. he glanced towards the window. "Sun's coming up. When it does, there's something I'm going to show you Laurie." He looked back at her. "You're a sight for sore eyes, honey," he said, his love for her in his every look. "Damn, but I missed you!"

"And how do you like my outfit, the absolute latest straight from Paree," Laura said.

"I don't give a good Goddamn what you're wearing or not wearin, as long as you're still my Laurie," he said and reached across the table to take her hands in his.

"I'll always be yours, Nate," she said softly, looking into his eyes. "You've got me all day. When you've shown me whatever it is, can you take me to bed and give me some real loving? Not just slam, bang, thank you ma'am like these horny little bastards. Like you did at home under that old tree in the meadow? "

"I'd purely love to, honey," he said.

She got up and went around to the other side of the table and slid under his arm and watched with him as the sun came up, flooding the room with golden light.

Bugles blew outside and there were the sounds of activity.

"Got no duty until this afternoon since it's my 'natal day'. That's morning parade assembling now. Every morning her highness comes out and inspects the troops," said Nate. "Come on, we can see them out of this window. It looks over the *maidan.*"

Morning sun from a clear blue sky shone upon the spacious parade ground that was visible from up high here in the barracks.

And Laura gasped as she took in the scene below.

It was an army, a huge army of every kind of soldiery she had ever seen or even imagined. There were foot regiments, all in perfect order, companies of horse and artillery and war elephants. There were large guns, cannons, gleaming in the sunlight. As she watched, a company of mounted lancers wheeled in perfect formation, their bright pointed lances moving as if they had all one mind. Over every regiment flew a bright pennon, snapping in the wind, a red banner with the image of the black multi- armed Kali upon it.

As Laura watched, huge guns, towed by elephants, were maneuvered in precision and the gun crews lit their fuses. In perfect unity, the guns roared out, just as a gigantic white elephant, decked in red and black and cloth of gold, with a red *howdah*, draped with pearls and gold fringe, carried the Maharani into view.

"Twenty five thousand men all together, Laurie and they want more. They pay a bounty to each man who can get a friend or a relative to join up," said Nate in her ear.

Outside the men cheered in one voice. It took Laura a few minutes to make out that they were shouting "Kali! Kali!"

"And if they are gathering black magical power," said Nate in that same low voice, "I reckon that it'll be going to help these fellows, and it's my guess that this bunch will be going up against the British, since the talk I hear is all hatred of the *feringhi*. The thing I don't know yet is *when*."

Alan removed his arm from Rosamunde's shoulder and she began to lay backwards. He grabbed her arm. "What are you doing?" he said angrily.

"But if you are going to take me, I have to–" she said in bafflement

"I do not *take* women, Rosamunde! I make love with them, with a woman who desires me as much as I want her! Not like this! Not with you! Do you want me to have sex with

347

you? Do you?" he insisted as she looked up at him, confusion on her face.

"No," she said at last "but, Alan, if you don't use me, they'll *know*, and I'll be punished and they will not give me to you again!" She was beginning to tremble. "And now that you've come I could not bear it, to know you are here and not to be able to see you! Oh, please, just take me!"

"No!" he said decisively, letting go her arm. "How will they know?"

"They can read it in the ruby," she began and before she could stop him he bent down and touched it and it reacted on him as it had on her. He gave a gasp and looked at her, all the colour draining from his face, so that under the dye he looked gray and ill.

She knew what he had seen. The General, who had kept her over an hour that night, was a man of depraved tastes and she had never been able to tell even Laura what he wanted from her.

He sat down abruptly on the charpoy beside her, muttering to himself.

She finally made out what he was saying: "I'll kill them all! I'll kill them all!" He then turned to her and pulled her against him. She could not tell if it was for her comfort or his. They said nothing but just held one another for the longest time. There was nothing sexual in their embrace at all, they were two frightened children in the dark, seeking comfort from each other. And she was consoled by the fact that what he had seen had not repulsed him, that he still wanted to touch her and still felt affection for her.

And Cathal, in need of comfort himself, wiggled up between them.

An hour or so later the torchlight had abruptly died. "That's good," Rosamunde had said, "because when the torches go out it means that the Maharajah has successfully bedded his bride and no longer needs to spy upon his guests."

"Filthy little degenerate!" Alan had sworn. He then said "I can still make illusions, Rosamunde, and I'll put what they want to see in that ruby. I just can't add to your misery by debauching you. I would never forgive myself," he stopped himself before he said "I love you too much."

Rosamunde lay on her side almost on her chest, turned slightly away from him. She was still deeply ashamed that she had to appear before him like this, for what she had told him earlier was not true. Even after nearly five months of nudity, of constant use by all sorts of men and performing in degrading, indecent dances she was still mortified, embarrassed and humiliated to be seen like this, particularly by Alan. To lay in this position was not very comfortable, given those horrible hoops in her breasts that were always in the way, but it hid most of her bosom and private parts from view. It had hurt when Alan had crushed her against him, but she would put up with any pain to feel that he still cared for her, no matter what she had become.

She was now stroking Cathal, who had been very silent ever since she had told then about Sinéad. "Will it fool them, though?" she asked now. "Enough to make them give me to you again?"

"I don't know," he said frankly. "If it does not perhaps we can tell them I am incapable of using a woman yet obtain much joy from just looking at your body. They seem eager to please me."

"Alan!" she said in protest.

"What is it they put in the food here?" he asked before she could protest further.

"It's some sort of an aphrodisiac, I think " she said. "A while ago, Laura and I were taking some rubies from the *Hakim* to the Room of Kali and on the way back we were accosted by two young *jemadars* who took us back to their quarters, with the eunuch's approval. They kept us busy all afternoon." Rosamunde flushed as she remembered some of the things that the imaginative young men had demanded of them. "They were able to use us for hours by sniffing up a dust, a black dust. And Laura says that the men who used us in the brothel were drugged."

"That's quite common in sex magic brothels," said Alan thoughtfully "The longer a man lasts the more power is generated. And with a magiced aphrodisiac a man may use more than one woman in a short length of time, again, gathering more power." He them recalled something else that she had said. "You said that you were taking some rubies

349

from the *Hakim*–?"

"Yes, Alan, he's an alchemist! He makes all of the rubies! I saw the athanor! I feel sorry for him, however, he's a prisoner too. His brother is the chief eunuch, Mahbub Al Khan, and the *Hakim*, Ahsamaallah Al Khan, is held here against his will. He seems to be a Wizard Healer of sorts, else wise most of us would be covered in whip marks. The Maharani keeps his wife and children locked up and threatens to put his wife to work in the brothel if he does not do as she says."

Covered in whip marks. Alan thought despairingly of her being whipped. These people were beyond evil. Everything he had ever read or studied or heard of: none of it had been as bad as this.

And how was he to get Rosamunde out of here? How was he to bear watching her dance in that lewd fashion, or watch that little deviate handle her? And to bear knowing that every day she was being repeatedly violated by man after man, with no regard for her pain, her feelings or her modesty?

Alan could not know it, but Nate Connelly, now cuddling a sleeping Laura against his side, was lying awake, wondering the selfsame things.

37

the room of kali

After more conversation Alan and Rosamunde had fallen into an exhausted sleep. He had wanted to sleep on the floor; she insisted he remain on the *charpoy* with her "Oh, what do the proprieties matter?" she said. "I'm completely undressed and when I leave you in the morning it will be to go to be used by a countless men. I've no reputation to maintain any more. And you look as if you need a good night's sleep."

In truth, she was worried about his health. After he had cast the spell of illusion on her ruby he had looked exhausted and had admitted to being dizzy. She had noticed how anxiously Cathal had studied him.

How were they to escape from this place if Alan had no magic to speak of? She had cherished dreams of him arriving and sending everyone to Hell in a burst of overwhelmingly powerful magic, of seeing him raze the *Mahal*, of ridding her and the other women of their slave jewelry, the rubies, and the spell against wearing clothing. Now it seemed as if all of those dreams were to come to naught.

But at least he was here, and if his illusion had worked perhaps she would be allowed to go to him every evening after the others had finished with her. Like Laura, he gave her strength. And he was *home* to her. She could talk to him of things dear to her heart She just wished that he would not have to see her perform in those filthy dances and be used as the prize in a game of dice and especially see her fondled by that little pervert. And she wished that she need not be naked in front of him. But it all had to be endured if she was to be near him.

She hoped to see Laura this morning before they had to go into the *Durbar*.

But she was alone in the wash room, with Pramoda Tandon, with no sign of Laura.

As usual the eunuch took every opportunity to humiliate her and squeeze and poke at her.

This morning, though, after the washing was done he left her hanging from the hook instead of moving her to the tables where the oiling was done.

He stood back, as if waiting and in a few minutes, the door opened to admit the Maharani and Hussaini. Mabel Clutterbuck trotted behind Hussaini.

Mabel sank to the ground in the attitude of submission while the Maharani studied Rosamunde. "You may speak, girl, for I shall be asking you some questions," she said.

The Maharani reached out and touched the ruby in Rosamunde's navel. A strange expression, almost of triumph, crossed her face and then she turned to Hussaini. "It as we thought it would be. Look here."

Hussaini, who today wore green trousers heavily embroidered with gold, left off fondling Mabel's hair and came over to touch the ruby. "Oh ho!" she said with a salacious grin. "That magician is a lusty fellow! Four times! And in the *ghosulkhana* too!"

"Did the magician enjoy you, girl?" the Maharani demanded. looking hard at Rosamunde. "He took you in the bath, on the *charpoy*, out in the garden and on the *chabutara*. Does he want you again?"

Rosamunde was stunned.. What had Alan put in that ruby? She could only manage a rather strangled "Yes."

"Do you see the power, Hussaini?" the Maharani asked. "Four times what is usually captured! Four times! Do all of the people in your far away country have magic?" she inquired of Rosamunde.

"Yes, highness," Rosamunde said hesitantly...

"That must account for it," the Maharani murmured as if to herself. She looked at Rosamunde again "From now on, girl, you shall spend every night with the magician, but only after you have been with as many of our guests and officers as want you. You have not been making enough effort to attract as many men as possible," she added, frowning.

Rosamunde felt a sickness spreading itself at the pit of her stomach. She had been hoping that no one would notice that she had been trying to avoid her other 'duties' than just that of dancing. She ought to have known that this was a forlorn hope at best, for eyes were everywhere, watching. What went on at the *Diwan* was bad enough but to deliberately put herself in the way of those who would want her....

And the Maharani knew this. She laughed softly as she looked at Rosamunde. "You shall hate that, girl, will you not? But you must try harder or not only will you taste the lash but you shall spend two full days with the *Bhutas*."

The Maharani had won. She knew that Rosamunde would do anything to stay away from the *Bhutas*.

"Encourage the magician, girl," said the Maharani. "Hussaini, let us make certain that the magician is well supplied with the Dust of Kali. Perhaps it is best that he does not know he is getting it."

Hussaini nodded.

"We are every close, Hussaini," said the Maharani as if Rosamunde and Pramoda Tandon were not even present. "But we still have need of more power and more men."

She then turned to the eunuch who had stood silently at attention. "Where does this one do today, Tandon?"

"She practices the new dance this morning and is fitted with the costume. Then she will be in the *zenana* for use until the *Durbar* and then will dance for his highness and his guests this evening."

"Chowki will dance instead and be my son's pleasure at the *Durbar*. This one will come to the room of Kali this afternoon. And I have decided that there will be a large bag of *mohurs* for any eunuch who keeps his women well supplied with men," said the Maharani.

Tandon's eyes gleamed with greed. Rosamunde felt sick again. She had to be fitted for a costume that was nothing but bespelled ribbons designed to show off her body, made by a *dazi*, a tailor, who delighted in groping the dancers, practice her lascivious dance, which involved watching herself in front of the mirror which was always revolting and also sleep with at least two of the musicians before hand. And with a bag of *mohurs* in front of his eyes, Tandon would be certain to bring as many men as was possible to her. And perhaps the greatest horror of all of those, the room of Kali.

353

Rosamunde was looking at herself in the glass. The 'costume' consisted of a wide collar of silver and rose quartz that came down over her shoulders. When she wore it, a spell on it made all the rest of her jewelry seem as if it too was silver. From a ring on each shoulder point on the collar came a ribbon of dark pink silk. One on each side crossed her chest and went under her breast, the left ribbon under the right and the right ribbon under the left, both of them crossing to form an 'x' between her breasts. This tied behind her back with long fluttering ribbons. A ring on the middle of the collar bore a third ribbon which went down her torso and stomach, splitting to go around the ruby and split between her legs in front.In the back it became a single ribbon again up between her buttocks and was attached to a center ring on the back of the collar, again with long fluttering ends.

Parminder wore a similar costume. They were to perform the Dance of the Roses, a new dance. To Rosamunde's surprise the Maharani was the one that choreographed the dances. Parminder was to perform her usual lewd dance, using artificial roses in a very suggestive manner, while Rosamunde performed a series of *arabesques, jetés* and *fouettés en tournats* about her, with one leg in the air as she went up and down on her toes and pirouetted. She had made herself some crude *pointe* shoes, with carefully placed darns and a toe box glued and reinforced with many layers of fabric. The shoemaker had been eager to help her as long as she paid him in the usual way and had given her a pair of very soft curly toed *juties* with which to experiment when he had been delighted with the payment.

The first time she had gone up on her toes the entire court had been astonished. Now they wanted to see it several times a week.

The costume seemed to draw even more attention to her nudity, she thought in despair as she studied herself. The ribbons drew the eye to what they outlined. Once again she wished that Alan did not have to see her like this. "Why do we have to bear the humiliation of exhibiting ourselves like this? What would be wrong with a minimum of clothing?" she asked Parminder, turning away from the mirror and going to sit beside her friend upon the floor.

"You have used the word that best describes it, Rose

of the World. It is for the humiliation that we feel, the anger and the despair," said Parminder. "The humiliation is immense. And too, the Maharani likes to show her power over us, that she make us degrade ourselves. She also likes to show the people in Jhaniput that she can take daughters and wives and sweethearts away and use them for her own purposes. She takes their sons for the army as well or if they are very handsome, for her bed men or dancers."

Rosamunde shivered. Hearing about the male dancers made her hope and pray that there were no male and female dances while Alan was present to see her have to perform in them. That had been the ultimate in shame and degradation.

As soon as she had been able to snatch a few minutes alone with Parminder she had told her of Alan's arrival.

Now the Indian woman said. "Might you tell your magician to visit the bazaar as soon as he may?"

"Why?" Rosamunde asked curiously.

"He must speak to the curry seller who has a stand near the House of Assignation, the public brothel in the city."

"*Another* brothel?" Rosamunde said in disgust.

Parminder smiled sadly. "Did you think this the only one? There are many men here who want a woman,"

"I am beginning to think that men are little better than beasts!" Rosamunde interrupted.

At the look on her face Parminder said gently, "All the men are not beasts, Rose of the World. Some of the men are kind and will use you carefully. Some will refuse you because they are married and will not commit *kufr* (infidelity) The curry seller is very kind."

"Is he kind to you, Parminder?" asked Rosamunde in a rather brittle voice.

Parminder's eyes filled with tears. "He is always kind to me," she said slowly and turned her head to look at Rosamunde. "For, you see, he is my husband."

All through her stint in the *zenana* Rosamunde thought about what Parminder had told her.

Parminder and the man she had married, Sishul Mehra, and his family were a natives of the city, although she had been sent to Bombay to be educated and to live with a childless aunt and uncle. Both of their families were of the military caste, the *Kshatriya*, the second highest *Varna* or caste. And both families, once prosperous, with high positions, had been ruined by the Riwats, through taxes, fines and outright persecution. Parminder's husband, once addressed as 'lord' was now forced to make a living as a curry seller so that his wife, children and his wife's elderly parents would not starve.

Parminder had been stolen from her family when one of the eunuchs had seen her dance at her brother's wedding. There was nothing her family could do about it, for anyone who protested the *Mahal's* stealing of a woman was silenced permanently.

Rosamunde felt desperately sorry for her friend. It was even worse for her as Parminder had been dragged from not only parents, siblings, in-laws and a husband but two children as well. She had been a captive of the *Kala Mahal* for three years now and her children were growing up without her. She had not seen them or her husband in all that time. What had happened to her was a tragedy for both families. It made Rosamunde realize all over again how truly evil this place was.

Rosamunde looked for Laura as she wanted to tell her about Alan, but Margaret told her that word was that Laura was with one of the officers as a special 'reward' and would be gone until much later in the day.

Rosamunde was disappointed, for she knew that she would be in ill condition when she came from the room of Kali to have any meaningful talk with anyone. Any of the women who visited the room of Kali were excused from all duties for the rest of the day, for they were in no fit case to entertain men. They were good for nothing, only semi-conscious, until the next day. A visit there was something that none of them looked forward to. Laura had said she'd rather be humped by a grizzly bear than go in to the room of Kali.

The room of Kali was the very same room in which they had received their rubies and the other 'gifts ' of Kali, a misnomer if there ever was one as if it were some sort of present to be forcibly prevented from having children or kept from being able to wear clothing.

Pramoda Tandon did not take her to the room of Kali. He did however, wash her again after her mornings 'work' and this time applied no oil at all.

The chief eunuch, a gigantic man named Mahbub Al Khan, came and threw her over his shoulder. He was a morose individual who only smiled when he saw one of the women being beaten. He much hated and resented women now that he was a eunuch and his only pleasure was seeing them hurt. He had once been a general somewhere, the whispers ran, and had been found with one of his employer's wives in a very compromising position. He had been castrated, broken in rank and cast out. The Maharani had found him, and made him her chief eunuch and consulted him on all military matters. He was fiercely loyal to her and to Kali. All of the female slaves in the *Mahal* were afraid of him, with good reason.

The room of Kali was made of black marble, mirror-like so that Rosamunde was forced to watch herself as Al Khan tied her to a most peculiar table in front of a large statue of Kali.

The first time that she had been in this room Rosamunde had not really seen the statue or her sur-roundings, for she had been too afraid of the black magic being performed. She had now become only too familiar with it.

The statue was of black stone, of a seated, full figured woman cross legged and naked. She had a multitude of arms, each of them either holding a weapon or the hand held in a scissor- like position or the finger pointing. In the language of hands the former was meant to indicate a weapon, while the latter signified inspiring terror. Around her neck was a necklace of human skulls and a red stone tongue protruded from her mouth. Her eyes were painted and seemed to stare right into Rosamunde's soul. The statue, too, wore a large ruby in her navel. This was Kali, the black one, here in her darkest aspect as devourer of worlds; she of death, destruc-tion, fear and the drinker of blood.

An altar stood before her statue and to either side of it a brazier was burning, an acrid stench that burned the eyes and the throat.

In front of the altar was a curious table. The head of

357

it, furthest from Kali, resembled a Christian cross, but the foot of it was split to form an upside down 'v'.

Al Khan threw Rosamunde on this table on her stomach. He roughly pulled her arms out to each one of the arms of the cross, using the rings in the jewelry to tie her down. He then wrenched her legs apart and tied them to the arms of the v, so that she was spread eagled, facing the statue.

He then maliciously poked and pinched and slapped her, including reaching underneath to torment her breasts, which already hurt from laying face down on the horrible hoops that pierced them. Rosamunde knew better than to react to anything he did, for that just seemed to drive him to further heights, much like the vile *tabla* player.

Just as Rosamunde began to feel that she could not stand another minute of this treatment and would soon scream, begging him to stop, she heard a door open.

The eunuch immediately took his hands from her body and said, bowing, "She awaits your pleasure, highness."

There were noises from behind Rosamunde, near the altar. Face down, Rosamunde could not see what was going on but she had now been in this room enough times now to know. The Maharani was stripping off her *sari* and Al Khan was anointing her with the oil of Kali.

A familiar, too familiar, fetid odor began to fill the room. The scent of the oil was sickening for it smelt of death and decay and evil. It was nauseating enough that the Maharani reeked of it. But only minutes later Rosamunde heard the sound of the Maharani's feet on the bare floor and she felt a puddle of oil poured first onto her buttocks and then onto her back.

The Maharani began to rub the oil into Rosamunde's flesh with hard, heavy strokes, leaving a trail of foulness. Rosamunde wanted to shudder, to draw away from that vileness for both the woman's touch and the oil were obscene. But not only was she tied tightly, but she knew Al Khan would now be holding a short whip with which he would have no hesitation in lashing her should she fight it or even show the slightest bit of distaste. She forced herself to lie still, but her stomach was rolling with nausea and dread and disgust threatened to choke her.

"Turn her," the Maharani told Al Khan.

He untied Rosamunde and turned her onto her back, retying her with quick efficiency.

Now Rosamunde could see what was going on and wished that she could not. The naked Maharani, gleaming with the stinking oil of Kali, stood over Rosamunde and from a *chillumchee,* a copper bowl usually used for washing the hands, poured a stream of the oil over Rosamunde's breasts and lower abdomen, where it trickled down between her outstretched legs.

The small, pudgy hands, so like her son's, began to massage her. "Such a beautiful body," she said to herself. "Such high firm breasts, such softly rounded hips and a tight *yoni,* such as men like. Had Kali made me thus I should have been *Padishah* of all Hind by marrying the most powerful of men. But Kali chose to give me power, not beauty and in the end that is better. I can make beauty such as this serve me. And I need not serve a husband to have power."

Rosamunde wanted very badly to be sick. the woman's touch and the repellent *wrong* feeling of the oil was vile beyond words.

But worse was to come. When the Maharani had fully anointed her, covering everywhere that was exposed, save her face and neck, she called the eunuch to her.

He well knew what came next and he was carrying a knife and another *chillumchee,* this one of black onyx. As Rosamunde watched he nicked a vein in his mistress's arm and let the bowl fill with her blood.

When the bowl was filled the Maharani touched the wound and a red light flaring from her fingers healed it as neatly as if it had never been there.

She then took the bowl and put it on the table between the V of Rosamunde's legs. The silver bowl, which should have been slightly warm, filled as it was with human blood, and held in the eunuch's large hands for some time but instead was ice cold.

The Maharani dipped her finger into the blood and began to trace arcane symbols on Rosamunde's body, down both thighs, on her abdomen, her rib cage, over and around her breasts, painting the nipples until they shone red. Then she took a handful of the blood and poured it between

359

Rosamunde's legs By the time she finished Rosamunde was shivering spasmodically from both cold and revulsion.

She lay there, dreading what was to come, as the eunuch then painted the same symbols on the Maharani, who seemed to revel in the process. The *wrongness* of the symbols, the feeling of darkness and corruption, threatened to overcome Rosamunde. If she lost consciousness for this part of the ceremony she would be harshly awakened by the eunuch. She had to be awake for what would follow.

The Maharani removed the bowl and gave it to Al Khan. She then came to stand between Rosamunde's outstretched legs, upon a little step stool, for she was too short to be in the proper position without it.

In a low guttural voice that Maharani began an incantation. It was in no language that Rosamunde understood and it was harsh and ugly.

As she chanted she rubbed her hands up and down the sides of Rosamunde's body where no symbols were painted, faster and faster until the friction was painful, Rosamunde had to bite her lips to keep from crying out.

The light in the torches began to glow bright red.

And the eye sockets in the skulls around the neck of Kali glowed red as well.

Shadows began to move on the wall, shadows of six arms beginning to move in sensual dance.

"She wakes," said the eunuch impassively.

With a shriek of triumph the Maharani threw herself on top of Rosamunde so that her navel touched the pigeon's blood red ruby imbedded in Rosamunde's abdomen. She grabbed the rings in the girls' breasts, pulling them painfully.

Rosamunde always thought that she was ready for what came next but it always ended in the same way: a convulsion of pain that made her arch up against the restraints.

And the statue's eyes focused and it *looked* at her.

The Maharani shrieked, but not in pain as she slid off Rosamunde's body. In her navel now gleamed the ruby, pulsating with the red light of power.

38

unicorn's horn

As the Maharani reveled in the power that filled her veins and prostrated herself in front of the altar of Kali, where the statue now writhed and looked out on the room with awareness in he painted eyes, Rosamunde lost her tenuous hold on consciousness. The sheer horror of the foul magic and the living statue that seemed the very epitome of evil always effected her, a Witch dedicated to the Light, far more than it did most of the other women, for she understood all too well just how diabolical this entire ceremony was.

She was unconscious for the ruby's restoration to its place in her navel after every scrap of power that was drained from it.

The Maharani stood over her body as Al Khan untied her. She, in sharp contrast to Rosamunde, seemed to glow with power and elation.

"Send two of my bed men to me, for I would couple now," she ordered Al Khan. "And do not take this girl to be washed. Take her instead to the room of the magician. I ordered the dust of Kali placed in large quantities in his *haziri* and *tiffin*, and he shall be needing a woman badly. A great amount of power will be generated if he uses her while she is adorned with Kali's oil and symbols. He will not be able to stop from taking her."

"Perhaps I should see, highness, that he has some sherbet and fruit with the dust in it as well," suggested the eunuch, swinging Rosamunde up onto his shoulder.

"An excellent notion," she approved. "He may have her all night. He seems to be a man of lustful habit, for he took her four times yester eve with but a touch of the dust in his food. Four times the usual power, Al Khan! If I had more like him and more women such a this one, we should be much nearer our goal." She looked suddenly thoughtful. "My son will be disappointed, but I think that we shall keep the magician in his room all night with this girl so that we may gather as much power as possible. This girl is very valuable, as valuable as a *mem-sahib,* for her shame is very great. She too, has a touch of magic and she generates more power than many of the others. We must impress upon her that she is to attract as many men as possible else she will be punished. And yes," she said, seeing the look on the big eunuch's face, "I shall let you have her to whip if she does not obey. And then she will go to the *Bhutas.* She generated much power there as well. I only wish –" She sighed. If only she could use the *Bhutas* all of the time on all of the women! But the *Bhutas* were difficult to control, even with the power of Kali. And the women so used, if left too long within that room, had a tendency to die.

"Go now," she ordered Al Khan. "Send my bed men. And take this girl to where she may do us the most good – in the bed of the magician Jehan."

It was with acute anxiety that Alan had watched Rosamunde being borne away over the shoulder of an enormous eunuch. All of the eunuchs here seemed to be chosen for their size, and Alan suspected, for their cruelty and hatred of women. They all handled her roughly and spoke to her brusquely, as if she were an object.

Rosamunde had seemed reluctant to speak about what had been done to her here. After that one outburst about how much she hated the attentions of the Maharajah she had spoken only of her friends, Laura and Parminder, and of the other women she had been enslaved with.

Alan had been completely horrified and sickened by what he had seen in the ruby. He had not imagined that a man could, in all good conscience, do such things to a woman, and do them with the glee he had seen in the General's face.

And almost worse had been the look in Rosamunde's eyes when she understood that he had seen her degradation. Such a look of hopelessness, of deep pain and despair he had never thought he would see. She had fully expected him to reject her; he could see that in her face as well.

And when instead he had embraced her and held her

against him he could feel her relief. He had wanted to tell her that it did not matter to him what they had done to her; he knew that she had been forced into it or perhaps she was even bespelled. He had noticed how quickly she obeyed every obscene thing the eunuch told her to do, particularly laying in that lewd 'position'. If she had not been bespelled perhaps she had been beaten so many times that she had to give in because of the pain or perhaps she had even been tortured. He could not even imagine what might have been done to her. He remembered what he had learned of tortures, sexual and otherwise, in Professor Williamson's class, tortures that were designed to compel the women's obedience in places such as this. It had made for sickening reading and lectures. And she had said that the *Hakim* was a Wizard Healer of sorts. A skilled but depraved Healer could erase all or most evidences of beatings and torture, so that the victim could be abused again and again.

He was so angry and revolted that he found he could not sit still, but paced the room like a caged animal. And he had been further enraged when he found out that he was locked into the room. He actually heard someone come and turn the key in the lock mid-afternoon.

Cathal had been very quiet since he had heard about Sinéad's death. He looked up at Alan's angry exclamation and said "Can't you unlock it magically?"

"No," said Alan shortly. "Remember it takes a *Magus Magistra* to undo a magiced lock and I am not even a *Magus Novititae* any more! And this one *is* definitely magiced. I can feel it. God damn it, why are they locking me in? They let me wander around this morning! Oh, God, Cathal, why did I have to lose my magic!" He groaned and sank onto the *charpoy*, and bent his head, winding his fingers in his hair. "I feel so useless – as if I am nothing!"

Cathal left the window and scurried across the floor to get up beside his Wizard, putting a paw on Alan's leg.

"I cannot bear to think what they are doing to her," Alan said passionately. "I keep thinking if I were only not so damned stupid we might have been married by now and setting up our home near the Laboratory. And she'd be happy and perhaps looking forward to our children instead of being brutalized and –" he could not go on.

Cathal started to speak but a noise at the door made them both look up as a key turned in the lock. The door swung open to reveal another large eunuch with Rosamunde over his shoulder. As if she were a carelessly disposed of package he dropped her on the bed beside Alan. "Her highness graciously gives you use of this slave for the rest of the day and the evening hours as well. You are not to perform tonight. Instead, her highness rewards you by giving you this slave."

His look was significant. Alan realized that he was being commanded to lay with Rosamunde as many times as he could. And if he had not purified every piece of food that had been delivered to him that day he probably would have fallen on her body like a ravening beast. A vast quantity of the aphrodisiac had been in everything, even the tea.

Even before the eunuch had left, locking the door behind him, Alan could feel the *wrongness* rising off Rosamunde's body.

"Phew!" Cathal exclaimed. "What is that stuff? And those symbols, those are evil, Alan!"

"She's probably been used in some sort of black ceremony," said Alan, studying the symbols on her body. "Perhaps to drain the power in that stone." He reached out and touched the ruby and no images came to him, for which he was profoundly grateful. "Yes, it's been drained. But we have to get this foulness off her, Cathal, it's hurting her and I doubt she'll wake up before it is cleaned off. Those bastards probably think that I would be so full of that aphrodisiac that I would be willing to lay with her in this condition."

"A bath?" Cathal suggested. Without waiting for confirmation from Alan he ran to the *ghosulkhana* to turn the spigot that filled the tub.

Alan studied the symbols drawn on her body; some of them he recognized from the text he had used in Oxford. He wished he had it with him now, not back in his rooms in Cheltenham. But others of them were completely strange, made in an esoteric tradition that was not his.

One thing was certain; they had to come off her, now. He did not like her colour, which gray tinged, nor the way her head lolled sideways.

When he picked her up with difficulty, for he still did

not have much of his strength back, she was like a floppy rag doll in his arms and he had to grit his teeth against the feeling of foulness that the oil gave him, right through his *achkan*. He staggered into the *ghosulkhana* and almost dropped her into the water.

"Here's some things I found in the cupboard," said Cathal eagerly.

He had found an English style bath sponge and some bars of soap. "*Savon de Paris?*" Alan read the wrapper in disbelief. These people certainly did not stint themselves! Imported mushrooms and now imported French soap. He shrugged off his jacket and rolled up the sleeves of the shirt underneath. He then knelt beside the sunken tub and rubbed the soap into the sponge and began stroking her with it, hoping to cleanse every trace of that vileness from her.

The soap smelled enticingly of white lilac and gave Alan such a longing for home, reminding him so much of the lilac that grew outside the drawing room windows at Summerhills, that tears filled his eyes. "Stupid!" he told himself. "It's the wrong time of year for lilacs!"

"It's not working!" said Cathal in dismay.

Alan looked down at her body in the water. Indeed it was not, instead the water and the soap and sponge were now befouled. The only change had been that the arcane symbols of blood were now smeared.

"I'm an idiot, Cathal!" Alan exclaimed. Carefully and gently he lay Rosamunde back against the edge of the tub and put the sponge aside. Reaching inside his shirt he pulled out the silver chain with the piece of unicorn's horn on it. He slipped the chain over his head and dipped the horn into the water.

Blue rings at once began to ripple out from it, leaving purity in their wake. The magic crept up on to her body, wiping away the filth as if it had never been. In five minutes she was cleansed of the dirty oil and blood and laying in a tub of warm water of crystal clarity.

Alan lay the bit of horn against the sponge and the soap as well.

Her colour was improving and she seemed to be more in a natural sleep.

Alan decided to give her a good bath with the soap

and sponge. He even washed her hair, removing all the traces of oil and hair pomade that she usually wore. He also slipped the chain with the horn on it over her head. He had noticed her wincing the night before, from those hideous breast hoops and thought that the healing powers of the horn would help her. All the while he worked his mind was going round and round, thinking that it might now be too late for them. For even if he could get them away from this terrible place, would she ever be able to bear a man's touch again? Or return his love?

When Rosamunde awoke she was warm and comfortable but appeared to be laying on grass, with sunlight warming her body. She felt extraordinarily well, even her breasts and other parts of her body, which nearly always hurt, felt well.

She was laying on her back and when she turned her head she saw Alan, sitting cross-legged beside her, looking at her with a most peculiar look, one of sadness, she thought.

Conscious of her body, she sat up quickly and put her knees up to her chest. "What am I doing here?" she asked in confusion. She usually awoke late at night, in the *zenana,* after a session in the room of Kali.

"Those perverts thought that I would make more power for them by laying with you when you were covered in that filth with which they painted you," he explained. "They laced all my food today with vast quantities of the aphrodisiac. They don't know that I have this," He held up the silver chain with the unicorn's horn on it, now back around his neck. "I used it on you, Rosamunde. It removed every trace of that foul brew. And I hope you don't mind, but I gave you a bath as well. I had to bring you out here in the sun to dry as I was not certain if I could use a towel with out causing bale fire."

"The eunuchs dry us with a type of scraper," Rosamunde said. "Oh, Alan, it feels wonderful to be free of oil! And my hair is clean, too! Thank you!" she tuned a glowing face to him. "I smell of lilacs!"

He relaxed visibly. He had been afraid that she would be offended that he had washed her, had been so intimate with her body while she was unconscious.

"The unicorn horn has made me feel better all over," she said. "I have not felt this well since I came here, not even after I have a session with the *Hakim*. Do you use the unicorn horn to purify the food?"

"Everything they give me," he answered. "Speaking of food, are you hungry? They've just delivered a laden table, and I've purified it and I had enough magic to keep it hot until you woke up."

Rosamunde was suddenly conscious of being very hungry indeed. But she did not know what to do, for if she stood up she would be completely exposed.

He read this in her face. "Rosamunde," he said gently. "We are both of us going to have to become accustomed to your state of undress. You cannot remain upon your stomach the entire time we are together or with your legs up to your chest. How will you eat?" And that rear view was just as distracting as the front view, he could have added.

She steeled herself and put down her legs and allowed him to help her off the ground and lead her to the table. As they were seated on small thin cushions on the floor there was little she could use to cover herself.

He tried his best to pretend that she was not naked, that he could not see her beautiful unclothed body. This was going to severely try his fortitude, loving her so much, and, he admitted, wanting her as well. But he could tell that she was in an agony of shame and embarrassment. Once again he cursed the people who had done this to her. He would not add to her pain and mortification by staring at her or acting in a lecherous fashion. He would be the perfect gentleman, no matter what it cost him.

Now he served her with some food: the inevitable chicken, a Mughal recipe called *Dopiaza* that combined many spices with chicken and onions and tomatoes, on a bed of *basmati* rice, and Indian cheese, *paneer,* with more mushrooms and peas, spices and yogurt. This time with shallow fired *paratha* bread, made much like *chupatties* but made with *ghee* (butter) in the ingredients so that it was richer flavored. He asked, "Were you able to speak to your friends?"

She had immediately begun eating as if she was starving. "Oh, this is much better than what hey give us in

367

the *zenana!*" Then she answered his question. "Only Parminder, when we practiced the new dance. Laura had been given to one of the officers and was not back by the time I was taken to the room of Kali."

Alan winced at the terminology. A woman had 'been given', as if she were a package or a piece of furniture. And Rosamunde said it almost casually, as if it were something she was well used to, and with a jolt, he realized that she *was* well used to this. She had been given to more than one man herself, indeed, she had been given to him for his use.

"Kaveri pointed out your friends to me, Rosamunde," said Cathal. His usual hearty appetite had deserted him and he picked at a plate that Alan had made for him.

"Kaveri?" Rosamunde asked.

"She's a mongoose," Cathal explained.

"Oh, she comes to the *zenana* sometimes. We pet her and give her food if we have any left," said Rosamunde. "She's very friendly and sweet."

"She told me that your friend Laura was taken off to be with a group of officers and then taken to the officer's quarters in the barracks. Mabel Clutterbuck was in the barracks too and in the stables. Kaveri says she is like a rabbit in heat."

"It makes me sick to see how she likes it here," Rosamunde confessed. "When we are in the *zenana* she boasts about how many she has had and how much they all like her!"

"Remember how awful her parents were, Rosamunde. My father explained that to me about Donald Clutterbuck, her brother, remember how he tormented me at school? Their parents did not love and support them as ours do. I was watching her before and after my performance and she lives for the approval of that Hussaini woman. It's very sad."

Rosamunde thought that Alan was too kind. Nothing could explain the eagerness with which Mabel greeted each man that was brought to her. Her eunuch told long stories about how many men she had taken and what she had done with each one of them and how she never cried or begged to be let off as other women did, and then were severely reprimanded for both shirking their duty and talking out of turn.

As the meal progressed Rosamunde became quieter. She hated to see this time with Alan end. All too soon Tandon would return, to take her to dance for the little pervert. She did not know as yet that she was to be Alan's all night. She also had to tell him of Parminder's strange request for him to go to the bazaar and talk to the curry seller.

She took another sip of tea and said, "Will they let you go to the bazaar?"

He looked at her. She was grateful to notice that he looked at her face, not her body. "I do need to go and get some more supplies for my magic act, beads and such. There was only so much I could carry on horseback. Is there another reason I should go?"

"Parminder says it is important that you go and talk to the curry-seller near the House of Assignation," Rosamunde answered. "She could not tell me why, just that it is important."

"Since the city is locked up tighter than a drum I don't see why they would not let me go, once they decide to let me out of here."

She blushed. "We are locked in so that no one will interrupt your time with me."

"And they gave you to me for the rest of the day and night," he said.

Such joy broke over her face that he was almost stunned. "I can stay here with you, until the morning?" she cried. "No dancing, no men?" she felt like crying in relief.

Cathal suddenly stood up and said "Someone's in the garden!" all on the alert.

"Stay here," said Alan, and rose, going to the window where he disappeared behind the semi-transparent curtains.

A murmur of voices was heard and Rosamunde, in case it was a eunuch, ran to the *charpoy* and assumed the position.

A few moments later Alan entered, and turned and bowed, to followed by the Maharajah, who was scowling and dragging a teary eyed Parminder by the arm.

"Why is that door locked?" he shrilled. "I was obliged to go all the way around outside and come through and unlock the garden gate!" He looked hot and cross. "And no one would tell me where you were!" he looked at Rosamunde as if it was her fault. "My mother lies with her bed men and refuses me entrance. Usually she will let me watch!"

"My countrywoman has been given to me for my use for the day highness. I was just about to... when my animal heard you," said Alan.

"Well,what am I to do when I wish to see toe dancing?" the petulant princeling demanded. He pushed Parminder away from him and she hit the floor, none too gently. "Teach this one to go up on her toes!" he told Rosamunde "Now!"

"Oh, you have my leave to sit up!" he added, even though I like you in that position a great deal. You will lay that way at the next *Durbar,* I can see everything so well! Is she good to couple with, magician? They tell me her *yoni* is very tight," he added wistfully. "We call her Serai, the house of accommodation, yet I have never been accommodated by her! It is not fair!" he mourned. Then turning back to Rosamunde, he ordered "Now teach this one the toe dance," he ordered, "Or I will tell my mother to give her to the *Bhutas*! She has been with them once before and well remembers it!" he added maliciously.

Rosamunde exchanged horrified glances with Parminder, who was now trembling. She could not teach her to go *en pointe* overnight! It took years of training!

"Teach her or I shall give you *both* to the *Bhutas!*" the Maharajah threatened.

"I wish I could just stay here forever, in bed with you," said Laura dreamily as she watched Nate dress. He was going on duty shortly and the eunuch would be in to take her back to the *zenana* and from there to her guard duty.

"I purely love the idea of being in bed with you forever," said Nate, "but I ain't too crazy about the 'here' part. Much rather be on that little farm of ours!"

"Hell, yes," said Laura and she stretched languidly. "Oh, Nate, honey, the loving's so good with you!"

He came over and sat down beside her, putting a hand on her hip bone. "Laurie, when we found out what kind of a place this hell hole l was I was scared that you wouldn't want to let me love you ever again. After all these bastards banging you..."

"One big difference, I love you and you love me and you take the time for me to get my pleasure. These skunks, it means about the same to them as blowing their damn noses or farting!" she said in disgust.

He chuckled. She was so plainspoken, just one of the things he loved about her.

When she had first come out of the mines the admiration he felt for her grit and spunk had turned to love. When he had proposed, she had insisted on him taking her to bed before she gave him her answer. She was afraid that her sexual experience there, since she had had no other experience, might have made her afraid or incapable of having relations. But he had been slow and gentle, he let her set the pace and tell him if she wanted to stop, and it had been good, and just got better every time. He was so thankful that this experience hadn't ruined her for loving. The way he felt about her, life without Laurie was not worth living. And even if she had been ruined for loving, he thought as he looked down at her, he'd still marry her, just to be with her and share his life with her, bed loving or not.

"When we get out of here, Laurie, you and me are finding ourselves a preacher and we're tying the knot," he now said abruptly. "We ain't waiting no longer."

"But you said you wanted to wait until we could buy the farm," she said, looking at him in surprise.

"While we were looking for you I bought it, I got me a windfall. Remember how I caught that wanted man out in Wyoming when me and your Pa was with the calvary?"

She nodded.

"Turns out he was worth five thousand dollars!" Nate said. "So I spent it all on the farm, with what we've saved it was more'n enough and your Pa said he'd give us a tidy sum for a wedding gift, for furniture and such, not that I can't build what we need. And I've got money put aside to cover the cost of a good stud and some mighty fine mares and then you and I can get to breeding our own little colts and fillies."

"Oh, Nate!" Laura threw her arms around his neck. She was so happy that she could have burst into tears. A few did trickle down her cheeks.

"Don't cry, honey," he said, wiping the tears away with his thumb. "Now, you got to find out if that feller you was telling me about is your friend's Wizard cousin, and if he is, I got to get joined up with him and we'll put our heads together and try and get up some plan to get us all out of here. It ain't going to be easy," he added.

Laura knew this. It was not over yet. But now she had to figure out a way for Nate and this Wizard to meet, without it seeming suspicious and then for them all to get out of this mess. As Nate said that would be far from easy.

39

succubus

"Highness, if I may speak," said Alan quickly, "It is impossible for this woman," he nodded at Parminder, still on the floor where the Maharajah had pushed her, "to learn this art. It is a skill given to her priestesses by our great goddess and not one taught to outsiders. A girl must be dedicated to the goddess before the age of five. And she must practice diligently every day for hours on end. It takes many, many years of study, and prayer, to do this!"

The Maharajah looked at him suspiciously. "Is this true, girl?" he said, looking at Rosamunde. "You may speak."

"Yes, highness, I began to learn this when I was but five," she said.

"What is the name of this goddess?" he demanded.

"The goddess ballet," said Alan "in our country, a powerful goddess indeed." He hoped that Maharajah was as stupid as he seemed, and would believe this.

"*Bah-lay?*" the Maharajah repeated. "I have never heard of her!" His tone seemed to imply that she could not therefore exist. But he was quite fearful of goddesses. He had sometimes been present at the Kali ceremonies and had felt that Kali had looked at him as if he were but a worm. "Oh, very well," he grumbled. "But I need to see some toe dancing and some of those great leaps. I can see everything when she leaps," he explained to Alan. "It excites me, and I am with a new bride this afternoon." Abruptly, he turned to Rosamunde, "You shall come with me and dance while I take my bride. It will excite me, for she is plain and has the figure of a plank. I do not know why all my brides are so ugly! And they scream so!"

"Highness, your excellent mother gave this girl to me for the entire afternoon and night..." said Alan, implying that the Maharani would not be best pleased if her son was to abscond with the slave that was supposed to be entertaining the magician.

The Maharajah paused and momentarily blanched for he was afraid of his mother's wrath, but he could not summon any enthusiasm to take his bride without some sort of stimulation. And his mother would also expect that he deflower her this afternoon; the Maharani would check that, he was certain. "I shall keep her but an hour, to dance while I take my bride and then I shall return her to you through this garden gate and no one shall be the wiser. I have the key! My mother need never know! And I shall leave this one" he pointed at Parminder "for you to lay with, magician. In fact, you may have them both when I return the toe dancer to you. Is that not generous of me? You will have many hours still to use Serai! *And* this Chowki! But for now I need this one!" he declared, grabbing Rosamunde's arm, hauling her to her feet. The offer of Parminder was clearly a bribe for Alan's silence.

Rosamunde exchanged a helpless glance with Alan and had to allow the Maharajah to bear her away.

"Does the *husoor* wish to make use of this slave?" Parminder inquired, when they had gone, not moving from the floor.

"The *husoor* does not wish to make use of anyone," Alan said on a sigh and offered his hand to Parminder to help her up from her sprawled position. "I should l like to talk to you, however. Why don't you sit down and I shall see if the tea is still drinkable. Would you like a cup?"

Parminder looked at him oddly, but sat down in Rosamunde's vacated place and accepted a cup of tea in not quite steady hands.

"Don't be afraid," said Alan, smiling at her. "I will not hurt you. Rosamunde said that she told you about me, since he called you Chowki, I assume that you are Rosamunde's friend Parminder."

"It is not you of whom I am afraid, *sahib*," she said, sipping at the tea which he had warmed up magically, "but the *Bhutas*."

"Call me Alan," he said, pouring another cup for himself. He did not really want it but he thought it might make her easier if they shared tea together. He was glad that he had asked them to bring an extra cup for Cathal. "What are these *Bhutas?*"

She gave a long shudder and the tea shook in her

hand. "They are terrible things! We are given to them as punishment when we do not obey. When I first came here I fought these people, for I wanted to go home, to my family, and I thought that if I was wild and unruly they would think that I was not worth the trouble and that they would let me go. Instead they put me in the *tykhara* with the *Bhutas* and left me there for the space of an afternoon." She had been looking into her tea cup as if remembering something terrible and now she raised her eyes to his face. The expression in her large brown eyes was one of horror. "They are creatures, Alan *Sahib*, that rape again and again and again and tear at one's flesh with horrible long claws. They have the breath of the grave and scaled bodies, but I could not tell you what they look like, for there is no light at all in that room with them. Their male members are huge and ice cold when they penetrate, and their seed is acid and it burns. And unlike a man they never tire of copulating and go on and on until the pain is so great," she broke off, her breast heaving and on the verge of tears. "Do you know of these, do you have them in your country? Rose of the World has told me that you are a great magician in your own country."

"I *was* a magician," he said. "And yes, I know of these creatures. In my country we call them Incubi. The name means 'that which lies upon' and their only purpose is to have relations with human women in order to sire demon spawn. They also have cloven hooves and sometimes forked tails as well. When they come to a woman who is awake and able to see them by candlelight or moonlight they generally take on the semblance of a husband or a lover. They can be defeated by the light of day – any strong, pure light. They are very difficult to control, however, even for a powerful magician." As he spoke his blood was running cold, had Rosamunde been given to those creatures? Was that the torture she had undergone to make her so obedient?

They could also become enraged if they were not allowed to impregnate a woman, but only have intercourse with her as filling a human woman with their demon seed was their chief purpose in life. There were not many Incubi found in the Six Nations for Repressors had done a good job of eliminating and controlling them. But they were a huge problem on the Continent and even the Inquisition could do little about them. However had the Maharani been able to capture Incubi and keep them contained? Did she realize the risks she was running? If they knew that she was the magician keeping them captive, and giving them infertile women they would tear her limb from limb if they ever escaped!

"I have many questions about this place and Rosamunde says that you have been here for three years. I am very sorry to hear that," Alan said. "You must miss your family and your home very much,"

Her eyes filled with tears at his sympathy. "I will answer you as much as I might, but I do not know everything," she said.

When Rosamunde was returned to Alan's room a little over an hour later she found Parminder asleep on the *charpoy*, and Alan at the low table, staring at nothing, an unreadable expression on his face. Cathal lay sleeping on one of the cushions.

"She was exhausted," Alan said, seeing Rosamunde glance at Parminder. "So I told her to lay down for a while. Are you all right?" he asked quickly, for there was a shadow on her face.

She sat down opposite him. "It was horrible, Alan! That poor child was no more than thirteen, barely a woman, and she was thin and underdeveloped but that is scarcely her fault! And I had to dance around the room while he used her so he could watch me and she screamed and cried. There was so much blood! It was just terrible! He slapped her for screaming and I nearly forgot myself and jumped on him to get him to stop but Tandon was in the room also and he was watching me like a hawk with his whip at the ready."

"He does like an audience, doesn't he?" said Alan in disgust.

"And then he made me lie on the bed with them and he fondled me," Rosamunde continued, "pointing out to his bride that the way I behaved was how she should behave, to *worship* him, to allow him access to her body and how much more womanly I was than she is, which was loathsome of the little toad! The worst part is, that if she does not become with child within a few months after he uses her constantly, she will be made into a slave, given to the lowest cast men and given a vile duty, such as a remover of night soil. And all through no fault of her own, for I would think that he is more than likely infertile and the problem lays not in his brides but in him! Men are so vile!"

"I hope that that blanket commendation does not extend to me?" he asked.

"Of course not," she said crossly. She was so incensed that for the first time that he had been with her she was not conscious of her nudity and was making no attempt to hide herself from him.

"It was clever of you to think of the 'goddess ballet,' " Rosamunde went on. "Elsewise Parminder would have been terribly punished. He is afraid of Kali. The goddess is one of the few things that will give him pause when he gets one of his ideas. Parminder is an excellent dancer, when she does not have to dance in a filthy and degrading manner, but she is not ballet trained and at her age it would be difficult for her."

"I had quite a talk with your friend Parminder," said Alan carefully. "She was able to answer some questions I had. Rosamunde, did they tie you up and give you to man after man?"

Her head came up sharply and she looked suddenly angry. "Why do you want to know that, does it excite you?" she demanded, her voice a little shrill.

"No, it does not, it makes me sick that you had to endure it! I am just trying to understand what is going on here and understand what you have had to suffer," he said, trying to keep his voice even and non argumentative. "Why are they doing this? That is what I cannot understand. What is all of this power for, and why restrain you like that?"

She had relaxed slightly at the sound of his voice and said, "Laura said it was to teach us the position and to humiliate and train us in obedience."

"The gathering of so much power usually has a purpose. I shall have to try and find out what it is," he said thoughtfully. He paused and said deliberately "Parminder told me about the *Bhutas* and what they do with them here. We call them Incubi in the Six Nations. I studied how to combat them at University." After another pause he went on,

377

"These Incubi of which your friend Parminder spoke, Rosamunde," Alan closed his eyes and swallowed hard. "Did you–were you–?" He did not know how to go on, for his imagination had presented him with a picture of her in the obscene embrace of a scaled, cloven hoofed being and, unlike Parminder, he knew exactly what one looked like.

The minute he had mentioned the *Bhutas* she had shot to her feet and gone to stand near the window through which moonlight was now streaming. She stood with her back to him, her arms wrapped around herself.

"Given to them? Oh,yes?" she said in a flat voice. "It was why I gave in, Alan, finally, after being locked in a black, windowless, lightless room with them where I could not see but felt every vile thing that they did to me. I don't know how long I was with them. At the end of that time the eunuchs came for me and threw me down at the Maharani's feet. And she asked me if I would now obey and accept the fact that I was just a slave for men to use or did I want to go back there? If I did not accept my fate, she explained that I would go back there again and again and that they would make certain that I stayed alive so that those things could use me as much as they wanted. That's why I finally gave in, Alan! Just the thought of going back into that room, I could not bear it! I fought them before, but those things–!" she gave a long shudder. "I groveled at her feet, Alan, and begged her to have me raped again and again, as long as it was by *men*. I promised to do any obscene thing they wanted and never raise a protest! I told her she could give me to ten men in a row and I would not protest!"

He had risen from the table and quietly went to stand behind her.

"And now I suppose that you despise me, that I jump to their bidding and whore for them," she went on, still refusing to turn and look at him.

"What did she do when you told her that you would cooperate with her?" he asked gently.

"Gave me to ten men in a row and then had me whipped for insolence. I then went to the *Hakim* and was healed so that I could go right back in to the brothel," she said in a now brittle voice.

"I don't despise you at all, Rosamunde," he said "How

378

could I? I think you are the bravest person I ever met. You haven't allowed this place to steal your compassion or your loyalty to your friends and in spite of the fact that you have had to give in to their demands on the surface. I think you are still fighting them underneath, still trying to keep what is yours"

She turned to look at him before he had finished speaking with a look on her face that said she wanted to believe him. "Truly?" she said on a whisper. "Truly, Alan?"

"Truly," he said and took her in his arms.

He wanted very badly to kiss her but he was afraid to do so. She had been through so much and she had never thought of him as a lover.

Her heart was beating wildly. She had always dreamed of his holding her, of loving her, but not like this. Not with her being a naked slave with the all too evident marks of her bondage pressing against his chest and causing pain to her. Was it only pity for her plight? But there was no pity in his voice. He actually sounded as if he admired her!

In spite of the pain caused by the horrible hoops in her breasts, although she could tell that he was trying to be careful and not hurt her, she leaned into him and relaxed in his embrace. If she could only stay in his arms forever, just like this, with no demands upon her. She would even put up with the breast pain.

When the torches winked out Alan insisted that the two women share the *charpoy* and he bedded down with Cathal on some of the cushions. He carefully inserted illusions into each of the rubies that the women wore, a process which drained him utterly. He was more than glad to seek his couch, even if that couch was but some thin cushions on a hard limestone floor.

He lay awake for a long time, wishing that he dared tell her how he felt. But he was afraid. She seemed to be certain that she was now ruined, that no man would ever want someone who had suffered this treatment as his wife or the mother of his children. And he was not sure how he could convince her otherwise. Would just loving her be enough?

He fell at last into an uneasy sleep and found himself dreaming of Alisande.

Lady Alisande ap Gwrraged was an Elfess, a golden haired Elf of Wales, one of those who looked after lost children and who were kind to persons who lived in poverty and tried to help them. In Wales, in the Black Mountains, they were known as the *Gwrraged Annwn*, and were considered water Faeries, although in actuality were Elves.

Alan had met her in the Hollow Hills. His family were all considered Elf Friends and were frequently invited to Oberon's kingdom.

On his eighteenth birthday Alisande had approached him and had given him an oak leaf, which among the Elves signified that the giver desired the recipient as a bed mate.

And when he had accepted, for she was beautiful and extremely desirable, that had begun a relationship that had still been ongoing when he had left for India. He had visited her frequently beneath the Hollow Hills and she had even magiced herself into his room and into his bed in Cheltenham. It had been extremely satisfactory to them both, although neither one was in love with the other. It was understood that if either one found another love there would be no recriminations, nor regrets, only good memories. She had taught him a great deal about loving a woman even though she was not human.

Now she appeared to him in the most seductive guise he had ever seen, clad in flimsy draperies that floated about her, first revealing and then hiding a body that seemed far more voluptuous than he remembered. She leaned over him, kissing and fondling, whispering in his ear and he reached for her, and something bit his ear – hard!

"Alan!" came Cathal's terrified voice. "She's trying to lay with you, that *thing*, she wants you to–"

Alan woke abruptly to find a vile caricature of Alisdande's beauty floating just inches above him. There was little doubt about what she had been trying to do. As he looked at her in horror, Cathal stood up on his hind legs and hissed at her, baring his teeth.

The image of Alisande changed and she turned on Cathal, her lips peeling back to reveal fangs and her hands becoming long, dirty claws. Beneath the remnants of a now filthy and tattered drapery cloven hooves showed as she reached for the ferret.

"No!" Alan shouted and threw up a Mage light of brilliant blue white.

The thing shrieked as she put her claws up to her eyes. All resemblance to Alisande faded as she was revealed for what she was, a hell-born Succubus. The name meant 'to lie down under' and like her male counterparts the Incubi, the Succuba sought to have human men impregnate them so that they could mother demons. Her flesh was scaled, she had a long forked tail and small horns sprouted from her forehead amidst a tangle of unwashed greasy hair, so long unwashed that its original colour could not even be guessed at. Her rank smell filled the room.

Thankful that he could still make a mage light, Alan increased the intensity until it was almost blinding and the thing fled, screaming with pain and frustration. The Light was the one thing that frightened her, for she was a creature of the Dark.

Alan collapsed back upon the cushions, his heart beating so wildly it felt as if it were up in his throat. He was covered in a cold sweat.

"I saw those in one of your books!" said Cathal. The ferret's teeth were chattering. "It was a Succubus! It was trying to seduce you!" He turned his eyes made large with fear towards his Wizard. "I could not wake you, no matter how much I shouted! So I *had* to bite you, I'm sorry!"

"Don't apologize!" Alan touched his still bleeding ear. "Anytime that happens, bite away!" he shuddered. "Those things drain one's life essence!. Once she succeeded in seducing me I would have been helpless to resist her ever again, and once she was with child she would have killed me. You saved my life, Cathal! Thank you!"

"If you had died I would have wanted to die too," said the ferret simply.

Alan sat up shakily. He had not felt this badly since first waking up from his long illness. He felt as if he might be sick. The thought of what he had escaped made him shiver all over.

He glanced over at Rosamunde and Parminder. The women slept in a deep, unnatural slumber. The Succubus had the power to make them sleep while she worked her wiles on Alan. The Mage light, if he kept it up, would turn that bespelled state into a good, natural, relaxing sleep.

"What are you going to do now?" the ferret inquired.

"Take a bath," Alan replied grimly. "I feel as if I had been rolled in foulness." He sighed as the familiar dizziness assailed him as he stood. "What else will there be, Cathal? What other horrors are in this place? Every time that I think it cannot get any worse, it does! And I am so ill-equipped to protect even myself, much less Rosamunde and her friends!"

the eye of the tiger

After his bath Alan went out on to the *chabutara* and sat there in the dim light with Cathal in his lap. When he left the *ghosulkhana* the two women were sleeping peacefully so that he was able to douse the mage light. There was no sign of the Succubus. She had completely disappeared. It was as if she had been but an evil dream.

But she was not a dream, and for the first time Alan was deeply afraid that there was nothing that he could do to help Rosamunde or himself. He had no weapons but the simplest to battle this evil. The sheer numbers of people in this place and the stringent measures to prevent any escape were appalling. Cathal had been all over inside the secret passages and had questioned the mongoose closely. The only exits were mouse sized or smaller. If he still had all his magic, Alan could have enlarged a mouse hole, unseen, and taken Rosamunde out that way. But such an alteration was impossible for him, and there was, as well, this spell on her that prevented her from wearing clothing. In all of his studies he had never read of such a thing. How was that to be negated? And those terrible rings in her breasts, how were they to remove those?

He felt completely helpless, alone, and utterly depresssed. To see what Rosamunde was enduring each day, or what was almost worse, to *imagine* the indignities, the abuse that she suffered, it was almost unbearable.

He sat up the rest of the night, Cathal sleeping in his lap, stroking the ferret's fur over and over as he tried to think what he could do. But nothing came to mind. He was empty of both ideas and magic.

Pramoda Tandon, with another eunuch, came for the

women in the morning, and delivered Alan's breakfast as well. Alan had no appetite; he did not know when he would see Rosamunde again or what woudl be done to her that day. Would she be brought to him again that night? Tandon only shrugged when Alan questioned him.

The door was left unlocked when Tandon left and Alan went out, with Cathal on his shoulder, to find the Nazir.

Of course Jehan could visit the bazaar, he said, especially if it was to obtain supplies to keep his highness amused. He even gave directions to the bazaar, though it was almost a straight walk down the hill. Jehan was not to spend his own money but to tell the merchants that it was to be put on the account of his highness.

It was a very nice day and the city not too far away. Alan decided to walk. He felt an urgent need to stretch his legs and get away from this place. If he stayed here this morning he would just think about what Rosamunde might be enduring.

He had walked about half the distance, when behind him came the soft thud of hooves and the creak of a cart and he turned to see a *bal ghari* carrying a load of straw, coming up, going in the direction of the city.

The driver was a man of middle years, with a graying, sparse beard and weary eyes, clad only in a very shabby *dhoti* and turban. He pulled up when he saw Alan and Cathal.

"You must be the magician of whom everyone is talking," the driver said, looking at Alan intently. "There are people who wish to speak to you. Come, ride in my *ghari*. I know to whom you must speak."

This was very mysterious but Alan swung up beside the driver, who moved over on the board seat to make room for him. "You seem to know a great deal," Alan began.

"And why should I not?" the man replied. "My daughter was stolen to serve as a slave for them. And do we never see her any more, only hear that she is now a woman of pleasure? Perhaps you know her. She is one of the dancers, Ananda Ohri, called Dharamasala by the evil ones."

Alan had to say no, he did not know her. He did not

recall Rosamunde having mentioned her. Dharmasala meant rest house. The renaming of the women to some degrading style was just another example of how perverted these people were as far as Alan was concerned.

The *ghari* driver sighed. "It is too much to hope for, to have word of how she goes on. I am Mukhul Ohri," the *ghari-wallah* continued. "If you do see my daughter will you tell her that I asked after her and that her mother and I send our love and every day her mother prays for her? We live for the day that she will come home to us."

"I will tell her if I can," Alan promised. How terrible for these parents, to know exactly what was happening to their daughter. He was suddenly glad that Stuart and Julia did not have to see or even know about their daughter's pain and degradation.

They passed two more men on the road and both of them turned to stare at Alan after the *ghari* had creaked its slow way past them.

"What you seek will be at the House of Assignation," said Mukhul Ohri. "You will have no trouble there with the demands of her highness." As he said 'her highness' he spat into the road in a gesture of contempt.

Alan had passed through more than one city or large village on his journey from Ranijhat and he had thought himself quite familiar with Indian cities. They were crowded, colourful and noisy, full of life.

But this city, Bulbupore, the capital of Jhaniput, was a closed, secretive place. Most of the houses that looked out, or should have been looking out on the rabbit warren of streets, lacked windows, as if the inhabitants had secrets to hide. An atmosphere of darkness, in spite of the bright sun, hung about it. People walked quickly, heads down, as if they did not want to be noticed. There were few women about and no sounds of children at play at all. Very few people looked up as the *bal ghari* creaked by and those who did look wore expressions of dull apathy.

They passed through the bazaar, which had the usual merchants, rug and jewelry and fabric vendors, with food sellers and artisans, but like the rest of the city it was as if most everyone had vanished. There were few people on the streets and there was no loud bargaining, and there was a total absence of any music. A large black statue of Kali dominated the square of the bazaar and her neck had been adorned with many garlands of marigolds.

Ohri brought them to a low house of sun bleached stone. "The House of Assignation," he said "Here you will find what you seek."

He had refused any coin or to tell Alan who wanted to speak to him or why. Alan was unaware that anyone other than the guards had noticed his arrival in the city. "There are many women here for your pleasure!" Ohri said in a loud voice as if he was afraid he being watched and then drove away without a backwards glance.

It was quite obvious what this place was, for a sign, painted with one of the positions from the *Kamasutra*, hung beside the door and in both Urdu and Hindi script it read "House of Assignation."

Alan and Cathal were still quite near the bazaar and their arrival had attracted attention, for a man rose from where he had been squatting behind a low table laden with brass bowls of food which simmered over charcoal braziers and walked towards them. It was the booth of the curry seller.

Cathal couldn't suppress a gasp as he came closer. He was an extraordinarily ugly man, a port wine birth mark disfigured his face and his lip was twisted so that he appeared to have a permanent grimace. He also limped heavily.

"I have been told I am to seek you," Alan began.

"Be quiet, fool!" the man hissed, coming close to Alan. "Come in with us as if you intend to enjoy the women! Do not give your feelings away, for they may be watching!"

He pushed them into the door and then down a corridor to another door that led into a courtyard where a fountain sent a spray of misty water into the air amidst a lush growth of plants.

A woman in a *sari* was sitting on a cushion at the edge of a fountain, idly feeding the fish that lived in the water. She looked up as the two entered and said "Sishul! Is this—?" hopefully.

"Yes, he is come at last," the curry seller said. The woman stood up. She was quite tiny and very plain of face and plump, but her face was kind and she said "Welcome! Welcome indeed! We hoped that you would come here! We have waited so long!"

"I don't understand," said Alan in confusion. "You have been waiting for us?"

"More specifically, for you," said the curry seller. "We have been waiting for you for fifty years!"

Alan was even further mystified.

The curry seller laughed at his astonishment. "You are the man with the eye of the tiger!" he said, looking into Alan's amber gaze. "It was prophesied long ago that you would bring down the House of Riwat and restore the rightful Maharajah to the throne of Jhaniput! When our spies saw you ride into the city we knew at once that you were the one, the one that we have been waiting for! Geeta, I will take him to the *Sadhu!*"

He bore a bemused Alan off, Cathal clinging to his shoulder, as the woman looked after them with hope in her eyes.

the sadhu and the curry seller

Alan noticed something strange as the curry seller hurried him through a maze of twisting hallways. The man had stopped limping. But he was not given an opportunity to speak as he was rushed faster and faster, deep into the bowels of the House of Assignation, always heading down on a slight incline.

At last the curry seller stopped and turned to Alan as they stood before a carved door. "In the days before the Rawits occupied the throne," he said, "this was a temple. They razed it, for it was a shrine to Vishnu, not to Kali. But here, underground, remains the heart of the temple. We have, over the years, made this place into a maze, to keep out prying eyes." He knocked on the door as he spoke and from inside, a voice called "Enter, Sishul!"

"He always knows that it is I," said the curry seller, with a crooked smile.

The door swung open into a blaze of light, after the dark corridors it was blinding and it took Alan a few moments for his eyes to adjust.

The light was coming from a small hole in the ceiling. It illuminated a man who sat cross legged in the puddle it created on the stone floor.

He was an incredibly ancient man with wizened features and a body that was deep bronzed and bone thin. He wore an immaculately white *dhoti* and turban and he was so clean he almost shone, even his bare feet were as clean as if he had never stepped on any ground. His eyes very wise and deep, almost lost in wrinkles and his beard was pure white as well.

"Come! Come!" he called to them in a surprisingly strong voice. "It is he for whom we have waited! Come and sit by me!"

"It is indeed he for whom we have waited, *baba-ji!*" said Sishul, bowing. "There can be no mistaking the eye of the tiger!"

The old man sat facing a statue of Lord Vishnu. This representation of the God was standing, with a crown on his head and his four arms held aloft. The upper left hand held a conch shell, a discus-like weapon was held in the upper right hand, a mace in the lower left and a lotus flower was held in the lower right. On the handsome stone face was an expression of kindness and intelligence. The statue had been painted sky blue. Alan felt drawn to the statue, feeling nothing of the repulsion he felt towards the many depictions of Kali he saw in the *Mahal*. It seemed to project serenity into the room.

Alan sank down beside the old man, falling into the same cross legged position. Cathal left his shoulder for his lap, acting like the pet he was supposed to be.

The curry seller went to one side of the room and bent over a basin, washing his face and then toweling it briskly. When he joined them on the floor, all signs of the port wine stain and the disfiguring twist to his lips was gone, revealing him as very good looking.

At Alan's look of inquiry he gave a dismissive wave of his hand "Beggar's tricks!" he said. "But such I have had to learn if I wish to survive here."

"And he is a fine figure of a man," put in the old one "if she were to see him as he truly is, handsome and whole of limb, the false Maharani would no doubt wish him for a bed man!"

"And as soon as she tired of me, I would be a eunuch!" the curry seller said with a grimace. He introduced himself as Sishul Mehra and the old man as the *Sadhu* Prabhat.

"I do not understand how you claim you have been waiting for me for fifty years!" said Alan in confusion, stroking Cathal. The ferret was tense beneath his hands. He would not speak unless Alan gave him leave. Too many people thought talking animals an evil. "I am only four and twenty and had no idea that I was ever coming here!"

"When I was but a young man," said the *Sadhu*, "I renounced the world and became a wandering Holy man, for Lord Vishnu called me to do so. He came to me in a vision, and he has continued to seek me out over the years. A very long time ago, or so it will seem to such as you young men, he told me of this place and the evil that was in flower here. He also told me of a man with the yellow eyes of the tiger who would be the instrument by which the evil ones were defeated. He would be *feringhi* and a magician of great power and that certainly is you," he finished.

"I no longer have great power," said Alan miserably. "If I had, these people would have been in Hell the first day that I came here. I now have less magic than a beginner in the craft. All my magic is good for at the moment is some illusions and amusing that royal toad in the *Mahal*."

Sishul gave a short laugh. He liked the description 'royal toad'.

"That which was lost may be found," said Sadhu Prabhat calmly. "Vishnu has promised. He has also promised the Sishul shall again sit on the throne of his ancestors."

"The throne of his ancestors?" Alan echoed. "But I understood that all of the rightful heirs to the throne were dead!" Rosamunde had told him Parminder's story of how the Rawits gained the throne.

"My grandfather, Kshitij Srivastava, was smuggled from the *Mahal* by a faithful servant, and a dead baby from the village left in his place. It was thought that he died of the poison fed to him by the *choga* bearer's daughter, she who bespelled my great grandfather into marrying her. Such as she was scarce fit to be a concubine to a Maharajah, never mind his wife!" said Sishul bitterly. "All these years we have kept our secret, waiting for you to come, Jehan! Even my wife does not know that I am of royal blood for I was afraid to tell her lest she be stolen away and perhaps tortured. As it came to pass, she *was* taken from me by those vile creatures and enslaved! And what good would it do for her to know herself a Maharani but also the wife of a poor curry seller?" His eyes were burning with a fierce intensity as he looked at Alan, as if all his hopes and prayers were bound up in the person of Jehan the magician.

Looking at his expectant, hopeful face Alan felt almost ill. He could do nothing to help them—nothing! "I don't think that you realize that I have no power left!" he said again. "I came here to free the woman I love from this horror and I cannot even do that, much less topple a throne!"

"Lord Vishnu will show you the way," said the old

man calmly.

"Forgive me, but I am not a Hindu," said Alan. "How can Vishnu–"

"Did you not say, yourself, once that surely there are many paths to God?" the *Sadhu* said, smiling at Alan.

"*How did you know that?*" Alan said in a stunned whisper, feeling as if a goose had just walked over his grave as a shiver crept all over his body. He had said that to Ravi, in private conversation, months ago.

"Vishnu whispers to me," said the Sadhu. "You must surrender yourself to the will of Vishnu, child, and he will restore that what was lost. Now, if you will become my *chela*, my pupil, for but a while, I shall teach you what you are needful of knowing."

Geeta looked up as she heard a noise at the door and the magician entered, followed by the curry seller, who was tenderly guiding the steps of the *Sadhu*. Sishul, who had restored his ugly disguise and was once again limping, helped the old man to a cushion on the edge of the fountain.

The *Sadhu* smiled benignly upon them all. "Have you the box, Geeta?" he inquired. She jumped up from her seat and fetched a small carved box from a nearby inlaid table.

"Here," he handed the box to Alan. "Vishnu provides. Give this to the lovely child that you love so well. In it the evil ones will see what they wish to see. She will be spared the pain of too much attention from the men at the *Mahal*."

Alan opened the box. Inside lay a ruby, the same size as the one in Rosamunde's navel. "Am I supposed to switch this with the other?" he said in confusion. "I don't think that I can! I don't have enough magic!"

"Vishnu provides," the old man said again. "Has he not already put words on your lips?"

Cathal gave a startled exclamation, quickly suppressed. That explained why Alan had been so calm when he had first seen Rosamunde and had realized what those terrible people had done to her. Cathal had never thought to see his normally hot-tempered Wizard so calm.

"Vishnu put words in my mouth?" Alan queried, shaken.

"And if you will but follow my teachings and do as I direct, Vishnu will also bless you with the return of your magic," said the Sadhu complacently. "He will guide you and nurture you."

The rest of the day passed slowly. Alan bought things at the bazaar that he could use in his magic act. The bazaar was surprisingly well stocked for a city that appeared to have no trade or commerce with any other. They then returned to the *Mahal* where Alan lay upon the *charpoy*, stroking Cathal, both of them busy with their thoughts, and disinclined to sleep even in the afternoon when many persons did so.

He needed to talk to Rosamunde. It seemed an age before she was at last delivered to him, for which he was grateful. He had been afraid that with the small illusion in her ruby they might deny him her company.

The door had scarcely shut behind Tandon when Rosamunde sat up on the *charpoy* where he had deposited her and said "Alan, what did you put in that ruby? They are over the moon about what they saw there, the Maharani and Hussaini both! She said that you are a most inventive fellow and very lustful, taking me again and again."

"What?" he looked at her blankly for a moment, his mind still on what the old Sadhu had told him. "Again and again?" he said as he realized what she had asked him. "The illusion was only for once, Rosamunde, and there was nothing perverted about it. It was all I could do to cast an illusion of one time and that wore me out. I had to put an illusion in your friend's ruby as well." A chill ran down his back. Was this Vishnu as well?

"The Maharani was very pleased at the frequency and the inventiveness," she said.

He looked at her in shock. "Rosamunde, I swear to you that I did not put anything strange or excessive in the ruby. For God's sake, I don't even know any perverted or odd positions, other than what I've seen here in these repulsive murals and statues! First of all words in my mouth and now this!" he added, almost to himself. He looked suddenly haggard and Rosamunde looked at him in alarm.

"You had better tell her what happened today, Alan," Cathal prompted.

"Let's sit down," he said and sank abruptly to beside the table, suddenly feeling as if his legs would no longer hold him up.

Tea waited on the table and he poured two cups and some into a saucer that had held bread for Cathal. Then he told Rosamunde all that had taken place in the city.

"There was a prophecy," he said, sounding more than a little depressed. "They seem to think that I will destroy the evil House of Rawit. The old man thinks that my magic will be restored to me."

"But that's wonderful!" she said, excited.

"Wait until you hear what he has to do to get it back," said Cathal.

At Rosamunde's look of inquiry Alan said miserably, "I have to surrender myself completely to Vishnu, Rosamunde. And I don't think I can! I could never even surrender myself completely in any of my own rituals, never mind one in which I don't believe!" He picked up the little box which the old *Sadhu* had given him. "I don't understand any of this..." he began and opened the box.

And the ruby flew across the table and attached itself to the one in Rosamunde's navel. There was a flash of brilliant blue light and something hit the floor.

She gasped. "Oh, Alan, what is it? For the first time since they put that thing in my stomach it doesn't hurt!" Cathal had gone under the low table when he heard the noise of something falling. Now he emerged, rolling another ruby. "I think you have a *good* ruby there now!" the ferret said excitedly. "Feel this one – it's foul!"

They could feel it without even touching it. As they watched, it began to disintegrate and was soon gone.

"Oh, I feel so full of Light!" Rosamunde said happily.

"The *Sadhu* said that will spare you too much attention from men," said Cathal.

"If only that is true!" she said, and the thought of male attention suddenly made her think of what she had been

393

able to learn from Laura when they had finally been in the *zenana* at the same time. "Alan, I must tell you–" she said urgently.

Rosamunde had been overjoyed to find Laura in their little corner of the *zenana*, by herself. "Maggie and Ivy are still cleaning rooms," she said in answer to Rosamunde's inquiry "and Hetty's still doing laundry. She had so many men lined up for her today that she got next to no washing done. She ain't able to scrub and screw at the same time, I reckon. It would be a mite difficult!! But Rose, honey, have I got news!" Her whole face glowed. "Nate's here!"

"And so is Alan!" Rosamunde said and for a minute or so all was confusion as with many interruptions and whispers of astonishment they exchanged stories.

"We got to get them together, somehow," said Laura determinedly when they were each done with explanations. "Nate wants to see your Alan and see if together they can't come up with a plan.It's too bad he lost his magic 'cause that would sure have made things easy! But you say that there is a dragon, an honest to God dragon coming?"

Rosamunde nodded. "I just don't know when."

"Thing is," said Laura, "I don't know if even a dragon could stand up to all of those big guns I saw and all those rifles and lances! Maybe a whole regiment of dragons, but not just one."

"I'll tell Alan about the army tonight," said Rosamunde. "I'm to go back with him after we're done in the *Diwan-i-Khas.*"

"The little pervert will be all over you tonight, Rose, because he didn't have you or Parminder last night. He was royally pissed. He said you are his two favorites to fondle. He grabbed at poor little Ananda and kept telling her how inferior she was. Poor kid's only a baby! Liked watching her get banged, though."

She sighed and said "Let me get my brain box to thinking on how we can get our men together. Did some snooping around and there ain't any way they could just bump into each other here in the *Mahal* and your Alan has no business going to the barracks. I'll ponder on it while toad face is squeezing my tits. It'll give me something else to think about other than killing the little bastard 'cause, that makes me too hot and bothered and the jackass thinks he's getting me excited!" She snorted.

Laura had been laying back on the cushions and now sat up. "Look sharp, Rose! Here come two *nauks,* with that 'I can't wait to hump me a woman' look on their faces!"

42

horse trading

Unexpectedly, Rosamunde was taken back to the *zenana* before she had little more time than to tell Alan that Nate was come and that they must meet. The royal toad had demanded a command performance and had been so obnoxious, even throwing a tantrum, that his mother had given in to his demands. He wanted to see the new dance NOW, not wait any longer. Alan was promised that he could have Serai for his use later, and that he too was to perform before the dance, after which he was to be dismissed. Rosamunde fretted, for who knew how long it would take to get back to him again and she had so much to tell him.

That evening was particularly trying.

"I am more than glad to be a maidservant and set to cleaning rooms," said Margaret, watching Parminder and Rosamunde put on the ribbon costumes they were to wear for the Rose dance, and Laura don her 'uniform'. "By this time of night most of the men have had a woman and there are only occasional visitors. But you three have to go and exhibit yourselves—"

Laura made a face and snorted expressively.

"But we's got to offer ourselves to any man who is in the rooms," Ivy said. "I had me a Rajah and 'his servants, this afternoon, one after another. They was all randy bastards!"

"And all the men at the river *ghat* seem to want nothing else!" said Hetty bitterly. "They swim, jump on me, swim again and come back for a second time! And then I am censured for not getting my washing done!"

The head laundry man, or *dhobi,* had informed her that she was not getting enough laundry cleaned in one day, adding insult to injury as he said this while using her body.

"Is there any chance of stealing some of them flame proof duds, Hetty?" Laura asked as she put the helmet on her head.

"No, because there are guards everywhere. I can only

scrub it. Men bring it to the *ghat* in baskets and take it away again. They watch me like hawks," Henrietta said. "I found out that all extra clothing is locked away, as is the fabric that the clothes are made from. And the men are cautioned all the time to not let us get our hands on their clothing. That is another reason that the eunuchs are constantly looking in while we are being entertaining. And at any rate, even if I could steal some of it, where would I hide it?" she queried, looking down at her body.

"The eunuchs check everywhere," Parminder said. "They look in all of the corners and under and behind everything daily to make certain that we hide nothing from them, food or clothing or coins. Sometimes guests will give me several *annas* afterwards, if they have been pleased. That money is taken from me immediately."

"Greedy bastards," said Laura. "It ain't as if we could buy our freedom with a few *annas!*"

"They are afraid that we will use money rather than paying for everything with our bodies. We dancers must pay the musicians when we practice with ourselves."

Henrietta looked disgusted. "What is it all for? Why are they doing this to us?" she burst out. "Just because they are perverted?"

Laura and Rosamunde exchanged looks. They had decided against telling any of the others but Parminder about Nate and Alan. The fewer that knew the better. But there was no reason that they could not know about the army.

"They're massing a big army to go up against the British," Laura said "and I'm willing to bet that all this power they're gathering in these damn rubies is to help them defeat the Company's soldiers."

"They think that they will be invincible," put in Rosamunde as Parminder finished tying the 'bows' on her ribbon costume.

"But if they have magic and our forces do not—" Henrietta began and then grew sick and pale as she realized what this meant. "We could be here forever!" she said. "All along I have been hoping that soon we would be rescued, that our forces would invade this horrible place, oh, God!" She buried her face in her hands.

Laura went to her side and laid an arm across her

shoulders. "Never give up!" she said bracingly. "There's always hope! Always! We all got folks who are looking for us and want us back!"

At this moment Pramoda Tandon came into their corner and they all had to fall to their knees. "Serai, Chowki and Pice, it is time that you assume your duties in the *Diwan-i-Khas!*" He looked at them critically. "The costumes are good," he said, looking at the ribbons, which had been tied over bodies oiled with saffron and sprinkled with silver dust so that they gleamed. "There are many important guests tonight, Rajahs and Nawabs and military men, even a Mirza of Delhi! The costumes accentuate your bodies, and be certain that you flaunt yourselves before the gaze of his highness's guests as they will wish to imagine what it would be like to lie with you. And you," he turned to Laura "tonight you and the other guard will be included in the dice throwing. As there are so many guests, more women will be needed so the guests are not obliged to wait. You others," he looked at Ivy, Margaret and Henrietta, "will prepare yourselves, for many more men will be visiting the *zenana* this evening, by order of her royal highness. We shall be taking strict count."

"And I just said nights were quieter!" Margaret thought in dismay.

It was quite late before Rosamunde was delivered to Alan. Earlier in the evening he had put on a magic show for the toad and his guests but had been dismissed shortly after he was finished and escorted back to his room. The Maharajah would not allow a common magician to sit with him when there were others of high rank present.

As usual the eunuch dumped her upon the *charpoy* and ordered her to assume the position. "Use her well, magician," he said , with a nasty leer at Rosamunde.

"I am all eagerness," Alan said, wanting to wipe that sneer off the man's face. As soon as the eunuch left Rosamunde sat up and said wearily, "It was an orgy tonight, there were many guests."

"I saw that when I did my magic tricks," Alan said. "Cathal's out with the mongoose, spying on them—"

"And all of them acted as if they hadn't had a woman

in years! I am so sore–" she broke off and blushed as she realized what an intimate thing this was to say to him. "If this ruby is magiced it didn't seem to work," she added a little bitterly.

"I've drawn you a bath. And here," he drew the unicorn horn over his head," wear this again, it will help."

"Will you help me get out of these ribbons?" she asked shyly, for they tied behind her and she could not reach them. They were twisted and tangled as well for the costume had stayed on while the men had their way with her. None of them had been gentle for the food they had been served had more than likely been heavily laced with the dust of Kali.

They went into the *ghosulkhana* and he quickly untied the ribbons, allowing the 'costume" to fall to the ground.

A steaming tub awaited and she slid into it gratefully. "No, stay," she said as he turned to go to give her privacy. "It's not as if you have not seen me in the bath before, and I have much to tell you."

The tub was deep; the water came up over her breasts. He sat on the edge of the bath, and handed her the lilac soap and a bath sponge.

The torches suddenly flared out. "He's retired," said Rosamunde on a sigh. "We don't have to worry about him spying on us," she added, leaning back as the unicorn horn finished up its work.

Alan look disgusted.

"He is getting worse," she said, closing her eyes. "He actually brought his little bride to the orgy and took her right there in front of everyone. The poor child cried and begged but it just seemed to excite him! Even Hussaini was busy with a man. She usually just sits and watches. This place is getting worse, Alan! And I found out why!"

Quickly she told him about the army.

"Twenty five thousand men!" Alan exclaimed in dismay. "Rosamunde, I learned in Ranijhat that there are less than 14,000 British troops in the Army out of about 300,000 total! Most of that number of native troops is in open revolt! And there are about 23,000 Queen's troops stationed in the Punjab, kept there to quell the Pathans. The odds are incredibly stacked in Jhaniput's favor! And if you add black magic to that mix, it will be a slaughter! What are they waiting for?"

He came to his feet and began to pace back and forth. "What are they waiting for?" he wondered again. "To gather enough power? For even more men?"

"Nate told Laura that many disaffected *sepoys* and *sowars* are joining up, as the pay is three times the seven *rupees* a month they are given by the British," said Rosamunde. "The food is better and they are allowed the use of all the women they want. In fact they are ordered to be with us at least once a day! And today the eunuch told us that many more men will be coming to the *zenana* at night. We are to be with as many men as possible or face punishment." She paused and squeezed hot soapy water from the sponge over her shoulders. The Unicorn horn had removed all of the silver dust and the oil from her body and eased the pain as well. "Alan, you have to get your magic back! Magic is the only thing that can defeat these people and you are an Adept!"

"*Was* an Adept!" he corrected. "I told you, I don't know if I can surrender myself to Vishnu! I could not do it in my own Druidic rituals, Rosamunde. To attain the highest level of mastery there is a ceremony in which one must give oneself over to the embrace of the God and I have never able to do it. I cannot tell you exactly what the ceremony is, because it is a sacred Mystery, but I cannot let go of my own consciousness and put myself under another's power! It frightens me to death! What if I was lost in that – what if I came back changed?"

"But others have done it," she said.

"Oh, yes," he said in near despair. "Grandpapa, Papa, Uncle Stuart, Grandfather Lyon, Sacha and I have no doubts that Alex was able to give himself. They all spoke of the wonder of it, of the unity with the power of the universe, but I have never been able to achieve it, and they probably all feel sorry for me or think I'm a shirker!" he finished in misery.

Rosamunde had never seen him like this. She had always thought that, unlike her, Alan had no self doubts, that he was strong and sure and confident, and that everything he did was perfection. He had sailed through his schooling and University easily, achieving mastery at all levels at an early age.

"But you are fully robed –" she protested, referring to the white robe given Druidic pupils upon attaining their Mastery. "I was at the robing ceremony!"

"I did not achieve the highest level, unlike everyone else in the family," he said. "And now the *Sadhu* wants me to give my consciousness to a deity I do not even worship! Something I know nothing about! If I could not give myself up to my own beliefs, how can I give it to someone's else's? It was bad enough disappointing the family, that I did not attain the highest level of mastery, but these people seem to expect that I am going to work a miracle! I don't think I can do it, Rosamunde! I just don't think I can do it!" He turned his back on her and she saw his hands, hanging at his sides, clenching into fists, his breath coming rapidly.

She rose from the water, and, soaking wet, went to put her arms around him. "Do what you can," she said soothingly and pulled his head down so that it was resting on her shoulder. "That's all we can ask of you." She realized what a burden this must be on him, everyone looking to him as their savior and even she was expecting him to rescue her from this place.

"I have been having nightmares about having to stay here forever, Rosamunde, watching you being grossly mistreated and having to entertain that little pervert for the rest of our lives," he said, choking.

"Brendan will be coming," she said. "Perhaps he can rescue us, if I cannot wear clothes ever again, perhaps I can go and live beneath the Hollow Hills. The Elves won't notice or care if I am always naked!" she said lightly, trying to lift his mood.

"Oh, Rosamunde!" he said despairingly and pulled her tightly against him.

She did not even squeak when the horribly hoops dug into her. He needed comforting too badly.

All the same, she felt nearly as much despair as he did. It seemed impossible to ever escape from this situation. Is this how they were to go on for the remainder of their lives, her a whore and him a captive entertainer?

Alan and Rosamunde had slept side by side on the *charpoy*. Once during the night he had awakened to find her cuddled against him, an arm over his chest. The nights were getting cooler now and she had probably felt the chill.

If it were not for her vile jewelry he could have pretended that this was their marriage bed and if he kept his eyes closed, pretended that thy were at home. But his other senses would not let him. The sounds and the scents coming in the open door on to the *chabutara* were too alien to his ears and nose. And he was all too conscious of the breast hoops and the bracelets. Every time he looked at those rings that had been used to tie her down so that she could service a multitude of men he wanted to do murder. He had noticed that she now walked in a particular swaying fashion that made the bells jingle. When he had asked her why she was walking so strangely, she had explained that this was what they had been taught, to entice men with a seductive gait and to make the bells ring out so that men would know a woman was available and near. Everything he learned about this place only made him more ill.

He stayed awake a long time, just looking at her, wishing that he could make all her pain and suffering end tomorrow.

He finally fell back into a disturbed sleep, still no closer to a solution.

Shortly after Rosamunde was taken away the next morning a note was delivered to him. It was written in formal Hindee script and informed him that *Daffadur* Gautama Sarin wished to meet with him to discuss perhaps buying his horse from him.

He almost crumpled it up and threw it away until he remembered that Sarin was the name being used by Laura's Nate.

The note had been brought to him by a slave girl and he instructed her to go and tell the *Daffadur* that the time mentioned was agreeable to him and that he would meet the officer in the stables. He had to also turn down the use of the girl's body, pleading weariness from excesseses the night before.

With Cathal on his shoulder, he was in good time for the meeting at the stables, noting, as Laura had, how many men there were everywhere and how determined were the battle preparations. The men trained assiduously at all aspects of martial combat. He heard rifle practice and gunnery, sounds that were not discernible from inside the *Mahal,* which was probably the result of magic.

The cavalry officer's horses and household horses of the *Kala Mahal* were housed more luxuriously than many of the peasants in the surrounding countryside. They ate from marble mangers and stood in oaken stalls with the finest of *bhoosa,* straw, underfoot. They were a handsome, high bred herd and thrust inquiring heads over the doors of their stalls as Alan and Cathal headed towards the stall assigned to Akhil.

"They know who you are," said Cathal in Alan's ear. "They are saying that you are the magician. They envy Akhil; they think to be a magician's horse must be an interesting life and better than being shot at or standing on parade for hours on end."

There was a large man in Akhil's stall, running his hands over the horse's legs. He looked up as he heard Alan approach and said in Hindustanee, "You are the magician Jehan? I am *Daffadur* Gautama Sarin. This is a fine animal. Would you be interested in selling him?"

"Perhaps, if the price is right," Alan said cautiously. "Now that I have come here to be Court Magician to his highness I shall have no real need of a horse." He was all too conscious of the *syces* working nearby.

"I should like to try his paces," The big man straightened up. Alan was tall, a few inches over six feet, but he had to look up to meet this man's eyes. Laura's Nate was broad shouldered and looked as if he would be a good man to have at one's side in an altercation. Alan liked his steady gaze and the gentle hands on the horse's flank. "Ride out with me," the *Daffadur* suggested and called for a *syce* to saddle Akhil and his own horse. "We shall discuss price when I have put him through his gaits, if I am pleased with him."

A few moments later they were mounted, Alan on the

Daffadur's black, a gelding called Sandhya, while Akhil was ridden by his prospective buyer.

They went to the main gait at a trot, the big man riding easily. Alan noticed what light hands he had and how he seemed almost a part of the horse. Alan considered himself a good rider but this man was a Centaur.

At the gate they were questioned by the guards, who told the *Daffadur* that as an officer in her highness's troops he was free to come and go but he would have to be responsible for the magician, as the entertainers were not allowed to leave without express permission, not since the puppet master had tried to run away.

"We but ride out," said the *Daffadur* easily. "Jehan is well pleased with his situation here and has no need to flee!" His strong white teeth flashed in a grin. "And why would he not be? Every evening his highness gives him another token of his esteem and he has the use of a beautiful *nautch* girl all the night! What more could a man want?"

The guard smiled back. This was true. He waved them out, the gate closing behind them with a resounding thud.

Once clear of the environs of the gate Nate at once put Akhil into a gallop and Alan followed suit, leaning forward over the horse's withers as Cathal clung to his neck.

They did not pull up until some distance from the city. The horses were scarcely blowing. Now, in nearly mid October it was cooler, almost pleasant.

"Whew!" said Nate in English, letting Akhil walk, "I hope we got to a place that we can talk with no ears listening in!" It was strange to hear an American accent coming from a Indian *Daffadur*, the casual English contrasting oddly with the more formal Hindustanee.

"I'll let you know if anyone comes even remotely near us," said Cathal. "We're safe now."

Nate looked at him in astonishment. "A talking critter!" he said.

"This is my familiar, Cathal," said Alan.

"Pleased to meet you, Cathal," said Nate. "I ain't never had a lot to do with familiars and Wizards. Heard of them, of course, just never thought I'd ever meet up with one. And Laurie tells me you've got a dragon too," he said to Alan.

"Yes I hope that he will be on his way here soon," Alan answered. "The sight of such a large armed force disturbs me, though. Have you found out definitely, are they going to attack the British?"

"'Pears likely," said Nate. "They ain't training for no Fireman's Muster on the Fourth of July, that's for damn sure. They've had a fellow they call a *Maulvi* and another they say is a *Sadhu* stirring up the troops, preaching hellfire and brimstone at them, to drive the *feringhi* out of India."

"A Muslim and a Hindu holy man, both," sighed Alan, much troubled. "With the large amount of magic they are securing from this brothel they will have an easy victory."

"The British don't use Wizards and such in their wars?" Nate queried. "There's no Wizards with the British cavalry or infantry?"

"None that I know of. You see, we Wizards must take an oath to do no harm, unless of course we are fighting Dark magic, and then it is our duty to destroy it. Unfortunately I have misplaced my magic, otherwise I should be quite happy to destroy these people."

Nate heard the bitterness in his voice and could see the strain he was under in the tense lines of his body and his hands tight on the reins. That tension was not transferred to Sandhya's mouth, but it was there nonetheless.

"The way I see it, we got to not only get our gals and the rest of these ladies out of this place but we got to do something about his army, even it's just to warn the authorities," said Nate.

"And how to do that is the problem," said Alan, as the horses continued to walk slowly. "We are not even certain how much time we have before they go on the attack."

Nate cleared his throat. "Found that out this morning – it's Guy Fawkes day. They think it's a big fat joke to attack on a British holiday. I bet you the first thing they're planning to do is to take back Delhi. They're also waiting for somebody real important to show up here."

Delhi had been back in British hands since September 20th, and William Hodson had captured the King of Delhi, Zafar, who was going to be set on the throne of India. Hodson had also executed most of Zafar's sons, the Princes of the last Mughal Kingdom.

405

"Guy Fawkes Day!" Alan repeated, completely appalled. "That's less than three weeks away on the fifth of November!"

43

chalangadong monastery

The wind off the mountains was cold. High in the Himalayas, in the land of Bod the peaks of the area known in Persian as the *Bam-I-dunya*, the Roof of the World, the Tibetan Pamirs, the summits of the world's tallest mountains, were always covered in snow and the wind brought snow chill with it.

The Pamir Highlands of the High Asia were the modal point for the mountain systems of Tien-Shan, Kun-lun, Karakorum, the Himalayas and the Hindu Kush, thus the name of 'the Roof of the World'.

Brendan paused in the large courtyard of the monastery and took a deep breath. When he had first come here he had found it difficult to breath as it was so high and the air was so thin. He had never been so high before. But now after almost six months he was well used to it. His scales did not feel the chill air nor was he bothered by the sheer deep gullies and ravines that would induce vertigo in humans.

He was so glad that he had been able to come here. He had learned so much. But he was beginning to have a nagging feeling that Alan needed him and paying attention to feelings and acting upon them was part of the training that he had received here.

The monastery was draconic and dedicated to the Dragon Lord, he who was called Ummu Khubar in Persian and Varnu in Sanskrit. The monastery was set up along Buddhist lines, for it had been founded at the same time, the 11th century A.D., as some of the great Buddhist monasteries in the area, and Varnuism had much in common with Buddhism.

It resembled a Buddhist monastery architecturally as well. It stood in a vast courtyard, surrounded by high walls, but with everything on a draconic scale. Nine great oblong terraces contained buildings of an enormous size, built of red stone, each rising from the other in ziggurat fashion. Each was topped by four needle thin towers of gold. There were white edged windows, a vast quantity of them, in each tier. Prayer flags in the five colours which represented the five different aspects of life, adorned the roof of the highest level and snapped in the breeze. Outside the walls lay a line of stubby little buildings, carved all about with representations of dragons, all painted in ochre. These were *chortan,* the resting place of the ashes of former Lamas of the monastery, and considered most holy, a fitting place for a supplicant to pray. Brendan had done that earlier, praying for guidance.

Even over the wind Brendan could hear a gong being beaten and the chanting of the nuns, many of who did little besides chant the Sanskrit mantra *"Om Mani Padme Hum",* this had been borrowed from the Buddhists and it was thought that this never ending murmur accumulated personal merits and expressed good for union with the Dragon Lord.

Brendan, feeling increasingly anxious about Alan, had asked for an audience with the Lama, Tenzin. He was now waiting for the Lama's secretary, Pasana, to admit him to the presence of the Enlightened One. He had been told to wait here in the courtyard.

He did not wait much longer. Pasana, a yellow Chinese dragon, a *T'ien lung* or Celestial dragon, wingless and bewhiskered, came up to him in the slow, stately fashion used here and bowed. Lakota had told Brendan that the Celestials of China were arrogant and rude, but Pasana had been here a very long time and had renounced the ways of the world and had cultivated serenity.

"The Enlightened One will see you now," he said "Had you not requested an interview he would have sent for you, for something of great import has been seen."

After six months Brendan knew better than to demand to know what had been seen. All would be revealed at the proper time. He inclined his head, indicating respect, and followed Pasana through the great red doors inscribed with golden dragons that led into the monastery.

The many corridors were maze-like and decorated with *mandala* paintings, carvings of demons, and representations of the Dragon Lord. Rather than stairs there were ramps for the ease of draconic users. They passed chapels, where silvery dragon statues were adorned with precious jewels. All the windows were shuttered. Light was provided by myriad 'butter' lamps whose small flames flickered as the dragons passed, sending long shadows across the walls. The gongs could still be heard, as could the chanting. It had bothered Brendan at first, but he had become used to it. Now he rather thought that he would miss the rhythm that underscored each day here when he went home.

They traversed a long curving ramp which ended in a room with wooden pillars which were covered in red silk. All the walls were painted here with representations of various birds and animals. Brendan had been astonished to learn that these had all been painted by dragons, for in his world dragons did not wield paint brushes.

In a niche at the end of this room stood a great golden statue with emerald eyes of a Chinese style dragon that held aloft a gigantic pearl. Incense burned to either side of this statue in brass braziers. As usual, there were several dragons praying in front of this statue. Two monks stood there, banging on a ram's skull with thin ebony stocks.

Brendan and Pasana went on by, merely bowing to the statue, for their goal lay up another level.

They paused outside another huge red door and took *khatags*, long white silk scarves, from an iron ring in the wall. These were to be worn into the presence of the Lama and then presented to him as a part of the ceremonial greeting from a lower born to a higher born.

They draped the *khatags* around their necks and Pasana opened the door, ushering Brendan into the Lama's ante-room.

An enormous arched window stood open to the bright crisp day, overlooking the high valley in which Chalangadong sat. Light reflected off the gold brocade which covered the walls and picked out the bright gold in the dragons carved and painted in high relief that adorned the edges of the green dais on which an extremely ancient dragon sat.

He was a Tibetan dragon, bright red in colour originally, but now somewhat faded from the weight of his years. He was very Chinese in appearance, with face whiskers and lacking wings, having three toes and a sharp leg spur on fore and hind legs. He was very long and even in resting his back arched and his tail, which looked as if it ended in a flame, draped off the end of the dais. He had only a few spinal ridges and no horns.

He also had a look of complete peace and utter serenity. Now he bowed his head as the two others advanced. They bowed low in return and then as soon as they were close to the dais, took the *khatags* from their necks and, holding them high up to their shoulders, offered them in one talon to the Lama Tenzin.

He reached forward with both talons and took the *khatags*, first from Pasana and then from Brendan, for Pasana was of higher rank than the Irish dragon. They waited for him to speak, which he did not do until he had draped the *khatags* about his own neck. He invited them to sit and then said to Brendan, "It is well that you have come to me, for there has been a seeing by the Oracle which much concerns you. We have a great task to accomplish and you are instrumental in that. It is not a task which can be accomplished without pain, however, for the portents are grave." He turned to Pasana. "Please ring the gong. The Oracle awaits my summons."

Pasana crossed the room to where an immense brass gong stood. A baton, with a sheepskin head hung from its supports and with this he struck it once. The note had scarcely stopped reverberating when a door in the back wall opened and a dragoness, one of the nuns, entered, on her hind legs. She held a plain glass bowl on a silver tray in her front talons.

She was a very small blue dragon, of Chinese extraction, a four-toed Imperial. She ws also quite young. Brendan had discovered that it had long been a custom amongst the dragon families in this part of the world that at least one of their eggs was dedicated to the temple even before hatching. It was a rare dragon family that did not have a monk or a nun in its numbers. She bowed low and put the bowl on the floor in front of Tenzin.

Pasana went to a cupboard and came back with a tall flagon full of an ink black liquid. This he poured into the bowl until it was nearly full.

"Look into the darkness, little one, and again tell us what you see," said Tenzin gently.

The dragoness bowed her head and said "I will

endeavor to do so, Highborn."

She bent over the bowl, her eyes staring into it, unblinking. Suddenly her eyelids twitched, her eyes became unfocused and her entire body stiffened, her tail standing straight out "Black, black, black, all that was Light is black," she said in a strange, high-pitched voice. "That which was Light is now given over to Darkness and must be purified. The eye of the tiger opens wide and looks upon the evil ones. With him the green dragon rises on wings to bring the Light back. A red tide washes over Hind and all shall go down before it. Death is everywhere and the innocents shall perish on both hands. The black one calls to her children but the Lord of Light cries that she will not succeed..." her voice trailed off and she suddenly slumped as her eyes came back into focus. Looking wretchedly tired she said "That is all that I see, Holy One. This dragon," she nodded at Brendan, "has a great task to do in company with a man who has the eyes of a tiger."

"Alan!" said Brendan. Tigers had amber eyes, as his friend did.

"There is also coming here a man of Hind, to seek your aid," said the Oracle to Brendan. "He will be here soon."

The only man of Hind Brendan knew that would be seeking his aid would be Ravi. "Most revered Oracle," said Brendan, "What is this blackness of which you speak? And the red tide? Did you see?"

She shook her head. "It is but images without clarity. But there is a very great darkness, centered in Hind. If not purified it could spread here to the land of Bod and it would spell doom for us." She shivered. "It is a very great evil, Holy One, and I fear it will be used for an even greater evil. It is power corrupted."

"Black magic," said Brendan. "I wished to see you, Enlightened One, because I have been feeling that Alan, my human friend, is in some sort of trouble. I feel as if I need to go to him."

"You have a part to play with him," agreed the Lama.

"I just wish I knew what it was," said Brendan rue-fully. The Oracle's vision was very vague.

"You have gained wisdom since you came to us," said Tenzin "Listen to your heart and it will tell you what is

411

needful of doing. Help may come unexpectedly. Your name shall be in our daily prayers. My blessings on you."

This was a dismissal. Brendan bowed and left the room, thinking of what the Oracle had said. He would wait for Ravi, if it was indeed him who was coming. He wondered what had happened in Ranijhat. He had had one letter from Alan and several from Cathal, talking about Alan's continuing illness. Brendan had been alarmed about that but assumed that it was a relapse of the influenza. He had received no mail lately at all and had had nothing from Rosamunde and Sinéad. He was uneasy about them as well.

Ravi felt as if he had been traveling for most of his life.

He had set off, deliberately riding east along the foothills of the Himalayas to avoid the conflict in Hindustan. He had started out on a horse from his father's stables which he had soon had to trade for a tough little hill pony. That too had been traded for a mountain guide and a yak once he had traversed Nepal and started climbing towards Tibet.

Between Katmandu and Lhasa he had to begin going up into the mountains in a part of the highest range in the world, nearly inaccessible to humans. Dragons flew to Chalangadong, so high up that in the distance one could see what the British had just declared to be the world's highest peak, Chomolungma, which the Royal Geographic Society was trying to name Mount Everest, over the protests of the man who was to be honored by this name, Colonel Sir George Everest. This mountain was some 29,000 feet in height and had never been climbed to anyone's knowledge.

Ravi had done more than a little climbing at home and had gone with Alan to the Caringorms in Scotland and the Pennines in Yorkshire, even the rugged Black Mountains of Wales. But he had never seen anything like these mountains here on the Roof of the World. Gray, grim, capped in snow and harsh against the sky, they were forbidding and a constant challenge.

There were few paths through them and even the yak that carried all their supplies found the going difficult and those creatures were bred for these mountains. Ravi was very glad that he had hired a Sherpa guide, a middle-aged man named Lobsang, who was calm, even-tempered and was the finest climber Ravi had ever seen. He was a genius at scouting out a route, finding a place where the yak could go and finding a good camp at night.

But he insisted that Ravi eat his own diet of *tsampa,* barley *momos* (dumplings) and butter tea with dried goat or yak meat. Ravi could not stomach the butter tea at first. His father had told him that the Tibetans spread the brick tea from China out upon the road for several days because it was not strong enough for them as it was and had to be trampled by passing feet and hooves.

Butter tea or *poo cha,* was made by boiling the tea for several hours. This infusion, so strong it could walk by itself, was then poured into a vessel of hollow bamboo. A handful of salt, a pinch of soda and a good lump of rancid yak butter was then added and it was churned. This resulted in a purplish liquid that looked like thick oil. Lobsang showed him how to blow the scum of butter off the top of it in order to drink it and laughed at his efforts to politely drink it without grimacing. Tibetan etiquette called for the cup of *poo cha* to be constantly refilled from a clay teapot and it was not uncommon for a person to drink forty cups of it in a day. It was all Ravi could do to swallow a few mouthfuls at first but the higher they climbed the more he found that it heartened him. It seemed to add energy when his strength was fading. So he gritted his teeth and drank it. In the morning Lobsang poured *poo cha* over a lump of *tsu,* which was yak cheese, yak butter and white sugar. This made a very thick breakfast drink.

One clear morning they awoke, emerging from a tiny tent, and saw that it was incredibly clear. Lobsang pointed to a peak in the not too far distance. "Chomolungma," he said simply.

It was a jagged triangle sticking into the blue bowl of the sky. They were near their goal. Somewhere in that not too distant landscape was the draconic monastery and Brendan.

A huge shadow passed over their heads. Lobsang gave a yelp and dived back into the tent.

Squinting against the sun, Ravi looked up and saw

light sparkle off green scales. "Brendan!" he said in relief, thinking what a fortunate happenstance this was. He watched as the dragon began to spiral downwards.

44

converging

It had been a wretched trip: getting lost, wasting time going miles out of their way, having to ford rivers swollen with the Monsoon rain, braving the many dangers of the jungle, and always having to search for food, Sinéad had, more than once, despaired of ever reaching their goal. She could not rest easy, for a part of her knew that Rosamunde was in terrible danger and needed her help. She was tortured by 'if onlys": if only Rosamunde had not married Raymond; if only they had not come to India; if only they had not been separated; if only Rosamunde had not lost her magic...her regrets were endless. And since she ws superstitious, she still blamed herself for cursing Raymond. That curse, she had become convinced, had brought down this disaster upon all their heads.

She was the only one amongst the companions who had any urgency to reach Ranijhat. The others seemed content to let the days go by. Hari was happy to have people again who enjoyed petting and playing with him. Bharat was grateful for the attention given him by Niaz, for the *jemadar* cut the best grass for the elephant and washed him whenever they came to deep water.

And Niaz and Molly, Sinéad realized one day, just after a perilous crossing of the Sutlej river, that they were falling in love with one another, in spite of the very real differences between them. He looked out for her, carefully helping her on and off the elephant, making certain that she had enough food and a safe, dry place for her to sleep. She in turn kept his clothes mended and clean and asked his opinion on everything they did. They both talked endlessly, of their childhoods, of what they wanted in life and in spite of the fact that they came from two different worlds their experiences and desires were remarkably the same. Each had lost their parents at an early age and had been brought up by relatives who begrudged their existence and had cast them out as soon as they were old enough to be on their own. Each wanted nothing more out of life than a home and a family of their own.

Only Isha wanted to get to Ranijhat, and that only so he could turn around and return to the jungle near Malabad. He rejected all overtures of friendship from the humans and when Sinéad took him to task for his rudeness, he said "Only my duty to Koda Khan keeps me with you, cat! If I had my way I should leave these humans to their fate!"

"And what would be your problem with humans?" she asked. "These two are as nice a pair as you'd ever be wantin' to meet! They're both kind to us animals and are goin' out of their way to share the food and see that we are taken care of, aye, and get pettin' an' lovin' too! In all the time we are after bein' together there's been never a harsh word nor a blow."

"You're a fool if you let yourself love them!" Isha interrupted. "They'll just abandon you when you least expect it! Something new will come along that will take their attention and without a backwards glance they will leave you!" His voice was angry and his black face was screwed up in a sour scowl.

"Is that what was happen' to you?" she asked shrewdly. "Some human loved you an' was after leavin' you?"

He glared at her, his bright eyes angry. "It's what happens to everyone who gets involved with humans!" he retorted. "This woman of yours that you are so eager to get to has more than likely forgotten all about you! Perhaps she even has a new *pet,*" he added, making the word pet sound as if it was a swear word.

"Just because some human was leavin' you it is not meanin' that they are all like that," said Sinéad. "Rosamunde will be after waitin' for me to be findin' her. I know it."

"They're all the same, swearing to love you forever and then–" He broke off and said "I had a human once that loved me, her name was Sarah and she was a *mem sahib.* I was her favorite, she played with me and fed me and loved me when she was little and then she grew up. Suddenly *Sahibs* and officers were more important to her and I saw less and less of her as the days went by. She ignored me or pushed me away when I tried to get into her lap, shrieking that I would ruin her dress or her hair. "Take this nasty thing away!" she said once to her *ayah*. And then she married and went to live in *Belait*. Others take us with them when they go to that far land. But she gave orders that I be taken into the jungle and left there. I had no experience of living in the wild. If it had not been for Koda Khan I would be dead today! He arranged for other langurs to teach me how to go on. And then you ask me why I do not trust or like humans!" he said bitterly.

"Yon was a light-minded, shallow female," said Sinéad. "but they are not all bein' so! It is in my heart that neither Niaz nor Molly would be like that. Just be givin' them a chance!"

Isha still wore that look of resentment on his face. He would not say one way or the other if he would even consider her words.

That evening Molly sought her out and said, "Sinéad, Rosamunde told me that a familiar was a good keeper of secrets and always listened well. I need to talk to someone." She looked troubled.

"Let's be goin' over here beneath this tree an' I'll be listenin' to you," the familiar suggested. Hari had gone hunting and Niaz had taken Bharat down to the river, where he would wash the elephant and attempt to catch some fish for their supper. Isha, of course, was sulking in a tree.

When Molly had made herself comfortable on the ground Sinéad climbed into her lap. "What is after troublin' ye?" she said.

A little absent mindedly Molly began to stroke her fur. "It's Niaz," she confessed. "I think, I think, I may be in love with him!"

"Is he after returnin' your feelin's?" Sinéad inquired.

"I think so," Molly said in a low voice. "I see him looking at me sometimes when he thinks I don't see him..."

"What's after bein' the problem then?" said the cat.

"How can you say that, Sinéad?" asked Molly reproachfully. "We are of different races and different religions. People are horrified at the thought of a man actually marrying a native woman. What would they say to a British woman marrying a native man, even it he actually would want to marry me," she finished. "It's probably against his religion."

"Ye're of age, neither of ye has nay relatives to object an' ye could become a Muslim, unless yer are bein' one of those fanatic Evangelical Christians," Sinéad suggested. "Would ye be throwin' away yer happiness for what people would be sayin'?"

"When I was a little girl my father, before he died, taught me that no one religion is better than another, that there is no right way," Molly said.

"Yer Da was after bein' a sensible man," said Sinéad approvingly.

"My life would have been so different if he had lived," said Molly. "Do you think that it would be wrong, Sinéad?"

"That I do not!" said the familiar emphatically. "I would be tellin' him how I was feelin'—"

"Oh, I could not do that!" Molly interrupted, horrified. "That would be most improper! No lady would ever do that!"

This business of proper ladylike behavior was what had gotten her and her Witch in trouble in the first place! Sinéad thought in exasperation. If only Rosamunde had told Alan how she felt about him they might never had had to leave home!

"And what if I am wrong?" Molly went on. "Suppose he does not care for me in that way? I should never be able to look him in the face again after confessing such a thing to him and being rejected by him!"

"But I would not reject you," came a soft voice. "For a long time now all I have dreamed of is to hold you in my arms."

Molly gasped and looked up. There, with several fish on a string, stood Niaz, a look of wonder on his face.

"Forgive me, I did not mean to spy upon you, but I could not help but overhear and what I have heard, *Iarla*, has filled my heart with delight!" Niaz went on.

Molly gasped, putting her hands up to her cheeks, which were now red with embarrassment.

"Get up and be goin' to him, ye foolish girl!" said Sinéad in a hiss to Molly and got off the young woman's lap, pulling at her skirt with her claws to pull Molly to her feet.

Sinéad pushed Molly towards Niaz and stayed only

long enough to see him take Molly in his arms and bend his head to kiss her before she left them alone to be private.

If only her own problems were that easy to solve!

It had taken Sacha far longer than he had anticipated to get permission to leave the country and travel to Russia. The Foreign Office, although they appreciated the fact that relations with Russia, peaceful, cooperative relations, were to be desired, was exceedingly reluctant to let anyone leave the country who was not in the service or the diplomatic corps. Anatoly Tcherepin was the Grand Imperial Wizard of Russia and his request for Sacha's magical help in a matter of urgency and delicacy was legitimate, but it was not until Sacha enlisted the aid of Chenevix and the Duke called in a number of favors owed that the wheels of the FO began to grind at all. Sacha had been reluctant to disturb the Duke where his Grace had so recently suffered another heart attack, but to everyone's relief, to be actually doing something towards rescuing their missing young people seemed to bring back the Duke's health as nothing else had been able to do.

Sacha was well aware that his mission was fraught with danger. The news out of India was still bad, in spite of a number of victories. On September 25th Lucknow had been relieved by the forces of Havelock and Outram, but the siege continued. Mutineers still roamed, killing and looting. Nana Sahib had disappeared, after being defeated at Cawnpore by Havelock back in July. Nana Sahib was considered to be an extremely dangerous man and the fact that he had vanished from sight filled some breasts with foreboding.

And in spite of his confidence in his own immunity Sacha could not help but be worried about the black ley lines. Not just their effect on him, but what they might have done to Alan and Rosamunde. He could discuss this with no one, for everyone else was too overwrought as it was. Sacha was well aware that the others, particularly Stuart, as he was a doctor, knew all too well what polluted ley lines could do to a Witch or a Wizard. But they had chosen to remain hopeful and optimistic and Sacha was not about to be a naysayer and quash their hopes. Miracles happened every day, and neither

Alan or Rosamunde were ordinary magicians.

It was a drizzly day in early October when Sacha finally left for Russia, taking tender leave of the entire family who had pinned all of their hopes on him. Cynara and Lakota had their own goodbyes. They had never been separated before and this would be a particularly difficult time for them as they were hoping to try for an egg. And Sacha's familiar, Anastasia, would not be able to go as she was due to have a litter of kittens any day.

They were able to fly directly to John O'Groat's in Scotland, as the etheric barrier extended around the entire group of islands that made up the Six Nations, including the Isles of the Blessed to the west of Ireland and the Channel Islands, still allowing travel and commerce between the nations.

From John O' Groats they would fly to Norway, after Cynara had eaten a good deal of firestone to allow her to stay aloft for a long time. Years earlier, in China, Lakota had discovered that drinking lime infused water allowed him to fly longer than with firestone alone and now it was standard practice for water to be treated with lime and given to dragons They could fly further with this addition to their diets, still not far enough to cross the Atlantic, but it eliminated the dangerous mid-air passing of firestone from rider to dragon in such areas as over the North Sea.

Cynara now flew much better than she had when Sacha had first brought her home. In the mines of New Spain, where she had spent her formative years, her wings had been tied down and she had taken some time to be able to fly. It was then a brand new experience for her. She would never be as strong as flier as some other dragons, but she had come a long way. It just took her a little longer to get where she was going. She was as anxious as was Sacha to complete their rescue mission.

Once they reached Saint Petersburg Sacha spent some time with Anatoly, plotting a route and making plans for any contingency. If Alan and Rosamunde were ill he would bring them back to Saint Petersburg, where the Collegium of Wizard Healers could treat them, if winter in Russia were not too far advanced.

It was not going to be an easy flight to India. It was over 1,000 miles just from Saint Petersburg to Taganrog near the Sea of Azov. From there they would fly southeast over the Caspian Sea, crossing the Ust-Urt plateau, over the Aral sea and then cross the Kyzul Kum Desert and then to Tashkent, with another stop in Samarkand before they left Russian territory, crossing the Hindu Kush through one of the passes or *kotals*, probably the *Kotal-e-Salang*. From there they could go to Ranijhat near Kashmir. This somewhat circuitous route was necessary for a supply of firestone to be readily available. Anatoly had arranged it for them. He had been a soldier before he became a Wizard and was able to give Sacha and Cynara valuable advice about the region, for he had been posted there once.

Sacha had visited the Hollow Hills before he had left Ireland and had asked the Elf King to give both himself and Cynara the languages necessary for this rescue mission. The Elf King had been glad to help, as he could do nothing else. Chenevix had provided Sacha with a hefty money belt and Stuart had given him a medical kit. Letters from everyone else, as well as clothing and supplies were in Cynara's breast harness. He had even packed a brace of pistols. They seemed ready for any eventuality.

The Russian part of the trip passed without incident. The firestone was plentiful and the supplies more than adequate, thanks to Anatoly.

Sacha was not worried about crossing the desert. Dragons loved heat and sand and moreover could find water anywhere. He was more concerned about crossing the Hindu Kush. They were high mountains, particularly to the west of Kabul, where several peaks were as high as 20,000 feet. This was too high for both him and Cynara. She was unused to heights like that where the air was cold and thin, as was he. He was much afraid that her wings would ice up. It would be a necessity to find a low pass to fly through.

After much study of the maps provided by Anatoly, Sacha and Cynara decided to stay away from the Khyber Pass. They had to avoid being seen by British forces as they were in India illegally and this most often used pass would bring them too near Mardan, Rawalpindi and Peshawar, all British strongholds.

Cynara stayed as high as she could as even her shadow passing on the ground terrorized the herds of horses, goats, sheep and cattle they passed over. Even the people in this part of the world were terrified when they saw her. Sacha could no longer imagine being frightened of a dragon. It had been too many years, and acquaintance with quite a lot of dragons since he had been in the least scared of one of the great creatures.

They had successfully passed the British outposts and had turned east towards Kashmir and Ranijhat, when, late in the morning, Cynara turned her head and said "There are people on the ground waving at us, Sacha. They are dressed in English style clothing! I think they are in some sort of distress."

Sacha wore binoculars around his neck. He took these up and looked where Cynara had indicated. A man and a woman were below them on the ground, alone, out in the barren, rocky mountain terrain. Both were older people and appeared to be in distress, as Cynara had said. The woman was waving a tattered shawl at them. She obviously knew what a dragon in the sky meant, that rescue might be at hand.

"Damn!" said Sacha. "We can't just leave them here! Find a place to put down safely, sweetheart. We'll have to rescue them."

He would gladly take thee people to Ranijhat, but nowhere else. His purpose was too important to be put aside. They would have to be content with that.

45

time passing by

The days fell into a pattern for Alan. Conscious of the time hurtling on towards Guy Fawkes Day he went every day to the bazaar and worked with the *Sadhu,* but to no avail. In spite of all the effort he put into the meditation and yoga exercises Prabhat patiently put him through, (the old man never became impatient or gave up), he could not obtain the final level of giving himself up that was need. Something always held him back, just as it had when he had attempted much the same thing during his Druidical training.

The Maharani and Hussaini were well pleased by what they read in her ruby, but to Rosamunde's amazement and relief there were not as many men choosing her as there had been. Their gaze passed over her and her suffering seemed to be limited to the nights in the *Diwan.* The ruby always looked as if she had entertained many men and the power level was high as well.

After returning from the House, Alan usually went riding with Nate. The Maharajah had given his permission for the magician to ride out with the *Daffadur* as Jehan had pointed out that he needed exercise.

The two men had become firm friends. They spent much time devising and discarding plans for escape and exchanging notes on what they had observed on the defenses in and outside the Mahal.

But they never discussed with one another how they felt about having to endure seeing the women they loved being daily abused and violated.

Once Rosamunde was returned to the Mahal she was, along with the others, put to work in the *zenana,* and the amount of men using them had increased significantly, many of them full of the dust of Kali. This was being used in increasing quantities. And again, to Rosamunde's amazement, the men overlooked her, and the eunuchs did not seem to notice that she often sat unmolested. Nor did the other women notice. Rosamunde could not but help feel guilty to see her friends still so abused when she was not. But this did not hold true in the *Dwan*.

There were more guests of an evening, all of whom were fed the dust as well. Every evening, after the entertainments were over, turned into an orgy presided over by the Maharani, who sat on her throne with its embroidered *gaddi* with a total lack of emotion on her face, as if she were not watching a complete debauch of sensuality.

Laura began to be taken to the private rooms of the Maharajah so that he could fondle her or watch Kumala Jha or another man take her as the royal pervert mounted his bride. Laura felt extreme pity for the girl, who was only fourteen. She was a *Rajkumari*, a Princess from a small state in southern India and her father, not a wealthy man, had not been able to contain his greed at the offer of the hefty bride price promised and had sold her to Jhaniput without a backwards glance. Her name was Jaswinder and her sensibilities were violated as well as her body. She never ceased protesting this treatment, earning her slaps from the Maharajah as well as endless sexual congress. He was determined to get her with child. She had six tall, strong brothers and many uncles on her mother's side, which was the reason Jhaniput had been so interested in her. What truly revolted Laura was that the little toad had not even married her properly. He would do that when and if she become pregnant, and not before. If after four months of unrelenting use she did not quicken with child, she too would be made a slave, taken to the brothel and given a menial, degrading job as punishment for failing her lord.

After a morning spent in the rooms of the Maharajah Laura too, was returned to the *zenana*. Like Rosamunde, who was very glad that Alan was always dismissed after his magic show, Laura was grateful that Nate did not see how she was used at the nightly binge. Neither of them got much sleep.

After the bacchanal in the *Diwan-i-Khas* each evening Laura was given to Nate and Rosamunde went to Alan, unless they had been promised to another first. The *Daffadur* Sarin was high in favor at the moment. His troop was the best trained, both in shooting and riding, for Nate was a dead shot as well as a talented horseman. His men could accurately aim and shoot from the back of a galloping horse. The horses were the best trained as well.

He took advantage of the royal favor by requesting Laura as often as was possible and ended in being given her for his exclusive use each evening when her duties were finished.

He much hated seeing the look on her face when she was delivered to his rooms each evening, usually looking worn and disgusted. She was very often bruised and sore as well. All the same, she always insisted that he make love to her, afterwards falling asleep in his arms to sleep like the dead, while he lay awake, his arms tight about her, fuming with anger. As did Alan, he wanted to murder someone.

Alan had a bath waiting for Rosamunde each evening and gave her the unicorn horn to wear as she bathed. He always stayed in the *ghosulkhana* with her and they conversed, usually a conversation about home, which was both comforting and sad. Then they went to sleep on the *charpoy*, laying far apart, sometimes with Cathal between them, but during the night, while sleeping, they always ended in moving closer to each other.

Alan had fallen into the habit of visiting Nate every evening after he was dismissed from the royal presence. No one had seemed to notice or care that the magician and the *Daffadur* were becoming friends. Alan's movements about the *Mahal* were not curtailed any more, for he too was in favor, only his movements outside the walls. Even his many visits to the House of Assignation were not remarked upon.

One evening in mid October he made his way to the barracks as usual. His heart ached and his temper boiled as he thought what Rosamunde would have to endure that night. There were many guests, all of them with glassy stares he associated with the use of the dust of Kali. He had seen them when he performed.They were still putting it in his food as well, but the potency of the unicorn horn was undiminished.

His part in the evening's entertainment always came early, just after the puppet show, but before the dancing. Rosamunde, he knew, was glad that he was not present to see the dances, which, Alan had found out from Parminder, had become increasing lewd and the male dancers were participating more often. His imagination as to what was being done to her was bad enough; he could not think how he would restrain himself if he actually saw her being debauched. And without magic all his anger would earn him would be a quick death under the lances of the guards who would be instantly summoned.

Nate was waiting for him, for they had made the engagement earlier, while riding. Nate had a supper spread out on the low table, and a *parchesi* board set up, for they found that occupying themselves kept them from thinking about what was being done to Laura and Rosamunde, even though they had never once discussed this aloud by tacit agreement.

Cathal who as usual had ridden on Alan's shoulder, saw the little ears of corn he so liked, and scampered down to the table top with an exclamation of pleasure.

Alan sat down heavily on a pile of cushions that served as a chair. "I shall never, ever, after this, wish to sit upon the floor again," he said wearily. "I shall fill my home with chairs."

Nate looked at him in concern. Alan looked not only incredibly weary, but hag-ridden as well. He was fine drawn and taut, his eyes shadowed.

"Take it that it ain't going well with the old man?" Nate said in sympathy, and filled plates for both Alan and Cathal. Now that he was riding high in the royal favor he could have almost anything he wanted, even extra plates, spoons and food. He always put aside some food for Laura to eat later, for she was not fed in the *Diwan-i-Khas*, but had to endure watching others eat and sniffing the enticing odors.

"I reach a certain point and then I simply cannot go on!" said Alan sounding hopeless. "The *Sadhu* is endlessly patient with me. If I had a pupil as stupid as I am, I should have strangled him long since! I daresay it is a good thing I never became a professor as did my father. I would have been in Dublin Gaol for murdering students." He took a long draught of a cup of fragrant tea Nate poured for him. He had little appetite but was forcing himself to eat. Cathal scolded him if he did not eat enough.

"All I can think about," Alan went on, taking a bite of a spoonful of Lahore style lamb, which was made with a curry blend, cinnamon and cooked with *chana dhal* or yellow split peas, tomatoes and chilies, "is how close we are getting to the day of attack. I think the reason for all of the increased activity in the brothel is because they need to raise a pre-determined level of power, rather like   raising a Cone of Power."

"What's a Cone of Power?" Nate asked, loading his plate with *Karahi* potatoes, with whole spices, saffron rice, and a *bharti* of roasted aubergines with spring onions. A big chunk of spicy *mossi roti* bread went with this, as well as an ample helping of the lamb.

"When Witches and Wizards wish to do a major working as they did back in my grandfather's day to repel Napoleon, they gather in Druidical Circle or Wizards' Circles and the Witches gather in their Covens and band together to make a huge amount of power. The sheer amount of magic from many magicians can actually be seen as a huge cone rising into he sky, with its base on the ground and narrowing to a point towering above it. It looks like a mass of swirling energy ranging from blue to violet in colour. It can be tipped and directed to where it will do the most good. Back then it was sent towards France with the message to Napoleon "You cannot come! You cannot cross the Channel!"

"Sort of like a twister; what you folks call a cyclone," Nate commented.

"Exactly," agreed Alan, taking more food as he received a look from Cathal. "But we tap the ley lines as well as other energies in nature to draw all this power and there are many of us. As far as I may tell there is but one magician here, the Maharani."

"The royal jackass ain't a magician?" Nate asked.

Alan smiled wryly. "One of the few things I can still do is read other magicians and believe me, he has no magic. Neither does anyone else here. She is the only one I can feel it from. A few of these people have some psychic ability, that man Kumala Jha is an Empath and Hussaini has a low level psychic talent. And when there is only one magician the same amount of power can not be raised as in a Circle or a Coven. But a magician can store power and infuse some inanimate object with it. This is precisely what most black magicians do, as they usually work alone. Many times they will put the power into a stone, or an amulet they can wear about their necks. I am willing to bet that is why that awful woman always wears a ruby on her forehead. That would be a secondary power storage for her. But since she has gathered so much power from the constant sex magic here, there would have to be a primary storage for all of that power. I daresay it is that statue of Kali in the room that Rosamunde and Laura have both mentioned. If either one of them had been able to remain conscious they would have no doubt seen the Maharani transfer the power from the rubies into the statue after she drained off as much as she needed for her own stone. I only wish that I knew what was wrong with the ley lines here and if these people could use them. Most black magicians do not use ley lines, as they are essentially looking for easy methods of gaining power and the ley lines are usually vessels of the Light and can be difficult to use without training, although some people have a natural affinity for them. My mother does, which is unusual amongst Witches. Ley lines can become corrupted, however. I wonder if that is what has happened here?" he sighed and looked at Nate, a somber expression on his face. "I feel so lost," he confessed. "I have no one to consult and no books to guide me. I've always had an extensive library and other Wizards to turn to and time is running out."

Nate felt very sorry for his new friend. Alan had an awesome responsibility for everyone was counting on him and in his own eyes he was a miserable failure. And Nate could tell that the harder Alan tried the more likely he was to fail, just because he and everyone else was so heavily relying on him.

"Maybe that dragon of yours will get here soon, before they do attack. I'm trying to find out where they aim to do that," said Nate.

"Oh, didn't you know ?" said Cathal, looking up from a piece of mango he was chewing with great enjoyment. "They intend to go into the Punjab first and destroy all the Queen's troops there, since that is where the most of them are located. After they have done that they intend to retake Delhi, annihilate the people holding out in Lucknow and then on to

Calcutta and destroy the East India Company, wiping out any British resistance on the way "

At the stunned look on the faces of the two men Cathal said modestly, "It's easy to overhear things when you are a small animal and no one thinks you can understand human speech! Kaveri and I spend a lot of time spying upon the General."

"I'd of placed a tidy bet that they'd go to Delhi first. They were some upset that the British took it back," said Nate slowly. "But a surprise attack on the Punjab, it makes sense. It's rough country, though,"

"And totally unprepared for an attack," said Alan. "Many of the troops are being shifted to Hindustan, to quell the Mutiny."

"The General also expects the Pathans in Afghanistan to join them," said Cathal. "I heard only today that he has been conducting secret negotiations with them."

"And the British will be squeezed right between the two of 'em," Nate said grimly. "It looks like everything hinges on that dragon of yours arriving in time, Alan."

"Yes, because no one can count on me for anything!" Alan thought bitterly. He hated himself at this moment.

When Rosamunde arrived that night she had news.

Alan insisted she get into the bath before she told him. She looked utterly worn, even walking rather gingerly. As usual, he dropped the unicorn horn around her neck, wishing as he did so that he could take her in his arms and kiss away all her pain.

She settled back in the water with a sigh of contentment, the unicorn horn beginning its good work immediately. "You cannot imagine how much I look forward to this!" she said, laying back against the tile sides of the immense tub and closing her eyes. "To get rid of all that nasty oil – I think that I shall hate the scent of musk forever. And to feel the healing, to be able to be with you, it is all that keeps me sane throughout the vile goings-on in the *Diwan -i-Khas!*"

"Was it worse than usual?" he asked, carefully. She did not like talking about what was done to her, but he was tortured by visions of what happened to her, that one image in her ruby of the General and the men who had come before him had stayed in his mind, tormenting him ever since he had seen it.

"It is getting worse all the time," she said, sounding strained. "Every night there are more guests and more men are brought to us in the *zenana*. The eunuchs are competing for bags of gold to make certain that the women in their guard take more men than any other group. Mabel Clutterbuck thinks she is in a competition with me and is always seeking me out to tell me how many she has had that day."

"And early next week there is to be a very special guest, I do not know his name as yet, but the Rajah of Ulladar spoke of him admiringly as a black magician." She did not tell Alan that the Rajah had been using her body as he spoke to the Maharani, who sat beside them, watching. It was horrible enough to be used like that, in front of all of those people, without that terrible woman watching, with her snake-like eyes, cold and unmoved. Rosamunde felt like a specimen under her father's microscope. "The Maharani is devising a special dance, a peacock dance, for Parminder and me. If we are very fortunate, she told us today, one of us will be chosen to sleep with the special guest, which is to be considered a very high honour indeed. It is one I can do without." She opened her eyes suddenly as a thought struck her. "Alan, since I am a Witch dedicated to the Light, what will happen if I sleep with a black magician?"

"I don't know," he said slowly. "If you had your full powers it probably would be very bad indeed. To tell you the truth, I have not read much about that as it is not something that usually happens, a sexual union between Dark and Light. I can't remember reading about it ever happening!" He looked helplessly at her. "I just don't know, Rosamunde!"

She said nothing more. He looked so distressed that she had not the heart to mention the dance of Kali that was to be performed.The Maharani had not decided if she or Parminder was to impersonate the black goddess in a dance in which her union with her husband and lover Shiva would be fully depicted.

46

meeting in ranijhat

Cynara began to spiral down easily. Where the two people stood was high and relatively flat. Cynara was a small dragon, not even twenty five feet in length. Since she was a Luna, moon-coloured, and as such was not a breed, but a genetic sport, Sacha had no idea if this was her full growth or if the ill treatment in the mines in her youth had stunted her adult size. They would probably never know what breed her parents had been as she had been in the mines since hatching.

Now, being small worked to her advantage for she was able to land well away from the people. A dragon always took care to land some distance from persons and property as the considerable wing span could damage or even kill and the gliding landing did not allow the wings to be folded until the dragon's talons had touched the ground.

The two people waiting below were obviously unused to dragons, for the woman ran forward before Cynara had completely folded her wings.

"Oh, please! Oh, please help us!" she called, tears streaming down her face. "You're English, aren't you? I know there are dragons in England!"

She came right up to Cynara's shoulder, her hands clasped in front of her in entreaty, looking up earnestly and myopically at Sacha as he undid the safety harness and swung his leg over the saddle, preparing to slide down onto Cynara's lifted front leg.

Sacha decided against making matters more complicated by telling her that he was a Russian living in Ireland and said instead. "Yes, we're from England. What are you doing out here by yourselves, ma'am?" he inquired as he stepped onto Cynara's front leg. She lowered him to the ground easily.

Her male companion had followed more slowly and came up to them just as Sacha touched the earth.

He was a clergyman, that much was obvious by his dress. But like the dark blue gown worn by the woman, his vestments were tattered and dirty.

"I told you that the Lord would provide, Maude, and He has! Even though He has chosen to do it in the instrument of a minion of Satan!" he said in satisfaction.

Cynara sharply turned her head towards him and said. "If you persist in naming me a minion of Satan, sir, I shall be very glad to leave you here to your fate! I attend church as often as you do!"

"You will do as your master bids you, creature!" the clergyman said, affronted that a beast would dare to speak to a man of the cloth.

"I am not her master. She is my friend and it is up to her who she will or will not carry," said Sacha firmly. "And I don't care for this Satanic drivel either. There will be no more of it, or I too will be very happy to leave you here!"

The man looked somewhat abashed as the woman begged "Please, Ignatius! We shall die if we stay out here any longer with no food or shelter! How can we continue to do the Lord's work if we die here?" She turned back to Sacha and said, tearfully, "I am Maude Holloway and this is my husband, Reverend Ignatius Holloway. We are fleeing from the murderers. We paid a man to guide us to Rawalpindi where there are British troops stationed. But he brought us only so far and then abandoned us, taking all of our goods with him! That was two days ago and we have had no food since and only a little water."

Sacha had discerned this for both of them had cracked and dried lips and a hungry look about them. He went to Cynara's breast harness and pulled out water bottles, which had been bespelled to remain cold and pure and a packet of Elfin journey bread that would assuage their hunger as nothing else could, and it was incredibly delicious as well. "I have plenty of food and drink," he said , and gave them each a cold bottle and a wedge of the journey bread, which looked like the finest cake, full of fruit and redolent of honey.

They had not exaggerated their plight. From the ferocity with which they attacked the bread and the bottles it might have been longer than two days since any form of sustenance had passed their lips.

Both the Reverend and his wife had fallen to the ground and were busily eating. Exchanging a look with Cynara, Sacha gathered stones for Wizard's fire, no wood necessary, and with additional materials pulled from Cynara's breast mesh harness, he was soon making tea. With water from another bottle he filled a small kettle and added a packet of dried vegetables, herbs and dried meat that would soon make a tasty, nutritious soup.

"Now we must thank the Lord," said the Reverend piously and knelt to begin a long prayer of Thanksgiving for their rescue. Thinking it would show the clergyman that they were not imps of Satan, Sacha knelt with them and Cynara bowed her head, both joining in the loud "Amen!" at the end.

"You have not as yet informed us who you might be, young sir," said the Reverend at the end of the long prayer, long enough to allow the kettle to boil for the tea and the soup to simmer, sending an enticing scent out onto the air. "And how it is that you are so serendipitously here to affect our rescue, sent by the Lord no doubt!"

"I'm Alexander Kustodiev," Sacha answered. "This dragoness is my friend Cynara. We've come here from Ireland to search for relatives who are missing in the Mutiny." He poured out the tea, including a dragon sized cup for Cynara.

"We were fortunate to not be killed!" Mrs. Holloway shivered. "Had we not been called away that fateful Sunday morning we too would have been slaughtered by the natives!"

"That was not fortune, Maude, but the hand of the Lord! " said her husband reprovingly. "The Lord has more work for us to do in this heathen country. That is why we were spared. Are you able to take us to Rawalpindi, young man?"

"Rawalpindi lies some ways behind us," said Sacha."Our way lays north, to Ranijhat near Kashmir. We can certainly take you there," he looked briefly at Cynara who nodded 'yes'. "But my mission is urgent. I cannot delay. Our relatives have been missing since May and I hope to find my nephew in Ranijhat and hope that he has had word of my niece who was at Malabad—"

"Malabad!" Mrs. Holloway cried. "But that is where our mission was located! Perhaps we know of your niece. Pray, what is her name?"

"Rosamunde DeLacey. Her husband was—"

"Lieutenant Raymond DeLacey!" Mrs. Holloway finished. "Oh, yes, we knew them well! The Lieutenant was a very Godly young man. He felt just as he ought on all important subjects and was always so grateful for any guidance and a faithful attendee of both the church services and our little lectures. I am afraid that your niece did not share his sentiments completely but then, she was very young and had this massacre not intervened I was hoping to set her feet on the proper path of Christian womanhood."

Sacha almost choked on his tea. He could imagine how Rosamunde would have taken that.

"But you said 'was', Mr. Kustodiev. Was the Lieutenant a victim of these vile mutineers?" the Reverend inquired.

"Yes, we received confirmation of his death while I was still in Ireland. But Rosamunde is officially listed as missing, so we have hopes that I will be able to find her," Sacha returned.

"And how will you do that, with these murderers still, no doubt on the rampage?" the Reverend said.

"He has me," said Cynara dryly, "And Sacha is a very powerful Wizard."

"As is my nephew in Ranijhat," Sacha added. "but a great deal of time has gone by and many things have happened."

"Do you know all of the latest news?" Mrs. Holloway asked eagerly. "We have heard little but rumors. Is Delhi still in rebel hands?"

Sacha was able to fill them in on the last reports he had read in the journals before he had quit Ireland. As he ladled out the soup he hoped that these people were not going to be an unnecessary complication. Already Mr. Holloway's smooth self satisfaction and smug assurance that he had been especially spared from the fate of so many other British irritated him. And he knew that Cynara disliked the man as well.

They would fly the Holloways to Ranijhat, and it was up to them to get to Rawalpindi from there, although Sacha had a feeling that much more time spent in their company, particularly the Reverend's, would soon make him volunteer a large sum of money to anyone who would take them off his hands and out of his company.

Niaz had found a wandering *Maulvi* who agreed to marry him and Molly, provided she promised to convert to Islam as soon as they were settled. The old man grumbled at Niaz's haste and had protested volubly at first, but had allowed himself to be persuaded. These were strange times, everything was in chaos and things were not being done in the right way. Niaz also promised that a proper ceremony would be made as soon as they reached Ranijhat. But he wanted to make Molly his and have the rights of a husband to care for her and protect her.

The *Maulvi* might not have been so agreeable if he realized that Molly was a *mem-sahib* but weeks of traveling in the open air had bronzed her skin and lightened her hair to a shade sometimes found in the women of Circassia. She was careful to speak only in Hindustanee, which had become more fluent in the past weeks, thanks to Niaz and Sinéad. The *Maulvi* heard her name as Mullee Frazee, rather than Molly Fraser.

Sinéad kept the other animals away from them on their wedding night. She was happy to see the next morning that both Molly and Niaz looked pleased and satisfied. They touched each other often, and kissed. It would be a good marriage, Sinéad thought. Molly was more than willing to bend to his ways, even the thought of a *zenana* did not dismay her, for she was shy and ill at ease in company. As long as he took no other wife, which Niaz said he would have no need or desire to do.

Sinéad had told Molly and Niaz about Isha's past and they had both been indignant that the monkey had been treated so badly. "You may tell him," said Niaz, "that we would be honored if he wished to make his home with us. And we hope that Hari and Bharat will remain with us as well. Bharat grows old and I shall willingly care for him in his old age. I am hoping to find some sort of employment in Ranijhat and our home will be open to all of them, and to you as well, Sinéad, if you do not find your Witch."

But Sinéad refused to even think of such a contingency. She *would* find Rosamunde. They *would* be together again. Anything else was unthinkable.

It was at the end of a long, weary peregrination that they at last saw the towers of Jhat city rising out of a mist one October morning. All were footsore and weary. To spare Bharat, they walked part of each day. By now, both Molly and Niaz were barefoot, their clothes in near rags, for Niaz's small store of *rupees* had long since gone. But they were happy in each other. Sinéad had promised to introduce them to Ravi, who might be able to find employment for Niaz.

And lately Isha had been accepting fruit from Niaz's hand; still wary, still watching how he and Molly treated the other animals. Hari considered them his new family, talking of 'my people' when he spoke of them and Bharat was quite reconciled to spending his final days in their care. Since Nirav, the Maharajah of Mahouts, was dead he could not ask for better people.

Sinéad wanted to run ahead and find Alan at once but she had a duty to these who had helped her get here and she stayed with them as they slowly traversed the banks of the Ajit, each feeling now, that they had finally reached their goal, an overwhelming exhaustion.

The sun was rapidly burning off the mist. It would be another blue, clear day. It was nearly ten o'clock and they were nearing the main gate, the Lahore gate, when Sinéad saw an enormous shadow pass over them and she knew at once what that meant. "Brendan!" she said joyfully. looking up and squinting against the sun, trying to see the dragon.

But it was not Brendan. The shadow wheeled and came back and a few moments later a Luna that Sinéad knew well landed near them.

"Sinéad!" Sacha exclaimed from Cynara's back. Behind him on the six passenger dragon saddle sat two persons Sinéad had hoped never to see again, the Holloways. However had Sacha taken up with those gowks?

"Cynara said that was you!" Sacha undid the safety harness and slid from Cynara's back. He ran forward and picked up the little familiar.

It felt so good to be held by a well known and loved person again. Sinéad purred loudly as Sacha held her up to his cheek and stroked her. "Oh, Sacha," said the little cat, "me darlin' Witch is bein' in the hands of slavers! I am after thankin' Bastet that you have come to help! Is Alan after bein' here too?"

"I was only arriving myself," said Sacha. "Introduce me to your friends, Sinéad and we'll go find Alan."

Introductions were made all around, Sacha horrifying the Holloways as he bowed to the animals as if they had been rational beings! They also looked with disapproval at Molly and Niaz, dirty heathen natives! And a talking cat! They were equally shocked to learn that Sinéad was Rosamunde's familiar and that Mrs. DeLacey was a Witch. It was little wonder, Mrs. Holloway thought, that she was not a good Christian woman, having indulged in naked orgies and unchristian practices all her days.

The landing of a strange dragon had not gone unnoticed at the *Moti Mahal* and a brace of guards, armed with lances, hurried towards them, with the Maharajah Zahallah and Ravi's two brothers, Chetan and Dhaval, on three of the Maharajah's highly bred horses. Like Bharat, these horses were skittish of the dragon until she greeted them pleasantly in Animal language.

A veritable babble broke out as everyone began talking at once. Sacha had just put his fingers to his lips to whistle for silence when another great shadow flitted over head.

Cynara gave a loud exclamation in Dragon which effectively silenced everyone. With her long dragon sight she ws able to see who it was. "It's Brendan!" she exclaimed joyfully.

In Jhaniput, the Maharani was critically studying her two primary *nautch* girls as they knelt before her in the Room of the Dance. "It is a difficult decision," she said, "for you both have dancing skills and have forms and *yonis* that will appeal to our very important guest."

With her stood Hussaini with Mabel at her feet.

Behind Hussaini's back Mabel made a face at Rosamunde and mouthed *"I have taken more than you have today!"*

Rosamunde hated the way Mabel thought that they were in some sort of obscene contest. Nothing she could say, or that Laura had said bluntly to the Clutterbuck girl, could convince Mabel otherwise. Every time she saw Rosamunde she made a point of listing off her quota for so far that day with an air of superiority that excited pity for what the girl had become in Rosamunde's breast.

Laura did not feel sorry for her. "She's a natural born whore," Laura had said. "Some women are like that, Rose. Pa tried to help a soiled dove in the camp we lived in once, tried to get her a decent job, but in two weeks she was back to whorin, she missed it. It's my guess that your Mabel is like her. She's happy with what she's doing and ain't nothing we can say that's going to make her else wise. I reckon when we're rescued from this place she'll end up in a cat house somewhere and like it, too."

Rosamunde thought that this was unbelievable and pitiful. Now she ignored Mabel's mouthings and paid attention to what the Maharani was saying.

They had spent the morning practicing the Peacock dance and being fitted for the costumes which were little more than beads and feathers. Their bodies would be sprinkled, after oiling, with a new iridescent blue powder, which mimicked the gleam of peacock feathers. Lewd things would be done with peacock feather fans. They were to dance in the *Diwan-i-Am*, the Hall of Public Audience, which was going to be lined with looking glasses so that the images of the dance would be endlessly reflected. They were to dance a mirror dance of preening peacocks. No one minding the inaccuracy that it was the male who sported the gorgeous plumage. None of the men present would care about seeing a nude man dance in a lascivious fashion, unless he were using a woman.

The Maharani studied them again." Chowki shall portray Kali," she said at last, "for she is the more voluptuous, the more like our Goddess herself. But Serai shall be given to our special guest, for the courtesans in his *zenana* more closely resemble her form and her *yoni* is very tight, which he prefers."

"You have been honored above all others, girl!," said

438

Hussaini , stroking Mabel's red hair as the girl leaned against her legs. "I would hope to be able to lay with him myself! He is a lusty man and will take you again and again, even without the use of the dust of Kali! He is very inventive as well and will have you do things you never could have dreamed of! I would that I could be there to watch! Most women would die to be able to boast that they lay with the Peshwa of Bithur, Dhondu Pant, the magician they call Nana Sahib."

And Rosamunde's blood ran cold.

dragon fire and peacock feathers

Brendan landed neatly in the small space left on the riverbank. The Maharajah Zahallah gave an exclamation of pleasure and satisfaction as he saw his son and heir on the dragon's back .

Brendan went at once to Cynara and, touching his snout to hers, said "I am glad you have come. I have a great task to do and I can use your help."

"I'll be glad to do anything I can," she promised.

"Come," cried the Maharajah, clapping his hands. "We will all rest and refresh ourselves and talk! " He gave orders for tables to be set up out of doors so that the dragons could join them.

An hour or so later explanations had been made, stories exchanged and even minor things such as both the Holloways and Niaz and Molly being bathed and outfitted in new clothing, were accomplished. A tired Bharat had been taken to the *sawaree,* for Ranijhat had several elephants, used for both hunting and work, as well as fighting. Hari had stayed near Molly and Niaz and had climbed into Molly's lap as soon as they had sat down at the table. She fed him bits off her plate and even Isha stayed near, accepting sliced fruit from Niaz.

Sinéad, grateful to have someone from her home, had refused to be parted from Sacha. She had been more than disappointed to find Alan gone and had been dismayed when she was informed just how long it had been since he had left in search of Rosamunde.

"And he's not been after fetchin' her back yet?" she had cried. "What is he thinkin' of?"

"He was left with very little magic after his illness," said Ravi. "He was *very* ill, Sinéad. At times we despaired of his life. And we have no way of knowing what has happened in Jhaniput."

Brendan was also horrified to hear just how ill Alan had been. To Sacha and Cynara's surprise though, he did not immediately talk wildly of taking off after Alan. The green dragon seemed to have changed, deepened in character and matured since he had been in Tibet. "As much as I want to help Alan, I can help him best by doing the task I was set by the Lama and the Oracle," he said. "And I am glad you are here, Sacha, you can help as well. You are not affected by the ley lines?"

"I don't seem to be, but I have not been here that long," he answered, stroking Sinéad to calm the little cat's agitation. She wanted to go after Rosamunde immediately.

"It would make my task easier if there is a Wizard here to read the ley lines," said Brendan.

While Niaz and Molly had sat respectfully quiet while the high born ones, as Niaz thought of them, were speaking, the Holloways had listened to all the talk of magic with increasing dismay. The Reverend's brow grew thunderous as the green dragon took over the conversation and all the humans appeared as if they were willing to take orders from him.

"Enough of this blasphemy!" he cried, smashing his hand, open palm down on the table so that all the crockery rattled violently. "If there is any rescuing of a white woman to be done it should be done properly by British troops, with the blessing of the Lord! Not these Devil's arts! Not under the direction of a reptile!"

Sacha looked at him in irritation. He had known that the man would be trouble. "Are you completely unaware that there is a great difference between white and black magic?" he began hotly.

The Maharajah Zahallah forestalled him. "I am certain," he said soothingly, "that you and your wife, Mr. Holloway, are tired and worn and in much need of some sleep. My guards will escort you to the suite of rooms which have been prepared for you. After all, you will play no part in the events to come and to see such things may even be upsetting to you. "He waved to the guards, who came forward and picked up Mr. Holloway, who was now gobbling like an enraged turkey cock and carried him off. The guards had been chosen for their size and strength and had no trouble in subduing him. Mrs. Holloway, after a frightened glance at the others, scurried off after him.

"I think," said the Maharajah calmly, "that the missionaries shall remain my guests for some time. We will not wish them to become more of a nuisance than they already are."

"Why were ye not leavin' them in th' mountains?" Sinéad muttered.

"Thank you," said Sacha in relief to Zahallah. He had lost all patience with the Reverend. He might be a man of the cloth but he was also a jackass.

Brendan was certain that he had to complete his task before they could set out for Jhaniput. He thought it best that he and Cynara rest before the task was undertaken and proposed the next day for it.

"What exactly is it we are going to do?" Cynara asked curiously.

"We are going to purify the ley lines," said Brendan, "with dragon fire. We shall burn off all the contamination and open the channels to the Light once more."

Early the next morning Cynara and Brendan, accompanied by Ravi, Sacha and Sinéad, flew up to a shelf high on the side of the mountain that loomed over the bulk of the *Moti Mahal*.

They had spent some time discussing Brendan's plan and even arguing about it. Sacha had tentatively touched the ley lines and had been appalled at the Darkness in them. It had effected even him, acting as a depressant. "They are more than polluted," he said grimly. "They are completely corrupt and it is a deep, old evil." He doubted that dragon fire could even penetrate it at all, much less burn it off.

Brendan was calmly confident. "The Lama has assured me that we shall have help when we need it," he said. "And the Oracle has said that if we but do our task in the proper manner we shall triumph."

Sacha was at last forced to admit that if sheer

confidence could carry the day, it would be Brendan who could do it. The Emerald dragon remained calm, cool and certain, in spite of all the objections.

Ravi had insisted on coming with them. He had spent some time the evening before with Niaz and Molly. He had offered Niaz a position in the small cavalry of Ranijhat and had personally showed them to a small house that they could call home, and had advanced Niaz a good sum of money so that they could set up housekeeping. Ravi was convinced, that given the state of Hindustan, it would be in Ranijhat's best interest to modernize and expand the army and for this, young officers were needed. Niaz, a British trained *jemadar* of cavalry, was a godsend.

Ravi was praying to Allah that what Brendan planned would work. He felt responsible for all that had happened to Alan and was willing to do anything he could to help, including being supportive and doing whatever Brendan needed him to do.

Cynara had been worried about sleeping the night before as the importance of what they were to do had weighed heavily upon her. But Brendan had given her a phrase to chant and although she felt foolish, she obeyed him and to her surprise, fell into a deep, dreamless sleep and woke the next morning feeling refreshed and ready for anything. She even felt more optimistic that what they were going to do would actually work.

Now she stood beside Brendan, with the other three to one side, taking deep breaths as he instructed her. She'd had eaten the last of the firestone that she and Sacha had carried and only hoped that it would be enough. She had never had as much flame as other dragons, for again, breathing fire was something she had not done in her youth. But Brendan seemed completely unconcerned and assured her that he had every confidence that she would be more than adequate for the task at hand.

Brendan lifted a talon and tapped the ground lightly. "Sacha, will you dig a channel here?"

"That is a particularly potent line, Brendan," Sacha warned.

"Yes, I know," said the green dragon. "All ley lines that come form mountains are powerful as mountains are generally sacred and have been worshipped and venerated for centuries as the abode of the gods. This one will serve our purposes quite nicely."

Sacha was still concerned. He had seen ill-trained mages overwhelmed by ley lines and the power this one contained was immense. It led from a very sacred place, high in the hills. All ley lines originated from sacred places and converged upon one another, usually meeting in pools of great power, the nodes. And this one led directly to a gigantic node.

But nevertheless he blasted open a channel with violet light and staggered with the pain of it.

And before the power, as black as midnight, could escape, Brendan had filled the channel with dragon fire, nodding to Cynara to join her flames to his.

Sacha was a Dracophilologist and had studied dragons all his life and thought he knew almost everything about dragon fire. But he had never seen dragon fire such as Brendan was producing. And as Cynara's fire joined with Brendan's it, too, changed.

It was a rich deep green, the green of healing magic and beneath his feet Sacha was conscious of heat as it burned into the channel, igniting the energies in the line rapidly, burning furiously. Cautiously Sacha opened himself to the line and felt and 'saw' the line burning so rapidly that already it was miles away and increasing its strength as it went. It was eating away the blackness as a prodigious rate, leaving cleanliness and purity behind and even as it burned deeper into the heart of the country the energies of Light began to fill it.

Brendan abruptly stopped the flame, signaling to Cynara to do the same and said "It will burn by itself now, there are other dragons from the Monasteries on the borders doing the selfsame thing, and in the south as well. I can feel them. Four points of fire will converge and all the ley lines will be cleaned."

"*Blagdos Christos!*" swore Sacha, reverting to Russian. "Brendan – how, why–? What *was* that?"

"There was a prophecy from an oracle at one of the draconic monasteries over one hundred years ago that in the year of the Fire Snake, the year in which John Company would fall, there would be a great cleansing in the land and that dragons would be the instrument," said Brendan. "Before we left Chalangadong the Lama explained to me that I did not come to the monastery by chance as I had thought, but it was ordained that I would come, long before my birth. And it was further foretold that having brought the tiger eyed man to Hind we would both be instrumental in ridding this part of the world of a great evil. What I did, that was the dragon fire of Lord Varnu that he allowed me to use as his conduit. The Gods have grown tired of the pollution of the land and the flourishing of evil." He lifted his head and looked east. "It is time to go and help Alan." he said "There is still much evil to vanquish."

On the day before Brendan began to cleanse the ley lines, early evening found Rosamunde and Parminder 'clothing' themselves for their dance performance.

"Just who is the Nana Sahib that they are all so excited about?" Laura asked as she watched her friends tie the blue beads over their bodies which had been heavily oiled and then sprinkled with the blue powder, making them gleam with the sheen of the male peacock's breast.

"He is Peshwa of Bithur, which is near Cawnpore," said Parminder. "He is the adopted son of the Maharatta Peshwa Baji Rao."

"I know what a Rajah is, and a Maharajah, but what's a Peshwa?" Laura inquired.

Parminder thought for a moment and said "You might think of it as a type of hereditary prime minister, a very high position in the Maharatta Empire at one time."

"And supposedly a black magician, from what I've been hearing." said Laura. "Christ, those costumes are God-awful!" she said as Rosamunde straightened up and faced them.

"They are completely indecent," said Henrietta, her lips tightening.

"Them's worse than naked," Ivy commented.

The peacock costumes were on much the line of the previous Rose costumes, blue beads outlined the breasts and went down between the legs, all connected to wide enameled collars. A single line of beads came up through the buttocks, but three strings of beads hung under each buttock cheek like a stranded pearl necklace and hung over each upper arm as well. A single strand passed low around the hips. Three peacock feathers hung from this strand on each side and the same amount of feathers adorned the blue and enamel helmet. The blue powder had been applied so that the eye was drawn to the breasts and to the private parts. Their bottoms were heavily dusted as well. Their eyes had been heavily outlined in kohl and smudged with the eunuch's finger, as, according to Hussaini, Nana Sahib liked that. He also liked red, red lips shining with betel juice. Over their eyes glowed more of the iridescent blue powder. The final touch was a collar of peacock feathers that stood up behind the head like a ruff. Each woman would carry two peacock feather fans that could fold and unfold. These would be used to accentuate the many obscene posturing and gestures they would make in the dance.

Since she had been taken from Alan this morning Rosamunde had repeatedly been told what an honor it was for her to be chosen to sleep with the Nana. She was not honored at all, she was afraid. She had sat up a good part of the night, talking with Alan, trying to figure out what might happen if she lay with a black magician. She could see by Alan's face that he felt hopeless and angry that he could do nothing to protect her and prevent this from happening. She had never seen such despair in him

She had tried to hide her terror from him but succeeded very ill, for her teeth chattered and at times she could not control the shudders which shook her body. The Room of Kali was bad enough, to be that near to black magic, but this, to be so intimate with a black magician–! And she had heard whispers of his cruelty to his bed mates; he was not easily satisfied and had perverted tastes, it was said.

Alan had, at her request, held her most of the night. Neither one of them had slept much. At Alan's query to the eunuch that morning, he was assured that Serai would be brought to him as usual. The eunuch had laughed, for he remembered a previous visit from Nana Sahib. "Once he has slaked his lust on a woman's body, he wants no more of her and will kick her from his bed! Never fear, magician, you shall still have her to use this night, no matter how many

446

times Nana Sahib wishes to use her!"

"You relieve my mind," Alan had said controlling himself with an effort that left him shaking. He would make certain that the bath, food and the unicorn horn were ready for her. Tonight she would need them more than usual.

All this passed through Rosamunde's mind as they finished dressing. Both Parminder and she dreaded this dance, for it was incredibly obscene and to have to watch themselves in the mirrors was going to be sickening. The Maharajah liked them to dance with downcast eyes, but this dance was for Nana Sahib, and he liked his dancers to look at him and mime passion as they danced, playing to him.

"Oh, you look beautiful!" came a voice and Mabel Clutterbuck was with them. "I wish I could wear costumes like that! The men must love it!"

"Jesus H. Christ!" said Laura in disgust. "Look, Lali, if you're here to tell us how many men you took today we ain't interested. In fact, we're getting goddamn sick of listening to you boast about how many times you've been screwed! Frankly, none of us gives a shit!"

"Laura!" Margaret protested, sounding outraged.

"Are you jealous?" said Mabel, putting her hands on her hips and thrusting those large breasts forward. "I don't ever hear of any men wanting you especially!"

"It ain't as if I've ever had any ambitions to shine at whoring," drawled Laura. "Why don't you just trot your little ass off and go find yourself a bunch of horny bastards. Don't know how you're standing it, your *Yoni* must have been empty for at least five minutes by now. Or is what I've been hearing true, you're sharing Hussaini's bed now too?"

Margaret and Henrietta both gasped. Ivy snickered.

"You're just jealous that they all like me so much and Hussaini is so good to me!" said Mabel. She did not deny Laura's accusation. "But I've come to tell Chowki and Serai that Hussaini wants them, she needs to approve their costumes before the dance, which *I* get to see and *you* don't!" She made a face at Laura.

"You're out there, little Missy," Laura said, lifting a piece of her armor and waving it at her "I'm on guard duty tonight."

Mabel looked as if she would like to slap Laura, but

given the fact hat Laura was both taller and stronger than her, she satisfied herself with a decided flounce as she turned away, calling to Rosamunde and Parminder, "Come, or I will have Hussaini punish you!"

"You shouldn't bait her, Laura!" Rosamunde said, *sotto voce*, as she and Parminder began to follow Mabel.

"I can't stomach her," Laura said, "Something about her makes me want to take her down a peg."

When they were gone from sight Margaret said in tones of horrified fascination. "Is that true what you said, Laura, that she is sleeping with Hussaini?"

Laura shrugged. "That's the rumor. Noori told me yesterday. Lali spends an awful lot of time with Hussaini and Noori also told me that Hussaini was originally purchased by the old Maharajah as a bedmate for his daughter as men found her so repulsive. Even he didn't want to sleep with her, even though there's a real big tradition of incest in this family. 'Course now that she's Maharani she can make any man she wants take her to bed. She must have to load them up with that Kali dust!"

Henrietta shuddered. "This place just grows more and more horrible every day; such depths of depravity! I don't know why it has not sunk into the sea or been razed by heavenly wrath like Sodom and Gomorrah!"

Nana Sahib was a sleek, stout, self- satisfied man. He wore a mustache, rather than a beard and was of middle height, and rather dark complexioned for one who was proud of boasting of pure Maharatta descent. His eyes were a bit too close together and his face full. His manner was arrogant and he was most elegantly garbed in *kinkawb* garments with ropes of pearls and diamonds about his throat and a mass of pearls and diamonds that looked like a lady's tiara on his head. He also wore his late adoptive father's sword of state, gorgeously bejeweled and said to be valued at three *lakhs* of *rupees*. He had an insolent charm and seemed to derive immense pleasure from looking at, and touching, the many naked women at the *Diwan-i- Am*.

When his eye lit on Hussaini he beckoned her to him

and said to the Maharajah and Maharani "I remember this woman well. When I was last here I told her that such a magnificent bosom should always be seen and I see that she took my words to heart."

"I have never covered my breasts since, excellency," said Hussaini.

"Good! Good! I also remember how much I enjoyed you in my bed," he said, reaching out and stroking her. "Your appetites matched mine well. I shall have to make certain that we are together again."

"I shall be honored, highness," said Hussaini, smirking. "I look forward to our joining with eager desire."

"Sit beside me during the entertainments so that I may touch you," ordered the Nana.

Rosamunde and Parminder, standing in an alcove while waiting to perform, watched this byplay. "Perhaps he will prefer her to you," whispered Parminder.

Rosamunde could only hope so. Mabel, abandoned at the very end of the low table, looked forlorn and a little sullen. She was Hussaini's shadow but had not been allowed to go with her to the Nana's side.

They had quite a while to wait. Alan was to perform first as well as the dancing troupe and the puppet master. The evening's entertainment was to be augmented by a snake charmer and a fire-eater, as the Nana was amused by these tricks.

Rosamunde only wanted it to be over with to be safe again with Alan, to feel the healing power of the unicorn horn and to wash this foul stuff from her body and lay aside the gaudy costume, which as Ivy had said, was worse than being naked. She was still terrified and sick. She had been unable to eat much, only forcing down some food when Parminder had reminded her that she needed her strength for the dance, which was lengthy, for if she fainted and disgraced the Maharajah he would have her whipped most severely.

Please, she prayed silently to anyone listening, *please, let it be over soon!* Since seeing Nana Sahib she had no trouble in thinking that everything said of him was all too true.

48

surrender

After his dismissal from the *Diwan-i-Am,* Alan went at once to seek out Nate. He had been paid the supposed compliment of Nana Sahib's offering to purchase him from the Maharajah, for the Peshwa had much enjoyed the magic tricks. Upon finding out that Alan was not a slave, the Nana offered him a princely sum to join his household in Bithur. When Alan politely refused, saying that he was happy in Jhaniput, the Maharajah beamed with approval and gave Alan a huge diamond ring for his loyalty.

All the while he had been performing Alan was as conscious of Rosamunde as if she was by his side. He could feel her fear, even her loathing of the dance she was to do. Facing the *Musnud,* where the Maharajah's party and their guest sat, he could see her and Parminder waiting in the alcove, gleaming in their indecent peacock costumes. She would tell him little about the dance, only saying, tight-lipped, that it was very vile and had been designed to please the perverted tastes of Nana Sahib. The Maharani and Hus-saini were, for some reason, much more eager to please him that any other guest

Rosamunde had not told Alan that she had been instructed to do anything Nana Sahib demanded of her with eagerness and delight, no matter what it was. This had only served to increase her terror. She doubted that she could feign eagerness and delight for any kind of sexual union, much less some aberrant behavior, especially with a black magician.

When he was at last dismissed, having to perform much longer than was usual, Alan took Cathal on his shoulder and headed for the barracks. Usually he went to his room first and changed from his performance clothing, but tonight he urgently needed to be with someone who under-stood what he was going through. He and Nate had never openly discussed how it made them feel to know what

Rosamunde and Laura were suffering every day, but Alan was always aware of Nate's unspoken sympathy and understanding. Tonight he needed this more than he did normally.

Nate threw open the door at Alan's first knock and at the sight that greeted him said "Jesus H. Christ!" and fell backwards, putting an arm to his eyes as if blinded by the light. "What are you all rigged out for, Christmas?" he said, blinking.

Alan had been given a special outfit for his performance for Nana Sahib, an *achkan* of black silk, heavily embroidered with silver thread over white silk jodhpurs that were also embroidered in silver down each side, embroidery so thick that the garments felt heavy. Silver curly toed *jutties* on his feet were encrusted with gems and the outfit was topped with a huge turban of white silk, with an enormous *sarpeche* of a sapphire holding aloft an aigrette of three white plumes. A multitude of pearls, diamonds and sapphires hung about his neck and rings sparkled on each hand.

Nate grinned. "They're going all out to impress this Nana Sahib, ain't they? I've seen whores in the fancy cat house in New Orleans with less fancy rig out than you!"

"I don't care what they make me wear," Alan said harshly. "I only wish that they were not giving Rosamunde to him! I tell you, Nate, I felt such evil coming off that man! He makes that daughter of Kali look like a Vicar's wife! And I don't know what being with him will do to Rosamunde. Good God, Nate, I've never been so frightened in my life! And I can do nothing, *nothing* to stop it!"

Nate sobered at once and laid a compassionate hand on Alan's shoulder. He could feel the tension in Alan, just through that light touch.

Cathal looked at Nate, his eyes showing his misery, as well. "She's so frightened," the ferret said in a low voice.

"Laurie told me," Nate answered. "She also told me about the Peacock costume and how god-awful raunchy it is. She said Rose don't want to do that filthy dance neither." He took his hand from Alan's shoulder and moved towards the low table where he poured out a cup of the waiting tea for his friend.

Alan took it absently, murmuring his thank yous, and drank it down, scarcely noticing that he did so as he paced

451

back and forth in agitation.

"I don't know how much more of this I can stand, watching her being tormented by these people!" he suddenly burst out. "Every night when they bring her to me she is in more pain, and her eyes, Nate! Looking into her eyes–" he broke off and could not go on.

"I know," Nate sad harshly. "My Laurie's the same way. Makes me want to kill someone to see her like that."

"I *could* kill someone, all of them, if I could only surrender myself to Vishnu and regain my powers!" Alan said. "Each day that I fail is another day she has to suffer all the shame and the horror of this place! God, I hate myself for not being able to help her!"

"Maybe you're trying too hard," Nate suggested. "'Pears to me you're wound up tighter than a clockwork and fretting over worrying about failing."

Alan sighed and sank down on the cushions at the table. "You're probably right, but when I think of what she is going through..." He put his head in his hands, but encountered the bulk of the turban and with an angry gesture, tore it from his head and threw it across the room.

Cathal slid off his shoulder and said. "You may try again tomorrow, Alan, with the *Sadhu*, but for now I want you to eat something! You've scarcely had a bite all day and I could tell that even the magic show tonight took a great deal out of you. Nate has gone to all the trouble of getting together this nice little supper and I want you to make a good meal! If tomorrow is the day that you *can* reach Vishnu, well, you will need all your strength. And besides," he added, "it would be rude."

"You're worse than my mother," Alan said, but took a plate and began to fill it, all the while, wondering as was Nate, who was worrying over Laura, what was going on in the *Diwan-i-Am*, and in what condition Rosamunde would be when she was returned to him and how long it would be before that happened.

It was very late and Alan had left him some time earlier when Laura was finally delivered to Nate. She was very much the worse for wear and even her armor was dented, and the peacock feathers in her helmet were ruffled and one was broken.

"Damn!" she swore, as she lifted off the helmet. "That means I got to go to that frigging plume maker tomorrow and get those things replaced! And of course I got to pay for it! He likes for me to kneel down, pretend I'm a mare and he's a stallion and likes for me to make like I'm trying to buck him off and neigh while he's taking me! It ain't dignified!"

Nate had been taking off her leg gyves and as she said this he took the one he had in his hands and with an oath bent it in half as easily as it had been cardboard. Standing up, he threw it against the wall where it made a tremendous clang. "That's another rat bastard I aim to kill with my bare hands!" he growled."There's a lot of these rat bastards, Laurie, that I aim to rip apart when the time comes! When I think of what they do to you every day, I just get so damn pissed!"

She put her arms around his neck. "It ain't as bad for me as is it for some of the others, honey. Rose, for instance. That poor kid was scared shitless today and after seeing that goddamned Nana I don't blame her one bit. Never saw such a nasty piece of work! Little beady eyes roaming all over us! The whole time he was watching the dances, and they were really raunchy tonight, he was fondling that Hussaini and damned if he didn't tell her to drop her drawers and he hopped on her right on the *musnud* and we had to listen to them thrashing around and groaning fit to beat the band. That little turd of Maharajah was watching them, drooling all down his shirt front and had his fat little paws all over me! One of these days he's going to forget his Ma's orders and screw one of us."

Nate crushed her against him. "I'm going to make this all up to you, Laurie, when I get you home. I'm going to treat you like a Queen and beat my brains out to make you happy until you forget all about this place and them goddamned mines too!"

Laura doubted that she would ever forget about this place. It, like the mines still did, would live in her nightmares for years to come.

It was early morning when Rosamunde was finally returned to Alan. He had bathed and changed when he had returned from Nate's rooms and had laid down upon the *charpoy* in what turned out to be a futile effort to get some sleep, Cathal curled up beside him.

It was almost dawn, he judged, when the eunuch opened the door and entered with Rosamunde over his shoulder. She ws limp in his grasp and when he tossed her onto the *charpoy* she appeared to be unconscious.

"I shall have to tie her into the position, magician," he said, "for she is much fatigued by the use the Nana put her to!" He gave a malevolent grin. "You should be honored that you are so privileged as to use the same slave as his highness the Peshwa!" He reached beneath the bed as he spoke and pulled out the ropes that were attached to the bottom of every *charpoy* in the *Mahal.*

"Leave that!" Alan said so sharply that the eunuch gave him a strange look. "I shall do it myself."

"As the *Husoor* wishes," said the eunuch. He bowed himself out.

"She looks terrible, Alan!" said Cathal in deep concern. "We had better get her into the bath!" He scampered off towards the *ghosulkhana* to draw the water.

She indeed looked terrible. Her colour ws ghastly and he thought she looked far worse than she did after her visits to the room of Kali.

Many of the beads, made of glass, had been broken and made her bleed. She had bled in other places as well and a huge bruise was forming on her right hip and leg. Most of the feathers were broken.

He took a penknife from his magic box which sat upon an inlaid table near the *charpoy* and wasted no time in cutting all the beads off her, allowing them to fall to the floor and scatter. Alan's hands shook as he worked, so badly at times that he had to stop and try and steady them. He was so enraged at what had been done to her that he literally saw red. When they were all off, and he had removed her helmet and the collar that had supported the beads as well. These he tossed onto the floor to join the beads! He slipped the unicorn horn necklace over her head and watched as it began its healing work at once. Little bits of glass that had been imbedded in her skin were pushed out by the magic of the horn and the cuts began to heal immediately. The bruise also faded.

"The bath is ready," Cathal's voice interrupted his black thoughts.

Alan picked her up and took her to the *ghosulkhana.* She felt light and insubstantial in his arms, scarcely seeming to draw a breath and for one moment of heart stopping terror he thought she was dead. But her breast moved ever so slightly. He was deeply afraid, because even the power of the unicorn horn had not awakened her.

Cathal watched anxiously as Alan put her in the water. Alan stripped off his *choga,* so that he could bathe her without getting soaked. Cathal gave him the lilac soap and the bath sponge.

As he had that first time, Alan tenderly bathed her all over, washing her hair and all the oil and cosmetics off her. His mind was seething with the blackest of thoughts and an overwhelming hatred for the man who could treat a woman, moreover a helpless woman who was forced to obey him and had no choice in the matter, in such a vile and cruel fashion.

He avoided touching the ruby. He was afraid to know exactly what Nana Sahib had done to her. And he had a feeling that she would not want him to know. It was the least he could do for her, to respect her privacy. And what he had imagined was bad enough.

By the time she was clean her colour was better and, as he had before, he took her outside. The sun would be rising shortly and he would let its rays warm and dry her.

He sat down beside her, noticing with concern and dread that she seemed to have lost more weight. She was not eating either. He often saw a haunted, lost look in her eyes that cut him to the quick. Even though Vishnu's ruby had lessened the attentions she was paid, there was still the nightly horror of the *Diwan-i-Khas* to endure.

Suddenly it was too much and Alan buried his face in his hands. "I cannot bear to see her tortured any more!" he cried silently. "Do whatever you wish to me, Lord Vishnu! Only end her suffering! Let me be the instrument of revenge against these people! Please! Take me!" Something deep inside him let go.

The sun came up, abruptly as it always did in the tropics. But the long rays should not have yet filled the walled garden with an incredible golden light as it did. Everything was outlined in glowing light, each leaf and blade of grass. Alan heard Cathal gasp but he could not look at the ferret for he could see nothing but the golden sun and it seemed to fill him up everywhere, running down into his fingers and toes, its warmth sweeping over him like a wave. Once again, power began to run through his veins and the feeling that he had been missing for so long, of a constant contact with the energies of the earth, seemed to burst into flower inside him.

Alan gasped and bent over, to fall flat on the earth. The feeling was almost overwhelming.

"Alan!" Cathal cried, terrified. And then he said "Oh my goodness!" as light seemed to gather over and around his Wizard and touched every inch of him. Alan seemed ablaze with light.

Afterwards, Cathal could not begin to even guess how long he sat and watched his Wizard being caressed by that golden glow. It embraced him as if he were a much favored child, and even touched Rosamunde, so that her stupor changed to natural sleep and her healing was completed.

When the light at last faded Alan sat up abruptly and looked at Cathal, an expression of joy and wonder on his face. "Cathal!" he said huskily. "I have my magic back, all of it!" He stood up as he spoke and said excitedly, "The dizziness is gone!"

He bent over Rosamunde and picked her up easily, carrying her into the room and laying her gently on the *charpoy*. "He even took care of her," he said quietly.

"He?" queried Cathal.

"Lord Vishnu," said Alan. "He spoke to me, Cathal! We were in a beautiful garden, his garden. He said that I shall be his avatar here on earth and that this great evil will end and very soon."

"How soon?" Cathal asked anxiously.

Alan looked at him and his face was glorified. "Tonight!" he said, "Tonight it ends!"

Rosamunde was warm and comfortable. She had been having the nicest dream. She was at home, with her family and it was all so clear and real.

And when she woke, her body felt relaxed, well, and rested, far better than she remembered feeling even after a session with the unicorn horn.

As she became more awake the memory of the previous evening came rushing back: the dance, the remarks that Nana Sahib had made, all lascivious and crude, and what he had done to her when the Maharani had given her to him.

From the first moment he had touched her, such a blackness, a feeling of being smothered in evil, had invaded her body that she thought she would drown in it. It had been very real pain racing along her limbs and in the very heart of her being. It had been difficult to breathe, and then he had hurt her very badly and had ordered her to do such things that even now she could not think of them without shuddering and wanting to vomit.

But there was no pain now and the feeling of blackness was gone. She sat up and looked down at herself. All sign of blood and the huge bruise, caused when had abruptly tired of her and had literally kicked her from his bed, were healed. The unicorn horn could account for that but she had fully expected to still feel that sense of Darkness today. She had thought she would never recover from it.

And then she realized something else.

Her magic was back.

"Alan!" she called excitedly. "Alan!"

A fresh breeze was blowing from the open door to the *chabutara,* causing the filmy white drapes to billow. Alan came through the drapes, pushing them aside. Cathal came after him.

She gasped at the sight of him. He was *glowing*! He looked like one of the *Sidhe,* the shining Ones!

"Rosamunde!" he said and hurried to her. He sat down beside her on the edge of the *charpoy* and took her hands in his. "I have magic again!"

For once she was not conscious of the shame of being

naked in front of him and she said. "Mine is back too! You did it, Alan!"

"No, *you* did it! When I saw what that bastard did to you something in me snapped and I was able to give myself to Vishnu. And Vishnu did the rest!" he said. "Rosamunde, you have but a day more to bear this! Vishnu has promised that it will all end tonight! He has promised me help, I spoke with him in his garden, so beautiful that you cannot imagine it– and it will end for all of us! We can go home!"

She wanted to cry with joy but there still seemed to be no tears left. She had to content herself with leaning her head on his shoulder and saying. "I thought it would never end. I thought that we would be here forever until we died, with no escape for either of us. I was beginning to wish for death."

"That will not happen. Vishnu will guide me and these evil people will be defeated. Now, I have breakfast saved for you and the eunuch will come soon to take you to be washed. I must go to the House of Assignation and talk to the *Sadhu* and to Sishul." he said. He wanted very badly to stroke her hair and then turn her face up to his for his kiss but something still held him back. It was still too soon to speak to her of love.

It was difficult to bear the touch of Pramoda Tandon that morning as he washed and oiled her. He spoke gloatingly of what Nana Sahib had done to her, both while still in the *Diwan-i-Am* and later in his room, for the whole palace was talking about it, he informed her as he poked and pinched and stroked more than usual. He seemed to think that violating the body, with his hands, of a woman who had lain with the Nana was a great honor for him.

"And his excellency the Peshwa wants to see you dance upon your toes tonight. He has already told her highness that he desires both you and Mistress Hussaini in his bed afterwards. Even now he shares his bed with the Mistress and Lali. He called for the Mistress when he had done with you and she took Lali along as the Mistress well knows his tastes. He often likes to have two women at once, as you well know!" he smirked.

Rosamunde could not help it. A shudder ran over her.

Halfway through the evening he had demanded a second woman and the eunuch on duty had brought in little Ananda. What had happened after that did not bear thinking about.

Tandon laughed as he saw her shudder. It was very difficult to let him handle her when she now knew that she could casually toss him against a wall. But she had promised Alan that she would not let them know her magic was back. She was thoroughly shielded now, and they could not discern it at all. Not until tonight. *"Tonight! Tonight!"* She kept saying to herself in a blaze of joy. And again, it was difficult to act cowed and submissive.

When she had been oiled and gilded, Pramoda Tandon hung her back up on the hook. "They are coming to see you," he said, seconds before the door to the 'slaughter house' opened, admitting the Maharani, Hussaini and her shadow, Mabel.

As they paused in front of Rosamunde, Mabel fell to her knees and as usual, leaned against Hussaini's legs.

Hussaini shone with pride, full of herself. The Peshwa had thoroughly enjoyed her and had told her so, saying that her breasts were even more beautiful than he remembered. Today, great golden tassels swung from tight nipple clamps, making her bosom even more noticeable than usual.

"Nana Sahib wants us dressed alike tonight, girl!" Hussaini said abruptly. "You shall be fitted for tassels like these, that and a gold belt low on the hips is all we shall wear. This morning he told me what he has planned for us. He is an inventive fellow! "And," she looked down fondly at Mabel, whose hair as usual she was stroking, "I have obtained his permission for Lali to watch. She has still much to learn about pleasing men. If she is fortunate he may even use her again as he did last night. She knows how honored she was by his attentions."

Was it just Rosamunde's imagination or did Mabel look and sound less eager than usual? Her tones as she said "Yes, Mistress," seemed rather dull and resigned, lacking the enthusiasm she usually greeted every utterance of Hussaini's.

The Maharani had remained quiet and now she leaned forward and touched Rosamunde's ruby. A variety of emotion flitted over her ugly face as she 'read' the ruby, gloating, greed and even, to Rosamunde's surprise, envy.

"You are fortunate, girl," she said in her harsh croak, "that a man like the Peshwa desires your unworthy body."

A curious grimace twisted her face. She had kept her finger for an inordinately long time on the ruby, looking at the scenes in it again and again. "You are very fortunate," she said again, huskily in a tone that was, could it be? – *jealous*?

With a jolt Rosamunde realized that the Maharani was in love with Nana Sahib and would like nothing better to be the woman whose image was caught in the ruby with his.

49

waiting

Everything seemed to be going their way. Midway through the morning Rosamunde was taken back to Alan and urged by Tandon to gather more power. Rosamunde was in alt to be taken back to him, to perhaps be with him for hours instead of in the *zenana*.

She told Alan of her discovery of that day, that the Maharani was in love with Nana Sahib.

"It makes her almost pitiful," he said. "I doubt that there is any emotion worse than unrequited love." As he well knew.

Cathal, on his shoulder, sighed to himself. He had argued with Alan that morning after Rosamunde had been taken away, that his Wizard should tell her how he felt about her. Alan had again refused and made Cathal promise that he would say nothing to her. Cathal could not help but think that humans were very stupid about some things. Why could they not confess their feelings to one another and why could they not discern that they loved each other when it was so obvious to others?

Rosamunde thought that nothing could ever make the Maharani pitiful in her eyes. Once again she thought how kind Alan was. "He will never return her regard. He worships beauty and a feminine figure and the Maharani is not what he finds attractive at all," she said.

"I hate having to ask you to endure this even one more day, but I cannot allow them to guess that we have power–" Alan said apologetically. "I would like to reverse the spells upon you right now and to keep you out of that brothel in the *zenana*."

"I can bear one more day," she assured him. "knowing that it will be over soon! Just knowing that I need not go to him again–"

"If I have my way," said Alan savagely "he'll be dead soon and the rest of them as well!" He thought of how excited

Sishul had been when he told them the news. The *Sadhu* had said that it was the outcome he had expected all along. And this afternoon he would tell Nate.

"Hot damn!" said Laura when Rosamunde told her the news when at last they were together in the *zenana* late in the afternoon. They spoke in low voices, privately, in their little corner. "You aiming to tell the others?"

"No," Rosamunde said. "The fewer who know the better...Alan spent the morning with Sishul, making plans, and he probably is telling Nate right now as they had an engagement to ride out together."

"Was beginning to think this was going to last forever, "Laura said on a happy sigh. "Ain't I glad it won't! What are you going to do, Rose, after it's all over? You and Alan going to get hitched?"

"Hitched?" Rosamunde repeated. staring at Laura. "Do you mean married? Oh, no, there is no – he's my cousin! He does not feel like that about me!"

Laura snorted. "Don't give me that! I been watching him at the *Diwan-I-Khas* and the first thing he does is look for you. And when the little toad is handling you he looks like he'd like to wrap his hands around the bastard's neck. 'Sides, he told Nate he loved you."

"What!" Rosamunde said, looking stunned. "But he's engaged, or as good as, to a girl named Christine Chapman at home! He's never felt that way about me!" she said again.

"Well, he does now," said Laura. "Things change, Rose honey, and maybe seeing you so manhandled made him realize what he felt. Some men have to be knocked ass over teakettle before that know their own minds. You told me you grew up together and he probably never thought of you as anyone but a kid sister."

"But I knew I loved him!" Rosamunde blurted out.

"Ha!" said Laura "You *do* love him!"

"Always," said Rosamunde in a low voice. "But Laura, even if he does love me, how could he ever want to marry me, I'm ruined! Society would judge me a whore!"

Laura made a rude noise. "Listen to me, honey, who

gives a damn what society says? Marriage is between two people, and men like ours don't give a damn about what went on in this hell hole. Me and Nate are going to be married. He says we're finding a preacher as soon as possible. It ain't like you got to confess this to some fresh faced kid who's asked you to marry him, not knowing what had happened to you here. Alan knows! And Nate says all he talks about is how he wants to spend the rest of his life making you happy! Believe me, I don't think it matters none to him! He just wants *you*, well used or not!"

Rosamunde looked doubtful. She suddenly wished that she could talk to Alan. But she would not see him again until tonight, and with what would probably go on tonight there would be no time for intimate talk.

Was Laura right? Would Alan still want her after seeing her like this? She looked down at herself. She had been given gold tassels and a low slung belt like Hussaini's. The clamps had hurt, but with Witchcraft she was able to make them comfortable to wear.

"Hussaini said that I was to come here and take men with you," came Mabel's voice. Behind her were the other members of their group, Margaret, Ivy and Henrietta.

Mabel wore breast tassels and the gold belt. "I am to lie with Nana Sahib too," she explained, looking for the first time that Rosamunde had seen her, apprehensive and a little frightened.

Laura muttered "Serves you right," under her breath, but Rosamunde felt a sudden pity for the Clutterbuck girl.

"They have not served supper as yet?" queried Henrietta. "They kept me at the *ghat* all day and did not give me a luncheon at all." She sank down on the cushions with a grimace. "Those horrible eunuchs kept bringing men to me! One after another!"

"Same for us maids," said Ivy. "Couldn't go nowhere or cleans the rooms without some man after me."

Margaret nodded in agreement. "It has gotten so we've no peace at all lately, just little bits of it such as this moment, and only because they have to feed us to keep our strength up!"

Rosamunde wanted very badly to tell them that it would soon be over, but she did not dare. Mabel might let something slip to Hussaini.

As the others had chosen seats on the cushions, Mabel remained standing, looking pleadingly at Rosamunde.

Feeling sorry for her, Rosamunde said, "Come here and sit beside me, Lali," ignoring Laura's grumbles.

Gratefully, Mabel scurried over and sank onto the cushions.

"Well, ain't you going to entertain us with how many men you banged today?" said Laura sarcastically.

"I did take a lot. Hussaini was pleased," said Mabel. "But," she turned a piteous look on Rosamunde. "I like regular coupling a lot, but the man, that Nana, it was horrible! What he wants is not normal! He likes to hurt! And I don't want to be with him again! Hussaini keeps telling me it is an honor to be with him. She *likes* what he does! I don't understand it! When I am with her, she doesn't like things like that!"

Henrietta gasped, for Mabel was unaware what she had revealed.

"You've got no choice my dear," said Margaret gently. "None of us do. I'm certain that they will take you to the *Hakim* if he hurts you. They can't afford to have any of us too damaged to use," she added dryly.

"And I 'eared tell that 'e'll soon be gone," said Ivy. "I 'eard that they're all of 'em 'cept the Maharajah, goin' away soon."

"Where?" Laura queried.

"Dunno for sure,but it sounded like it was north" said Ivy, "When I was cleanin' the General's room 'e was talkin' about it to one of 'is men. He was usin' me when 'e was talkin'. Me Hindoo is ever so much better now an' I can understand a lot. And when they're usin' a woman they seem to think it makes 'er deaf!"

Laura and Rosamunde exchanged glances. This seemed to confirm what Nate had been told, they would be attacking to the north, in the Punjab.

"Hush!" said Henrietta suddenly. "Here come the eunuchs with the food."

464

Rosamunde looked at herself in the mirror. She wore nothing except her slave jewelry, the belt and the heavy tassels and gold *pointe* shoes she had made herself. When the Maharajah had told Nana Sahib of the *nautch* girl who could dance on her toes the Nana had been intrigued and had demanded to see it. He had been particularly interested in the fact that she was the same dancer he had enjoyed the evening before, both in the dance and in his bed.

Rosamunde fervently hoped that anything that Alan did this evening would come soon, before she had to go to the Nana.

"It will be over soon," Parminder whispered, leaning towards her. They had been taken to the Room of the Dance for a practice session and had shared the room with the other female members of the *nautch* for a brief period. Rosamunde had whispered the secret to Parminder.

They would also be sharing the floor with the male dancers that evening, and that was not all that they would be sharing. Parminder told Rosamunde that the male dancers were fed the Dust of Kali all the day long so that they would be in a state of painful arousal by dance time and would be certain to give an exciting performance. "One feels sorry for them," Parminder said. "Most are little more than boys, chosen for their physical beauty", for their resemblance to the *maithuna* statues, whose male figures were largely adolescent looking, almost effeminate. "And they are kept drugged much of the time. And to keep them so, in pain, needing release, is as cruel as what is done to us. But from what you tell me that if all goes as planned, all of this will end tonight! And it is your man who makes this all possible!"

"Alan is not my man," Rosamunde replied uncomfortably.

Parminder looked at her with the same disbelieving look Laura had given her. "With a little encouragement from you, Rose of the World, I think that he would like to be your man," said Parminder slyly.

Why did everyone keep telling her that Alan loved her? If it was true surely she would be able to see it? Surely he would have said something, done something that would let her know? The Alan she remembered was impatient, in a hurry. In such intimacy as they had shared he would have revealed his feelings to her! She had never felt any hint that he wanted her and he had even turned her down when she had offered herself to him. Men, in Rosamunde's experience, did not turn down the offer of a woman's body unless they were completely disinterested. She did not realize that she still had a great deal to learn about love.

The Maharani too, stood in front of a mirror being adorned in her usual red silk *sari* by various of her hand-maidens. Like all of the other women save herself and Hussaini, they too were naked.

On the Maharani's sumptuous bed, hung with the finest silks, Hussaini lounged, clad only in her gold belt and tassels, for once not wearing her gauze pantaloons.

Like all of the fabric in the *Mahal*, the silks of the Maharani's bed had been magiced so that they would not burn when one of the slaves touched them. Therefore, Hussaini was able to keep Mabel beside her. Reflected in the mirror the Maharani saw Hussaini feeding grapes to Lali.

"You pamper that one too much," said the Maharani harshly. "Is it true you have taken her to your bed?"

"What if it is?" Hussaini shrugged. "You were the one who taught me that anything that pleases you is permissible as long as it delights you. And you no longer want me as a bed mate since you can now command any man you desire to couple with you. But most of the men here do not want me. They are afraid of me and my whip! So I must take my pleasure where I can."

The Maharani thought with a sudden pang that she could not command *any* man she wanted to her bed. The only one she really wanted looked at her as if she was invisible. She had never before wanted to be beautiful, but she was even willing to give up some of her power if only he would look on her with desire.

Hussaini saw all this on her face, for once, too easy to read. She smiled to herself. She was still fond of Kalidassa and the news she had been told to give her would please her former bed mate no end.

"His excellency the Peshwa called me to his chamber this afternoon," she said.

"Did he bed you?" the Maharani grated.

"Of course, but he had another purpose as well," said Hussaini, stroking Mabel's hair and popping another grape into the girl's mouth. "I like the way those tassels look on you, Lali. Does it not excite you to wear them? We will wear them often. I shall have silver ones and jeweled ones made for you, to match mine."

"Well?" the Maharani demanded impatiently.

"The Peshwa wants you to come and watch tonight when he is bedding the dancers and Lali and I. And then he wants to bed *you*. He wants to blend power with you, in the Room of Kali before the awakened statue." She did not add that the Nana had expressed his distaste at having to lay with such an ugly woman, but that he considered it completely necessary to totally empower himself with all of the magic that he would need for the success of the campaign against the British. He had been defeated by them once at Cawnpore and he would never suffer such shame again. This time he would be invincible and would sweep victorious through all of Hind.

The Maharani's eyes glowed. What a coupling that would be, and perhaps, if he saw how well their power blended and how much she could transfer to him through the use of her body, this would be the first of many encounters, perhaps even the prelude to a marriage.

Another fantastic outfit was delivered to Alan that night, this one entirely of red, with black and gold embroidery. The fussy little *Nazir* delivered it himself and told Jehan the magician that he must do everything differently tonight. "For the Peshwa," he said worriedly, "unlike his royal highness, does not care to see the same entertainment repeated and her highness has impressed upon me the importance of keeping his excellency happy!"

"I do not think," said Alan gravely, "that the Peshwa will ever forget the show he will see tonight. I have many new tricks planned, ones he will not expect."

"Excellent!" said the *Nazir* in relief. The Maharani had threatened him with castration if the Peshwa was not pleased or showed signs of boredom. "If they are of your usual cleverness, all will be well pleased."

Alan doubted that anyone would be pleased at what he was going to do that night, other than the slaves.

The *Diwan-i-Am* although a much larger area than the private audience chamber, was crowded to overflowing. At the Nana's last minute suggestion, an invitation had been issued to all officers above the rank of *havildar*, which meant that Nate would be present. Alan was glad, for Nate had expressed a wistful wish to "see the fireworks" and Alan was happy to know that Nate would be at hand in case he was needed.

The puppet show was first, the puppet master much relieved that at long last he could offer up a new show.

Again Alan was conscious of Rosamunde. He could see her waiting as usual in her alcove with Parminder. This time, however, he could almost taste her excitement.

Alan outdid himself that night. With the new power at his disposal the illusions were finer, the tricks more complicated.

Cathal walked a high wire held up by unseen hands, while juggling balls of light. Remembering the Arabian Nights Entertainment he had read as a boy, both in the early 18th century French translation and an English edition of 1840, Alan conjured up a lamp, and a giant Djinn that came from it as a trail of coloured smoke when he rubbed it. Unicorns sprang from his finger tips and danced to music that came from nowhere. Flowers, real flowers, rained from the ceiling and he put a small pot on the floor and made an immense peepul tree grow from it, sprouting leaves and fruit as it shot towards the ceiling. From his box sprang a troupe of monkeys, who gathered the fruit from the tree and gave it to the spectators who exclaimed in awe that it was real fruit that they could eat, and it was delicious!

The Maharajah was jumping up and down in excitement. No one, *no one,* had a magician like his! Even the Nana had been impressed!

"Wonderful! Wonderful!" the royal toad shouted in his shrill voice that went so oddly with his amphibian appearance. "Magician, you have pleased us mightily! Name a boon that I might grant you!"

"I am a simple man, highness, and desire little beyond what you have so generously granted me," said Alan, with a bow. "But if it please your highness, might I stay and watch the dancing?"

the avatar of vishnu

Since the exalted guest could not be expected to sit with the lowly entertainers, Alan stood to one side as the first dance began. This was Parminder; her dance, as usual, was extremely obscene and danced to a rapid, sensual beat. Alan thought of how Sishul had lamented his wife having to expose herself in such fashion and watched in disgust as both the Maharajah and Nana Sahib stared lasciviously at her gyrations. Nana Sahib sat between Mabel and Hussaini, with an intimate hand on each of them, while the Maharajah, not to be outdone, although considerably less adept, was fondling Laura and Noori.

Alan had a heightened awareness of everything. He could feel not only Rosamunde's emotions (excitement at what was to come, overlaid with dread of the coming dances) but Parminder's disgust at what she was doing, and Nate's anger at seeing Laura fondled by the royal pervert. He was even conscious of Mabel's fear and the lust of both the royal party and many of the officers present.

As he stood, watching the dance he became cognizant of a sense of power beneath his feet, a feeling he had not felt since he had left the British Isles. Apprehensive as to what he would find, he opened himself to the ley lines and was almost thrown off his feet by the power he felt there. And it was clean, bright power of the Light, not a even the slightest taint of Dark remained in it!

Alan almost reeled. What had happned? Had this been Vishnu as well? He came close to shouting aloud when he realized what limitless power was now his to use, and use it he would!

But something held him back from immediately beginning the retribution he wanted to deal out to these people. He stood still during Rosamunde's toe dance. He had never before realized that the beauty of ballet, a graceful art he had always enjoyed, could be made so vile. He could sense her shame and felt such empathy for her that it was painful. Not only was she shamed, but angry at her art being so perverted.

Nana Sahib applauded loudly. He liked the leaps and movements as much as did the Maharajah and commented loudly in approval of the breast hoop bells and the tassels she wore tonight. "I trust she shall be back in my bed?" he said to the Maharani, who had abandoned the *gaddi* tonight to sit near the Nana.

She nodded yes, never taking her eyes off him.

"*No, she won't! Never again!*" thought Alan fiercely.

Rosamunde was called to the *musnud* and told to place herself in the attitude of submission between Nana Sahib and the Maharajah, so that they might both touch her.

The *Nazir* hurried to the *musnud* and bowed low. "We have a special dance for your highnesses tonight, the Union of Kali and Shiva, fully depicted, for your delight!" He raised his hands over head and clapped twice.

A dark curtain at the back of the room parted and six eunuchs appeared, dragging a type of sledge on which sat a large statue of Kali. Without having been told so, Alan was aware that this was the Kali sculpture from the Room Rosamunde had told him about.

A multitude of marigold garlands hung around the statue's neck and braziers of incense burned on either side of it.

First of all came the girls of the *nautch*, who had been coated with black powder from head to foot. It gleamed as did black pearls. They all carried a marigold garland and each performing a writhing, sensual dance, beforehand, at first in unison and then singly, adorned the statue with more marigolds.

The music was wild and fast, the drumbeat thundering. It heightened as two figures suddenly ran out onto the floor, one from each side of the statue.

One was Parminder. She too had been coated in black and attached ingeniously to her shoulders and back were two sets of extra arms. She was the exact image of the statue of Kali, save for the marigolds. As she came to a halt and stood in a sensuous, swaying posture, she thrust her tongue from her mouth and twisted it sideways. It had been dyed bright red.

The other figure was a young man. His body had been palely painted so that he looked as if he had been smeared with cremation ashes. His throat was painted blue. He, too, wore extra arms, holding weapons and wore skulls and a serpent around his neck. It was a large, living snake. Alan could see its tongue flicking in and out. Slowly, it had probably been drugged.

The young man wore his long matted locks twisted in a coil as did the representations of Shiva that Alan had seen, and wore also the sign of the crescent moon and of the Ganges. Like Parminder, he wore bracelets, anklets and armlets, and a broad collar of rubies. A tall crown, like the roof of an Indian temple, sat on his head, and, like Parminder, he was naked, without body hair and in a state of arousal. His eyes seemed dazed and sweat beaded his forehead. Full of the Dust of Kali, Alan guessed.

The music changed. It became wilder and more sensuous. The two began to dance, but not so much a dance as a frenzy, coming closer and closer to each other.

Alan became conscious of a strange tingling that seemed to be building from deep inside his bones. He looked down at his hands and noticed that they seemed covered in light, and as he watched, his clothing changed colour, the red and black of Kali disappeared to be replaced with sky blue, and silver embroidery. Something began to fill him up, not taking over his body and soul but rather sharing it, a benign consciousness that he knew would do him no harm but needed his help to manifest itself here on earth. As he looked up he seemed to be seeing out of two pairs of eyes, his own and another which saw deep into the souls of all those present.

At the *musnud*, the souls of the Maharajah, his mother, Hussaini and the Nana were black, polluted things. Rosamunde's, Laura's and Noori's shone in a bright white light, while Mabel was dimmed and grayish.

Something made the Maharani take her attention from the two figures on the dance floor, now coming closer to a complete union, and her eyes met Alan's and the eyes of the other entity that shared his consciousness.

A look of utter horror crossed her face and she gasped, choking, trying to tell the others, who were paying little attention to anything but the sexual mania of the dance. Both Hussaini and Rosamunde had their eyes closed, Hussaini in pleasure as Nana Sahib stroked her and Rosamunde so that she would not see what he ws doing, as if not looking would make it less real. Mabel was staring at the table top apathetically, free of the Nana's attentions, now that he had Rosamunde to touch and abuse.

But both Noori and Laura saw him and their eyes opened wide in shock. He could only imagine how he must appear for his back was to the highly polished marble walls and he faced the *musnud*, which had a backdrop of an erotic mural. But a quick glance down at his hands revealed blue hands laid over his in ghostly image.

Others began to notice what was happening and there were cries of awe and fear, some even getting up and running from the room as hurriedly as they could, terror on their faces.

The music ceased abruptly and discordantly as the musicians saw the apparition before them. The dancers stopped and stared. All of these eyes turned towards Alan at last attracted the attention of the rest of them at the *musnud*.

The Maharajah screamed, a shrill sound, and began to scramble backwards trying to get away from what he saw. As Alan had instructed her, Rosamunde jumped to her feet and gestured to Laura and Noori to join her. She even dragged a stupefied Mabel, who was staring at Alan, mouth ajar, with her. Cathal ran to stand with them as well.

Hussaini, roused from her sexual pleasure by the cessation of the Nana's strokes on her body, saw them run away and shrieked. "Where are you going, slaves? Get back here!" She reached for her whip, but it writhed away from her as Alan saw what she meant to do and pulled it to him in a burst of violet light. It turned to ashes in the air and fell to the ground.

Nana Sahib was braver than the Maharajah. He stood and said angrily, "What is the meaning of these tricks magician? How dare you—"

"Silence!" The voice seemed to come from everywhere, and it tumbled the Nana and the others to their knees.

"The magician but acts as an avatar for me, lowly ones!" the voice continued. "You know who I am. Your evil is to end tonight! Look no longer on Kali the Black One as your protector! We are most displeased with her. Lord Brahma himself sent me here to punish you. Behold the image of Kali you have so often worshipped! She turns her face from you, Dipti Rawit!"

All eyes turned to the statue. Its head was turned to the side, the eyes were closed and the tongue had been drawn into the mouth.

"Shiva, he who is the god of fertility, is most displeased as well, for the women enslaved here are meant to be wives and mothers and by denying them their fertility and their husbands you have done a great wrong, Dipti Rawit! You have also murdered, stolen and committed acts of impiety. For this you will be punished, and punished most severely."

Seeing her whole world falling down around her the Maharani lost her fear and surged to her feet. She shrieked "No! I will not let anyone, man or God, take from me what I have worked so hard to obtain!"

She stood and with a gesture, threw a wall of black energy at the manifestation of Vishnu.

It broke around Alan as a wave broke upon rocks. An answering pulsating violet light grabbed the Maharani and took her by the throat.

"A fitting punishment—" said Vishnu. "Magician, you decide."

"I shall give her to the *Bhutas* as she has given so many other women!" Alan said savagely.

"Let this be so," said Vishnu. "She shall be used by them until l she dies of it, and then she shall go to *Naraka*, hell, and there, Dipti Rawit, you shall be punished until such time as you are reborn, the lowest of the low, an Untouchable, with always full knowledge of what you once were. And each life time shall be a misery to you until you reach true atonement." She disappeared from sight as he spoke, dematerialized to reappear in the *tykhana* with the *incubi*, who fell upon her with bestial lust, and killing intent, for they bore a long grudge against her.

Nana Sahib took this moment when Alan's attention was on the Maharani to launch his own magical attack. An expression of surprise was upon his face as he reached for the black ley lines and found them gone.

"I want to do this myself!" Alan said in his mind to Vishnu. "He shall pay for what he did to her!"

The God, approving, withdrew to a nearby statue.

Nana Sahib was a formidable black magician. He had refined the art with training from his adoptive father and came from a line of sorcerers, most of who had been responsible for the pollution of the ley lines.

He smiled as he saw Vishnu withdraw from his avatar. "Your illusions have no defense against me, magician. You have a certain skill in magic, bazaar tricks, but you are as an ant who fights an elephant, the ant cannot possibly win. And I shall step upon you as the elephant steps upon the ant!"

He launched a huge mass of red and black power at Alan, moving incredibly fast.

This was even more quickly countered by a violet wall that swallowed up the red and black energies.

Nana Sahib engaged again and again Alan countered until black and violet energies were flying back and forth so quickly that to those watching it was as if they were mere blurs. Thunderclaps sounded as the energies met and the air was full of electricity. It was a true Duel Arcane.

Hussaini, from where she had tumbled to the ground, watched this for but a moment, and then she was on her feet, and grabbing at the Maharajah, pulled him to his feet. "Take his countrywoman hostage!" she hissed to him. "Take out your sword and threaten to cut her throat!" she pointed to where Rosamunde, now joined by Parminder, stood with the other women in the alcove where they had so often waited to dance.

The Maharajah gulped in fear and stared at the women. He looked about for his guards, but nearly all had fled, terrified by the sight of the God incarnated and now the Wizard's Duel, which was doing extreme damage to the walls, floor and ceiling of the room as the two magicians dodged and feinted.

"Go!" yelled Hussaini. "Are you a coward? Do you wish to lose your throne and these women you can fornicate with? Go!"

Alan was dimly aware of fighting having broken out between Nate and several of the guards who had tried to go to the aid of the Maharani earlier. And outside the walls he could hear shouting as Sishul, with men from the village fought the guards at the front of the palace. As planned, he had cast a spell on the barracks so that the vast quantity of men there could not break out or help in any way. Even as he skillfully fought Nana Sahib, Alan was aware that they were still vastly out numbered, even with all of the magic at his disposal, unless Vishnu intervened and somehow rid them of the army.

With Hussaini's derisive prodding the Maharajah unsheathed his jeweled sword and rushed forward, intending to grab Rosamunde.

But she was ready for him. With a burst of magic she pushed him away from her, sending him stumbling backwards.

But he stumbled near Laura and reached out and grabbed her. Before she could react he had taken her enameled collar in one hand and pulled it tight up against her throat so that she was in danger of choking. With his other hand he put the sword to her throat

"Let her go!" screamed Rosamunde, lifting her hand menacingly, trying to aim at him, yet protect Laura.

Laura, struggling and cursing, was trying to kick backwards into a most vulnerable part of his anatomy. The little toad was surprisingly strong.

Hussaini laughed and ran forward to pick up a mace discarded by one of the guards who had fled when Vishnu manifested himself. She swung it experimentally and smiled as she realized that even a ceremonial mace was a formidable weapon. As a tremendous crash and noise came from the direction of the dueling Wizards she ran forward, with the mace lifted, aiming for Laura's face.

But she never made it. A long thin stream of fire took her and caught her and sent her shrieking to the ground, burning fiercely, just as Nate came running up behind the Maharajah and with one deep stroke, ran him through with his bloodied sword. Rawit's pudgy fingers retained their grasp upon Laura's collar as he fell, dead, to the floor, but Nate reached out and grabbed her away from him.

Rosamunde whirled in the direction of the fire's origin and gasped. There in the wide double doors, was standing Brendan. So fierce was his aspect and so terrifying was the mere sight of him that the last few men who had still fought dropped their arms and ran.

Alan, meanwhile, had sent Nana Sahib to the floor with a violet rope that circled his knees and then snaked up to his throat. With hands pulling ineffectually at the ever tightening pressure on under his chin the Peshwa glared with pure hatred at Alan, unable to speak.

"What dost thou wish to do with him?" said Vishnu speaking formally. "Wilt thou have thy vengeance complete by taking his life?"

Alan shook his head. He did not feel exhausted as he should have, but instead full of power that was lifting and sustaining him. "A worse punishment, my lord. I shall strip him of even the smallest of magics, make him repulsive to any woman so he shall never be able to hurt a female again, for none will ever wish to lay with him. I shall banish him to a far land, where he will live a hand to mouth existence without magic or friends and sycophants to succor him."

"A fitting punishment," the God approved. "which shows much wisdom."

Alan walked widdershins about the kneeling Peshwa and began to inscribe arcane symbols in the air, saying a spell to himself as he went. When this was completed, a circle of glowing violet, edged with purest gold hung about Nana Sahib and the black magician cowered away from this as if it would burn him.

Nate, watching with Laura still in his arms, swore ever afterwards that he heard the rustle of great wings and saw shadowy forms with burning swords as Alan pronounced the final incantation and lifted his hands over Nana Sahib.

The black magician gave a great choking gasp. A huge miasma of blackness rose from his body to the ceiling, where it was eaten by a pure white light that seemed to come from four directions.

And his face changed. It became that of a demon, vilely ugly and repellent. He was diminished in size as well and his body became as ugly and twisted as his soul had been. When Alan loosened the violet light he fell to the floor and lay there, sobbing, a broken man. Then he disappeared.

Alan looked towards Rosamunde, who had mercifully given Hussaini a death blow, for even though the Mistress's death was just, Rosamunde had been unable to watch the woman burn to death, the same death she had given to Untouchables with the bale fire.

Rosamunde turned as if she felt his eyes upon her and smiled tremblingly at him. She had never killed before and even though this was a blessing, a mercy killing, it still affected her profoundly. Her appetite for vengeance was not what she had thought it would be all during her long captivity.

Alan tuned to the statue of Kali and raised his hands. A violet wave of energy gathered itself and fell at the statue, meeting the stone hard and exploding it into thousands of pieces.

And as it did, in the entire *Mahal,* and the city, all of the rubies and all of the slave jewelry fell off every woman who had been enslaved.

Behind Brendan there was a tumult of cries and Sishul appeared, a pike with a blood stained tip, in his hands as the dragon moved aside to admit him and his rag tag army.

"They are all dead!" he shouted, flourishing his pike He took in the evidence of the battle in the room and grinned at Alan delightedly. "Well done, my friend! Well done!"

"Alan," said Brendan. "Cynara and I melted the cannons and destroyed the armory. We spoke to the horses and the elephants and the hunting cats they have for war and they will not fight. Cynara and Sacha are keeping the men under guard as well."

Sishul had spied Parminder and he dropped his pike and ran to her. She saw him at the same moment and with a cry of utter happiness, ran towards him. As she ran, the extra arms fell from her back, all the Kali trappings disappeared and the black dust coating her skin vanished. As she leaped into his arms Sishul whipped the cloak he wore around her and held her as if he would never let her go.

Nate had already doffed his *achkan* and covered Laura with it. He had his arms tight about her as well.

Alan walked over to Rosamunde, free now of the breast hoops and the other jewelry, the mark of her enslavement. They lay on the floor at her feet where they had fallen and Alan kicked them aside as he stripped off his coat and gave it to her. And throwing caution to the winds he took her into his arms as well. Cathal ran up his shoulder and nuzzled Rosamunde.

A black and white streak came down from Brendan's back as the dragon came forward amidst the rubble caused by the Duel Arcane.

Rosamunde and Alan were almost knocked off their feet as a determined little cat launched herself at them. "Me Witch!" shouted Sinéad, as she landed on Rosamunde's shoulder.

There were sounds of a happy ferret as well, as Cathal leaned from Alan's shoulder to rub noses with the best friend he had thought dead.

Rosamunde screamed in delight and pulled the cat into her arms to share in the circle of Alan's grasp. "Oh, Sinéad! Oh, Sinéad!" she said joyfully, rubbing her cheek on her familiar's soft fur while the little cat purred loudly. There would be time later to find out the hows and whys of Sinéad's reappearance for now it was enough that her familiar was back with her and they were all free. The horror was over. Now they could all go home, together. She looked up gratefully at Brendan, who had come up and dropped his head on Alan's shoulder. With one hand on Sinéad, who was now between them with her friend Cathal, and the other on Brendan's snout, as Alan's arms tightened around her, Rosamunde leaned into their embrace and felt their love, feeling for the first time in months as if it were possible to become happy once more.

Alan had questions of his own. How had Brendan come here at just the right time? And Cynara and Sacha, and the familiar, where had they come from? But for now, he had Rosamunde in his arms and she was safe and he would make certain that no one ever hurt her again.

51

one small step

While Alan held Rosamunde so tightly the God had disappeared, leaving no visible trace behind.

At first all was confusion but in a very short length of time everything began to be organized and Sishul was completely responsible for this. He announced his identity to the stunned men who had fought with him, who then overwhelmingly burst into excited and pleased exclamations. Parminder looked incredulous but managed a smile as the others cheered and clapped their hands.

If the present circumstances were any indication, Sishul would be an energetic and able Maharajah, for there was still a great deal more to do to cleanse the *Kala Mahal* and Sishul set about it right away.

The eunuchs were rounded up and locked away. Most of them would more than likely be executed for the torments they had visited upon the helpless women in their charge.

The bodies of the Maharajah and Hussaini as well as the guards and servants that had fought on the side of the Rawits were dragged out and put in a huge funereal pyre. The slave jewelry was gathered up and Sishul offered it and the many jewels they found all to Alan. "For without you, this evil would never had ended," he said earnestly.

Alan refused them. "Use them to rebuild, and some settlement should be given to each woman who suffered here. Although those rubies were made by an alchemist, they are still valuable and would give anyone who needs it a fresh start." Sishul was much struck by this idea and agreed to it at once.

People from the city had begun to stream into the *Mahal*, looking for children, wives and sweethearts who had been stolen from them. It was heartwarming to see the reunions.

Geeta arrived with a *bal-ghari* full of women's clothing and for the first time in a long while, all of the women were decently and modestly clothed.

For some space of time all was utter confusion again. Alan was reminded irresistibly of the Dublin Dragonport at Christmas time when people and dragons were coming and going for holiday visits.

Leaving Rosamunde with Laura and Sinéad, who seemed to be very content to be in each other's company, Alan went about the palace with Sishul and Nate to obliterate any trace of the remaining evil. Willing hands helped pull down the erotic hangings and statues, most of which Alan turned to dust. The erotic murals became pastoral scenes and the black walls were turned to a soft pink marble with the help of the ley lines.

"In my great grandfather's day," said Sishul, "this was known as the *Bagh Mahal,* the *Garden Mahal,* for the gardens were numerous and open to all to enjoy. The gardens shall bloom again and the gates shall be opened once more so that people and trade may come and go as they wish." He was full of plans for the betterment of his people, and every trace of this long evil was to be eradicated.

"Did you ever think you'd be a Maharani?" Laura asked Parminder as they sat in a large group of some of the freed women, and Parminder's relatives, including her children who could not get close enough to their mother. Her mother and father watched them with tear filled eyes and trembling smiles. They had never thought to see this day.

"I cannot still believe it," she answered, looking dazed. "I have always known that Sishul was special but I never imagined that he was the holder of the throne!" She put her arms about her three children and held them tight.

"What will happen to us now?" Margaret said, worriedly. She kept looking down at herself, stroking the fabric of the skirt and blouse she now wore, as if finding it hard to believe that she at long last wore clothing again.

"Alan says that with two dragons available we may take you anywhere you like, even up to Mardan to your husband, Margaret," said Rosamunde. Geeta had given her a pale blue *sari* and Sinéad had curled up in the lap of this garment, she had not stopped purring since she and Rosamunde were reunited and Rosamunde had not stopped petting her. They were profoundly happy to be restored to one another. They were a part of one another and each had felt maimed and lacking while they were parted.

"Will our husbands and families want us back?" said Henrietta in a tight voice.

"All these folks seem real glad to have their kids back," said Laura. "The husbands too, and Nate's damn glad to have me back. He says we're gonna be married as soon as we can find a preacher."

"Natives and Americans!" Henrietta's face seemed to say. "What else could one expect?" She on the other hand was completely afraid of the future. Could she possibly not tell Hugh what she had been doing these past months? But what if he found out later and realized that she had been lying to him? Which ever path she trod was a dangerous one.

"Are you not afraid as to what your husband will say?" she asked Ivy, who had been looking rather soft-eyed as she thought about her Albert.

"Me Bert's Mum was a whore," she said . "An' I was about to go on the stroll when we was married. 'e'll not care, I opes 'e's still alive!"

Henrietta stared at her in shock.

Mabel Clutterbuck was the only one silent, the only one not looking forward to returning to home and family.

She supposed that she would be returned to her aunt in Delhi, who would never let her forget that she was ruined goods.

She did not feel as if she was ruined, on the contrary, she already missed being what she had been and she hated wearing clothing again. Everyone else had exclaimed over how 'wonderful' it was to be clothed once more. Mabel wanted nothing more than to rip the skirt and blouse from her body and go and find a large group of men who would take her, one after another, all eager for Lali. She loved being Lali, the Red One, the naked one, she did not want to go back to being Mabel, clothed, corseted and celibate. She needed the admiration and the sex act as if it were a drug. How was she to bear it? Her face had reverted to it's old sullen look and she sat a little apart from the others. Perhaps she could run away again and, if she was fortunate, be sold into another brothel. She was also going to miss Hussaini. The Mistress had been good to her.

"Rosamunde," said a voice and she looked up in delight. She put Sinéad on her shoulder and came to her feet and ran forward to throw her arms about Sacha.

He hugged her tight against him. "We've been so worried!" he said, dropping a kiss on her hair. He laughed a little and said "But I would not have recognized you if I had not seen Sinéad in your lap! Here, let's restore you to what you should be." He took his arms from about her and stood back a little. "Sinéad, you'll have to stay on the floor for just a moment while I cast this spell."

"I'll take her," said Laura, holding out her arms for the familiar.

Rosamunde gave the little cat to Laura and said "Uncle Sacha, this is Laura Fitzroy. Do you remember her? From America?"

He did indeed remember her."You've grown up a bit since then," he said "I remember your Father as well, Lowell Fitzroy. Is he here?"

"Nate, that's my intended, Nate Connelly, says Pa'll be here soon. He sent him a message just after the goings-on here ended," said Laura.

"Will ye be after doin' th' spell and stop yer yammerin' so that I can be goin' back to me Witch!" Sinéad said crossly.

"As you wish, my lady!" Sacha grinned and took out his wand. "*Restituere!*" he pronounced and touched the wand to the top of Rosamunde's head.

It was as if she was enveloped instantly in a cyclone of violet light. In minutes it began to dissipate, whirling down to the floor, and leaving Rosamunde's skin and hair restored to its natural colour. The curl was back in her silvery locks and the hair clip sprang open and fell to the floor for it could not contain their exuberance.

"Whew!" said Laura, blinking at the transformation. Her friend had been a beautiful native girl, but restored to herself she was spectacular. It was a good thing, Laura reflected, that the Maharajah had never seen her thus, for he would have taken her to his bed, his mother be damned. The pale skin and hair made the violet eyes so much more obvious.

"Thank you, " said Rosamunde gratefully to Sacha.

Mabel was staring at her, her mouth agape. She well knew who Rosamunde was and she was suddenly angry that she had never been told. But it all seemed part of everything bad that had happned lately. She was perhaps one of the few persons in Jhaniput who regretted the passing of the Rawit regime.

There would still be a great deal to do the next day. The female slaves had to be sorted out. A good many had come from the city and were back with the families, but many had come from elsewhere, for Wazid Ali's net had been cast far and wide. The Mutiny was going to make returning them to their families difficult. Cawnpore, Lucknow, Delhi, Meerut and other cities were either in the hands of rebels or were in ruins.

As much as Alan wanted to return to Ranijhat and from there home when he was certain that Rosamunde was suffering no ill effects from her captivity, he was forced to admit that he had a duty to help these women return to a normal a life as was possible. Having Brendan and Cynara at their disposal would make it easy to go abroad and try and find the families of the former slaves. Once a family was located the woman could be returned. In cases where the family had disappeared or had been killed in one of the many conflicts, Alan and Sacha could take them where they wished to go and provide them with a sum of money and the ruby that they could sell. Some of the *mem-sahibs* would be taken to Bombay where they could be put on ships for the British Isles.

All this took a good deal of planning and it was quite late into the next evening before Alan and Cathal were free to return to their room, not even having had a short respite since the incredible events of the preceding evening, for there had just been to much to do. Cathal had made himself useful writing lists, directions to homes and taking names of women who needed help.

Upon entering the room Alan lit a mage light on the tips of his fingers, and went directly to the *ghosulkhana* and before getting into the bath, used a restore spell on himself and returned to his natural looks. He would be glad to lay aside the turban as well, it was a fashion he would never be able to take to as normally he would not even wear a hat unless it was completely necessary.

Cathal, yawning loudly, had almost nodded off on the edge of the bath. "I'm so glad this is all over," he said, head between his paws as he waited for Alan to finish bathing. "And I'm so glad Sinéad is still alive!" He gave a little wiggle of delight.

"I presume she told you how she happened to be here?" Alan inquired. At Cathal's nod he said "You may tell me tomorrow, for now all I want to do is to get into bed." But with a pang, he realized that there would be no Rosamunde to share the *charpoy* with him. The women who remained were to be housed in the *zenana*, which had been one of the first places to be completely refurbished. Sacha had helped with that. It was now a decent, pretty place, with no reminders left of the brothel it had been.

But when Alan went to the *charpoy*, he had a surprise.

There, curled up with Sinéad, sound asleep was Rosamunde. She wore a silken garment of some sort and looked so beautiful, looking as she should be, that his heart turned over with love for her. Why was she here?

As he stood there, staring down at her, she stirred and woke. She smiled at him sleepily .

"What are you doing here, Rosamunde?" he said.

"I didn't want to be alone," she answered. "Laura is with Nate and Parminder is with Sishul and Sinéad and I wanted to be with you and Cathal, not by ourselves. This is the one room in this palace that does not hold bad memories for me."

Sinéad looked up and yawned loudly, showing her little pink tongue. She gave Cathal a look and he nodded.

"And we've been after thinkin' me and Cathal, that it is bein' time that the two o' yez need to be havin' a talk!" the familiar announced.

"Enough trouble has been caused by the fact that you cannot seem to discuss with each other how you feel about one another," said Cathal. "Rosamunde, Alan loves you and wants to marry you," the ferret said to her.

"And me Witch has been lovin' ye all her life! It near broke her heart it did, when ye did not make an offer for her at her come-out ball!" Sinéad informed Alan.

The two humans stared at one another, aghast.

Rosamunde was the first to speak "You can't love me," she protested, sitting up. "Not after this, not after I've been used by so many men,"

"Nate loves Laura still, and Sishul wants Parminder as his wife," he said, hope surging up in him. She had loved him that long?

"But what about Christine Chapman?" Rosamunde cried.

"Who?" Alan looked blank.

"The girl In Cheltenham that everyone thought you were going to marry!" she said in exasperation. "Peter's mother told my mother—"

Alan gave an unsteady laugh. "I scarcely remembered! Rosamunde, Christine was betrothed to a good friend of mine who worked with me at the laboratory, Iain MacCausland. He went to America for a course at Columbia University and asked me to look after her while he was gone. Her father had recently died and they could not be married because of her mourning period. She had to go and live with her aunt and uncle who Iain felt, were unkind to her and he wanted me to watch out for her and make the relatives know that someone was keeping an eye on them. It was fortunate that I did so, for they treated her miserably until I put the fear of my magics into them. She and Iain must be happily married by now. There was no romantic nonsense between the two of us, why, all she did when I called upon her was talk about Iain! But what about Raymond?"

She looked down at her hands, which were tightly clasping the edge of the *resai* which she could now keep over herself. "I married him because I could not have you," she said in a small voice. "And when I thought that you were going to marry Christine I could not bear to see you with her and I chose Raymond as the best of a bad lot of suitors and for the very reason that he was posted here in India."

"I'm an idiot, " he began.

"Ye are bein' that!" said Sinéad sharply. "And why are

ye standin' over me darlin' Witch like that when it's sittin' beside her wi' yer arm about her ye should be?"

Rosamunde was a little nervous in his embrace. He thought that she felt tense. He thought he knew why and lightened the hold he had about her shoulders and dropped a rather chaste kiss on her brow. It was not what he wanted to do.

"Cathal is right, you know, I do want to marry you," he said gently.

She was silent for so long that he began to be frightened. "Rosamunde?" he asked hesitantly. Sinéad started to speak but Cathal hushed her. "This is their problem to work out," he whispered, "We've done all that we can."

"I love you, Alan," she said at last. "I always have and I daresay I always will. But I don't know if I am able to be anyone's wife, I don't know if I can bear being intimate, being a real wife in every way. Right now I can scarcely bear the thought of being touched in an intimate fashion, much less–"

He removed his arm from about her. "I can wait, Rosamunde. I am more than willing to wait until you are ready. I completely understand why you feel that way, indeed, it would be amazing if you did not. Remember that I love you and I will never stop loving you. I can wait forever, if needs be."

She looked at him with troubled eyes. Earlier on in the day Laura had spoken to her again about marrying Alan and Rosamunde had confessed to her friend how she felt about intimacy

Laura had looked at her oddly. "He loves you, honey! That makes a lot of difference. I thought the same way after I came out of the mines and when Nate proposed I made sure he took me to bed before I gave him my yes. And it was good. You ought to sleep with Alan and see how different it is when the man loves you and has tenderness and concern for your pleasure! It's a hell of a lot different!"

Pleasure? Rosamunde could not associate the word with what had been done to her. She had never felt anything but pain. It seemed an utter impossibility, even with Alan. And to marry him, feeling as she did, would hardly be fair to him.

But she still craved to be near him. Now she said. "I

don't mind if you hold me, I, I...quite like it. But the other," she swallowed hard. "It would remind me – may I stay with you tonight? Would you just hold me?"

He would take her on any terms. He opened his arms and she crept into them, shivering a little. He lay back and pillowed her head on his shoulder as the two familiars crowded in closely. He wanted to kiss her, to stroke her hair, but he felt that even that small gesture would be too much for her at the present. He was going to have to cultivate patience and a sense of humor and take a great many cold baths. It was a small step forward that she was even willing to be held like this.

52
sorting out

Alan left quite early the next morning, roused from sleep when Brendan poked his head in the door of the room from the garden outside and said, "Time to rise, Alan. There's a great deal to do today."

Cathal and Sinéad awoke as well, the ferret yawning and the cat stretching with an enormous yawn. Rosamunde still slept and Alan hadn't the heart to awaken her. When Sinéad started to poke at her Witch with a paw, Alan said quickly, "Let her sleep, Sinéad. It has been a long time since she has been able to sleep uninterrupted. Watch over her today."

When he had awakened, she was still cuddled against him. This wanting to be close gave him hope, and remembering her confession of love of the night before he was able to leave for the day's work with a lighter heart. There was indeed a great deal to be done and he had not as yet had a chance to talk to Brendan. He hoped that the day's events would allow him time to be with Rosamunde again.

Rosamunde awoke some hours later, rested and refreshed. She missed Alan immediately and sat up looking about her, wondering where he was.

"Brendan was after comin' an' takin him off a while back," Sinéad explained from the table top where a tempting breakfast lay. "He was thinkin' of us, though, this food has been magiced to stay hot and it's all our favorites!" She was busy shredding some kedge with her paw as she spoke.

It wasn't a dream, Rosamunde thought in gratitude as she saw her familiar. She had Sinéad back, she was wearing a nightgown, the horrible breast hoops and the other slave jewelry was gone and today was hers, no more duties in the *zenana*, no more dancing for the royal pervert, no one would touch her or use her body, it was all over.

"Sacha was comin' by too," said the familiar, "He was after leaving a package for ye, said the Elves were 'givin' it to him afore he was leaving Ireland."

"And I slept through all of this?" Rosamunde said in wonder. It had been a very long time since she had slept so deeply or so well, with no evil dreams or abrupt awakenings. She had become, all too often, used to being dragged from sleep for her 'duties'.

"Alan said I was to let ye sleep," explained Sinéad. "Are ye wantin' to open your package?" She asked hopefully. Like most cats, she was very curious.

"Breakfast first," Rosamunde decided, "and while we eat I want to hear what happened after they took me from the *Hirren Mahal* and how you ended coming here with Sacha, Cynara and Brendan at just the right time."

The tale took some time in the telling and then Rosamunde had to tell Sinéad what had happned to her. It was a relief to tell this old and trusted friend some of what had happned, but there were still things of which she could not speak, not even to her familiar.

Sinéad, having talked to both Brendan and Sacha, was able to explain to her Witch why she had lost her magic. The polluted ley lines had stolen it from her. Sacha had theorized the only reason Alan had not been completely drained was his status as an Adept. He had more power to lose than Rosamunde, and he had Druidical powers as well. And Rosamunde had not practiced her magic as much in recent years.

The morning tea had grown cold and had been reheated by magic several times as they talked and they were still sitting over the breakfast table when a knock came on the door and Laura entered.

"Had a hard time finding you!" the American said. "Thought you'd be in the *zenana* with the rest of 'em. Did you spend the night here? With Alan?" she inquired with interest.

"Not the way you think, Laura. I could not take your advice," Rosamunde said, looking away from her friend.

"And what advice would that be after bein'?" Sinéad asked.

Laura had easily adjusted to talking to an animal and she answered, "I told her to make love with Alan, to see the difference there is when she's with someone who loves her."

"'Tis a good notion," the familiar began but Rosamunde said sharply "No! I cannot! Why can you two not understand that? Just leave me alone about this! Alan understands! He did not press me, nor even suggest such a thing!" She stopped, an angry flush on her cheeks and refused to meet their eyes. Her gaze lit upon the package, laying on a chest against a wall that had contained a mural of lovers locked in lascivious embrace and now showed a scene of elephants in a procession.

She arose form the table and crossed the room to get it. "Let's see what Sacha bought me."

Laura and Sinéad exchanged glances but said no more as Rosamunde took the string off the silvery paper that made up the package and opened it.

A riot of colour burst out of it. It was a wardrobe fit for a Queen.

Laura gasped. "Jesus H, Christ!" she said "However did all of those clothes fit in that little package?" She went towards the pile of garments and fingered a beautiful green gown. "Never felt anything like this," she said, and added wistfully, "Never saw anything so beautiful."

"Try it on, Laura," Rosamunde urged. She had found a gown of her favorite Parma violet colour.

"Rose honey, I ain't nowhere near your size in gowns. I'm too broad in the shoulder, long in the arm and you've got a tiny little waist," said Laura patiently. "And I'm taller than you, even this *sari* is halfway up my legs!" she said ruefully. "Ain't no way that gown is going to fit me!"

"It's magical, it will fit," Rosamunde said. "Go ahead, Laura, please!"

Laura shrugged. She was certain that it would not fit but she decided to humor her friend.

To her amazement it fit as if it had been made for her. And what is more, the skirt stood out in the fashionable bell-shaped silhouette without benefit of crinoline or hoops. It was a beautiful emerald green with long sleeves, cuffed and collared with lace and a row of gold buttons marched down the pleated bodice front.

"I wish that Nate could see me in this!" she exclaimed.

"He can. I'll give it to you, and as many of the others as you want," said Rosamunde. "In fact, there are so many gowns here that I shall give one to each of the Englishwomen. They will be more comfortable in them than in the *saris*."

"That's uncommon generous of you," said Laura. "Don't know if I could stomach giving away anything this pretty! Let's see what else is in that pile!"

There were cobweb fine undergarments and stockings, gowns of all colours and dainty slippers; more than enough for all the Englishwomen. There were no bonnets. Elves seldom ever wore hats, but there was enough lace to make caps.

At the bottom of the pile were two green gowns which made Laura gasp with delight. They were covered in *diamenté*, with short balloon sleeves and sparkling veils folded with them.

"What are these for ?" she asked Rosamunde. "They're mighty fancy! What are they made from? "

Rosamunde had a strange look on her face. "They're made from spider silk and the sparkle is the dew of the morning," she said quietly. "They're wedding gowns, Laura."

"Wedding gowns? But they're green! That ain't a lucky colour for a wedding!" Laura protested, thinking Rosamunde's answer a trifle poetic. "But, my, ain't they fine!"

"The people who made these gowns would never think of green as unlucky. White, the colour we wear to wed in, is their colour of mourning," Rosamunde said.

The Elves never did anything by chance. They had foreknowledge of events. Rosamunde had heard many times the family story that Oberon and his Queen had gifted her uncle Simon with the exact amount of Elfin cloaks he ended in needing during his travels in Russia. Two wedding gowns! Rosamunde felt that one was meant for Laura, for although they were both exquisite, Laura seemed drawn to one especially, just as she had been drawn to the green dress, and just as the women she would offer the gowns to would be drawn to one particular dress, the one that would make them look their best.

And Rosamunde wanted very, very badly to stroke and try on the other wedding gown. It was calling to her, although not in words.

The Elves had obviously meant it for her, a beautiful green gown for her marriage. But she was afraid of marriage and the intimacy it implied. And she was afraid of the gown. It seemed to be pushing her in a direction she did not want to go, for she was not ready for it.

Later that afternoon with Laura's help, Rosamunde visited all the Englishwomen and gave them their choice of gown, with under things, stockings and slippers. Everyone received a length of lace for a cap or head scarf. It was amazing how the gowns lifted the spirits of each woman and made them feel more confident about what lay ahead of them. Telling their spouses and families what had befallen them was going to be an ordeal, but looking their best, in a gown of their own country's style, gave them a much needed lift in spirits

"Only that Lali ain't pleased about her dress," said Laura, as they headed back to Rosamunde's room. "She was buck naked when we found her and didn't even want to try the dress on. I told you, Rose, she's a natural born whore. I'll bet anything she'll go looking for a whore house to work in as soon as she leaves here. Did you hear her say she misses the men?" Laura snorted.

Rosamunde shuddered. She could not understand Mabel Clutterbuck. How could someone MISS what they had been subjected to? Why did she want to remain naked at all times? Rosamunde looked down at her violet dress, made with high neck and gigot sleeves, and trimmed in fine lace. She felt so happy to have it to wear and be decently and modestly covered again. She said as much to Laura, who shrugged.

"We ain't all alike, Rose, and if that's what she likes, being naked and banged by a bunch of men folk, then I guess that's what she ought to do. We can't make her think like we do. She'd make a godawful wife. The fellow who married her would have to be dragging her out of the cat house every day."

Rosamunde thought that she would never be as accepting of these differences as Laura was, she found Mabel and her liking for whoredom totally repugnant.

"All the Clutterbucks are strange," Alan said later when he and Rosamunde took their dinner with Laura and Nate and Laura had regaled them with the story of Mabel. "There were only two of them that were ever any good, Hezekiah, now known as "Harry" and Hamlin and they broke with the family. Donald and Rufus, the ones who teased me at school, ended up in prison. I heard Donald was due to be hanged, like his father, for murder. What you tell me of Mabel does not surprise me," he said dismissively.

"But what will become of her?" Rosamunde said. Sacha had left for Delhi armed with a list that afternoon and Mabel's name, along with others, and the direction of her relatives were on that list. Sacha would contact as many of the families as he could and then return for the women who had friends and relatives left in Delhi and reunite them.

"That's up to her, honey," said Laura. "She'll have the money from the ruby. She can set herself up as a madam if she wants! Let's talk about something else rather than that little piece of tail! Alan, Nate told me you invited us to Ranijhat. I'd like that fine. Never rode on a dragon afore, and I knew Nate'd want to go the minute he told me about the fine horses there!"

Nate, rid now of his bushy beard, revealing a dark, rugged face with a distinct American Indian look about it, said "And Sacha tells me there's a preacher there who can splice the knot for us, Laurie. You Pa should be here soon and we can all go and have these good folks and your Pa stand up with us. I ain't taking no chances on losing you again!" He dropped his big hand over hers and the look they exchanged smote Alan to the heart. If only Rosamunde would look at him like that!

Later, when Nate and Laura were alone in their room, he said, "I'd like to see those two get hitched."

Laura snorted. "So would I, I think a heap of Rose. But the poor kid was so banged around here, Nate, in more ways than one, that she's all tied up in knots over having sex

494

with anyone, even someone who loves her as much as he does. I told her to go to bed with him and see how it felt but she won't do it."

"It's going to be hard on him," said Nate thoughtfully, watching her get undressed for bed in deep appreciation. "If it was us and I couldn't touch you, well, it'd be damned hard."

"I hope it is damned hard!" said Laura mischievously. "All this bedroom talk–!"

"Come here, woman!" he said , and reached for her.

Again Alan found Rosamunde waiting for him. And again she wanted to be near him and just wanted him to hold her. But she shied away from the cousinly kiss he planted on her brow, and again shivered in his embrace as if she wanted to go but could not make herself leave the shelter she craved.

This was going to be the most difficult thing he had ever done.

Within a week that *Mahal* was empty of the former slaves. Most had been reunited with family. Sacha had located Margaret's husband, who had come to Delhi with the relief force of the Corps of Guides, and found Ivy's husband as well. Albert Higgins had been wounded, but was very glad to find his wife. Like Major Broadbent, he was happy to have her back, alive and well. There were no recriminations from either one of them.

It was a different case with Colonel Montmorency. He was horrified and appalled at what Henrietta had become and went on at length about his own feelings until Sacha took him outside and with a nice right, laid him out on the terrace and then gave him a stern talking to.

Finally, shame faced, the Colonel went to his wife and offered to try and work things out. When he left them in Delhi, Sacha was not certain whether or not they would stay together, but at least they were going to try.

At Laura and Rosamunde's request Alan went to Bangalore and found Ameera's purchaser. He was glad to sell her and the new born babe when he saw the sum that Alan offered. Ameera was returned to Sanjaya, who had been desperately searching for her since he had escaped from the carnage of Delhi. Unsa and Neha proved to be happy in their new situation, in fact Unsa was to marry her master.

And the best news of all, was that Wazid Ali had been caught and hanged, not as a slaver but as a suspected mutineer. He had fallen afoul of the vindictive Sir Theophilus Metcalfe, a junior magistrate of Delhi, who was fast becoming noted as a bloodthirsty instrument of revenge towards the mutineers. The four Pathans had shared his fate. Sishul had raided Ali's slave emporium in the city and freed all the unfortunates there.

And, sadly, Rosamunde had found out that the other members of the Fishing Fleet had died, Susan Midthorpe in Meerut with her father, cut down by his own troops, and Lavinia Baldwin in the horror of the Women's House in Cawnpore.

Sacha had flown to Bombay and, using Chenevix's influence, sent a telegram home to Ireland, telling all the family that he had found the missing ones and that they were safe and well. Messages came back from Ireland expressing joy and hope that they would soon be home.

The large army was dispersed, some to find other employment and a small force to stay on in Jhaniput after swearing loyalty to the new Maharajah.

Within a fortnight all was sorted out, and after watching Sishul take the throne of Jhaniput, they were free to leave. Laura's Pa had arrived, and after a joyous reunion readily agreed to go north and see his little girl married.

And every night Rosamunde had shown up in Alan's bedroom and asked to stay with him. She never failed to ask. It never became an accepted matter. Every night he had welcomed her, and held her all night as she slept. He, however, did not sleep very much.

She had placed the Elfin wedding gown at the very bottom of the canvas bag she would be using as a portmanteau, afraid even to look at it. Her emotions were all in a tangle. She tried to stay away from Alan, but being alone at night frightened her and she had no nightmares when she was with him. Even Sinéad could not end her bad dreams as

Alan could with just the lightest touch. In his arms she was safe from the terrors of the night.

So matters stood when they bade farewell to Sishul and Parminder and set out for Ranijhat.

53

wedding in ranijhat

Rosamunde liked Ranijhat at once. The atmosphere, the scenery, the very air, was all so different from Jhaniput that they might have been in another country altogether The people in the city were cheerful and friendly and the Maharajah and his family were kind and free of the vices she had come to expect from those in a *Mahal*.

However, she was stunned to find the Holloways in residence. She had assumed that they had been killed in the Mutiny.

And right from the beginning they began to cause trouble.

First of all, they were appalled that Rosamunde had not gone into mourning, full blacks, for Raymond. And where did they think Rosamunde was going to be able to obtain mourning? Sacha had asked.

When Nate asked Reverend Holloway to marry him and Laura the missionary was horrified that a white woman wanted to marry a man with dark skin and refused to perform the ceremony until the Maharajah Zahallah told them sweetly that he was more than happy for them to remain his guests indefinitely... As the Holloways wanted to go somewhere where they could again spread the Word of God, the Reverend reluctantly agreed to wed Laura and Nate. Zahallah would not allow the Holloways to preach Christianity in Ranijhat. Every time they tried they found themselves locked in the suite of rooms, politely but firmly removed from the vicinity of the objects of their proselytizing.

Mrs. Holloway was horrified when she discovered that Rosamunde went to Alan's room every night and slept with him. Of course, she assumed the worse and at breakfast one morning went into a long tirade against the immorality of such a state of affairs, branching out into the fact that Laura and Nate were cohabitating as well, without benefit of clergy.

Their ceremony would not be for some days as the Maharajah was delightedly planning a huge celebration, complete with food, fireworks and music.

Her voice becoming shrill and harsh, Mrs. Holloway ranted vehemently. She was disgusted that both these young women, who should have known better, were not only defying all the laws of God and man but had chosen to lay with men of inferior races. She was particularly incensed with Rosamunde, who was of a good family and raised in a Christian country since Laura, being an American, was little better than a savage. And how could Rosamunde lower herself to have an incestuous relationship with a half Chinese when she had been widowed only a short time before and had been the wife of such a good Christian as well?

Alan stood it as long as he could. Sacha had advised him to ignore the woman for she was naught but a bigoted ignoramus, but the sight of Rosamunde, visibly wilting beneath this verbal onslaught cut him to the quick. His lips opened to say something scathing to her but Lowell Fitzroy forestalled him.

Laura's "Pa' was a big man, not fat but hard with muscle and very tall. He was normally quiet, not given to much speech, but what he said was pithy and to the point. He was heavily tanned with deep lines about his eyes that spoke of a lifetime spent in the sun. Like Laura, he had auburn hair but his eyes were a steely gray.

Now they narrowed as he looked at Mrs. Holloway and his square jaw tightened. When he spoke, he was not loud, but his voice made an impression on every one in the room. "Can't say as I care for your opinion of Americans, Missus, and if what my Laura does sets right with me, I reckon you ain't got no cause to squawk about it. Couldn't ask for a better son-in-law than Nate here and he'd be my choice for my girl if'n it was up to me. An' as for these other two, I'd be right careful what I said to a Wizard, 'specially one who's got a dragon. No man worth his salt is going to sit still and listen to his lady bad-mouthed and looking at Alan here I'd guess he's pretty close to turning you into a weevil or a rattle snake. Can't say as I'd blame him none."

Both the Holloways looked startled. Ravi said quietly , "May I remind you both how much you owe to Alan's family?

499

If Sacha had not rescued you in all probability you would be dead now. And you are tolerated here, that is all. You would do best to hold your tongues, both of you."

"Yes," put in Sacha "I am beginning to regret that I saved you from death. Cynara and I could easily return you to where we found you,"

"You Hindus have no notion of morality!" thundered the Reverend. "What these young women are doing is *wrong*— that is the truth with no bark on it!"

Zahallah rolled his eyes. The Holloways had never understood the difference between the many religions of India. To them, everyone in the country was a Hindu and therefore a heathen.

"Excuse me," said Rosamunde in a choked voice and ran from the room in the direction of a *chabutara* that looked out over the mountains.

Sinéad jumped down from the table and followed her.

Alan jumped up as well, startling Cathal, who had been listening to Mrs. Holloway with an expression of astonishment on his masked face. It took him a moment to run after his Wizard.

Alan found Rosamunde standing at the rail, staring sightlessly at the beautiful scene before her. Now in early November the wind from the hills was cold and rather strong, but she did not seem to notice it. It lifted and played with her hair and tugged at the bell skirt of the blue floral silk she wore, another Elfin gown.

Without turning around she said as she heard Alan come up behind her "Is that how everyone will see us, as immoral? They assume that we are having sexual relations!" Her voice was tight and brittle.

"People always think the worst, Rosamunde, and they thrive on scandal," he said soothingly "particularly narrow minded bigots like these Holloways. Everything to them is black and white."

"What am I to do, Alan?" She bent her head over the railing she clutched so tightly. "I need to be with you. You are the only one who can keep away the nightmares! I've tried sleeping by myself and even napping I begin to dream and it is always awful!" She turned around to face him and her face was anguished. "I realized as Mrs. Holloway was talking that we cannot go on like this. When we go home and on the journey there I shall have to be by myself again."

The two animals were watching anxiously, their gaze going back and forth between the two humans. Sinéad was not jealous that she could not supply Rosamunde with the comfort she needed. She only wanted Rosamunde to have what made her happy.

How much Alan wanted to take her in his arms! But it was only at night that she did not become as a statue in his embrace. Only when she was frightened of the hideous dreams she had, would she cease to be tense.

"There's an easy solution," he said carefully. "Marry me, give me the right to comfort you at night without scandalizing people."

"But I can't be a real wife," she said, her eyes full of pain.

"I told you that I can wait," he said.

"But your marital rights," Rosamunde protested.

"I don't believe in that nonsense," Alan said firmly. "Rosamunde, it has to be mutual. Until you tell me that you want me to make love to you all I shall ever do is hold you, and that I shall do only when you want me to. I give you my word."

"But what if I never–?"

"If and when that happens is when we will worry about it," he said. "When we are home again there are Wizard Healers who might be able to help you forget the worst of what has been done to you."

She was torn, for when she thought about losing the comfort of his arms at night when the nightmares began, something akin to utter panic swept over her. He always seemed to know when she was at the beginning of some vile dream and would awaken her from the horror and then hold her against him until the terrors had subsided. She felt safe in his arms, safer than anywhere else, even safer than with Sinéad.

But what sort of life, what sort of marriage, would it be for him? It was not fair to burden him with a woman who could be no real wife.

"Please, Rosamunde," he said, seeming to know what she was thinking, as he so often did, "I shall take you on any terms. I love you."

"Say yes," said Sinéad softly. " 'Tis the best thing ye can be doin'."

Cathal; nodded. "Brendan will agree," he ventured.

She allowed herself to be persuaded and agreed to a double ceremony with Nate and Laura.

Laura was in alt that they would be brides together. "I was going to ask you to be my bridesmaid but this is better!" she exclaimed. "Ain't it lucky that those friends of yours put two wedding gowns in that package?" For Laura had every intention of wearing the green gown. She loved it so that even the fact that green was considered unlucky could not deter her from wearing it. "And anyway," she said to Rosamunde. "I ain't exactly entitled to wear white!"

These words made Rosamunde miserably aware of what should have been. If she had not let propriety stand in her way and had confessed her love to Alan, she could have been at home, preparing joyously for their wedding, in a white gown,the colour of purity, which she would be able to wear proudly, with all her female relatives and her friends about her as she prepared for the nuptials. Her father would give her away and all the family would be happy for both of them, unlike her marriage to Raymond, which had been attended by sadness, for they knew she was going so far away from them, married to a non-magical stranger.

What was done, was done, though, as the Maharajah Zahallah liked to say. She must do her best to be happy and enjoy the festivities Zahallah was planning with child-like glee.

As the short time until the double wedding closed in Rosamunde began to suffer from painful headaches and was often dizzy. She spent a good deal of every day lying upon the *charpoy* while Alan sat beside her, stroking her forehead with lavender water.

'Wedding jitters', Laura called it. When Alan detected

a fever on some of the worst headache days, Laura said it was not surprising, given all that Rosamunde had been through. "Sometimes people just sort of collapse when they've had to be strong and brave for a long time, and then it's all over," she said when Alan was anxious. " Rose has damn good cause to be sick. She'll perk up when we head home."

Even the *Hakim* seemed to agree with this diagnosis. "She seems to be a young lady of nervous habit," he said after an examination. "And to such, a radical change such as marriage can be overwhelming and manifest itself in many forms of ills." Both Alan and Rosamunde hoped that this was so as the headaches were debilitating and painful even for Alan, who could not stand to watch her suffer. Even the headache powders in his Wizard's bag did not seem to help.

"You make beautiful brides, both of you," said the Maharani Jyoti shyly, in her careful English. She had asked her eldest son what he knew about English marriages and had been excited to find that the bride was traditionally helped to dress by friends and family, not just servants. Both Laura and Rosamunde had spent time in the *zenana*, becoming acquainted with the Maharani and her daughters and they had also become very fond of one another.

Also present was Molly. Rosamunde was glad to see her again and happy for her that she had been married to such a pleasant young man. Molly had been afraid that Rosamunde would despise her for having married a Muslim, but Rosamunde was not prejudiced in that regard in the least. Only the Holloways had cut up stiff about it and had been shocked when every one attended a Muslim ceremony uniting the two again as Niaz had promised the wandering *Maulvi*. Molly was even now taking instruction in Islam.

With Molly came Isha and Hari, now well-loved members of the Ul Mulik household. To Sinéad's satisfaction Isha was a different monkey. He had learned to trust again and had given his heart to Niaz and Molly. The familiar was certain that he would not be hurt again by humans. Niaz and Molly would love him and their other animals always.

Sinéad introduced her animal friends to Cathal and the

two dragons and enjoyed watching their awe at the sight of the dragons.

Even Bharat was present. He was going to carry the bridal couples through the town in a magnificent *howdah* in a small procession. The elderly elephant was much enjoying his retirement and the sweet grass and spoiling he received from his human friends.

The Maharani Jyoti gave each young woman who was to married a long double strand of pearls to wear, which ended in a huge diamond. This was Ranijhat's wedding gift to each of them.

Rosamunde's stomach was churning as they put the finishing touches on their wedding finery. She had shown Laura how the Elves pulled their hair up into a special knot that their new husbands would loosen before they retired to the bridal chamber. The veil of spider webs fit around the knot perfectly and fell to the floor from the top of the head, shrouding each bride in a shimmering cascade of shining, diaphanous fabric. The Maharani and her daughters and the female servants all sighed in awe at the beauty of the veil. The gowns sparkled as well, the wide skirts catching the light and seeming to be every shade of green in the spectrum, changing constantly, like the surface of the ocean.

"Why are you so nervous, honey?" Laura said as they waited for their escorts. Laura's Pa, of course, was to give her away, and Zahallah had begged for the honor of escorting Rosamunde. Ravi was to be Alan's best man, while Sacha would perform this office for Nate. Ravi's sisters were to be bridesmaids. The whole family had fallen in with the idea of an *Angrezi* wedding and had done every thing that they could to make it a successful occasion.

"I don't know," Rosamunde said. "Nothing is going to change. But Laura, I do feel rather ill," she admitted.

"Were you sick like this when you married Raymond?" Laura queried.

"Yes," said Rosamunde, remembering that she had spent the entire morning before that service throwing up.

"It's just wedding jitters, honey, like I said," soothed Laura. "You'll be all right once it's over, just you wait!"

"Aren't *you* nervous, Laura?" Rosamunde asked, her teeth chattering a bit. Why was she so nerved up? This was

Alan she was marrying, *Alan,* not a stranger she barely knew!

Laura grinned. "I ain't got a nerve in my body, Rose honey. I can't wait to be Mrs. Connelly, all nice and legal."

A knock came on the door, it was time to go. Bharat would carry them on a circuit of the city and then they would return to the *Diwan-i-Am* for the weddings.

Sacha said afterwards that it was the most lugubrious wedding service he had ever seen. The Reverend Holloway performed the sacrament as if he had been officiating at a funeral. He left no one in any doubt that he completely disapproved and had performed the ceremony under duress.

Nate and Laura refused to let the dour Reverend douse their joy in being married. Alan and Rosamunde were quieter. He seemed far happier than did she. They exchanged rings for it was a tradition in both their families for the man to wear a ring as well. Reverend Holloway had protested this, for to him, the woman's ring was a symbol that the woman belonged to her husband and was bound to submit to him and defer to his better judgment. A man did not need such a symbol. He was further horrified when Alan insisted that the word 'obey' be struck from the service. He did not want Rosamunde to obey him. Theirs would be a marriage of equals.

Nate enthusiastically kissed his bride while Alan kissed his bride on the cheek. Rosamunde's hand had trembled and felt hot in his and he frowned as he kissed her, for her cheek was warm as well.

"Are you getting another headache?" he whispered as they turned to walk down between the rows of guests who had come to the *Moti Mahal's Diwan-i-Am* to see the *Angrezi* weddings. It seemed as if the whole of Jhat was there and all very enthusiastic.

Rosamunde nodded miserably. She was beginning to feel very dizzy and said, "Alan, I'm so cold!" Suddenly, she was shivering and looked wretched.

Alarmed, he stopped and put his hand to her forehead. Cold? When her hands felt so hot to the touch?

"Rosamunde! You're burning up!" he said in horror.

His look of complete consternation was the last thing she saw before she fainted.

home thoughts from abroad

For the next several weeks Rosamunde had only brief periods of lucidity during which she was completely exhausted between paroxysms of illness. First she would feel incredibly cold, and shiver spasmodically, in spite of the fact that her temperature was increasing. These shivering fits lasted as long as an hour and then were followed by a vicious headache, a feeling of suffocating heat and dry, burning skin. This stage lasted from two to six hours. Lastly came the sweating. It was profuse, but it heralded a declining temperature, leading into an exhausted sleep that went on for two to four hours. When she awake from that she was somewhat rational but it seemed to those caring for her that another paroxysm of shivering came very soon on top of the cessation of sleep.

The *Hakim* confirmed Alan's worst fears when he said "It is what you *Angrezi* call malaria, Alan *Sahib*, but I think not the worst kind which causes death. She will recover, with the help of Allah, but it will be a long road." He was treating her with the help of the cinchona bark, known as Peruvian Bark, with full instructions as to use that Stuart had included in the emergency medical kit. "Just in case", he had told them. Alan was very thankful that his uncle had been so cautious.

Alan could not comprehend how this had happned as both of them had gone to a Wizard Healer who was well used to tropical diseases and the spells put upon them should have prevented this. "I don't understand it!" he said to Sacha midway through her illness, as they were both at her bedside.

"I think I do," said his uncle. "Didn't you tell me that Vishnu removed all the spells that were on the women, the slave jewelry and the no clothing spells and such?"

"Oh, damn!" said Alan. "Why didn't I think of that? *All* the spells were probably removed, even the disease prevention spell! How could I be so stupid as to not think of that?" He looked at Rosamunde as he spoke. She now lay in the exhausted slumber that followed a paroxysm.

"You didn't think of it because you are very nearly as tired as she is," said Sacha gently.

For Rosamunde wanted him by her side every moment. She seemed to know, even in the grip of fever and delirium, when he was not there. Even Sinéad, who had refused to leave her Witch save for food and trips to an earth box, could do little other than watch for the signs of paroxysm and purr to somewhat soothe Rosamunde. She would not lie quietly unless Alan was holding her hand or better yet, lying by her side where she could clutch at him with fever hot hands.

Even now as they spoke, Alan held her hand, and wiped her forehead with a cool cloth, kept that way by magic. He warmed the *charpoy* when she was shivering and cooled it when she was hot.

Laura insisted on helping with the nursing. She proved deft and exceedingly competent at moving Rosamunde, sponging her when the fever was high and doing all the many things that needed doing for someone as sick as her friend. She was a calming presence for Alan as well. With her sturdy good sense and ever hopeful outlook. She had seen a great deal of malaria when she was in New Spain and was able to predict the course of the illness as well as the *Hakim*. She also understood the use of the Peruvian Bark better than he did, for it came from South America, where she had been enslaved.

With a thin tendril of violet light Sacha reached out and touched Rosamunde briefly and carefully. After a moment he said "There are no spells on her at all, Alan, not a one. There are signs of eight having been removed."

The removal of spells left a residue behind that could be read for about six months by a *Magus Magistra* such as Sacha.

"Eight?" Alan repeated, looking at Rosamunde in consternation.

Laura, who had been folding new clean cloths for the sponging at the side of the room, said "We talked about that once, me and Rose. She told me she had what she called a contraceptive spell on her afore she even came out here and the tropical sickness spell too. Then in the *Mahal* we had another contraceptive spell, a spell that stopped our monthly bleeding," she began to count off on her fingers, "the keeping bare spell, the slave jewelry, and Rose had two of them, one for them frigging tit hoops, and the spell for the little toad's game of statues. I make that eight all right," she said.

Two contraceptive spells? That rang an alarm bell in Sacha's mind but he could not mentally track down why this was so. "That explains how she got sick," he said. "Bless Stuart for not placing all his dependence on spells!"

"That bark'll do the trick, Alan," said Laura kindly. "I saw it bring a lot of folks back from the brink. This damned malaria runs three to eight weeks at a time."

"Three to eight weeks!" Alan echoed in dismay.

"But I'm willing to bet she's over the worst of it now. She'll still be sick for a while but I think she's beginning to come out of it," said Laura soothingly. "You watch, already the episodes are further apart, not so much so as you'd notice it particular-like, but just a little bit."

Alan could not see that. He had never seen anyone so ill. He was terrified that she would slip away from him, when he had only just won her.

But in the end, Laura's prediction proved true. Three weeks saw the end of the worst of it. "Rose is a lot tougher than she looks," said Laura, when the *Hakim* expressed surprise that such a frail looking female had shaken off the disease, as he saw it, so easily.

Alan thought there had been nothing easy about it. When late one night he was half asleep by her bedside and she spoke his name, he was overjoyed to see her clear gaze and the light of reason in her eyes, unclouded by the debilitating exhaustion and fever.

"How do you feel?" he asked eagerly, awakening Sinéad, who had been sleeping by her Witch's side, with Cathal close beside her.

"Tired," she said slowly, "Weak. Alan, did I dream it, did we get married?"

"It wasn't a dream, these are wedding rings on our

fingers and you can call yourself Mrs. Stillfield," he said, and raised his left hand to show her his ring.

She said nothing, only looking at him with an unreadable expression. She had lost weight during her illness and her violet eyes seemed enormous in her thin face. She now closed them and turned her head restlessly in the pillow. "I want to go home," she said suddenly. "I want to sleep in my own bed, and see Papa and Mama and the rest of the family, Oh, Alan, take me home, *please!*" She turned back to face him and opened her eyes shaded with anxiety. Her voice was full of longing. "And you'll stay with me, you won't ever leave me?"

He took her hand in his. "I'll never leave you, ever!" he promised. "And as soon as the *Hakim* says you may travel we'll go home, as fast as we can."

"Thank you," she whispered. She wanted very badly to cry but there still seemed to be no tears in her. "I would like to sleep some more. Could you hold me so that I don't dream?"

He agreed to this at once and the little animals moved aside so that he could stretch out beside her after he had kicked off his boots. He took her in his arms and pillowed her head on his shoulder as Cathal and Sinéad snuggled up against them. Sinéad began to purr and they all fell asleep.

When Laura came in some time later to check on Rosamunde she found them like that and as Rosamunde seemed to be sleeping a natural, healing sleep, Laura left them alone.

Alan wanted to get her home as quickly as possible but his proposal of flying up to Russia, over the mountains and from there cross Scandinavia and the North Sea was vetoed by both the *Hakim* and Sacha.

The *Hakim* though that the cold air in the mountains would be bad for her. Sacha agreed. He remembered how cold it had been when he had come to India over those high mountains.

"And besides," added Sacha, "it's nearly December, Alan! There's probably been snow in Russia since the end of October and perhaps even more in Scandinavia. No one in his right mind flies over the North Sea at this time of year. It's frigid, incredibly windy, and it takes a lot out of a dragon even in the summer. We've passengers to think about as well, and they aren't used to dragon-back." He looked at Nate, Laura and Lowell as he spoke, for they were to come back to Ireland. Nate wanted to see the horses there and Alan was certain that his family would want to meet the people who had helped save Rosamunde. They also were to wait there for a shipment of horses that Nate had purchased from Zahallah, which would take some time.

It would have to be the Southern route, they decided. The *Hakim* even thought that the sea air would be good for Rosamunde.

Accordingly, Sacha and Cynara flew south the next day to find out when an English ship with good accommodations for passengers would be sailing for home, either from Calcutta or Bombay.

Alan concentrated on helping Rosamunde return to health, bullying her lovingly into eating and drinking plenty of milk, supporting her when she began walking again, and taking her out into the fresh air, wrapped in a magiced blanket, to sit on the *chabutara* and look out over the forest and the mountains. He watched her very carefully, as, slowly, she began to regain her health. But she said, and he was certain of this as well, that she would not be really well until they were at home. It was all she wanted, all she longed for.

Rosamunde was touched when Ram Dass brought to her something he had rescued from Malabad, something he had almost forgotten about. It was the little trunk that had stood at the foot of her bed and in it were her treasures: her best jewelry, which to her were the pieces that had been given to her by loved family members, her diary, pictures of her family, her little enamel clock that she had put away since Raymond disliked the way it ticked, and an extra set of crystals and harp strings for the *telyn* that Ram Dass had also rescued. Alan was able to mend the broken frame and restore the little harp to its former beauty. Soon she was well enough to sit up on an ottoman like piece of furniture and play and sing Irish airs in her sweet voice.

Ram Dass thought that the looters had left the chest behind because they could not open it. The outside, of course, had healed itself from the rifle butts and clubs that had been used upon it, for it was a potently magical trunk. Rosamunde was very glad to have it and her *telyn* back. She cared nothing for the clothing that had been lost. Ram Dass was also able to give her news of the servants. She was sad to hear of the death of Alam Din and the others, but glad to hear that Sita and her *syce* Kashan had been spared. Ram Dass had even brought her little mare, Devika, back to Ranijhat and the mare was to go to Ireland with the horses Nate had purchased, as was Alan's gelding Akhil, who had been returned from Jhaniput by a servant of Sishul's and Parminder's.

All the same, Alan was still concerned about his new wife, for she was very quiet and played nothing but the most heart rending, melancholy songs upon the *telyn*. Alan even caught Laura standing outside Rosamunde's room one day, silently crying as she listened to Rosamunde play and sing in Gaelic.

"It'd tear your heart out!" she said when Alan offered her a handkerchief. She wiped her face and blew her nose furiously. "Here I thought she'd be happy, to be married to you, Alan, and to be going home, but listening to that, she sure as hell ain't happy yet!"

Rosamunde was playing the poignant and beautiful Londonderry air with all the pathos imaginable. It was said to be a Faerie tune from ancient times. As they listened to the Gaelic, which Alan was not about to translate for Laura, as the lyrics were to the version of the song known as '*The Confessions of Dervorgilla*' and began "Oh, shrive me, father" and went on more heartrendingly from there, Rosamunde began to sing in English Thomas Moore's setting, "*My Gentle Harp*".

My gentle harp, once more I waken
The sweetness of thy slumbering strain.
In tears our last farewell was taken
And now in tears we meet again.
Yet even then, while peace was singing,
Her halcyon song o'er land and sea.
Though joy and hope to others bringing,
She only brought new tears to thee.

"Jesus H. Christ!" Laura muttered.

A shrill feline voice interrupted this, fortunately in Alan's view. "I'm hearing a dragon coming!"

Alan opened the door as Rosamunde put down the *telyn*. She sometimes still needed support when walking and he knew she would come to her feet quickly when she heard that Sacha had returned, hopefully with news of a ship leaving for home.

She smiled gently at him when he came into the room. "You always know when I need you," she said. "Sinéad said she hears a dragon." She was holding on to the back of the furniture as she spoke. As he had worried, she had indeed stood up too quickly. He took her on his arm, and led her, followed by Laura, out to front of the *Mahal* where Cynara had just landed.

Nearly everyone had gathered outside, in spite of the chill air. Alan threw a warming spell around Rosamunde, since other than the sheltered terrace, she had not been outdoors at all.

The two dragons were eager to nuzzle her hair and express their joy at seeing her again and that she was getting well.

And Sacha had excellent news for them. "In a week's time," he said, "a British ship, a passenger ship called *Pearl of the Orient,* sets sail from Bombay. I secured three cabins, one each for the married couples and one Lowell and I can share, and there is a dragon deck as well, capable of a three dragon load. The *Pearl* carries nothing but passengers and is considered a luxury ship. I was quite impressed with the cleanliness and spaciousness when I looked her over. There are stewards to wait on the passengers and even a doctor. She's well used to carrying Witches and Wizards and there are accommodations for familiars. She travels by the way of the Cape of Good Hope so we shall be on her all the way to Southampton. I've already sent a telegram home, telling them when the *Pearl* expects to arrive in England."

Rosamunde's eyes shone like stars. Home! At one point she had never thought to see it again. She clutched at Alan's arm, trembling in her joy, Sinéad's furry face rubbing against hers as she sat on her Witch's shoulder. They were all going home. They would not be home for Christmas but spring would be beginning when they arrived, and at the thought of the soft green glory of spring in Ireland Rosamunde felt something like wings rise inside her. No more heat and dust, only misty green. Lilacs, daffodils and country flowers, green, green meadows dotted with white lambs, no more palm trees or bullocks, but oak and beech and birch and best of all, her dear, dear family.

55

poisonous tongues

Sacha had been wrong about the *Pearl of the Orient* carrying nothing but passengers, she was also a mail ship, The *RMS Pearl of the Orient, RMS* meaning Royal Mail Steamer. India to the British Isles was not her usual run, that was Singapore to San Francisco, but since the Mutiny she had been especially commissioned to carry refugees home and carry urgent mail from survivors as well.

She was relatively small, only 207 feet, but she could carry as many as 115 passengers and had a crew of 82. She had three masts and two paddle wheels amidships. She was fast, ten knots an hour. This was not as fast as the sailing ships, the tea clippers, which could make as much as 18 knots for a short run, but it was a steady ten knots with the combination of steam and sail.

It was nearly 4,000 nautical miles from Bombay to Southampton in Britain. There would be stops at Cape Town, at Fernando Po, an American base off Cameroon, St Helena, and Gibraltar before finally reaching Southampton. They would be nearly two months at sea. This was far better than the time they had made coming out to India, but the *RMS Pearl* was several steps above the elderly East Indiaman and the little steamer from Suez.

It was also far more luxurious. A large dining salon stood on the upper deck, there was a "Ladies' Only" salon, and the cabins, although far smaller than the sumptuous rooms in the *Moti Mahal* in Ranijhat, were comfortable and well planned.

Both couples were advised to have new passports made out for the ladies as their marriages had been so recent, and they did so at the British Isles Legation in Bombay. It felt odd to Rosamunde to write her name as "Rosamunde Stillfield." But it enabled her to share a cabin with Alan and therefore she would be able to sleep at night, since he kept her safe from evil dreams.

They hadn't much baggage, any of them. Sacha always traveled light, two sets of everyday buckskins and a dressier one with fringe and beads were all he ever wore. And the others, except for Alan, had lost most of their belongings in the Mutiny.

But they were not alone in this. The *Pearl* was full of refugees from the Mutiny. The woman and children had only been evacuated from Lucknow on November 19th and from many other areas all over Hindustan people were still straggling into the ports. Many of them were near destitution and had no money to purchase a berth home particularly on a ship like the *Pearl*, which cost 100 guineas for the trip to Southampton. Alan used Chenevix's letter of credit and set up a fund so that refugees could take up the many empty berths in the *Pearl* and even granted them a sum of money for clothing and other accoutrements. Sacha contributed to this as well, for he had a large fortune of his own.

Brendan and Cynara would be the only two dragons on the large dragon deck towed by the ship. Due to the dragon deck being magiced for buoyancy it was not a drag on the ship's speed.

Rosamunde bore the flight from Ranijhat to Bombay very well. She was so keyed up by excitement that Alan was anxious and insisted on putting her to bed as soon as they boarded ship. The bed was far larger than the narrow bunks on the other ships they had journeyed on and Rosamunde was happy to see that there would be room for Alan and the familiars as well, although small pull-out couches were provided for familiars. The *Pearl* was used to magical passengers; it even employed a Wind Wizard. The doctor, however, was not a Wizard Healer, but he was experienced in dealing with malaria and at Alan's insistence, came to see Rosamunde when the ship had put out to sea.

He was a young man, by the name of Charles Murgatroyd and was very brisk and competent. He gave her a clean bill of health, for the moment, but cautioned them that malaria could recur sometimes unexpectedly. He advised her to see a Wizard Healer when they reached home, as a spell could purge the disease from her system.

"Often wished I had magic," he confided as he closed up his little black bag, "Those fellows can do so much more with magic than I can!"

"My father is a Wizard Healer," said Rosamunde, smiling at him.

"Well, there, you're all set then!" he said with an answering smile. "Now, Mrs. Stillfield, try and get as much fresh air as you can until we head into rough waters. They set up chairs on the deck for ladies and I shall put your name down for one if you like. The wind can be a little strong as it blows from the north east this time of year, but it is invigorating. Just wrap up well."

"I would like that," she said.

"I'll make certain that she does not overdo it, Doctor," said Alan. "I don't want her getting sick again. Perhaps she should try and sleep now? We came a long ways dragon-back yesterday."

"Yes, she'll need plenty of rest. You look as if you could use some rest yourself, Mr. Stillfield," said the doctor. "Come and see me if you need any sleeping powders."

But of course, Alan would never take sleeping powders as he felt he must be easy to rouse if Rosamunde needed him.

At the beginning, the voyage was almost idyllic. At this time of year, the Indian Ocean could be home to tropical cyclones, causing the dangerous *tsunamis* that could swamp ships and cause catastrophic damage on land. But the weather was largely fair, allowing Rosamunde to sit out on the deck, in company with husband, friends and familiars. Sacha, with Nate's help, took on many of the dragon duties in order to let Alan stay with Rosamunde, who fretted if he left her alone too long.

Sacha viewed this with concern and hoped that she would soon get over this dependence on Alan. It was not good for either one of them. Nate, with whom he discussed this, seemed to feel that when Rosamunde was really well again she would find her way, right now she was still of an invalidish habit, and still weak, although she was much improved over what she had been. Sick folks, he assured Sacha, took fancies to or against things and what the women had been through in Jhaniput was enough to make anyone clingy.

Laura liked to sit with Rosamunde and 'watch the pass' as she termed it. Nearly all the passengers took a daily or even twice daily turn on the deck, and from their chairs the two friends could see the many women and children, many of them widows and orphans, that walked past them on the upper deck.

"Never seen so much black in all my born days," said Laura one bright morning as a large group of women in badly dyed, much mended black garments walked by, shepherding a group of children, all of whom wore black as well. "The English sure make a fuss out of black mourning clothes."

"But people go into mourning in the United States, do they not?" Rosamunde inquired. Sinéad was curled at her feet, snoozing in the sun.

"Not where I come from, honey," said Laura. "Out on the frontier you're damn lucky if you get a set of work clothes and a Sunday go to meeting outfit. We're even lucky if there's a meeting to go to on Sunday, preachers being as scarce as hen's teeth. And it's a long way to go sometimes, to a place where you can get dry goods or sewing supplies, much less somewhere you can get black clothes. What's wrong, honey? You got a headache?" She noticed that Rosamunde was rubbing her forehead.

"Slightly," Rosamunde admitted. "The water is so bright..." she sighed. "Do you think Alan and Nate will be back soon, Laura? They've been gone so long!"

"They just went to get us some tea, Rose, and they were going by to check on the dragons. They'll be back in a minute." Laura said soothingly.

"Sacha and your father are down on the dragon deck. They can look after the dragons and we could have ordered tea from the steward," said Rosamunde, sounding a trifle petulant. She rubbed at her forehead again.

"Men folk need to stretch their legs, honey. It isn't until they get old that they take a liking to setting in the sun," Laura pointed out.

Rosamunde had not told anyone that on getting out of bed that morning she had felt dizzy, and walking up to the deck on Alan's arm she had been unable to look at anything too closely, for it had a tendency to slip sideways. She was not going to be sick again! She would not let it have its way with her again. She was going home and she was going to be well when she got there. She wished it were not so chilly out here on the deck, but Laura did not seem to feel the cold.

Another group of black clad women came onto the deck, and seated themselves in a group of deck chairs a little distance from Rosamunde and Laura, pointedly ignoring both the young women, one of them going so far as to turn her chair about so that her back was to them.

Rosamunde stiffened, the headache beating behind her eyes now. "That woman has given us the cut direct!" she said, affronted. "Pray, who does she think she is?"

Laura chuckled. "Don't go all society lady on me, Rose! That lady is a Mrs. Prouty and her late husband was a bishop. He was killed by natives in their mission near Agra. She's full of piss and vinegar water and she told me to my face that I'm–how did she put it–, Oh, yes, "a disgrace to Christian womanhood" because I'm married to a black man. You're associating with me, I reckon, so obviously you're cut from the same cloth and approve such goings on."

"Laura, that's horrible!" Rosamunde said, appalled. She clenched her hands on the blanket to hide their trembling.

"I guess I'll be glad when we get home. There's been so much marriage between blacks and Indians and white people at home that most of the time you can't even take a guess at what anyone's kin folks was. You British think too much about the colour of someone's skin, not you and Alan and Sacha, but a lot of the others we met did," Laura said frankly.

"No one in our family will treat you and Nate like that," said Rosamunde quickly.

"I know they won't, honey, and I don't mind Mrs. Prouty. She's just an ignorant old piss ant, is what she is and I don't pay her no never mind."

Just at this moment the Bishop's relict's voice rose above the other noises on the deck and pronounced: "And the Captain, if you may imagine such a thing, had the complete temerity to ask me to speak words of comfort to a woman who was ravished by natives and now finds herself in the family way! As if any decent Christian would wish to associate with a female who has had knowledge of a man outside marriage! And to be increasing from an encounter with a native! Such women are the same as a woman of the streets, unfit to be in the same room with their betters."

"She would have down better to put an end to herself!" came another's shrill voice. "She can never show her face in decent society again! Why we would be polluted by the mere association with such a befouled creature!"

It is my fervent belief," stated Mrs. Prouty viciously, "that such creatures are promiscuous by nature and claiming that they were forced is only a justification for what they secretly wanted all along! Promiscuous Jezebels, all of them!"

There were shocked gasps from her auditors, shock tinged with avid salacious curiosity.

"Such women are little better than prostitutes and if we obeyed the injunctions of the Bible as we had ought to do, they would be stoned," Mrs. Prouty continued. "It is our Christian duty to at least shun them for their sin."

Laura said under her breath. "Self righteous old bitch! Why don't you go back and actually read the Bible and see what Jesus said about Mary Magdalen?"

A clacking sound disturbed her and she looked up to see Rosamunde with her teeth chattering wildly, arms about herself, staring at her. Her eyes were bright with rising fever. "Laura," she got out, "Don't let them stone me, please, Laura..."

"For God's sake!" Laura said, alarmed, and jumped up to put her arms around her friend. "I'm right here, honey and Alan's coming. Nobody's going to stone you!"

"But I'm a whore, Laura," she said in a whisper."I'm promiscuous, just like my mother..." Her eyes looked beyond Laura to stare at something her friend could not see.

"Sinéad! Wake up!" Laura said harshly, pulling the blanket that covered Rosamunde's legs up around her shoulders. "Go get Alan, *pronto!*"

Sinéad woke abruptly and hissed, her fur standing on end. She sprang down from the chair only to run into Alan who was coming around the corner with a laden tea tray. When he saw Laura trying to comfort Rosamunde and how his wife shivered convulsively, he dropped the tray in a crash of crockery and ran forward to take her into his arms and take her back to their cabin, shouting for Nate and Cathal, who had followed him closely, to run and get the doctor.

There followed a period which none of them could remember in later years without a shudder.

Rosamunde was far more ill this time, with higher fever and delirium. She had one idea in her head, that she was going to be stoned for promiscuity and all her ravings were this same endless refrain. Even Alan had trouble soothing her. She relived every horror of Jhaniput over and over.

Dr. Murgatroyd told Alan that it was not unusual for someone as ill as his wife to have a fixation, often a morbid one, while in delirium. Without telling the doctor all the horrors of Jhaniput, Alan did tell him that she had been raped. Much of her raving was in Gaelic, for which Alan was thankful. There was too much attention being paid to Rosamunde by the other ladies on board, who seemed eager to hear every detail of her illness, a morbid curiosity that Alan found revolting.

"Then I am not surprised at this fixation she has developed," Dr. Murgatroyd said quietly when Alan told him of this. "There are certain females on this ship, Mr. Stillfield, who seem to delight in making the sufferings of women like your wife much worse, by their supposed Christian piety. Mrs. Prouty and her coterie are particularly loud in their condemnation of any woman who had the misfortune to be violated during the Mutiny. One of the women below decks, who is with child from a rape, tried to kill herself the other day after hearing a diatribe from Mrs. Prouty about how she was now unfit to inhabit the same planet as a good Christian. I told Mrs. Prouty where she might take her piety but it seems to have made no impression on her, even the Captain speaking to her has had no effect. If she does not cease I shall order her locked in her cabin and dosed with laudanum. I realize of course, that it is a combination of grief and fear for the future that must be driving her but I cannot not allow her to have such a grave, even dangerous affect on others."

"Why don't I give her laryngitis?" Sacha suggested sardonically.

"While I cannot sanction such an action, sir," said Dr. Murgatroyd, with a tired smile, "it would certainly be helpful."

"Consider it done," said Sacha.

Save for Laura and Sinéad, who sat with Rosamunde, now in exhausted sleep, they were all in Sacha's and Lowell's cabin, conferring with the doctor over what was to be done for Rosamunde.

"I am concerned about what will happen after Cape Town is reached," Dr. Murgatroyd said. "I know for a fact that there are no Wizard Healers in Cape Town and she needs to see someone with magical healing skills as soon as possible. I am also worried about what will happen when we reach the Atlantic and then the Bay of Biscay. The waters are very rough this time of year and I don't like to think of her suffering from *mal de mer* on top of malaria. I am aware that she is held to be a good sailor, but her constitution is much weakened."

"Brendan says he can fly her home from Cape Town," Cathal said suddenly. Everyone turned to stare at him.

"That's too far!" Sacha said at once. "He'd have to fly a long way over open water. No dragon could carry enough firestone to do that. It's why we have dragon decks. Even if he hugged the coast of Africa, most of it is savage and unexplored and much of the coast is in the hands of countries of the Inquisition, Brendan would be shot down on sight if he was too low and if he ever had to land, you would all be put to death for being magical."

"Brendan says that he learned things in Tibet that can make it possible and that he can now fly over two hundred miles an hour," said Cathal.

"That's impossible!" said Sacha disbelievingly. "The fastest dragon ever clocked only achieved 115 miles per hour. The average is much more like 75. Lakota is very fast and he can only do 100 miles an hour or so."

"Brendan is certain that he can do it," Cathal insisted. "Please, for Rosamunde's sake, go and talk to him and see what he has to say. We can't take any chances with her life!"

Sacha suddenly remembered the Brendan of Ranijhat, the calm confident dragon who seemed to be able to tap into some esoteric energy that Sacha had never seen before in all of the years that he had been working with dragons.

"I'll try anything rather than lose her," said Alan briefly. "I'd trust Brendan with my life, with both our lives."

Two days later they put in at Cape Town. There was some dragon traffic in this area (mostly mail between the very limited settled areas and carried by the small Welsh Reds) and they were able to obtain the supplies that Brendan told them they needed.

First of all, firestone, and both Alan and Sacha were surprised by how little Brendan claimed he would need.

"At the monastery they taught us how to prolong the effects of firestone," Brendan explained. "That is why I can do this for Rosamunde."

He also planned to carry his four passengers, Alan and Rosamunde and their familiar, in a breast harness, not unlike that of an ambulance dragon. They would be well wrapped against the cold and Rosamunde would be placed against his breast so that the heat from his body would keep her warm. A canvas top and sides would make the litter almost as if it were a little tent. A saddle was useless, he explained, as he would be going so fast that they would be swept from their seats by the force of the wind he would create.

Brendan carefully planned his route. They would halt at Fernando Po, fly across East Africa, stop at Madeira, (which had belonged to Britain since the end of the war with Napoleon) and from there, the most difficult part, the longest distance, to Chenevix Duchis in Dorsetshire. Stuart and a Wizard Healer familiar with tropical diseases could meet them there. Going to Dorset would be quicker than traveling all the way to Ireland and it would still be 'home' to Rosamunde as they had spent a great deal of time there since they were children. And it was closer to London, where specialists could be found.

Since a joint American/British effort of magic had allowed the laying of telegraph cables in most places, the family could be telegraphed from Cape Town and warned of their arrival. The message had to be very brief, however, and in the end all Sacha had space for was *"Arriving early - Dorset - Rosamunde ill - malaria."*

Only a day after their arrival in Cape Town Brendan set off, with the four of them encased in the tent-like breast carrier.

It was with extreme trepidation that Sacha watched Brendan spiral up into the air. Following directions in the emergency medical book they had put Rosamunde in a state of stasis. She would not get worse, but she would not improve either. This spell could only be used for five days at the most for after that it became dangerous. There was a real threat of the patient slipping from stasis into coma and from there to death. Brendan was confident that he could have them home in that length of time

As he stood with Cynara, Laura, Nate and Lowell, watching the dragon spiral up into the sky, Sacha wondered if he would ever see any of them again. This was an incredible long shot.

Soon Brendan had gained height and was just a speck to his human watchers. Cynara with her long dragon sight, suddenly said "Oh, my goodness!" and stood up on her hind legs as astonished dragons often did.

"What is it, sweetheart?" Sacha queried.

"He took off like a rocket!" she exclaimed. "I've never seen anything like it! The speed is incredible!" She turned her long neck and looked at the humans. "He just might do it, he just might! If he can sustain his flight from Madeira to Dorset, they will make it!"

56

sir quentin davies

Rosamunde was having such a pleasant dream. It was so vivid and so real, without the distortions that marred so many excursions in the land of Nod.

She was in her room at Chenevix Duchis. She recognized it at once without even looking around her. The room had been hers since she was a little girl. It was in one of the older parts of the house, with a plaster ceiling with painted medallions of wildflowers. Honey coloured wainscoting was halfway up the walls and a carving of flowers and small animals ran around the top of the wall. She had always loved to lay in bed on a frosty morning, for they spent almost every Christmas at Chenevix Duchis, and looked at the animals and the flowers. A little mouse peeked out from some wheat sheaves, a hedgehog sat beneath a poppy, a cat played with a bunch of grapes. Her great grandfather once told her that these had been carved by monks and she liked to think that the spirits of the monks and the animals were protecting her.

The fireplace, which was burning with her favorite apple wood, was surrounded with Delft tiles of blue and white. She remembered spending hours studying these, looking at the windmills, canals and houses of Holland, and the wooden-shoed people, so different from her world.

She lay in a roomy tester bed, with a fine canopy of crocheted lace. The bed was of light wood, in the now old fashioned Chippendale style, with a matching escritoire, a dressing table, chairs and tables. The chairs and a little sopha in front of the bright brass fender on the fire were upholstered in a misty blue and the carpet was blue and gold . She had worked the fire screen her own self and examples of her needlework, mostly florals and birds, hung on the blue walls.

The sheets smelled of lavender and the comforter was of wadded blue silk. She was cozy and warm and she could hear the hiss of sleet against the windows, as well as the ticking of her little clock and the crackle of the fire. It always made her feel safe and secure to be warm in bed and hear the sleet on the windows, knowing she need not be out in it and everyone she loved was safe and warm as well within the old walls of the house.

Sinéad lay beneath her hand, sound asleep. Rosamunde did not want to awaken for the dream was too real, too much what she had longed for. She was afraid to wake up and find that she was still someplace she did not want to be.

And then someone turned a page in a book.

Rosamunde turned her head and saw her father sitting by her bedside. Spectacles on his nose, he was reading a tome entitled *Infectious Tropical Diseases*.

He was quite engrossed in this but he felt her eyes upon him and looked up and smiled at her. Carefully marking his place he said "You're awake at last. How do you feel?"

"Papa, this isn't a dream?" she said slowly.

"No, my darling girl, you are at Chenevix Duchis in your own room." Stuart rose and came to her bed and bent over her to drop a kiss on her forehead. He then felt her forehead with a practiced hand and taking a watch from his waistcoat pocket, took her pulse. "No fever, good strong pulse," he said in satisfaction.

"What happened? How did I get here?" Rosamunde inquired. She felt weak and tired, but she had to know, for the last thing she remembered with any clarity was the ship they had boarded in Bombay.

"You became ill again just before the ship made Cape Town and Brendan flew you home from there."

She looked at him in disbelief. "But a dragon can't fly that far over water!" she said.

"It seems that Brendan can. He learned quite a few things at the place in Tibet, amongst them, flying at incredible speed and making the most of the firestone he chewed," Stuart answered. "We owe him your life, Rosamunde."

"Where's Alan?" Rosamunde demanded, trying to sit up in bed. "He promised that he would not leave me alone." Her movement woke up Sinéad, who yawned and stretched, showing her little pink tongue.

Stuart put out a hand and gently pushed his daughter

back down amidst the soft, down filled pillows. "I gave him a sedative and put him to bed," he said.

"But why isn't he here with me?" she said. "I need him!"

"He needs his rest more, Rosamunde. When I think he is sufficiently restored I will let him join you, but not until then. And yes," Stuart added. Seeing the look on her face, "I know that you are married, that it is perfectly permissible for him to be in here with you, but he is on the verge, in my opinion, of a nervous collapse, at the very least utterly exhausted, and needs to spend a great deal of time in his bed, alone and sleeping uninterrupted. You both need building up and good food."

"Now," he continued briskly, "there are a few things you need to know, Rosamunde. I had Joseph Lane down from London and between us we purged you of the malaria, so you need not worry about that again. And Sir Quentin Davies is arriving tomorrow to see you as well."

"But is he not an *alienist,* Papa?" Rosamunde said.

"Yes, my dear, and after what was done to you in Jhaniput you badly need to talk about it. Sir Quentin can help you come to terms with it and help with those bad dreams."

"Alan told you about Jhaniput?" Rosamunde said in a small voice, seeming to shrink in upon herself. "And you still love me, Papa?"

"Why would I not love you?" he retorted. "Do you think that any of us blame you for what was done to you; that we consider it in any way your fault?"

"But Papa, I'm ruined, I'm no better than a whore. I cannot understand why anyone can even look at me without shuddering! " she said, her hands tightening on the silken comforter.

Sinéad had listened to them talk back and forth without comment. Now she said, rather blightingly, "Sure, and that's foolish talk! Does not Alan love ye so much that he held ye in his arms all the way from Cape Town without a thought for any one save ye? And were they not all crying with joy when Brendan landed here and they saw ye again? And was not yer Ma sitting beside ye all night, stroking yer hair even after Alan was telling her about Jhaniput? And even yer grands have all been being in to see ye!"

"They all know?" Rosamunde said, her eyes fixed painfully on her father.

"Only your mother and I know the full extent of what happened, my dear," said Stuart gently. "The others know that you were sexually assaulted. It will be up to you as to what you want to tell the rest of the family. Everyone is here save the children. When Sacha wired us that you had malaria I judged to best to keep them away. They are a noisy group and you need quiet. It would have distressed the little ones to see you so ill. But they are constantly scrying for news of you."

Stuart would never forget the sight of Brendan spiraling down to land in front of the Ducal mansion. The dragon had made an incredible journey but his only thought had been his passengers. And both Alan and Rosamunde had been more dead than alive. Even the familiars were in a state of utter tiredness.

Alan would not even change his clothes until he had seen to Rosamunde's comfort and given her over to the care of Dr. Lane and Stuart. Then he waited anxiously in the library with the other family members until Stuart and the assisting Wizard Healer, knowledgeable about tropical fevers, had treated her.

Then Alan had requested a private interview with Stuart and Julia, telling them of all that he had learned and seen of what had happened to Rosamunde at Jhaniput. By the end of this recital he was in tears, with Julia's arms about him. That was when Stuart decided to put his nephew / son-in-law to bed and treat him as another patient. Alan, after scant recovery from a serious illness, had been living on his nerves for far too long. Stuart bullied Alan into taking a sedative and let Tatya put him to bed. She and Simon stayed beside him until they saw him sleeping deeply, and left him in Cathal's capable paws. The familiar would let them know if there were any problems.

Now as Rosamunde once more said that she had to have Alan beside her, that only he could take away the nightmares, Stuart said "I never thought I would have to accuse you of selfishness, Rosamunde, but you cannot continue to use Alan as a buffer. His health will not stand for it. I know that you have been ill, and ill-treated as well, but now you must learn to deal with what has happened, which I hope that Sir Quentin willhelp you in."

"But the dreams," she said on a whisper.

"Have you had a bad dream recently?" her father asked.

"No," said Rosamunde slowly, wrinkling her brow.

"In stasis you would not dream of course, but you have been out of that state for two days now and mostly asleep," Stuart explained. "You also had a very special visitor, Rosamunde, Oberon himself. He brought you a gift."

He rose and went to a small table with a door beneath the single drawer. Opening the door, Stuart reached in and pulled out a crystal flask.

"I would give a fortune to know how this is made and how it works," he said, holding up the flask so that Rosamunde could see it. "If we only had this to give to all patients in delirium or hysterical, what a blessing that would be! And you are uncommonly fortunate, my dear, that the King of the *Sidhe* thinks enough of you to share this Elfin secret."

"What is it?" Rosamunde asked.

"Your grandfather, who can read Elfish script, says a good translation would be "No Evil Dreams". Oberon explained to us that but one drop of this will guarantee you a deep sleep with pleasant dreams. However, this is not something you may take indefinitely as there is not a lot of it here and Oberon tells me that even for the Elves it is difficult to make. That is why I shall have you working with Sir Quentin. An alienist may help you control and banish those dreams. Now, I am going to give you a dose and send you back to sleep until it is time for dinner. And yes, if Alan is awake and sufficiently rested, I shall allow him to come and see you. Your mother is going to come in and sit with you, as well. I'll call her now."

Stuart gave two tugs to an embroidered bell pull as he spoke and then turned to the bedside table where a water pitcher stood beside a crystal glass, kept cool by magic. He poured a glass of water, and added one small drop of the Elfin fluid to it.

Instantly, it turned a lovely blue and a sweet spicy fragrance filled the room.

Stuart helped her sit up and drink down the contents

of the glass. It was delicious, tasting of fruit of some sort and sweet with honey. It left a delightful flavor upon the tongue.

As Rosamunde lay back down amongst the pillows Julia entered the room and with a glad cry, hurried to Rosamunde's side.

The last thing that Rosamunde remembered before she slid into sleep was Julia's arms about her and her head being pillowed on her mother's breast as Julia wept tears of thankfulness to have her daughter returned to them.

Rosamunde liked Sir Quentin Davies at once. He was of medium height and spare of figure, in his late fifties and had a shock of graying dark hair that reminded her of Lyon. He wore spectacles and a short beard and had very kind eyes under heavy gray brows. He listened intently to everything that Stuart told her about his daughter and then asked to be alone with Rosamunde.

He sat down at her bedside, and took a pocketbook and pencil from inside his coat and flipped it open. He smiled at her. "Your expression is a little fearful, Mrs. Stillfield. Have you ever worked with an alienist ?"

Rosamunde shook her head. "I'm not really certain what you do," she confessed.

"In simplest terms, doctors such as I help people cope. We help you get to the root of your problems and help you find solutions," he said. He had a very soothing voice, deep and mellow. "Years ago, it was the practice to actually manipulate the memory through magic, to erase traumatic events, but we have learned better now. It is far better to help the patient learn how to deal with and manage suffering and pain, for the memory of the stress can return unexpectedly and it is often far worse than it was originally."

"What do I have to do?" Rosamunde inquired. She was still nervous. She did not know if she could even speak about Jhaniput to this doctor, as kind as he was. She had been unable to say anything to her parents about it.

"We'll just talk," he said, smiling at her. "Make yourself comfortable now. Why don't you tell me how you happened to go out to India?"

After an hour with Rosamunde, Sir Quentin joined Stuart and Alan in the library for a glass of Madeira. Stuart had promised the rest of the family to let them know what Sir Quentin had said.

One of the talents that made Sir Quentin so successful in his profession was that of empathy and it had allowed him to 'read' Rosamunde.

"She is very deeply ashamed of what was done to her. She feels defiled and dirtied and blames herself for letting it happen," he told his listeners. "There is a great deal of guilt and anger there as well."

"But she could not have prevented it!" Alan cried. He still looked tired but was in far better shape than he had been. "Even had she all her magic I doubt that she could have prevailed against the level of black magic in that awful place! I had to have the help of a God to do so."

"I shall wish to hear all about that as well," said Sir Quentin. "As we talked, it became obvious that she expects some punishment for her sins as she thinks of them."

"When she was delirious on the ship she worried that she was going to be stoned for lewdness," Alan said angrily. "Our friend Laura told me that they over-heard some old biddy of a bishop's widow saying that women who had been raped by natives ought to be shunned or stoned as harlots, that they were no longer fit to be with decent Christians. It seemed to prey upon Rosamunde's mind to an incredible degree."

"Hearing this merely reinforced her own opinion," said Sir Quentin. "Society does persist in blaming the victim of a rape, as if it were her fault and from what you tell me, Mrs. Stillfield spent nearly six months being violated repeatedly by a multitude of men."

Stuart closed his eyes briefly and clenched his fists, unable to even think about his daughter being so used, it made him want to hurt someone very badly.

"I shall want you to tell me, Mr. Stillfield, your own observations. I think this is going to be a long and wearing task. Her anguish runs very deep. I also think that it will help if she could talk to someone, preferably another woman, who

531

has gone through this and has come to terms with it."

"Laura will be here shortly," Alan said eagerly. "She was with Rosamunde at the *Kala Mahal.* "

Sir Quentin shook his head. "The friend who shared her enslavement? No, Mrs. Connelly is too close to the situation. We need someone who has been in a similar but different circumstance. I shall have to make inquiries..."

"I think I know someone who might know of a woman – Professor Williamson at Oxford," said Alan suddenly. "Sex magic is his subject."

"Of course!" Sir Quentin approved. "I shall wire him at once."

"I shall go and see him at once," Alan amended. "Brendan says that he is well rested now. We shall leave this afternoon while Rosamunde is sleeping and we can be returned before she even misses me. I will lay odds that Professor Williamson is acquainted with some one who will be able to speak to Rosamunde."

57

helena

Chenevix Duchis lay in the Dorset Uplands between Cerne Abbas and Maiden Newton. From Dorchester, some miles to the south, it was less than ninety miles to Oxford to the north in Oxfordshire, so it was not even that to the University city from Chenevix Duchis.

Brendan flew fast and low, going northeast, and passed over Salisbury Plain where soon many magical peoples would be gathering for the Winter Solstice at Stonehenge. Almost every year since he was little Alan had attended this festival. Witches danced, there were bards and celebration as well as the sacred rituals of the Druids for the shortest night, which of course meant that the days would now lengthen. He doubted that he would attend this year, for he could not leave Rosamunde. She was barely well enough to leave her bed as yet.

It was amazing how effortlessly Brendan flew now. He ate but little firestone and glided through the air as if he were swimming in it. In no time at all they were above the city of Oxford, its towers obscured by the mist of a very light snow falling.

It was the Christmas holiday, but Alan had taken the precaution of scrying his old professor and making an appointment to visit him at his home, just outside the city.

Professor Williamson had told him that there was a landing place suitable for dragons quite near the house and Brendan spiraled down to this. The snow that had fallen and was still coming down was very light. Not even an inch had accumulated as yet.

After the heat of India the snow felt wonderful. When Brendan landed Alan remained in the saddle for a moment, tilting his face up to the sky and letting the snow caress him. At this moment he felt as if he would never complain about winter again. Cathal, who had ridden in the front pocket of Alan's flying suit, stretched his paws out to the lightly falling flakes.

Brendan said the he would be quite happy waiting in the field. There were trees for shelter and he would more than likely take a nap.

The Williamson house was set amongst trees on a spacious lawn. It was a good sized, two story dwelling with turrets, a Wizard's Tower and a mansard roof. A large porch wrapped itself around the house and this was littered with toys. As Alan, with Cathal on his shoulder, climbed the front stairs, the door opened abruptly and what at first seemed a horde of small children shrieked in delight. A boy of about ten clutching a bag of dragon treats said breathlessly "Please, sir, may we go and see your dragon?"

"Of course," said Alan, "His name is Brendan and he likes children," he said as an older woman came up behind the group which on second glance proved to be only six children.

"You must be Mr. Stillfield," the woman said, smiling at him. "I'm Mrs. Williamson, and these are our grandchildren. You are not to pester the dragon to give you a ride!" she said, raising her voice as the children, bundled into winter coats, streamed towards the field where Brendan waited.

"They won't be able to persuade him" Alan reassured her, entering the hall and stamping the snow from his shoes on a mat provided for that purpose. "If I have time I shall be glad to take them up before I return to Dorset." He introduced Cathal to Mrs. Williamson.

"That would be very kind. They are all dragon mad, Dragon Day does not come often enough as far as they are concerned! And with Christmas and the Solstice coming they are in alt all of the time." She led Alan into a small room that had a rack and pegs for outdoor clothing. "You may leave your flying suit here," she said "and I shall go and tell my husband that you are come. I'll be back to take you to him in the library."

Alan stripped off the flying suit and with the aid of a convenient mirror smoothed his hair and twitched his cravat into place.

It seemed a very comfortable home, casual and easy in manner. The furniture was not new and from the evidence about the children, like in his family, were not banished to an austere nursery above stairs.

Mrs. Williamson returned in a few moments and said "Would you care for some wine or tea, Mr. Stillfield? And some refreshment for you as well?" she asked Cathal. "Our familiars like my milk punch." Cathal agreed eagerly to this.

"Tea would be most welcome, thank you," Alan said. "It was a chilly flight. If it would not be too much trouble, my dragon would probably appreciate a cup as well."

She smiled at him. She was in her late forties or early fifties, he would guess, tall and slender and very fair with bright blue eyes and a charming face that was quite lovely. "We haven't a dragon-sized tea set but I daresay a pudding basin would do in a pinch," she said.

"Thank you. Brendan will appreciate it," he said, with an answering smile as they went through a drawing room where a Christmas tree stood, gleaming with mage lights and glass ornaments and under a preservation spell. Christmas greenery of fir branches, holly and mistletoe hung everywhere.

"It is a little early to decorate as yet," said Mrs. Williamson, noticing his glance. "But the children enjoy it so that we gave in and allowed them to fill the house with Christmas greenery. They shall only be here until Boxing Day. It is difficult to believe that it is scarcely a fortnight away."

They crossed a hall and she opened a paneled door that led to her husband's library.

It was a relatively small room compared to the vast library at Chenevix Duchis but completely filled with books on every wall, from floor to ceiling. With just a cursory glance Alan recognized many arcane titles that could be found in the family libraries in Dublin. On a perch in one corner sat a large owl, the professor's familiar. She was fast asleep.

Nigel Williamson had changed very little in the last four years, a little grayer, perhaps. He rose to his feet as Alan approached his desk and shook hands. "You're not looking particularly well, Mr. Stillfield," he said critically. "Has this to do with the problem which you think I may be able to help you?"

"I shall fetch the tea," said Mrs. Williamson, and

whisked herself from the room.

"I don't know where to begin," Alan said, sinking into a basket chair opposite the desk and running his hands through his hair.

"Begin at the beginning," the Professor directed.

Accordingly, Alan started with Rosamunde's marriage to Raymond, and his illness and trip to India to visit Ravi.

"I remember Mr. Chopra or should I say the Prince," said Williamson, "even though I did not have the pleasure of teaching him. A great dragon-ball fan as I remember."

Cathal was able to fill in many of the blanks that Alan did not know, things that he had learned from Sinéad.

During this somewhat lengthy recital Mrs. Williamson came in with a young housemaid who carried a laden tea tray. The professor's wife dismissed the housemaid but stayed to dispense the tea and listen herself.

Alan faltered when he came to the foulness of Jhaniput, looking more than a little embarrassed in Mrs. Williamson's presence.

"My wife is well aware of sex brothels and what goes on there, Stillfield, you needn't scruple on her account." said the Professor dryly.

"I can tell the worst of it," offered Cathal.

"Only if I can't manage," said Alan with a smile of thanks for his familiar. He plunged bravely into the rest of his story, telling of the condition of the women and the use of Incubi and the Succubus who had attacked him.

By this time the owl, named Minerva, was awake and listening and another familiar, a tabby cat, had joined them. All were hanging on his every word.

Alan finished with Vishnu's intervention, its aftermath and then told them of Rosamunde's state of mind and the recommendations of Sir Quentin Davies. "So you see, sir," he concluded, "I thought that if anyone knew someone who might be able to speak to Rosamunde as Sir Quentin wishes, it would be you."

"Had anyone else told me this tale I should have doubted their veracity. It seems a tale from the Arabian nights, an avatar of a God, a draconic monastery, Incubi and Succuba, evil Maharanis...had I not known that such did exist," he exchanged a look with his wife, who nodded slightly.

536

"I know the very person you need, Mr. Stillfield, and you may take her back with you to Dorset this very afternoon."

Rosamunde was sitting up for the first time since she had come home. Wrapped in a warm dressing gown and fur lined slippers, with a comforter over her legs and a shawl around her shoulders, she sat in front of a blazing fire in the hearth of her room. Sinéad and her sister Aithne, who was Julia's familiar, slept in front of the fireguard.

Rosamunde had been receiving visitors all day long, her parents, her grandparents, René and Diana, her great grandparents, the Duke and his Duchess, Lucie now more or less permanently in a an invalid chair, and her great great grandparents, Lyon and Ninon, as well as Alan's mother Tatya. Her uncle Simon had been obliged to go back to Dublin for the end of term at Trinity, but he was flying back within the next few days. Diana and René were going back to Dublin as well, to escort all the children to Dorset for the Solstice celebration and Christmas.

Julia made certain that Rosamunde was not overwhelmed by any of her guests and noticed carefully when her daughter seemed to tire. Rosamunde was still far from well; it would take a long while before she was completely recovered. Dr. Lane did not want her making the journey to Ireland as yet. He felt it best that she remain at Chenevix Duchis until the weather improved. There was next to no snow in Dublin, although everyone still remembered the terrible winter of 1845 when snow and sleet and arctic temperatures had blanketed much of the Emerald Isle.

Of course, she had missed Alan, but Stuart had told her that he had sent Alan on an important errand and that Rosamunde would have plenty of the company of those who loved her, who could keep the memories at bay. She had to be content with this.It had hurt when her father told her that she was selfish and a glance at Alan told her that he was not, as Papa had said, in the best of health. Rosamunde was ashamed of herself and resolved to try and not hang on Alan's sleeve as much and let him get the rest he deserved. This was a very difficult resolution to keep. She wanted him by her at all times.

She watched anxiously, though, as the early winter
dark drew in and a maid-servant came in to draw the
draperies. Only Julia sat with her still, doing some white
needlework, handkerchiefs for Christmas, while Rosamunde
dozed on and off. She felt neither like reading nor needlework.

When at last there were footsteps in the hall,
Rosamunde looked up eagerly. This had to be Alan at last!

Julia, looking at her expectant face thought that
Rosamunde had been lit up from the inside. Whether her
daughter realized it or not, she was deeply in love with her
husband. And unless the present situation could be resolved
Julia saw nothing ahead but heartbreak for both of them.

It *was* Alan, but he had an unknown woman with
him. Two familiars trotted behind them, Cathal and a tabby
cat. Sinéad and Aithne woke up and stared at the strange cat.

Alan made the introductions. "Aunt Julia, Rosamunde, Aithne and Sinéad, may I present Mrs. Helena
Williamson and her familiar Portia? They've come from
Oxford with me just now. Mrs. Williamson has some things
she would like to discuss with Rosamunde."

Julia put aside her work in a basket. "Then we shall
leave you. Aithne, why don't you and Sinéad take Portia to
the kitchen and have cook give you a late tea?"

Sinéad did not want to leave, but when Julia gave her
a severe look, the little cat gave way and trotted out of the
room with the other cats and Cathal. Julia followed them.

Alan stayed only a moment more and told Rosamunde
that Mrs. Williamson was the wife of his Professor at the
college of Merlin, the very one who had taught him all about
sex brothels and that she would understand what had happened to Rosamunde far better than most people. As he spoke
Mrs. Williamson removed her hat and her wrap and took the
chair so recently vacated by Julia.

The door had scarcely shut behind Alan when
Rosamunde burst out "I don't see how *you* can help me! Just
because your husband teaches courses in sex magic? How can
you possibly understand?"

"I can understand very well, my dear," said Helena
Williamson cooly. "You see, I was a prisoner in a sex magic

brothel in Persia for over four years and I was used by literally thousands of men."

Rosamunde could only gape at her.

"We were kept each in a tiny windowless cubicle, just big enough for a bed, chained to this by a slave collar that had a focus stone in the middle of it. For all that time I saw no one but the men who used me, those who disciplined us and the magician when he came to drain the power from the stone," said Helena Williamson. "I later found out that there were some twenty other women there. We were somewhat drugged all the time, not enough to render us unconscious but enough so that we would not fight what was done to us. I tried to kill myself at least twice, first by hanging myself by the collar, but it was magiced to prevent that. When I stopped eating I was forcibly fed through a nose tube. I was also severely beaten. I bear the scars to this day."

"How did you get there?" Rosamunde asked, wide-eyed.

"I had been Christmas shopping in London on Bond Street and I hailed a hackney. When I entered, it filled with a gas that made me pass out. When I awoke at last I was in Persia, naked and chained to that table. My magic was nullified by the collar and I could do nothing to help myself. That was one of the worst things, that helplessness to prevent anything that was done to me."

Rosamunde found herself agreeing with this.

"The sex magician, was the Vizier of a small Caliphate, employed agents in London to be on the lookout for women like me, foolishly alone. They particularly liked fair women, as they are uncommon in Persia."

"How did you escape?" Rosamunde asked.

"I did not. I was rescued by my husband. Nigel was certain that I had not run away with another man as some people suggested to him. He knew I would never leave him or the children. We had two at the time. He searched for me for four years and when he found me, destroyed, with the help of several good Wizard friends, the brothel and its owner. So you see my dear, I well know exactly what you have gone through and are still going through. And we have another thing in common, husbands who love us deeply. What your Alan feels for you was so readily apparent in everything that he told us this afternoon."

She paused and said, "I imagine that you feel as I did when first I came home from that evil place, dirty, degraded and guilty. And angry at what had been done to you, you probably even wondered why it had to happen to you, what had you done to deserve this? Later on one wonders if somehow one *does* deserve it."

Rosamunde nodded, this was exactly what she had been feeling. *Oh, this woman understood!*

"When I first came home I felt as if everyone who saw me somehow knew that I had been used by camel drivers and thieves everyday, again and again for four years. I felt as if they could tell just by looking at me. I remember once that Nigel said to me "It's not tattooed on your forehead, woman!" But I felt as if it was. I felt too vile to make normal human contact, I did not even wish to see my children for fear that I would somehow pollute them by my presence. And most of all I could not believe that Nigel still loved me and wanted me for his wife and wanted to have more children with me. I thought that every time he looked at me he would see those thousands of men in his imagination. But he did, we had three more children and now we have grandchildren as well."

"But how could you let him," Rosamunde said in a whisper, and clutched her shawl around herself.

"Touch me intimately? Make love to me?" Helena finished for her. "I had to face the fact, my dear, that either I be a real wife to him or I had to let him go. You shall have to face up to that as well. I do not think that you will ever break your husband's love or loyalty to you or his spirits and patience but you may end in breaking his health."

"My father said the same," Rosalind admitted. "But how do I stop thinking about it? How do I go on and stop feeling the way I do?"

"It is not easy; it will probably be the most difficult thing you have ever done. It is just this, we make our own happiness. It is your choice as to whether you let what has happened to you colour your entire life. This may sound cruel, my dear, but you are not the first woman this has happened to nor will you be the last. You are not unique."

"But what if anybody found out, what they would think of me?" Rosamunde cried.

"And did everyone you met approve of you *before* you went into that brothel?" Helena countered. "You will find that many people, especially amongst magicals, will understand, and those that will not are not worth bothering with. And think of this, there is no earthly reason why you have to tell anyone! If you let them make you feel badly about yourself it will only be your fault. As Nigel told me once "The hell with them!"

"I can't tell Sir Quentin the worst of it, about Nana Sahib and the General and some of the other things," Rosamunde confessed. "Everyone keeps telling me that I must unburden myself to him, but I am too ashamed!"

"Would you like to tell me?" Helena suggested. "It does help, you know. And nothing you can tell me will shock me, as every possible deviation and perversion in the world was done to me in that brothel, I am shock proof."

Suddenly Rosamunde wanted very much to tell someone, someone who, like this woman, would not look at her in shock or horror, who would make no judgment upon her.

Slowly, hesitating at first, she began to talk, and before she had finished, telling for the first time all the details of what the General did to her regularly and exactly what had happned that night with Nana Sahib, she was crying, crying real tears for the first time since Akbar had raped her.

By this time Helena's arms were about her and she was sobbing into the older woman's shoulder.

"You needed that," Helena said as Rosamunde's sobs died away. "I daresay it will do you a world of good. I am going to give you my direction and you may write to me or scry me or even come to see me if you badly need to talk or need some support from someone who understands. I think you will find now that working with Sir Quentin will go easier, and he will be able to help you, I have no doubts."

She had taken out a handkerchief and was dabbing at Rosamunde's face. "But my dear Rosamunde," they were by now on Christian name terms, "you are going to have make a difficult decision about that husband of yours. If you cannot face being a real wife and let him make love to you, you had best let him go. Living a half live is not good for either of you. If you cannot support laying with him it is better to end it and let him find someone else and have a normal marriage with loving and children. Think about it, long and hard. He seems to understand what you went through and what you feel but you cannot expect him to wait forever. Think about losing him, never bearing his children or him taking a mistress. Think of everything you would gain or lose by divorcing him."

"I can't lose Alan!" Rosamunde said in fear. "I love him, I have loved him all my life!"

"Then if you don't love him enough to have a true marriage, you must love him enough to let him go," said Helena gently.

After Helena left, Rosamunde sat a long time by the fire. When Julia looked in to tell her that Alan and Brendan had taken Helena back to Oxford, Rosamunde told her mother that she wanted to be alone for a while. Julia went away, giving Rosamunde a little hand bell to ring if she needed anything.

Rosamunde stared into the leaping flames. She thought of life with and without Alan. She thought again of Laura's advice. She thought that Alan would wait for her, but how long? Would he return to the Elfin lover she had found out about? She found that she could not stand the thought of Alan with an Elf, or with anyone else. And when Helena had spoken of children, something within Rosamunde twisted. She wanted children badly – Alan's children.

But it was too soon, far and away too soon. She had to have a little more time, time for the memories to fade, time to regain her health and strength. She felt too fragile at the moment to be making changes or any major decisions. At the moment even deciding what she wanted for breakfast exhausted her. She would have to explain this to him and hope that he understood.

58

union

Rosamunde had made up her mind to get well. This was not as easy as it sounded for it was far simpler to slide into a cocoon of cosseting, to spend the winter days tucked into her warm bed, dreamily watching the fire, to spend hours and hours in sleep and to procrastinate about any decisions.

But she had given a great deal of thought to what Helena had said, and had come to the conclusion that she did not want life without Alan. She loved him and without him her existence would be a poor, pale thing. She felt more alive when near him and longed for him when he was not with her.

And she could not be a proper wife to him if she was not well. She still shied away from the thought of physical intimacy, but with returning health and strength, many letters and scrys to and from Helena, and thrice weekly sessions with Sir Quentin, every day she was able to put more of the memories of Jhaniput behind her. She was sleeping better as well, with fewer nightmares and waking more refreshed.

Alan was true to his word. He neither pressed her or showed any impatience. Never did he try to demand the privileges of a husband and as her health improved, Rosamunde began to wonder why he did not. She had always been used to men trying to force themselves upon her. She was not certain that she wanted such attentions but it began to hurt a bit that he did not want to kiss and hug her at least.

She spoke of this to Julia as they sat in front of the fire on a February afternoon. Outside, the sky was beginning to look like spring, with a warmer slant of the sun and a sky pale blue in colour. Very little snow remained on the ground as the climate of Dorset was not a particularly snowy one at any rate.

Alan had gone out. He spent hours riding the Duke's horses and went around to the farms with the Duke's bailiff. Lambing had begun and he always came home with stories of the sheep and the shepherds and their dogs.

"Rosamunde, don't you realize that Alan is holding himself on a very tight leash?" said Julia looking up at her daughter from the green Beltane robe she was embroidering for David, who seemed to be growing out of everything these days. "He loves you very much and, quite bluntly, wants you. One kiss or hug and he's more than likely go up like a bonfire! Why do you think he's spending so much time out in the cold and doing so much physical activity? Why he looks so strained and fine drawn at times?"

Rosamunde looked startled. "I didn't realize," she began. "Men are so different than we are; we don't care about such things."

"Perhaps you don't, but I certainly do!" Julia interrupted her. "And being away from your father all this time, it's been difficult, to say the least!" She stabbed her needle into the leaf of a branch of hawthorn she was embroidering, rather angrily.

Stuart had been obliged to return to Dublin for his duties with the police and in particular his patients at the Free Clinic could be neglected no longer. Of all the family, only Julia and Alan remained at Chenevix Duchis with Rosamunde. Even her great grandparents were gone to Bath so that the Duchess might partake of the benefits of the waters there.

"Rosamunde, perhaps this is none of my business, but what were the relations between you and Raymond? Don't you have a memory of what it is liked to be loved and cherished in bed?" Julia asked curiously, laying aside her work. "I know what you suffered in that horrible place was very, very bad, but can you not remember, for Alan's sake and for your own, what being loved was like? You always spoke of how much you wanted children. You will never have any if you do not allow your husband your bed!"

This was plain speaking indeed. And Rosamunde, equally plain spoken, feeling as if she was violating a confidence, told her mother exactly how it had been between her and Raymond and the promises he had extracted from her as to telling no one about their problem.

"Oh, the young idiot!" said Julia when Rosamunde had finished her miserable confession. "If only he had come to

Stuart or some other Wizard Healer! Does Sir Quentin know about this?"

"I couldn't tell him," said Rosamunde. "Raymond made such a fuss, it was difficult even to tell you, Mama."

"Does Alan know this?" Julia asked, leaning forward.

Rosamunde could only shake her head and added, "Laura is the only other person who knows."

"Little I wonder you are so reluctant," said Julia half to herself "when all the memories are of brutality..." She looked at Rosamunde again. "Alan ought to know, Rosamunde. He has the right to know." Privately, her opinion of Raymond, which had never been high, went down quite a bit. From what Rosamunde had left unsaid, which told Julia more than if she had come right out with it, Raymond had blamed his wife for his problem. That one sentence: "...he said I was too beautiful..." was very telling.

Julia would also lay odds that Stuart had been correct in that Raymond being non-magical had also caused a rift between them. For Julia had received an earful from Aithne after Sinéad had poured out her heart to her sister, who in turn had told her Witch all that had gone on in the bungalow in Malabad, including the episode of the letters. It had been a bad match from the beginning, but Rosamunde was being extraordinarily loyal to Raymond's memory, or was it simply not speaking ill of the dead?

"You must tell him about your marriage. I think perhaps he is holding back for fear that you are still mourning Raymond." she said aloud to her daughter.

Rosamunde looked startled for a moment. "Do you really think so, Mama? I'm not mourning him, and I feel guilty about that."

"Don't!" said Julia briskly. "It is a sad thing that he had to die but believe me, I know it is very difficult to mourn someone you no longer love. I mourned my father very little. He was a bully and a domestic tyrant. I never even went into blacks for him and married your father less than a six month after my father was murdered. And didn't the eyebrows go up over that! Didn't you tell me that you had decided to ask for a divorce?"

"Yes," Rosamunde said, looking down at her hands. "We did not suit. I should have never accepted him. I thought

I could change him and we could be happy..." her voice trailed off.

"Too many women make that mistake," said Julia. "You can only change someone if they want to be changed. It sounds as if Raymond was quite happy with himself the way he was. And he seems to have thought that he could change *you*. You need to tell Alan all of this, Rosamunde, and discuss it with Sir Quentin and perhaps your friend Helena as well."

Rosamunde knew she was right but it would be difficult, as difficult as it had been admitting to Alan that she had always loved him and had only married Raymond to escape the sight of him married to Christine Chapman. And she might have never even admitted that without the prompting of the familiars.

As if Sinéad had known that her Witch was thinking of her, the door to Rosamunde's room opened suddenly and Sinéad and Aithne entered, followed by a footman with a laden tray.

"Excuse me, ma'am," said the footman, placing the tray on a table in front of the hearth, "but the familiars were telling Cook that as it was a raw day you might want a little chocolate and Faerie cakes, fresh from the oven to tide you over until luncheon is served."

"I shall get fat if this keeps up!" laughed Julia.

Rosamunde was suddenly hungrier than she had been in quite a while. The chocolate looked and smelled enticing and the Faerie cakes, feather light confections with tiny currants, were still warm. She would definitely eat for she would need all her strength to talk to Alan. Mama was right, she owed him an explanation. He had done so much for her and been so patient. When he came back from the lambing they would talk.

But Alan had not gone to the lambing. He had ridden out towards Batcombe Hill, a rather bleak and desolate area of the Dorset Downs where the road ran north to Holywell, and eventually to Yeovil and Ilchester.

But his goal was to none of these places. He left his horse in Batcombe village, which was under the Northern slope of the Chalk Downs, and then, on foot, climbed to the steep summit, until, buffeted by a strong wind, he found what he was seeking.

Of honey gold Hamstone, an ancient limestone mined at Ham Hill in Somerset, the Cross-in-Hand stood three feet high. Hidden in the verge, it was an elderly monolith that had been there, some said, since the time of the Romans in Britain; others said since the 4th or 7th century. Still others said that it marked the site of a peace offering between four ancient Kings, who crossed hands here when the area was still called Wessex. Local legend had it that the Cross-in-Hand marked the grave of a murderer who sold his soul to the Devil.

Many claimed that they could see the shape of a hand grasping a bowl at the top of the monolith, and perhaps that it was an early Christian monument or even an earlier pagan one.

But Alan knew what it really was. It was the portal to another world.

He lay his hand lightly on the honey gold stone and, opening himself to the ley lines, said a Word. The Cross-in-Hand sank into the ground, revealing a stairway cut into the earth.

Without hesitation Alan stepped down. As soon as he was deep enough, the Hamstone slid back into position, leaving no sign that it had ever moved.

As usual, an Elfin steed waited for him. They always seemed to know when he was coming. He mounted the mare and almost at once they were at their destination. Alan had no idea how far the Elfin steed traveled or even how long they were on the journey, for here in the kingdom of the Elves, time and distance were irrelevant and had no bearing on time and distance in the world above.

And here it was high summer.

Alisande's cottage stood in a green dale, beside a crystal brook. Flowers bloomed everywhere, all of the Elf maiden's favorites blooming at once. Tulips were beside roses, daffodils near larkspur, irregardless of the season. Over the thatched roof hung a thick cascade of roses, while wisteria, heavy with purple blooms, guarded the door. By the slant of the sunlight (and where did sunlight come from, underground?) it was late afternoon, the dark blue shadows lengthening and the sunlight turning the grass to gold.

Alan felt badly that he had not come to see her since his return to England. Their association had been a relatively long one, nearly seven years, and it had been more than good. He owed her a farewell and an explanation.

As he dismounted, he saw a movement in the garden and then watched as Alisande stood up. She wore a broad brimmed hat, unnecessary here where one did not even tan unless one wished to do so, but she looked very well in it and a dark pink gown that looked vaguely fashionable. She carried a basket full of flowers which would soon adorn the house.

She was as tall as he was and her hair was the colour of ripe wheat. It spilled down her back almost to her waist. Her eyes were every bright green and she was so beautiful that had she appeared in the world above she would have caused a riot.

"Hello, Alan," she said in a low musical voice. "I was wondering when I would see you."

"Alisande," he said a little awkwardly, "I should have come to see you before this. I've been negligent...you see, I was married while out in India."

She smiled. "I know all about it. The entire Court is abuzz with what you did in India! I understand that Rosamunde, your wife, has been very ill. That was surely on your mind. And we made no binding promises to each other. We always knew the day would come when you or I would marry." She gave him a radiant smile. "It so happens that I am to be married myself, to Jair Goldenhand. I think you know him?"

"The goldsmith? Yes, congratulations, he's a fine chap," he said sincerely and went forward and gave her a light kiss on the brow.

"When you left for India I was at a loss," she said, "And Jair began to come around frequently and before I knew it I realized that I was in love with him. I hope that you and your bride will come to the wedding." She looked him in the face, her hands still light on his shoulders. "What is wrong?" she said abruptly. "You are worried, and not happy. Come!" she took his hand and led him into the cottage. "I shall make us some tea and you shall tell me why a new bridegroom looks so miserable."

When the lengthy tale was done, and he felt no compunction in unburdening himself to her; he could not have kept anything from her if he tried, she said, "I am going to tell you just what you must do."

"You don't think it's hopeless, then?" he asked, He felt a sudden surge of optimism.

"I do not," she said firmly. "You have still to hear some revelations that will surprise you," her green eyes looking as if she was seeing visions far away, "But do as I tell you, persevere, be patient, and above all, *love* her and you shall have your heart's desire."

Rosamunde left a message for Alan to come and see her as soon as he returned. He did not come until luncheon was being served and brought her tray up to her and ate with her in front of the fire, in company with Cathal and Sinéad.

Dr. Lane had prescribed a glass of port for her each day as it was considered 'strengthening' and under the mild relaxant of this beverage she was able to tell her story not without many halts and moments of embarrassment, with impetus from Sinéad and many sips of port.

Alan was a long time silent when she faltered to a halt, staring at his glass of ruby port in which the flames of the fire danced.

At last he said. "My poor darling! The only thing you've ever known is those miserable bastards in Jhaniput. Little wonder that–"

"Alan!" she said recklessly, downing the last of her port in a gulp, which would have shocked the Chenevix butler as a fine port was meant to be sipped and savored. "I want to be your wife–I do! I want to stay married to you and have a real marriage! Will you come to me tonight?" she added, before the port wore off and she lost her courage.

He put down his glass and took her hands in his. "Are you certain, Rosamunde? Are you absolutely certain?" he asked, looking into her face so intently that she thought perhaps he could read her mind.

Nervously, she wet her lips and slowly nodded, "I'm

certain," she said. She noticed how tired he looked and felt guilty that perhaps she was doing this to him.

"Will you trust me enough to put yourself completely in my hands?" he asked. "You may cry halt at any time if you do not wish to go on, but I want this to be a pleasant experience for you and I think that I know how to go about it for your enjoyment."

Enjoyment? It was a word that she would have never used for that particular activity, but she nodded again and said "Yes, I will trust you."

"Well, 'tis after bein' time!" said Sinéad in tones of thankfulness.

In spite of her brave words Rosamunde was so nervous that she could eat very little supper that evening. She was still eating on a tray in her room and did not appreciate Sinéad making a joke about how she should have had oyster stew for supper as it was considered an aphrodisiac. She was glad that her familiar would leave the room when Alan came.

He did not keep her waiting, but shortly after supper, he tapped on the door and came in, holding the door open for Sinéad to go out. The little familiar was obviously reluctant to leave her Witch, acting as if she wished to oversee the entire business.

"Cathal will keep her busy," Alan said, correctly discerning Rosamunde's worry.

He was wearing a dressing gown and carrying a small bottle, which he put on the bedside table.

She had the covers pulled up to her chin and her knees up to her chest. "What do you want me to do?" She asked nervously. "Shall I take off my nightgown? Shall I assume the position of usage?"

"Forget everything you ever learned in that vile place, Rosamunde. That had nothing to do with love. I am going to love you, which bears no relationship to what they did there. But I would like you to take off your nightgown."

She nodded, her eyes large in her face. He had seen her naked before, she reminded herself. Nonetheless it was hard to shed the gown. She had clung to clothing as a protection, as a safety line since she had left Jhaniput.

To her surprise he did not leap upon her as she thought he would. Instead he told her to lay upon her stomach. He pulled the sheets up so that her legs below the knee and about half her back, up to her shoulders, was exposed.

"What are you going to do?" she asked nervously, afraid of something depraved.

"I'm going to give you a massage," he answered.

"Like the Elves do?" she asked in surprise.

"Just like the Elves," he replied. "You're very tense and a massage will help you to relax. I'll just be touching your back and your feet and legs, and remember, any time you want to stop, just say so."

She heard him moving about and then there was the lightest touch on her shoulders and smelled something incredibly beautiful. "It smells like summer!" she said.

"It's an Elfin lotion," he said, "a floral effusion that they use in massage."

She was very grateful that it was not a musk oil.

Whoever had taught him to do this had taught him well. His fingers were skillful and as he lightly touched her back and shoulders she felt the tension, even the anxiety about this encounter, ebbing slowly away.

He moved onto her feet and lower legs and she relaxed further. She had almost fallen into a doze when he suddenly doused the mage lights, leaving the room in darkness except for the now lowering firelight. She heard his dressing gown drop onto the floor and he slid under the sheets beside her, pulling it down over their feet and pulling up the comforter.

"Time for sleep," he announced.

"But aren't you going to–?" she faltered.

"Not tonight, there's no hurry. All I am going to do now is hold you and kiss you a little, if you don't mind."

"No, I don't mind," she said, remembering how safe she felt when he held her in his arms. She did not even mind that she was naked, and he was also, she realized as he drew her against him.

The kisses were feather light on her brow, cheek and neck, and as he kissed her he stroked her hair.

Still relaxed from the massage, she fell into a deep, dreamless, healing sleep.

This pattern continued for a long while, night after night, and she came to look forward to his coming and the massage that drew all of the tension and worry out of her. Afterwards they slept together, quietly and peacefully. When she asked timidly, when he would actually take her he said "When you can say 'make love' instead of 'take'."

During the day he took every opportunity to kiss her and touch her, holding her hand and putting an arm about her waist as she began to more fully recover and they took walks in the sheltered walled gardens. It was almost like being courted.

But he never rushed her, never made demands. It was always as she wished. The slightest hesitation on her part and he backed away.

She was beginning to crave his touch as much as she craved his presence. She wanted his arm about her, and his lips on hers. She wanted to be held against him.

New feelings and longings were beginning to awaken in her as the end of February drew near and spring began to advance.

Spring and the touch of his hands at night awoke something, a longing that she did not understand and one evening when he finished with the massage, which had become deeper every night, and encompassed more of her body, she was left with a feeling of incompleteness, that she wanted something more. Parts of her body that had never felt anything but pain now tingled in anticipation.

When he had doused the mage lights and took her in his arms she said in an urgent whisper, "Alan, please, I want, I need,– it aches–oh–please, make love to me!"

It had happened at last. Wordlessly, he kissed her, a deep lover's kiss, and she made what sounded like a purr in her throat.

A little while later, there was a soft cry, but it was not one of pain.

Afterwards, she lay in his arms and said dreamily, "Is it supposed to be like that?"

He laughed, feeling absurdly happy. "Like what, *mo mhúirnin bán,*(my fair darling)?"

"Well, enjoyable!" she said.

He laughed again, putting his face in her hair and tightening his arms about her. "I hope it will one day be ecstatic for you!" he said. "You will forget every terrible thing that happened to you and just be happy."

She knew, however that she would never completely forget Jhaniput, no matter how far back she pushed it in her memory. But being loved like this would make up for a great deal.

And three days later when Laura, Nate and Sacha arrived after a rough trip in heavy winter seas, Laura took one look at her friend and a grin split her face. "Jesus H. Christ!" she said. "You finally took my advice, honey! Now you just got to follow my lead and get a bun in the oven too!" She patted her stomach. That's what happens when you spend a lot of time alone with your man! I think I got knocked up when we were in Ranijhat."

Rosamunde looked eager. She hoped that she too, would soon be carrying a child.

But five years later there was still no sign of a pregnancy and, after many, many consultations with all sorts of physicians, they knew that there never would be.

the home that wasn't

London - December 1863

Nicholas Frayne sat in the window seat, watching the drizzling rain stream down the dirty glass. The seat was hard, for there were no cushions, and, like the entire building, it had seen better days. The paint on the window panes and sill was peeling and the view was of a barren courtyard where the children here at St. Mary's Home for Little Wanderers took their exercise. No one would be going out of doors today as the rain was constant and the wind was both cold and raw. Some of the nuns thought that it might turn over to snow later.

Nicholas always thought of St. Mary's as 'the home that wasn't a home'. He supposed that the nuns tried their best, but anything more un-homelike could hardly be imagined. There were few diversions or toys or books, or pictures on the walls. All the walls were a dull brown, easier to clean, Mother Superior said, and the floors were covered in strips of dark gray drugget. Life was governed by bells, one to rise with, one to wash by, one for breakfast, one for prayers, one for going to lessons, and so on during the day until the last bell rang at night to go to one's narrow cot in the dormitory.

"Perhaps this time we'll be adopted," said his sister's voice timidly.

Nicholas turned to look at her. Nicola was four years younger than he was, which made her six.

"Don't be stupid," he said roughly "No one ever wants us. They keep us for a day or so and then send us back."

But Nicholas knew that it was not *them* that was not wanted, it was *him*. Nicola was a sweet child with dusky ringlets, sea-blue eyes and dimples. He knew that he was sullen, for the nuns repeatedly remonstrated with him and punished him for this character trait.

He boiled with anger all of the time and he did not know why, even though some of it was probably what had happened to them since their parents died.

But the anger had become particularly bad in the last two years or so. He had a terrible temper that manifested itself in fighting and fits of destructiveness. And as much as he was contrite and even tried to mend his ways he could not seem to control it, as many times as he was punished or as many times as the nuns had him on his knees, praying for guidance.

Many people had wanted to keep Nicola but she had hysterics and ran away repeatedly when they were separated. He was the only family that she had ever known for she had been very little when first their parents and then the much older brother who was like a second father to them had died.

Then had started the ordeal of going from one horrible relative to another, many of whom were cruel, indifferent, or begrudging. After the last uncle and aunt, who had been not only abusive, but seemed to think that the children were to be used as unpaid servants and worked to death, they had ended here two years ago.

This couple who had come to look them over today would be the tenth occasion they had been sent out to see if they might be adopted. Again, Nicholas had no hopes. Try as he might, he knew that he would do something that would make them hate him. It was inevitable.

The Mother Superior of St Mary's, Mother Mary Judah, looked at the young couple sitting on the other side of her desk and said "I will say it again, Nicholas is a difficult boy. Perhaps he has some excuse for these children were treated horribly by some of the people who had them in their charge. There were all sorts of abuse from starving to beatings and I suspect even abuse of a *private* nature. It is a great deal to ask of anyone to deal with such problems, much less persons as young as yourselves and inexperienced with children."

Alan Stillfield smiled. "My wife and I, Mother Superior, are both the eldest of large families. And Rosamunde is twenty-five and I am nearly thirty, not nearly as young as you seem to think us." He felt Rosamunde's fingers curl around his as he spoke.

"We cannot have our own children, Mother," said Rosamunde. "The doctors are adamant about that. When we heard that you had two children of a magical family here we thought at once that they would be perfect for us. Part of Nicholas's difficulties might be that he has never been placed with a magical family before."

"For some reason it is a great deal more difficult for a non-magical family to raise a magical child than it is for a magical family to raise a non-magical one," said Alan easily. "We are more than willing to take the chance. And the children will have a great deal of family to love and to guide them."

"Yes," said the Mother Superior, looking down at the papers that lay in front of her. "You come highly recommended and our investigations, forgive me, but we must be so careful about where these children go! indicated that you are more than suitable as adoptive parents. I understand that you are heir to a Baronetcy, Mr. Stillfield. Pray, how does your father feel about the fact that your adopted son cannot inherit the title?"

"As your investigators no doubt found out, ma'am, my father is adopted himself, and I have two younger brothers who may inherit the title: indeed my brother Jack's wife recently had a son. Our entire family has encouraged us in this adoption," said Alan.

"We particularly hoped to find magical children to adopt," Rosamunde put in. "But it is not easy to do so. Wizards and Witches tend to have large families and if children are orphaned there is usually someone eager to take them in. Magical children scarcely ever end in an orphanage."

The Mother Superior still looked troubled, the lines in her old face deep. "Very well," she said at last. "I hope that it will work out, for all of you. These children need a real home. They ended here because no one else would take them in. Nicholas has quite a reputation. They are not even Catholic, but Church of England, but we never refuse any child that is sent to us. I am a little hesitant to send them for a two week's visit so close to Christmas, as holidays make

Nicholas even worse for some reason. For the sake of peace here I would just as soon have him gone."

Rosamunde already felt a deep sympathy for Nicholas and this only deepened it. Imagine not being wanted at Christmas! She squeezed Alan's hand again and felt an answering pressure. He thought just as she did.

The Mother Superior rang a bell and in a few moments another nun ushered the two children into the room, each with a pitifully small bundle of personal belongings.

The boy did look sullen. Without the scowl he would have been a handsome boy, with black hair and very blue eyes. He was tall for his age, but too thin and his clothes showed that he had grown rapidly lately and his clothing had not been replaced for his wrists stuck out from under the sleeves of the jacket and his trousers were too short in the leg.

The little girl was thin as well and anxiety shadowed her eyes, so like her brother's. She was in a too short shabby dress and a patched pinafore. Her stockings hung down around thin legs. They were holding hands and the boy's stance indicated both protectiveness and wariness.

"Nicholas and Nicola, this is Mr. and Mrs. Stillfield, who are interested in adopting you. They will take you to their home for the usual fortnight and you shall see if you shall suit one another," said the Mother Superior, wishing that Nicholas would not look so forbidding.

Rosamunde got out of her chair and in a rustle of pink silk skirts, knelt in front of the two children. "Hello, Nicholas and Nicola. I hope we are going to like one another very much and will wish to be a family."

Nicola looked at her with wide eyes and said "Oh, you're so pretty!" Almost all of the people that had wanted to adopt them had been much older and did not look like a Faerie princess.

Alan said hello as well, not attempting to shake the boy's hand, but letting him maintain his distance.

A few moments later they were in a cab. Having ascertained that they wished to return to the place he had brought them from, the cabby clucked to his horse and they started off. It was still raining, a steady drizzle.

"Perhaps no one told you where we are going," said Alan, looking at the two who sat so close together on the seat opposite him and his wife. "We live in Ireland, outside Dublin. It's a nice big house, with gardens and plenty of places to play. If you decide you want to be our children, you'll have many cousins and other relatives to play with." He looked at the two with his Othersight and what he saw appalled him, especially in the case of Nicholas.

"Nicholas, have you ever studied magic?" he asked abruptly.

Nicholas shook his head. Magic! What had he to do with magic? This man was an idiot!

"Has no one ever told you that your father was a Wizard?" Alan asked gently. "And your older brother, Peyton, was an excellent Wizard as well? I knew him at Oxford."

This gained Nicholas's attention. He had adored his brother and his loss had been a greater grief than the loss of their parents, for Mr. and Mrs. Frayne had been very involved in society and scarcely ever saw the two unexpected additions to their family. But Peyton had always taken time to play with them, and pay attention to them. Nicola did not remember him at all. Nicholas had been not quite six when he died and now the memories were fading.

"No–sir," He answered, remembering to add that 'sir', the lack of which would have had one of the nuns laying a ruler across his hand until it smarted.

Magic was positively boiling inside the boy. He should have learned to shield and ground by now and how to control the tugging he was feeling from the natural energies all around. "Do you often feel angry, and as if you wanted to strike out at someone?" he asked.

Nicholas looked at him, startled. How did he know this?

Alan smiled at the look on the boy's face. "I'm a Wizard, too," he explained. "And my wife is a Witch. Our whole family, with few exceptions, is magical. When we get you to Dublin I am going to make certain that you have a few lessons in magic."

Lessons in magic? Nicholas thought in wonder.

A further wonder was waiting. The cab pulled up and the cabby's voice sang out "'ere ye be, guv!"

When they climbed out of the carriage Nicholas's eyes ran out on stems and he felt Nicola gasp and back up against him.

Dragons, at least ten of them, sheltering under a canvas cover. They all looked at the cab with interest, turning their head on long necks.

Nicholas felt at first hot, then cold all over. He knew what this place was, for he had heard people speaking of places like it. It was a Dragon Park, where people left their dragons when they had business in parts of the city that were too cramped for dragons to land.

Ever since he could remember he had been mad for dragons. When he was smaller his brother had given him a wooden dragon toy and this had been his most treasured possession until the relatives they first went to had taken it away and thrown on the fire.

"Are we going to ride on a dragon?" he demanded, his face changing from its usual surly expression to one of eager expectancy.

"We do most of our traveling dragon-back," answered Alan. He exchanged glances with Rosamunde. The boy's interest in dragons might be a way to ease him into the family.

Nicholas watched breathlessly as an emerald green dragon detached itself from the group and came forward. He noticed the saddle and the harness and everything in him thrilled to the thought that he was going to actually ride a dragon.

"Are these the children?" the dragon asked as he halted in front of them. He bent his face towards them. "Hello, I'm Brendan," he said pleasantly.

Nicola was rather afraid of something so big. Her hand slipped from her brother's as he went forward eagerly to see the dragon up close.

A comforting embrace dropped around her shoulders and the pretty lady said, "You don't have to be frightened, Nicola. Brendan would never hurt you. He would die to protect you. But he is big, isn't he? Perhaps you'd like to sit in front of me when we fly? I'll hold onto you, if you like. You'll be strapped in, and there is a handle on the saddle you can use if you like."

Nicola nodded, never taking her eyes off the dragon. She *was* afraid, but she could see that Nicky wanted to go and she was not going to be left behind, separated from him. She liked the feeling of the lady's arm about her, though. The lady smelled nice, like flowers, and Nicola leaned into her embrace.

On the back of the dragons' saddle was a wicker hamper of sorts and now the top of this flew open, and two heads appeared.

Now it was Nicola's turn to be delighted. "A kitty!" she said at the sight of the black and white face. She did not know what the other little animal was, but she loved anything small and furry.

"These are our familiars, Sinéad and Cathal," said Rosamunde, indicating which animal was which. Alan stepped forward and took the two little animals down from the basket and put them on the ground.

"And sure, they're after being a likely looking pair!" Sinéad pronounced. "I can be smelling the magic on them!"

"What's a familiar?" asked Nicholas, staring at the sight of talking animals.

"We're Wizard's helpers," Cathal explained, looking puzzled. As Sinéad did, he sensed the magic on the children and could not understand why a young Wizard of Nicholas's age did not know about familiars, in fact, the boy should really have a familiar of his own by now.

"Nicholas's magical education has been much neglected," Alan explained, as he tucked the children's belongings in the breast harness. "We'll remedy that at once."

Nicola had bent down to pet Sinéad and said shyly "I love kitties!"

"You'll find many cats at our home," said Alan encouragingly. "Brendan, can we make it back before dark?"

"I think so, if I go a little faster on the second leg of the trip over the Irish Sea. I shall go slowly at first until Nicholas and Nicola become accustomed to dragon flight." He smiled at the children in such a friendly fashion, in spite of his very large white teeth, that even Nicola was not quite as nervous. Sinéad's purr, with its touch of magic, was having its effect upon her, calming and soothing.

Nicholas was practically shaking with excitement as

Alan showed him how to mount Brendan's foreleg and from there climb into the saddle. He showed him how to check the safety harness and how it fastened.

"Always check the harness and fasten it securely, Nicholas," said Brendan, turning his head to look at his young passenger. "I will not take you up if you have not checked it and are not secured in properly. I will not take a chance that you might be injured or fall from the saddle."

Alan put Nicholas in the front seat. He himself would sit behind the boy so he could keep watch over him. Next would go Nicola with Rosamunde behind her. The two familiars would go back in their traveling basket. Rosamunde gave both children grayish cloaks that fastened with a leaf brooch at the throat. She and Alan donned some of these as well and Nicola was amazed when she saw that the pretty silk skirt was split so that the lady could sit astride the dragon.

Despite his longing to fly Nicholas was still nervous and clung to the handle that could be pulled out. Nicola grabbed her handle and closed her eyes, leaning back against Rosamunde and grateful for the arms that came around her.

After walking out onto the grass that surrounded the Dragon Park Brendan launched himself into the air with a thrust of his mighty legs and a strong downward sweep of his huge wings. Unfurled, they were even larger that Nicolas had imagined. Unlike his sister, he kept his eyes open, not wanting to miss anything.

In spite of the fact that he loved dragons so much, Nicholas knew very little about them such as how they flew, how fast they were...the people they had lived with had no interest in and very little to do with dragons. He had never seen a book about dragons or had anyone to answer his questions. Now he noticed that the dragon did not go straight up into the air, but went up in slow circles, like a spinning top coming to a rest.

When the dragon reached a height above the top of the tallest trees, he gave another thrust with his wings and they were suddenly above the lowering clouds and into blue skies. It looked as if they were flying above layers of slightly lumpy blankets. The earth had disappeared.

"These are stratus clouds we are flying over," said

Alan's voice in his ear. "They are low lying clouds. We are only slightly above a mile in the air."

"How can he see where he's going?" Nicholas asked.

"Dragons have a wonderful sense of direction, an instinct for where they are that means they can fly in a heavy fog, snow or rain. The only weather in which they cannot fly is in a thunderstorm, because of the danger of lightning strikes," said Alan. "They don't get lost unless they've been caught in a windstorm that has turned them around."

Since they were going slowly, Brendan tuned his head and asked "Shall we make a stop on the Isle of Man for some tea, Alan? I don't want Nicholas and Nicola getting saddlesick on their very first flight. It is a long way to fly, two hundred and eighty air miles."

"Good idea," Alan approved. "The Arch Druid can give us tea and perhaps we can show the children his sea horses."

"Nicky?" came Nicola's voice out of the darkness "I like it here. I want to stay."

They were tucked into the nursery of a large, old fashioned house called Dragon's Rest. They were a little old to be sharing a room but Alan and Rosamunde had wisely decided that they would be less nervous about this new place if they were able to remain together.

They had stopped at the Isle of Man and met a jovial, friendly man who was the Arch Druid of Man. He wore a beard and a white robe and Nicola thought at first that he was Father Christmas. He gave them a lovely tea with oh, so many good things to eat. Then he took them to the seashore and blew a horn shaped like a shell. The sea foam became agitated and from it appeared the heads of white horses. They leaped from the sea, showing that they had no back legs but instead had the tails of fish. The Arch Druid explained that when he drove them on land in his scallop shell shaped chariot they flew through the air.

Then they had flown on to Ireland. The sky by now was clear and they could see the rich green land below. In no time at all they were landing near a house of three stories, made of a light stone and looking as if it had been there forever. Ivy covered the façade and the roof looked as if it was a castle. The children could not know, but Dragon's Rest was indeed a very old house, parts of it had been built in the eleventh century and its' most recent reincarnation had taken place, before Alan and Rosamunde purchased it, had been back in 1722.

Modernizing and decorating their home had taken a long time and Rosamunde had kept herself busy with it and it managed to keep somewhat at bay her longing for a child. But when it was finished and one doctor after another had said that there could be no children because of the two contraceptive spells, and the fact that they were two different types of magic, they had listened to Lady Diana's advice and begun to think of adoption.

There was only one problem; they both wanted magical children and those were not easy to find. Lady Diana had many connections with various charities and had put out feelers to try and find magical orphans. And at long last they had. It had taken six months for all the paperwork but now the children were here and Rosamunde very much wanted them to stay.

Alan wanted them just as much. The thought of no children was insupportable. He had looked forward to teaching his son about magic and dragons and watching him grow and develop and see a daughter dance and participate in the rituals of her Coven.

When they read the Frayne children's histories, it had been decided that they would be very slow and careful with these children. They would keep things quiet so that they would get to know one another and introduce them to the rest of the family slowly. They might be overwhelmed at first, Dragon's Rest was a large house and they had many servants, as well as red dogs, familiars, horses, and a dragon.

Nicola was in alt almost at once, from the moment they set foot in the house. Everyone was so kind and she fell in love with the two red dogs, the familiars, a litter of kittens, Sinéad's latest, and even a litter of ferrets, for Cathal had recently taken a mate. She liked the big, light rooms with mullioned windows and old fashioned furniture. Even in December there were flowers everywhere and instead of the cabbage and carbolic smell of the orphanage there was a delightful odor of lavender and beeswax. Unlike some of the places they had lived it was immaculately clean.

A smiling country girl named Maeve was to be their nursery maid. But the lady and her husband came to say goodnight to them when they had been tucked into bed after a full afternoon and early evening of exploring the house and the bright nursery filled with pretty furniture and pictures on the walls, with cases full of books, and a few toys. The lady promised that they would go into Dublin the very next day and buy new clothes and toys. When the beautiful lady dropped a kiss on her forehead and tucked her in, just as Nicola always imagined a real mother would, the little girl's cup of happiness was near to overflowing. That was when she told Nicky, as soon as they were alone, that she liked it here and wanted to stay.

"You always like every place," he said sourly. "Just wait, we'll be back in London before you can imagine. They'll not want us either. No one ever does."

"I do not like every place!" she said. "Those Robinsons were horrid even in the carriage when they took us away, Nicky! And the Smiths, they just wanted us as slaves, you said so yourself and Uncle Ebeneezer and his wife were horrid too!" She paused a moment and with a suspicion of a sob in her voice, said "Please, Nicky? Won't you be good this time? I do like it here!"

Nicholas wanted to be good. He wanted a real home as much as she did but there seemed to be a demon inside him, one he could not control. Already he could feel its influence building up. Tomorrow would probably be their last day here.

"Nine tenths of what is wrong with that boy," said Alan to Rosamunde as they prepared for bed, "is his magic struggling to get out. If he had been properly awakened, and taught to ground and shield and given an outlet for his powers he would be a different boy. "

He was pacing up and down as he spoke. Rosamunde watched him from their bed. He looked enthusiastic as he gestured with his hands.

"Will you take him to the Druidry?" she asked.

Alan shook his head, "Christmas hols," he said. "No, first thing in the morning I will take him to Grandpapa. I already scryed Amberwell. We'll have the awakening ceremony. Our vicar will be there to bless his magic and between us we'll give him a first magic lesson and teach him to ground and shield. It's criminal neglect, Rosamunde! Even non-magicals should have realized that the children of a Wizard should have magical training, even though their mother was non-magical and the relatives they went to were all hers. Nicola is just old enough to start her magical training but Nicolas is at least two years behind. If they want to stay with us I shall enter him in the Druidry for next Michaelmas Term and tutor him myself if needs be to get him ready. But Grandpapa has already volunteered. I think he misses teaching since he retired. We shall see a great difference in Nicholas once he is properly grounded and has shields."

Rosamunde hoped so. She was already nurturing tender feelings towards shy little Nicola and something in her reached out to Nicholas as well. She could understand, far better than anyone else, what being abused was like.

Jhaniput was five years behind her, but she could still suddenly be reminded of it at any time. It was easier now to put the memories behind her. She now enjoyed being intimate with her husband. She had even begun to dance again after a long time of not being able to do so. She had also at last rejoined her Coven, a must if she was to have a daughter who must be trained up in the traditions of Witchcraft. She had even danced several times sky-clad, finding that much of her self consciousness had disappeared. Her lack of body hair was not an embarrassment, for three new members had the blood of the Selchies, the seal folk, and they had no body hair either. Hers had never grown back, for as all magicals knew, in order to negate the effects of a potion, one had to know what had gone into the original potion and that had not been found out. All that Rosamunde knew was that it was yellow in colour, smelled foul and stung the skin.

Now she hoped that Alan was right. She wanted these children and wanted them badly but the decision to become a family had to be mutual.

60

home at last

"Nicky, wake up!" A small, imperative hand pulled at Nicholas's shoulder and dragged him from sleep. "Come look! It's so beautiful!"

Nicholas yawned and rubbed his eyes. Nicola's glowing face hung just above his and she tugged once more at his arm.

"Come look!" she repeated again and ran to the window, where she stood on tiptoe to look out.

He climbed from bed and joined her, lifting her so that she could perch on the wide window ledge and then scrambled up to join her.

The old nursery faced east and the sun was now rising in gold and pink. Gold touched the edges of small blue clouds on the horizon and sent gilded streamers across a lake that lay below their vision in the park that surrounded Dragon's Rest. There had been a slight frost in the night and every tree limb was gilded as well. Above the little clouds the sky was clear and began to turn a crystal blue as the sun rose further. In the park the children could see small deer beneath the trees and on a terrace directly below a peacock screamed and spread its incredible tail, it, too, in a glow of rising sun.

"Isn't it beautiful?" said Nicola, her face radiant "Did you ever imagine that there could be such a beautiful place? It's like heaven!"

Nicholas looked at it with a lump in his throat. It *was* like heaven. But they would not be allowed to stay. There would be some reason why these people did not want them as usual, more than likely his fault. Even if he could be good they would find him sullen or obstinate and Nicola would scream if they punished him. Adults did not like children who screamed and were sullen.

They sat in the window quite a long time, watching as the sun revealed more and more details and the sky cleared completely.

Maeve found them there when she came upstairs with a tray of milk and bread.

"Come along, then," she said in her musical voice. "This is but a wee *bricfesta* until ye are being all washed and dressed and fit to go down to the breakfast parlor."

"You mean that there will be *more* food?" Nicholas asked rather suspiciously as he climbed down from the window, helping Nicola down as well. Almost every place they had lived, including the orphanage, had featured only a glutinous porridge and some thin milk for breakfast. Asking or expecting anything else brought punishment or, from the nuns, a simple statement that there was nothing else.

Maeve looked at him puzzled. "And would ye not be wanting more food and dining with himself and herself? And isn't himself telling us that he's going to take ye wi' him to be feeding the dragon this morning? And there's after being kittens and wee ferrets to be fed as well."

They were to find out that the servants usually referred to the Master and Mistress as himself and herself, not in any derogatory sense, but in affection.

Feed the dragon! Nicholas's stomach felt painful. He was to see the dragon again!

Nicola had seated herself at the small table and chairs in front of a peat fire, which as Nicholas sat down, flared up at a Word from Maeve.

" 'Tis magiced," she said at his look of surprise. "Once we are learning the Word, all of us servants can be making a fire as easily as naught."

"This is so good!" Nicola paused in taking large bites of bread and butter. The bread was fresh and the milk was thick and creamy. Maeve showed her that in some little covered dishes on the tray were several kinds of jam and fruit preserves and told her that all the fruit and jam was made right here at Dragon's Rest and the milk and butter came from their own cows.

Indeed, it was far from the usual fare they had become accustomed to and they were tempted to eat voraciously. But there was just enough to whet the appetite.

The children hurried through washing and dressing which was another surprise, for the water was actually hot and the towels thick and fluffy with sweet smelling soap.

Maeve brushed their hair but clucked over the state of their clothing. "Never ye mind," she said encouragingly, "Herself will be takin ye to Dublin and making certain that ye are having all that a little gentleman and lady are after needing."

Maeve took them downstairs to where a tall young footman waited in the hall. He smiled at them and said *"Dia duit ar maidin,* young master and miss. I'm Aindriú and I'll be taking ye to the breakfast parlor. 'Tis being a big house but ye can be asking anyone of us if ye are getting lost or turned around. 'Tis a grand place for hide and seek. All the young folks in this family are liking fine to play here."

They followed him through what seemed a maze of halls, but everything was light and clean and smelled good. There were many windows and from them they could see nothing but parkland, trees and gardens, now somewhat desolate in early winter. They had never been in a rural situation before and it seemed very strange not to see rows of houses or streets full of traffic.

The breakfast parlor proved to be a sunny room with pale yellow walls, and at the breakfast table, as yet bare of food, were the Stillfields, and the two animals the children had met the day before.

The children were warmly greeted and told that the animals would be fed first while the human breakfast was being prepared.

Rosamunde took Nicola with her to a little room off the breakfast parlor, sun-filled and cozy, where two baskets, one of small ferrets and one of kittens, lay. Sinéad and Cathal accompanied them.

A footman appeared with a great-coat for Alan and Nicholas's shabby, outgrown coat. They then went out a back door onto a terrace and went along a graveled path.

"Do you know much about dragons?" Alan asked conversationally as they walked.

Nicholas shook his head. "Nobody ever had any books and the nuns don't know about dragons. I think they're all frightened of them. But dragons are good, aren't they?" He quickly looked up at Alan and just as quickly looked down again, wary and tense.

"They're *very* good. They help us in many ways. They carry the Royal Mail, provide transport, for dragons can go where the railway cannot and guard their families. Dragons are also one of the best companions you can ever have. They're very clever and love puzzles and games such as dragon-ball. Have you ever seen a match, Nicholas?"

Nicholas shook his head. Sometimes he read about dragon-ball in the newspapers that the nuns used to light the fires. He thought it would be the most thrilling thing he could ever see.

"Trinity University is of course, on Christmas Holiday," said Alan, "but they still have scratch matches that do not count towards a University Blue. The dragons love the sport and often talk their riders into one. I shall scry my father and ask him if there is a scratch match I might take you to. He's a professor at University and is on the dragon-ball team as well."

Nicholas had another lump in his throat. He could not believe that all this was happening. How long would it last before they didn't want Nicola and himself here any more?

Alan stopped at the end if the graveled path. "If you don't mind, Nicholas, I'm going to give you a temporary ground and shield before we go to the dragon pen. It is warmed by ley lines and until you learn to ground and shield for yourself they may affect you badly. You're very magical and you should have been learning to control your magic at least two years ago. That's why you feel so angry at times. It's your magic struggling to get out and it is uncontrolled at this point."

Nicholas stared at him. Once again he was surprised that anyone actually knew why he felt the way he did.

"Do you mind if I use magic on you, Nicholas?" Alan asked. "I cannot do it without your say so."

"Will it hurt?" Nicholas blurted out.

Alan laughed. It was a kind laugh. Nicholas did not feel that this man was making game of him. "No, it might even feel good."

"All right," said Nicholas and screwed his eyes shut, bracing himself for he knew not what.

To his surprise a warm feeling seemed to pass over him from head to toe and that restless churning inside him that built up every day until it exploded in temper was suddenly quieted as if it had been turned off by a spigot.

He opened his eyes just in time to see Alan put a decorated piece of wood away in his breast pocket. "That's my wand," Alan explained as he saw Nicholas's eyes. "You'll have one yourself one day."

"This spell is only temporary," Alan continued, smiling at him. "But you'll feel better now until we can teach you to ground and shield for yourself. We'll go and do that right after breakfast."

As they resumed their walk Alan began to tell him more about dragons and spoke casually of giving him some books about dragons that he could keep no matter what happened.

While Rosamunde took Nicola into Dublin to buy clothing and toys, Nicholas was able to ride the dragon again. He had been astonished to learn that dragons liked grain and fruit with milk and honey for breakfast, not chunks of raw meat as he had imagined. Brendan, whom he found it easy to talk to, explained what dragons liked to eat.

Alan told him that dragons needed milk and cream, as it was important to their health that they have calcium frequently as it helped their bones stay healthy. Brendan quite obligingly showed him a small stream of flame as well.

Then they flew to another large home called Amberwell, where he met a man he liked at once, a tall man with silver streaked hair. Nicholas recognized his accent as French, for one of the nuns, Sister Marie Cecilia, was from the Channel Islands and she spoke French quite a bit.

There was a Vicar present as well and after a small ceremony of magic in Wizard's Latin, and a blessing by the Vicar, Nicholas suddenly felt as if his world had steadied. The churning inside him was also gone and he felt no urge to strike out.

The nice man, whom Mr. Stillfield said was his grandfather and the Nicholas could call him 'professor', then taught Nicholas how to ground himself and shield. This was necessary for every Wizard, he explained, because not only did they draw energy from nature and the ley lines, but they were also having it drawn from themselves.

"A Wizard is a receptacle for magic, both giving and taking," said René. How criminal that this boy had had his magical beginnings so very important, ignored for almost too long!

"Can I be a Wizard?" Nicholas asked breathlessly.

"Of a certainty," said René. "I shall teach you this very day how to make a mage light as this is always the first lesson, no?"

And before they left from Dublin where they were to join Rosamunde and Nicola for luncheon, Nicholas had learned to make a mage light.

"The potential is very high," said René to Alan as they watched Nicholas, delighted with what he could do, make a light over and over. "I shall be glad to teach him, *je vous assure*, until he is ready for the Druidry."

"If they decide they want to be ours," said Alan. "We're both very keen, but they have been placed ten times before and it has never worked out. I do think that a great many of Nicholas's problems will have been resolved by what he just learned, but there is still the abuse and his wariness. Nicola is more inclined to trust, but she is younger than Nicholas and remembers less of it. They both suffer from nightmares and she sometimes has screaming fits. I tell you, *Grandpère*, the files on these children made sickening reading. That people could do things like that to innocent children! And most of these people were never even prosecuted! The law allows discipline of children that would make a sailor quail in fear! They said that Nicholas had to be beaten because he was intrinsically 'bad'! I noticed this morning that he flinches away from normal contact. It's not going to be easy."

"But you and Rosamunde are the perfect ones to make them whole, *n'est-ce pas?*" said René. "I only wonder how many other children there might be that have been so neglected and abused even as these magical ones."

His grandfather's words remained in Alan's mind long after they had left Amberwell and gone into Dublin.

Nicholas had the nightmare that night again. Replete

with a delicious supper, and the proud possessor of several books on dragons, some new clothes and some carefully chosen toys, he expected to sleep as well as he had the night before, when exhaustion had claimed him once he lay down in bed.

They had both been assured that anything they were given was theirs to keep even if they decided not to stay here. Perhaps it was anxiety that this might not be true, or perhaps he had been overexcited, for there had been three dragon flights that day and then the toy shop, where he had been allowed his choice. In spite of that, he only chose two things, the things he wanted the most, for at the orphanage they were only allowed two personal toys, for some children did not have any toys, save what the nuns could make. When they went back any others would be taken away.

One toy was a perfect little sailing ship that was suitable for sailing on a pond, while the other was a wooden dragon, that was a great deal like the one his brother had given him, save that this one was an Irish Emerald, like Brendan, and the first one had been a black Highland Dhu.

Nicola chose a beautiful porcelain doll that had come with a suitcase full of clothing, and a sweet faced velveteen cat that she had taken to bed with her, after carefully putting the doll into a nightgown and cap and putting her to sleep in a doll bed.

Alan and Rosamunde were in their sitting room in their bedroom suite discussing how the day had gone with the children,

"I was prepared to buy out the entire toy shop if they wanted it," said Alan. "But they seemed reluctant to take even what they finally chose."

"They've lost so much, and I think they are afraid of losing anything they are given," Rosamunde said thoughtfully. "It's just awful, Alan, to think that a little girl has never had a doll! All little girls should have a doll and little boys should have a sailing ship or a ball and hoop or some sort of toy!" She paused and said in a determined voice" Ever since we saw St. Mary's and I saw how much that is needed there I have thought of nothing else, I want to make these orphaned children happier. I want to make certain that they have toys and a safe, happy place to go if they lose their parents or for them to go if their parents are bad people. I sent the nuns at St. Mary's quite a large cheque today as they are seriously under funded. I could see that in one short visit. And even if Nicholas and Nicola want to stay with us I want to adopt more children who need us. This is a big house and what better to do with all these rooms but fill them with children? And who can understand better than I what it means to be abused and ill treated?" She added passionately, "Perhaps I ended in Jhaniput so that I would do this work after knowing what it is like to be abused and mistreated. I would like to think that there had been a reason why I was there."

The first cry came then and they heard it clearly as they were but a story down from the nursery in the newer part of the house.

"That's Nicholas!" said Alan, starting up from his chair. Closely followed by Rosamunde, he ran down the corridor and up the stairs until they burst into the nursery.

Maeve had already come from her room and was trying to both calm Nicola, on the verge of hysterics, and wake Nicholas, who was thrashing about in his bed and screaming, shouting "No, no! Leave me alone!"

"Go make some tea, Maeve, if you please," said Rosamunde and sat down on the bed beside Nicholas and took his wildly flying arms in her grasp. "Wake up, Nicholas," she said gently, but firmly. "It's only a dream, wake up. You're safe, we're here with you and nothing will harm you. Wake up now."

Alan took a tearful Nicola in his arms. She said "You won't beat him because he made a noise? He doesn't mean to, it's his bad dream." Her teeth were chattering and she was stiff in Alan's arms. "He doesn't mean to," she repeated.

"Why should I beat him because he had a bad dream?" said Alan reasonably. "We cannot help our dreams, Nicola."

"Children should be seen and not heard," she said, her blue eyes overflowing with tears.

"Not in this house," said Alan. "Children laugh and play and sing here."

She looked at him doubtfully, but he coaxed her to lean against him and picked up the velveteen cat. "You didn't tell us what you named him," he said, seeking to divert her.

Meanwhile, Rosamunde had managed to waken Nicholas, who looked at her at first wildly and then began to stammer that he was sorry and hadn't meant to make any noise. "I'm always bad," he said .

"You are not bad for having a bad dream!" Rosamunde said. Would you like to tell me about it? Sometimes talking about a bad dream helps, I know. I used to have a lot of bad dreams at one time. I don't any more because I had people that I could talk to about them."

"It's too awful, you would say I made it up," he said, pulling away from her.

"Nothing you can tell me, Nicholas, will make me think badly of you," Rosamunde explained. "You see, the doctor at the orphanage guessed what had happened to you, and it was not your fault. That man was very evil and he is in prison now where he belongs. You were not the first child that he hurt. And you see, I was in a similar situation myself where people did bad things to me, so I know what it is like to have people that are bigger and stronger than you are and make you do things that you don't want to do that hurt you."

She was conscious that Alan had picked up Nicola and gone to sit in front of the fire, where he was rocking and soothing the little girl. Silently, she blessed her husband. This would give her some privacy with Nicholas, who might be reluctant to speak of the horror he had undergone in front of his little sister. Rosamunde had noticed that he was very protective of her.

"I want very badly to be your mother, Nicholas," 'Rosamunde said softly "and you can tell me anything. I won't be horrified, or blame you."

"You really want me?" he said. "Nobody ever wants me. They say I am bad, and sulky."

"You feel better now after you've been shielded and grounded, don't you?" she asked.

He nodded and wiped away a tear that trickled down his face.

"I don't think you'll be mad and destructive ever again, particularly if you continue to learn how to use and control your magic. If you want to be our son we'll make certain that you have magic lessons. There is a school near

Tara, a place you'll see when we go there shortly for the Winter Solstice celebration. It's called the Druidry and it is where you can learn more magic and meet other boys who are learning to be Wizards. Nicola will probably go to my old school where she will learn Witchcraft. We've all sorts of wonderful plans for you and none of them include beatings, or being made to work like slaves or hurting you in any way. Please, Nicholas, believe me. We want you and Nicola to be our children, just as if you were born to us."

He wanted to trust her so badly and then it occurred to him if he told her what that man had done, both to him and to Nicola, who thankfully did not remember much of it, and she did not flinch or show disgust or say that it was his fault, perhaps he *could* trust her.

So haltingly, slowly, in a low voice, he told her. And before it was half done she had her arms around him and he was crying. He could feel that she was crying too. She did not reject him or tell him that he was bad or wicked as one woman had, or accuse him of lying, since the man who had hurt them was a respectable member of society and would never do the terrible things that Nicholas had accused him of doing.

And he could feel her love, real love, mother love. He was *wanted*. It was going to be all right. Somewhere inside he relaxed and let go of the pain and the anxiety and the anger. Whatever happened, they were now loved. They had come home for good.

Epilogue

Dragon's Rest, Ireland - Lá Bealtaine Eve, 1869

Nicholas Stillfield paused just inside the wide doors that led out onto the terrace of Dragon's Rest manor and looked from there to the emerald green lawn, now dotted with lawn chairs and blankets, little tables and people, many people, all of whom he loved dearly.

His parents were there as well as their American friends, the Connellys and their children, who were visiting this summer from America. Nicholas' uncles, Ellery and David, were there, his cousins Lewis and Margery, Uncle Jack's children, his uncle Alex, too, with a young lady of whom everyone was wondering if they were going to make a match of it. Nicholas hoped so; he liked her. Her name was Jane and she had joined in all of the games that afternoon, laughing as much as any of the others. Also present were Nicholas's siblings.

And tonight, Beltane Eve, when they all gathered to light the fires and begin the rituals of this High Sabat he would see the rest of his family that he loved so well, aunts and female cousins, who were now busy in the kitchens baking for Beltane, grandparents and great grandparents and so on into the greats.

"Come on, Nick!" said a voice a trifle impatiently behind him. "Sam said he'd teach us to play baseball like they play in America! Perhaps we'll be able to use these cricket bats if he can't find the American bat he brought with him."

Nicholas turned to look behind him. Looking rather eager, his twelve year old brother Julian was frowning a little. He was going to be tall, even the adopted children in this family seemed to run to height, and he had honey-blonde hair and gray eyes.

Looking at him now, Nicholas found it hard to believe that four years ago he had not wanted Julian or his older sister Felicity to join their family. It had been perfect as it was: himself and his sister Nicola, and their adoptive parents,

Alan and Rosamunde Stillfield. He had been more than a little jealous, until Rosamunde let him read the file on Julian and Felicity.

They had been in a perhaps even worse situation than he and Nicola had before they had come to Dragon's Rest. Julian and Felicity had been dragged around the country by a drunken, abusive, non-magical father who had offered his daughter to men in pubs in exchange for drink, and beaten his son because he looked like the Witch mother who had died at his birth. They had lived hand to mouth, begging, and eating from dustbins.

Nicholas's sympathy had been touched as Rosamunde knew it would be and he made an especial effort to be nice and helpful to the new members of the family. His sister, Nicola, was thrilled to have an older sister in Felicity, who was now fifteen, and they had all welcomed Cary last year and just lately, little Phebe. Now Nicholas never thought of the others as anything but his brothers and sisters.

"Let's go get Cary out of the tree house," Nicholas suggested to Julian. "If Luke Connelly can play baseball at his age, Cary can too." Luke Connelly was the youngest of the American children. He was seven, and Cary was eight.

Julian agreed to this and the two boys set off together for a large tree in a nearby copse that held an equally large tree house.

Out on the lawn the adults saw them go off together, Nicholas's arm draped companionably about his brother's shoulders.

Laura Connelly leaned back in her wicker chair and said, "Did you ever think, Rose, that you'd have six kids?"

Rosamunde, holding golden-haired Phebe, who was only two, in her lap, shook her head. "And there's no end in sight."

"That's true," put in Alan, sitting beside Nate Connelly, with whom he had been discussing Sam's extreme love of baseball. Sam, at eleven, was the Connelly eldest and looked a great deal like his father. Next came nine year old Tabitha and then Luke.

"Next month we are going up to Scotland to see about

adopting another little boy named Alasdair," Alan continued. "He's nine and magical and his grandparents were non-magical. They thought he was possessed of the devil and were very cruel to him. The grandparents were extremely religious and thought they were beating the devil out of him. Fortunately they died about two years ago and he was put in one of our orphanages. But he needs a family and most people do not want to adopt a child who had been so abused."

"You're the one of the few," Laura put in, looking at Phebe, who would not be parted from Rosamunde for a moment. The little girl's short life had been filled with violence and from the first she had seen Rosamunde as a shelter. The only word she said so far was "Mama".

Rosamunde noticed Laura's look and said "She's much improved. She was used to spent all her time screaming and I could scarcely leave her for a moment. Now she will go to bed in the nursery by herself, but she does want me as soon as she wakes up. The girls especially dote on her and she is responding to them. She is very leery of men yet, but that is improving too. She actually held her arms out to Alan yesterday."

"I confidently expect her next word to be Papa," said Alan.

"How many orphanages do you have now?" Nate asked, watching the children and older relatives streaming to the field for baseball, watched a horde of familiars; cats, ferrets, owls and hedgehogs. Brendan shared the edge of the field with Ellery's Erianne, David's Stella and Nicholas's one year old Varian. They would start flying together this summer.

"Five. The one in Wales is opening this autumn," said Rosamunde. "Grandfather Chenevix has been very, very generous. They're all named the Lucie Chenevix Home for Orphans after Grandmother Lucie who died just after we adopted Nicholas and Nicola. They're all staffed with young people, both men and women, who truly enjoy and understand children. We've been very careful with the staff we have appointed, which is one reason that there are not more orphanages. And there is always at least one magical person on staff so that we can recognize magical children and their particular problems."

"I don't know how you do it, Rose!" said Laura."Four's enough for me! The last Connelly child is right here," Laura patted her stomach, which was still flat in the American denim trousers she wore, for they had gone riding earlier and she refused to sit a sidesaddle. "She'll be making her entrance in November. I hope it's another girl 'cause me and Tabbie are outnumbered right now."

Congratulations were in order and the talk then turned to catching up with news of absent friends.

Laura's Pa, Lowell Fitzroy, was working on a telegraph project in western Canada. Alan told them of a recent letter from Ravi. He had married a *Rajkumari* from the Rajput, a distant relative of his mother's. His family was in good health and spirits. Parminder and Sishul had written that the old *Sadhu*, much revered and beloved, had passed away, leaving his blessings on the now peaceful and happy state of Jhaniput. Rosamunde heard from Molly on occasion and she was happy with her husband and their two children. Niaz was now a Major in the army of Ranijhat. They still had the animals that Sinéad had known and others as well. Margaret Broadbent and her Jim had retired, but after one winter near London had gone back to India and settled in Jhaniput, where Jim was a military adviser to Maharajah Sishul. Albert and Ivy Higgins owned a pub in Bethnal Green, in London now and were doing very well. They had heard nothing of Henrietta.

"But one of the strangest fates of all," said Alan, "is Mabel Clutterbuck's."

Laura snorted. "I ain't got any doubt about that!"

"You mean that red headed gal who didn't like wearing clothes?" said Nate. "Thought Sacha was taking her back to an aunt in Delhi."

"She only stayed there one night and then ran away," said Alan. "We were curious as to what became of her. Rosamunde's parents are friendly with her brother Harry and, according to him, she just dropped out of sight. So we asked Chenevix's agent in India to try and find out what had happened. She's in Bombay, mistress of a bawdy house."

Laura snorted again. "I knew it! That one was a natural born whore!"

"According the Grandfather Chenevix's agent she has

dyed her skin and is calling herself Lali, a half caste," Alan continued. "The brothel is called "The Painted One" and she wears only some bell and bangle jewelry and floral designs painted on her body."

Laura looked disgusted, while Rosamunde was troubled. She had never understood Mabel's predilections and never would.

Nate was more forgiving. "If that's what makes her happy," he said lightly. "She ain't you, Laurie."

"Never could abide that girl!" said Laura. "And speaking about people I ain't able to abide, whatever happened to them missionaries that married us?"

"The horrible Holloways," said Rosamunde, bouncing Phebe in her lap at which the little girl gave a gurgle of laughter, her first.

When the fuss over this had died down Alan said "The Holloways did not stay long in India as they were singularly unsuccessful in converting any one."

"God, I wonder why?" said Laura sarcastically.

"After being recalled back here for a while, they were then sent to New Zealand, where it is thought that they were captured and eaten by cannibals," said Alan trying to suppress a smile. "Of course, they never found any trace of them or their remains."

"Hell, all they had to do was look for cannibals with a stomach-ache from all that Christian piety!" said Laura. "Bet you they were full of Holloways!"

"But the odd thing is," said Alan quietly "this little boy, Alasdair, is their grandson. Their daughter ran away from home and ended in marrying a Scots Wizard. When his parents died, Alasdair was sent to live with them, between missionary stints, when they were back here in the Six Nations."

"Only you two," said Nate, "would take on the grandson of a couple of rats who were so damned mean to you both."

"God, what if he grows up to be a parson!" said Laura with a roll of her eyes.

They all laughed and looked out at the baseball game, a noisy, merry affair.

Alan and Rosamunde exchanged a glance. They were

very glad to see these old friends and seeing Laura again had not brought back nightmares of Jhaniput for Rosamunde.

She was happy and busy now, with the orphanages, a very satisfying marriage, a large family and her Witchcraft to keep her busy. All of the children were turning out well. Nicholas was going to go into Dracophilogy and Julian's bright green aura had determined that he would be a Wizard Healer. Felicity wanted to teach and Nicola wanted to go to one of the new women's colleges and study history. It was too early to tell with the others yet, but whatever they chose to do they would have the love and support of their entire family.

Rosamunde often wondered if any of this would have happened if she had not gone to Jhaniput. Would she and Alan be married now? Would they have adopted the children? Would she have the deep understanding of their problems that made her so skilled in dealing with abused children?

Probably she would never know. But it had come not to matter that much any more. Helena Williamson had been right, it had been her choice to be happy, to have a busy and useful life instead of dwelling on what had been done to her and wallowing in self-pity and guilt over something that she could not have prevented.

And looking about her now at husband, children and friends, she was certain that she had made the right choice.

THE   END

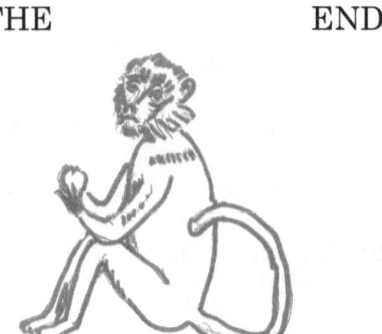

From the pen of

G.M.S. Altman

(continued)

Dippel's Oil

John Calvin Ramsey was a genius, a computer technician extraordinaire who tolerated his mundane public life only because he held loftier aspirations. One day he planned to be the most powerful man on earth, someone with all the money anyone could ever want and the long life to in which to enjoy it. For that reason, John Calvin was on a quest: to find one very special man who he knew held an ancient and monumental secret.

He longed to find this man and spent countless hours pouring over arcane documents, internet sites and tracing history from the 17th century to the present.

He was ready to pledge himself as his most obedient, diligent, loyal, and grateful student.

And then John Calvin was going to kill him.

ISBN: 978-1-888071-17-7 Trade Paperback $14.95 336 pages

HELENENTHAL BOOKS

www.galtman.books.officelive.com

ISABELLA LEAGUE
Fantasy Novels

Jongleur

The year is 1811 in an England where Wizards and Witches practice their magic and dragons carry the Royal Mail.

It is up to a young English Witch and a French émigré Wizard to thwart the black magic of the Jongleur and his unholy allies of the Unselighe Court before they succeed in ridding Britain of white magic and magicians – and making the British Isles a conquered land.

ISBN: 978-1-888071-16-8 Trade Paperback $19.95 626 pages

Land of the Firebird

When Professor of Dracophilology Simon Stillfield is asked to go to far away Russia to help set up a dragon post like that in the British Isles, his first impulse is to refuse. To his knowledge, there are few dragons in Russia besides the feral Ice Dragons of Siberia. But when a disappointment in love makes him long for a change of scene, Simon, his dragon friend Lakota and familiar Janus embark on a strange adventure in a distant, largely unknown land.

When a young boy Simon has befriended is kidnapped by an Ice Dragon, Simon must attempt a rescue, and face Russian Witches, Rusalka, and an evil Necro-mancer who seems bent on killing him — for an unknown reason. It will take all of Simon's resources — magical and otherwise — to confront danger, death — and love.

ISBN: 978-1-888071-18-4 Trade Paperback $16.95 422 pages

Dragons' Pearls

The dragons of China, ancient and wise, were angry. Not only had the dragon temples fallen into disuse with no offerings or worship, but no dragon adviser sat by the Emperor's side in the Forbidden City. And now something more terrible was happening – for both the dragons and for China itself: someone was killing dragons with magic, selling their flesh and bones for profit and stealing their pearls – the fount of all their wisdom and knowledge – even the power to fly – that they wore under their chins.

When one of the great Celestial Dragons came to the scholar of dragons, Dr. Quong Lee, for his help, the elderly man could only think of one person to help him battle this black wickedness – and the dragons – and his country. He needed not only a dragon expert, but a magician – for there were no White magicians left in China.

ISBN: 978-1-888071-19-1 Trade Paperback $16.95 324 pages

Murder Moon

When in the autumn of 1844 the blood red moon rose over the Six Nations of the British Isles, the magical population of Witches and Wizards were facing perilous times. For those magical persons of unstable character, or those who suffered from a long stress, were liable to commit mayhem, violence – and murder.

Stuart Delmar, a Forensic Wizard with the Bow Street Police in London, was abruptly ordered back to his former home in Dublin, Ireland. Armed with magic, and the help of his brilliant familiar, the cat Dr. Foster, Stuart begins his search for a clever and vicious murderer.

Time was running out – there were too many suspects, too many alibis and the woman he is coming to love is in danger of going to the gallows for a crime he was certain she had not committed.

ISBN: 978-1-888071-20-7 Trade Paperback $16.95 468 pages

HELENENTHAL

BOOKS

www.galtman.books.officelive.com